LE TEMPS VIENDRA

A NOVEL OF ANNE BOLEYN

VOLUME II

SARAH A. MORRIS

Also by Sarah Morris

Fiction
Le Temps Viendra: a Novel of Anne Boleyn, Volume I

Non-fiction
*In the Footsteps of Anne Boleyn (*co-author Natalie Grueninger)

https://www.facebook.com/ LTViendra
https://www.facebook.com/sarahmorrisauthor
www.letempsviendra.co.uk
Twitter:#LeTempsViendra

Spartan Publishing

Published 2013

Copyright: Sarah Morris

The moral right of the author has been asserted

978-0-9873841-9-5

Spartan Publishing
www.spartan-publishing.com

This book is dedicated to my Aunt Sylvia, who was a great supporter of my writing endeavours, but who sadly died on 6 July 2013, and therefore never got to read Volume II of *Le Temps Viendra: a Novel of Anne Boleyn*. I hope that somewhere beyond the veil, she is smiling down on this final chapter in the life of Anne Boleyn.

With love, Sarah.

Acknowledgements

Many people have inputted into the writing of this book. In no particular order, I am indebted to the following: Emma Raphael (http://www.raphaelhistoricfalconry.com/home.php) of Raphael Historic Falconry, who ensured technical accuracy in those scenes in which Anne is out hawking with the King; Bess Chilver, Historical Costumer, who kept me straight on all the details relating to forms of address and the often complex nature of Tudor costume at the Henrician Court; Heath Pye (AKA *Rhys the Bowman*) who guided my hand in relation to the scene in which Anne and her ladies are playing archery in the garden at Whitehall Palace; Professor Aidan Halligan, consultant obstetrician and gynaecologist, who I consulted regarding the medical aspects of Anne's stillbirth in the summer of 1534; Erica Stewart, counsellor at SANDS (the Stillbirth and Neonatal Death Society), who kindly gave her time in helping me understand the likely physical and emotional impact that the stillbirth of 1534 would have had upon Anne Boleyn.

To all my enthusiastic Facebook and Twitter fans, who shared every exhilarating, and sometimes painful, steps in bringing Anne's story to life and, of course, for their never-ending bounty of support and commitment for the final product; and finally, to Natalie Dormer who helped me wrestle with the question of 'When did Henry fall out of love with Anne Boleyn?' by sharing her very unique perspective of having walked in Anne's shoes for over two years, whilst filming the Showtime series, *The Tudors*.

CONTENTS

Part Five

'Remember me when you do pray, that hope doth spring from day to day'

Anne Boleyn

Chapter One

Windsor Castle,
1 September 1532

'Madame.' Just barely discernible through the heavy mantle of sleep, I heard the woman's voice speaking to me in gentle tones. I was vaguely aware of a hand resting lightly on my shoulder, softly shaking me awake. 'My Lady, Viscount Rochford is here.' My eyes flickered open as I was drawn swiftly from unconsciousness by the compelling familiarity of that sweet, melodic voice. To my utter amazement, I found myself looking into the beautiful, blue eyes of a friend I thought never to see again. With a frisson of excitement and a surge of energy, I lifted myself up onto one elbow, sweeping the tousled mane of hair from my face, I scanned the room. I couldn't believe it! After two long, desolate years stranded in a colourless twenty-first century, I had finally come home.

I was lying in a huge four-poster bed ornately carved from the finest English oak. The intertwined motif of honeysuckle and acorns wrought into its wooden frame was a symbol adopted privately by Henry and Anne; the honeysuckle denoting love and devotion, and the acorn, fertility and new life. It was in an exceptionally finely decorated room which was familiar to me, yet in my disorientation at having been sucked back so violently into the sixteenth century, I could not yet identify where I was. However, I could again admire the vivid richness of the Tudor decor that once I had found so gaudy and which, in time, I had come to appreciate for its uplifting vibrancy. The bed frame itself was painted and gilded with gold leaf; the hangings were made of crimson cloth of gold, richly embroidered with borders of purple velvet and emblazoned with a whole array of badges that I assumed related to Henry and Anne.

I sat up in bed excitedly, swinging my legs about until they were tucked underneath my body and I was kneeling on the mattress. In sheer joy and exuberance I grasped the counterpane which lay scrunched up around me; it was a beautiful thing made of crimson and white damask, embroidered with a border of cloth of gold and edged with a narrow fringe of Venice gold and lined with russet sarcenet. I held it against my breast and raised my face to the heavens in nothing short of ecstasy. For a moment, I forgot completely about my modern day life, and about Daniel. It seemed that I was again caught hopelessly in the mesmerising world of Anne Boleyn, overjoyed that I would see her face again, that I would behold Henry's magnificent presence; that I would know his love and adoration once more. How naive, looking back, that I should be so utterly carefree when already Anne Boleyn's halcyon days were beginning to draw to a close. As I was soon to find out, there would be unbelievably trying circumstances ahead that would test my resilience and courage to the limit.

Yes, I knew exactly where I was,

'Windsor!'

Anne's life had moved on since I had last tread reverently in her shoes. She now occupied the queen's apartments at Windsor Castle and was mistress in her own, very splendid, regal, household. Yet I still did not know where I had landed in her story—what was the date? Thankfully, I did not have to wait long to find out. As I turned about, I saw my beloved Nan standing before me smiling, as she clasped her hands to her breast in unadulterated delight saying,

'Oh, my Lady…Anne…you look so radiant! Today will be truly glorious! Just think…a marquess in your own right—no other woman in the land holds such privilege!' Her eyes suddenly welled up with tears of joy. My devoted friend went on, 'To think how far we have come…you have come, since you first told me of the king's intentions toward you. Do you remember? The day his majesty was invested into the *Ordre of St. Michel* and we escaped from the drudgery of the queen's chambers and went walking in the gardens at Greenwich?' I smiled for how could I forget! I felt my own swell of emotion surge up and threaten to overwhelm me, for Nan could not possibly know what I had been through to get here; and from my reading of history, I knew only too well the trials and tribulations that Henry and Anne had endured to reach this day of triumph. Through Nan's words, I knew the date with certainty; my study had served me well. It was Sunday, 1 September 1532, the day that Anne would finally be raised to the peerage in preparation for the meeting between Henry and King Francis in Calais that autumn.

Francis had known Anne when she was maid-of-honour to his first wife, Queen Claude. Now, as befitting her elevated status of queen-in-waiting, Anne required a formal title of her own. The realisation was truly bittersweet, as I knew that this moment would define the pinnacle of Anne's power and influence with Henry.

'My Lady have I said something to upset you?' I smiled at her reassuringly, 'No Nan, you have not offended me, I was just reflecting on the enormity of this day. You are right, his majesty has taken on the might of Rome, the self-righteous pomposity of the clergy, and the stubborn pride of many of his leading noblemen so that he may have me by his side as his queen.' I swallowed hard as I felt the full force of the burning resentment that a multitude of folk at court and across the land must have harboured in their hearts toward Anne. It would always be easier to blame her, rather than Henry, for the fires of hell which many now believed raged across England. Yet, for the sake of the day and for the happiness of my friend, I brushed aside these melancholic reflections.

'Come Nan! You say that Viscount Rochford is here? Then let us not keep my dear brother waiting. Fetch me my dressing gown!' Nan swiftly retrieved an exquisite black satin nightgown which was lined with black taffeta and edged with velvet. I slipped my arms quickly into the sleeves as Nan fastened the gold clasps at my breast.

I knew that by 1532, the Boleyn faction was almost at the height of its ascendancy and that in December 1529, nearly three years earlier, Anne's father, Thomas Boleyn had been created Earl of Wiltshire and Ormonde, thus her brother, George, was now Viscount Rochford. I was almost beside myself with excitement for I longed to see George's beautiful face again. I knew that Anne and her brother were kindred spirits and shared a deep and unspoken connection forged in the misadventure of their youth. I believed that he was the only person alive who unconditionally accepted Anne for who she was; this was their unshakeable bond. I had desperately missed his easy charm and carefree nature.

As I made my way to leave the room, I caught sight of myself in a mirror. I had seen Anne's face many, many times before and yet she never failed to take my breath away. I smiled gratefully at my reflection, the reflection of an extraordinary woman in whose eyes I saw a familiar, fierce loyalty and pride. I also saw something else, something new that I could only guess had come about as a result of six difficult years fighting for her place at the king's side. Alongside Anne's usual aura of courage and determination, I detected a subtle fear mixed into the palette of her emotions, no doubt imperceptible to most. I recognised a haunted look, the look of the hind who knows well that she is chased by wolves. It was slightly unnerving but I breathed in deeply, settling my nerves before Nan opened the door of my bedchamber and I stepped into the room beyond. I was so overjoyed to see the magnificent sight of my brother clad entirely in striking crimson red and standing right before me that I noticed little else. Completely forgetting myself, I rushed forward throwing my arms about his neck and kissing him excitedly on the lips. In my exuberance, my brother must have been quite startled for he stepped back, and holding me by the shoulders at arm's length, laughingly asked,

'Dearest sister, to what do I owe was such a heartfelt welcome?' He raised an eyebrow as if to tease me for my childish ebullience. I wanted to tell him how much I loved him, that such a precious and beloved brother no woman could ever hope for, when I suddenly became aware that we were far from alone. We were standing in the queen's privy chamber; a large, light and spacious room that connected the queen's audience chamber with the privy bedchamber from which I had just emerged. The room was flooded with light afforded by a large oriel window adjacent to where I stood with George. Further along the same wall, two mullioned windows overlooked the small courtyard below.

It was a lavish room partly covered with wainscoted oak panelling, and set about with decorative pillars which were worked in the grotesque style and painted in rich reds, blues and gold leaf.

An elaborate frieze depicting religious scenes was set around the upper third of the room, while the walls were hung with fine tapestries and oil paintings, many of which were of significant, dynastic importance.

A large, stone fireplace dominated the left side of the room and remained unlit in the warmth of the late summer. Yet I must confess that despite the dazzling grandeur of this chamber, I was more startled by the number of people who were gathered there.

When I was last in Anne's world, I was permitted only four ladies in waiting according to my rank and status: Margery Wyatt, Nan

4

Gainsford, Mary Norris, and Joan Champernowe. A maid, Eliza, an equerry, George Zouche and a single page of the chamber had all been generously appointed by his majesty to wait upon me. The rest of the time I spent in the quiet company of my dear Lady Mother who oftentimes acted as chaperone. As I surveyed the room, I realised just how high Anne had been elevated at court and the exalted position she had come to occupy as consort-in-waiting. I found that attending Anne were eight ladies of noble birth, all of whom I recognised from my previous time at court—although none had ever sought to frequent my private chambers before.

Amongst the gathering there was the diminutive thirty-six-year-old Eleanor Paston, Countess of Rutland, the daughter of Anne's cousin, Bridget Haydon; near her was the kindly twenty-three-year-old Dorothy Stanley, Countess of Derby. The countess was one of the youngest of seventeen children born to the late Duke of Norfolk and the much younger half-sister of Anne's mother, Elizabeth. I knew that because of the age gap, Elizabeth Boleyn acted largely as a surrogate mother toward Dorothy, looking upon her as a daughter and loving her well. Far less pleasant however, was the sight of the rather dour and formidable Elizabeth Wood, Lady Boleyn, who was clearly in the middle of dealing with one of Anne's chamberers when I burst through my bedchamber door. Lady Boleyn was Anne's aunt who, despite the family connection, made it clear that she disapproved of her chit of a niece. Her imperious and brittle manner toward me and Anne had been difficult to tolerate, and I sensed that Anne was hurt by her aunt's disdain and rejection. However, her contempt only served to raise Anne's intemperance against her stuffy aunt.

I was also acutely aware that Lady Boleyn would be one of the five women to attend Anne when she was first committed to the Tower in 1536, to spy on her and report her every word to Master Kingston. There was no love lost between these two women, so it was not surprising that the sight of Lady Boleyn made me recoil in distaste.

To my left was the seemingly ever sour-face of my brother's wife, Jane Boleyn, Viscountess Rochford, who beheld the sweet and easy affection between Anne and her brother with pursed lips that spoke volumes of her childish jealousy. Finally, near the door leading through to the distant presence chamber, were two ladies who had evidently been in discourse with one another and who looked at me with turned heads. The first was the middle-aged wife of Arthur Plantagenet, uncle to the king. Her name was Honor Grenville, Lady Lisle. Although ambitious, I found Lady Lisle to be a cheery and pragmatic character who was ever wont to ingratiate herself into the Lady Anne's good graces. Finally, next to Honor was another dear friend, Bridget Wiltshire, Lady Tyrwhitt, whom I first met at Allington Castle on that idyllic day when a group of us, including my sister Mary, Margery and Sir Thomas Wyatt, had whiled away the hours picnicking in the golden sunshine. It was the day when Sir Thomas Wyatt had fatefully stolen a trinket from the pocket of my gown which, some weeks later, had caused my first serious altercation with Henry.

Bridget was almost exactly Anne's age and had grown up in Stone Place in Kent. Hence the Boleyns and the Wiltshires were neighbours and shared a common fealty. I met her on subsequent occasions when she visited my mother and me at Hever. It was during these visits that I learned that Bridget, like Margery Wyatt, had been a long-standing childhood friend of Anne's. Our paths also crossed often at court for Bridget had long been in the service of Katherine. She and I passed many happy hours together in pleasurable dalliance with the gentlemen of the king's chamber when they stopped by to pay their respects to the queen. This was before Henry removed me from waiting upon his wife, and although our friendship remained firm, this arrangement meant that we saw each other less often.

It was clear that today was to be an intimate affair, with Anne surrounded only by members of her extended family and close Kentish friends. I surveyed the faces of those present and was delighted to see my dearest friend, Margery, as ever smiling at me reassuringly. I was glad for the other ladies looked somewhat taken aback; I suspect they considered my behaviour toward a gentleman rather inappropriate—even if that gentleman was my precious brother. I quickly gathered myself together, clasping my hands lightly in front of my stomach and raising myself to my full height, as Anne was often wont to do when she needed to regain her composure.

I felt the familiar sensation of her hand guiding me. Having walked in Anne's shoes for over a year, I was well used to the feel of her body, the way she moved, her mannerisms and inclinations. I remembered that the first time I found myself in her world, I'd been distinctly aware of our separateness. It had taken several months for the boundary between my sense of self and Anne's to dissolve. Yet by the time I had fallen ill with the sweat, I had become so distant from my own persona that I often went for extended periods knowing nothing of the other Anne's presence. However, on this occasion, the transformation would happen much more quickly. My brother thankfully cut across the awkward silence as he said,

'Sister, the king has requested that I come hither with this message; that his majesty wishes you to attend his private mass this morning in his privy closet as thanksgiving for this day' George was exceptionally formal in the presence of my ladies, yet out of their sight, he winked mischievously.

'Thank you, brother.' I said equally formally, nodding my appreciation. George turned to go, acknowledging first his wife, then the other ladies present, before he swept out of the room with an uncommon grace.

I turned instinctively to Margery and said calmly,

'I wish you to help me dress. Please attend me to my wardrobe so that I may choose my gown.' I knew that below my privy bedchamber, connected by an outer spiral staircase, lay my wardrobe, and with Anne's elevated status, I expected this to be quite extensive. However, I guessed that this arrangement was as true of Windsor as it was of all of Henry's great houses, so I was thankful when Margery nodded and led the way from my privy chamber through a small connecting door which led us down several turns of a stone staircase until we emerged in the room below.

The chamber occupied the same footprint as the privy bedroom above it. There were a number of windows running along one wall with bars that were meant to protect the costly garments stored within. On the opposite wall was a large fireplace, which unlike those of Anne's privy chambers above was already lit, providing a warm, dry atmosphere, best suited to airing the delicate fabrics of Anne's expensive trousseau.

As we entered, two gentlemen were busily occupied making alterations to one of Anne's gowns. I was now familiar with the way the royal household was organised, and I knew well that one of these two gentlemen was probably the yeoman of the wardrobe responsible for the care, upkeep and delivery of the queen's gowns to her privy chamber. The other was a servant of lesser rank, a groom or page, who assisted his master with his work and learned his art. Straightening themselves immediately, both men self-consciously dusted off their clothes and adjusted their doublets awkwardly. They were startled by our appearance and had probably never had impromptu visits from Lady Anne. Slightly embarrassed, Margery sensed my discomfort, and ever the protective friend, spoke up immediately dismissing both gentlemen from the chamber.

Once they had disappeared, I felt I could finally relax and let out a heavy sigh of relief, at last alone with a true friend whose presence always managed to chase the shadows away. I wanted so much to take hold of her and give Margery the tightest of embraces, for like my other friends, I had missed her so much. I knew that this further show of emotion would seem misplaced to those for whom nothing had changed. So I resolved to keep my own counsel and allow Anne's regal sense of grace and dignity to take over, and keep my exuberant joy locked away privately in my heart.

For the first time, I was able to view this functional, yet intriguing, room that served the queen. It was plain and undecorated, with several large presses stacked in frames along the walls which allowed the flat storage of precious carpets, tapestries and garments. Most delightful were the presence of ten or so mannequins, which were charmingly referred to as 'babies', used to display a variety of Anne's gowns. I looked at Margery and smiled conspiratorially for I knew that we shared the same love of fine things and fashion. Looking at these beautiful clothes, all I could say was,

'Oh! Margery,' Two words which filled me with deep appreciation. I moved forward from the doorway, sauntering between the mannequins, my hand trailing behind me, constantly brushing across various expensive fabrics that had been styled into a glittering array of exquisite dresses; silks, velvets, cloth of gold and silver; garments trimmed with furs such as miniver, sable and even ermine. I came to rest in front of a particularly stunning gown of crimson velvet, its bodice and skirt edged with soft ermine and the long straight sleeves trimmed with the same. If this wasn't breath-taking enough, the bodice and kirtle were covered in jewels that had been sewn into the material in intricate designs. As the light from the nearby window fell upon it, the gown glittered, the whole effect casting a myriad of miniature rainbows which danced around the room. Margery stood next to me as she explained,

'It is truly beautiful. The great wardrobe delivered it yesterday in time for today's ceremony. You will look every inch the queen consort; his majesty will be so proud of you.' I smiled at her, my heart suddenly racing at the thought of seeing Henry again. Then a morbid thought struck me; I knew that the higher Anne was raised, the greater the bitterness and resentment harboured by her enemies. For every courtier who rejoiced in her good fortune, there was at least one other whose eyes would flash with jealousy and hatred. My opulence today would only serve to inflame those sentiments. I voiced my concerns aloud,

'Yes, no doubt. Yet there will be many who will conceal the burning outrage in their breast; people who offer no goodwill toward me.'

'It may well be so, Anne, but let them grumble! It is how it is going to be!' I stared at my friend for she had just uttered the words which Anne briefly adopted in 1530 as her ill-fated motto: *Ainsi sera, groigne qui groigne.* I smiled at her quizzically as Margery raised her eyebrows as if sharing a private joke. We both appreciated her play on words and found ourselves laughing openly; I enjoyed her wicked sense of humour and admit it was a blessed relief with so much tension simmering at court.

'Let us make haste, my dearest friend. I must be with the king shortly and time is slipping away.' I said as I turned to make my way up to my bedchamber, leaving Margery to organise my clothes so that I could be made ready for the most important day of Anne's life so far.

Just before 8.15 am, accompanied by four of my ladies, I made my way to the king's privy chamber on the north side of the castle. With every ounce of self-restraint, I conducted myself into the king's presence as a vision of dignified and glittering majesty which I hoped was befitting Anne's hour of glory. I felt breathless with anticipation, a heady mixture of desire, excitement and anxiety rising up from my belly. I longed to be reunited with my love and after nearly two years, it was about to happen.

A palpable buzz was in the air, for there was much excitement at court that day at the prospect of the historic events that were to take place. First, there would be the grand ceremony to invest Lady Anne as Marquess of Pembroke. I knew that never before and never again would a woman be raised to the peerage in her own right; it was a defiant and emphatic gesture from Henry who wished to leave no one in any doubt of the great love he bore his lady, and his intention to make her his queen. After the ceremony, the king was to process to High Mass at St George's Chapel where Henry and Francis, represented by the French ambassador, Gilles de la Pommeraye, would swear to the terms of a treaty between England and France. It was to be the dawn of a new era in English policy and would set the scene for Anne and Henry's triumphant journey to Calais that autumn.

Many members of the king's privy chamber had already gathered inside the king's chamber. Anthony Knyvett stood close to the entrance as a gentleman usher to ensure that no unauthorised persons came into the king's presence. Several gentlemen had already gathered around the king including: my brother, George; Anne's first client, Sir Thomas Cheney whose wardship of another lady Anne I had helped secure from Wolsey in 1528; Sir Henry Norris, ever at the king's side as his trusted groom of the stool, and Anne's cousin, Sir Francis Bryan. Two others, whose identities I would later learn, were the cultured and generous Sir Peter Carew, who would accompany Henry and me to Calais, and the twenty-one-year-old Francis Weston, who had only that year been appointed as a gentleman of Henry's privy chamber. I could not take my eyes off him for I knew that his fate was entirely bound up with Anne's and that one day, they would both lie under the same cold earth within the Tower precinct.

With the announcement of my arrival, these men parted like the Red Sea to reveal the king's majesty towering above them all. I sank immediately into a deep and generous curtsy—for the sight of Henry after so long completely took my breath away. The king was sumptuously dressed in a jerkin of white satin and lined with purple satin and taffeta; the gown had a square collar, decorated with a broad garde, or border, which was embroidered with Venice silver. Beneath his jerkin, Henry wore a doublet and hose of matching white satin; the former was quilted with a garde of white velvet embroidered with Venice gold and lined with fustian. White stockings, shoes, and a cap that was decorated with a fine white ostrich feather completed the dazzling spectacle before me.

Henry had gained some weight since I last saw him; his face a little rounder; his girth somewhat more substantial. Yet his youth had not entirely deserted him and his charismatic magnetism sparked the familiar tingling of electricity up and down my spine. The king was clearly jubilant. I knew that there were few, if any at court, who dared look the king in the eye—except Lady Anne. That time was no exception for I could not take my eyes off the king. As always, Henry seemed unperturbed by Anne's boldness and greeted me with an enormous, warm and generous smile.

'Anne, sweetheart you look simply breathtaking!' The king moved forward offering me his hand so that I may rise to my feet; I noticed him surveying me covetously, as if I were the most precious of his possessions.

'Sir, in most humble wise that a heart can think, I am truly grateful to Your Majesty for the great honour you do me this day and I remain now, as ever, your true and loyal servant.' Henry raised my bejewelled hand to his lips, gently planting the most delicate of kisses there; all the while holding my gaze with an unnerving depth of desire. I knew from history that opinion concurred that in September 1532, the love between Anne and Henry remained unconsummated. However, in that moment, I could feel the enormous sexual tension between us, gripping me with fiery desire. In a few short months, Anne would submit to the king and give over her body completely, which I assumed would be the result of an unstoppable tsunami of passion that would overwhelm them both. I did not yet realise that the truth of the matter would be much more calculated and very different to how I imagined.

For the present though, Henry led me by the hand from his chamber into his adjacent privy closet, colloquially known as the 'kneeling place', a small, but sumptuously furnished room with carpets, cushions and a kneeling desk for the king to use for his private devotions. Under a royal blue cloth of estate embroidered in gold with the words *Dieu et Mon Droit* were placed two X-framed chairs upholstered in rich blue velvet, fitted with gilt nails and fringed with gold. These seats of authority were reserved only for the king and his consort, as I realised that Anne was already queen in all but name.

At the doorway, I turned to the Countess of Derby who carried my book of hours which I took from her as I noticed that a similar vellum-bound book, which belonged to the king, was already laid open upon the kneeling desk before us, a quill and ink pot resting beside it. Henry would often work on his private papers whilst listening to mass which was made possible by a wooden grill cut into the wall, which separated the king's oratory from the more public closet beyond where the king's chaplains would gather to celebrate the service.

I took my seat on the right side of the king; only Sir Henry Norris and the Countess of Derby accompanied us inside for the oratory was the most private of rooms and tiny in comparison with the king's other magnificent chambers. In the closet beyond the grill, Henry's private chaplain began the service in Latin. A sweet fragrance of incense gently wafted through the lattice fretwork evoking in me a sense of ritual and profound peace that was almost hypnotic. I opened my book of hours and began to thumb through its pages, stopping from time to time to read the religious texts or admire the beautiful illustrations contained therein. Henry was watching me intently and eventually spoke,

'Do you know that today marks a renaissance for England?' I looked across at the king and frowned at him quizzically, clear that I wished him to continue; 'Now the clergy have submitted to our will, and our brother King Francis aligns with us in a new treaty against our common enemy, the Emperor; and now that he has recognised you as my intended queen, you and I will soon be able to set aside all doubts and worries; and from the fruit of your womb we shall establish a new and legitimate Tudor dynasty.'

I swallowed hard but managed a smile at the enormity of expectation that was bearing down upon Anne—and me. Yet I did not have much time to think on it, for the king reached across and took from me the book which was lying open in my lap. Picking up the quill from his kneeling desk, Henry dipped it in the ink before flicking through the pages and finally coming to rest his hand beneath a sorrowful picture known as *The Flayed Christ*. I held my breath for I recognised the delicate illustration immediately; the last time that I had seen it, I stood behind a glass cabinet in the British Library. This delicate and opulent sixteenth century object had been on display in the exhibition celebrating the 500 years since Henry VIII ascended to the

English throne. It was the book that I had been looking at when I received a text from Daniel telling me that he had finally left his wife; it was the last thing that I saw before I had lost consciousness and found myself once again in Anne's world.

The image represented Henry's metaphor for a man who struggled with many sorrows, sorrows that he himself felt he had endured in order to reach this day. I knew in that moment, before it even happened, what Henry would do next and I knew the words that he was about to write. I sat in complete awe as I witnessed history written down before me, as the king scribed in French the following:

'If you remember my love in your prayers as strongly as I adore you, I shall hardly be forgotten, for I am yours. Henry R. Forever.'

Henry smiled at me, his face alight with love and adoration as he passed the book back into my hands. As I took it from him, I knew what I must do; I turned to the miniature of *The Annunciation*. It was a powerful message of the Angel Gabriel proclaiming to the Virgin Mary that she would have a son, the Saviour. Suddenly, I saw the symbolism that both Henry and Anne had used in this exchange. It struck me for the first time that whilst on the surface these were words of love and romance, at a deeper level, Henry and Anne were declaring a contract of faith. Henry had to endure great personal sacrifice and opposition to raise Anne to be his consort; the *quid pro quo* was that Anne must deliver her side of the bargain—a son and heir.

Despite these weighty thoughts that had already begun to quash the heady romanticism I brought back with me into the sixteenth century, I indicated to Henry, somewhat flirtatiously, that he should pass me the quill. Dipping it in the ink pot, I remembered well the iconic words that I must write in Anne's familiar hand:

'By daily proof you shall me find to be to you both loving and kind.'

How strange that history was being defined by events in the future. Henry, who had been leaning over me reading the words, grinned at me mischievously, before reaching for my hand and, for the second time, drawing it to his lips in appreciation of my gesture. As the priest moved on to the consecration, we knelt to cross ourselves and as I did so, I prayed more fervently than ever that this time things would be different for Anne. Yes, I still hoped that events would transpire to hold a different outcome; that she would, in time, give birth to a healthy, male child.

After the service, walking side-by-side, we shared our hopes and dreams for the day, for the new friendship between England and France and of our intended trip to Calais. As we moved from Henry's privy chamber through a succession of increasingly more intimate and private rooms, the general buzz of the court faded away, only gentlemen of the chamber were allowed to follow us into the heart of the king's inner sanctum. Eventually, in the presence of only a couple of the king's closest confidantes, Henry finally raised something that had clearly been on his mind,

'Anne…' The king paused, somewhat uncertain as to how to broach such a delicate subject, 'your father spoke to me yesterday of our imminent intention to marry. He urged that we should proceed with some caution; that there remain… difficulties…difficulties that are yet to be addressed which might seriously affect the validity of our union.' I stopped dead in my tracks, suddenly overwhelmed by a feeling of irritation that I could only guess reflected a long-running, deep frustration for Anne, borne out of a difference of opinion between father and daughter about her relationship with Henry; in particular, when and how it should be validated. Before, I had chance to alter the outcome, I sensed Anne's volatile intemperance surging to the fore, seizing hold of my being as she began to speak through me again; I found myself snapping at Henry in reply,

'Difficulties; if we waited for there to be no difficulties,' I heard myself emphasize the last word somewhat sarcastically, 'you and I would never be married!' Folding my arms defiantly in front of me, I paused before adding impatiently, 'To what "difficulties" does my father refer this time?'

Henry glanced towards Sir Henry Norris and my brother, who were the only two gentlemen remaining in attendance and who had followed us as far as the king's privy bedchamber. For a moment I saw irritation flash in his eyes. I wondered just how often had Anne reprimanded the king in front of others, undermining his fierce male pride and chipping away at the foundation of his tolerance for Anne. However, on this occasion the king's great love for her won the day; he retained control of his emotions and replied calmly,

'Anne, you know well that Archbishop Warham is dead and Thomas Cranmer is not yet back in the country, let alone consecrated as our new Archbishop of Canterbury. When Cromwell's Act of Appeals is passed, establishing our royal supremacy and breaking all judicial links with Rome, and when Cranmer is elected head of our church here in England, nothing will lie in our way.' Henry turned to gaze out the window across the Thames and the Berkshire countryside beyond. He paused, weighing up his words before continuing, 'Your father is right, we should do nothing that would upset the Vatican and interfere with Cranmer's appointment; we must dissemble and play our cards close to our chest.' Henry turned his head to look at me and sighed heavily. 'I have decided that we should postpone our marriage until the New Year when all will be well and you and I can finally be lawfully wed.' Henry came over to me, taking both my hands in his, imploring me to see sense with his searching gaze. However, in that moment, I felt something snap in Anne; the years of patience, perseverance and endless prevaricating finally taking their toll. I should have shown more humility, but the fire of Anne's temper had already taken hold; I snatched my hands ungratefully away from Henry, brushing him off as I began to speak boldly, quietly at first, yet with simmering rage,

'You want to postpone the wedding?' I shook my head as I looked away, unable to comprehend what must have seemed to Anne to be a cruel joke; the prize once again ripped away from her when it had been so nearly in her grasp. Then I cried aloud, entirely forgetting myself and the gentlemen present. 'No! I am sick of waiting. Can't you see that I have given up the best years of my life as a woman, waiting for you to be rid of Katherine! I could have been long married by now and have children of my own, which are the greatest consolation in this world a woman can have. But no! I have kept myself a maiden believing that you wanted this—you wanted this as I wanted it!' I turned away from Henry and speaking in increasingly fiery tones, pacing about, my left arm resting on my hip, my right swiping through the air in fury. I pushed on, emboldened by Anne's overwhelming indignation. 'But I see that I am deceived!' I swung about to face Henry as I continued my tirade, 'Do you not see how the Pope plays you and my father like puppets? Why do you still care what the Vicar of Rome thinks? I thought you had accepted that he had no jurisdiction within your

15

realm—that *you* are the supreme head of the church here in England? Please don't tell me do you still believe popish, superstitious nonsense, that somehow the Pope's displeasure can touch such a mighty king as yourself and that he has the power to damn your soul for all eternity?'

By this point, I was entirely lost in Anne's fevered tirade; it was if I was a bystander witnessing David setting forth to slay Goliath. However, what I said next was incredible for I could not have been more outrageous if I had stepped up to the king and slapped him in the face in front of the whole court. 'You and my father are supposed to be men of great courage, are you not?' I spat defiantly. 'So where is your courage now, for I do not see it?' I knew that in speaking these words Anne had purposely cut at the very heart of Henry's manhood and I saw him flinch from the blow.

I recognised a black thunder gather in Henry's eyes, his jaw clenching in growing anger. Yet even I was disbelieving of what happened next; for Henry's rage was no match for Anne's stormy, white hot fury. Suddenly, I blurted out, 'No! If this is how it is to be then I want no more of it! I see that you have been playing with me and that we will never be wed. Leave me alone, Henry; I am going back to Hever and I never want to see you again!' In that moment, I thought that I—and Anne—had rashly thrown away everything. As I turned about on my heels full of anger, fear and pride, I saw my brother's face as he stood by the door looking completely aghast at what he had witnessed me say to the king.

'Anne! Please don't go!' I was shocked to feel Henry grab hold of my arm and swing me about until he held me fiercely by the shoulders, his face betraying a confusing maelstrom of emotions: his own hurt pride, self-righteous anger and pure blinding fear; the latter—luckily for me, dominated them all. I realised that despite my outrageously bold accusations which would have seen better men than me thrown into the Tower, the king's fury was instantly diffused by my threat; that more than anything else, Henry was clearly gripped by an overwhelming sense of panic that he would lose his lady, his love, his hope and the one person in the world who treated him as an equal.

Holding me in his strong grip, the king briefly turned his attention to my brother and Sir Henry Norris who remained in silent attendance, shifting their weight uncomfortably and keeping their eyes downcast, clearly wishing they had been anywhere but there that day. Henry nodded curtly in their direction and dismissed them from the room. Gladly, both men made a swift exit, but as the door to the king's privy bedchamber opened momentarily so that they may pass, I could see a number of courtiers in the privy chamber beyond who stood silently, staring in our direction. I knew that in my temper, I had spoken more loudly than I meant, and that they had overheard much of what had passed between Henry and me.

I confess, that as my anger began to abate, I felt a little abashed at the ferocity of my outburst. I was, yet again, painfully aware of the sharpness of Anne's tongue when she was provoked. I knew that in so many ways, this would play such a significant part in her undoing and I longed to be able to mellow her nature, yet in my heart I knew she was a wild creature. It was the quality in her which Henry both loved and loathed in equal measure. Yet for the time being, his heart remained her captive slave and with the departure of both gentlemen, the king turned his full attention upon me as he said imploringly,

'Anne, sweetheart, I beg you to dispel your unreasonable thoughts. You know well that I am your only Henry and that above all things, I long to be yours just as much as you wish for the same. Yet lack of discreet handling of this matter at this late hour might undo all that we have worked for, for so many years.' Henry squeezed my shoulders just a little more tightly as if to emphasise the veracity of his words as he went on, 'you are a greater comfort to me than all the precious jewels in this world and I will, by God's word, make you my wife. But please, my love, you must trust me and your father for we both look to protect you and your good name so that there can be no question of the true legitimacy of our children.'

As the king finished speaking, I felt the deep sincerity of his words. My anger began to dissolve away and I felt the fight go out of my body; as I did so, I nodded my understanding. Henry let go of my shoulders, taking both my hands in his and bringing them to his lips where he held them; his face was only inches from mine, his eyes glistening with emotion. 'Are we perfect friends again, Anne?' I found it difficult to speak but I nodded again in affirmation. We placed our arms about each other, our faces pressed close, cheek to cheek as the king whispered tenderly, 'Good sweetheart, continue the same, not only in this, but in

17

all your doings hereafter; for thereby shall come, both to you and me, the greatest quietness that may be in this world.' We stayed there for what seemed like the longest time as our bodies melted one into the other and the deep longing that we both felt began to mend the tear I had made in the fabric of our relationship. After a few minutes, Henry spoke softly as he said, 'Come with me, my love, for I have something that I wish to show you.' Pulling away from me, he took me gently by the hand as we smiled tenderly at one another, desiring only to heal the other's pain, as the king led me through his bedchamber and into the most secret part of the king's lodging.

We moved deeper into the king's private chambers, to a wing of the castle built as an extension to the privy chambers at the turn of the sixteenth century by Henry's father, Henry VII. These new rooms, which consisted mainly of the king's study and private library, afforded a much greater degree of privacy away from public life. The Henry VII Tower, as it was known, had panoramic views to the north and to the inner courtyard to the south. Most importantly, it ran perpendicular to the queen's side; the two sets of apartments joined at the angle of the 'L' in another bedchamber; one which Henry would summon me to on many future occasions when he wished to make love to me. I knew well that all of Henry's great houses reflected a similar arrangement. Looking back, I remember how sensual I found it when we first started to share a bed; night after night I would be 'invited' to prepare myself for his majesty. Henry would come to me attired in his nightgown, which would soon be cast aside as we would fall passionately into bed, the outpouring of six years of longing, years of contained sexual tension driving an inexhaustible flow of erotic energy.

But on this occasion, as soon as the door to his private study was closed, Henry led me over to his desk, where a series of ornately carved coffers of various sizes and inlaid with gold, had been laid out side-by-side. 'These are for you,' said the king folding his arms in front of him, one arm bent up, his fingers stroking his closely trimmed, auburn beard. I knew he was toying with me. I must admit the boxes themselves were incredibly beautiful and I could not even begin to imagine what might lie within. I decided to play along with Henry's game; I knew he relished the role of generous benefactor and, in any case, I found it difficult to rein in my ever mounting curiosity. Already, the memory of our altercation was fading, as it always seemed to do for the king and me. The relationship between Anne and Henry was tempestuous, there was no doubt about that. Yet as intense and stormy as our arguments were, they were soon forgotten. If anything, the relief that we had weathered the storm drove us to a greater level of mutual tenderness and intimacy; it was as if such arguments reminded us both of what we stood to lose and the fragile beauty of our love.

This was one such moment of reconciliation; from behind my eyelashes, I played the dallying maid, abashed at the bounty and generosity of her lord. With a wry smile, Henry gestured to me to open them. I gently lifted the lid of the most ornate casket. I heard myself gasp, lightly touching the fingers of one hand close to my breast as if it might help me catch my stolen breath; one after another, I opened each box to find the most dazzling array of jewels. I had known many riches since my sojourn in Anne's world, but seeing these exquisite works of art all together was truly beyond my wildest dreams. I looked up at Henry who stood at the end of the table, his arms folded, smiling at me proudly, delighting in my reaction. I recognised all these pieces, for I had seen them worn before.

'Katherine's jewels?' I asked in an aporetic voice. Henry did not immediately reply, but picked up a splendid carcanet which lay on a white velvet cushion beside a matching bracelet. I did not count them, but I suspected that it had at least some eighteen tabled rubies set with a number of smaller diamonds and pearls. He placed it round my neck as he spoke,

'They are the queen's jewels and Katherine no longer has the right to keep them; they are yours now, my love.' With that, the king fastened the clasp behind my neck. Laying a hand on each of my shoulders, he leaned into me and slowly began to kiss my neck with sensual passion. I yielded immediately to the searching insistence of his touch and his kisses, more vulnerable than ever in the light of our recent row. Despite our persistent longing, we were both acutely aware that time was against us, and that within the hour, I must formally present myself to his majesty in front of the entire court to receive Anne's Letter's Patent as Marquess of Pembroke. Reluctantly, we separated as Henry ran his fingertip lightly down the side of my temple, my cheek and along the line of my long and graceful neck, before I melted once again into his arms. Oh, that strong and generous embrace in which I had longed to lose myself for so many months! As I drank in the warm and familiar lavender and orange flower fragrance of his skin and clothes, he spoke again, 'I want you to wear these today, Anne. I want the entire court to know that very soon you will be Queen of England.'

'Queen of England.' I had always wondered what it must be like to be exalted to such dizzying heights. In Anne's world, the king and his consort were divinely anointed as God's representatives on earth; as queen, Anne would have enormous influence politically, socially, and most powerfully of all, in religious affairs. I had always sensed Anne's strong engagement with her own destiny; an upbringing by the side of queens and princes, and a fierce political acumen that had long prepared her for this role. In that moment, I felt no fear, only Anne's enormous pride and determination to fulfil her duty and fulfil the destiny to which she had been born.

Upon returning to my chambers, it did not take my ladies very long to make the final preparations in my attire and appearance for the ceremony which lay ahead of me. Already dressed in my exquisite crimson gown and adorned with the magnificent carcanet that had been placed about me by the king, my ladies brushed my lustrous chestnut hair so that it flowed freely in a cascade of gentle curls across my shoulders and down my back. I was to leave my head bare, for the king would soon place upon it the coronet of my peerage. Before I left my bedchamber, I cast a final glance at Anne's reflection; she was a truly dazzling sight bedecked from head to foot in a glittering array of precious jewels. Unfortunately, I could not fail to notice the rather po-faced Lady Boleyn who stood in attendance at the doorway of my chamber, as she stared disapprovingly at the jewels displayed so resplendently around my neck. I brushed her mean-spiritedness from my mind, determined that Anne would enjoy the day she had waited so long to see. I knew the enormous emotional toll such waiting must have exacted on her; for her pain, in so many ways, had also been mine with Daniel.

Just before 10.15 am, I left my privy apartments in solemn procession led by Thomas Wriothesley, Garter King-at-Arms. Behind me came Lady Mary Howard who was already in Anne's service, despite her tender age of fourteen. As Anne's younger cousin, I knew that Mary's future would see her married to Henry's illegitimate son, Henry Fitzroy; and in time, she would also be elevated to occupy the position of one of the leading ladies of the land as Duchess of Richmond.

There was no doubt that this noblewoman had been graced with a perfectly proportioned oval face, delicate features and dazzling grey-green eyes. In a short space of time, I became very fond of Lady Mary; she was the antithesis of her mother, who was a long-term friend and staunch supporter of Katherine, and who made her distaste of Anne perfectly clear. The Duchess of Norfolk was a woman much embittered by the blows she felt fate had unfairly dealt her. Her father, the third Duke of Buckingham, was beheaded by Henry for treason in 1521, and she had found herself trapped in a loveless, and some said occasionally violent, relationship with my uncle. The duchess was one of those people who constantly seemed to be at war with the world, and whilst I knew Elizabeth Howard's approval of Anne's status was important, I declare that I liked her not. Yet somehow, miraculously, the diminutive Lady Mary had managed to develop a sweet temperance, entirely at odds with that of either of her acerbic parents. I would also learn that, around Anne, her cousin would develop a strong inclination towards the reformed faith. In the many months ahead, Lady Mary would often gladly read from the bible to me, and together we would discuss important matters of theology. It would be a sweet friendship and in many ways, I would always feel very maternal toward her.

As I walked, I sensed the kindly presence of this young child behind me, carrying the coronet of Anne's marquisate on a crimson, velvet cushion. Following Lady Mary were the Countesses of Derby and Rutland, who between them, carried the twelve foot long crimson velvet mantle, trimmed with ermine that would be placed around my shoulders. Perhaps I should have been more circumspect, knowing so well the trying circumstances which still lay ahead. As our procession left my privy chambers at Windsor Castle, I sensed Anne's delight and sheer exhilaration in her moment of glory.

Full of regal dignity, our party made its way along the thirty metre long queen's presence chamber past lower members of court, who would not be permitted into the king's presence chamber to witness the ceremony, doffing caps, making curtsies and bows in deference to lady Anne. Once outside the presence chamber, we turned left walking half way along the even grander watching chamber before taking a doorway on the right which led along a light and airy gallery. It was at this very point approximately four years ago that I had encountered Katherine on her way to chapel. It was here that we faced each other for the last time in a most bitter and cutting exchange. It seemed incredible to me that I witnessed it; that Katherine had long been banished from court, and in the intervening time, Anne had become the premier lady in the land in all but name.

With my eyes fixed steadfastly on the back of Thomas Wriothesley, the Garter King-at-Arms, led us down this long corridor until we entered into the king's great watching chamber. With much swishing of skirts and petticoats, we swung left and walked along the entire length of this imposing hall, which was hung with a series of priceless tapestries and dwarfing even the mighty yeoman guards who were positioned along our processional route.

As we approached the heavy, gilded, oak doors which led into the king's presence chamber, I could hear the excited buzz of an expectant court and knew that with the exception of Anne's most implacable enemies, all who held sufficient status would be gathered within. Even for them, this was history in the making, and their appetite for gossip was insatiable. This young girl, who had returned from France at the age of twenty, had within six years, risen from obscurity on the back of her own wit and graces to steal the heart of a mighty prince, seizing the coveted position at his right hand side. In the process, she caused the country to be turned upside down. As I stood just out of sight of the gathered crowd, awaiting my announcement, I felt immensely proud of my heroine, for she was a self-made woman; no man had brought about this astonishing elevation, not even her father. At best, he may have introduced Anne to court and supported her relationship with Henry, but Anne was far too astute to be only a pawn in such games. I believed that history's tendency to see Anne's father as the cause of her rise— and fall—was to do great discredit to her own shrewd intelligence and ambition, and in particular, her strong sense of destiny. Thomas Wriothesley stepped forward to announce the arrival of Lady Anne Rochford to the king and all those gathered, as we glided into his presence with great dignity and grace.

For the most fleeting of moments, I experienced a series of flashbacks; to my standing in what was left of this chamber at Windsor Castle in my modern day life. I was drawn here during my days of mourning for my lost life. Tracing Anne's steps as well as I was able, when I had arrived at Windsor one gloomy spring morning—only to be engulfed in an enormous throng of tourists at the castle gate. But I quickly slipped through the crowds as I knew exactly where to go. Moving swiftly from room to room, ignoring all the later, gaudy renovations, I soon found myself alone in the garter throne room—as Henry's presence chamber came to be known. Most visitors gave this room little time, blissfully ignorant of the great events that had transpired here. When I found myself alone that day, I recalled the great banquet that Henry held for me in 1528; the echoes of laughter and music filling my mind as I saw us dancing and making merry; I felt a certain sadness at how we had spent our joy, carelessly, as if it would last a lifetime. Although I was yet to experience it, I had also envisioned Anne's auspicious day; for I knew that in this very room, nearly 500 years earlier, she had been created the Lady Marquess of Pembroke, the turning point in her story with Henry.

And so I found myself there, on that very same day, as I had imagined. The scene was much changed for the chamber was packed to capacity; a sea of eager faces craned their necks to get a first glimpse of Anne in her brilliant ascendency. As I entered the room, the sun fortuitously broke through the clouds outside, flooding the dull interior with golden sunlight. I wondered if this sudden illumination would be taken to be a felicitous sign to those who saw Anne as the bringer of light, appointed by God to establish the true gospel in England. Whether this was the case or no, I was making an impact with my appearance, for I heard several people gasp; I literally lit up in a dazzling spectacle of refracted light from the multitude of jewels which adorned me.

As we made our way toward the king, I recognised many of the English nobility, all elegantly dressed in their ceremonial clothes. Yet of all the people present, I craved above all others to see only one, my beloved mother, the only mother I have ever known. As I approached the dais, I finally caught sight of her. Standing at the front of the assembled throng, I saw her radiant face light up with a beaming smile that silently spoke of her enormous pride in her younger daughter. Although I felt I must maintain a solemn dignity, I tried to convey through the light in my own eyes my love for her, and my deep appreciation at her constancy and devotion. I was also somewhat surprised and delighted to see by her side, my elder sister, Mary. She looked flushed with excitement, ever the voluptuous English rose. I wanted so much to rush over and scoop them both up in my arms, but of course I could not.

Reaching the foot of the dais, Thomas Wriothesley bowed low to the king, who was flanked on either side by the Dukes of Norfolk and Suffolk, neither of whom I was particularly delighted to see, nor had either man changed much since I last saw them. Keeping pace with the king, Charles Brandon too had gained just a little weight and a few extra grey hairs in his beard and hair; my Uncle Norfolk appeared increasingly gaunt and hawkish. My father stood to the fore of a small group of leading noblemen to the left of the canopy of estate, next to the man I would come to know as Giles de La Pommeraye, the French ambassador.

Having bowed to the king, Master Wriothesley stepped aside, leaving me standing in front of Henry, who had not taken his eyes off me since I entered the room. I came forward to kneel upon a large, blue velvet cushion, embroidered and fringed with gold, placed on the floor in front of me. With my eyes downcast, I slowly raised my head and found Henry towering above me in awesome majesty. With his throne behind him, the king was framed by a rich blue velvet canopy, one of the finest, most richly embroidered pieces of fabric that I had seen in the castle. It had been worked intricately with gold thread, wrought into a pattern of twisting vine leaves and edged with a border of geometric design; just above the throne, was the royal coat-of-arms: a red Welsh dragon and white greyhound supporting the royal shield of England, itself quartered into a pattern of a golden fleur-de-lis and English lions. The shield was surmounted by a gold crown with the letters HR VIII worked in gold thread.

Although surrounded by the entire court, Henry and I only had eyes for each other, and throughout the whole ceremony, we remained locked in a delicious intensity, full of hope and expectation. I was vaguely aware of Master Wriothesley stepping forward once more and handing my letters patent to a man that I had come to know well, Stephen Gardiner, who had since been elevated to his bishopric. I was unsure of this gentleman when I first met him at Hever Castle, my intuition warning me that he was a man not to be trusted. Subsequently, when I returned to my modern day life, I had the opportunity to read all about him and found that my instincts had been correct. Bishop Gardiner was indeed a man who set his sails according to the direction in which the wind was blowing. He had already shown himself to be a turncoat in the matter of Henry's divorce from Katherine, first supporting the king and then swinging behind Katherine, only to realise that he was foolishly on the losing side. Luckily for him, Stephen Gardiner managed to salvage some shards of trust from the wreckage of his disloyalty. Henry took him back into royal service, but I knew that he would never trust his servant in the same way again. I was also painfully aware of the bishop's true devotion to the Roman Catholic faith, and on that account alone, he was never a real friend to Anne.

In a deep, clear voice, he began to read aloud the patents which conferred upon Anne and her offspring the title of Marquess of Pembroke, in her own right. It took just a few minutes, and when that part of the ceremony was completed, Henry stepped forward, coming down from his dais and extending his hand toward me. I took the king's hand as he raised me to my feet, indicating with the other that Dorothy, Countess of Derby, and Eleanor, Countess of Rutland should step forward with the ermine trimmed mantle. Breaking our steadfast gaze for the first time, the king took it from them, before unfolding its heavy folds and resting it about my shoulders. With a nod from Henry, Lady Mary then came forward and the king took the gold coronet between his hands, and with great reverence placed it upon my head. In full view of the entire court, the king leaned forward and kissed me gently on the lips, sealing once and for all, Anne's exalted position at court.

As he stood back, I felt the full weightiness of Henry's expectation bear down upon me. I saw the fierce pride shining from his eyes. Yet, I also truly understood how naive I had been in my initial excitement and exuberance of seeing him again. For when I had fallen unconscious and travelled back to my modern day life, my love for Henry had been frozen in time. We were at the height of our romance, carefree and with few expectations. I entirely failed to understand that in my absence, a full four years had passed for Henry and Anne in their world. Anne and her faction had brought down a man that the king once loved well, Cardinal Wolsey. Together they had faced the full wrath of the Holy Roman Catholic Church, the indignation and resistance of the English clergy, the disapproval of many of Henry's leading nobles, and of course the stubborn martyrdom of Katherine, who had ceaselessly picked away at Henry's conscience. The king faced them all with his usual might and resolution. However, all these events came at a cost, and although Henry entered willingly into them in the pursuit of his love and of a legitimate male heir, I realised that an unspoken debt had been mounting up at Anne's door. I also saw that nothing was ever unconditional for Henry; the king would now expect all the debt to be repaid—in full. Chillingly, I would have to pay for it with my blood.

After the ceremony, I thanked the king in a clear and strong voice for all to hear, and in a fanfare of trumpets, I made my way back to my chambers, whilst the king processed to St George's Chapel at the side of Giles de la Pommeraye, his honoured guest. They were followed by much of the court, all of whom were eager to play their part and bear witness to the rest of the day's spectacle.

Back in the privacy of my bedchamber, Margery and Elizabeth Wood were helping me take off my ceremonial robes and coronet when there was a knock at my door and my mother entered followed by my sister, Mary. Both were full of smiles. I was overjoyed to see them, finally able to throw my arms about them both and smother them in my love. When I at last released them, I sat myself down on a nearby stool. Margery began to work on my hair, which was worn up under a gabled hood, adorned with eighteen brilliant diamonds, for the great banquet which was to follow. Lady Boleyn stood close by, assisting Margery when necessary, whilst I indicated for my mother to draw up a stool and sit next to me. I could not help but notice that she had aged visibly since I last saw her, and I worried for her health. In contrast, Mary, as ever, was full of ebullient energy, dancing playfully around the room to the sound of imaginary music; she was clearly excited about the celebrations to come—dancing with gallant gentlemen. As she practised her steps, she was the first to speak,

'Oh Anne, it was marvellous, wasn't it?' I realised it was more of a statement than a question. 'You looked amazing. Did you see the king? He could not take his eyes off you!' Then she stopped for a moment 'But what about the Duke of Suffolk; did you see the look on his face when his majesty kissed you in front of the entire court?' I did not, so I looked at Mary with my eyebrows raised, for I was now immensely curious.

After Wolsey was brought down in 1530, I was aware that my Lord of Suffolk saw no further merit in the ascendency of the Boleyn faction. He resented my pre-eminence and influence with the king and crucially, we shared no common ground in matters of religion. So, the temporary alliance with Charles Brandon had rapidly deteriorated, and by 1532, I knew that he bore Anne—now the Lady Marquess—no good will. I could only imagine how the king would have insisted on Charles' presence that morning, and that the duke would have complied with great reluctance. My sister, however, was in full flow 'But really, who does he think he is? I have never known such pomposity...and hypocrisy...I mean just look at how he carried on with the king's sister in France; they were all over each other and made little attempt to hide it!' She leaned her body and cheek against the nearby bedpost, idly tracing the pattern of honeysuckle and acorns with her finger as she continued, 'Well, at least the Duchess of Suffolk wasn't here, she hates us all so much she would have probably had one of her infamous tantrums and stormed out!'

Before my mother could stop her, Mary launched into one of her very funny impressions—for which she had a talent. She began mincing around the room, her nose stuck up in the air, clearly imitating Mary Tudor's imperious manner and notoriously foul language. Margery and I both collapsed in peals of laughter, tears soon streaming down our faces at my sister's outrageous parody. As the matriarch of the family, my mother clearly felt it was her responsibility to conduct herself in a dignified manner, although I noticed that even she was chuckling, hiding herself behind her clasped hands, which she had brought up to her face to cover her mouth. Finally, she spoke,

'Oh Mary, you must stop!' I sensed this was more from a deeply ingrained sense of propriety rather than a genuine desire for my sister to desist; for in truth, I suspected that the relationship between Anne's mother and the duchess was far from congenial. I knew that being fiercely protective of her children, Elizabeth Boleyn would not have appreciated Mary Tudor's intransigence; she felt much aggrieved by the obvious snub toward her youngest daughter—as Mary Tudor continued to refuse to attend court in Anne's presence, or yield her position as first lady of the land.

As our laughter died down and we wiped away our tears, I noticed that Lady Boleyn remained unmoved, staring at us with surly disapproval. Mary, too, must have noticed for suddenly, she piped up,

'Aunt Elizabeth, what vexes you so? Why, you look as if you've been sucking on sour lemons!'

'Mary!' exclaimed my mother who was not prepared to tolerate such rudeness, even if, in my opinion, the comment was much deserved. For a moment, my mother glared at Mary with stern disapproval, before she turned her face toward her sister-in-law and said kindly, 'Elizabeth, why don't you and Margery see that Anne's ceremonial robes and coronet are conveyed to her wardrobe for safekeeping.' Lady Boleyn looked much aggrieved, but before she had chance to retort, Margery nodded, indicating to Lady Boleyn that she should follow her. The two ladies gathered up my robes and coronet and left the room. When the door to my bedchamber closed gently behind them, my mother spoke again, this time addressing both of us in a solemn voice,

'Mary, Anne,' she said looking at each of us in turn, 'I know your aunt is a difficult character; she has neither your looks, nor your grace or wit, and I fear for that she harbours a spiteful jealousy in her breast. You must realise that both of you have all these qualities in abundance and that these bring you many admirers. You in particular, Anne,' she turned towards me nodding her head emphatically as if to emphasise the point, 'are gaining great power and status; something that I fear your aunt craves but alas, will never have. Yet unfortunately, Elizabeth Wood has neither the humility, nor the good grace to accept her place in life. Nevertheless you should be kind to her. Let me say this to you child,' my mother directed her words solely toward me, 'your great fortune is a blessing, but you should well know that until you bear the king a legitimate son, your position will never be safe. There will always be those about the court who will envy all that you have and try and take it from you. Mark my words, sometimes the bitterest enemies arise as serpents from within one's own nest.'

We lived in a man's world, but my mother was no fool. Being a Howard girl, she understood only too well what men—and women—would do for their hour of glory. It was a chilling reminder, and I resolved yet again to check my temper and to extend kindness to those who may otherwise seek to destroy me. Yet, for someone like Anne, who valued loyalty very highly, such an undertaking would be an almost impossible task. I confess, to my own detriment—and Anne's—in the months ahead, I would often fail in my endeavour.

Chapter Two

Greenwich Palace,
4 October 1532

As September progressed, summer's golden mantle gradually ceded to the earthy tones of autumn. During the day, the land remained bathed in the gentle warmth of an Indian summer, which was pleasant to all. It also gave cause for rejoicing, for not only had the harvest been excellent, but such calm weather would make our crossing to Calais all the safer. For that I was exceptionally glad as I suffered terribly from sea-sickness in my modern day life, and prayed to God that Anne was made of sterner stuff.

Thus, on the morning of Friday, 4 October, St Francis' Day, a cavalcade of over 2,000 courtiers finally set forth from Greenwich Palace. Henry had decreed that the 300-strong royal party should travel separately to the main body of the court; ever fearful of disease, the king wished to avoid the plague which had lately sprung up in cities such as Rochester. Thus, we would first travel by barge to Gravesend, then by ship onto the Isle of Sheppey, before travelling overland via Canterbury and onwards to Dover.

Whilst awaiting our departure, I watched the main cavalcade begin its journey from the south-facing windows of the queen's privy apartments. It passed out through the gatehouse on the south side of the palace precinct and snaked its way up Castle Hill, there to join the main London to Dover road. It was a truly magnificent sight, so many ladies and gentlemen of Henry's court bedecked in rich fabrics, furs and a dazzling array of jewels. The procession was flanked at intervals by Henry's yeomen of the guard, so distinctive in their vibrant red, gold and black livery. Each one carried a halberd at his side, and from time to time, the early morning light would catch the steel edge of its axe-shaped head, casting from it a flash of brilliant white light. Thus, the whole procession shimmered like a rivulet of water, which stretched as far as the eye could see. I had never beheld the like of it before; the spectacle of an entire Tudor court on progress was an awesome sight.

Presently, we too were on the move. Having been summoned by the king, I left my chambers accompanied by my thirty or so ladies, who had been appointed to attend on me during the Calais trip, and made our way through the palace toward the privy stair. There, our barge waited to take us on the first leg of our journey. By that time, I was much used to travelling in this manner, and I understood why those who could afford it preferred this mode of transport. There was nothing more delightful or comfortable than travelling in a sumptuously furnished barge as it glided along the shimmering surface of the Thames. It was endlessly fascinating to watch the many fine sights of Tudor England slip silently by; or at other times, to be entertained by Anne's fool, or serenaded by a minstrel, who would amuse us all by playing well the game of courtly love.

As I arrived that morning at the steps of the Water Gate, there was a good deal of commotion; a whole flotilla of barges was required to convey the three hundred-strong party on its way. The air was filled with shouts as the boats were directed one by one to manoeuvre into position and collect their prestigious passengers. It did not escape my notice that on this occasion, the king had placed the queen's barge at my disposal. With my heart almost bursting with pride, I took my place under a canopy of arras and cloth of gold, whilst I was followed on board by a number of my ladies, including: Margery, Nan, Viscountess Rochford, my sister and the Countesses of Rutland and Sussex.

Soon, we were cast off from the shore as our oarsmen quickly slipped into a steady and hypnotic rhythm. Just ahead of us, the king's barge led the flotilla eastwards along the Thames with royal standard fluttering in the gentle breeze, and the sound of the wind snatched greedily at the heavily embroidered fabric. I lifted my chin taking in a deep breath of clear, fresh air, relishing the chill of that glorious autumn morning, the river breeze pinching at my cheeks with her icy fingers. I was filled with a sense of vibrancy and anticipation at the enormous adventure which lay ahead as, for the first time, Anne was stepping onto the international stage as Henry's consort, in all but name.

We made progress at a steady pace, dictated by a drummer aboard a nearby barge, whose distant beat floated across the surface of the water compelling the whole procession to move as one living, breathing entity. Once underway, a young gentleman—probably no more than twenty years old—stepped forward. He held in his right hand a fine looking lute and making a gracious bow, he introduced himself,

'My Lady Marquess, I have been sent thither from his most gracious majesty to entertain you and your ladies on your journey with sweet song and gentle music.' My ladies giggled, for there was no doubt that this man had a handsome face and an unusual, magnetic aura of playful sexuality. I was amused and realised that I had not seen him before. Yet my ladies seemed to know this man well, for they were relaxed and at ease in his company. I sensed that Anne also knew him, but I had not yet seen him at court over the previous few weeks and I wondered why. Never the shy or retiring type, Margery spoke up, and in doing so, revealed the identity of this mysterious courtier.

'Why Master Smeaton you have returned from the country; 'tis a good thing for we have missed your dulcet tones and sweet music.' I gasped inaudibly for this revelation had caught me by surprise. So this was Mark Smeaton, another of the unfortunate men who history foretold would die for Anne on the scaffold. I knew he had shamefully confessed to adultery with the queen, and yet in all the time that I had known Anne's story, I had never been able to blame him. For under torture, how could one judge a man who was in terror for his life? Who knew what treachery or bribery had been used against him to extract his confession. Had Cromwell and his cronies promised him a quick, clean death by the axe instead of the barbaric hanging, drawing and quartering that befitted his low status? Had this prized the confession from a young man who had no powerful family to protect him?

What I do remember most about Mark from that first meeting though was his smooth, velvety voice and chocolate brown eyes which, despite his lowly birth, burned with boldness and dreamy romanticism. He cast a glance at Nan, who was sitting close by me, chuckling in a fit of girlish giggles, much flushed by the brazenness of this dashing gentleman. He winked at her flirtatiously, and I watched as my friend's pale complexion blushed scarlet in response to his coquettish behaviour. I felt somewhat abashed, as I realised that I too had been stirred by his maleness. I saw immediately that although Anne and Mark were a world apart in terms of their position in life, they shared the same impish spirit and enticing sexuality. They both exuded fiery passion and communicated it in the language of emotion and of the heart. I understood the dangerous chemistry that might exist between the two of them, chemistry that could be so fatally misconstrued by those men of logic, or by those who simply sought to use it brutally against them.

I raised an eyebrow and sat back in my seat, tilting my head to the side, as I appraised this rather cocky young man full of devilish charm. He grinned back at me and building upon my newfound knowledge, I eventually asked him,

'And so you think to join us and accompany us to Calais?' There was playful challenge in my voice.

'Oh no, my Lady; I am bound wholly unto his grace who has presently conferred upon me the position of groom in his grace's privy chamber.' He went on, adding mischievously, 'I begged his majesty to desist from sending me to entertain you ladies. He looked about with an elfish spirit, before going on, 'Yet alas, Madame, I see that it is a burden which I must bear.' With that he clasped his free hand against his heart in a dramatic gesture which feigned great melancholy. It was clear that Master Smeaton delighted in female company, and revelled in being the old fashioned troubadour and the centre of attention.

'Then you must play and sing for us, Mark. For it is as Margery has said, we have missed your fine talents.' I teased him, indicating with a playful flick of my wrist that he should commence. Mark dutifully sat down and, taking the lute in his hands, began to create the most exquisite melodies. He had an extraordinarily fine singing voice and considerable musical ability, yet, he also had a wicked sense of humour, and how we laughed! He spent much of the twenty mile journey spontaneously creating new verses to well known songs in honour of each of my ladies, verses which both flattered and teased them mercilessly. Oftentimes, this caused the lady in question to lower her head coyly, or blush furiously, whilst her companions collapsed in delicate gales of laughter.

Eventually, it was my turn, and I sat back in my seat staring Mark straight in the eye, daring him to play his game with me. Mark paused, lifting his eyes heavenwards as if to seek inspiration. Suddenly, his face was alight, clearly pleased with himself that he had found the perfect tribute. Yet when he sang, it was a sonnet whose words were familiar to me and unlike those of my companions, I had heard it before:

'What word is that that changeth not,

33

Though it be turned and made in twain?
It is mine answer, God it wot,
And eke the causer of my pain.
It love rewardeth with disdain:
Yet is it loved. What would ye more?
It is my health eke and my sore.'

For a second time, Master Smeaton managed to take my breath away, for he had sung for me a famous poem that I knew had been written by Tom Wyatt. In my modern day life, historians had much debated the answer to this riddle which was of course: ANNA. Had Thomas penned this epigram in honour of the woman whom he had loved so entirely and who had rejected his advances? It was obvious that my ladies also knew of Thomas's great affection and unrequited love, as they began to giggle, although somewhat nervously. I mused that if a lowly court musician knew of this infatuation for Anne, then it was not difficult to understand how, when the axe finally fell in the catastrophic events of May 1536, that Thomas Wyatt too would be sucked dangerously close to the vortex of the collapsing Boleyn faction.

Somewhat perturbed by these thoughts, I was pleased to reach the end of our river journey. The whole court had transferred to a cavalcade of horses, which had been brought ahead from the stables at Greenwich, and now awaited us on the banks of the Thames. I was delighted to be riding Starlight once again. She was a vision of magnificence, dressed in her trappings of black velvet, fringed with gold. Together, we must have looked an impressive sight, for I had chosen an exquisite black velvet gown which was studded about the bodice and sleeves with hundreds of precious pearls and a shimmering kirtle of cloth of gold beneath my skirts. The false sleeves were full, edged with gold thread work, and clasped together along their length by aiglets, also made of gold and studded with precious diamonds. Similarly, the edge of my low, square-cut bodice, skirt and French hood were fashioned in the same rich and decorative style; clusters of precious pearls mounted between gold links, each one set with a single square-cut diamond.

With the queen's jewels at my disposal, I had hundreds of priceless items to choose from. In the end, I selected a heavy carcanet to hang about my neck and an eye-catching brooch that Nan had pinned to the front of my bodice. A multitude of rings and a rich girdle of gold finished the outfit. I fully intended that Anne's distinguished status would be clear to all whose eyes fell upon 'the Lady Marquess'.

Starlight moved along easily with her usual smooth and ambling gait, lulling me with her steady rhythm, giving me a chance to reflect on all that had happened over the previous few weeks.

I had arrived back in Anne's world in the midst of a whirl-wind of triumphant celebration. It was clear that after a long period of stalemate in which Anne and Henry had battled to find a way through the religious and canonical complexities of divorcing Katherine, events were now moving at a breathtaking pace. I had lost myself in Anne with frightening speed, picking up from where I had left off, and greatly relieved that no one seemed to notice any change in her.

For the first few days, I was so utterly delighted to find myself again in the midst of the glittering Tudor court that I had shamefully paid little thought to my twenty-first century life. I had not reflected on Daniel's last message; nor was I overly concerned about what might have caused me to lose consciousness and pass across the horizon that seemed to separate this world from the other. Had another aneurysm burst? Had this been a fit as I had been warned to expect? Was I even still alive? I had no answers to these questions, nor was I inclined to dwell upon them. In truth, I relished being reunited with my family and friends, and had since spent many a happy hour in their goodly company, walking in the privy gardens, dancing, singing, gambling, playing archery and of course, hunting.

As we made our way along, I mused on how much had changed for my friends since I was last in Anne's world. Within my closest circle of confidantes, I knew from my reading that Margery was widowed in 1530, and the following year remarried Sir Anthony Lee of Quarrendon, thus becoming Lady Lee. I was soon to realise that my loyal friend was also pregnant once again, as she had begun to let out the laces of her gown. Thus in the autumn of 1532, Margery was awaiting the birth of her seventh child, due early the following spring.

The family of the beautiful and intelligent Joan Champernowe had also grown since I had last seen her. Following the birth of Honora in 1526, there were two more little girls; Anne born in 1528, who she christened as my namesake, and Mary born just two years later, in 1530. Sadly, I was never to see Mary Fiennes, Lady Norris, again. As I had poured over my history books in the twenty-first century, tracking down the fate of all those who I had come to know and love, tears rolled down my cheeks when I read that Mary died in 1530, aged thirty-six. She and Sir Henry Norris had had four children: William, Edward, Henry and Mary, who were now motherless. I was already missing Mary's sweet presence and I knew I was not alone, for I had seen sadness in Sir Henry's eyes that I had not known when I had last been in his company. It did not surprise me as he was a loyal and committed husband and father who had ever loved his gentle wife.

With Anne's elevation, it was clear that she had developed a new and expanded sphere of influence at court. Many ladies and gentlemen, particularly those of the reformed faith, were quickly drawn into the ever widening circle of her friends and clients. Of course, a good number of those who found an allegiance with Anne, and the Boleyn faction, were related to her through marriage or blood; indeed, I never failed to be amazed at the complex web of linkages which existed in every nook and cranny of life at the Henrician court.

After alighting on the banks of the Thames, we made our way from the little town of Gravesend toward Stone Place, and the home of Bridget Wiltshire, Lady Tyrwhitt. When I had arrived back in Anne's world in September of that year, I learned that Lady Bridget had been widowed for a second time in August, 1532. I often overheard my ladies gossiping about how soon after her husband's death, Bridget had so quickly fallen head-long in love with another gentleman of the court, Sir Robert Tyrwhitt. For a short time, it was the scandal of the court as many had commented on the unseemly speed of the relationship. Whilst her late husband's body hardly had time to turn cold within his grave, just a few short weeks later, Lady Bridget and Sir Robert were married.

I knew Bridget's second husband Sir Nicolas Harvey well as he had been much about court when I had last walked in Anne's shoes. Sir Nicolas was a true and honest man, who had long been in the service of the king, and proved that he was not only a faithful servant, but a strong partisan of reform—and of Anne. As a result, the king's grace had shown him a great deal of favour, and Bridget and Sir Nicolas had fitted easily into the Boleyn's expanding circle of supporters. But with Sir Nicolas dead, I was anxious about meeting Sir Robert. I inferred from my ladies' gossip that he was great friends with my Lord of Suffolk, and by implication, it was unlikely that he would be any friend of mine.

As the royal party pulled up outside the fine Tudor mansion known as Stone Place, we were greeted by Lady Bridget, who stood placidly by the side of her new husband. Although Stone Place had been inherited by Bridget when her father had died some five years earlier, Sir Robert had clearly already claimed his matrimonial right as head of the household and so led the greeting of the king with great effusion. However, I could not fail to notice that his reception of me was both cursory and stilted; how quickly he had turned his attention back to the king. And whilst I had been prepared for Sir Robert's perfunctory salutation, I was far from expecting Lady Bridget's frosty acknowledgement. As I made to hug my friend, she brusquely avoided my embrace, instead dipping into a formal curtsy as she inclined her head, before stepping aside and indicating that I should follow the king and her husband, both of whom who were already walking ahead together, toward the great hall.

I confess that I was deeply confused, for I did not know what I—or Anne—had done to deserve her obvious displeasure. I knew that it was not the time to enquire, surrounded as we were by so many persons of the court, several of whom would be eager to see and hear of my discomfort. So, I made toward Henry, who was in hearty discussion and laughter with Sir Robert and the Duke of Suffolk. As I approached, I watched the latter two men embrace lustily, as long lost friends. Then, for a split second, as Sir Robert pulled away, he cast a glance in my direction. His glance was full of disdain and confirmed in an instant all that I had feared; that behind the hospitable veneer, he hated all that I stood for, and that he would forever be my implacable enemy.

After the initial greetings were completed, the king, Sir Robert and a number of Henry's closest friends of the privy chamber retired to the principal parlour to discuss business and matters of state. This gave me precious time alone with Lady Bridget, and soon we found ourselves walking side-by-side in the long gallery and through its windows, I watched as the last of the afternoon sunlight faded rapidly, casting long shadows across the floor of the chamber. Several of my ladies remained close by in attendance, yet I wanted privacy with Bridget. I gestured to them indicating that they should remain at a discreet distance. Margery was amongst them and, of course, being close Kentish neighbours, she knew Lady Bridget well. I noticed how she eyed our friend cautiously. I suspected that she also felt that something was amiss, and ever protective of me, I could make out traces of anxiety etched across her forehead. Once we had found our own space, I stood still for a moment then turning to face my friend I asked gently,

'Bridget, I am sorry for the loss of Sir Nicolas,' then I added generously, even though I did not feel it, 'Yet I see that you have made a good match in Sir Robert. I must congratulate you.'

'Thank you, Madame. Robert is a good and honest man.' My friend's reply was tense and reserved as she looked at me with a hint of unfathomable haughtiness about her.

'Oh come now, Bridget…what is the matter… is something wrong? Have I offended you in some way that I do not understand?' After much consideration, Lady Bridget finally spoke again,

'I think that it is improper that the queen and the princess should be handled so cruelly.' She looked at me defiantly, knowing all too well the implication that she was making. At first, I had laughed aloud, for I thought this was a joke. When I had last known her as Sir Nicolas's wife, she had often been the first to speak abrasively about the Spanish queen and her proud, defiant daughter.

'Oh, Lady Bridget!' was all I managed to say through my laughter. If it wasn't for the seriousness on her face, I would have sworn that she was teasing me. Yet Bridget continued to stare at me impassively, and I knew at that moment that she was deadly serious. My laughter quickly died away, as I realised my error and with similar gravity, I asked, 'Since when have you cared for Katherine or the Princess Mary?' Bridget did not reply, but rather lifted her chin audaciously in mutinous challenge. Suddenly, I understood all.

'Ah! Now I see.' I folded my arms in front of me and sensed a dangerous and gathering storm. In effect, Lady Bridget had boldly challenged Anne's morals, virtue and dignity. The message was clear, that she had no right to be at the king's side; she had risen above her station and taken—against God's laws—a husband from his wife, a father from his daughter. I had tried to be gracious to my friend in the face of a chilly, if not outright hostile, welcome, but suddenly, I felt something snap inside me. It was always the point of no return when

38

Anne's infamous temper was suddenly unleashed, and this storm broke with fury. 'I see that this is all about Sir Robert, is it not?' I did not wait for a reply. 'It is clear that your husband is no friend of mine and has shamefully poisoned your own mind against me; I, who has ever been a loyal and true friend unto you. But let me remind you, Madame,' in my anger, all congeniality was lost and I addressed my friend in the most formal manner, 'that if he is no friend of mine, then he is no friend of the king's grace. I would advise your husband to tread very carefully for...' I moved one step closer to my friend and with menace, I said, 'whether your husband likes it or no, I will soon be Queen of England and I will be able to crush him just as quickly as the king has raised him up.' Almost the moment that these words had come forth from my mouth, I regretted them. For in the flash of fiery temper that had seized my body, the words had tumbled forth, taking on a despicable life of their own. In an instant, they ripped the heart out of our relationship, leaving the trust between Lady Bridget and me shattered and in pieces about us. I watched the colour drain from Bridget's face. For a moment, there was a flash of genuine fear, before a cold anger replaced it and, if it were possible, I saw my friend harden against me even further. For a few seconds, Bridget stood there in front of me, motionless, before she dipped into a brief curtsy and said,

'Madame, if you will excuse me. I find that I have some urgent household business I must attend to.' Bridget then turned about upon her heels and flounced indignantly out of the gallery. I stood looking after her. I confess that I was shocked at what I had said and already regretted it terribly. But I felt Anne's pain at the betrayal of her friend. As she was often inclined to do in these situations, through me, Anne had lashed out in thoughtless retribution. It would cost her—and me—dearly. In months to come, Lady Bridget and I would cautiously make efforts to repair our relationship, although it was never to be the carefree easy friendship that it once was. Many, many months into the future, the fallout from this day would indeed come back to haunt me, with fatal consequences.

Chapter Three

The rest of our stay at Stone Place had been an awkward one; although for the sake of Henry, who remained in excellent spirits, and for the sake of appearances, I did my utmost to brush aside my cares and present a facade of joyful celebration. Even at a discreet distance, Margery had witnessed my altercation with Bridget, and I confessed all to her as soon as we were alone. She did her utmost to reconcile the two of us in the short time that we rested at Stone, yet to our shame, both Lady Bridget and I were two fiercely proud individuals who found it difficult to offer or accept the olive branch of peace.

The king and I took our leave of Sir Robert and his lady wife the following day, and the royal party made its way on horseback toward the port of Gravesend. It was a relief to see Stone Place slipping away into the distance. At Gravesend, we boarded a sailing ship that took us to the nearby Isle of Sheppey, an island lying just off the mainland of Kent, where we tarried for a full three days as the guests of my client, Sir Thomas Cheney. It was good to see Sir Thomas again; he was a genuine and generous host, a far cry from the frosty reception that I had received from Sir Robert. And whilst the bitter taste of the fallout with my friend remained stubbornly with me, three days of glorious hunting, dancing and feasting did much to assuage my heavy heart. In truth, it felt like the beginning of my triumph of Calais; the king had never been more devoted and I was once again firmly at the centre of his world—loved and adored above all others. I even sensed that back then he was still truly in awe of me, and I would oftentimes find him staring at me silently, in sheer wonderment. I would smile back at him coyly or flirt with him sensuously, or challenge him boldly; so expressive were Anne's dark and bewitching eyes. On such occasions, the king would usually lean into me and whisper in my ear that he 'loved me entirely' and that I was 'a woman not made of ordinary clay'.

With renewed optimism, we set out on the next leg of our journey, crossing back to the mainland by ship before travelling across Kent, towards Canterbury and the home of Sir Christopher Hales, Henry's attorney general and a good friend of Master Cromwell. We were to stay with Sir Christopher for just one day and so in honour of our host, the king decreed that only a small and intimate party would dine together including: the king and I, Sir Christopher, Master Cromwell, and Lord William Sandys, Henry's Lord Chancellor.

I had met Master Cromwell and Lord Sandys on many occasions and as we sat down to dine, it was the former who drew my attention. I knew that I was sitting opposite the man who would ultimately destroy Anne and the entire Boleyn faction. It was a peculiar feeling, for in 1532, Thomas Cromwell was still a staunch ally and ever gracious toward me, as any client should be toward their sponsor. The Boleyns shared much in common with him on matters of religious reform, and in return for Cromwell's service, my father promoted his interests tirelessly with the king. I also sensed Anne's great esteem for his stance on the Roman Catholic Church, his intelligence and the tireless way in which he worked to further the cause of the king's divorce from Katherine. I alone knew how vehemently he would turn against Anne during those fateful days of 1536. Yet despite myself, I was deeply intrigued by this rather thick set and unpretentious man. As Cromwell listened attentively to the king, I studied him and reflected on his physical appearance and demeanour.

In 1532, Cromwell was forty-seven years old, but remained in the most robust of health. He reminded me of a wily, old fox, close-set dark eyes, long straight nose and marked furrow lines across his brow which spoke of his shrewd diligence and stubborn tenacity. It was patently clear that Thomas Cromwell was not a sentimental man, and like many men at court, he possessed a ruthless streak which served the king well. It was difficult not to be impressed by Master Cromwell's intellect and his clear and incisive mind, which would bring the Roman Catholic Church to its knees in England; and to Henry's immense pleasure, was about to bring him all that he desired—absolute supremacy in his kingdom, and the woman he loved by his side. I knew too that he was often talked about at court, not least because he was resented by those noblemen who considered him an upstart, who had reached well beyond his station in life.

Thomas Cromwell was born in Putney. A self-confessed 'ruffian', he left England as a young man travelling between France, Italy and the Low Countries, first as a mercenary and then later building a network of contacts with merchants in countries, which in my modern day life, I knew as Belgium, the Netherlands and Luxembourg. He ended up working as an agent in Rome for the English cardinal, Christopher Bainbridge. At some point, Thomas Cromwell metamorphosed from a hardened thug into a cultured and well-grounded gentleman. During his time away on the continent, he mastered the art of hunting and hawking, and learnt several languages fluently, an essential factor in Cromwell's meteoric rise at the English court. Henry welcomed ruthless men around him, to carry out the more unsavoury tasks of governing a kingdom, but outright, brutish thuggery would not be tolerated; there should be a facade of sophisticated charm and goodly learning. No one was more adept at this than Master Cromwell.

Thomas returned to England some twenty years earlier, married and honed his intellectual capacities by training as a lawyer, where his talents soon came to the attention of Cardinal Wolsey. Cromwell subsequently entered his service, and by the time of Wolsey's fall in the autumn of 1529, Thomas had become one of the cardinal's most senior and trusted advisers. It was a mark of the man that he was quick to leave his master to his fate, literally riding to court to carve out a new career as part of the king's most intimate circle, whilst Wolsey's world collapsed catastrophically around him. By 1530, Henry appointed Thomas Cromwell to the Privy Council and in the two years that I had been away from Anne's world, Thomas had made himself utterly indispensable to the king. But it was Master Cromwell's ability which elevated him ever further into the king's good graces. He was hospitable and gracious with his words, though he was not a man of great charisma, relying instead upon his fierce intellect and shrewd political nous to advance his own, and the king's, agenda.

It was a rather strange relationship that I would have with Thomas Cromwell. With all my knowledge of what lay ahead, I decided that he was a man to keep as a friend. I had no idea how long I was to remain in my current state; when, if ever, I might be sucked back again into the twenty-first century. If it were possible to change anything that might make a difference to Anne, it would be to preserve the alliance that had existed between the two of them since Cromwell first appeared at court.

Although I did not know it then, by the time I was to arrive back in the sixteenth century for the third and final time, the die would already have been cast; Anne's fate would be sealed, and I would be too late to help her.

Suddenly, I realised that I was being addressed by Sir Christopher, who sat to my right.

'Madame, may I congratulate you on your elevation to the peerage. Master Cromwell has told me all about the ceremony at Windsor and how your great beauty and grace bewitched the entire court.' He turned towards the king, raising his goblet as he spoke again, 'Your Grace, may I propose a toast to your good health and that of the Lady Marquess. May your trip to Calais be a triumph.' Henry raised his goblet high and spoke with great ebullience,

'To my most beloved cousin, the Lady Marquess …' he turned to look at me, inclining his head in my honour and smiling at me with radiant appreciation, before he turned back to the table and continued, 'and to our trip to Calais, may God give us safe passage and deliver unto us a successful outcome; not only for me, but for my kingdom.' We all raised our glasses in turn, accompanied by many smiles and words of goodwill. Henry then addressed Lord Sandys.

'I trust Lord Sandys that all is in order for my meeting with Francis. It will be good to see my brother again and we have much to talk about for the Saracen threat still menaces our borders, and it is our God-given duty to ensure that the infidels do not gain a foothold in Christendom.' Henry took another swig of his wine before continuing to cut up and eat mouth-sized bites of the venison as he listened to his Lord Chancellor's reply.

'Your Grace, everything is in order. On 16 October, his grace, the Duke of Norfolk will ride forth to meet with Anne de Montmorency to agree to a time of Your Majesty's meeting with the King of France; we are to propose, Monday the 21st day of October. Afterwards Your Majesty will accompany King Francis to Boulogne to meet with the Dauphin, the Duke d'Orleans and the Duke d'Angouleme, both of these latter gentlemen being close brethren of the King of France, as you know. Your Grace will tarry there for four day as a guest of the French king. If our plans are accepted, the Friday thereafter, Your Majesty will escort King Francis to Calais; two miles out of which you will be met by the Duke of Richmond and a great number of noblemen who did not accompany Your Grace to Boulogne. King Francis will hence come forth to Calais. I have arranged that he will stay at Staple Hall at the expense of the merchants of Calais,' Henry nodded in agreement, 'which as you know is a princely residence that will be well prepared for his grace. A great number of entertainments have also been organised that will culminate in my Lord of Norfolk and my Lord of Suffolk being invested in the *Ordre de Saint Michel*, whilst the Grand Master of France and the Admiral of France will, in return, be made Knights of the Garter. This has already been negotiated with the French.'

Lord Sandys was impeccable in his speech and meticulous in detail. An elderly man of sixty-two, he had long been a close and beloved friend of the king. When I first met him, I warmed to him instantly as, remarkably for a courtier, he seemed to have few vices and was uncorrupted by greed or the need for power. I did not know what he thought of me in his heart, but I knew that he had always showed me great kindness and seemed to accept my presence at the king's side.

I looked at the king and noticed Henry was still nodding his approval. I also had been planning something in honour of this momentous occasion, and I knew it was the time to make plain my plans. I was not surprised when Henry told me that no French noblewoman of equal birth would agree to meet me on French or English soil; a fact well recorded in history. Although I could sense Anne's deep sadness and indignation, with her natural sense of flair and high drama, I knew that she could still steal her moment of glory. I knew not whether my plans had already been designed by history, but I knew what to do, and set about designing a fantastic masque with Henry's yeoman of the revels. I turned to Henry as I spoke,

'Your Majesty, I have been planning a very special surprise for you in honour of Your Grace and King Francis.' Henry sat back in his chair nonchalantly, one elbow rested against its wooden arm, the other arm bent up stroking his neatly trimmed beard thoughtfully; he smiled at me indulgently and indicated with his hand that I should continue. 'I have in mind a masque that I wish to perform with my ladies at the banquet, the one planned for the Sunday night. I have been working on the design for our dress. We shall be most gorgeously apparelled in cloth of gold.' I leaned forward placing one elbow on the table, resting my chin upon my hand as I flirted playfully with my love. 'I have fashioned a dance which methinks will be most pleasing to Your Majesty and King Francis. With your permission, Sir, I would like the masque to be my entrance and meeting with the King of France.' I raised my eyebrow playfully and waited for a reply.

After a few short moments, Henry nodded his head courteously and said, 'You have my permission, my lady.' I knew he loved my sense of drama, and that once again my spirit had aroused him. He held my gaze far longer than it was necessary, his eyes conveying his lust, already undressing me in his mind's eye. I knew that he was imagining the softness of my skin and the gentle swell of my breast under his touch, and I too felt myself flush with desire. The tension of our sexual energy was palpable within the room and I sensed our three dinner companions shift slightly awkwardly in their seats as with every passing day, Henry and I were ever more careless about who saw the passion that we shared for one another. I was also aware that gossip at court was rife—in England and abroad; tongues were wagging and ambassadors were speculating whether the king and I had already married and consummated our relationship. Yet I knew the truth of the matter; Henry's sexual appetite for me was rapacious and I yearned to feel him inside me. It was not that the king was any longer the handsome man of his youth, but I found his power intoxicating. He was a deeply charismatic alpha male, and at the most primitive and instinctive level, my female sexuality could not help but respond in kind. I knew from history that within a few short weeks, Henry and Anne would, after six long years, become lovers. But what I found so fascinating about the story in which I found myself as protagonist, a story I knew so well, was that I had no idea when I would finally lie with Henry. Yet this was one part of the tale which has remained a secret stretching across the centuries, something which only Anne and Henry knew the truth of in their hearts. I found myself slightly overwhelmed that soon I would know that very same truth for myself.

Chapter Four

The Port of Dover,
Kent, 11 October 1532

I was awoken early on the morning of our departure for Calais by my sister, Mary. The wind had changed direction in our favour and so to capitalise on our good fortune, Henry ordered our immediate departure for the continent. Shortly before five o'clock, I found myself riding in a torch-lit procession as the royal party snaked its way from the ancient and indomitable fortress of Dover Castle towards the harbour where a flotilla of ships waited to transport us across the Channel.

It was still pitch black, and riding atop of Starlight, I was barely awake. The wind on that October morning was insistent, and although I was wrapped up in warm furs and fur-lined, kid-leather gloves and boots, it cut through me like an icy blade. Lit only by the full moon, a path of glistening moonlight cast itself across the surface of the water, almost as though God himself was lighting our way toward the impenetrable blackness of the English Channel lying beyond. The air was salty and fresh, and way below the castle, I could hear the swell of the water clawing insistently against the chalky, white cliffs.

I was both excited and apprehensive at the reception that lay ahead of me. Anne last set foot on French shores some eleven years earlier, before being recalled from the French court by Sir Thomas Boleyn in 1521. King Francis knew Anne well. But what exactly he knew about her and her time in France, I wondered. I believed that unlike Mary, who had gained a scandalous reputation, Anne remained chaste in the face of the infamously licentious French court. I mused on what I would learn at Calais and what secrets might King Francis hold?

As I rode along, I was flanked on one side by my mother, now the Countess of Wiltshire, and on the other by my beloved and gentle sister; both of whom I knew loved me dearly. I felt safe. However, there remained one niggling thought, my argument with Lady Bridget. I should have known better, and remembered its significance from my avid reading of history. I could not shake off the feeling that the incident would have far reaching ramifications for Anne. Frustratingly,

I could not put my finger on why. I determined to resolve the issue by writing a letter to Lady Bridget as soon as we were settled on board.

A little while later, I was at Henry's side as we stepped onto the deck of the *Swallow* and were greeted by the Lord High Admiral of the English fleet, the thirteen-year-old Henry Fitzroy, Duke of Richmond, the king's acknowledged, bastard son. Of course, at such a tender age, this role was largely ceremonial, nevertheless, I watched Henry's chest puff out in pride as he greeted the precious young duke. I looked about me and was warmed by the flicker of torches that lit the deck; the full moon allowing me to make out the indistinct outline of the main mast which towered above my head. Filling my nostrils was the smell of wood and pitch, and from underneath my feet, I felt the gentle lilting of the vessel in the relatively calm swell of the harbour.

Henry and I were followed on board by my mother and father, a number of my ladies and the Duke of Suffolk. Whilst the king stayed on deck to talk with Charles Brandon and my father, I was escorted towards the stern of the ship and the relative comfort and grandeur of the royal quarters.

Once inside the cabin, I could hear the cacophony of shouts from sailors outside as they prepared the vessel to depart. When we did so, a thunderous peal of guns rang out from the two forts guarding the south-western side of the harbour, as they saluted our departure. I was relieved to discover that Anne was at home on the high seas. She seemed unperturbed by the rolling of the ship as we left the harbour and headed out into the choppy waters of the English Channel. I settled myself comfortably at a beautifully carved English oak desk. My mother and my ladies similarly made themselves at home, and there was much excitement and gossiping about the dancing, flirting and magnificent celebrations to come. A breakfast of ale, bread, ham and honey was delivered to us; however, I could not eat, for I had a task to complete. At my request, Margery, who was attending me as one of my chief ladies-in-waiting, delivered a crisp parchment, ink pot and quill to the table, as I turned my attention to how I might heal the rift that had arisen between us. Presently, the words began to flow with a life of their own and Anne guided my hand once more.

Madame,

I pray you, as you love me, to give credence to my servant this bearer, touching you or removing and anything else that shall tell you of my behalf; for I will desire you to do nothing but that shall be for your wealth. And, Madame, that what all times I have not showed the love that I bear you as much as it was indeed, yet now I trust that you shall well prove that I loved you a great deal more than I made feign for; and assuredly, next to mine own mother, I know no woman alive that I loved better: and at length, with God's grace, you shall prove that it is unfeigned. And I trust you do know me for such a one that I will write nothing to comfort you in your trouble but I will abide by it as long as I live; and therefore I pray you leave your indiscreet trouble, both for displeasing of God and also for displeasing of me, that doth love you so entirely. And trusting in God that you will thus do, I make an end. With the ill hand of

Your own assured friends during my life,
Anne Rochford

As I signed my name, I felt satisfied with my efforts and summoned Margery to my side, and said,

'Margery, please make sure this letter is conveyed directly to Lady Bridget.' I looked at her earnestly as I went on, 'it is my singular desire above all else to see us reconciled. I also wish you to convey through the bearer of this message, my invitation to Lady Tyrwhitt to come to court presently and attend upon me as my chief lady of the bedchamber.'

'Very good, Madame,' replied Margery. As she turned to go, I grabbed at her wrist adding with some urgency,

'Margery, pray tell Lady Bridget that I am greatly sorry for our troubles and that soon we shall be perfect friends again.' Margery smiled at me and squeezed my hand reassuringly, before turning to leave. I watched her disappear to find a bearer to convey the letter safely back to English soil as soon as we had landed at Calais.

Although the matter still troubled me sorely, I resolved to put it out of my mind and throw myself entirely into the great festivities and celebrations of the next three weeks. I looked out through one of the tiny wooden windows, and with a joyful heart, I could make out the very first light of dawn as it cast its rays across the eastern horizon. I suddenly longed to taste the fresh, salty sea air, and to watch the breaking of this glorious, new day. Indicating to my ladies that I wished

48

to be alone, I made my way out onto the deck of the ship, picking my way across the many coils of rope and barrels which lay thereabouts, as I moved towards the bow. I gazed upwards and in the half light saw the vast outline of the great sails which were full and straining against the wind, and listened to the song of the ship as it groaned and creaked its way through the surf.

Once outside, the fresh and spirited breeze quickly chased away any remnants of heavy sleep. Henry was nowhere to be seen, and I assumed that he and the other gentlemen had retired to the king's cabin. As I reached the bow, I came across Charles Brandon, who stood looking out to sea. I almost mistook him for Henry as he looked uncannily like the king. I thought about slipping silently away and leaving the duke to his thoughts, but I was curious. It was rare that I was alone with the Duke of Suffolk, and I wondered if I might use this opportunity to forge a connection of sorts between us. Standing a few steps behind him, I spoke up,

'My Lord Suffolk, I see you too have chosen to enjoy the fresh air.' Charles Brandon turned his head and eyed me quizzically, always suspicious of my motives. The early tentativeness between Charles and Anne had given way to a familiar, but polite, disdain that the Duke rarely made an effort to conceal—except in Henry's direct presence. Charles stared silently at me for several seconds, before he turned his head back to gaze once more toward the coast of France. 'You look deep in thought, Your Grace. What vexes you?' Charles cast a second glance in my direction, as if I were an irritating fly that refused to go away. Eventually, he wistfully looked out once more toward the horizon, before he said,

'When I sail across this water, I find myself thinking of my youth which I fear has long departed; the times that I have accompanied the king to France for the glory of battle. Forsooth, what English man could be happier than when fighting for the honour of his king and his country?' For a moment Charles became animated in much the same way as Henry did whenever he spoke of war. I so wanted him to tell me more of such monumental events, and although he seemed reluctant, I tried to carry the conversation,

'Pray tell me, Your Grace what do you remember of those times?' Charles heaved a heavy sigh, before he replied,

49

'Everything was so much simpler then; you knew what was in men's hearts. There was an ancient order of things, a truth that was never questioned.' I knew of course immediately to what the duke referred; the religious and social upheaval that was cutting across English soil in the wake of the Reformation. From my twenty-first century perspective, I was aware of just how monumental this change would be, and I also knew he rightly blamed Anne as one of the principle protagonists in this revolution. Intelligent men, like Suffolk, sensed the enormity of the shift too—even if they could not see into the future as I could. I knew that they were already aware of the schism that would in time come to divide the country and cause so much bloodshed. I recognised in the duke, man's eternal fear of change, and yet I could not help but challenge it. Boldly, I spoke my mind,

'But Your Grace, surely change is a natural part of life and that old, outdated ways must eventually make way for that which is new and fresh and pure.' I suddenly felt myself flash with irritation, 'Is it not right that every man or woman should have the right to know their God directly that…'

'Your Grace, the king wishes to see you in his cabin.' I spun around to see my father standing several paces behind me, his face hardened and resolute. He had heard my words, dangerous words that despite my great favour with the king, perhaps more wisely might have remained unspoken. I turned to look back at Charles Brandon, who stared at me with cold dispassion. After pausing for a few moments, the duke dismissed himself, acknowledging my father and I as he said curtly,

'My Lady Marquess, My Lord,' before he strode off with some irritation toward the back of the ship, from whence I had come. When he had gone, my father moved in close to me; he spoke in a tense whisper so that he should not be overheard.

'Anne, you may soon be the Queen of England, and have in all matters the king's ear, but remember that our beliefs are still heresy in this realm. It would be wise not to speak of such matters; do I make myself clear?' I heard a deep uneasiness in my father's voice, and whilst I felt truculent that I had been scolded like a child, I knew in my heart the truth of his words and nodded my head to convey my understanding. I looked out wistfully toward the coastline of France which had begun to loom ever larger on the horizon. Despite my father's solemn warning, I sensed Anne's excitement; for this was a homecoming of sorts; a return to a place of many happy, carefree memories; of a country and court which had in so many ways groomed Anne for the position that she now occupied as queen-in-waiting at the side of one of the most powerful kings in Christendom.

By ten o'clock of that same morning, our grand flotilla was poised to enter the harbour at Calais. It was a vibrant and colourful spectacle. In the crisp morning sunlight, every ship was hung about its sides with a myriad of St George's flags, flying at least two flags of the royal standard each, all fluttering gaily in the gentle, morning breeze. Attended by those gentlemen and ladies of the court who had travelled on board the *Swallow* with us, Henry and I stood on the deck, as I marvelled at the sight of the magnificent, medieval town of Calais, and the many people who had gathered to greet us.

As we made our approach, the seamen on board our ship set about skilfully navigating our vessel past the castle of Rysbank, an ancient stone fortress that guarded the entrance into Calais' natural harbour. I took the opportunity to drink in the sight of the only remaining jewel of English sovereignty that still remained as part of the French mainland; a remnant of the vast empire of England's Plantagenet dynasty that had once reigned across not only England, but much of northern and western France, as far down as the southern region of Aquitaine.

Calais was surrounded by an area known as 'the Pale', some twenty square miles of territory of low-lying ground to the west, and higher ground to the east. Beyond the town were a number of small hills and several wooded valleys, many of which were dotted with tiny villages. Over the 200 or so years that Calais had been occupied by the English, the marshy area to its west had been drained and cultivated; a vast network of watercourses, dykes and canals could be seen stretching back from the town, keeping the earth from becoming waterlogged and providing rich, fertile pastures for growing crops.

The magnificent town of Calais commanded the picture. Set just a little back from the harbour, which was lined with quays and jetties, the town was fortified by enormous city walls with a series of towers along its length. On the right hand side of the town was a tower known as the Water Gate, which guarded the entrance to the inner harbour of the citadel. However, it was the Lantern Gate, the principal gate of the town that dominated my first impressions of Calais; a huge, central, stone tower with the enormous wooden gates built to resist hostile advances. Beyond those walls stood the churches of Our Lady to the left and St Nicholas to the right, whilst the exquisite medieval structures of the Town Hall and Staple Hall stood centrally, directly to the south of the Lantern Gate. I would spend four of the most delicious, intense and joyful weeks of my life here, the memories of which are indelibly etched in my mind.

In front of the Lantern Gate, by the side of the harbour, a splendid procession of knights and soldiers formed to accompany the Mayor and the Lord Deputy, both of whom waited patiently on the quayside to greet us. Henry glanced across at me and smiled, for he too had seen that most of the townsfolk had gathered to welcome our arrival. There were many cheers of 'God save the king!'

After setting foot on dry land, I was both relieved and truly elated. Henry took me by the hand and led me proudly by his side, whilst all about us a thunderous roar of cannons signalled the safe arrival of the king and his consort. Anne was finally home.

Calais was part garrison, part trading town, the last English outpost before the rest of the continent. Within its fortified walls was a grid-like network of narrow streets, packed tightly with fine medieval houses owned by affluent Calais merchants. Every so often these streets would open up into spacious squares used for trading, recreation and the gathering of its townsfolk; the most important of these, of course, was the central Market Place. On that day, it was hung with a multitude of colourful banners and flags to welcome the arrival of the king.

Once we had been greeted by the town's Mayor and Lord Berners and the king's deputy, the royal party rode in magnificent procession toward the mighty Lantern Gate; there carved proudly, although as it would turn out slightly over-confidently, was the inscription in French which read: 'Then shalle the Frenchman Calais winne, when iron and leade lyke corke shall swimme.' In a little over twenty-five years' time, I mused that Calais would finally be lost to the French. I could not help but imagine the great glee with which the new French conquerors would finally erase those words for all time. However, that was the future, and unimaginable to a mighty king like Henry, who worshipped the great warrior King Henry V, and prided himself on his resounding victories against the French.

Passing beneath the gate, we rode down Lantern Street and into the breathtaking central Market Place led by the Mayor and Lord Berners; the king following behind, a picture of gracious majesty, whilst I rode at his side. I remember that day so vividly; my heart was bursting with pride to be finally riding alongside my love as his legitimate consort on what could only be described as Anne's first state occasion. From time to time, I even heard someone shout, 'God bless the Lady Marquess of Pembroke!' It seemed that the people of Calais had already taken Anne to their heart in a way that, sadly, was not often the case on the other side of the Channel. I did my best to carry myself with regal dignity but my heart was simply overflowing with joy and the deepest gratitude for the warmth of our reception. Here, in the heart of the English Pale, I felt like a queen. All my cares about Anne's future, which so often stalked me like menacing shadows whilst at the English court, seemed finally dispelled in the midst of a sea of good wishes and rejoicing.

Our procession made for a glorious sight to the ordinary townsfolk who hung out of pretty, little Tudor windows above us that jutted out over the narrow streets to watch us pass. Behind the king and I rode the premier nobles of the land; the Dukes of Richmond, Norfolk as Lord Treasurer of England and the Duke of Suffolk. A little further back rode Stephen Gardiner, Bishop of Winchester and the Bishops of London, Lincoln and Bath. Adhering to the strict hierarchy of Tudor society, then followed the Earls of Exeter, Derby, Arundel, Oxford, Surry, Rutland and my father, the Earl of Wiltshire and Ormonde. I glanced over my shoulder to see our procession stretch back almost as far as the eye could see, including: more knights such as my brother, Lord Rochford, Sir Thomas Wyatt, and my clients, Sir Thomas Cheney and Sir John Wallop, and three of my father's brothers, Sir William, Sir Edward and the youngest brother, Sir James Boleyn. Unfortunately, the latter meant the presence of Elizabeth Wood, Lady Boleyn, whom I wished with all my heart I could have left behind in London.

Once in the Market Place, I looked about in awe at the fine Tudor/Flemish architecture of the buildings; my breath clear taken away by the magnificent sight of the Staple and Town Halls, which stood side-by-side, dominating the southern side of the square. They were beautiful buildings indeed, and a testament to the rich, long and prosperous history of this vital trading post. We crossed the square to the right of Staple Hall, before turning into the long and narrow High Street which ran east to west through the town, toward the towering edifice of the church of St Nicholas; a magnificent Gothic building where in the fourteenth century, the young Richard II was wed to his eight-year-old bride, Isabella of France.

To celebrate our arrival, the court and the townsfolk of Calais paused at the church to hear a Solemn Mass. In front of the strikingly beautiful altar, I knelt in prayer at Henry's side, giving thanks for our deliverance. An hour or so later, we left the church to a deafening peal of bells that sang out their mighty song of celebration, before the king and I were finally conveyed to our lodgings at the Exchequer; a fine mansion directly opposite St Nicholas', which had been newly enlarged and refurbished for our coming.

The king was to tarry at Calais for a full ten days before riding out to meet King Francis. On the sixteenth day of October, my Uncle Norfolk, accompanied by the rather dashing twenty-three-year-old, Edward Stanley, Earl of Derby, and a great number of gentlemen, would meet the Grand Master of France some six miles from Calais on the twenty-first day of the same month at Sandingfield, three miles within the English Pale.

The king shared everything with me during those heady days including his plans for the refortification of the town; he also discussed his thoughts about the meeting with King Francis, and how he wanted to show me off to all the French court on their return from Boulogne. He asked my opinion on opulent fabrics and cloths that were brought to him for his inspection, and of course, as ever, Henry showered me with a bounty of jewels purchased from grateful, local merchants. We also spent a good deal of time discussing the refurbishment of Whitehall. The king had ordered no expense was to be spared in completing the remodelling of Wolsey's original palace. Messages arrived regularly, updating Henry with the progress. We often scoured the plans together, discussing and debating how works should progress. The two of us would never be closer.

On the third evening after our arrival, I found myself playing cards in my privy chamber with Henry, my brother and his wife, Lady Rochford. Like all the rooms on the queen's side, this chamber was richly hung with cloth of gold and arras; the tapestries which surrounded us depicted dramatic scenes from the fall of Troy. The floor was laid with expensive carpets that had been shipped from Greenwich. These were strewn with roses, lavender and other sweet herbs; the scent of which was diffused by currents of warm air emanating from the welcoming fire which had been laid in the large, stone fireplace.

We were playing one of my favourite games, Primero, a sort of sixteenth century version of poker. I found that since I had been in Anne's world, I had a knack for it and often beat the king sorely. There was much laughter around the little table as we played; great cries of disbelief and playful accusations of skulduggery were cast about when one of us acted out a particularly convincing bluff, or snatched victory from an overconfident opponent. In the background, Mark Smeaton unobtrusively serenaded us gently on a virginal with tender songs of love and chivalry, whilst we were served fleshy, sweet cherries, grapes and pears—a present from Anne de Montmorency, Grand Master of France. The king was in truly excellent spirits, for we had enjoyed three glorious days of hawking, gaming and dancing. Henry had given me the world; how could a girl not fall so utterly head over heels for such a man? A man that had raised me—and Anne—so high that none other than the king himself stood above me.

In my happiness, all I desired was the happiness of others. It was with this earnest wish in mind that I cast a glance at my sister-in-law, Jane Rochford, who so often seemed miserable and greatly put out. Jane was a tiny creature of slight frame, unfeasibly narrow waist and a bosom not much raised. Like my dear friend Nan, she had fashionably pale skin which was as translucent as porcelain, golden hair and crystal clear, blue eyes; her beauty was only flawed by the fact that those eyes were set a little too wide apart and gave the permanent impression of her being slightly startled at her surroundings. Otherwise, her face was a slender, oval shape, whilst her nose was perfectly proportioned and she had full, rose coloured lips.

I knew that history had given Lady Rochford a notorious reputation for slandering her husband and Anne at their downfall, allegedly accusing them of the heinous crime of incest that sealed their fate and allowed Henry's image to emerge untarnished from those bloody days of 1536; for who could indeed accuse a king of purging his court of such demonic behaviour? I had known Jane for some considerable time and was well acquainted with her rather difficult, and often prickly, temperament. Yet I admit, I was often perplexed; for she did not seem to be the evil and heartless woman that I had become acquainted with from my understanding of history. I could not help but muse on what had caused her to turn her back on her husband and sister-in-law in their darkest hour; had she indeed been so wildly jealous of their close relationship as to be driven to vindictive retribution? Or, had she been afraid; intimidated by Cromwell during his intense, relentless interrogations of her? In truth, it was not hard to believe either one.

I knew full well that George loved life, and although he took pains to hide it from me, he was as active in his private life as he was in his public one. I was aware that he adored sexy, vivacious and challenging women and loved to live life on the edge, often riding it as if it were a team of wild, unbridled horses. To love life, sex and women as much as George did, should never be a crime. The only crime was that he was poorly matched with a woman who was hopelessly ill-equipped in temperament, needs and sex drive to ever satisfy him or command his attention. And oh, how she longed for his attention! Jane was a complex character, for beneath that rather conservative facade, I always sensed there was a different woman longing to be unleashed; this was the Jane that yearned to be bold, daring and perhaps even shocking: I sensed she envied her sister-in-law's carefree sexuality, fierce courage and spirit. I could see easily how she armoured herself against the world, how uncomfortable she was with her sexuality. I wondered if she had been neglected as a child and therefore had come to crave the attention and spotlight which had for so long eluded her. Perhaps she had thought that with her marriage, she would become important, the mistress of her own household, adored by her husband and surrounded by doting children. However, Lady Jane had been married to George for nearly seven years and must have been acutely aware that she had never captured his heart; and no precious children had followed.

Sometimes, I would touch gently upon the subject with her, but up until that day, she brushed me aside as if it mattered little, as if she did not care. Yet I sensed her pain, a deep cavernous, raw pain. It was easy for me to see, just as it is always easy to see another's pain when it has haunted your own soul for so long a time. Every time I looked at her, I was reminded of Daniel and the agony of his stubborn refusal to give himself to me when I had laid myself bare and vulnerable before him. Even though I knew Anne loved George more than life itself, I was now determined to help my sister-in-law in any way that I could.

For the time though, I turned my attention back to the game; Jane and my brother had already turned in their hands in defeat; and in the case of my dear brother, with more than a little disgruntled, but good-natured, frustration. It was between the king and me. I smiled playfully at Henry from behind the hand of cards that I now held up to my mouth like a fan. I was flirting outrageously and I knew it! Beneath the table I ran my foot seductively up the outside of Henry's leg, trying my best to distract him; I knew it would make him hard with desire. I giggled as I watched the king attempt to keep a straight face. It was clear that he was trying to concentrate as there was a good deal of money placed on the table in wagers. However, in truth, the king was in so jocular a mood that he cared little about the wager and thoroughly enjoyed playing along in earnest with my little game. His grace looked at me and raised an eyebrow, trying to weigh up whether my bravado was true or no. In return, I too raised an eyebrow in elfishly reply, mirroring his gesture, yet holding my counsel and saying nothing. Finally, after careful consideration, the king placed another ten pounds on the table,

'Primero!' he said proudly as he laid his cards before him. I frowned, faking my disappointment, as I watched the king smile in satisfaction and reach to take the winnings that were already piled high on the centre of the table. Ever bold, I reached over and swiped at the king's knuckles with my cards, causing him to pause in confusion before I too turned my hand over and said with some delight,

'Chorus!' Henry threw up is hands and cried out in mock despair, for he knew that I held the winning hand. Despite this defeat, soon we were all laughing raucously as my brother shook his head exclaiming,

'Anne, how do you do it? You are the luckiest minx I have ever known; I shall be bankrupt if I keep playing you at this game!'

'Bankrupt indeed, my lord!' chimed in the king. He turned to speak over his shoulder to the keeper of his privy purse, Sir Henry Norris, who stood close by in attendance. 'Sir Henry, be sure to give my Lady Marquess her winnings!'

'Thank you, Your Majesty,' I replied playfully. I was about to speak again, when the arrival of the Duke of Norfolk was announced.

'Ah, Norfolk. Come thither and rescue me from your niece, lest the Privy Purse be soon empty!' Henry said sitting back in his chair still chuckling good-naturedly from our frolics and banter. My uncle's entrance was perfect timing, for I had a mind to speak alone with Lady Rochford, who rather unusually seemed genuinely happy and relaxed. I wondered whether I might take advantage of this and see if I could get to the bottom of her usual, intractable sadness.

'Uncle Norfolk, it is indeed perfect timing, for Lady Rochford and I have plans for the masque to be celebrated on Sunday next. Perhaps you might continue playing with his grace and I am sure,' I said indicating to my sister who stood close by, 'that Lady Mary Rochford would be happy to stand in for Lady Jane.' My uncle bowed to the king and inclined his head politely toward me before saying,

'It would be a pleasure Your Grace … my Lady Marquess.' Henry smiled at me and nodded his agreement as I rose from my seat and offered it to my uncle, who gave me only the most cursory of acknowledgements.

'Lady Jane, would you accompany me? I think to take a walk in the gallery.' Jane rose; we both curtsied to the king before she followed me. We were attended at a distance by several of my ladies as we meandered our way through the queen's presence chamber. I began to speak, 'Jane, it is good to see you looking so happy. It seems that Calais suits you. It is a pleasant town, do you not think?' Jane turned to smile at me and I mused on how much more pretty she looked when she did so. She replied,

'Indeed, Madame. I think it is the most agreeable town that I have ever known and it is good to see his grace in such fine health and good spirits. He loves you dearly.' I smiled at the truth of her words as we continued to walk along. 'But tell me Jane, has my brother been buying you gifts?' I nodded towards the beautiful carcanet with diamonds and sapphires which hung about her neck and which complemented the pretty blue gown she was wearing about her tiny frame. Jane raised her hand and touched the carcanet, as if reminding herself of the treasure which adorned her, before she replied,

'Yes my lady, he thought it befitting of the great celebrations ahead of us.' She smiled wistfully, as if there were some sadness behind her words, so I probed gently beneath the surface of her happiness,

'How is everything between you and George? I paused then said, 'You know he loves you Jane, don't you?' Jane looked away; her happiness dissolving in an instant and I knew that I had reminded her of a painful truth that she clearly wished to forget. 'Come now, Jane. We are sisters, are we not?' I stopped for a moment to face my sister-in-law as I added, 'I want to help you if I can.' She hesitated, unable to meet my gaze for a moment. I knew she was aware of how close I was to my brother and that she was weighing up the wisdom of confiding in me. I reached across and gently laid my hand on her shoulder, which caused her to look at me straight in the eye. She decided to speak her truth.

'My Lady... Anne... I want so much for George to love me, to treasure me more than anything else in this world. Indeed, I would give my life for him. I adore him!' I watched her eyes began to fill with painful emotion as she continued, 'yet I fear that he loves me not. I try to be a good wife, but George... well he... oh, it is difficult to speak of it, my Lady!' I saw her cast a nervous glance towards my ladies, who still followed us within earshot of our conversation. I sensed her shame and her need for privacy. So, I waved my ladies away indicating that they should keep their distance, before I took Jane by the hand and led her into the long gallery where it was quiet, and I urged her to continue,

'It's all right Jane, I will not judge you.' I said softly, sensing that she longed to share the burden of unhappiness. Suddenly the tide of her misery broke through her defences and she began to weep.

'George is a man of great passion and lust. I fear that what he asks of me...in bed...is sinful in the eyes of God.' I guessed immediately to what Jane referred; that George's sexual appetite was rapacious and that his open minded attitude to sex was too much for my self-conscious and conservative sister-in-law to bear. I was about to speak when Jane went on, gulping air in great sobs, 'I cannot satisfy him and so...so...he has found solace elsewhere.' I fully understood her misery; the man she adored had spurned her and lay with another woman. Not only was she ashamed at what she had had to endure in bed with her husband, but all her best efforts to please him had been thrown back into her face, as she

59

had watched George turn his back on her and seek emotional and sexual fulfilment in the arms of another. I put my arms around her small body, which I sensed longed so much for tenderness. I comforted her as I whispered softly,

'Shhh, there's nothing wrong with you. It is just that my brother is a man of lusty appetites and I fear for all the goodness in his heart, he sometimes thinks little beyond his own pleasure.' I paused before taking her delicate chin in my hand and turning her face toward me, I added, 'unfortunately men can be selfish creatures'. I spoke from bitter personal experience, if nothing else from my time with Daniel, and from what I knew lay ahead for Anne, 'and it is a woman's lot in this life to endure it as best as we are able.' This was certainly true for the sixteenth century wife, who was in the eyes of the law, society, and God, the property of her husband. Thank God at least that had changed.

In that moment, I realised that I was blessed to have tasted a kind of freedom virtually unknown to the women that who surrounded me.

For several minutes, I hugged Jane tightly as I absorbed the desolate years of private shame and isolation that were released in a flood of tears; then I said quietly, 'Console yourself Jane. I will speak to my brother and see if we can't make things better for you.' She did not say anything in reply, but nodded her head in understanding. All I needed to do was find some time with George and resolved to do so as soon as I was able.

Chapter Five

Calais, France,
16 October 1532

That perfect time came two days later when the king and I went out hawking together accompanied by a small party of close friends and confidantes which included: Sir Thomas Wyatt, Sir Henry Norris, my brother, Lady Rochford, my cousin Mary Howard, and finally my beloved mother, Elizabeth Boleyn. Many of the other great nobles and gentlemen, including my father, had left Calais that morning accompanying my Uncle Norfolk to meet Anne de Montmorency within the English Pale to finalise the arrangements for the forthcoming meeting between Henry and Francis.

The earth was flush with a palette of autumnal colours on that October morning and I had dressed to compliment Mother Nature's mood, choosing a gown of plain crimson velvet, the sleeves turned back with miniver; the false sleeves and underskirt being fashioned from rich crimson cloth of gold. As ever, I was bejewelled with a stunning array of fabulous pieces. These included a bracelet, gifted to me from the king since our arrival in Calais, and also a beautiful pendant brooch that was pinned to the front of my gown, set with the cipher 'AB' in gold, and from which hung three, large, teardrop pearls.

As we were to spend the day hawking, we were attended by a number of the king's falconers and cadgers; the latter of which carried six or seven hooded birds on a large wooden frame slung about their shoulders. One of the birds we took that day was a rare and fabulous white gyrfalcon imported from Russia, the most expensive of birds, presented to me by the king's master falconer, Robert Cheseman, on Henry's behalf. He was a magnificent creature, his breast unblemished and white as pure, virgin snow. I had fallen in love with his aloof beauty almost immediately that I had laid eyes on him. I named him Shadow. The king warned me that such birds were notoriously temperamental, highly strung and difficult to fly, which aroused my curiosity even more. I empathised with the nature of this wild and unyielding creature and was determined to fly him for myself.

I had learned much about the ancient art of hawking and falconry since I had walked in Anne's shoes. Peregrine and gyrfalcons were the most prized and expensive birds, yet the king preferred to work with native goshawks, sparrow hawks, and merlins. Henry was a practical hunter and chose to hunt with birds that filled his larder. The hawk was affectionately known as 'the cook bird', and after a day in the field with these exceptional hunters, we often returned with an abundance of rabbits, hares and ducks for the table. I was most acquainted with the merlin, a small type of falcon, which because of its size, was well known as the bird of choice for a lady. These birds were hugely expensive though, and greatly prized by the nobility as a symbol of status and wealth. As we paraded through the town, the king carried the most splendid of his hawks called Espagnol or 'the Spanish one' upon a gloved hand for all to see. He looked so very handsome to me that day; every inch a magnificent prince dressed in a riding coat of black satin with two cut borders of black velvet and a russet partlet also of black velvet and lined with black sarcenet.

Once we reached an area of open ground, several miles south-west of the city walls, Henry turned toward me and said,

'My Lady Marquess, do you not think that this is an ideal spot for hawking?' I was touched that he asked my opinion on something which in truth he knew full well the answer. Nevertheless, I graciously replied,

'Yes indeed, Your Majesty. Your Grace has chosen well.'

'Would you care to enter your bird first, my lady' the king offered gallantly, but I had other things on my mind. I wished to talk with my brother, and so I replied,

'If it pleases Your Majesty, I would very much like to watch you work Espagnol for it is always such a great pleasure to see Your Grace's skill with such a magnificent bird.' I smiled warmly at the king, and in return, Henry inclined his head in acknowledgement of my compliment.

'Then so be it! Master John,' the king called out to one of the royal hawkers who attended us that day, 'come thither with Espagnol for I wish to fly him.' As the king was handed a fine hawking glove embroidered with red silk, I turned my horse about and retreated a distance, sidling up next to George. Thankfully, he had been concerned with giving instructions to his gentleman servant, so was already separated somewhat from the rest of the party. As I came up alongside him, he dismissed his serving man and I was able to speak to him with the degree of privacy that I had hoped for. I watched as the king took his hawk onto his glove, before I greeted my brother warmly.

'Good morning brother! I have not had a proper chance to speak with you this day. I trust all is well?' My brother replied with his usual air of bonhomie,

'Thank you kindly, *Madame la Marquise*. I am indeed well, and you, I must say, look beautiful this morning,' he said leaning over in the saddle, speaking the last words softly and with great affection. I smiled coyly in return; George ever had a way of making a woman feel desirable if it was his inclination. With some sadness though, I thought for a moment upon his wife, Lady Rochford and the misery which she felt from my brother's rough neglect. I suspected she longed for such a compliment and it spurred me on to raise the delicate issue which I could not defer any longer. Whilst the king inspected his hawk, I took the opportunity to speak.

'George, I need to talk to you about an important matter,' before he had chance to say anything I went on, 'it is about Jane.' Now my brother raised his eyebrow; clearly, his curiosity was piqued for it was the subject that rarely came up between the two of us. 'She is sorely aggrieved for she thinks that you care not for her.' George made to speak, but I held up the palm of my hand to silence him, for I had a mind to continue. 'No, George. First, you must listen to me. I know how it is between you in Jane, and in truth, neither of you is to blame. It is a sad fact that you are poorly matched.' I sighed looking at my brother in earnest. I felt empathy for both of them, yet I knew that I must speak to him of things that he would rather I did not know. 'Jane is not a bad woman but one who is ill-equipped to cope with your lusty appetite. I fear that you ask things of her in bed that she cannot in all good conscience give herself over to.' Suddenly my brother flushed scarlet with shame, for he was not used to his sister addressing him about such intimate matters. Despite his discomfort, I pushed on. 'I know that she cannot fulfil your needs and that you lie with another; she has told me so herself.' Now George turned his head away, for he could not meet my gaze. He cared little for the opinions of others, except one; to be admonished by the older sister, whom he loved and admired above all others, was difficult for him to bear. I forged on with all the compassion and love that I could muster, for his sake, and Anne's, I needed to be tough on him without reserve. 'Dear brother, you must realise this; very soon your sister will be the Queen of England. You must know that the Boleyns have so many enemies who will use anything that they can find against us to bring us down from our high favour. Until I have borne the king a son, we are all vulnerable. Do not make your wife our enemy on account of your selfish and foolish desires. George, I beg of you be a good husband to your wife; treat her kindly and with respect, and if you do have to find your pleasure elsewhere, for God's sake be discreet and be careful; do not bring ill repute on our family.' When I had finished, there was the longest silence between us. For the first time since I had been in Anne's world, I had taken my brother to task, but only out of the great love that I bore him. I knew the dangers that lay ahead for my beautiful and often irresponsible brother, and I wanted to keep him safe; I wanted to keep Anne safe. I still hoped that I could change the course of history.

My brother and I had no more time to speak, however, as the hunt had suddenly begun. Beaters with hounds flushed a petrified rabbit out from the undergrowth. Judging the moment precisely, the king removed the bird's velvet hood and slipped it from the glove, allowing Espagnol to take flight. From our high vantage point, we watched the hawk lock onto its prey and swoop down upon it with deadly accuracy. The hawkers shouted as they rushed towards the kill to retrieve it before the hawk could tear it apart and spoil it for the table. The rest of our party cheered and applauded the king's good fortune, before Henry turned and smiled at me, his face alight with boyish excitement. How often in those early days did he turn to me to bask in my acknowledgement and approval of his valiant manhood! I took it for granted then. Despite all that I knew, I still thought that it would never end and now, in truth, I wonder if it was all a dream; I wonder if he ever really loved me.

George finally looked me straight in the eye and nodded his understanding. When I turned around, my mother had silently come up next to me atop her beautiful black mare. As she looked between me and George, I knew that she sensed something significant had occurred between us and I was grateful that she did not ask about it. As it turned out, she had something else on her mind.

From our mounts, we watched as the hawker covered the prey with rough cloth, coaxing Espagnol back onto his hand and feeding it the rabbit's liver in reward for its work. As the first kill was bagged, and Henry's hawk returned to his fist, my mother finally spoke,

'The king looks well and happy. How are things between you?' I answered in truth,

'Very well, indeed. The king shows me daily ever greater affection.' I paused, waiting for my mother to continue. I sensed her line of questioning was leading somewhere, yet I knew not where.

'Has he spoken anymore to you about marriage?' I suddenly understood my mother's concern. With some heaviness of heart, I looked down to the ground and shook my head gently. It was enough for Elizabeth Boleyn, who understood that since my row with Henry at Windsor, he had spoken nothing more of it, and due to my fear of provoking another vicious argument, I had avoided the subject entirely. Yet in truth, I sensed Anne's yearning to bring to an end six long years of waiting and uncertainty; six long years of endless prevarication. At thirty-one years of age, Anne was not getting any younger, and I sensed her creeping anxiety that time was running out to give the king his son and heir. Yet what my mother said next entirely took me off guard, for she had always been cautious with regard to my physical relationship with Henry, urging me to maintain my good name and maidenhood above all else. As I looked up to meet her dark eyes, she spoke softly yet with intense gravity,

'Anne, unfortunately men do not often show the same measure of decisiveness in matters of the heart as they do in issues of power, wealth and revenge.' There was something in the way that my mother spoke, the way she looked at me which left the statement pregnant with unspoken meaning. I frowned at her and asked,

'What are you saying mother?' Elizabeth Boleyn paused for a moment, never taking her eyes from mine, and then continued,

'Sometimes a man needs to be left with no choice; sometimes we need to make that decision for him.' I shook my head almost imperceptibly in some confusion, for my mother appeared to be speaking in riddles and I did not understand to what she referred. For the briefest moment however, my thoughts were interrupted by the king who called across to me,

'My Lady Marquess, I believe it is your turn to enter your bird.' I briefly looked up at Henry who was awaiting my response. It was if I were in a dream, for my mind was still whirling with my mother's words and their hidden meaning. I saw Henry nod at me, encouraging me to choose which bird to fly. I turned my head once more and spoke to the falconer, who awaited my instructions.

'Bring me Shadow.' One of my servants stepped up and handed me my doe-skin hawking glove, embroidered ornately with crimson silk and gold thread. In short order, the falconer passed the bird up to me. Shadow stepped onto my glove, and stretched out and flapped his mighty wings; it was the first time that I was to fly him. I paused and admired his beauty, yet all I could hear were my mother's words ringing in my ears. I suddenly caught sight of a rook circling close by, the perfect quarry for Shadow. With my right hand, I slipped off his crimson velvet hood and for a few seconds only our eyes met. I sensed his steely resolve to have his way and make his kill. Something within me stirred in that moment, and as I slipped him from glove, I watched the chase begin as the rook took fright and began his climb on the breeze in an attempt to make his escape. Shadow followed, rising with astonishing speed and grace to circle nearly a thousand feet above us. More powerful in flight, he climbed above his prey until the rook eventually began to tire and lose height. Shadow knew instinctively that the game was nearly won. He put in a few short stoops to confuse the bird before it made a last, desperate attempt at escape. Breaking free from his circling, in one long flight and without hesitation, Shadow pitched into a vertical dive and took but a few seconds to descend upon his startled prey, crashing into the back of its head with a 'thwack' that could easily be heard echoing around the little valley as he killed the rook on impact. In that moment, I understood everything that my mother had tried to tell me; that the time for prevarication was done; I must take matters into my own hands and carve out my own destiny. Anne needed security, and my mother was telling me in her own way that it would be the consummation of Anne's relationship, and the king's child within her belly, that would finally bring an end to this never ending stalemate. I was startled that the final push came from Anne's mother. Yet the die was now cast, and I resolved to act decisively before we returned to England.

However, before I could do so, an unexpected twist of events occurred; although seemingly fleeting and insignificant, the king made a vow that would forever haunt his soul—and mine. It was four days later. I had stolen away some quiet time from the never ending round of pleasant pastimes and courtly pursuits that had been underway since we had arrived at Calais. Attended only by two of my closest friends, Margery and Nan, I had hidden myself away in one of my most privy of chambers, and was deeply engrossed in reading a copy of the reformist writing of Jacques Lefèvre d'Étaples entitled, *The Epistles and Gospels for the Fifty-two Weeks of the Year*. It was a translation which had only been recently and rather skilfully completed by my brother. He had gifted it to me just one month earlier to celebrate Anne's elevation to the peerage as Lady Marquess of Pembroke. Perhaps for the hundredth time, I turned to the dedication that he had lovingly inscribed for me, and which prefaced the work. Clearly Anne had encouraged him in this endeavour and there, graven in plain letters, was a testament to his great love and affection for his sister. Although badly water damaged, this little book and George's note to Anne would survive into my modern day life. I marvelled at it for the longest time, glad that the obvious devotion between these two siblings would survive long after their flesh had disintegrated into dust, as it was without doubt a sweet love that deserved to endure. By that time, I had almost memorised the words.

To the right honourable lady, the Lady Marchioness of Pembroke, her most loving and friendly brother sendeth greetings.

Our friendly dealings, with so diverse and sundry benefits, besides the perpetual bond of blood, have so often bound me, Madame, inwardly to love you, that in every of them I must perforce become your debtor for want of power, but nothing of my good will. And were it not that by experience your gentleness is daily proved, your meek fashion often times put into use, I might well despair in myself, studying to acquit your deserts towards me, or embolden myself with so poor a thing to present to you. But, knowing these perfectly to reign in you with more, I have been so bold to send unto you, not jewels or gold, whereof you have plenty, not pearl or rich stones, whereof you have enough, but a rude translation of a well-willer, a goodly matter meanly handled, most humbly desiring you with favour to weigh the weakness of my dull wit, and patiently to pardon where any fault is, always considering that by your commandment I have adventured to do this, without the which it had not been in me to have performed it. But that hath had power to make me pass my wit, which like as in this I have been ready to fulfil, so in all other things at all times I shall be ready to obey, praying him on whom this book treats, to grant you many years to his pleasure and shortly to increase in heart's ease with honour.

I was lost in my thoughts, allowing my fingers to trace across the writing, which was still clear and vivid, before suddenly the door to my chamber opened and Lady Fitzwalter, one of my ladies, announced,

'My lady, the king is here to see you.' As she finished speaking, she stepped aside and dipped into a low curtsy. Henry entered the room. Whilst Nan and Margery followed suit, I made to rise in similar fashion before the king stopped me, holding up his palm to indicate his wish that I remained seated. Ignoring the ladies about me, he spoke with great tenderness,

'Do not rise, Madame, stay just as you are.' I could tell immediately from the softness in his voice and his warm informality that the king wished to be alone with me. I nodded briefly to my ladies who swept silently from the chamber.

It was early evening and the king was casually dressed, clad only in his hose, tights, boots and a finely embroidered lined shirt that was open at the neck. I guessed that he had passed through the private gallery connecting his privy chamber to my own, thereby avoiding the public gaze. I watched as Henry walked towards me with fierce intensity, never taking his eyes from mine. When he reached me, I laid the book I had been reading down before he took my chin gently in his hand and turned my face up toward him. Finally, Henry spoke his voice imbued with great wonderment, 'You look so incredibly beautiful.' The king then smiled, not this time to me but more to himself as he sighed and shook his head in wonder,

'What bothers you so, my lord?' I asked equally softly. The king shook his head slowly again before he said in reply,

'Tis nothing, Anne. For how could anything be wrong when you are in this world and at my side? Yet forsooth, I declare I know not what spell you have cast upon this heart of mine which remains bound unto you above all others.' Despite these great words of love, I shuddered momentarily, for I knew of the accusations of witchcraft made against

Anne during the terror of 1536; how the king in his anger and self-pity may have looked back on these intense feelings for this woman who had, most unusually, enslaved his heart. He must have felt strangely bewitched by her magnetic allure. After a few moments of silence Henry went on,

'As you know, I leave for Boulogne tomorrow and I find that I'm missing you already.' For a moment, my love hung his head in sadness in a rare display of raw and tender vulnerability. I reached up and took his hand in mine, squeezing it gently, reassuring him of my presence. He turned to look at me once more before he spoke again, 'Anne Boleyn, I love you with all my heart. There is no other woman in the world like you—you are life itself; I do not think that I could breathe without you in my world.' Henry then sank to his knees looking up at me with searching intensity as he said, 'Swear to me you will never leave my side…' I made to speak but before I had a chance, Henry went on, '…and I swear to you as God is my witness that come what may, from this day forth, I am bound to follow, love and to serve you until the very end of time itself.'

There it was; the vow that was to bind these two lovers together for all eternity. It had come out of the blue; yet with a flash of lucid insight, I suddenly understood all the feelings that I had had about Daniel, our relationship, and why I felt Anne's presence so keenly in my modern day life. It had all been borne of this moment. I had indeed been living this never-ending love story with Henry. The king pushed my knees apart so that he could come close into my body and lay his head against my breast. I held him in my arms for the longest time. I knew that tears of wretched longing and the raw tenderness of the deepest love were flowing down his cheeks. I kissed the top of his head and felt only great pity and compassion for his soul as, for the first time, I realised how it had wandered restlessly across time, reliving his love story with Anne over and over, without end. I felt ever more mired in responsibility, which in truth, had not been mine to take. If I could give the king a son then history could be rewritten. Henry would not have to betray Anne, nor break his vow. Perhaps then the two of them could finally be free. Perhaps I could finally be free.

On the morning of 21 October, the king took his leave of me in my

privy chamber at the Exchequer. Meeting with his royal cousin was always a matter of ostentatious display, and Henry rose magnificently to the occasion. He was dressed opulently in rich, russet velvet with borders of goldsmith's work and a myriad of the finest quality pearls sewn into his costume. As he left our lodgings at Calais, his grace was accompanied by an impressive escort of 140 velvet-clad gentlemen of the court, forty guards and a vast retinue on 600 horses.

With the king's departure, the palace fell into relative quiet, and I retreated gladly into my private rooms. My encounter with Henry a few days before had left me badly shaken; I felt as if a spell had been cast from which there was no escape, as I found myself slipping deeper into a dark hole of despair. Since then, I had been haunted by the knowledge of the fate which lay ahead for Anne. Once more, I was faced with the monster of betrayal, which I had steadfastly refused to confront since I had arrived in Anne's world for the second time. The oppressive responsibility of my role bore down heavily upon me as I was tortured by the prospect that my own soul would be bound to repeatedly experience the bitterness of deceit by those who claimed to love me—perhaps across all time.

Much troubled by these thoughts and desiring my own company, I had excused myself from my ladies and sought refuge upon a window seat in the queen's garden chamber, next to a fine mullioned window that looked out onto the queen's privy gardens below. For almost half an hour, I had been trying to concentrate on the book which I held in my hands, and yet stillness would not come. Frustrated, I tossed it to one side and leaned back in defeat against the window; my eyes coming to rest on the most vibrant and beautiful tapestry that was hung on the opposite wall of the room. I was amazed when I first saw it at the Exchequer, for I had recognised it immediately. It was the tapestry that depicted the marriage of Henry's sister, Princess Mary, to the aged Louis XII of France in 1514. I remembered how I had seen it in my modern day life during my last pilgrimage to Hever. By some amazing quirk of fate, in the twenty-first century, it had come to rest at the Boleyn family home. I remembered well how I had stopped in profound amazement as I recognised the face of the young woman whom I had come to know so well; it was the face of Anne Boleyn, depicted as one of the ladies in attendance upon the new queen. I had mused that it seemed fitting that the tapestry should begin life here at the Exchequer in Calais for it must have been here that the Princess Mary had first rested on her way to Abbeville to marry the King of France.

However, as I was mired deeply in these reflections, there was a gentle knock at the door of the grand chamber in which I had sought refuge. My sister, Mary, entered.

'May I join you, Anne?' Mary spoke to me softly with her usual gentle smile, as I indicated that she should take a seat beside me. I continued to gaze at the tapestry, somewhat lost in my own world. Since I had arrived at Calais, the more I had looked upon this beautiful work of art, the more I had been assailed by a montage of images and fragmented conversations, all memories that I strongly suspected were Anne's own recollections of the events that she had witnessed when she first arrived in France at the tender age of thirteen. It was clear that I was becoming ever more connected to Anne's consciousness, her past as well as her present. In those memories, I sensed how carefree had been her world at that time, unencumbered by weighty matters of marriage or dynastic duty. How in that moment I had envied her! In the silence, I sensed Mary studying me intently, for I knew that my melancholy was tangible. Ever maternal, it did not take her long to touch upon the matter. 'Are you well, sister? You have been so quiet since the king's departure and I am concerned for you.' I did not look at her but continued to stare at the tapestry and wondered where on earth I would begin to explain what troubled me so sorely. Despite myself, I said,

'Do you remember it, Mary?' I nodded towards the tapestry as she followed my gaze. I spoke wistfully almost as much to myself as to my sister. 'Was it not such a gloriously happy time? We were so young, so full of life and nothing really seemed to matter at all.' I knew that my sister was also depicted in the scene, and that she would indeed remember it well.

There were a few moments of silence between us before my sister tentatively enquired, 'Are you not happy? Are you sad that you are not yet married to the king as you thought to be, here in Calais?' I knew that there had been talk of a Calais marriage but that had long since disintegrated into ashes, blown away in the turbulence of political uncertainty. My sister reached over and put her hand reassuringly upon my shoulder as she went on, 'I beg you Anne, do not fret, for the king simply adores you and could not live without you. As we speak, our great friend and most loyal supporter, Thomas Cranmer, returns from the continent to be consecrated as Archbishop of Canterbury, and Master Cromwell works tirelessly to ensure that legally no one may challenge the validity of your marriage to the king. When all this is said and done, Henry will make you his wife.' Mary always saw the best in people; oh, I could not imagine how painfully her heart would be broken by the tragic events which would befall her family if fate was to take its course. Suddenly, I was overcome by an earnest desire to try and warn her, to toughen her up and protect her in case the course of history couldn't be changed. I shifted in my seat, turning to face her, before I spoke with great seriousness.

'Mary, sweet sister, you must listen to me; as our mother has said, we Boleyns make a nest in a bed of vipers and...' I paused for a moment not knowing how to explain what I should not know, 'You must not speak of this to anyone, but if I cannot give the king a son then, then things may happen—terrible things—and if they do, promise me this,' I took both her tiny hands in mine and squeezing them tightly, entreated her to listen carefully to my every word. 'I cannot be more specific, but if what I speak of comes to pass, then you will know that what I have spoken of now is the truth, and you must, dear sister, get away from court as quickly as you can and stay away; do not think to return, for you have children to think of and our mother will need you more than ever.' Mary's eyes flashed with fear as she replied,

'Anne, you're frightening me! 'Terrible things! Of what do you speak?' Suddenly, there was another more forceful knock at the door. But before it opened, I had chance to say to Mary, 'Think nought of it anymore, but remember my words and promise me you will do as I say. Promise me!' I could see that she was deeply perturbed but I felt compelled that, come what may, Mary would be safe; that of all of us Boleyns she deserved it, for there was not a malicious bone in her body. Mary nodded her head. Yet fear was plain in her eyes. I let go of her hands quickly and turned towards the door as I said assertively, 'Enter!' Our aunt, Elizabeth Wood, Lady Boleyn stepped inside, her hands clasped rigidly as ever in front of her stomach, as she announced,

'My lady, Master Farlyon has sent word to say that he is ready for the rehearsing of the masque and awaits your presence.' Even though I had not been able to confide all my fears to my sister, I realised that it had also been a blessed relief to share some of the load that had borne down so heavily upon me in recent days. As we made to leave, I saw that Mary looked shaken and I resolved, for her sake, to bury my cares once more and throw myself into the great courtly celebrations which were planned for Sunday, 27 October. Henry was to return from Boulogne with Francis in less than two days' time. I needed Anne to be at her glittering best, for he would expect her to shine like a diamond, captivating the court above all others as his intended wife and queen. I could not let him, or Anne, down.

Chapter Six

The Exchequer, Calais,
Sunday 27 October 1532

The first that I had heard of the king's return was a blast of 400 shot, fired from Newenhambridge, a small garrison that lay just about a mile to the west of the town on the main Boulogne to Calais road. This was followed by thirty at Block House, 300 fired from the Rysbank Tower in the harbour, and finally, as the king approached Calais itself, a great round of 2,000 shot was fired, reverberating seemingly endlessly around the town's narrow streets and marketplaces. With Henry's return there would be great rejoicing and celebrations; I could lose myself once more in my fairy-tale, happily deluding myself that the love between Anne and Henry would last forever. It was easy to do so, for Henry had returned in fine spirits. I was summoned to the king's presence chamber not long after his arrival at the Exchequer. Following a formal greeting, during which I and my ladies curtsied low and I had commended myself unto his majesty, we fell into each other's arms in a rapture of love and happiness. Henry led me into his privy chamber where, with great excitement, he told me that Francis had promised not only to wage war with him against the Turks, but that the French King would unreservedly support our marriage. He pledged to send forthwith a message to the Pope with reassurances that, backed by France and England, his Holiness had no need to fear the Emperor's wrath. Henry was one step closer to fulfilling his heart's desire—his union with Anne and the fulfilment of his dynastic aspirations.

The king was present when, later that day, Francis sent the French provost from his lodgings at Staple Hall with a gift of a large, flawless diamond in honour of *Madame la Marquise,* which I graciously accepted. When the provost had left, Henry took the jewel in his hand and held it up to the light, examining it closely. After some time, he nodded his head in goodly satisfaction and turned to me, announcing that he would have his goldsmith, Cornelius Hayes, fashion it immediately into a pendant as a remembrance of our triumph at Calais. This fine stone, he commanded, was to be 'tabled' and set centrally between the entwined initials of 'H' and 'A', wrought from pierced

74

gold. I would wear it often thereafter as it reminded me of the happiest of times and would keep it close to my person until the very day that I was arrested at Greenwich when, like everything else that I owned, including my life, I surrendered into the king's hands.

Yet such unhappy times seemed so far away as the court awoke on that Sunday morning to a fine and bright day. There was an expectant buzz about the palace for today was to mark the pinnacle of the celebrations of our trip to Calais. After dinner, Henry set out with his retinue to the Staple Inn where bull and bear-baiting had been arranged for entertainment in the large central courtyard. The inn was renowned as the finest and most handsome residence in the town, lying due south of the Market Square almost opposite the Pryncen Tower, on the southern wall of the citadel.

I had agreed with the king that I would not show my face to Francis until the grand masque to be held after supper that evening. I remained behind at the Exchequer with my ladies where there was great excitement; my sister, Lady Rochford, Dorothy, the Countess of Derby, Lady Fitzwater, Lady Wallop and Lady Lisle were all due to accompany me in the masque for the king and his honoured guest. As before, when Nan, Mary Norris and I danced afore his majesty during the picnic at Windsor Lodge, I had been responsible for much of the choreography, which we rehearsed tirelessly until our feet had been blistered and our muscles ached. On Sunday afternoon, these six ladies spent most of the time in my privy chambers, gossiping and giggling, trying on their costumes and practising their dance steps, whilst officers of the king's wardrobe made last minute adjustments to their garments. Nothing less than perfection would do.

Late in the afternoon of Sunday, 27 October, we were conveyed by torchlight in some secrecy to the Staple Inn, where a sumptuous banquet was already well underway. It was a magnificent three- storey structure, the central archway surmounted at the first level by the coat of arms of the Staple Guild of Calais, and above that on the upper floor, was displayed the royal coat of arms. As we passed beneath the gatehouse and into the enormous central courtyard, we could hear the general hum of excited chatter coming from the inn's great hall. Eager guests were being served from an astonishing array of over 170 dishes, including a huge variety of meat, game and fish. The masque, which was just getting underway, included as ever music, dancing, singing and acting, with many of the latter parts played by the king's professional actors. These same actors often performed allegorical plays which paid homage to their sovereign lord. Such masques were hugely popular at Henry's court for they provided a great spectacle of entertainment and allowed noble lords, ladies and gentlemen to participate, and show off their fine mastery of courtly pastimes. Tonight the banqueting hall of the Staple Inn was alight with speculation, for amongst the English nobility were many of King Francis' noblemen, all of whom were eager to catch the first sight of Anne Boleyn; some of whom remembered the lady from her time at the French court, some twelve years earlier. There was intense curiosity to see the woman who had risen from relative obscurity to capture the heart of a king.

I had stayed hidden from view since King Francis' arrival at Calais, which had heightened expectations enormously, and allowed me to create a sense of drama. Yet I had to confess that as my ladies and I waited to begin our performance, my heart thundered in my chest; a mixture of excitement and terror surged through my veins. Would I do Anne justice and hold an entire court spellbound? I could not resist the temptation to take a peek of what lay beyond a curtained doorway, and with the finger of one hand, I surreptitiously drew the curtain back just a couple of inches to catch a glimpse of those who would be our audience.

It was a celestial vision that literally took my breath away, for the walls had been hung with silver and gold tissue and adorned at intervals with gold wreaths that literally glistened with precious stones, reflecting the warm light from nearly twenty silver chandeliers, each one bearing nigh on 100 wax candles. The light cast from those magnificent chandeliers lit up the faces of several hundred courtiers as they ate, drank and made merry with old friends and new. To complete the glittering spectacle, on the far side of the room close to the dais where the two kings dined, was an enormous seven-tier buffet, gleaming under the weight of the Tudor gold plate. It made an impressive display of princely wealth and status.

The evening's revels were well underway, and would soon reach their climax with our dancing. I strained my neck eager to catch my first sight of King Francis, who sat at the Henry's right hand side as his guest of honour. Henry was dressed in violet cloth of gold, the most noble of colours, reserved exclusively for the king and his immediate family, and one which I, since Anne's elevation to the peerage, had also been granted permission to wear. What was most eye-catching about the king that evening was the magnificent collar of fourteen rubies and fourteen diamonds that hung about his shoulders; the smallest ruby being the size of an egg. These stones were separated by two rows of pearls; hanging down from this collar was another rare and precious stone that I recognised immediately as the Black Prince's ruby. It was one of Henry's favourites; a magnificent jewel, the size of a goose's egg. It had been given to Edward of Woodstock, the Black Prince, in 1367, and even worn by Henry V in his crown at the Battle of Agincourt. It had been in the possession of every English king ever since and I longed to tell Henry that in the twenty-first century, it would be set into the Imperial Crown of England, perhaps one of the best-known jewels in the world. By wearing it that day, Henry was reminding Francis of England's magnificent victory against the French at Agincourt, almost to the day, 117 years earlier, in 1415.

I had seen enough and let the curtain fall back into place, then turned to face my ladies who were chattering with nervous excitement. They had all been chosen to dance that evening on account of their fair looks and accomplished graces. First amongst them all was my sister, Mary, then came my mother's youngest sister, Elizabeth Howard, and the third was Lady Fitzwalter, Anne's aunt. Elizabeth had a petite frame, a perfectly shaped oval face, and like Anne, she had an abundance of glossy, chestnut-brown hair, but in her case striking grey-green eyes. Four maids of honour, including Lady Mary Howard, were also present to escort us into the hall. I smiled as I watched their happy exuberance when my sister caught my attention and broke away from her conversation with Jane Rochford and Mary Howard to make her way toward me, her face alight in eager anticipation.

'Oh Anne, you look truly beautiful! As ever, methinks that the king will not be able to take his eyes from you this evening.' Indeed we were all gorgeously dressed in loose, gold laced over-dresses fashioned from cloth of gold, with sashes of crimson satin, ornamented with a wavy pattern in cloth of silver, were tied about our waists accentuating our feminine silhouettes. The four maids of honour looked resplendent in the same colour with tabards of cypress lawn—a rather delicate and transparent material which showed the detailing of the dress beneath it. We were to be Greek goddesses, descended from the heavens themselves to entertain the court—desirable, untouchable, divine. Tonight, I intended to be Henry's goddess incarnate.

'Thank you, sister. You, too, look beautiful.' I said in reply. 'Have a wonderful evening but make sure you do not steal the heart of a French nobleman for I will not lose you to the French court!'

'Ladies, your masks!' I said, indicating that we should tie our masks into place and prepare for our grand entrance. The yeoman announced the arrival of seven muses, goddesses beyond this earthly realm, come forth to dance for the delight of his most gracious majesty and his honoured guest. Anne would now bask in the adoration of not only the king, but an entire court. The curtain was pulled aside, and maintaining my hidden identity in amongst my ladies, Anne stepped into the hall to take her place at the centre of Europe's most prestigious stage.

From behind my mask, I watched Henry's response to our dancing, flashes of pride, love, lust and desire on his face. I also watched King Francis lean across to his royal brother and make a comment—was he asking which of the ladies was *Madame la Marquise*? When our dance of seduction came to an end, all seven of us dropped to the floor, our eyes downcast in reverence. The room burst into thunderous applause, as I lifted my face to see Henry and Francis clapping enthusiastically. Henry gestured to Francis that he should take to the floor to partner a lady and lead the dancing that was to follow. My ladies tactfully withdrew to find their partners elsewhere, among them some of the leading noblemen of the French court, including the King of Navarre, who had been claimed by Dorothy Stanley, Countess of Derby. I stepped forward to offer my hand to Francis who had swept onto the dance floor, a picture of princely countenance. He took my hand graciously with a gallant flourish, raising it to brush my soft skin delicately with his lips, as he said in a voice that was heavily accented with Parisian French,

'Madame, may it be my good fortune to accompany you in this dance!' I knew that Francis was a notorious lover of beauty and of the flesh, and from behind my mask; I saw his lusty appreciation of my feminine guiles. I curtsied as I replied flirtatiously in fluent French,

'Your Grace, it would be a great honour to dance at Your Majesty's side.'

Many of the courtiers took to the floor for the pavane, the most stately of dances, designed to enable the great ladies and gentlemen of the court to process in a manner which allowed them to see and be seen. With King Francis by my side, we danced changing places or circling about one another, toying carefully with each other's sexuality as we did so. Francis had a reputation as being affable, courteous, generous, with a wicked wit, but these were eclipsed by his tendency to selfishness, frivolousness and infuriating inconsistency. There was a palpable and predatory maleness about him which undoubtedly accounted for his notoriety at court. Like Henry, Francis was a charismatic alpha male, and I could see why women would find him irresistible; he had power, charm, good humour and wealth, a potent force for stirring the senses. I cast a glance out of the corner of my eye at this king that Anne knew so well. I was curious to drink in the appearance of the man who had played a significant role in her early life, who had been Mary Boleyn's lover for a time, and who had become Henry's greatest rival.

King Francis I of France was well built, thirty-eight years old and at six foot six, towering even above Henry's magnificent physique. He was very handsome, of dark colouring, a closely cropped beard and moustache and warm chocolate brown eyes. However, his rather long-pointed nose somewhat marred his appearance; Henry once laughed aloud as he recounted the story that he had heard through the English ambassador to the French court that one of King Francis' courtiers had infamously said that the king 'had the largest nose of any man in France, except his jester!' There was no doubt that despite the rich fabrics and costly jewels which bedecked Henry and the English court, Francis and his French noblemen were a picture of sartorial elegance, with the French aristocracy still defining the epitome of high fashion. He was dressed in blue cloth of silver which glistened in the flickering candlelight with a doublet which was overset with a multitude of precious stones and rich diamonds. Gossip about the court was that it had cost the king an unbelievable thirty million pounds. As the king led me with great skill and style around the banqueting hall, he could not help but enquire about my identity. I smiled and teased him saying,

'Is not the beauty of the masque that I can be whoever you wish me to be, Your Majesty?' as I tilted my head somewhat coquettishly, goading Francis to rise to the challenge.

'Forsooth, and if that were so Madame, then I would choose a lady who moved with the grace, and spoke with the tongue of a native born Frenchwoman... which to my great joy, I find that you do.' We turned to face each other, the music coming to an end as Francis bowed and I curtsied low before him. Before I had chance to reply, I caught sight of Henry moving towards us, his arms outstretched and open in warm welcome as he said ebulliently,

'Dear brother, does the lady please you?' Francis smiled and said, 'She is divine... and speaks like an angel. Tell me, brother who,' he turned to face me raising a single eyebrow playfully, 'is this lady?' With that, Henry stepped behind me and with a single pull undid the silk ribbon of my mask, triumphantly revealing me to Francis and the entire French court. Francis cried out, no doubt in feigned surprise. I was sure that he had known me well all along.

'Ah! *Madame la Marquise*! It is truly an honour, my lady.' He once again took my hand and in front of the entire court, kissed it, acknowledging to all his recognition of my status at Henry's side. The room was still applauding our performance and our unmasking as Henry whispered in my ear,

'You look stunning. I am so proud of you!' he said gently kissing my cheek, I smiled coyly at him, basking in his adoration. Henry extended both his arms open again indicating that the two of us should continue in our conversation, and whilst the music recommenced, Francis offered me his hand and together we walked towards the fine oriel window which looked over the inner courtyard below, for here we could be afforded greater privacy to talk. When we had finally seated ourselves on velvet cushions, I took a moment to cast a glance around the room. The atmosphere was deliciously vibrant; with the coming together of the two courts and the evident goodwill between both monarchs, there was much jubilation, the forging of new friendships and in some cases, the cementing of old alliances. The air was filled with the scent of sweet beeswax and fragrant herbs, whilst the general hubbub was punctuated with the occasional sound of raucous laughter and spirited melodies which joyfully accompanied the dance.

With a gold goblet in his hand, I watched as Henry moved about the hall, stopping to talk animatedly firstly with my brother and Sir Henry Norris, before moving on to speak with the young Duke of Richmond, whom I noticed was deep in conversation with my cousin, Mary Howard. I knew that in time they would be married and that Anne probably played a significant role in bringing about their union; I now understood why. Anne was deeply fond of her young cousin and used her influence to secure Mary Howard the best possible marriage; and what marriage could be more advantageous than to the king's acknowledged, albeit illegitimate son, one of only three dukes in the land. Francis suddenly cut through my thoughts. He had abandoned any attempt to speak to me in English, for he was well aware of my fluency in his mother tongue, yet I had not anticipated what he would say next.

'It does not surprise me that the king desires you above all others, for you cannot have forgotten that there was once a time when I pursued your favour with the same fervency.' My head snapped about to look at him. Suddenly, I was trying desperately to understand the implications of his words. I had always assumed that Anne had remained chaste at the French court. Was King Francis now telling me that in fact she had slept with him—had become his mistress?

'I ... I...' I did not know what to say, and must have looked aghast. Francis began to laugh, oblivious to my discomfort and confusion,

'I tried everything I knew to get you to be my mistress, and yet Madame,' he put his hand on his heart as if to feign great sorrow and wounded pride, 'you spurned me without mercy! I only suspect that you have given the King of England a similarly hard time?' It was both a statement and a question, and I when said nothing but smiled somewhat enigmatically, Francis chuckled and nodded his head knowingly, 'Yes, I thought so. Madame, you are an unfathomable mystery, and I wish my royal brother all the luck in the world in trying to solve the puzzle that is Anne Boleyn.'

The king rapidly moved on to other matters, and for over an hour, we were deeply engrossed in conversation that was sometimes playful and flirtatious, sometimes deadly serious. Flashes of fragmented memories that had come to me over previous weeks slotted into place as Francis recounted the happy times of our youth. I had sworn my allegiance as a friend of France, and Francis reiterated his commitment to Henry that he would support our marriage and any backlash from the Emperor. At the end of the evening, when Francis had taken his leave, and Henry escorted him back to his lodgings at Staple Hall, I could not forget his words. I had now heard it from somebody who had been there, that Anne had emerged pure from her time at the French court: she—and I—would go to Henry's bed a virgin, untouched by man.

We made our way back to the Exchequer under cover of a starry sky. The streets were deserted, save for the litters which had carried the ladies home, and a steady stream of mostly drunken courtiers whose good-natured laughter and songs could be heard echoing through Calais' empty streets. As we approached our lodgings, I cast a glance out of the window of our little carriage and admired the resplendent Gothic facade of St Nicholas' Church. It was illuminated by the silvery-blue light of a full moon which cast menacing shadows from the gargoyles that had been placed about the building a few hundred years earlier to protect it against evil spirits. As we passed underneath the main gateway of the Exchequer, I heard the great bell of St Nicholas chime midnight, but I was not tired. The exhilaration of such an intoxicating evening of dance, wine and courtly love had left my ladies and me bubbling with excitement, and full of gossip: who had flirted with whom, what kisses might have been stolen, and who was the most handsome bachelor that evening.

I alighted in the main courtyard and, accompanied by my ladies and maids of honour, we laughed and chatted our way up the great processional stair, through the queen's great chamber, eventually finding ourselves in the 'raying chamber'; a room which led directly into the queen's bedchamber, used as Anne's dressing room. It was a goodly sized chamber covered in wood panelling and painted with various royal and heraldic symbols on three separate panels, the central one depicting the royal coat of arms and the king's motto, *Dieu et mon Droit*. There were two decorative panels on either side, one with the initials *HR* and the other, *AB,* which I guessed had only been recently painted in preparation for our visit. There were a number of fine and sturdy pieces of furniture along with several mannequins or 'babies' as they were called, of the type I had first seen at Windsor Castle, and which currently displayed a variety of my most favoured gowns. A lit fire had kept the room warm and welcoming, and a number of candles augmented the soft glow from the flickering flames in the hearth.

I sat in a chair whilst Lady Wallop knelt at my feet to remove my shoes and stockings and listened with some detachment as my ladies good-naturedly teased little Mary Howard about the obvious attentions of the young Duke of Richmond. Yet in my mind, I was elsewhere. Although I had spent precious little time at Henry's side during the course of the evening, I had not failed to notice how avidly he had watched me, and felt the palpable and growing sexual tension that existed between us, pulling and clawing at our sensibilities, impelling us toward the inevitable expression of our desire. Whether it was a finger traced across the back, or a momentary linking of hands, or the gentlest breath against a cheek, it might as well have been the deepest and most passionate of kisses, for it stirred me so intensely. I could see in Henry's eyes that he yearned for me with every fibre of his being; sometimes they were hard and intense as if he wished to devour me, sometimes dreamy and wistful, hypnotised by desperate longing.

Since the conversation with my mother whilst out hawking, I could not forget her words and admit that I had thought much upon them ever since. I knew it was time for Anne to force Henry's hand, and as Lady Lisle unpinned from my hair the many fine jewels which were threaded through it, I sensed that I had taken a step from which there was no going back. I heard my ladies laughing and talking animatedly and my sister, perhaps more effervescent than most, swirling about the room, replaying the moment when she had danced with Francis' son, the young and very handsome, fourteen-year-old dauphin. Yet I was lost in a memory of the last dance that I had with the king before he had taken his leave of me and the evening had drawn to a close. It was a volta, full of intensity and intimate contact. When the dance finished, Henry took hold of both my hands and brushing his cheek against mine whispered breathlessly, 'I want you, Anne Boleyn.' I had paused for a moment trying to catch my breath. It was not the exertion of the dance that left me so, but that I knew that what I was about to say would catalyse a force of nature which I would be unable to stop. I felt fate compelling me on and before I could change my mind, I replied, 'then...why... don't you... take... me?' There had been a moment of pure stillness between us, as I knew the words struck the target with force enough to cause Henry to draw back slightly. He stared at me, his face just a few inches from my own, searching my eyes in an attempt to fathom if I was serious or no. I raised an eyebrow and flashed those beautiful, black eyes of Anne's at him provocatively, before dipping into the deepest of curtsies and withdrawing; my gaze lingering upon that of the king's in a way which invited only one response. I knew that he would come to me that evening and that our love would finally be consummated.

My thoughts were suddenly interrupted by a loud knock at the door that connected directly to the king's bedchamber. I looked towards it, as did all my ladies, whose gossip and chatter suddenly ceased. Mary froze in the midst of a great whirl of movement. I indicated to Dorothy, Countess of Derby, that she should open it. She moved forward, acting immediately upon my request. There standing half undressed in only his open silk shirt, stockings and shoes was the King of England looking somewhat dishevelled yet deliciously intense, and dangerously sexy. He lifted an arm, leaning one elbow above his head against the doorway, and in the other, he held a fine silver-gilt goblet which contained a full measure of wine. He said nothing, but I knew exactly what he wanted as I said softly,

'Ladies, please leave us.' My sister was the last to leave as she flashed me a look of recognition to wish me *bon courage,* and closed the door softly behind her. I moved forward taking one deliberate and provocative step in front of the other, until I stood just three or four feet from the king; my hair hanging loose about my shoulders, my feet were bare, yet otherwise fully dressed. Henry took the last swig of his wine as his gaze rose to meet mine. His breathing was rapid and shallow, belying the adrenaline that I knew must be coursing through his veins, for I too had felt my pulse quicken as a flush of desire spread deliciously through my groin. We were as the hunter and the hunted; I was both afraid of the strength of Henry's desire and at the same time, I longed for him to show me the pure, unadulterated power of his maleness. Time stood still in that moment until I tilted my head to the side as if to say, 'and what are you waiting for?'

Suddenly, in a pyroclastic explosion of passion, Henry threw aside his goblet, sending it clattering across the wooden floor, before he lunged forward toward me. Our bodies collided as the king pushed me back forcefully against the wall, and I felt my breath ripped from my body as I fell into the wooden panelling behind me. With one hand, Henry pinned my arms above my head, whilst with the other, he grasped voraciously at the curves of my body, as we devoured each other in a frenzy of deep, searching kisses. I heard him groan,

'Oh God! I need to be inside you…' With his free hand, he grasped at my loose gown pulling up the hem of my dress. Willingly, I lifted my left leg and hooked it about his waist, allowing him to run his hand along the outside of my thigh, grasping at my buttock before he thrust his still fully clothed body hard against my own. For several minutes we remained there, intertwined in an almost violent raping of the other's senses; grinding our bodies against each other simulating intercourse, luxuriating in the deliciousness of our passion, arousing our senses to ever heightened levels of intensity, clawing, devouring, needing each other as if our lives depended upon it.

Henry finally let go of my arms, and for a moment, I grabbed each side of his face, holding us suspended in the midst of our lovemaking as I whispered provocatively,

'Do it now! I want you inside me now.' Henry grabbed me and spun me around, colliding with a sideboard that abutted against the wall next to us, lifting me up by my buttocks until I was perched on the edge of it, whilst I obligingly clasped my legs around his waist. I was fighting for breath, entirely submerged in a firestorm of desire which was engulfing us both, burning away years of frustration and unspent sexual energy. Blindly, I reached out behind me to steady myself, sending various items of gold and silver plate flying through the air and crashing unceremoniously to the ground. I was vaguely aware that beyond the doors of my raying chamber, my ladies must be hearing the violence of our union. Yet I knew that they dare not enter.

I then became aware of Henry pulling down his hose. I reached behind him, grasping at his bare buttocks, craving to feel him penetrate me. I cried out as he ripped his way through my vagina, momentarily unable to breathe, as a searing pain tore through my groin.

Henry thrust mercilessly hard and deep, at times seemingly oblivious to my presence, lost deeply in his own vortex of erotic lust. I watched his eyes cloud over as he was approaching his climax and so, with all the strength I could muster, I pushed him off me, holding him for a moment at arm's length. With fierce determination I hissed at him,

'The bedchamber. Let us go to the bedchamber.' I slipped off the sideboard and made my way towards the bedchamber that lay beyond, where we would have a little more privacy from prying ears. As I did so, Henry came up behind me, clasping his arms about my waist. I melted into them, groaning in desire as he ran his hands across my breasts, my belly, my hips, all the time kissing my neck and nibbling at my ear lobe; his body was pressed closely against my back as I allowed my head to rest back onto his shoulder, surrendering myself entirely to his will. As we walked in tandem, step-by-step toward my bedchamber, the king began to tear at my dress, literally ripping it from my body and sending the precious stones and pearls which had adorned it, pinging in all directions, bouncing like raindrops falling during the fiercest storm across the oak floor. By the time we reached my bed chamber, the king had divested me of all my robes; I was entirely naked before him.

I turned about, pulling at Henry's shirt while he kicked off his stockings and shoes, leaving only his magnificent collar of diamonds and rubies which he had been wearing throughout the evening. I smiled at him seductively tracing my finger from stone to stone. The king looked down at my hand before taking the collar in both of his, lifting it from his shoulders and placing it about my neck. It was my turn to look down upon it, marvelling for the briefest of moments that between my breasts lay the Black Prince's ruby. How strange is life, that in the twenty-first century, I would see this stone so many times in the crown jewels of England—yet never for a moment could I have ever believed that I had worn it, a very long time ago, so close to my heart.

When I looked up again at Henry, he began to kiss me evermore fervently, before suddenly exploding once again into even greater unbridled passion and suddenly picked me up so effortlessly in both his arms before throwing me down upon the bed. Within moments, he was between my thighs and once more inside me, dominating me entirely. This time I could not stop the inevitable. The King of England would have me and together we were submerged into our rhythm of love; the feeling of each thrust sending a luscious tingling bursting through my entire body. Henry began to gasp and call my name. I tore at his back and buttocks, clasping my leg around him, urging him deeper. This time there would be no care for the consequences; I would have Henry's child in my body. Finally, my lover cried,

'Oh God, Anne! God, I'm going to come!' Nature seized hold of us both and carried us together in a torrent of unstoppable energy toward our climax. Together, we arched our bodies, pressing our hips together as Henry exploded inside of me, both of us crying out loudly oblivious to who might hear the consummation of our relationship. When it was finally over, we both collapsed back on the bed, breathless from our exertion. I could feel waves of after-shock travelling through my body one after the other; a luscious feeling of profound physical contentment merged with relief that finally, the deed was done.

Henry was never the most tender of lovers, but he was enthusiastic, passionate and never afraid to assert his dominance, something that I found enormously sexy. Anne may well have been a virgin but in my twenty-first century life, of course, I was not. I could not deny that I was no shrinking violet in the bedroom. Thus perhaps I would do things to Henry that some of his other sixteenth century lovers would never entertain. I knew that there were times when the king would look momentarily taken aback at my open and brazen sexuality, only for the very same expression to melt away into delight as he experienced the pleasure of our lovemaking. Like everything else in our relationship, in the bedroom, I was Henry's equal.

We slept very little that night, our groans of ecstasy and playful laughter echoing around the silent palace into the early hours of the morning. Finally, a little before seven of the clock, the king kissed my forehead, bid me 'good morrow' and slipped away from my bedroom to prepare for the day ahead. Monday, 28 October was to be the last day of King Francis' visit to Calais. There was to be the glittering ceremony that morning, when Anne de Montmorency and the Admiral of France were to be made Knights of the Garter, in return for the honour bestowed upon my Uncle Norfolk and the Duke of Suffolk by the King of France just a few days earlier. The rest of the day was to be followed by courtly entertainments arranged for the delight of both of the sovereigns, their nobles and lords. As there were no ladies of the French court present, I would again keep to the privacy of my chambers.

A short while after the king had departed, I threw the covers off my bed and slipped into my favourite black silk, taffeta-lined night gown, throwing a velvet-lined cloak over my shoulders and returned to my rooms. When I stepped into the chamber beyond, I could not help but giggle softly, the evidence of our tempestuous lovemaking was scattered everywhere around the floor. It was as if the room had been ransacked by a madman searching for something that he had been unable to find. Two of the 'babies', the mannequins, had fallen awkwardly, whilst gold and silver plate lay strewn haphazardly upon the floor. All around my feet were scattered pearls and precious diamonds that had been torn from my costume, the latter of which lay in tatters as a trail from one side of the room to the next.

As I surveyed the damage, there was a delicate knock on the door of my privy apartments. I knew this must be one of my ladies.

'Enter.' The door was opened rather timidly and I was met by my friend, Nan Gainsford and my sister, Mary, who both entered cautiously before quietly closing the door behind them. As I stood there surrounded by this scene of devastation, I watched them look about the room with a mixture of both horror and amusement. Mary spoke first,

'God's blood! I have never seen the like!' she exclaimed, as she picked up the hem of her skirt and tiptoed toward me making her way amongst the wreckage of our lovemaking. When Mary reached my side, I saw a flash of concern across her face. Reaching out to brush my hair from my shoulders, she said with great disquiet, 'Oh my word! Did he hurt you, Anne?' I saw that she was looking intently at my neck and shoulders. I shook my head, confused as to what she was referring as Mary laid her hand upon my shoulder and turned me about to face a mirror on the wall close by. I took two or three steps closer to it, scooping my hair up with one hand to reveal my bare neck and shoulders; to my horror they were covered in a mass of bites and bruises. I ran my finger down the left side of my neck, turning my face this way and that to examine the extent of the damage. Finally, looking back toward my sister and friend, I finally said,

'I am fine, sister. But let us clear up this mess before someone arrives who I'd rather not see it.' Then I added, 'Nan please have my chamberers prepare me a bath and light the fire; it is a chilly morning and I feel the need to soak my tired and aching muscles.' With that, Nan nodded her understanding and immediately disappeared to convey my command. When the door to my raying chamber closed behind her, without airs or graces, my sister and I began the task of making right the worst of the carnage when she eventually spoke,

'Are you really all right, sister? Did he hurt you? It's just that...that,' she paused awkwardly clearly searching for the right words which would not offend me, 'I sent the others away, but Nan and I stayed next door… in case you needed us. We could not help but hear… I wondered if… if he had taken you by force.' At that moment, I understood my sister's look of perpetual concern. So fierce had been our lovemaking that she had thought that Henry had ravished me. I turned to look at her, smiling and shaking my head as I said,

'Oh, no. No, Mary, the king did not force himself upon me.' I walked up to her, taking both her hands in mine as I went on, 'it is just that it has been such a very long time that, as you well know, I have kept Henry at arm's length. You, sweet sister, know more than anyone how passionate his majesty can be!' Mary smiled and a look of recognition crossed her face. I saw her shoulders fall as the tension was released from her body. I was reminded yet again of her gentle, caring soul and was touched deeply by her concern for me.

Nan returned with three maids in tow, two carrying a large wooden bath, and a third who set about kindling a glorious and welcoming fire in the hearth. A little while later, I sank gladly into the hot, steamy water scented with rose petals and lavender, washing away the smell of sex which had clung to me from the night before. As I lay there, my mind could not help but drift back to the events of the previous evening. I felt aglow from the nectareous memories of Henry's ardent desire for me and the promise he whispered to me in the still of the night; as soon as we returned to Dover, we would be betrothed. I was well aware that as we had already consummated our relationship, this was *de facto,* in the eyes of the law, Anne and Henry would be man and wife—assuming Henry's marriage to Katherine would ultimately be dissolved; as I knew it soon would be. I saw how history continued to work both for and against Anne, but in that moment, I cared little for anything except the delicious and searching intimacy that I had finally known with the king.

Around us the Exchequer was beginning to stir. In the main courtyard below, visitors to court had already begun to arrive. Servants bustled this way and that, and several more of my ladies began to appear in my chambers, amongst them Margery, who was first to arrive, followed by Lady Mary Howard, Elizabeth Wood, Lady Boleyn, Lady Wallop and Lady Lisle; all of whom I suspected were eager to find out what had transpired between the king and me. However, I did not have a mind to speak of it, for these memories were still too new and too precious to carelessly give away. And so I was dressed by my ladies, keeping well my counsel, requesting only that they dress me in a high-necked partlet which would hide the worst of the tokens of love which the king had imprinted upon my delicate skin. Thankfully, I was almost completely dressed by the time my mother appeared at the door.

'Mother, good morrow!' I said brightly, genuinely happy to see her, as she put her arms about me and kissed my cheek,

'Good morrow child.' She turned to Mary, repeating her welcome with a kiss and an embrace, before she said to us, 'You both looked beautiful last night. Your father and I were very proud of you.' It was a rare compliment for my sister, who these days was so often overshadowed by Anne's glittering presence and therefore starved of parental approval. I watched her glow from our mother's praise, drinking it in as if quenching her thirst after the longest drought. My mother then turned her attention back to me, and was about to speak again when she caught sight of the marks upon my neck, the ones which were too high up to be hidden by the partlet. I watched her as she paused, studying my neck for a moment, before raising her eyes to meet mine. I knew the question that was playing on her mind, but she dare not ask me in the presence of my ladies, and so I said,

'Come mother, I think to take the air before I break my fast. Would you walk with me in the privy gardens?' My maids brought forth furs in which we might wrap ourselves against the morning chill. Accompanied by my sister, Nan, Margery and Lady Mary Howard, all of whom followed us at a discreet distance, my mother and I went down the queen's stair and into the queen's privy gardens on the north side of the Exchequer. It was yet another fine and bright morning, the naked silhouette of sleeping trees cast in stark relief against a bright blue sky, whilst the cold air made our breath visible as we spoke. We walked along together in silence for a few moments, admiring the beauty and freshness of the morning before finally my mother asked,

'What happened?' I knew immediately to what she referred. Elizabeth Boleyn, Anne's mother, was the only mother I had ever known and I relished the intimacy and trust that we shared. I wanted her to be the first to know what had transpired between the king and me. I sought for a moment to find a way to convey the matter truthfully, but with as much delicacy as I could muster.

'I have given myself into the king's hands,' I said to the countess who was looking at me with some concern. Stopping for a moment, I linked my arm with my mother's, drawing her closer to me as we continued to walk. We crunched our way along the gravel path, and in a voice that could not be overheard by my ladies, I added, 'The king has commanded that arrangements will be made for out betrothal as soon as we land in Calais.' My mother's face lit up in great delight,

'Is it true, Anne? Is this the will of his majesty?' I could see a flash of sheer relief pass across her face. Like any mother, she had worried endlessly for me, that my reputation would be ruined and that ultimately I would be cast aside by the king with nought to show from our relationship. Elizabeth Boleyn was no meek or submissive woman, but she knew the practicalities of the world in which she lived; that women needed the status, wealth and protection of a man to take her proper place in society. I nodded my head and smiled back at her, happy that I could bring her such joy. Elizabeth Boleyn clasped her hands together at her breast and looked heavenwards as she said, 'Then God be praised that such a thing will soon come to pass!' She paused for a moment before adding thoughtfully, 'Did the king say anything else?'

'Only that we should speak little of it; his majesty remains keen to see the return and consecration of Thomas Cranmer as Archbishop of Canterbury, and to see Master Cromwell's Act of Appeals passed through Parliament before the king can finally be divorced and officially married.' My mother understood the need for discretion, yet was bursting with happiness and pride for her beloved daughter. Suddenly, my mother stood still, her brow crumpling into rivulets of pain, her hand held against her chest, slightly out of breath. 'What is it mother? Are you all right?' I said with great concern, as I put my arm around her shoulder and assisted her to a nearby stone seat.

'I'll be all right in a minute, child. I just need to get my breath.' She smiled at me feebly before she added, 'it must be the shock and the wonderful surprise of your news.' I sat down beside my mother, my arm still about her shoulders as I searched her face intently.

'You are not well. Has this happened before?' I probed, noticing that I felt enormously protective of her. My mother took a few moments to answer, and as her breathlessness began to subside she replied,

'Just once or twice; sometimes I find it hard to catch my breath. It is of no great concern. We have far more important things to think about now,' she said, smiling at me bravely, clearly wanting to underplay any concern I might have for her health. 'Now, we must find your father for he will be delighted to hear of these developments. Come Anne, let us tarry here no more.' With that, our little party made its way back into the Exchequer, my mother leaning just a little more heavily on me than usual for support. Although I did not know it then, I had witnessed the first signs of the illness which would—not long after Anne's own death—carry the Countess of Wiltshire to her grave.

Chapter Seven

Dover, St Erkenwald's Day,
14 November 1532

For just under two weeks, the worst storms in living memory raged across the North Sea and English Channel, tearing relentlessly at the little town of Calais and making a return journey to England impossibly dangerous. Approximately half the ships that tried to make it to Dover were turned back to Calais or shipwrecked on the inundated shores of Flanders; mercifully, relatively few were lost to the sea. When the winds finally abated, the royal party were yet again thwarted from returning by a dense fog that descended upon the town, lingering eerily for the next two days, keeping us confined to our lodgings.

At Henry's command, we departed from Dover by the flicker of torchlight at midnight on Tuesday, 12 November. The fog began to lift as we stood on the deck of the *Swallow* watching the mighty walls of Calais' fortress merge into the blackness of the night, and we made our way into the Channel to face the long and gruelling twenty-nine hour crossing. It was 5 am on Thursday, 14 November when our ship, accompanied by several others of the royal fleet, finally entered the harbour at Dover. We were all irritable and exhausted, for despite the relative luxury of our accommodation, the ship was cramped and smelly with little room for exercise. Although our sailors had fought valiantly, unruly weather had sent the Swallow rising and falling interminably upon the choppy swell of the English Channel and many of my ladies had been sick. I was never more grateful to see Dover's white cliffs, or to set foot on land which did not sway under my feet.

Once we had disembarked, our party reformed on horseback and wended its way through the cramped, sleeping streets of the little harbour town, before slowly making our way uphill toward the mighty fortress of Dover Castle. The castle had been founded shortly after the Norman Conquest in the eleventh century. However, it was the ambitious building project of King Henry II, straddling the twelfth and thirteenth centuries, which gave the castle its formidable, central keep and an appearance which has endured into my modern day life.

In the twenty-first century I had visited Dover on several occasions, so I knew how the town had gradually encroached upon the hillside to the west of the castle as woodland had been replaced by roads, pavements and houses. As we rode along, I marvelled at how we approached the castle along the very same road that led up to the main westerly gateway to the fortress. I looked up to see the very first embers of light aglow on the eastern horizon, and considered the building which towered above me. In size, might and its position upon a high rocky outcrop of land, Dover Castle always reminded me of Windsor Castle. Yet unlike Windsor, which was a much loved and well used family home, the fortress of Dover was inconvenient in its layout. Apart from its main function of defending against war, it was largely only used for ceremonial purposes and for occasional important visitors stopping off on their travels between England and the continent.

We entered the castle's precinct by passing through the western gateway, known as Constable's Gateway. I shivered, partly as a result of the cold, partly because the remnants of the fog which clung to the higher ground made for a ghostly spectre as it swirled about the many ramparts and ditches of the outer bailey. Henry led the way until we emerged into the precinct of the inner bailey. I raised my eyes upwards toward the formidable facade of the enormous square keep that housed the royal apartments. If I had not been so bone tired and chilled to the core, I might have recoiled from the sight of this most austere of palaces, but I knew that the fires would be burning, with a hearty breakfast prepared for the king and his courtiers. I yearned to warm my body in front of the hearth and to lay my head upon a steady pillow. As we dismounted, the king turned toward me and said,

'Sweetheart, it has been a long journey,' he took my hands in his and kissing them tenderly he added, 'and I see that you are cold and no doubt tired.' He spoke over my shoulder to the Countess of Derby, who had dismounted her horse close behind me and said, 'Lady Derby, see to it that your mistress is given a goodly breakfast and is well rested.' He then turned his gaze back to mine before adding softly, 'and when you are refreshed, I command that you come to my apartments, for I wish to parley with you. Bring only one of your ladies in attendance.' He raised his eyebrows at me and I knew full well that he referred to our betrothal agreed amidst the greatest secrecy possible. 'I shall be

94

waiting for you,' he added before kissing me softly upon my lips. I smiled, despite my exhaustion as I was overflowing with the love that I felt for his majesty and nodded my acceptance of his most gracious invitation. With that the royal party swept inside, leaving the dawn to break on this feast day of St. Erkenwald.

I could not help but pray for the blessing of this Saxon saint. At thirty-one years of age, after six long and difficult years of struggle, Anne was finally on the brink of her marriage to the King of England.

By 10 o'clock in the morning, my ladies and I had rested and broken our fast. Having washed away the sticky, sweet smell of pitch and vomit that seemed to cling to me from our sea journey, I was greatly refreshed and being dressed by my ladies in my finest attire. As they worked busily about my person, pinning and lacing my gown into place, I looked around my cosy but rather small bedchamber and reflected upon why Dover Castle was not popular as a royal lodging. It still retained its outdated medieval layout. Six-foot-thick walls prevented significant changes to the structure of the royal apartments, which were laid out over two floors; on each floor, two large, vaulted chambers ran side-by-side, dominating the central part of the keep. On both levels, one chamber was used as the great hall, or presence chamber, in which the king or queen held audience, whilst the other was reserved as the monarch's privy chamber. Extending beyond these two great chambers was a series of smaller rooms built into the walls of the keep. I was now standing in one such room, my principal bedchamber, in front of a crackling fire which had been lit before my arrival. These rooms would be stark indeed if they had not been covered in rich tapestries and vibrant paintings, with open fires blazing in every hearth, and a myriad of candles chasing away the gloom.

My ladies were busy making the final adjustments to one of my favourite gowns; the bodice, sleeves, skirt and its long train were fashioned from cloth of silver, whilst the underskirt and false sleeves were made of royal blue velvet which were lined and turned back with expensive ermine. With the last item of clothing pinned into place, I turned to the diminutive Lady Mary Howard and said,

'Ladies, would you please leave us. I wish to talk to the Lady Mary alone.' Dutifully, they both made a gentle curtsy and left the room.

Once they had closed the door behind them, I asked Lady Mary, 'You have looked sad these past two weeks in Calais. What troubles you so child?' Lady Mary had picked up my French hood which had been adorned with a beautiful billament encrusted with diamonds and sapphires. She hesitated for a moment with the hood held in her tiny hands, her eyes downcast as if feeling the pain of my question. I reached over and laid my hand on her arm, gently encouraging her to speak her mind. She said nothing, and so I spoke for her, voicing out loud what I felt must surely be on her mind. 'Do you miss the Duke of Richmond?' I was well aware that during our time in Calais, the young duke had paid the Lady Mary considerable attention. However, Henry Fitzroy had left for Paris at the side of King Francis. Along with the fifteen-year-old Henry Howard, Earl of Surrey, they were to complete their education, as Anne had once done, at one of the most sophisticated courts in Europe. Keeping her eyes demurely lowered, Lady Mary nodded before raising her gaze dolefully to meet mine. 'Do you love the duke?' I enquired. In my modern day life, it would not be a question that I would seriously pose to a fourteen-year-old. But I knew well that in the sixteenth century, Lady Mary Howard was of an age to take a husband, and would indeed shortly be expected to do so. Suddenly, Mary Howard broke into a sweet smile, clearly thinking of her beloved, as she said,

'Oh yes, my Lady I think I do love him!' In her eyes, I saw the youthful exuberance for the innocent love that they clearly shared.

'And does the duke love you?' I asked. Lady Mary nodded with a great beaming smile lighting up her face. Nervously, she looked for a moment over her shoulder towards the door, checking that we were alone before she leaned forward and whispered excitedly,

'I believe he does, for he has told me so.' I smiled at her, saying nothing for a moment but indicating that she should proceed to place my French hood upon my head. Having done so, she set about wrapping about my neck a carcanet of matching diamonds and sapphires, whilst at the front of my bodice she pinned into place the brooch with the initials *HA* set centrally with the large table diamond which had been given to me by King Francis in Calais. I watched her silently at work, her nimble fingers working quickly and precisely. When she had completed her task, she raised her eyes from the brooch to meet mine. I smiled wistfully at her as I finally spoke again.

'Oh, Lady Mary, you are so very young, yet I see the duke has captured your heart.' I watched as she blushed scarlet; I did not doubt that Henry Fitzroy had been the first male to stir her female sensibilities. 'Do you think to marry him?' I knew that history had deigned it so, but I was curious to know the Lady Mary's mind without the ambitious interference of men.

'The duke boldly proclaimed that he desired it above all else... yet, I fear that his majesty will not think that the young daughter of an English duke is worthy enough for his grace. I have no doubt that he has in mind a great and advantageous match with some foreign princess.' She sighed sadly, clearly resigned to a lifetime of thwarted love as young people are so dramatically apt to do.

'Perhaps...perhaps not...' I replied enigmatically. Mary Howard looked at me quizzically. 'If you are in love, and it is what you wish for, then I shall speak to the king, let's see what we can do.' Suddenly, Mary's bright blue eyes widened in excited delight.

'Oh, Madame, do you think it might be possible...?' It was heartening to see such great happiness and faith in the power of love, so I put my arm around her and whispered conspiratorially,

'Anything is possible, Lady Mary. You should never forget that we may be the weaker sex, but a woman has great power when she learns how to wield her feminine guiles.' She smiled once more as I added, 'now, you must help me with the rest of my jewellery, and then I have something to ask of you.' Clearly still giddy from my pledge to help her, Lady Mary gushed,

'Anything my Lady Marquess, I will always be your true and loyal servant.'

'Then, I ask that you accompany me into the king's presence this day. What you witness, you must, thereafter, keep entirely to yourself. No one must know of it; it is the king's express and solemn command.' I saw Lady Mary gulp in trepidation; I knew that the towering frame of the king, and the mere thought of incurring his wrath was enough to turn her knees to jelly in terror. She looked confused, but there was not time to explain more, so I said in some haste, 'Come! Help me finish dressing. His majesty awaits me.'

Accompanied by Lady Mary Howard, I ascended one of two stone spiral staircases in the castle leading into the great hall of the king's apartments, on the second floor of the keep. The chamber occupied the same footprint as the one in the queen's apartments below. It was a large space, some seventy-foot in length, dominated by a vaulted wooden ceiling embossed with roundels painted with lapis lazuli, crimson red and gold leaf. The walls were decorated with vibrant hangings of deep, crimson red, shot through gold thread worked into a design of a clambering rose bower, whilst on the far side of the chamber, a single, large fireplace warmed the room and a series of candleholders, holding ten or so flickering candles each, were positioned at intervals along its length. At the upper end of the chamber was a dais over which was hung a rich canopy of estate, a piece of regal furniture that had travelled with the king from Greenwich to Calais and now back to England; beneath it sat the king upon a gilded throne.

Henry was deep in dialogue with my father and Uncle Norfolk, attended by Sir Henry Norris and Francis Weston, who hovered discreetly, ready to serve his majesty upon his command. The room was abuzz with courtiers and officials, several of whom waited for their opportunity to present themselves to the king to receive instructions, deliver petitions or seek justice. With my hands clasped before me and my head held high, I made my way toward Henry. As I did so, the sea of nobles and gentlemen began to part as a hush descended upon the room; all heads turned to look in my direction. I was a picture of glittering majesty, my attire and abundance of jewels surpassing all except the king himself. Alerted to my coming, Henry broke off his conversation with my lord father and my Uncle Norfolk; sitting back in his throne, his eyes full of pride as I reached the foot of the dais and dipped into a graceful and deep curtsy.

'Ah, my Lady Marquess, I see that you are fully rested and have finally come to us. It pleases me greatly to see you.' I rose to my feet as I replied,

'Thank you, Your Majesty. I hope I did not keep Your Grace waiting too long.' From his throne, Henry towered above me, his magnificent broad shoulders hung with a beautiful surcoat of white cloth of gold, edged with chocolate brown, sable fur. The king then turned his attention to the waiting crowd and announced in a clear voice,

'We shall hear mass in my privy chapel with my Lady Marquess in order to give thanks for our safe return to England. I command that none shall accompany us.' Then he turned, throwing his words over his shoulder, he said, 'Except you, Sir Henry. You will attend us along with Lady Mary.' With that the king descended from the dais and proudly took me by the hand, followed by Sir Henry Norris and Lady Mary, we walked in procession together to the chapel of Thomas Becket.

The chapel itself was built into the walls of the keep, in the south east tower of the building. Clearly, the king had arranged all that was necessary in advance, for waiting in the adjacent sacristy was not a priest, but Thomas Cromwell. The chapel was a miniature church, with a tiny nave and chancel, and was dedicated to the eponymous archbishop, who was murdered in Canterbury Cathedral by four of Henry II's knights, only a few years before the said king had begun his reconstruction of Dover. I was immediately enchanted by this little place, and so delighted that Anne was to be betrothed to her prince in such romantic and beguiling surroundings.

Henry indicated that we should move into the nave, and as we stepped across its threshold, Henry turned to Master Cromwell and said,

'Master Cromwell, do you have the contracts?' The king's secretary nodded toward a table which had been set up against one wall. Upon it was placed a parchment already inscribed with writing, which I assumed described the pledge that we were about to make to one another in the presence of witnesses which, in the eyes of canonical law, would bind us as man and wife.

'All is ready for you, as you can see, Your Majesty,' said Thomas Cromwell extending his arm and indicating toward the table. The king then turned to Sir Henry and Lady Mary and said gravely,

'Sir Henry, Lady Mary, what you witness here today must not be spoken of to a living soul. Do I make myself clear?' I looked across at Lady Mary, who was as white as a sheet, and managed only to whisper,

'Yes, Your Majesty.' Sir Henry assented to the same, and turned to me, taking both my hands in his as he said,

'Anne Rochford, Marquess of Pembroke, in the presence of these witnesses I, King Henry VIII of England, France and Ireland, hereby consent to be contracted to you from this day forth in marriage, as your lawful husband.' For an awful moment I froze, for I did not know what to say, or what was expected of me. However, I felt Anne's indomitable spirit stir within my belly, and I knew that I could not go far wrong if I repeated the same and so, gazing intently into Henry's eyes, with a great intensity of joyful emotion, I proclaimed in earnest,

'King Henry VIII of England, France and Ireland, my sovereign lord and master, in the presence of these witnesses I, Anne Rochford, Marquess of Pembroke, hereby consent to be contracted to you from this day forth in marriage, as your lawful wife.' I gulped back emotion, feeling tears of joy stinging at the back of my eyes. Suddenly, we both broke into broad smiles, as Henry leaned forward and kissed me tenderly upon the lips. Pulling away from me, he then turned toward Master Cromwell, extending his arm with an upturned palm as he said,

'Master Cromwell...' who then reached within his coat and withdrew a small box covered in crimson velvet and handed it to the king. Henry looked at me mischievously, knowing I would be eager to see what lay within. Opening it up, I saw within a huge diamond ring with the cipher 'HA', the king took my right hand and slipped it upon my ring finger. I watched him complete the task, before raising my eyes to meet his gaze, as he gestured toward the table, 'My Lady, let us sign the contracts.' Together we moved over to the table, and I watched as Henry took the quill in his hand, signing with his rather scrawling, flattened signature; the king then handed me the quill, and I did the same. Outside, I heard the church bells of St Mary in Castro ring out within the castle precinct. It was eleven am on Thursday, 14 November, and I was now *de facto* Henry's lawful wife and Queen of England.

Chapter Eight

London,
Late November – Early December, 1532

Winter was finally upon us. A sudden hoarfrost cast its icy magic across the land as we finally approached Greenwich, on horseback, from nearby Eltham Palace, some eleven days after the royal party first landed at Dover. The king was keen to leave Dover Castle as soon as we were rested, for there had been no connecting doorways or staircases allowing the two of us to secretly share our bed at night. Nevertheless, his majesty was determined that we would take our time on our return to trip to London, enjoying the goodly hospitality of his subjects along the way.

Our progress wound its way leisurely through the Kentish countryside: first heading north along the coast, and stopping overnight at a priory in the heart of the ancient town of Sandwich, then heading east and inland, staying first at the medieval city of Canterbury, as guest of my Lord Feneux, then to the Lion Inn in Sittingbourne, along the historic London-Dover Road. I also asked the king's indulgence to call upon Sir Robert and Lady Tyrwhitt at Stone Place on our way back to the capital. I confess that I did not relish a reunion with Lady Bridget, but I felt compelled to see her face to face, to know for myself how she had received my letter of peace.

Perhaps reflecting on the folly of their indiscreet handling of the king's lady, or perhaps mollified somewhat by my words of reconciliation, Sir Robert and Lady Bridget welcomed me on my return with greater humility and warmth than I had received on my first visit. Sadly, I sensed that their goodwill towards Anne did not run deep, and what had actually been achieved was a stilted truce of sorts. The friendship between Lady Bridget and I would remain somewhat uneasy until the day she was to die, just over twelve months later. However, I admit that the animosity between her husband and me lingered long after, for I could never forgive him for turning my dear friend against me. When the king and I left Stone Place the following day, it was with Lady Bridget's heartfelt assurance that she would come to court shortly after Christmas, and take up her post as chief lady of the bedchamber, when Anne's household was formally appointed.

I relayed the news of my betrothal to my family, as well as to Margery, who I treated like a sister. My father said little, but smiled at me, taken my hand and kissed it, never taking his eyes from mine. I knew that as a dutiful daughter, I had so far brought him more than he could have ever desired, and for that he appreciated me deeply. My mother and sister wept tears of joy, whilst Margery put her arms around me and hugged me close. It was ever the way with Margery; as if she was standing in my very own shoes; she knew the great burden of responsibility that now bore down upon me, and I sensed yet again her desire to protect me from harm.

Despite Anne's great triumph at Calais, and her subsequent betrothal in Dover, I began to sense an inkling of disquiet in my breast. It was a feeling, which over the coming months, would evermore take root and fester within my body, becoming a constant spectre that increasingly haunted my every waking hour. Even in those very early days, when she should have been basking in her hour of glory and unfettered from worldly concerns, I had already noticed fleeting, yet ominous, changes in the mood of the king. Although subtle in the beginning, occasionally, I would catch Henry unawares as he stared at me. Whereas before I would only ever be met with love, admiration and awe, I had begun to perceive a chilling menace alight in my husband's eyes. Sometimes, I felt that it was if he was looking upon a stranger, his enemy even. Yet, there was also confusion. I watched his mind struggle with a metamorphosis in our love that he could not understand. I sensed that with the signing of the betrothal contract, some otherworldly power had unfathomably begun to dissolve the hypnotic spell which had held Henry enthralled by Anne's charms for the past six years. As soon as Henry caught my eye, he would smile benignly or look away. I did not think in those days that even the king himself fully knew his own mind, but nevertheless, I could not chase away my fears.

Shortly after our return from Calais, on 1 December, the king took me to the Tower of London to inspect the works being undertaken to the queen's apartments ahead of my intended coronation the following year. Much to my amazement, Henry also took me to view the vast array of treasures housed within the jewel house, close to where the new lodgings were being feverishly remodelled.

Once inside, I was met by the sight of a large hall lit by only two relatively small windows, which were in turn protected on the outside with iron grilles for maximum security. The walls were covered in plain white plaster; there was no ornate decoration, no rich tapestries and no ornately carved fireplaces. However, that mattered little, for the sight that met my eyes was beyond compare; it was if I had entered King Solomon's goldmines. All about me was a magnificent display of an amazing number of priceless crowns, circlets, coronets, sceptres, rings, bracelets and jewelled swords, all displayed on huge oak tables and sideboards. Even on this rather dull, grey, winter's day, by the flicker of torchlight, the room literally glittered with gold.

I heard myself gasp aloud, much to Henry's amusement. Whilst the king stood within the doorway alongside Master Kingston, I walked forward throwing my arms out, turning around and about on myself, taking in all of that which lay around me. I could not believe that I was able to touch such treasures. I moved about the room, running my hands across a myriad of priceless objects, holding up to the light golden crowns, circlets and collars inlaid with enormous diamonds, rubies, sapphires and clusters of pearls. The exquisite beauty of the workmanship was beyond my wildest imagination, and after several minutes during which all I had managed to gasp repeatedly was, 'Oh my God!, Oh my God!' I finally turned back to look at Henry, who was standing feet astride, arms folded, chuckling with delight at my unbounded, childish exuberance.

'Your Majesty, I simply don't know what to say! I have never seen the like before.' Even as I spoke, my eye was caught by a large, ornately carved chest which was placed centrally against the far wall, opposite the entrance. It was covered in brightly coloured heraldic emblems and glittering in gold leaf. I looked at the king askance, as a slight frown across my forehead belied the question which now played upon my lips. 'Pray tell me, Your Majesty, what lies within this great chest?' I enquired as I took a few tantalising steps towards it, running my hand across the carved, gilded veneer and feeling beneath my fingertips the cold surface of an ornate golden lock that secured its doors. The king toyed with me for a few moments, one arm folded across his chest, the other stroking his close-cropped beard, finally, gesturing to Master Kingston,

'Master Kingston, please open the chest for the Lady Marquess.' Sir William dutifully selected a golden key which slipped easily into the lock, turning without effort. Henry then added, 'You may leave us now.' Master Kingston inclined his head toward me and then the king, before he disappeared from the room, closing the inner door behind him. Still smiling at me, Henry indicated with his hand that I should open the chest. My heart was fluttering as I knew that whatever lay within was precious indeed. Standing before it, with delicious anticipation, I placed my hands upon the heavy lid and heaved it open, the hinges, old and worn, creaked in complaint as I did so.

Directly in front of me were some of the most pulchritudinous pieces that I had yet seen. The most eye-catching of which was a resplendent crown made of gold, set with some eleven great, pointed diamonds around a thick gold rim; in between every diamond was a knot of pearls, rubies and emeralds. The crown was fashioned with eight bejewelled golden crosses which rose proudly from its base, each one set at its centre with an enormous ruby, sapphire or emerald. I picked up the crown reverently and turned it about in my hands. Set between the diamonds about the rim I read the name *Edith of Wessex*, each letter graven in coloured enamel. It was truly the most exquisite piece of medieval regalia and so rare; how I longed to steal it way and keep it safe from the marauding vandalism of Oliver Cromwell, who I knew, in over 100 years, would have it sold off or melted down for pittance during the English Civil War.

I had forgotten myself entirely, when suddenly I became aware of the king approaching. I snapped my head around to look at Henry, who was almost by my side. The king smiled at me, his eyes alight with our little game, as he reached up and took my English hood carefully from my head. I then watched, bewitched, as he took the crown out of my hands, and with a gesture that I had not for a moment anticipated, placed it reverently upon my head. There was silence for a few moments between us before he said,

'This crown once belonged to Edith of Wessex, wife of St Edward the Confessor. When I have you crowned as my queen, I will have Thomas Cranmer place the crown of St Edward upon your head, as it was placed upon mine.' With that the king took me by the hand and led me to the far side of the room where a large, gilded mirror was hung upon the wall. There, he stood behind me with his hand upon my shoulders. I gazed upon myself—upon Anne, as tears welled up in my eyes, for here was the sight I had always longed to see—which I knew in my heart that Anne had always longed to see—a beautiful woman whose raven hair and bewitching black eyes were set off magnificently by the glittering spectacle of the golden crown; and Anne every inch a queen.

'Tell me again, Anne. Precisely what did the king say?' asked my father, sitting opposite me. I had been entirely lost in a memory of the recent past, as I dined alone with my parents in my privy chambers at Greenwich. I had not done so for quite some time, and had desperately wished to be alone in their company, so I organised an intimate evening, with only my aunt, Elizabeth Wood, Lady Boleyn and Lady Rochford to attend upon us. It was very much a family affair. My only great sadness that evening was that my sister, Mary, had to return briefly to her country seat to supervise her children, and to ensure that all was running smoothly before returning to court for the Christmas festivities. Nor was my brother able to be with us that evening as he had been called to attend upon the king's grace, who had been closeted up for much of the afternoon, first with the Privy Council, and then with Master Cromwell.

Sir Thomas frowned at me as he broke a piece of bread apart as I recounted to my parents all my adventures of my outing to the Tower, all that I had seen and heard, and of course, my private moment alone with the king when he had placed a crown upon my head. I took a sip of fine, burgundy wine from a goblet of delicately carved Venetian crystal, savouring its deep aromatic flavours before I placed it carefully back down upon the table and finally replied,

'His grace said that he would have me crowned with the crown of St. Edward the Confessor.' My mother stared at me as she placed her hand lightly upon her breast as if to catch her breath, and then shook her head in bewilderment, before she said with some confusion,

'But that crown is only used to crown the sovereign themselves!' She looked at her husband and added, 'Thomas, if this is true then methinks that England will have never seen the like before.' My lord father sat back, interlacing his fingers upon his full belly— for we had dined upon several rich courses. He considered this for a few moments, before proclaiming,

'You are right, Madame,' then said to me, 'It is clear that his majesty wishes to elevate you to the highest possible honour, Anne. I confess…' it was then my father's turn to shake his head and shrug his shoulders in some disbelief, as he continued, 'that even I had not anticipated this great turn of events.' I found it difficult to suppress a wry smile, for clearly Sir Thomas Boleyn, a great diplomat, an intelligent man and shrewd courtier, had entirely failed to recognise the depth of the king's desire and his true intent. My father had also failed to notice the look that had passed between my mother and me in that moment. We loved the men in our lives dearly, but with one glance, we shared the same mind, our eternal amusement at the overinflated opinion that most men hold of their own abilities.

Oblivious to our good-natured mirth, the Earl of Wiltshire lifted his goblet, indicating to Lady Rochford that she should refill it with wine. As Jane reached over to do so, my attention was diverted toward her. I could not help but notice that there was an unusual radiance about Jane of late. I watched her with some curiosity; her eyes flicked up to meet mine, a delicate smile toying at the corner of her lips. I realised that since our return from Calais, my sister-in-law seemed of particularly good cheer and I wondered, hoped even, that my brother had taken my advice to heart and was paying his wife greater attention and showing her the affection she deserved. I winked back at her surreptitiously as she withdrew from the table. I decided to change the subject, and so picking up a piece of sweetmeat between my thumb and forefinger, I turned my attention once again to my father and asked,

'And Master Cranmer, have we heard of his progress?' My father took a swig of wine, before dabbing his lips with the napkin draped across his left shoulder, and replying,

'I heard that Cranmer left Mantua on 19 November. I expect we shall see him here early January.' I knew that Anne must know Thomas Cranmer well for he had been in the service of the Boleyn's for a number of years. Indeed, it was Thomas Cranmer who had first suggested to the king that within his own realm there was no higher authority than the king himself, and that the Pope's meddling in English affairs was contrary to the laws of God. I had yet to meet the man who would remain a true and loyal servant of Anne's to the very end, even when so many others would desert her. History records that he was the only person to remonstrate with the king after her arrest in a futile attempt to uphold her good name. Undoubtedly, this was at some considerable risk to himself. For this, he had already won my undying affection. I always greatly admired this honourable man of unswerving moral principle, and I eagerly anticipated meeting him.

After a few moments, I added thoughtfully,

'Master Cranmer does us a great service, for I hearsay that he seeks neither great offices nor riches, and comes with some reluctance to answer the king's bidding, that in truth, he does this for God and for the cause of the Reformation in England.' We finished our meal, and the hour was late. My father raised himself up to his feet and replied,

'It is true, child. Thomas Cranmer has the true light of God burning brightly within his breast, and he knows well that it is his duty, as it is yours, to break once and for all the vile and filthy grip that the Bishop of Rome holds in this realm.' I too rose from the table, soaking in Thomas Boleyn's words. I embraced my mother and father in turn, kissing them lightly upon the cheek, before they bid me good night.

I was left alone with Lady Rochford and Lady Boleyn to help me undress alone, privately reflecting that with Thomas Cranmer back in England, the trio of Cranmer, Cromwell and Anne would finally be united on common ground. The three together would create an unstoppable force, catalysing enormous religious change, and fatally undermining the foundations of the Holy Roman Catholic Church in England. Together we stood precariously placed before the dawn of the Reformation in England.

A little while afterwards, I found myself in the intimate surroundings of my raying chamber, which faced the great privy garden at Greenwich, looking out toward the Church of the Observant Friars. Despite the late hour, the garden was eerily illuminated by a blanket of virgin snow which had fallen incessantly earlier that day. I stood in my fine linen night gown, my hands and nose pressed against the cold glass, my warm breath made visible against its chilled panes, mesmerised by the night sky that was filled with great, heavy snowflakes which were whipped about by a fierce wind that was howling about the palace precinct, before falling silently and without complaint to the ground.

'Madame, you should come away from that window, for you are hardly dressed and will likely catch your death of cold.' It was Elizabeth Wood, Lady Boleyn, chastising me as ever she was wont to do with the least provocation. I knew she found my ascendancy increasingly irksome and intolerable, and her petty, small-mindedness caused her to criticise me at every opportunity. I confess, without shame, that I loathed it when she was to attend on me, and had often begged my father to have her removed from court. However, he had always firmly refused, persuading me against my better judgement that we should keep family close about us. Oh, my poor Uncle James, to be landed with such a disagreeable woman, when he himself was so gentle and kind, I envied him not and determined to have her removed once and for all as soon as I was queen, when my father would no longer be in a position to argue with me.

The rare and expensive silver-gilt clock in my chamber struck ten o'clock. It was a sweet and delicate chime. I drew away from the window, allowing my maid to close the heavy, purple and red velvet linen-lined curtains, shutting out the worst of the wintry weather. I confess that I had slept there very rarely since my return form Calais. Instead, I been called by Henry to the king's bedchamber virtually every night, something that no doubt Lady Boleyn greatly disapproved of, for I was sure that in her eyes, I was still unmarried and but a wanton strumpet. However, I cared little for her opinion, as I knew it was only borne from intense jealousy.

I made my way back into the room and stood before the glowing fire, slipping first one delicate arm and then the other into my black taffeta nightgown, which was being held up for me by Lady Boleyn. Jane came in front of me and was just fastening the gown about my person, when there was a knock on the door. I was not surprised, for it had become a nightly ritual; a gentleman of the king's privy chamber would make his way to my bedchamber to inform me that the king awaited my presence. I nodded to Jane to open the door; yet when she did so, I was greatly surprised to find my brother on the other side.

'My Lord Rochford, what a pleasant surprise.' Usually it would either be Sir Henry Norris, Francis Weston, William Brereton or Sir Francis Bryan who would be waiting to deliver the king's message. I could not help but notice that George looked somewhat uncomfortable with his task, nevertheless, he greeted me with an elegant bow, and spoke proudly as he announced,

'Madame, the king requests your presence and has sent me to conduct you thither.' I smiled at my sweet brother who looked so very handsome as he stood there shimmering in the flickering candlelight, clad in a matching doublet and hose of black velvet shot through with finely embroidered silver thread work. I nodded my thanks to Lady Rochford, and indicated to Lady Boleyn that she should accompany me with George toward the king's chambers.

The privy gallery in which we found ourselves was deserted, save the flickering candlelight which cast gentle, dancing shadows about the corridor. Grave faces of severe and august kings and princes stared down to watch my nightly procession to the king's bed; otherwise we were sealed away from the world, just George and I with Lady Boleyn following in attendance. I slipped my arm through my brother's, and we began to meander slowly along the silent gallery. I thought back to Jane and her radiance, and had not been able to resist asking,

'How are things between you and Jane? I noticed that she looked so happy tonight.' I paused for a moment, thinking of how to phrase this as delicately as I was able. 'Have you been paying her more attention of late?' I knew that my brother would understand my intimation, yet again, I noticed my lusty, young brother blush before answering,

'It is not easy sister, for all the reasons that are known betwixt us... but yes, I am being a good husband to her, as you requested.' I smiled and squeezed his arm gently, showing my deep appreciation for his efforts which, in truth, came not through desire for his wife, but to please his sister.

It was but a short walk before we passed through the king's study and raying chamber, both of which lay deserted. I shivered a little for the fires about the palace were shrinking back to their dying embers, and the chill of the wintry night had begun to encroach through the palace walls. Finally, we entered the king's bedchamber, where I was usually received by the king, yet Henry was nowhere to be seen. I turned toward my brother and was about to speak when George anticipating my question explained, 'The king awaits you in his most secret bedchamber.' My brother pointed to a small oak door set within a large donjon that jutted out from the main, northern edifice of the palace onto the Thames. Several times the king had led me up the narrow, vice-stair that led to his fine privy closet on the upper floor, but never had I been in the intimate privy bedroom on the floor below. We halted in front of the entrance, and for an awkward moment, I watched as my brother looked to the ground clearly finding it difficult to say what was on his mind. I took his hand in mine and asked gently,

'What is it, my Lord? You look sorely troubled.' Slowly George's eyes rose to meet mine, and with great concern etched across his face he said quietly, almost in a whisper,

'Is he … is he kind to you?' For a moment I was puzzled and then it dawned on me that George found it difficult to think of me naked in the king's arms. He knew only too well how a man, let alone the king, could legally treat a woman as his property; I suspect he also knew in his heart of what cruelty Henry was capable. I was deeply touched, for no one, even in my modern day life, had a care for me in the way in which my brother did that day. I let go of George's hand and took his face between both my palms, turning his head to look at me squarely, as I said,

'Dear, sweet brother, worry not, for the king is a most kind and gentle lord unto me.' For a moment, I entirely forgot that several paces behind me in attendance was my aunt, Lady Boleyn, and without a second thought, just as natural as could be, I lifted myself up on my tiptoes and placed a tender kiss upon my brother's lips. It was an innocent demonstration of my enormous love for him, yet suddenly, I remembered her presence and broke away awkwardly, straightening my nightgown and lifting my shoulders back; hoping to brush off what I feared my prickly aunt would seek to use against me. In a more clear and resonant voice, I added formally, 'Thank you, Lord Rochford and good night.' I turned to Lady Boleyn to dismiss her, meeting her disapproving gaze with my own fierce defiance.

When they had departed and I was left alone. I passed directly ahead, along a short corridor and into the first floor room, the king's private bedchamber, where the King of England waited to make love to me. These were precious moments, for I loved Henry with all my heart; away from the public stare of the court, in bed we could just be two people, a man and a woman; two lovers stripped bare of all the trappings of state, equal in the eyes of God. I came to adore those moments of searching intimacy, when Henry and I were bound together in flesh as one.

I soon came upon a heavy oak door fitted with an elaborate golden lock, already partially ajar. Soft light from within illuminated the short gallery. Through the gap, I could make out part of the chamber clad in linen-fold panelling, whilst the ceiling was finely moulded, painted predominantly in lapis-lazuli and studded with a multitude of tiny, golden stars. I reached out with my right hand and pushed open the door, finding myself in a relatively small room, perhaps twenty-five feet by fifteen feet. At the far side of the room, two small octagonal towers formed deep recesses encased with decorative, latticed windows, whilst against the left hand wall was an open fire, the flames bright and alive, flickering in the hearth. The king's bed, against the right-hand wall, was covered in rich, red and gold hangings, the tester emblazoned with the royal coat of arms. Upon an inviting throw of dark sable fur, the king was stretched out on the top of the bed, his legs crossed at his ankles, his arms clasped behind his head. He turned his head to look at me, as I walked through the door.

'Your Majesty' I inclined my head. Henry lifted himself up on one elbow, one knee bent as he turned toward the doorway.

'Ah, Anne, at last, come here, I need you to be a woman to me tonight.' I took a step forward and joked with the king that it was ever thus, every night, when suddenly Henry raised his hand and stopped me dead in my tracks; he clearly had decided on another plan. 'No, wait! Stay just when you are.' I settled back into my centre, my head slightly inclined, a seductive smile toying enigmatically at the corners of my mouth. I watched as Henry's eyes narrowed covetously, before he whispered assertively, 'Take it off. His finger flicked in my direction and I knew that he wished me to remove my gown. I lowered my eyes, untying the belt of my dressing gown before I let it slip slowly from my shoulders and fall in a crumpled heap at my feet. I was well aware that the delicately worked, linen nightgown I was wearing was almost transparent, and I wondered if Henry was already aroused by the outline of my soft curves, just visible beneath the sheer fabric. The king spoke again softly, 'No, I mean take it all off.' I knew well what his majesty meant, but I was the mistress of the art of seduction. Henry loved to devour my naked body with his eyes, and so I played his game, deliberately and slowly undoing the white ribbon at the front of my gown before I let it slip first off one shoulder and then the other, until it too fell to the ground. I stood before the king entirely naked, my dark raven coloured hair in sharp contrast with even Anne's olive skin. I watched as Henry sighed with deep appreciation, his eyes taking in every inch of my body and its fleshy delights.

The king quickly swung his legs about, sitting astride on the edge of the bed, he reached out his arms and beckoned me forward. I swayed seductively into his embrace, standing between his legs, his head coming to rest pressed between my breasts. I held him close to me for a few moments, before he turned to look up at me and our gaze finally met. Henry then began to speak, and he did so, he moved his mouth to encircle my right nipple, 'I have had a tiresome day, Anne.' I stroked Henry's head as he kissed and sucked at my right breast. Somewhat breathlessly, for I was already aroused, I asked,

How so, my lord?' Henry did not look up at me, but continued to bury his face in the soft flesh of my bosom, occasionally releasing himself to speak in short staccato sentences,

I had to spend all afternoon with the Privy Council…listening to that old fart Lord Sandy…ramble on…about God knows what.' Finally, the king broke away for a moment from kissing my chest and looked up at me, his eyes misted over with burning desire, before he added, 'I confess, I could not get you out of my mind; thinking about you lying naked next to me and what I would do to you tonight. I tell you, Anne I had to spend the rest of the council meeting with an enormous erection!' With that revelation, both Henry and I burst into gales of laughter, as we collapsed into each other's arms.

After several minutes, as the hilarity of the scene ebbed away, the king grabbed me once more, this time by the buttocks and drew me close to him again. We began to kiss, deeply and passionately, Henry reaching up to snatch at my lips with barely contained animal instinct. I felt his hand run up the inside of my thigh, whilst the other still pulled me firmly toward him. Suddenly, he put his fingers inside me and I gasped, my head falling back as I struggled to catch my breath at this most searching intimacy. Still kissing my breast and belly, the king whispered, 'My lady, your heart is tight and wet.' I found I could not reply, so lost was I in an ever escalating desire to have him inside me. Almost as if he were reading my mind, Henry quickly stood to his feet, coming about me until his front had been pressed against my back; his arms encircling my body from behind me. We were both breathless, caught up in a whirlpool of hungry lust and desire. Henry gripped my waist with his left hand whilst he took my long, loose hair and wound it around his right. Leaning in even closer, he whispered in my ear dangerously, 'Do you want it?' I was entirely lost in the moment, cognisant only of the sinuous strength of this man that would have me and my overwhelming desire for sex with him. Eventually I managed to whisper in return,

'Yes, yes, I want it now.' Henry was clearly in the mood to dominate me entirely. So with that strange mixture of ferocity and tenderness that only comes when love is mixed with raw, animal sex the king said,

'Then bend over and open your legs and let me take you like the dirty whore that you are.' It was a private game we often played at the height of our arousal, one dominating the other with lewd and lascivious words; and when the deed was done, those two people dissolved into oblivion and all courtesy and gallantry was restored. I obliged willingly to the king's request, soon feeling the exquisite pleasure of Henry inside my body, as he entered me like a savage animal, thrusting relentlessly until orgasm brought its relief.

Afterward, we crawled into bed together as I snuggled under the crook of his shoulder, Henry's arm wrapped about me, our bodies pressed close together. Outside, winter gripped the capital, as blizzards drove heavy snow into great drifts that were several feet deep. Yet inside, I was cocooned within the arms of my prince, and although I would not know it for several weeks to come, that night, within my belly, a new flower of the Tudor dynasty was finally conceived.

Chapter Nine

Greenwich Palace, London,
24 December 1532

The vicious blizzards which had rampaged across London and southern England on the night I conceived my darling Elizabeth had entirely abated by the following morning. Heavy snowflakes continued to fall in a muted ballet for a further two days, casting deep swathes of soft snow across the countryside which made travel to and from court impossible. The king had been irritable on account of it, fearing that his nobles, lords and ladies would be unable to return in time for the great revels that had been meticulously planned for the twelve days of Christmas. More than once, I heard him snap at Master Cromwell, reminding him unnecessarily that only on account of war—which there was none—grave illness or childbirth, could anyone dare not to show their face at court. Thankfully, on the third day, warmer air began to blow from the south west, bringing with it dark, brooding rainclouds, as overnight heavy rain dissolved the snow and ice within a matter of hours.

A few days later, the Tudor aristocratic and gentry classes began to arrive at Greenwich. By Christmas Eve, the palace was packed to capacity, abuzz with gossip, speculation and excitement. People knew that developments were afoot, although unclear of the details. The greatest changes in the king's twenty-three year reign were already gathering pace. Katherine had fallen from grace, and Anne resided ever more closely at the king's side. Rumours abounded of Cranmer's forthcoming appointment as Archbishop of Canterbury, and what this and Cromwell's Act of Restraint of Appeals, would mean for religious life in England. The question on everyone's lips that Yuletide was: would Anne preside over the festive celebrations as queen? Indeed, had the king already wed her in secret? Would Queen Katherine be banished to a nunnery? Would her daughter Mary be received by the king and his lady? Whilst the court hummed with speculation, I knew the truth of the matter. For the first time since the king's attentions had alighted on Mistress Anne, there was to be no more skulking behind the scenes for

114

the sake of appearances. This Christmas the doors to Anne's gilded cage would be thrown open and she would fly freely, soaring above the court, as graceful and majestic as the white falcon that was soon to become her emblem.

In my modern day life, I had known only too well what it was like to be the other woman at Christmastide. To be the centre of Daniel's world, that is, until the family's expectations for the Christmas holidays would tear the man that I loved from my arms, leaving me feeling abandoned and used—a convenience of sorts. I knew exactly how confused and frustrated Anne felt every long and lonely Christmas between 1527 and 1531—to be doted upon behind closed doors, yet rejected when it really mattered. For those few short months, I sensed the great joy that Anne held in her heart for her new found pre-eminence and freedom, but this was not the only source of her joy. Like Anne, my periods came regularly, a short cycle, every three weeks; I was three days late. I suspected that Anne was pregnant.

When I awoke that Christmas Eve, I was concerned that my sister had not yet returned to court. So, after breaking my fast and hearing mass in my private closet, I made my way to my parents lodgings, situated just beneath my own, on the ground floor of Greenwich Palace. I wished to enquire if they had heard news of her coming. Thankfully, I was accompanied that day by four of my closest friends and allies; Margery, Mary Howard, Nan and Jane Rochford; they would never think to use what happened next against me.

As I neared my parents' apartments, I heard raised voices from behind the door which was slightly ajar. I signalled to my ladies silently, with my raised palm, that they should remain as they were. I took a few steps forward, leaning close to the crack in the door, so that I might hear more clearly the heated exchange that was taking place. I heard my Uncle Norfolk raise his voice in indignation, arguing with my father,

'I do not like the way the wind is blowing, Boleyn. You know full well that when I agreed to put Anne before the king, it was not with a mind that I should be treated no better than a kitchen boy and nor,' there was a pause as if the duke was jabbing his finger in the air towards Sir Thomas, 'did I expect your daughter to prompt the king to dismantle the very fabric of our religious faith and church in this country, and play into the hands of that cod's-head, Cromwell, who would see us all cast into purgatory. There is but one true faith in England, and I will not see it destroyed by the meddling of a foolish woman. Get your daughter under control, my lord; otherwise you will have me to answer to! Do I make myself clear, Boleyn?'

As I listened to my Uncle Norfolk become ever more fiery in his speech, talking about Anne as if she were just some silly little girl, I felt her familiar white, hot fury begin to burn with a dangerous force all of its own. I was livid that my uncle should talk about me, a queen in all but name, with such contempt. Consumed by anger and thinking little of the consequences, I pushed open the door to the main parlour of my parent's privy apartments. My mother was nowhere to be seen, but in front of me was my father seated at a table, a mixture of anger and fear written upon his face; whilst standing over him, leaning forward with both sets of white knuckles pressed upon the table was my Uncle Norfolk. Sir Thomas may have felt fear, but I feared no one, and spoke boldly to the duke, making both men start at my unexpected appearance.

'You make yourself clear, Your Grace, but think upon whom you speak.' My voice was icy cold and dangerously calm. As I spoke, both men turned toward me with some surprise for they had not anticipated my presence. I was furious, and yet my voice did not waver. 'I like not the tone in which you address my father. And as for the other matter, that of religion...' I took a few steps forward my hands clasped at my belly, my head held imperiously high, knowing full well that I should not say what I was about to, but I was full of hatred for this man, and I was consumed with Anne's innate instinct to cause him pain. 'I predict this, my lord; that the Holy Roman Catholic Church is finished in this realm, the Pope will be cast out and the king will rightly take his place as supreme head of a new church in England. People will be able to talk directly to their God, and if I am to play a part in that happy outcome, then I will have fulfilled my destiny upon this earth.' I saw my father blanch at my audacity, although no doubt secretly, he greatly aspired to the vision. As I spoke, I watched the duke's jaw clench in ever mounting scorn, and for a moment, I wondered if he would draw his dagger and thrust it into my belly right there and then. Protected by the king's love and devotion, my uncle knew I was untouchable, and so

I watched the slight twitch in the muscle of his jaw, the only sign of a searing rage that burned within. The duke stood up tall and eyed me coldly for a few moments. He straightened his doublet before taking a few steps in my direction until we were but a foot apart, face-to-face, our gaze unflinching, one locked with the other in defiance. Finally, my Uncle Norfolk spoke with barely concealed venom,

'Now, it is my turn to give you a prediction, Madame. I predict that you will be the ruin of this house. And let me tell you this,' glancing towards my father, then turning back to me, adding ominously 'when you go down, do not think to take me with you, for I will wash my hands of you without mercy.' He stared at me coldly before saying, 'Good day to you, Madame.' With that the incensed duke swept out of the room, nearly knocking over the pregnant Margery, who had been waiting dutifully with my ladies just outside the door. When he had gone, there seemed to be an acre of silence which filled the space between my father and me.

As my rage subsided, I felt both shame and fear take its place. I raised my eyes to Sir Thomas, whose expression heightened my remorse. It was if in that moment, there was nothing more that could be said between us—the damage had been done. Rather pathetically, not knowing what else to say, I tried to speak, but the words would not come, and I had to clear my throat before I managed to croak,

'I have missed my sister, have you heard from her? When will she be back at court?' I watched my father bury his head in his hands; I knew he was aware of my remorse, and I suspect sensed the futility of bringing me even greater discomfort. Rubbing his face as if to wipe away the memory of the altercation that he had just witnessed, he answered me wearily,

'Mary sent a messenger that she should be here today.' I nodded my appreciation and turned to leave as my father suddenly added, 'Anne, please, I beg you do not make enemies so lightly, the king loves you but…' Holding up my hand to stop him mid-sentence, I said, 'I know, I know. We are not safe until I have given the king a son. I will try my hardest, on both counts, I promise.' It was a sincere promise made from the bottom of my heart, yet, I knew intimately Anne's intemperance and that when slighted or angered, an otherworldly force overtook all rational thinking and swept me up in a tempest, which was beyond my control. Sadly, I would find that it was not a promise I would always be able to keep. With the end of our conversation, I bobbed a respectful curtsy to my father and left him alone with his troubled thoughts.

Later that day, feeling somewhat subdued from my earlier quarrel with my Uncle Norfolk, I retreated from the hurly-burly of the queen's public rooms into my privy chamber. Yet with the palace full to capacity, many ladies had gravitated to my private chambers to attend upon me. My position as queen was not yet official, so my household had yet to be formally appointed; although every day, ever greater numbers of petitions arrived on Master Cromwell's desk. The king decreed that the response should be that the queen's side would be appointed shortly, and all must wait upon that time. Nevertheless, great and noble ladies, many of whom had attended me at Calais, came that Christmas to pay court to the star which was still in its ascendency.

Even though I had desired solitude, it proved impossible. As custom demanded on Christmas Eve, the room was being dressed by several of my maids with festive branches of yew, laurel, holly and ivy. With the late afternoon light fading, tapered beeswax candles were being lit about the chamber, whilst my maids attended to the roaring fire. I rested against the stone window frame, staring wistfully at the two figures clad in warm furs as they walked together in the queen's garden below. Nan and Master George Zouche were so very much in love, I had given my friend my blessing so that she could escape from her duties for a short while to be alone with the man to whom she was betrothed. I watched them snuggle close, walking arm in arm, as Henry and I had done on so many occasions; I was so happy for them, and in many ways began to long for the simplicity of their life.

About me, I was aware of some of my ladies talking in hushed tones, others embroidered, whilst I watched little Lady Mary Howard buried deep in the book of the good Lord. Under Anne's influence an evangelical heart was beating ever more strongly in her young breast, quite at odds with the rest of her Catholic Howard family; it was something I am sure my Uncle Howard did not look kindly upon. Nevertheless, it was clear that she defied him regardless. I reminded myself of the pledge I had made to her, to speak to the king again of a union betwixt the Duke of Richmond and herself. Thinking on how I might approach the subject, I turned to gaze out of the window. I had settled myself alone in a window seat, looking out over the orchard and great garden to the south, with the steep, gabled end of the Church of the Observant Friars just visible to the west. Beyond the palace precinct, I could make out the rooftops of the modest houses which made up the tiny village of Greenwich. From where I sat, I could see into the future, to the modern day bustling 'village' of Greenwich and the place that in the twenty-first century I called home. I wondered, for the millionth time how I was in my modern day life; had time stood still as it had done before, or had life moved on and would I be sucked back to find myself starting out on a future with Daniel as he had promised ?

Suddenly, I was jolted back in time by a familiar voice that I recognised immediately,

'*Madame la Marquise?*'

'Oh, Mary!' I snapped my head about, delighted to see my sister, who had just arrived at the palace, for her cheeks were still glowing and ruddy from the cold outside. 'God save you sweet sister, I thought you were never going to come.' I extended my right arm out to take her hand in mine, and with my left hand, indicating that she should seat herself beside me. With a great rustling of her deep, pink damask gown she did so, and I went on, 'Tell me, how art thou?'

'I am well, sister, and please…I crave your forgiveness for my tardiness. There was so much more to do than I had thought possible! It is difficult now that William…is…' She hesitated, stumbling over that which clearly still caused her some pain. Suddenly, I felt incredibly guilty, as I realised how wrapped up I had become—the whole family had become—in Anne's story, and how little attention was paid to a woman who demanded so little for her own happiness. I reached across and gently squeezed her hand supportively and said,

'I'm sorry Mary. It has been four years since William's death and you are still alone.' William had died of the sweating sickness during that fateful summer of 1528, when Anne had come close to losing her own life. Mary had been widowed with two children, Catherine aged four and little Henry, aged just two. I knew that both of them had been fathered by Henry, although he would never speak of it; for to admit as much would be to endanger our own union on the grounds of consanguinity.

After I had returned to the twenty-first century for the first time, I had read again how Anne had secured Mary a pension of one hundred pounds a year after her husband's death, and had also taken on the wardship of the infant Henry, at some point securing him an education in a well-respected Cistercian Monastery. I knew that Mary missed him, but like most well-to-do Tudor parents, she expected to see little of her children and was pragmatic enough to see the practical benefits of the situation for her son and his future. Nevertheless, Mary was a woman with a warm heart, who relished the protective and loving attention of a man. I was also well aware that if I did not find her a husband, sooner rather than later, history had deigned that it would be her own rashness in making an unsuitable marriage without the king's permission that would cast her out from her family. As I looked into the soft brown eyes of my English rose, I said,

'We must find a new husband to take care of you.' As I spoke, I saw a look flash across her face. For a moment, I could not place its meaning; then cocking my head to the side I probed, 'You have not met someone have you, sister?' Mary answered just a little too quickly,

'No. No, there is nobody.' I drew back, eyeing her suspiciously, but she smiled at me brightly offering no further information. My intuition was telling me that Mary was not being entirely truthful. Suddenly, I was afraid for her and for the wrath of the king and her family, which would come bearing down upon her should she bring disgrace upon the Boleyn name. Needing to warn her, I spoke firmly but quietly, so none could hear.

'Mary, you must listen to me. Idle dalliances with whoever pleases you can no longer happen. You are about to become sister to the queen; the king has raised us high and many resent us, ready to accuse and defame our good name at the slightest opportunity. We must be beyond reproach—me, you and George.' I watched Mary cast her eyes down to her lap; I could not tell if she were ashamed, guilt or angry with me for upbraiding her. However, as with George, I was sure that I needed to be firm for her own good, as well as that of the family. So, I forged on. 'I am sure that I do not need to remind you sister that you must not take a husband without the king's permission.' I tried to be as understanding as possible as I pushed for her acknowledgement. 'You do understand, don't you?' Mary did not look up at me, but toyed absentmindedly with the book of hours clipped about her waist. Eventually, she nodded, yet I was not satisfied, and was about to speak again when suddenly Francis Weston appeared before us.

'My Lady of Pembroke, Lady Carey,' he acknowledged each of us in turn with a bow, 'Madame,' directing his words to me, 'the king requests your presence in his privy chamber forthwith.'

'Thank you, Master Weston.' I smiled, nodding my understanding. I was not happy to break away from this conversation for in my heart, I already feared the worst; that Mary had taken a lover and was hiding it from the family. Had she already fallen for the charms of the lowly Master William Stafford? Despite my desire to stay and probe the matter further, I could not keep the king waiting, and so rather too abruptly for my liking, I took my leave of my sister, vowing to myself that we would touch upon the subject again. However, life was to move at an ever more rapid and all-consuming pace, and fatefully we were to never speak of the matter until much, much later—when the die had already been irrevocably cast.

Chapter Ten

Greenwich Palace, London,
25 December 1532

On Christmas morn, the inhabitants of Greenwich Palace awoke to a light dusting of snow, as if the Gods themselves had sprinkled sugar icing across the land, turning it white as far as the eye could see. There was an enormous sense of excitement and anticipation for Christmas Day marked the end of Advent, a period of fasting and preparation against the coming of Christ into the world, and the beginning of the great celebrations of the Twelve Days of Christmas. As was customary, Henry had commissioned a seemingly never ending round of entertainment for the royal family, foreign visitors, ambassadors and his courtiers. These included; feasting, mummers plays, carolling, dancing, masques and a great tournament to be held on New Year's Day.

On the previous day, when his majesty had commanded my presence, I had found the king's grace in his privy closet, attended by Master Cromwell and his Lord Chancellor, Lord Sandys. He had wished to go through with me the rather unusual arrangements for the following day; for although I was not queen and could not be formally recognised as such, for the first time, I would be present at all the official celebrations as the king's guest of honour, taking pre-eminence above all others. In truth, I would be acting as Queen of England in all but name. The day would begin as every Christmas Day, with mass celebrated before dawn in the presence of the king in the chapel royal. Thereafter the celebrations would commence, culminating in a grand feast and dancing that very evening. Of course, Christmas Day represented one of the great feast days of the year. Against the backdrop of networking, politicking and alliance building, it was an opportunity to impress upon all one's wealth and status. Thus, the entire court prepared itself to be decked in its most opulent finery.

As the king's consort-in-waiting, much was expected of me in this regard and so I had ordered a sumptuous gown of cloth of gold, trimmed with ermine for the occasion. Billaments of diamonds, rubies and clusters of pearls adorned the edging of my French hood and square-cut neckline, whilst a similarly bejewelled girdle hung about my waist. My skirt was full with a long train, my sleeves turned back with ermine, and about my shoulders was fastened a mantle of purple velvet, also lined and trimmed with the same fur.

Thus, I was dressed when I came before the king at six o'clock on Christmas morn, finding Henry waiting for me in his privy chamber. It was a large room, approximately thirty feet by forty feet, facing north onto the Thames. The chamber was already quite crowded with many of the king's most eminent nobles including, my Uncle Norfolk, the Duke of Suffolk and my father. All were ready to process to the chapel royal, dressed in their most sumptuous robes. The king greeted me warmly with outstretched arms, planting a kiss upon my lips as had become usual in public between us. He looked magnificent, majestic in a gown of purple damask, with a purple velvet garde embroidered with gold cord and fringe. Beneath the gown, his doublet and hose were fashioned from purple velvet, cut upon cloth of gold; the former had been fastened down the front with buttons of gold set with diamonds, and upon the garde of the sleeves were tiny gold flowers set with clusters of pearls. As if this splendour were not sufficient, Henry wore the great crown of state upon his head. At first, I was not able to take my eyes from it; a breathtaking golden headpiece, the rim fashioned into repeating fleur-de-lis and golden crosses, richly studded with pearls, rubies and emeralds; four arches met centrally and supported a small, golden orb surmounted by a bejewelled cross.

Only Henry was ever permitted to directly touch the purple velvet mantle lined with ermine that was to be placed around his shoulders. So, with the folded garment covered with gold tissue and carried on his outstretched arms, Sir Henry Norris reverently stepped forward. I watched my love unwrap the delicate covering, taking hold of the mantle himself and fix it about his person.

Accompanied by a procession of his nobles, the king made his way from his privy chamber through a narrow gallery and into the presence chamber beyond which was richly hung and bedecked for Christmas, a truly glorious sight. The room was full of courtiers, all eager to catch a glimpse of the king—and Anne. I walked solemnly behind Henry aware of the many eyes that fell upon me. I was nervous, but no one knew it for my eyes were fixed proudly ahead. I sensed that by Christmas 1532,

Anne fully accepted the estate to which she had been called and was used to the many bows and curtsies directed toward her. For many, this would seal their opinion that shortly there would be a new queen in England.

Greenwich was unusual in that it was a straight and direct route to the king and queen's holy day closets, which were on the far side of this gallery at first floor level, above the chapel's antechamber, and looked directly down into the main body of the chapel royal.

Henry then entered his closet accompanied by several of his peers and gentlemen of the privy chamber, and I was directed into the adjoining queen's closet, with an equal number of my ladies who were some of the noblest women of England following in my wake. However, three of the most senior of these ladies were notably absent: the king's sister Mary, Queen of France, who steadfastly and rather vainly refused to accept Anne's pre-eminence; the second was Princess Mary who I had not wanted at court and who therefore remained in neglected seclusion at the Palace of Beaulieu; finally, there was the Duchess of Norfolk who, by her outspoken condemnation of Anne, had been banished to her country estate.

Having spent a good deal of time at Greenwich, I was intimately familiar with the pleasant space in which I was received. Each closet was spacious, well lit, and lavishly decorated allowing the king and his consort to be seen by the court, and yet to be able to rest within undisturbed by courtiers or clergy alike. I knew that Henry often attended to business whilst the service went on below him. But I sensed Anne was more fervent in her religious devotions, and I always found myself drawn to give myself more fully to the mass. I never ceased to be mesmerised by the beauty of the chapel royal, nor the hypnotic godliness of the sweet singing voices that filled such a divine space.

On Christmas Day, a chair of estate was placed behind a prie-dieu that looked upon the nave below. Surrounded by rich hangings and kneeling beneath the canopy on a cushion covered with cloth of gold, I spent much of the service praying for the child that I was carrying in my womb.

After the service, Henry offered me his bejewelled hand and we processed side-by-side through the thronging crowd back to his majesty's privy chamber. As his grace's most honoured guest, I inclined my head this way and that, acknowledging the good wishes of Henry's courtiers as we passed by. In the midst of our progress, Henry whispered to me,

'I think to invite the Lady Mary for Twelfth Night; it would be good to see her here at court.' Even then, I always recoiled at her name— Mary. She would ever be the perennial thorn in Anne's side. Oh, I know she was only a child, and with a clarity that has come only from facing my own death, I see now her innocence. Anne had destroyed her cosseted world, humiliated her fierce Spanish pride, and separated her from the mother whom she adored; how could she do anything other than hate me— yet, despite my brittle exterior toward her, I had wanted her so much to love me. However, the truth was that I found it virtually impossible to have her around me for any length of time. Her disdain and haughtiness was intolerable and would test the patience of a saint— and I knew well that Anne was no saint!

In my modern day life, I experienced first-hand the power of a child from a previous marriage to disrupt the tender shoots of a relationship between a man and a woman, driving a wedge between them. In the sixteenth century, I had also come to know the frustrating intransigence of a sulky teenager. I was aware that Anne was not just resentful of Mary's existence, I also felt her fear. She sensed Henry's continued attachment to his only daughter, and until Anne had borne the king a son, Mary would always be there to remind him of his past.

So, as the king had spoken, my head snapped about and I must have glared at Henry. It was a primitive and instinctive reaction, but I did not want her to be anywhere near me—near us. Henry must have seen the anger alight in my eyes, for he had gone on to whisper,

'Keep smiling, Anne.' The king clearly did not wish for a scene in public, so I wisely held my tongue until we were in the king's privy chamber. Although a number of the king's gentlemen of the privy chamber remained in attendance, wary of my rage, Henry dismissed several courtiers, along with my father and the Dukes of Norfolk and Suffolk.

I was indeed simmering with fury. It was our first real Christmas together and everything had finally been going so well. I simply could not understand why he wanted to bring his daughter to court, she who hated me as much as if I was Beelzebub himself! The king beckoned me to follow him into his private study as we passed through the same oak doorway by which I had entered his privy bedroom, just a few short weeks before. Henry and I were accompanied only by Sir Henry who, once within the privacy of the study, accepted from his majesty the imperial crown and taken it from the room, closing the door quietly behind him. I stepped forward, my palms turned upwards in exasperation as I cried plaintively,

'Why? Why do you want to bring her here? You know she hates me. She will make Christmas a misery for us. No, she will make Christmas a misery for me! Do you not see that?' I brought the palm of my right hand up to cup my forehead in frustration, whilst the left rested indignantly on my hip. Sometimes, I utterly despaired of a man's ability to think about anyone but himself. The king unbuttoned the ermine-lined mantle from about his shoulders and laid it across a nearby chair. He looked at me, and in that moment, I saw a dangerous resentment flash across his face; I thought he was about to berate me for my cold-hearted selfishness, but he merely sighed heavily, and took my delicate hands in his, raising them gently to brush them with his lips as I felt compelled to speak again.

'Sire, Henry... I'm sorry to snap at you and on Christmas day of all days, for we should be alight with the love of Christ.' Then I added softly, 'You do know I love you, don't you?...And I want so much to love the Lady Mary... but it is true, she does hate me and I fear that her stubbornness will never allow her to accept me as your wife and your queen.' Henry studied my eyes intently for a moment weighing up the veracity of my words, before taking me fully in his arms, holding me close against his chest as he stroked my head and spoke softly,

'It is true; Mary has her mother's contumacious pride. But she is my daughter, and I will not accept her disobedience in such matters. I promise you, she will bend to my will or she will know her father's displeasure.' He lifted my chin with his hand and kissed me softly upon the lips before adding, 'Yet, I see you are right. This Yuletide is for great celebrating, we shall see what can be done with Mary in the New Year.' I smiled feebly, deeply grateful for Henry's understanding.

After we had talked a little, I made my way forlornly toward my own privy chamber to prepare for the great celebrations ahead. I felt an enormous tension drain out of my body knowing that I would not have to deal with the Lady Mary that Christmastime. Anne once famously said that she would be the death of Mary, or Mary would be the death of her. I had already tasted the bitter poison of their mutual hatred, so it was to my great relief that when I returned to my own lodgings, a delightful surprise awaited me—a surprise which allowed me, for a while at least, to forget all about my intransigent difficulties with the stubborn Spanish princess.

Margery met me at the entrance to the queen's privy chamber, she was aglow. At seven months pregnant, the laces of her gown were well let out, yet, I sensed there was more to her delight than either her pregnancy or my return. I did not have to wait long to find out what else was afoot, for rather excitedly my friend announced,

'There is someone here to see you, Madame.' I smiled quizzically, as Margery stepped aside and with a sweeping gesture of her arm indicated toward a woman standing in the centre of the room who was in deep in conversation with Nan. A number of ladies waited in attendance, but this particular woman had her back turned toward me and with her hood in place, I could not make out the identity of my mysterious visitor. Nan reached out and touched the lady's arm indicating with a nod of her head that I had arrived. The woman turned to look at me. It was the bright smile of my dear friend Joan Champernowe, who I had not seen since my arrival back in Anne's world, and who now greeted me with enormous warmth.

'Oh, Joan!' I exclaimed with delight. I held my arms open wide and together we rushed forward and fell one into the other. Tears stung at the back of my eyes as I realised just how much I had missed her presence; how much just seeing her brought back so many happy memories of those friends who had taken me under their protective wings when I first came to court in Anne's shoes in 1527; memories of the high jinks we shared whilst doing everything we could to escape Katherine's bitter hostility. 'Oh Joan,' I repeated over and over, hugging my friend, which was more than a little difficult as, like Margery, she was yet again heavily pregnant. 'It is so good to see you. I have missed you so much! Have you come for Christmastime?' Still holding each other, Joan pulled back and replied,

'Yes, Madame, I am here for the whole Twelve Days of Christmas, although, as you can see,' she let go of my arms and clutched her swollen belly, 'this little one will soon be upon me. I'm afraid I will have to return home after Twelfth Night to take to my chamber until, God willing, I am safely delivered.' So lost was I in my happiness to see my friend again that I failed to notice that standing quietly close by was another woman with whom I was not acquainted. Joan glanced to her left and said, 'Madame, I hope you do not mind, but I have brought my cousin to court. My Lady, may I introduce you to my cousin, Katherine Champernowe.' For a moment, I stared agog at the woman who, since first knowing Joan, I had longed to meet. Struggling to regain my composure and remember my manners, I inclined my head saying,

'Mistress Champernowe, it is indeed a great pleasure to me that you should visit us here at court. You are most welcome.' Kat was already a mature woman of thirty years of age, just one year younger than Anne. In the same way that one can instantly warm to someone we have never met before, but who reminds us of an old friend, I had immediately fallen for her kind and gentle nature. I was also acutely aware of the pivotal role she would play in Elizabeth's life.

Like Anne, she had dark, almost black, hair swept up in a French hood and deep brown, chocolate coloured eyes. Kat would never be described as classically beautiful, but she was a good-looking woman of fierce intellect and accomplished grace. She radiated humility and a quiet self-confidence that was a rare and precious quality; her understated good nature would make her many friends and few enemies at court. Like many decisions I was to make, I never knew if my choices had been preordained by what I had already read from history, but from the moment I met Mistress Champernowe, I knew only too well why Anne needed her to look after her precious Elizabeth. Kat sunk into a deep curtsy and in a voice lightly inflected with a rolling Devon accent she replied,

'Thank you right kindly, Madame. It is a great honour for me to meet you.' With that she raised herself up to her full height once more, her eyes shining with a mixture of kindness and admiration. Instantaneously, a flash of recognition took hold of both of us; it was like a spark, one that would ignite an ardent fervour of mutual respect and loyalty that will remain for many a year to come, protecting my darling Elizabeth long after my body is buried in the cold ground. I wanted to say so much to her in that moment, but I knew that the conversation that I wished to have must only be between the two of us, alone. So I merely nodded my head at her and then turned to the rest of my friends, Nan, Margery and Joan, opening my arms wide as we came together, scooping Kat up into our bond of friendship, as I said,

'My dear friends, it is more than I could ever have wished for to see us all here for Christmas and…' I then reached out placing my left hand on Joan's swollen belly, and my right upon Margery's, before continuing, 'Just as we celebrate the birth of Christ, so we are soon to have two new little ones amongst us, God willing.' I looked upon the smiling faces of my friends, who were clearly sharing in my delight. There was one sorrow that I could not forget though. With mixed emotions, I added, 'As we enjoy each other this Christmas time, let us not forget our dear friend Mary Norris who we all miss dreadfully and who now keeps God and the angels company.' My friends nodded in agreement as we shared a few moments silence. We did not pray for her soul, for as believers in the new religion, we all knew that Mary was already at peace in heaven. All of us were aware that events were moving apace, and that time marched on inexorably. I knew in that moment, Anne was standing on the brink of one of the most momentous years in her all too short life.

My friends looked weary from their journey so I chivvied them along, and said to Nan, 'Take Joan and Mistress Champernowe with you and ensure you find them some suitable lodgings at court, make it at my express command.' With a respectful curtsy, all three ladies took their leave of Margery and me. I slipped my arm through that of my friend and together we ambled toward my privy closet, as I spoke once more. 'Margery, let us kneel together and give thanks to God for this day for I am, *the most happy*.' With wry amusement, I found myself tripping unconsciously over the words that would later become Anne's motto. I had not thought to say them, rather they had arisen as a genuine expression of the sentiment that I had felt on that Christmas Day. My modern day persona understood Anne's feelings very well; the pure unadulterated joy of finally being recognised as the legitimate partner of the man she loves was all that Anne had come to hope and dream for—what woman would not be happy?

Margery followed me through the doorway to my privy closet. Like many of the Tudor closets that I would come to know in Henry's great houses, the lower half of the walls were clad in a mixture of linen-fold and wainscoted panelling and the upper half were painted with life-size murals depicting religious scenes. The queen's closet at Greenwich depicted the story of Anne's favourite Apostle, St Paul. The ceiling was a masterpiece of Renaissance art work; moulded batons, roundels and grotesque work all gilded in gold leaf, the regular geometric pattern punctuated at regular intervals with painted red and white Tudor roses. Margery and I walked across the floor which was covered in red and white chequer board tiles and knelt reverently upon two large, red velvet cushions placed upon an expensive Turkey carpet in front of an altar. Silently, we gave thanks to God. When our prayers were complete, I crossed myself and rose to my feet and beside me, my heavily pregnant friend struggled to do the same. Seeing her difficulty, I reached out and took hold of her arm, assisting her to stand once more.

'Thank you, Anne.' When we were alone, I commanded that Margery should always address me by my Christian name, for we were ever as sisters.

'Think nought of it. Forsooth, methinks that it will not be long before you will have to repay the kindness.' I made the comment lightly, toying with my friend mischievously. For a fleeting moment, Margery continued straightening her skirts as if I had said nothing of consequence. However, when the full meaning behind my words began to register, I watched a creeping look of recognition arrive upon my friend's face. She had made to speak, but no words had come forth; clearly she was still processing what I had said. Margery then whispered excitedly,

'Are you pregnant, Anne?' I said nothing, but broke into the widest of smiles. Afraid we might be overheard, I glanced over my shoulder to confirm that we were still alone, before I replied, 'Oh Margery, I am but a few days late.' Of course, I knew history had already determined my fate and so perhaps with more confidence than I might have otherwise had, I went on to effuse, 'Yet, I do believe I am carrying the king's child!'

'Oh, glory be to God!' Margery took both my hands and exclaimed in hushed tones, 'Oh, Anne, I am so happy for you—and so soon. I will pray with every fibre of my being that it is a healthy son for this surely must be a sign of God's great pleasure to take you as his wife.' I forbade Margery to speak of our conversation to a living soul as I had yet to tell the king and dared not do so until I was absolutely sure of my condition. I would wait until the great celebrations of Twelfth Night when it would be beyond any doubt that I was indeed with child. That Christmas would prove, on so many fronts, to be a momentous one. For at the very moment that I tasted Anne's greatest happiness, that very same evening, I was introduced to the woman who would prove— unwittingly as it turned out—to be the catalyst of Anne's tragic downfall. I was to meet the colourful and controversial Lady Elizabeth, Countess of Worcester.

That evening, I found myself once more at Henry's side in joyful procession through a palace ablaze with torches and candles. All the court gathered for the Christmas Day feast in the banqueting hall, which I came to regard as a living, breathing, theatre in which we were all players. When not in use, the space stood forlorn, stripped naked of its costume until it was once more transformed into the next magical wonderland; thus it was a room of infinite possibilities. Oh, how I remember the sight that awaited us as I had proudly walked into the hall that evening on Henry's arm. The room was already bursting to capacity with the king's most loyal and devoted courtiers, each one earnestly seeking to impress upon his majesty and their peers, their prowess and suitability for service. A roll of drums and a fanfare of trumpets greeted us. Henry was determined to emphasise the brilliant ascendency of Anne's star and so had ordered that there be a classical theme for the festivities, featuring Henry as Jupiter, the god of gods, and Anne as his Venus, the goddess of love and beauty. To this end, we were dressed in costume fashioned with a classical twist, the fabric made from cloth of gold, white velvets and satin, and upon our heads were festive laurel headdresses painted with gold leaf.

A spectacular canvas formed a false ceiling across the hall upon which were painted two, larger than life figures, Jupiter and Venus, both in gold flowing, white robes, mirroring our own. They stood facing each other, their arms extended afore them, each one helping to support

131

a figure of a baby boy. About the central characters, a host of angels and cherubs proclaimed the arrival of the Christ child with a flourish of mythical trumpets. The entire spectacle was surrounded by painted wreaths of holly and ivy set about with Tudor roses. It was the perfect fusion of the king's dynastic aspirations with Anne, as well as a celebration of the spirit of Christmas. The rest of the hall was bedecked with garlands of fresh green holly, yew and ivy, along with boughs of sweet smelling pine with the cones woven amongst them, painted in glistening gold. Above us, were four great chandeliers decorated with hundreds of the finest crystal drops that sparkled in the light cast from a similar number of lighted beeswax candles, and in the enormous and elaborately carved central hearth, the festive Yule log burned. Once the royal party had arranged themselves at the top end of the table, the king raised his fine golden cup in a toast speaking in a strong and clear voice,

'My lords, ladies and gentlemen, you are most welcome here with us on this Christmas Day. May God bring you good health and prosperity and great fortune for our kingdom. We, as your sovereign Lord, wish you a hearty and very merry Christmas!' With that he nodded his head and raised his goblet to one and all; many cries of good wishes and, 'Merry Christmas, Your Grace!' ran loudly out around the hall in reply. Briefly nodding his head, a second fanfare of trumpets erupted at the king's command, and with it Will Somers, the king's fool, made a grand entrance as the Lord of Misrule. Henry placed a mock golden crown upon his head to great applause and cries of, 'Long live Your Grace!' The entire court bowed or curtsied in submission to Will, including Henry. By that time, I had learned much about the *Feast of Fools* and the role of the Lord of Misrule, both of which had their origins in medieval society. For a brief period of time, the rigid order of the Tudor world would be turned upside down. During the Twelve Days of Christmas, it would be Will's role to keep up the pretence of reigning over us all, whilst encouraging great feasting and revels in a decorous and harmless manner. All would pay homage to him, as if he were Henry himself. Oftentimes, when the court was soaked in alcohol, there was great hilarity as roles were reversed and the lowly Will Somers ordered such great noblemen as my Uncle Norfolk, Charles Brandon or even the king to do his whimsical bidding. Being deeply mischievous, I too had grown very fond of Will's hilarious antics. I gladly submitted myself to his command, at one point serving him with wine, which I had to take away and replace three times afore he was satisfied; on another, condescending to dance with him instead of the king.

The dining itself was the most lavish that I had so far experienced in Anne's world. The *Boar's Head Carol* which welcomed in the centrepiece of the feast; a boar's head, garnished with rosemary and bay leaf, set about with green garlands and carried by four men on an enormous golden platter. Twenty-four glorious courses followed, including: swan, goose, venison and a peacock which had been skinned, roasted, and then placed back inside the cured skin with feathers and all. And when the dining was finally complete, the elderly Earl of Shrewsbury entered the hall holding his white stave of office, preceded by a large silver gilt wassail bowl carried by two burly pages. It was another moment of high tradition, with deep roots reaching back to Anglo-Saxon England. At the doorway, he paused and cried out for all to hear, 'Wassail, wassail, wassail!' In great and merry unison, the entire court replied in kind, before the earl and my Uncle Howard approached the king. Henry indicated that the Lord of Misrule should be the first to drink from the wassail cup, before he too took a hearty swig and passed it into my hands. Thus, it moved about the room, from the highest to the lowliest of the king's courtiers accompanied by minstrels singing a jolly wassail carol.

The feasting eventually melted into dancing and soon Henry and I were leading the court in a festive galliard. The atmosphere was raucous, full of laughter and carefree flirtation. Each time I wound this way or that, passing from one gallant gentleman to the next, I would always end back in the arms of my love. Lifting me high in the air, his eyes alight with love and adoration. Anne was still the centre of his world. I was still his Venus back then, setting the court alight with my enigmatic grace and quirky beauty.

As the dance ended, Henry encircled his arms about me, holding me tightly from behind and nuzzling my ear and neck in front of the entire court. When I finally broke away giggling, I playfully led the king around the hall by the hand. Together against a backdrop of music, dancing and the hurly-burly of general merry-making, we wound our way around the room, stopping to greet and wish Merry Christmas to our friends and family.

At one point my attention was grabbed by a particularly boisterous outpouring of laughter from a small group of ladies and gentlemen, including, my brother; Francis Weston, Sir Francis Bryan, William Brereton, Jane Rochford, Joan and Katherine Champernowe. It appeared that entertaining them all was a woman with whom I was not familiar. I tugged lightly on Henry's sleeve, catching his attention for a moment, as I said rather distractedly,

'Forgive me, My Lord, I want to wish my brother a Merry Christmas.' Henry nodded, equally unconcerned, for he had been watching the Lord of Misrule taunt his old friend the Duke of Suffolk—much to the king's great amusement. As I threaded my way through the crowds that melted away in my presence, I heard Henry's hearty belly laugh sound out about the hubbub. I soon left it behind me, arriving at George's side as the tight knit crowd that had captured my attention opened to greet my arrival. My brother, still chuckling with mirth, was the first to speak.

'Ah, my Lady Marquess, you know the Lady Elizabeth Somerset, Countess of Worcester, do you not?' It was a rhetorical question, and I could only assume that the paths of Anne and the Lady Elizabeth had crossed before. However, I had to bluff my answer, for it was the first time that I had met her whilst walking in Anne's shoes.

'Of course,' I replied with an air of feigned confidence and a slight inclination of my head, to which the Countess replied, proffering a deeper curtsy and thankfully an explanation for her absence at court.

'Madame, you must forgive me for my neglect of you. As you know, I was recently delivered of my fourth child. It was a difficult birth and it has taken me some time to recover. My Lady, I can verily say...' I was aware that the Countess continued speaking. However, while she did so, I was lost in my own drama. When George had spoken the lady's name, it had been entirely familiar to me and I was quite badly shaken at the mention of it, for the Countess of Worcester was infamous as being Anne's first accuser in those terrible days of 1536.

In the few short weeks that followed, I subsequently found out that Elizabeth Somerset, Countess of Worcester was just four years younger than Anne. Her figure was Rubenesque, that is to say, full and voluptuous, her above average height only adding to the considerable potency of her personality. In her own way, she was like Anne, a force of nature, a woman who could not easily be overlooked when she walked into a room. Her face was round, her nose long and straight, whilst her cheeks and décolletage were very often flushed red, reflecting the heat of her inner fire which consumed and digested life and its experiences at a voracious rate. Lady Elizabeth possessed a mane of thick, dark blonde, curly hair, which she tamed by plaiting it beneath her hood. I would soon come to know Elizabeth directly, rather than through the vague and incomplete imprint of her life that was all that was left of her within the pages of my history books. Lady Somerset, I learned, was no submissive, shrinking violet; quite the contrary.

Given her role in Anne's demise, I had always thought to dislike her. I imagined a spiteful, sour woman, one of life's perennial victims, whose friendship was bitter and prickly. Yet the reality of it was so very different. Lady Elizabeth was in every way a passionate lover of life. She had a prodigious appetite for food, wine and men. I do not say that she was unfaithful to her husband, but rather that she was a sensuous, earthy creature who gave of her passions, her energy and her attentions rather too freely for his liking. In fact, it soon became obvious to me that it was difficult not to like the Lady Elizabeth. She was gregarious, fun loving and her rather brazen and bold antics clearly appealed deeply to Anne's sense of playful mischief. In spite of myself, the countess was to become somebody who I would consider as a friend, and she soon fitted in easily with the young, dynamic and vibrant Boleyn faction.

'... and so, in short, Madame, it is a blessed relief to me to be returned to court.' I came back to my senses as Lady Elizabeth concluded her speech, of which I had heard very little. I was curious indeed to know more about her, but the countess would have to wait. I had other things on my mind. I smiled at her graciously, expressed my delight that she had regained full health and that her child was well as I then turned to the woman to whom I wished to speak alone.

'Mistress Champernowe, I wonder if we might get a little better acquainted, perhaps you would care to walk with me?' Kat Champernowe nodded her acknowledgement as together we took our leave of the group, leaving them to their merry dalliance and laughter. The two of us began to weave our way around the edge of the dance floor. From time to time, we paused and watched the dancers swaying this way and that, twirling about amid seductive glances and courteous gallantry. For a few moments, I was thoughtful, my hands clasped behind my back, before finally, I turned to Kat and enquired,

'I believe that we are of a similar age, are we not?'

'I believe so, Madame.' I nodded before probing more deeply,

'Forgive me for asking, but I cannot help but wonder what has brought you to court now, after all this time. Joan has often talked of you and your contentment with country life.' I tipped my head to the side as I spoke, searching Kat's face. I was fascinated by her easy self-assuredness and then I was taken aback by her reply,

'Why, I am here because of you, my Lady.' Kat held my gaze with unnerving penetration. It was as if she had been certain that I had expected her coming, and she searched my face for some sign of recognition of that fact. A slight pinch of confusion must have appeared between my eyebrows as I sought to understand her meaning. Kat continued, 'Madame, Joan has told me,' she leant in slightly, lowering her voice so that we could not be overheard, 'that you embrace the new religion, and you have been instrumental in bringing the word of God into this realm—and into the king's understanding.' She paused and chuckled to herself momentarily, before going on. 'I must confess my Lady that I do not fully understand why I am here either. But if I may speak the truth,' she hesitated again before I nodded earnestly, urging her silently to complete her story, 'I have never intended to seek position, nor honour, at court. Yet lately, I have not been able to shake off the feeling that I needed to come and meet you and serve you in any way that God sees fit…and so Madame, please forgive my audacity, but I humbly offer you my eternal affection and loyalty.'

For a few moments, it was my turn to be speechless. I felt tears unexpectedly sting at the back of my eyes and a tightness take hold in my throat. Such genuine commitment and selflessness was a rare commodity indeed. I felt humbled to witness the long lost moment in which Anne Boleyn had sealed a pact with Mistress Champernowe, one which would endure to the end of Kat's life. Of course, I could not speak of what I knew, that she would be, in so many ways, the mother that Anne's daughter—my daughter—would never sadly know. At the time, I could not recall from my acquaintance with history the exact time when Kat would be appointed into Elizabeth's service; was it before or after Anne's downfall? If it were before, then surely Anne would have a say upon Kat's appointment. However, if it were after, then without doubt she would need the support of an influential person at court to secure her position. I knew immediately to whom she must be introduced—Master Cromwell. Regardless of Cromwell's role in Anne's demise, he shared our religious inclinations, and on those grounds alone, would likely support the placement of Mistress Champernowe into Elizabeth's service—particularly if he saw her as an ally. With this in mind, I then enquired,

'Tell me, are you acquainted with Master Cromwell?' As I spoke, over Kat's left shoulder, I watched my brother take the hand of the Countess of Worcester and lead her onto the dance floor to join in a lusty volta. Something nebulous and fleeting tugged at my senses as I watched them dance. However, I was deeply engaged in my conversation with Kat, and whatever vague notion had formed momentarily, it soon dissipated and I was speaking again to my companion, who replied,

'Indeed Madame, I know Master Cromwell from his travels to the West Country; he was lodged under my father's hospitality for a while.'

'Then may I suggest that you keep on good terms with Master Cromwell for methinks that his influence grows ever more at court, and shall remain so for some time to come.'

I dared not say that I might not be around to fulfil my obligations, instead, I thanked her sincerely for her allegiance, and spoke in what probably sounded like riddles; that the time would come when I would need to call upon her services—but that it was not yet. I urged her to use the intervening time to return to her home in Devon, after Christmas, and order her affairs. I knew full well that once Kat was recalled, she would henceforth have a long and demanding service at court.

Chapter Eleven

Greenwich Palace, London,
Twelfth Night 1532

That glorious Christmas passed in a blur of colour and pageantry. After the bitter hostility that had existed between Katherine and Henry over the previous years, the king once again had a consort by his side that he loved and admired. Henry was merry once more, and the whole court reflected his great joy. Katherine was by then but a shadow; the king had even pointedly rejected her New Year's present of a fine golden cup. I admit that while she lived, her shadow always remained a spectre that haunted my relationship with Henry. It is so curious to think how I had longed for her complete and permanent demise, to never hear her name spoken again. Yet the perversity of it is—and I did not see it at the time—that while Katherine lived, Anne was safe.

At the end of the celebrations, the most sumptuous and celebrated feast day of the year descended upon us, Twelfth Night. It was also the feast of the Epiphany and, like Christmas Day, the day started with a Solemn Mass in the presence of the king, and an enormous banquet was prepared for the evening. Henry was determined that the gloom, which had hung over the court in recent years, would be swept away to be replaced by a new dawn. As a mark of the scale of the celebrations, temporary kitchens had to be erected adjacent to the banqueting hall on the tiltyard at Greenwich, just to service the lavish entertainments.

After mass, I returned to my privy apartments, walking a while with my brother in the privy gallery which, like most privy galleries at Henry's great houses, could only be accessed from the king or the queen's privy chambers at either end; thus it was designed for private, royal use, a place to talk intimately with invited friends, councillors and ambassadors. However, unlike the galleries at Hampton Court and Whitehall, which both looked out over the privy gardens, the gallery at Greenwich had its great range of mullioned windows facing the huge inner courtyard that lay at the heart of the palace. I paused, looking out one of the windows, observing the busy comings and goings of courtiers and servants, who crisscrossed the cobbled surface below.

My brother and I were engaged in light-hearted conversation; George, as ever, entertaining me with many stories arising from the drunken ribaldry of the previous twelve day's festivities. It never ceased to amuse me that my brother always seemed to be close to the thick of it, ever a magnet for outrageous behaviour for which I felt duty bound to chastise him, yet, I adored him regardless. George was in the midst of his story when two gentlemen approached us from the king's end of the gallery. One I knew well, and would trust with my life, Dr Edward Fox. Both gentlemen took their caps from their heads and bowed low before me. I spoke first, not able to contain my delight at seeing such a trusted friend.

'Dr Fox, this is a great and unexpected pleasure! How art thou?'

'Madame, verily the pleasure is all mine. I'm happy to say that I remain in good health and I trust that we find you in a similar state?' Dr Fox smiled at me with enormous warmth.

'I am well indeed, Sirs.' I glanced towards Edward Fox's companion, who looked perplexingly familiar, but I was sure that I had not met him before. Seeing my curiosity, Edward Fox introduced his associate.

'Madame, we have come directly from the king, who instructed us...' Dr Fox indicated towards himself and the unknown gentleman, '...to come presently to find you and pay our respects.' Then he added, 'My Lady Marquess, I understand that you are acquainted with Master Cranmer through your father?' I nodded my affirmation, for I knew it to be the case, suddenly realising why the gentleman looked so familiar. Thomas Cranmer's portrait had survived the test of time, and I knew it well. Dr Fox continued. 'However, these are...' Edward Fox cast a nervous glance about him, before lowering his voice beyond earshot of my ladies, '...extraordinary times and as I understand it, Master Cranmer has been recalled from the Imperial Court for a great purpose indeed. God be praised!' Edward Fox's enthusiasm was touching and I had not forgotten how he had kept his word to me. When I had first met him at Hever, he pledged to do everything within his power to dissolve the king's marriage to Katherine, so that I may become Henry's wife and queen. He had not let me, or Anne, down.

When I had been dragged back to my modern-day life, I fervently re-read my history books to find out what had happened next to Edward Fox. There I found the evidence of his loyalty to Mistress Anne; it was he who had brought Cranmer to Henry's attention. Cranmer had argued to put aside the legal case in Rome in favour of a general canvassing of opinions from university theologians throughout Europe. It was Edward Fox who had subsequently coordinated the research effort to produce the *Collectanea Satis Copiosa* and *The Determinations*, historical and theological support for the argument that the king exercise supreme jurisdiction within his realm. He was one of a tight-knit group of reformist clerics who were fiercely loyal to Anne Boleyn.

I remember my first meeting with Thomas as if it were yesterday. From the very first day, the man had lived up to my expectations; he was thoughtful, steadfast, caring, and as it would turn out, incredibly brave. I have ever loved him well, as he has loved me. Thomas Cranmer was forty years old when I met him first in the gallery at Greenwich. He was a well-built man with strong facial features—a long, straight nose, wide mouth and large, dark chestnut coloured eyes that shone with kindly wisdom. His hair was thick, wavy and dark brown and was more often than not hidden beneath a black velvet cap. Like any cleric inclined toward the reformed faith, Thomas Cranmer dressed simply, most often in a white gown, a plain white cape and black scarf. It was not so much what you saw when you met the future Archbishop of Canterbury that you remembered, but how he invariably made you feel— safe. Even Henry, who in his increasing mental instability in years to come, blowing hot or cold over one person or another, saw something in his trusted archbishop that calmed and soothed his vacillating moods; the king would always remain loyal to Cranmer, even protecting him against the sanguinary vultures that circled about the court, and who so often bayed for his blood.

Henry and I had been eagerly waiting for Cranmer's return. He was a creature of the Boleyn's and much favoured by my father. However, Thomas had clearly gained much store with his majesty through his incisive thinking that had opened up new possibilities for obtaining the king's divorce. If Anne had been instrumental in Cranmer's appointment to the See of Canterbury, it took very little to persuade Henry that Thomas should be his next archbishop. I knew that this was the man who would end Anne's interminable waiting. I drew myself up to full height, and with great effusion, offered my hand and said,

'Master Cranmer, it brings me so much pleasure to see you safely returned to England. I cannot deny that the king and I have been most impatient for your return. How was your journey?' Thomas Cranmer leaned forward, taking my hand gently in his and kissing it reverently, before he stepped back and replied in a rich and gravelly voice,

'It was smooth enough, Madame. Yet, it is good to be returned home.' I turned briefly to my brother and Dr Fox, as I requested,

'Gentlemen, permit me to speak alone with Master Cranmer for a few moments?' I indicated to Thomas that he should walk with me and together, we made our way slowly down the sunlit gallery. For the first time, I had the opportunity to become acquainted with the man who would henceforth play such a significant role in my life.

'Have you just arrived at court, Master Cranmer?' I asked.

'Indeed Madame. I had instructions to present myself immediately to his grace upon my return.' He turned and smiled at me, a twinkle in his eye, and added, 'I find the king's grace in merry spirits; it seems you bring him great joy, my Lady.' I smiled before replying,

'I hope it is so. But tell me Master Cranmer, I hear that you were reluctant to return and take up the great office which the king hath offered you.' It was a statement rather than a question. Thomas Cranmer reflected on it for a moment, considering my words and his reply. Finally, he looked at me directly in the eye, replying,

'It is true Madame. When I first received the news from the king's grace, I wished I could have thrown it into the fire and drunk not from this cup of poison…for I have never been a man of great ambition. I have thought long and hard upon it, but now I see that it is the will of God.' He paused for a moment, before turning to face me squarely and said, 'You may love the king, Madame, I do not doubt it. I see that you sense your own destiny is one which also calls you forth, despite the trials and the perils that rail around you, of which you are aware. I doubt not that there are times when you wish for your freedom.' Once more, I felt tears well up unexpectedly in my eyes. It was rare for another to see beyond the great opulence and splendour of my current estate and to touch upon the fear that stalked me daily. Thomas Cranmer's perception of what lay behind my facade had taken me quite by surprise, and he was wise enough not to even try to pacify me. Instead, he went on, 'and so I have seen it is my duty to be here to support you and Master Cromwell in any way that I am able, for the true word of God will be heard in this land.' With that, Thomas Cromwell suddenly knelt before me, and taking my hand once more, he kissed it in humble submission. Although his form was entirely blurred to me, as my eyes filled rapidly with tears that flowed silently down my cheeks, I felt a strange mixture of joy and fear. I felt that we were all pieces on a giant chessboard; the hand of God was about to move his bishop into place and I was about to take out the queen.

After meeting with Thomas Cranmer, I was unable to contain my excitement, and desperately wanted to share my joy with the king. However, there was more than that; I was now two weeks late. Sure that I was pregnant, I could not keep my secret any longer from Henry. So, resplendent in a gown of rich purple velvet, with voluminous sleeves trimmed and folded back with ermine, and a kirtle fashioned from cloth of silver, I triumphantly made my way through the public chambers at Greenwich. I felt bullish that day, and wanted the whole world to see Anne at her brilliant best.

With the full train of my skirt sweeping elegantly behind me, I was followed in regal procession by the Countesses of Worcester and Rutland, Lady Mary Howard and my beloved Nan. From my own privy lodgings, which faced south towards Duke Humphrey's Tower, we turned left, passing through a short gallery before entering the queen's watching chamber. By then, everybody recognised that a new queen in England was imminent, and many had thronged to the public chambers of my apartments to pay their respects and homage or, to petition for my favour. Yet that day, I needed to speak to the king, and my aura must have said as much; '*Noli me tangere, for Caesar's I am*' and so we passed unimpeded, as the crowds parted like the Red Sea amid many bows, curtsies and words of hearty greeting.

I walked briskly through the queen's watching chamber, through a gallery at the top of the grand stair, and through the king's watching chamber. Continuing through the square chamber that connected the king's presence chamber to the holy day closets of the chapel royal, I finally and with great ceremony, stepped before the king.

Henry was seated upon his throne, being entertained by jugglers and acrobats, all of whom performed with music to the hearty applause of those who were gathered there. Like many of the king's public chambers, it was about sixty feet in length and some twenty-five to thirty feet wide. The floor was tiled in red and white, and the oak ceiling was carved and painted with lapis lazuli in geometric patterns and decorative roundels, highlighted in gold. Directly opposite the huge, imposing gilded doors, was the king's throne beneath a green velvet canopy of estate, its edges bordered and tasselled with gold thread work. Behind the throne hung a huge tapestry worked in gold, blue and red thread, depicting the royal coat of arms. Henry's throne was carved and gilded with gold and upholstered in finely worked gold embroidery, whilst underneath his feet was a huge red and gold Turkey carpet upon which no one but the king was allowed to tread.

I walked forward proudly and with purpose. As I did so, the attendant crowd gradually became aware of my presence and their acknowledgement of me quickly caught Henry's eye. I watched, as with a flick of his wrist, he silenced the musicians and the acrobats melted away, as if they were mere wisps of smoke, cleared by the gentlest of breezes. A hush descended upon the room as I came before the king's grace, and sank into a deep and elegant curtsy.

'My Lady Marquess, this is an unexpected pleasure.' The king sat forward, legs apart, one elbow resting upon one knee, whilst he stroked his auburn beard thoughtfully, clearly pleased at my presence. I rose to my feet, and in a loud and clear voice, made my request.

'Your Grace, might I request a private audience with you.' I watched as one of Henry's eyebrows raised in peaked curiosity. The king rose, whilst he nodded in my direction that I should follow him into his privy chamber. A short gallery connecting the two rooms acted as a kind of airlock between the king's public and private persona. As we passed through it and the privy chamber beyond, both sets of doors were closed, and the hubbub of the crowd and the jaunty music faded into the background. Henry walked ahead of me, toward a large cabinet next to the entrance to the king's bedchamber, on the far side of the room.

'How now, sweetheart? Did you meet with Master Cranmer?' he said as he opened the cabinet and took out one of the Tyrolean boar spears that I had presented to Henry as his New Year's gift.

'Indeed, Your Majesty. Although, I must apologise, as I could not contain my excitement and so very much wanted to share it with you…' I paused momentarily, before gushing, 'Oh Henry, I think finally we shall be together, really *be* together, no more uncertainty, no more Katherine!' I took a few steps forward as I so wanted Henry to take me in his arms. The king must have sensed my desire, for he turned around, resting the spear which he had been trying out for weight and balance against the cabinet, before scooping me up in his strong embrace.

'Yes, my love. Yes, very soon I shall have my divorce, and you will be my wife and queen, and we will have many sons together.' With that he picked me up playfully and spun me around, laughing joyfully. Finally, Henry let me go and turned back toward the boar spear, picking it up once more and examining its finely carved handle. He was clearly keen to try them out in the hunt. Suddenly, the king looked at me with mischief in his eyes, as he said eagerly, 'Let us go hunting tomorrow, Anne. I wish to see how these perform,' as he spoke, he lifted the spear, looking down its length towards its razor sharp, steel head.

I clasped my hands behind my back, tracing a pattern in the carpet with the tip of my foot, and in a nonchalant way, I replied,

'Mayhap, it is not a good idea for a woman in my condition.' For a few moments, the king continued to examine the craftsmanship of the spear, apparently oblivious to the meaning of my words. Then, as with Margery, I watched him turn to look at me thoughtfully,

'A woman in your condition?' Distractedly, the king replaced the spear against the cabinet, and with his full attention upon me, I replied,

'Yes, Henry, a woman in my condition … I am with child, Your Grace.' I swear that such a loud whoop of joy had come forth that the entire court must have been roused to suspicion. Henry's face broke into an enormous grin, as he picked me up once more and twirled me around and around, until I had scarce been able to stand up straight. Finally, the king declared,

'You are with child...and so soon. Anne, it is truly auspicious … God is on our side and *I am* to have a son!' As he spoke, he took my small, bejewelled hands within his and squeezed them as if willing my body to finally give him all that he desired. I was a tempest of mixed emotions that day; to see the king's great joy, to feel his overwhelming love for me, was intoxicating indeed. And I hoped that I could defy Anne's destiny, and that this time, the outcome would be different.

Chapter Twelve

Whitehall, London,
25 January 1533

So much changed after I told Henry of my pregnancy, in ways which I had not really anticipated. Oh, he continued to adore me, perhaps even more fervently than before, for I was then *de facto;* the chalice carrying the king's future hopes and aspirations for the Tudor dynasty, and the security of his kingdom. I was ever aware how this responsibility weighed heavily on Henry's mind, and I see now, looking back, that he had believed in me completely. The king had placed his faith in Anne in the face of so much opposition, and was utterly convinced that she would not let him down.

Of course, he was terrified that anything could happen which might endanger the child, and so Henry forbade me to hunt, hawk or even ride. This confined me for weeks at a time to whichever palace precinct the court found itself in. For a vigorous and healthy woman like Anne, these restrictions were akin to torture; my body often ached to be free, particularly in the early days before my swollen belly finally curtailed any aspirations I might have had to escape the sometimes stifling boredom of my privy chambers.

What was even more difficult, for the both of us, was how our physical relationship almost disappeared overnight. When I first suggested that we make love, Henry virtually recoiled in horror at the suggestion. I admit that I completely failed to realise that such a practice was generally reviled and viewed as dangerous to the health of the baby. I was invited to share the king's bed much less frequently and many a night, I would find myself lying alone in my chambers, resenting what felt tantamount to rejection. My modern day knowledge told me that our precautions were unnecessary, and I think that the very first seeds of my jealously were sown during those long and lonely nights spent alone. How could it have been otherwise? I knew that history judged my husband to be an infamous philanderer, and although I tried, dear God I tried, to trust him, far too often my imagination would run away with me. When no message arrived from the king of an evening, I would retire sulkily to my bed chamber and see vivid montages of naked lovers falling into Henry's arms and occupying the space that for so long had been unequivocally mine.

Following my announcement, other events accelerated at a breathtaking pace. Henry became ruthlessly determined that our son would be born in wedlock, from the womb of a consecrated queen. Oftentimes, the king would recount that he had worked long into the night, in deep discussion with Cromwell, regarding plans for the consecration of Archbishop Cranmer, and refining the details of Master Cromwell's brilliantly conceived Act of Appeals. This act would put on the statute book a statement of the royal supremacy, finally breaking all judicial links with Rome. Of course, this would serve remove Katherine's legal right to appeal to the Pope in the case of her divorce, thus leaving the way open for Henry to have the case settled once and for all in his own dominions. It was clear by then that no one would stand in the way of the king's will.

And so it transpired that a week after Twelfth Night, the court relocated to the palace of Whitehall. Greenwich had been unoccupied for some time, and desperately needed cleaning; the stench, even in the most sumptuous parts of the palace had become overwhelming. In our absence, as was common practice, I knew the place would be cleaned, repaired and repainted as necessary, so that it would be ready for the king's return. However, in January 1533, Henry also had another good reason to move the court. Whitehall was located adjacent to Westminster and Parliament; the latter being due to open on 4 February. The whole court was abuzz, for there was important business that needed to be concluded and quickly.

To expedite this, the king and I took up residence in London's newly refurbished palace. Other key players were also given lodgings close by. Cranmer and Cromwell were now utterly indispensable to the king; and so Cranmer was moved into a house on nearby Canon Row, between the palaces of Whitehall and Westminster; whilst Cromwell was appointed chambers in Westminster itself. Both were at the king's side daily, and after the archbishop concluded his business there, he would invariably visit me on the queen's side, often saying mass in my privy closet.

It was clear that in those weeks Parliament toiled ceaselessly to pave the way for the final act in the drama of *the king's great matter*, and that it was Anne herself who had instigated the appointment of Archbishop Cranmer after the death of William Warham, the previous August. When, in my presence, Thomas thanked the king for his elevated position, Henry matter-of-factly replied that it was to Anne that he owed the greatest thanks. And so, the archbishop-in-waiting and I were to become the firmest of friends. Indeed, after his arrival in England, I quickly began to lean on Thomas heavily for advice in many spiritual matters. It was Cranmer, for example, who guided my hand in the appointment of those reformers who would be my chaplains as queen; Hugh and William Latymer, Edward Crome, William Betts, Nicolas Heath, Nicolas Shaxton, Matthew Parker and the man who attended me in my final hours in the Tower, my almoner, John Skip.

On the previous day, Friday, 24 January, the news of Thomas Cranmer's appointment to the See of Canterbury as the premier prelate in the land was finally made public. That evening, I received a visit from the king in my privy chambers. I was watching my ladies practising their dance steps, as Mark Smeaton and another court musician accompanied them with bright and joyful music. I was seated on a stool, clapping along to the beat the tambour, whilst at my feet, was a lady I had come to know as Mistress Savage. Although I was fond of Anne Savage, I was missing my dearest friends dreadfully.

After the Christmas celebrations, Joan Champernowe left court with her cousin, Kat, in order to prepare for the birth of her child. Margery had done likewise; whilst Nan had taken her leave of me to return home and make preparations for her wedding to Master Zouche. I wished them all well, and with tears in our eyes, we said our goodbyes; my pain only eased by my surety that both of my friends would survive the dangerous undertaking of childbirth. Yet for me, the timing was dreadful. I was only too aware that very soon Anne would finally be married to the king; 25 January loomed large in my mind. I began to wonder if history was wrong. The day was but twelve hours away and although Henry and I talked of marriage often, the king had yet to mention a date. There was so much uncertainty, and I desperately wanted them to be with me, my pillars of strength.

I remember that there was much hilarity and laughter that evening. In practising the dance, steps were often misplaced, and playful fun was made of the unfortunate lady responsible. However, when the king swept into the chamber, all ceased immediately; each person acknowledging Henry's arrival with a deep bow or curtsy. I stood to my feet more slowly, before doing the same, as humble submission dictated. Having righted my posture, I could see that the king's grace was accompanied by Thomas Cromwell, whilst William Brereton was in attendance as Henry's groom of the privy chamber.

'Ladies' the king nodded respectfully to me and my ladies, 'Please leave us.' Each one obediently retired to the queen's presence chamber, leaving the four of us; me, Henry, Cromwell and Brereton alone. 'Sweetheart' the king came forward and kissed me in greeting, then continued, 'it is time.' I frowned, deeply confused by Henry's meaning. Seeing my bewilderment, Henry went on to explain, 'We cannot delay proceedings any longer, now that you are carrying our child. We must marry, and I have decided that we will do so tomorrow before dawn.' Although I knew that this moment had been fast approaching, as ever, I found my breath stolen away, this time by the suddenness of Henry's convictions. Henry smiled at me, 'You will come with just one lady at five of the clock, tomorrow morning. Be discreet, for you know well I am not yet divorced from Katherine and all of us…' I noticed how he threw a steely glance at Brereton to make clear his message, 'must keep our counsel on the matter.' He then turned to Cromwell and began pacing up and down, hands clasped thoughtfully behind his back, as he went on issuing instructions. 'Cromwell, I need you to make all necessary arrangements. We cannot use Cranmer to officiate; I need him kept at a distance from our union, so that he may be seen to sit impartially in judgement upon the matter of my divorce.' Henry paused before declaring, 'At an hour before the appointed time, fetch Dr. Lee who resides in the palace, he can take the service. And let us congregate in the Lantern Room, the ceremony can be conducted there.'

Suddenly my heart skipped a beat. For a few seconds, all seemed to move in slow motion. I knew that Anne and Henry's marriage had reputedly taken place in the upper chamber in the newly completed Holbein Gate that straddled King Street. Was history about to change its course for the first time? For a fleeting moment, I was terrified of the unknown, and yet wildly excited that perhaps this was what I had been waiting for—the first shifts in the sands of time. In short order, my hopes were dashed by Cromwell who quickly interceded by saying,

'Your Grace, if you recall some repairs and repainting have been ongoing in your privy closet. May I suggest instead we hold the ceremony in your library in the upper chamber of the Holbein Gate? All works have been completed there, and at such a distance from Your Grace's main chambers, the utmost secrecy is assured.' Henry considered this alternative option for a moment, as I wrestled with a wildly beating heart that threatened to leap from my chest. The king nodded his satisfied consent and with that, all was agreed. I had just hours to prepare for my wedding to Henry. We were soon to stand before God and seal our fated union in the eyes of a church which was itself dying and waiting to be reborn.

At a little before five o'clock the following morning, I made my way from the queen's privy lodgings in Whitehall, toward the long, privy gallery that connected the king's private chambers with the Holbein Gate at its west end. It was midwinter, and at such an early hour the palace was deserted and eerily silent. All I could hear was the haunting screech of the night owl as she went about her last hunting forays of the night. I shuddered, for I too felt hunted that day.

After the king left my apartments the previous evening, I had called Mistress Savage to me and explained that I was to be married to the king in the greatest secrecy the following morning, and that I wished her to be the one to accompany me to the altar. She listened with breathless incredulity, and thought that surely I was teasing her. I had to reassure her that my request was genuine, and that I needed her to go discreetly about the task of preparing me and my dress for the following day. I gave her my instructions for the gown that needed to be fetched up from the queen's wardrobe. Margery would normally have made such arrangements, however, in her absence, Anne slipped quietly out of my chambers to carry out my bidding.

In the meantime, my thoughts soon turned to my beloved family. Everything happened so very quickly that in the end, I did not even have time to tell any of them of my momentous news. All of them, even my father, who was at that time invariably by the king's side, had left court for a brief period after the Christmas festivities ended. For shortly after I had told Henry of my pregnancy, I had alerted my family to my happy condition—to their great delight. My father made it clear that pressing business in the country should be handled immediately as matters would move quickly in London once Parliament resumed at the beginning of February, and it was imperative that we be united as a family. I wanted so much to speak to my mother that night. Of course, there was no way of reaching her at such short notice. Suddenly, I felt very alone and fearful that the step I was about to take would seal, once and for all, my worst fears for the future; my initial outpouring of joy was replaced by a deep, penetrating and haunting fear that I was but a lamb to the slaughter. There was no one in whom I could confide, no one to reassure me that all would be well, not even Cranmer, who in such a short time had come to understand me as if we had known each other for all eternity. By the time the hour arrived, I was gripped with an abhorrent sense of foreboding. All I had wanted to do was flee from the palace and turn my back on everything that Anne had strived for.

There seemed no escape, no last minute reprieve as Master Brereton arrived at the appointed time to escort both me and Mistress Savage along the 200 foot-long privy gallery, toward King Street and the Holbein Gate. As we made our way in silence, enshrouded by darkness, only William's torch threw out a welcome sphere of light that illuminated our way. The palace was icy cold as the torches, candles and fires in Whitehall had long been put out the previous evening in a guard against fire. I felt every sinew of my body brace against the chill.

We soon arrived at the door of the king's privy closet, a room also known as the lantern room, on account of a large and ornate lantern that was hung inside the chamber. We continued in silence through that deserted closet, only the swishing of our skirts and our insistent footsteps breaking the deafening silence around us. Many fine paintings hung upon the walls, as they still do today; although, I will never see them again. Glimpses of faces etched eternally in regal repose, each one emerging briefly in the passing light, only to be subsumed once more by the inky blackness as we glided by.

I was familiar with the layout of this extensive gallery, as I had spent a good deal of time with the king in this, his inner most sanctum, with its sumptuous interior design. The privy gallery was clad in linen-fold panelling, the ceiling decorated with fretwork consisting of low battens in a geometric design, and on the floor was thick, rush matting that was replaced at regular intervals. Without sunlight, the resplendent colours of the gallery were muted into shades of grey, with only brief flashes of its vivid glory apparent to the naked eye. Our quest took us past all five of the king's most secret rooms, each one laid out, one after the other, along the southern wall of the gallery. Henry's dressing room came first, followed by his privy dining room, bedchamber, study and finally, his bathroom. Then, just over half way along the length of the gallery, we came upon the great stair that led down into the great garden below. I had used the stairs many a time during the day, when I walked out with Henry to enjoy the fresh air and fragrant Tudor gardens. But, in the dark early hours before dawn, pricked with cold and gripped with fear, everything seemed so sinister; even the stone steps seemed to slip away into a hungry and cavernous abyss.

I glanced over my shoulder at Mistress Savage, who was following close behind me. I desperately needed her reassurance, for up ahead was the door that connected the gallery to the Holbein Gate. I began to panic. In my head, I heard myself crying out to somebody, anybody that might care to hear me, 'I don't want to do it! Please help me! Please save me!' Yet, I was not able to confide my fears to anyone.

When we finally arrived at the doorway, Master Brereton paused while he sought the key that would open the door to my life as queen. I looked out of one several windows running along the gallery, but it was still dark, and all I could see in the flickering torchlight was the reflection of my own shadowy apparition, half cast in darkness. Staring back at me, as ever, was the face of Anne Boleyn; this time though, it was a face etched visibly with fear, despite which, Anne looked hauntingly beautiful. For my wedding, I chose a gown of rich, black velvet set flatteringly against a kirtle and fore-sleeves made from cloth of gold; the wide, angular sleeves themselves turned back and trimmed with soft, chocolate brown, sable fur; the edge of the skirt being finished with the same. Showing from beneath my low, square-cut neckline was the finely embroidered trim of my chemise, worked delicately in black thread, whilst the neckline of the gown itself was decorated with thick, barley twist adornments made of gold thread, interspersed at regular intervals by repeating sets of two expensive seed pearls, sown one above the other. Similar pearls also finished the edging of my black, velvet French hood and studded the false sleeves of my gown. More than anything that day, I needed my talisman, and so, about my neck was strung a single gold chain and a double chain of pearls, the iconic gold letter 'B' resting at the base of my throat.

My brief reverie was broken, as I heard Master Brereton's key turn easily in one of the many ornate, golden locks fitted to all the doors of the king's privy chambers. William opened the door, and leading the way, stepped into the first floor gallery beyond. This part of the gallery connected the privy gallery directly with the tiltyard gallery on the west side of King Street. However, we were not to pass this way, instead Master Brereton indicated with an outstretched arm that we should turn to the right at the end of this short passage and ascend a narrow vice-stair that would take us to the upper chamber of the gate.

I felt sick and paused to gather my strength before I lifted up the edge of my skirts, and steadied myself against the cold stone surface of the spiral staircase. The staircase would normally have been illuminated by a series of windows set into the outer facing walls of the octagonal tower that encased it. However, it was some way before dawn, and London remained largely asleep. I wondered what someone making their way along King Street outside must have thought if they perchance looked up and witnessed our clandestine party climbing the turret of the Holbein Gate at such an early hour.

I was aware of Mistress Savage bearing the long train of my gown, and Master Brereton following behind as I completed several turns of the staircase before light from the upper chamber leaked out and cast shards of illumination onto the steps in front of me. I heard Henry's voice emanating from the room above; he was in conversation with another man. I strained to hear what was being said for, judging from the tone of the exchange, there seemed to be some tension between the king and the man to whom he spoke, a voice I recognised as belonging to Dr Roland Lee, the king's chaplain. I had heard Dr. Lee questioning the king about the provision of a marriage licence. He knew that technically the king was still married to Katherine. I held my breath, for to question the king thus required considerable courage. However, Henry had decided to play the game with humour, dismissing Dr. Lee's concern with laughter and a hearty rebuff that, of course, he held such a licence but that it was elsewhere in the palace, and could not be fetched at this hour. There was a moment's silence and I was sure that the priest did not believe the king's words. Henry reassured his chaplain that he would take upon his own shoulders all responsibility for what was about to come to pass. With that I found myself at the doorway to the little chamber, and pushed open the door.

As part of Henry's most secret lodgings, only the most intimate of the king's companions would ever hope to see this part of the palace. Ordinarily, the king used this room as his library, and so about its walls were many cabinets containing rare and expensive books. Directly opposite the entrance to the room was a small stone fireplace, lit to give a hearty welcome. Thanks to the heat emanating from this, and several lit candles placed about the room, the chamber was warm, and to my relief I felt some of the tension in my body begin to melt away. At either end of the chamber were two large windows, each flush with the wall and carved from stone into eight elongated Tudor arches; all were in-filled with mullioned glass. In daylight, these windows gave magnificent views up King Street towards Charing Cross, and down toward Westminster. That day, however, the large oak table which Henry would normally use to work upon had been moved in front of the window and made into a temporary altar, adorned with two enormous silver gilt candlesticks placed on either side of a crucifix. It was pitch black outside, and all I could see in the window was the reflection of these items and those who had gathered to witness our union.

In front of the altar stood Dr. Roland Lee, holding a bible in front of him. As we approached, Henry turned toward the doorway to see our coming. He looked truly resplendent in the flickering candlelight wearing a jerkin, and a long, pleated skirt, fashioned from cloth of gold damask and slashed across the breast and sleeves. The slashing allowed the white chemise beneath to puff through the doublet, whilst the fabric itself was decorated with geometric patterns of gold thread work, punctuated with clusters of pearls and diamonds set in gold mounts. The low, wide neckline also revealed the high-necked chemise worn beneath, as was much the fashion of the time; this chemise was trimmed around the collar with more gold thread work, studded with precious jewels. Worn over all of this, Henry carried magnificently on his broad shoulders, a thigh-length gown of black velvet embroidered with Venetian gold, its wide collar trimmed with the rich, chocolate brown sable fur, similar to that adorning my own dress. Upon his grace's head was a black velvet cap worn at an angle, the rim adorned with clusters of pearls and finished with a single white ostrich feather.

We were not alone. As I expected from my knowledge of history, Sir Henry Norris and Thomas Heneage were present as witnesses to our marriage. Henry broke into a satisfied smile upon the sight of his bride and reached out toward me, and said,

'My Lady, come thither and be my wife.' I moved forward, taking my place at the king's side; I could have sworn that every single person in the room must have heard my heart thunder violently in my chest as Roland Lee began the marriage ceremony in Latin. In truth, I heard very little of it, vaguely aware of the drone of his voice uniting Henry and Anne as King and Queen of England. I felt so terribly hot, and utterly paralysed with fear. I remember how I looked across at Henry, the man I loved with all my heart. I wanted to take him by the collar and scream at him, 'Why are you doing this when you think to murder me?' Of course, anyone who would have heard my thoughts would have thought me insane, for in that moment I was the woman who had everything— wealth, power, fame, the adoration of a mighty prince and his child in my belly. But I saw none of this; just a bloody sword and Anne's decapitated body. I wanted to stop it all!

As Dr Lee began to read from the Gospels, I found myself detached, in some otherworldly place, driven there by my own fear. Running through my mind was an unbroken montage of scenes from Anne's life. For a long time, I had access to Anne's memory and in that moment, broken fragments and disjointed recollections fused into one continuous stream of consciousness in which I saw how every moment had led perfectly to the next; how every meeting, every choice and every conversation had brought Anne to this point. In the most powerful way imaginable, I was reminded of Anne's destiny. There was something in the knowing of this, the way it touched my heart, my very soul, which caused a tremendous sense of calm to swiftly descend upon me. It was a pure state of grace, as if my shoulder had been touched by the hand of a guardian angel. I sensed that a greater power guided and protected me, and that despite whatever may come to pass, I would be safe. I did not truly understand it, as I do now, but it was as if by the grace of God, the curtain was briefly drawn back and I had glimpsed Paradise.

And so, Henry and I were finally married in a small, intimate chamber before dawn, in the heart of Whitehall. Anne Boleyn was England's new queen. God, it seemed, had been a relatively easy convert. All that remained was the rather more tricky business of making her so in the eyes of England's nobility and its people.

After the nuptial mass that bound us as man and wife, the wedding party melted away into the dark of the palace, leaving no trace that anything out of the ordinary had come to pass. I returned to the queen's lodgings with Mistress Savage and changed back into my bedclothes, so as not to arouse suspicion when my maids arrived just after dawn. The fear which had toyed so cruelly with my deepest vulnerabilities was now replaced by an unshakeable serenity and I knew without question that I was loved unconditionally by a God that would never forsake me, that I was somehow part of a whole in which I must play my part. As I sat on a window seat overlooking the Thames, watching the rising sun set the London skyline ablaze in a glorious palette of red, pink and grey, I felt that all was well, and for a time, could see only beauty in all that surrounded me.

On the day of our wedding, the king instructed me to come to his privy chambers after I had broken my fast as he had a gift for me. Rather enigmatically, he added that I should attend in the clothes that I had been wearing for the wedding ceremony. I obeyed the king's command and attended by Mistress Savage, Lady Mary Howard, and the Countesses of Worcester and Rutland, I presented myself in the king's private lodgings at Whitehall. The large rectangular chamber, approximately sixty feet by thirty feet, looked out upon the large, cloistered privy garden on the west wall and a huge fireplace dominated the room on the east side. The fireplace was a true Renaissance masterpiece: carved from stone, the elaborate decoration extended from floor-to-ceiling, four columns, arranged into two pairs were stacked one above the other and repeated on the other side to frame the design. Grotesque carvings were set against a series of roundels, and included figures of Charity, a mother with children on the left, Blind Justice on the right, and a battle scene set between them.

That chilly January morning, an enormous fire blazed in the grate; the walls were hung with fabulous tapestries and a number of intriguing paintings. However, one such painting of epic proportions was in the process of being removed from the wall at the far end of the room. Overseeing this scene of domesticity was Henry in deep discussion with a man who was modestly dressed and unfamiliar to me; although I could not hear what they were saying, my ear was drawn to his rather unusual accent, a harsh, rather staccato rhythm that jarred against the usual flow of a native English speaker.

'My Lady Marquess of Pembroke, Your Majesty,' a yeoman of the king's chamber announced our arrival. Henry, and the man at his side, turned about to greet me.

'Ah, my Lady Marquess, please come thither,' said Henry beckoning me forward. 'You have not met Master Holbein, have you sweetheart?' I was taken aback. Of all the people in the world, of all the things that I thought Henry would wish to show me, I had not for a moment thought to meet the man who through his fabulous paintings and sketches had single-handedly kept alive the court that Anne had known in her lifetime, through to the twenty-first-century. In my modern day life, I had spent many hours poring over the sheer genius of Holbein's work, mesmerised and entranced by the life-like quality which he captured in his sitters. It was if I had known these people for myself, as if I could reach out and touch their soul and know the secrets of their heart—even 500 years later. I also knew well from my history books that Anne had been a great patron of Holbein. He returned to England from Basel in 1532, and by early 1533, Holbein was once again influential in court circles and along with Thomas Cromwell, I would be an avid promoter of his work.

I stepped forward and the king took my left hand and kissed it gallantly in greeting. With his other arm outstretched, Henry focused my attention once more on Master Holbein. Like any lover of Anne Boleyn in my twenty-first century life, it was a great sadness to me that no contemporary portrait of Anne by Holbein had survived the decimation of the Boleyn faction. Yet in the months to come, I would learn that many such portraits would be painted by this Renaissance master, and during the hours that I would sit for him while he captured Anne's mesmerising allure, I would quiz Master Holbein fervently about the details of his life.

During our first sitting, he revealed that he had been born in Augsburg, which in the sixteenth century was part of the Holy Roman

Empire, and in my modern day life, lies in south-west Bavaria, Germany. He was only four years older than Anne, born around 1497. His father, Hans Holbein the Elder, had also been a successful painter, and passed this gift to his son, who picked up his first pencil in earnest at the tender age of two-and-a-half; and by the time he was just six years old, his rare and unusual talent was already evident.

Hans Holbein was a small, stocky man with strong facial features, a square jaw line and piercing, light blue eyes. He was blessed with a thick mass of light brown, sandy coloured hair, which was cut rather severely into a short fringe across his brow, the natural waviness of his hair showing itself in his close-cropped beard and moustache. It was Master Holbein's fiery intensity that I found truly compelling. When he painted you, he became lost in his work, enraptured by the creative process and hungry to tell the story of that which was hidden in and behind a human face. Holbein had always dealt in the currency of realism, and I would come to understand why; when he painted you, it was if he was reaching inside you with his pencil to pluck out and reveal the 'real' self from behind the mask of a person's persona.

With Henry's introduction, Master Holbein removed his cap, bowing low before me, as I replied,

'No, but I have heard much about you Master Holbein, and I think your work exquisite. I am most pleased to make your acquaintance.'

'I thank thee most humbly, Madame.' Holbein replied, before Henry cut in, eager to share his surprise with me.

'Madame, I have commissioned Master Holbein to paint your full length portrait, as a gift from your sovereign lord.' Henry meant 'wedding gift', for he raised his eyebrow knowingly as he emphasised the word 'gift', but clearly he did not wish Master Holbein to know of our happy estate—at least, not yet. I was beside myself with excitement to know that Anne would be painted by Holbein, and that I would witness the birth of a long, lost masterpiece. I suddenly understood why Henry had commanded me to come to his chambers in my wedding gown; he wished me to be painted as a new queen, newly married and pregnant with a new Tudor prince—it was to be a commemorative portrait. There was to be no delay; Master Holbein had already arranged the tools of his trade in the king's closet, where Henry directed him to make the first sketches of Anne's true likeness.

I did not know what instructions the king had given Master Holbein, so, I stood rather self-consciously whilst the great master set to work. Henry was but two rooms away in his privy chamber, attending to the usual demands of the day. He told me that he was to meet with Master Cromwell and that Thomas Audley was to be appointed as Henry's new chancellor the following day, Sunday 26 January. Arrangements needed to be made, and there was important business to attend to. Henry assured me that he would return when all was complete, for he wished to check on our progress.

I found it hard to relax or to maintain the type of regal and enigmatic pose that I felt I owed to this momentous occasion. It was fair to say that whilst Master Holbein was ever his impeccable and professional self, I could tell that his creative genius was frustrated by Anne's stiff reserve. I wondered if he sensed a more passionate creature, full of fire and fury, with a fierce determination that simmered beneath the surface. Even I became cross with myself; I remember that I pondered on why it is that when we try to be ourselves, 'ourselves' becomes ever more elusive? Where had my serenity gone? After an hour, I was at the end of my tether, my gown felt hot and uncomfortable and I was sure that my cheeks were flushed uncharacteristically red. Then suddenly, I sensed that I was being watched, and turned my head about to face the doorway. There, leaning nonchalantly against the door frame was the king. I do not know if he saw my discomfort and understood intuitively the painful irony of my situation, but a smile of appreciation played upon his lips, and I saw in his eyes an enormous love, which had instantly touched my beating heart. I remembered who I was; a woman adored by this man whom I, in turn, loved to distraction; that I was now a queen and, by the right of the child within her belly, was fulfilling all that was expected of her. Suddenly, I felt every sinew of tension dissolve as my eyes alighted upon my love. I came alive, and in 'forgetting' myself, everything that Anne was; sexy, enigmatic, determined, passionate, proud and fiercely loyal came flooding forth.

Master Holbein had not seen the king in the doorway, and knew nothing of what had occurred silently between me and my beloved. To most people no appreciable change would have been evident, yet to the artist's eye the shift was seismic. It was as if the sun had finally broken through the storm clouds on the greyest of days, and the glory of Anne

Boleyn shone brilliantly, lighting up the room. With unbridled excitement, Master Holbein suddenly exclaimed,

'Madame, that is it! Do not move; let me capture your eyes, your beautiful eyes, for now they are finally talking to me!'

No more needed to be said. I was a woman first and a queen second, and through Henry's eyes, Anne's Venus was unleashed. After the sketches were completed, I waited for several weeks with baited breath for the unveiling of Anne's portrait. However, before that time arrived, I was to witness, and take part in, several truly historic events that together would sweep England up in their wake, and change the course of its history forever.

Chapter Thirteen

Whitehall, London,
8 February 1533

A few days before parliament opened in Westminster on 4 February, my lord father and lady mother returned to court. They were, by then, parents–in-law to the King of England, and as such, were lodged in splendid apartments on the ground floor of the palace, close to my own regal chambers. George had also arrived back in Whitehall, and like many of the king's most intimate gentlemen of the privy chamber, he was also lodged on the ground floor, this time in the privy gallery range, beneath the king's own chambers.

I was so excited to see my family again, and fell into the arms of my mother, barely able to contain my momentous news. All three listened with a degree of breathless incredulity, as I recounted the secret, pre-dawn wedding ceremony conducted by the king's chaplain, in the presence of only a scant number of witnesses. George, typically, made gentle fun of me, raising his eyes to the ceiling as he exclaimed how it was impossible to turn his back on his sister for one moment without finding that she was either betrothed or wedded to the King of England, or mayhap carrying his child! It was a great joke between us, and one that we would share privately for many months to come.

Then, on the morning of Saturday, 8 February, exactly two weeks after Henry and I were married, I was visited by my parents and brother in my privy chamber. George was in fine spirits and had come to invite me and my ladies to watch him play tennis with the king later that morning. There was a flurry of excitement amongst the ladies in attendance with the prospect of watching two intensely competitive, testosterone-laden males battle for victory was a pleasant diversion from the often sedate pace of life expected of a noblewoman at court.

Bets were already being taken on the outcome, when a page of the chamber announced the arrival of Thomas Cranmer. Thomas swept into the room, clearly delighted by the unexpected presence of my parents. Having acted as my father's chaplain from the early days of Anne's ascendency at court, the two were particularly firm friends, and shared many common values and beliefs. I too was delighted to see my client and friend; I had not done so since before my wedding day, for pressing matters of state had sadly kept Thomas entirely occupied. Thus, he remained ignorant of the historic event which had lately occurred.

The archbishop-to-be swept a bow. Taking his Canterbury cap from his head, he greeted each of us each in turn, kissing my hand in an ancient act of fealty, and embracing my father in an obvious expression of the mutual respect and warmth that existed between them. My father was keen to speak with Cranmer in the privacy of my closet, away from the ears and eyes of the court, and, once assured of our privacy, was keen to acquaint Master Cranmer with my change of circumstance.

When I first considered telling Archbishop Cranmer that I was pregnant, I feared our new friendship would be fractured by the wrath of his religious indignation, even though I was already contracted to the king. But I soon found out that I would never again fear Thomas' judgement as I now understand that Cranmer was a simple and charitable man of unswerving loyalty toward Anne and the king. By that time, I knew Anne with the same familiarity as I knew my modern day persona; she was neither saint, nor sinner, and I would be forever grateful of Thomas' straightforward acceptance of her human imperfections and fallibilities. Archbishop Cranmer welcomed the latest news with characteristic, understated joy, insisting that he say the mass for me and my family in my closet, where he called upon God to bless the new queen and the child that she carried within her belly.

Despite the dark days which always seemed to stretch interminably through any English winter, my disposition was decidedly sunny, how could it not be? Anne was in her prime and pregnancy appeared to suit her robust constitution, which daily flourished on account of the child that grew within her womb. From modest beginnings, the Boleyn's had reached the zenith of their power, and I sensed Anne's great pride in the close-knit family that gathered protectively around her.

There was yet more joyous news that morning. I received a letter from my dear friend Margery, who had been brought to bed two weeks earlier than anticipated, and had given birth to a healthy son, which Sir Anthony and Margery named Henry in honour of the king. From my reading of history, I knew that little Henry Lee would one day become a great nobleman and champion of Anne's daughter, Elizabeth, which filled my heart with gladness. There would only be a matter of months between their birth dates and I speculated that Elizabeth must have felt close to the son of one of her mother's dearest friends. Oh, I so often I wanted to take my friends by the hand and tell them of all the good things that lay in the future for them and their children—but I could not. That day, I was determined to celebrate the great fortune which seemed to bless us all in those first few months of 1533.

Accompanied by a bevy of some of the wealthiest and most desirable women in the land, I made my way from the queen's privy chambers toward the leisure complex, which was near completion on the edge of the great St James' Park. I held the hand of Lady Mary Howard on my right, and that of my sister-in-law, Jane Rochford on my left. Amid a show of sisterhood, with much playful banter and giggling, I led a chorus of song in which all my friends gladly joined in. Our sweet singing voices echoed up and down the long gallery, and on a couple of occasions, we passed young, eligible gentlemen of the court, each one standing aside, bowing and doffing his cap, while smiling in appreciation of our beauty and high spirits. Flirtatious glances between the young gentlemen and some of my younger maids caused them to collapse in a fit of girlish giggles on more than one occasion.

Despite the great closed tennis play not being quite completed in terms of interior decoration, the court convened there around the king for it was Henry's wish to play *jeu à dedans*; indoors, we would all be sheltered from the rather cold and dreary weather of that February morning. As we crossed above King Street, using the first floor gallery of the Holbein Gate, I caught sight of the great play through the window that looked south towards the King's Gate and Westminster.

The great play was a magnificent building in its own right. When I had first seen it, it immediately reminded me of the great hall at Hampton Court, which I had seen many times in my modern day life. The building measured approximately eighty feet by twenty-five feet, and ran parallel to, and abutted against, the edge of King Street on its west side. It was five bays long and buttressed to the string course, above which rose a row of crenellations. A series of decorative spires rose up from each buttress and gold capped onion domes surmounted four narrow towers positioned at each corner of the building. I looked up to the golden weathervane mounted on top of one such dome which was imprinted against the skyline and told me of the south-westerly breeze that was keeping the harshest of the wintry weather at bay.

When I arrived with my ladies, there were already a number of courtiers present, including my father, who indicated that I should come and sit next to him in the dedans which had become my usual place. The majority of spectators were standing in the side galleries, but I was led to a small number of chairs that were set out in the penthouse for the Lady Marquess and her companions. Gathered around me were some of my closest friends and staunchest allies; William Brereton, Francis Weston, Sir Henry Norris, Sir Francis Bryan, Thomas Heneage, Thomas Wyatt and my ladies; Lady Mary Howard, Lady Jane Rochford, the Countesses of Rutland, Worcester and Surrey, Lady Fitzwater and Anne Savage.

I sat next to my father amidst a buzz of expectation and excited chatter, as ever more bets were placed upon the outcome of the game. It was far from a foregone conclusion. Before I had walked in Anne's world, I had assumed that the king would always win; gracious courtiers never daring to snatch victory from his hands. But I soon learnt that what Henry wanted most, whether it be the joust, at the tables, or on the tennis court, was true and fierce competition. Yes, Henry wanted to win, but only on account of his skill, athleticism and prowess. Nothing was more irksome to the king's grace than a hollow victory. So every single person gathered that day knew that we would witness a battle *royale* to snatch the coveted prize of glory.

Once seated, I spoke up boldly to my friends, declaring that I was placing a considerable sum of money upon the king for victory. My brother was already in the service end of the court, close to the dedans, and heard my deliberate, good-natured, taunt. He turned about, looking over his shoulder and raising his eyebrows as if to scorn my treachery. He looked so very strong and handsome that day, stripped down as he was to his shirt and hose, his fine, muscular body visible beneath his open neck shirt. The king was similarly dressed, in gloved hands, in which he carried one of his treasured rackets, the handle garnished with passamayne lace of gold and silver.

I had long since learned that real tennis was a game that required experience and tactical skill, such that very often an older player could outwit a younger, faster, more hard-hitting opponent. I had watched the king play tennis many times, and it was apparent that it was a sport over which he had gained considerable mastery. Often I had seen him clinch victory with a shot of surprising placement and ruthless accuracy.

George opened play that day by serving well, hitting the ball sweetly against the service penthouse. The king undercut it on the return, such that it dropped down sharply from the back wall requiring my brother to make the first of many energetic lunges to secure its return. Whilst the onlookers became increasingly absorbed in the play, clapping and cheering various heroic feats of athleticism and skill, after a while, I leaned in slightly toward my father, and although I had kept my eyes upon the game, I asked him quietly,

'How goes it in Parliament, father? Is there any resistance to the Act of Appeals?' Sir Thomas also continued to watch the game, as an explosion of applause accompanied the king's direct hit onto the wire grille that separated the dedans from the main court, thus winning the point outright.

'Everything seems to be progressing smoothly. There appears to be very little resistance to the bill…mayhap with one or two notable exceptions.' I nodded my understanding, at the same time clapping in appreciation of a particularly elegant return of play from the king. There were a few minutes of silence between us, as we watched the players change ends. The king made to serve, before I probed further.

'What of Master Cromwell, does he foresee any difficulties?' There was a gasp as George returned a serve and struck the ball cleanly, such that it ricocheted off the wire grille directly in front of where we were sitting, winning the point. My father applauded politely, then added,

'Of course Cromwell works tirelessly to persuade those who may be struggling with their conscience toward of the merits of voting for the bill.' I looked at my father with a raised eyebrow. I wondered what forms of 'persuasion' Master Cromwell was apt to use. However, my father seemed unmoved and added, 'Unfortunately, there are still some who cling to the old ways.'

'Such as?' My father turned his head in my direction, nodding toward Eleanor Paston, Countess of Rutland. The young countess was seated beyond me, excitedly cheering on the king, who had just scored a devilishly good strike at the winning gallery.

'The Earl of Rutland; I spoke with his lordship yesterday and found him somewhat reluctant to accept that Parliament had any competence in matters spiritual.' I sighed, exasperated by the stubborn intransigence of even those who claimed to be our supporters. I was reminded, yet again, of just how slippery the ground was for the Boleyns. I must have conveyed my frustration with a frown that pinched at my forehead, for my father continued to speak, while apparently turning his attention back to the game; a game in which Henry was beginning to show the upper hand. 'Do not concern yourself, Anne. I showed him the sharpness of my tongue and I think not that he will vote against his majesty.' I knew that the Earl of Rutland's temper was almost as infamous as Anne's, and imagined how my father would have browbeaten him into submission. I had just turned my attention back to the epic battle that was unfolding on court, when my father abruptly stood up, whispering in my ear before he departed,

'Anne, there is someone who wishes to speak with you.' I turned around, when a gentleman of the court with whom I was acquainted took my father's seat.

'Master Vaughan, what an unexpected pleasure!' My voice was laced with irony as it was difficult to warm to Stephen Vaughan, for he was one of Cromwell's strong men, who kept his eyes and ears about court delivering to his master a constant stream of 'information'. Thankfully, as part of the same underground evangelical faction at court, I had nothing to fear. I had gleaned from previous conversations that Anne had approached Master Vaughan to act as a go-between betwixt herself and Cromwell in order to assist others who found themselves persecuted for their faith. I suspected Master Vaughan's arrival meant that another reformer required Anne's assistance.

'My Lady Marquess,' Stephen Vaughan removed his cap and nodded in deference toward me.

'How may I be of assistance' I turned my attention back to the game, speaking under my breath so as not to draw unnecessary attention to our conversation.

'There is a reformer by the name of Thomas Patmore, the Parson of Hadham, in Hertfordshire. Unfortunately, Master Thomas has been incarcerated some two years in Lollard's Tower.' I shuddered at the thought. I had learnt of this place; it was a prison for heretics situated within the walls of Lambeth Palace. I did not like to think upon being locked up in such a foreboding place, but nevertheless asked,

'Just for his beliefs? He has committed no other crime?' I broke into genuine applause, as Henry snatched another point from my brother. I watched the king wipe the perspiration from his brow and adjust the neckline of his shirt, as if to let in air to cool his heated body.

'Aye, Madame, just for his beliefs, nought more.' I glanced at Master Vaughan before nodding my understanding. My look said it all; I would seek to intervene with the king on behalf of the pastor. Stephen Vaughan saw no more reason to speak. The message had been transmitted and we both knew what was to be done. He placed his cap back upon his head before slipping unobtrusively back into the crowd.

It surprised many when Thomas Patmore was suddenly released from Lollard's Tower without further charge or punishment. People rightly speculated that there were strong supporters of evangelic reform close to the king who had begun to prevail on him in such matters, and that at the heart of this circle of influence was the Lady Marquess of Pembroke. Indeed, even amongst the great nobles of the land, there was, by then, no one closer. Courtiers knew that to influence the Lady Anne was to influence the king, and evermore, they flocked to petition for Anne's good graces and assistance. I had truly reached dizzying heights; it was a gloriously happy time.

Chapter Fourteen

Whitehall, London,
13 March 1533

During the first half of 1533, Henry and I became exceptionally close. A mood of great celebration was tangible about the court, even though many did not know exactly what was being celebrated. The king's *joie de vivre* was infectious, people had seldom seen his more ebullient. To those privileged few who were close to the king's grace, the reasons were clear. Henry was finally within reach of everything that he had so desperately wanted for the last six years. At the beginning of that momentous year, all the cards seemed to be falling into place: Katherine was banished from court and forgotten; the Act of Appeals was progressing smoothly through parliament; there was peace in the land; our marriage and my pregnancy served to cement this vision of a happy ending.

By mid-March, I was twelve weeks pregnant and despite Anne's famous slight frame, my ladies had not yet needed to let out the laces of my gown. I was deeply thankful that I appeared to be unaffected by the morning sickness that so often plagued many of my ladies who, through lack of contraception, frequently endured near annual pregnancies. Yet I had been troubled by an extraordinary tiredness that hitherto had been unfamiliar to me. Sleeping seemed to affect little difference, but I found it helpful to take the air in the palace gardens. This I did often in the company of my mother and several of my ladies in all but the very harshest of wintry weather, being well wrapped up by the finest furs that my considerable personal wealth could buy.

The cold, frosty mornings nipped at my cheeks and fingertips, then gradually gave way to the milder beginnings of spring. As the sun regained her strength, she began to rouse the life energy which had lain dormant across the land for the preceding months. I truly felt a part of Mother Nature's cycle of rebirth. With the first flush of daffodils, whose sunny appearance heralded the return of the longer days, I was deeply aware of my own Tudor rose, budding within the protective confines of my slender body.

That morning, George joined me in the palace's privy garden to bid me farewell, for the king had commissioned him to travel to France on a diplomatic mission, the purpose of which was to secretly inform Francis of our marriage, and to convince the French king to assist Henry in reconciling his differences with the Scots. As a budding diplomat of considerable talent, George was exactly the right choice.

Whilst waiting for the tide on the Thames to turn in his favour, my brother and I spent our last hour together walking in the garden. It was abutted on the east side by the window of the king's presence chamber, on the south by the privy gallery, on the west by a range of courtiers' lodgings, and on the north by the great courtyard. Beyond the tranquil haven of the garden itself, various noises of everyday life floated over its walls. These emanated both from the various offices of the palace to the north-east of the garden, and the hurly-burly of Westminster life, on King Street to the west. The space was the epitome of Tudor fashion. As we walked arm-in arm, I glanced upwards to take in the intricate and vibrant detail of the distinctive grotesque work adorning the structures around us. Beneath it a pleasant cloister ran around all four sides of the garden. It was highly decorated, for the loggia had been painted with flowers of diverse colours, the king's coat-of-arms and tables of antique work wrought with fine gold.

Like all formal Tudor gardens, the space was geometrically divided, the edges of each bed bordered by a low fence painted in stripes of alternate Tudor white and green. In the centre of each bed, an ornately carved and painted pillar was surmounted by a different heraldic beast; each one clasped within its paws a golden flag upon a similarly gilded pole. It was a stunning sight, brought to life that morning by the crisp, clear light of that budding spring day.

However, not unlike my mood, storm clouds were gathering in a sky, which had been hitherto quite flawless. It was a typical, blustery March morning as I nestled closer to George for warmth, clutching my fur mantle around me to keep out the chill. As the two of us crunched our way along the garden path, I felt a heavy weight of sadness settle like a stone in my stomach. I knew I would miss my beloved brother dreadfully, and I ached in anticipation of the loss of him at a time when, more than ever, I needed his good cheer and unswerving loyalty.

George cut across my thoughts as he asked,

'How art thou, sister? Pregnancy does seem to suit you.' I lent my

168

head against my brother's shoulder, as I answered,

'I'm a little tired but otherwise I'm quite well.' George came to a halt momentarily, releasing himself from my arm as he turned about to face me, taking both my hands in his, as he continued,

'Promise me that while I'm away you will take good care of yourself.' He chuckled before adding, 'Methinks I know you only too well. The confines of your condition will no doubt drive you to distraction, but you must not make mischief for yourself, nor cause any undue stress to the child.' He reached out and delicately stroked my cheek with his gloved hand. I raised my eyes to meet his, as my brother spoke again, 'Promise me, won't you Anne?' I nodded my head silently, confirming my tacit agreement to George's request. I was feeling dreadfully sorry for myself, unable to find cheer in either my condition, or George's successful appointment to the embassy bound for France. For a moment, I became absorbed in the joyful warbling of a robin that was perched on the edge of the marble fountain standing at the centre of the garden. A few moments of silence passed between us, before I finally turned to look back at George and said,

'And will you promise to make haste to London as soon as you're able. I cannot bear to think of not having you at my coronation; for how could the day be complete if you were absent?'

'You know that if I can, I will be there, don't you? To see you crowned the Queen of England will make me the proudest brother that ever lived in this realm.' As he spoke, he moved over to me and put his arms around me in the tenderest of embraces. It was ever thus between us; we were physical, tactile creatures who lived and breathed through our sense of touch, and it sickens me now to think that such pure and innocent love could be twisted to such sinister ends. Like any two people that share a profound connection, my brother sensed that something more lay beneath my silence, a disquiet which he then sought to understand.

'Is there something else, Anne? What troubles you so?' I watched as the first drops of water fell from a slate-grey sky into the fountain, pricking its surface with ever greater ferocity as the heavens quickly began to open. My ladies, who had accompanied us outdoors, ran to take cover, calling to me that I should do the same. George began to pull away, making for the protection of the loggia, expecting me to follow. I remained statuesque, mesmerised by the droplets of rain agitating the surface of the water, and by the robin, which had ceased its song and then flitted into the air, taking flight to find its own refuge. I raised my face to the heavens to see a cascade of droplets falling effortlessly from the sky, the cool water running in rivulets down my face, before George urged me to take shelter.

'Anne? What is it? What's wrong with you?' I slowly turned my head to look at him and spoke quite loudly above the noise of the incessant, heavy rain. I knew that we were cocooned in our own watery world and no one could overhear us.

'What if it is not a prince?' I placed one hand upon the front of my belly, as if to emphasise my concern. 'Anne, what are you talking about? Come on, we must get out of the rain or you will catch your death!' George beckoned with his hand that I should come towards him, but when I did not move, he strode purposefully up to me, taking me by the hand insisting, 'Come! At least get out of the rain. Our lady mother will tear strips off me she finds out that I've let you get soaked to the skin.' With that he took hold of my hand and led me undercover of the cloister. My ladies were gathered close by, adjusting their gowns and shaking off the water which had sought to drench them. I looked at my brother plaintively, and he understood that I needed him to acknowledge my question. 'Anne, is not your union with the king blessed by God?' My brother did not wait for my response, but forged on convinced of the courage of his convictions. 'It is indeed thus, and therefore, sweet sister, you have nothing to concern yourself with. You will give his Majesty a man child and...' George then took my face between both his hands, as if to emphasise the point, '...and I promise you that I will return long before your coronation.' I smiled feebly at my brother's welcome commitment.

Suddenly, one of George's pages appeared in front of us carrying a message for my brother,

'My Lord, the tide has turned and your barge awaits you.'

'Thank you.' My brother acknowledged his man with a nod, before turning toward me. 'It seems the hour is upon us and I must tarry here no more. Now...' George gave me one last hug, as he whispered in my ear, 'Remember what you have promised me; I will not let you down and even though I may not be here in body, you are always in my heart.' George pulled away only to see a solitary tear run down my flushed cheek. He removed his glove and wiped it gently away with his thumb, before planting a final kiss upon my forehead. My brother then instructed my ladies to return me to my chambers and help me change my clothes, before he turned with a swish of his long, fur-lined gown and, all too soon, disappeared toward the great stair, where his barge was tethered, cruelly waiting to take my dearly beloved brother away from me, just when I needed him most.

Later that day, Henry and I dined alone in the king's dining chamber. His majesty was awaiting my arrival as the sun went down over St James' Park. It was to be one of our intimate dinners, served by flickering candle-light, and attended by only a couple of the king's most trusted gentlemen of the privy chamber, Sir Francis Bryan and Sir Thomas Heneage. The privy dining room, like every room that ran along the south side of the long gallery, was of a modest size, designed to create a greater intimacy for the king as he went about his most private affairs. In mid-March the fires were lit about the palace, as the last of the wintry chill still encroached upon the land at nightfall. Thus it was so in the king's dining room, the flames casting willowy shadows upon Henry's face as he greeted me, and indicated that I should sit opposite him. Although Henry welcomed me warmly, I was intuitive enough to sense immediately that he was a man sorely preoccupied.

'How now, my Lord? You seemed vexed. What troubles you so?' Sir Thomas held a large, silver gilt basin embossed with elaborate antique work afore the king. Sir Francis then stepped forward with a ewer of classical design, pouring water from it into the basin so that his majesty might wash his hands. The king sighed heavily, shaking his head almost to himself before replying,

'Do not think to trouble yourself, sweetheart. All will be well.' The basin was then offered for me to complete the same. As I washed my hands, I pressed the king again. Henry once famously said that 'if his cap knew his own thoughts, he would throw it into the fire'. He was not a man to divulge the secrets of his heart easily. But Anne was Henry's intellectual equal, and although I was only a woman, and so never allowed into the king's council chamber, we shared everything: our hopes and dreams, our frustrations and fears. I hated it when the king held back from me, even if it was as a result of his love, which sought to protect me.

'Sire, you know I am of a stout heart. Do not seek to protect me. If such events touch upon my person, I prefer to look my perils directly in the eye. If it pleases my lord, allow yourself to share the burdens that weigh so heavily upon you.' Outwardly unmoved by our conversation, Sir Thomas and Sir Francis removed the basin and ewer, placing them on the buffet. Sir Francis stepped forward and poured the king's favourite table wine into the finest, coloured, Venetian glass. Henry sat back in his chair for a moment, one arm extended, strumming his fingers upon the oak table at which we sat. Eventually, he looked at me weighing up carefully his words. After a few moments, he spoke again,

'The papal bulls concerning Cranmer's appointment to the archbishopric have not yet arrived.' Leaving the one arm extended on the table, with the other, he stroked his auburn beard, as Henry was apt to do when he was struggling with a difficult problem that preoccupied his mind. 'We are most anxious that they should arrive, for everything hangs on this, everything that we have wanted, everything that we planned. I need Cranmer as Archbishop of Canterbury, for when it is done, the bottleneck in Convocation and Parliament will be released and we can finally proceed with our divorce against Katherine.' Although the king did not say it, I knew that what most exercised Henry was his fear that our child's legitimacy would forever be in question, should it be born before his marriage to Katherine was dissolved—the clock was most definitely ticking. Although Henry's voice was steady and calm, the tension behind the words was palpable. Henry knew that the stakes were high. Cranmer's appointment as Archbishop was no small matter and he also knew that it was far from a foregone conclusion that the Pope would support Cranmer, a known reformist, to become the premier prelate in England.

It was impossible to tell Henry of my certainty of events that would come to pass in the very near future, but I did my best to assuage his anxiety—I flattered his ego.

'Sir, Your Grace's ability to dissemble with the papal nuncio on all matters relating to Rome surely means there should be no suspicion or cause for alarm in the Vatican. Forsooth Sir, is it not true that the papal nuncio has been ordered to please Your Majesty in all things in order to avert any further breach with Rome?' Henry took hold of one of his personal silver knives, an exquisite object with an amber handle, adorned with silver piqué work and studded with rubies and diamonds. As he did so, he reached over to a platter and speared some venison, which he returned to his plate and began to eat—as etiquette demanded —with his fingers. Acknowledging the veracity of my words, he raised his eyebrows and inclined his head to one side. I knew how proud Henry always was of his ability to hoodwink his opponents and falsify the truth of the matter, so I forged on, as I could see my argument was making ground. 'Surely there is little to concern us, Your Grace.' I finished my speech with a disarming smile that wove its own magic on the king. I then took my own knife, more delicate in design but equally beautiful, and selected some beef for my plate. After considering my words, Henry lifted the napkin which was draped over his left shoulder and dabbed at his mouth before replying,

'God's blood, you are right, Madame! I have God on my side and we should make plans.' Henry raised his glass to me in a toast, his face ablaze with anticipated glory, as he proclaimed, 'Anne, methinks it is time we started to appoint your household. You are my queen and all shall know it—and pay deference to you, as you rightly deserve.' I gladly reciprocated, raising my own glass high. I asked what suddenly was forefront in my mind. I knew Anne needed people about her whom she could trust. I felt certain that I must do all that I could to influence the appointments to her household. As I set down my glass, I found myself twiddling with the narrow, spun stem, staring into the deep, crimson liquid and tentatively enquiring of his grace,

'Might I select who attends upon me, Sire?'

'Madame, you will have your say in key appointments, those who will serve you directly and be closest about your person.' I smiled back graciously, overjoyed that I would be steering my own ship, that I truly would be mistress in my own household. The king then skewered a second piece of meat from a different platter, before adding,

'You should consult with your father who might also guide you. I will parley with Master Cromwell so that he, too, may assist you in the process, until you have your own secretary to do likewise.'

And so the rest of the evening was passed shaping England's history—and ours. We discussed the historic events which just a few short months ago had seemed so far out of reach. I excitedly shared my ideas for Anne's household. The king decided to present me to the court as queen at Eastertide and together, we made the first tentative plans for Anne's coronation, which the king determined would be one of the most sumptuous and memorable affairs of his twenty-four year reign.

I temporarily lost my brother that March morning, but would soon gain a household of two hundred to attend upon me. I was so proud of Anne. Daily, I drew upon her incredible strength and self-possession, and through her I learnt perseverance, self-belief and a relentless tenacity to see every course through to the end. Unfortunately, not all 'endings' would be as sweet as the one I tasted that day.

Indeed, the great satisfaction I enjoyed at the anticipation of appointing my own household was short lived. What Henry had not stipulated was that some appointments would be made directly by the king. This would prove somewhat irksome, but on the whole of little consequence. Oftentimes, I actually found those preferred by the king brought with them a wealth of knowledge, cultivated through years of service to the crown, which served me well. However, one such appointment would haunt me to this very day. Little did I realise it then, but within a few short weeks, I would come face-to-face with the woman who would seek to destroy Anne and the Boleyns—Mistress Jane Seymour.

Shortly after ten o'clock in the morning, I threw open one of the windows in my privy chamber so that I could hear more clearly the joyful peal of bells that rang out across Westminster from the Collegiate Church of St. Peter, better known as Westminster Abbey. It was the perfect spring morning. As I leaned far out of my window, I felt the welcome warmth of the sun upon my face; closing my eyes and lifting my chin in the air, I inhaled deeply and was rewarded by the sweet smell of summer beginning to infringe upon the earth. A clutch of my ladies gathered excitedly around me, opening a number of other windows to get a better view of the great flotilla of ships and barges that were on the Thames, many festooned with bright banners and flags to celebrate the day's momentous events.

It was a day of rejoicing for those reformists at court. The much awaited papal bulls had finally arrived from Rome on 26 March, and just four days later, Cranmer was to be consecrated as Archbishop of Canterbury. Not that Thomas himself was on any one of those barges. Rather more humbly, he made his way on foot from his lodgings in Canon Row to the old palace of Westminster, where the service was to take place. I received Thomas the previous evening when, at my request, he conducted mass in my privy closet and afterwards, I had the opportunity to give the new archbishop my own sincere felicitations, wishing him well for the day ahead.

With the arrival of the bulls, Henry was in majestic form. As he predicted, the great backlog of work in the Convocation of Canterbury and Parliament began to clear due to action in both houses. With Cromwell's assistance, the king had already set in motion feverish plans that would culminate in a divorce court hearing, anticipated for the beginning of May. I was full of the joys of spring. Despite some unwelcome interference from the king, my lord father and Master Cromwell over appointments to my household, I eventually relented with good humour, deciding to lose some battles to win the war. I began to appoint courtiers to all the principal positions within my household that were outside of the king's direct stipulation, as many of those appointments as possible were staunch Boleyn supporters, or passionate reformists, who aligned themselves with the Boleyn faction. Nevertheless, the king was assiduously present to observe the taking of their oaths of allegiance to the new queen.

Of the appointments made directly by the king, Thomas de Burgh, Lord Borough, as chamberlain was the first. Three years older than Henry, Thomas had long since been in the service of his majesty and Parliament. Lord Borough was not an easy man, he was a strict disciplinarian, particularly with his children, who I was to learn, all lived in fear of him. He had a reputation for being notoriously unforgiving. However, he was zealously committed to the cause of the Reformation and affiliated himself unreservedly with Anne's ascendancy. For a time at least, he was a formidable ally.

The second was Lord Burgh's vice chamberlain, Sir Edward Baynton. Sir Edward was considerably older than the king and had served his sovereign lord for many years as both a courtier and a soldier. Henry liked him well and insisted upon his appointment. I was less than convinced. It was well known about court that he was a personal friend of Katherine's; through his appointment, I feared a viper in the nest as Sir Edward could be easily persuaded to act as an imperial spy by my sworn enemies. I did not want to be afraid of sinister shadows lurking in my own household, and had balked at Henry's suggestion, as I felt as if I were fighting for my very survival. I confess that I even had a row with the king over the matter. The discord simmered between us for two days before my father stepped in, and against my better judgement, had assuaged my fears by pointing out that Sir Edward was also a strong supporter of religious reform and would be unlikely to rock the Boleyn boat. It was on this basis that I finally accepted his appointment with good grace.

The final appointment from the king was that of William Coffin, my master of the horse. Slightly younger than Henry, he had long been a courtier and gentleman of the privy chamber, serving his sovereign for the last eighteen years. There was great affection between them, Henry even taking an active interest in William's marital affairs. It was Henry who persuaded Margaret Dymock, at the time a wealthy widow, to marry William after the death of her first husband. In truth, William would serve me faithfully enough, but his wife made it clear that she loved me not. She was one of those self-righteous, brittle women who thought of me as nothing more than a strumpet and a whore who had displaced the king's rightful wife. Of course, I would never hear any of this from her lips, but those who did love me took pains to make clear her opinions of me. I loathed her harsh judgement, but detested even more her spinelessness in fawning over the king, who plainly was as much to blame as I for Katherine's marital misfortunes. In time, our mutual dislike would become legendary at court, and so it was, that when I was cast into the Tower, Henry, rather cruelly knew exactly who to put about me to report upon my every word. I cannot forgive him for such an unkindness.

At Master Cromwell's specific request, a certain John Uvedale was transferred from the position of secretary to the Duke of Richmond, to that of my own personal secretary. Experienced in the ways of royal service and familiar with the role, Master Uvedale was also close to Cromwell and shared our reformist tendencies. He seemed the perfect appointment, and in truth I could not think of anyone better qualified for the role. In the game of court politics, I also wanted deeper ties with Master Cromwell, through the acceptance of his preferred candidate.

In an attempt to cement the alliance between Cromwell and Anne, I also made a personal plea to the king for Thomas to be appointed as my high steward. He would principally work at the right hand of the king, but within the queen's household, and Thomas would have responsibility for working directly with me on all of Anne's major policy decisions. I was very conscious of the adage, 'keep your friends close and your enemies closer' and whilst in 1532 there was not even a hint of discontent between Anne and Cromwell, I was determined that the bonds that we would build would thwart the hand of destiny.

My first appointment was my father's younger brother, Sir James Boleyn, who I appointed queen's chancellor. I was particularly fond of Uncle James, for never was there a more genuine and loyal gentleman. His career and fortune had both been eclipsed and tied to that of his elder brother, Thomas, though I never once heard him complain about lack of land or the incomparable fortune of my father, for Uncle James was a man of modest needs and never shared his elder brother's simmering ambition. While he adored my father, I often mused upon the tension which must have existed behind closed doors with his prickly wife, Elizabeth Wood, Lady Boleyn, whose jealously and bitterness towards Sir Thomas' prestigious family must have driven an uncomfortable wedge between them. It was the measure of the man that if such discord did exist, Sir James never gave a hint of the true state of affairs that existed betwixt him and his wife.

Another appointment which had taken little thought was that of George Taylor. Master Taylor had been in Anne's service for several years when I returned to Anne's world in 1532. He was a deeply humble man, uncomplicated and ruthlessly honest. Trained as a lawyer, George Taylor would always apply himself to any task with fastidious efficiency and dogged determination. As receiver general or treasurer, Master Taylor was responsible for handling my finances and keeping account of cash and items of value passing in an out of my household. Like my Uncle James, he craved neither title nor power in a court where ruthless self-promotion was epidemic; furthermore his allegiance was beyond question and thus, I trusted him completely.

When it came to the appointments of my chaplains and almoner, along with consulting Thomas Cranmer, I also sought the advice of Dr William Butts, the king's physician. He was a Cambridge man from Gonville College, and held a deep interest in the reformist cause. It was Dr Butts who had treated me for my ailments at Greenwich in 1528, not long before I had been drawn back into my modern day life; he had since become established as a man of affairs at court. The king trusted his physician implicitly, and I quietly admired the way William made the most of his position of intimacy and influence with his majesty to further the cause of the reformed faith. After Henry proclaimed that I would put about me my household, I called Dr Butts into my presence to seek his recommendations for those worthy gentlemen who could fulfil certain key religious positions. William listened attentively to my wishes to set about me those who embraced the wholesome doctrine and infallible knowledge of Christ's gospel, and who would also assist me in setting high standards of piety, honour, equity, justice and measured frugality; all of which I wished to be associated with the name of Anne Boleyn. Without hesitation, Dr Butts put forward the names of William Latymer, who helpfully was on very good terms with Sir Edward Baynton, William Betts, John Skip and Nicolas Shaxton;

the latter of whom would act as my almoner.

With the key administrative and religious positions accounted for, I then set about appointing the female members of my household. These would be the noblewomen who would attend upon my person. Any squeamishness that I might have once possessed about the inequality of hierarchy had long since vanished. I had become a creature of Anne's world and negotiated its territory with ease. How strange that such an ordinary girl from twenty-first century Greenwich could feel so at home in my extraordinary position! For I was, by then, at the pinnacle of Tudor society, save the king himself. I never faltered, nor questioned my exalted status. If anything, it felt as if a distant echo of a life, long lost, had always called to me, and that finally, I had remembered who I really was, and who I was always meant to be—Anne the Queen.

That morning, as my ladies excitedly buzzed around me, chattering and pointing at some of the splendid sites before us upon the River Thames, I suddenly felt a hand gently rest upon my right shoulder. I turned to see the face of my dear friend Margery, who had finally returned to court after the birth of her son. She looked at me and smiled before standing upon her tiptoes to peer over my shoulder at the magnificent pageant below. I reached up and rested my hand on hers in a gesture of intimate friendship, as I watched her characteristic, girlish enthusiasm. I was delighted to have her back at court, and immediately appointed her in the official position of mistress of the queen's wardrobe.

Amidst this scene of great animation, I reflected on the assembly of some of England's finest aristocratic women, all of whom by their right and rank had been appointed to attend me within the privy chamber. Present that day were a number of my newly appointed ladies-in-waiting including: my sister Mary, who had returned to court following a summons by my father; my sister-in-law Jane Rochford; Anne Savage, who alone of my ladies would share the secret memory of my marriage to the king; the Countesses of Rutland, Derby and Worcester; the pretty, sixteen-year-old Countess of Surrey, who had been married for just over one year to Anne's cousin, Henry Howard; and finally my beloved friend Nan, who had proudly returned to court wearing her wedding ring as Mistress Zouche. By some quirk of fate, we had married our respective beaus within a few short weeks of one another.

At the same time, a bevy of eligible young maids were also within my charge. Some of them were present that morning including: Norfolk's young mistress, Bess Holland, who the Duchess of Norfolk despised and who, as 'the other women', I had a considerable degree of empathy for; Grace Parker, who was Jane Rochford's sister-in-law; the diminutive Lady Mary Howard; and most intriguingly for me, Anne's younger cousin, who had been newly brought to court with Anne's elevation, Margaret or Madge Shelton. Unlike my ladies-in-waiting, who were wives of peers and who all had specific duties attending the queen's person during her most intimate tasks, my maids were all daughters or grand-daughters of peers; all were unmarried, most of a tender age, and whose placement in the queen's household was primarily intended to groom them for an advantageous match at court. The maids would be supervised by the same formidable woman who had once supervised me and Nan as maids in Katherine's chambers, a certain Margaret Foliol, also known as Mistress Stonor. Anne was older than most of the other maids, and with my worldly experience, was not at all fearful of her stern demeanour, which caused many of the younger ladies to cower in her presence. Mistress Stonor took her role as mother of the maids seriously and ruled with an iron fist; for it would ruin her own reputation if a young girl got herself into 'trouble'.

I turned my attention from my ladies and glanced down at my belly. I was then fourteen weeks pregnant, and felt the tightness of my gown as the first swell of my abdomen began to make itself known. I rested my hand there for a moment, in awe of the life that flourished within me. When I looked up, my gaze locked with Nan's, who stood at the other end of the gaggle of ladies, most of whom were still preoccupied with the events going on outside our windows. She smiled at me warmly, reading my mind. Our silent connection was broken by a page of the chamber entering the room to announce,

'Your Grace, Lady Bridget Tyrwhitt seeks an audience you.' I turned my head immediately to look at Margery. My curiosity was definitely piqued, and I raised an eyebrow quizzically to convey my uncertainty as to what this reunion would bring. I had last seen Bridget on our return from Calais, when the king and I had stayed briefly at Stone Castle, the guests of Lord and Lady Tyrwhitt. Then, two weeks earlier, following the king's announcement that I should appoint my household,

I had penned a letter to my friend, inviting her to come to court and take up the position of chief lady of the bedchamber. This was my pledge to her as we sailed to Calais, and despite some trepidation, I was as determined to heal the rift between us, and so had kept my word.

I thanked the page before making my way from my privy chamber into the great presence chamber which lay beyond. With the many historic events unfolding at court, in the Privy Council and in Westminster, there was a great hum of expectancy in the public chambers at Whitehall. It was clear to all that the household of the Lady Marquess of Pembroke was being rapidly augmented, although no official announcement had been made of Anne's elevation as queen consort. Rumours that Anne was already pregnant and had secretly married the king had reached a fever pitch. So, when I entered my presence chamber at Whitehall, the room was filled with a goodly number of courtiers, all of whom sought an audience with Anne, or had gathered to be spectators and watch events unfold.

I swept into my presence chamber in the most beautiful gown, its radiance I imagined mirrored closely my own elevated spirits. The gown was made of cloth of gold, contrasted against a kirtle of white satin, embroidered over with pearled, gold acorns and honeysuckles, whilst matching sleeves were tied with ten pairs of aiglets of gold, being turned back and finished with miniver. To set off the glittering splendour of the fabric, I chose two exquisite pieces of jewellery: the first was a brooch pinned to the front of my gown, one set with the enormous diamond which had been given to me by Francis I at Calais; the second piece was an extremely expensive girdle of crown gold, which was hung at the end with a fine, gold and diamond encrusted pomander. In addition, I had asked one of my ladies to set my diamond and pearl ornamented French hood well back upon my head that morning. I wished for Anne's dark and lustrous locks to show themselves off splendidly in contrast to the lighter, shimmering gold and white fabrics of my dress.

The magnificent queen's presence chamber at Whitehall had similar dimensions to many of the large public chambers in the palace, and matched that of the king's, to which it was directly connected by a doorway at the low end of the hall. In times gone by, there had been many a night in which I had pored over the plans for Whitehall's refurbishment with the king. I saw for myself the original layout of Wolsey's palace and knew that the current presence chamber on the queen's side occupied part of the palace which had once made up Wolsey's privy apartments. In the glorification of the king's majesty and that of his newly elevated consort, all this had been swept aside, and a grand new chamber had been designed to mirror the king's apartments.

The chamber itself faced east, a great oriel window illuminating the high end, with a second great window at the low end of the chamber. The walls were hung with fabulous gold arras, whilst the floor was tiled with a repeating pattern of large black circles, set with a central red diamond on a white background. A great swathe of antique work covered a renaissance style moulding that ran around the cornices of the ceiling and down decorative pillars set into the walls. Despite the rich ornamentation, there was very little furniture in the chamber, save for a large oak buffet consisting of five magnificent tiers, all set with a huge amount of gold plate, which the king had transferred to Anne just before Christmas, and a richly embroidered cloth of estate, beneath which was the throne. A valuable x-framed chair covered in red velvet, fringed with gold took pride of place upon a rich, Turkey carpet.

As I entered the room followed by my ladies, I immediately caught sight of Lady Bridget Tyrwhitt standing directly afore the cloth of estate. I made my way toward her, choosing not to raise myself above her upon the dais, for I wished to set the tone for our relationship as one of warmth and genuine friendship. When Bridget caught sight of me, she dipped into a deep curtsy. I did not stand proudly before her, but instead reached out my hand, as an olive branch. Lady Bridget's face was downcast, but my hand caught hers and she looked up to me. I was determined to show my great love for her, and so I smiled warmly, sweeping away with a single gesture all the difficulties that had passed between us, as I said,

'Lady Bridget, you are most welcome at court and it brings me great joy to see you again.' Lady Bridget accepted my hand and rose to her feet. I still saw in her eyes fleeting shadows of doubt and reserve, and with great congeniality replied,

'My Lady Marquess, it is indeed a great honour that you have bestowed upon me, to welcome me back to court as your chief lady of the bedchamber. I commend myself heartily unto you, and I trust that you will accept my renewed pledge to be honourable and loyal in my service onto Your Grace at all times.' It was a public show of reconciliation, and my generous preferment of Lady Bridget would confer great status upon her at court. With the formalities of our public reunion complete, I embraced my friend and then linked my arm about hers, as if to make my way with her back into my privy chamber. Suddenly, a second page stepped forward and announced,

'Your Grace...Sir Francis Bryan craves an audience.' For the second time, I was somewhat surprised, but in truth thought little of it, imagining Sir Francis was coming with a message from his majesty, as was so often the way. I smiled at Lady Bridget and patted her hand, begging her pardon that I must attend to Sir Francis momentarily. Lady Bridget withdrew, nodding her deference as she did so. I then stepped forward, this time to stand upon the raised dais in front of the queen's throne. Drawing myself up to my full height, I turned about to see the gallant Sir Francis Bryan sweeping down the centre of the chamber, courtiers parting to make way for him as he approached; there was no doubt that he was a man of magnificent presence and a certain charisma that was strangely captivating.

As he drew close to the canopy of estate, Sir Francis swept into a deep and elegant bow, and as he did so, I caught sight of an unremarkable and diminutive lady, who was following submissively in his wake. I had not seen the lady before, and yet for the most fleeting of moments there was something about her countenance which unsettled me. However, my attention was drawn immediately back to the magnetic gentleman of the court who waited patiently afore me, for my acknowledgement. After a few brief moments, I spoke.

'Sir Francis, good morrow!' Francis lifted himself up to his full height, seemingly pleased with himself, and I was immediately curious to understand the nature of his visit.

'My Lady Marquess, I have come forth directly from the king.' With an outstretched arm toward the king's presence chamber, he announced, 'The king's majesty has appointed—for Your Grace's pleasure—an additional maid of honour to wait upon you.' It was not the first time Henry had acted to appoint a lady to my household without my consent. So far, the king's actions had been little more than mildly vexing, and I wondered what had motivated his majesty to make this particular appointment. Whilst I was thinking on it, Sir Francis forged on, '...Your Grace, it is my pleasure to introduce Mistress Jane Seymour to you, who before the king himself, has already pledged to serve you faithfully and with all honour.'

As Sir Francis finished speaking, he stepped aside, and with another sweeping gesture, indicated that the young woman, who so far had stood quietly behind him, should come forward and present herself. With the announcement of her name, everything around me seemed to stand still and I was frozen in a gestalt of time. I could hear nothing but the thundering of my heart in my head, see nothing but Sir Francis' proud smile and the figure of Mistress Seymour stepping forward and sinking into the deepest of curtsies afore me. It was if, in one catastrophic moment, the entire facade of the fairytale that I had been so diligently constructing around me was viciously torn down. I stood, unmoving, in shock. I could hardly breathe. One solitary woman, who indeed was no great beauty, stood before me and yet, I could see nought but the *Four Horsemen of the Apocalypse* careering toward me with death in their eyes. A huge surge of panic suddenly seized me and sent every rational thought spinning from my mind. This time when the explosion came, it was not through Anne's tempestuous anger, but through my blind fear. I alone knew the threat that Mistress Seymour posed to the very life of Anne Boleyn. In that moment, I forgot myself entirely.

'No... No...No!' I heard myself cry out, each time louder and with greater passion. The playful exuberance, the warm smile and the lightness of my soul was entirely obliterated in the instant that I heard her name. It may well have been my fear that catalysed my reaction, but Anne was by then part of my soul, and her legendary intemperance was also becoming mine. I realised suddenly that I was virtually shouting at Sir Francis, 'No! I will not have that woman in my household. Get her out! Get her out!' I turned to Margery full of helpless fury, as I repeated the same. 'Margery, get her out of here! Get her out of my sight!' Of course, the room had fallen into a deathly silence, and all heads turned to witness my outburst. I was utterly lost to myself, consumed with fear, fighting as I had never done before for my very survival. I remember the faces around me; how Sir Francis looked aghast at my entirely unexpected and incomprehensible response; how Mistress

Seymour's eyes had widened in dismay and horror that she was being slighted and so publicly humiliated; how Margery's brow was furrowed in concern and confusion—for clearly she too did not understand the vehemence of my reaction.

For a moment, I stood looking from Sir Francis to Margery, waiting for someone to act, for someone to help me. However, their shock was too great; my fear becoming dangerously mixed with fury at their inaction. One man had done this to me, and in my crazed logic, I already imagined that he intended to take Jane as his lover. Oh, how foolish I had been! To this day, I think that what I did next, made what would happen in the future, far more likely than if I had drawn no more attention to the entirely forgettable Mistress Seymour.

Unable to tolerate my outrage and fear for one moment more, I tore down from the dais, sweeping past Mistress Seymour, who remained nervously dipped in a curtsy, her face raised to watch my furious exit. Without stopping to consider the wisdom of my actions, I stormed out in a tempest of rage toward the king's presence chamber at the low end of the room, and as I flew through it, I nearly knocked aside Tom Wyatt, who had been heading toward my chambers—for what purpose I knew not. I confess that I barely noticed him. Like a missile locked onto its target, my tunnel vision was solely set upon finding Henry.

The king was deep in conversation with Thomas Cromwell and did not notice my entrance. I suspect that some of those courtiers at the low end of the chamber had been within earshot of my outburst within my own apartments, and as I swept into the hall, several heads already began to turn. Caught somewhat off guard by the abruptness of my entry into the king's presence, a yeoman of the guard somewhat belatedly made haste to announce my arrival to the king and court. With that, all heads turned and Henry looked up from the conversation that he was holding with his right-hand man. I saw the king make to welcome me, when his face had suddenly crumpled in confusion at my anger, which was no doubt more than clearly evident by my demeanour. In so many ways, I'm ashamed to think of it now, for Anne's rage had ripped out every shred of sensibility and even common courtesy from my being. I had not even deigned to dip into a curtsy before my sovereign lord, nor wait for his permission to speak, before I exclaimed fearlessly,

'I will not have that wench in my household! You must get rid of her!' As I spoke, I caught sight of my father out of the corner of my eye, standing over to my right, a look of sheer horror written across his face. But I was consumed with a white hot fury and could not see the folly of my action. Oh yes, I saw the king's eyes narrow and flash with his own temper, before he stood abruptly from his throne. I was not cowed as Henry said in ominous tones,

'Madame.' It was a command. With one curt word, the king strode angrily towards his privy chamber, clearly wishing to continue our 'discussion' in private. I was undaunted by the king's obvious displeasure and followed him in haste, even slamming the door to his privy chamber after us—and in front of the face of Sir Henry Norris and Thomas Heneage, who as their duties dictated, were both following in attendance.

'How can you do this to me? Why do you seek to appoint a woman to my household who loves me not?' I stood before the king, my arms outstretched plaintively, decrying what I perceived as a terrible injustice. 'I will not have her in my household. I don't care who it offends!' Letting one arm fall to my side as I spoke, indignantly, I swept the other about, cutting through the air and punctuating it with my disdain. Of course, the king had no real understanding of my fury and resistance. He suddenly turned about to face me, slamming his fist down upon a nearby table, rebuking me loudly in a fearsome rage that stemmed from Henry's wounded pride.

'Madame, do not ever think to speak to me like that in front of the court again. God's blood! I am your sovereign lord and I will not be humiliated by anyone, much less a woman—even if that woman is you!' I must admit that I jumped involuntarily as the king's fist had thundered down upon the table. I do not think that I had ever seen Henry so incited as he was that day; even though our quarrels—and our reconciliations—were already becoming legendary at court. My husband was in full flow as he began to pace in front of me, jabbing a finger in the air to emphasise his displeasure, 'Let me tell you this Madame, I will appoint whom I wish to this court, be it in my household or yours...' The king's voice dropped in volume, taking on a menacing tone as his spat out his words, '...and let me remind you to whom you owe such high favour. It is I who has raised you up to the exalted estate in which you find yourself, and believe me, Madame, I can take it all away just like…' with that the king had clicked his fingers in front of me to emphasise the fragility of my position, '…that. Do not think to meddle with my affairs Anne, forget not that everything is different now; you are my wife and queen and I expect you to behave like one!' With that Henry turned and made to move towards his most secret of chambers. I caught hold of his arm as he passed me, realising suddenly the danger of my temerity. The king halted momentarily, turning to face me, but he was in no mood for reconciliation. Holding up his palm and shaking his finger at me he said, 'No, I will hear no more of it. I have appointed Mistress Seymour to your household and that is my final word. I suggest you return to your chambers and crave the forgiveness of Sir Francis and Mistress Jane, who no doubt will have taken much offence at your discourtesy.' With that, the king turned about and swept out of the room, closing the door firmly behind him.

I stood motionless for some time. Only two yeoman guards, positioned at the entrance to the king's most privy apartments, had witnessed the smouldering wreckage of my tempestuous emotions. Of course, Henry and I had argued before, sometimes quite passionately; but something changed that day. I had never so vehemently and publicly slighted the king's majesty; in fact, no one at court had ever dared to tread on the ground upon which I had just so foolishly walked. As my fury melted away and left me standing alone on the deserted battlefield, I began to see with a clarity that only comes with a cool head, how I had so badly misjudged the situation. I saw immediately how even if the king wanted to grant me my wish, he could never do so, for everyone would know that he had submitted to the will of his wife. It was not so much that he might offend his companion, Sir Francis, but that such an about-turn would strike at the very heart of his kingship— Henry's unquestioned and absolute authority.

With the privy gallery to the queen's chambers inaccessible to me, I had to swallow my pride, and with my head held high, walk back through the king's presence chamber, through a sea of shocked and disapproving faces. It was an uncomfortable journey. A potent cocktail of emotions carried me back to my chambers, stirring up my mind with a montage of erratic thoughts as I played back the king's cutting words. Underneath my anger and fear lay pure confusion, a confusion of what

Henry wanted from me now that we were man and wife; a confusion which, in truth, I think I never truly resolved. He had sought me—had sought Anne—because she was an exotic creature, his intellectual equal, someone with whom he could debate matters of politics, religion and literature. He had hunted Anne down precisely because she was wild and mysterious, a woman of fierce intellect and free spirit, who would always speak her mind. Yet once he had her, he wanted her to be everything that she was not, and could never be. He wanted to possess, dominate and smother her. As I made my way back defiantly to my chambers, I reflected on all this, and as I did so, a renewed sense of indignation began to swell in my breast, making me stride ever more purposely toward the queen's side, cutting a swathe in the crowds as I went.

By the time I arrived, I was even more furious with Henry than I had been before. Entirely consumed by my anger at the unfairness of it all, and the fickleness of men, I completely failed to notice that Sir Francis and Mistress Jane awaited my return; embarrassed, confused and paralysed by my behaviour. I brushed past my ladies, for I could not bear to face any of them, and went directly to my bed chamber, closing the door behind me and making it abundantly clear that I wished to be alone. Finally, all the tension of the encounter, the alchemy of rage, fear and shock, caused me to crumple exhausted to the floor. There I lay for nearly an hour, sobbing at the king's betrayal, the rawness of my wounded pride, and the sheer sense of impotence that subsequently engulfed me.

Whilst I indulged in my own self-pity, I completely failed to give any thought to the fact that even though the king and I would be reconciled through our great love, the embarrassment I had caused my ally, Sir Francis, introduced a cancer that would eat away at the bonds of kinship and loyalty between us. I strongly doubt that Jane ever held me in her good graces; but that after that day, there would always be a frosty dislike between us and a lack of trust that, fatally, would never be bridged. What was worse, I had planted a thorn in Sir Francis' side, one which would niggle away at him and eventually drive him wholly into the arms of Anne's enemies.

Chapter Sixteen

Greenwich Palace, Greenwich,
12 April 1533

A shaft of coloured light fell upon my bejewelled hand. For a moment, I glanced down upon it, seeing that light refracted from a huge, square-cut jewel set upon a ring that I wore on the index finger of my right hand. The ring came direct from the king's goldsmith, Cornelius Hayes, who once again worked his magic, crafting a singularly exquisite piece of jewellery that bore my new motto in blue enamelling set around the central stone, *moost happi*. Yet this was not my primary concern. My hand rested upon a black, velvet-bound version of Tyndale's New Testament, first published in 1526. As Anne, I owned a goodly number of pious works, including a variety of beautifully illuminated manuscripts with decorative borders in the French Renaissance style. Whilst for my own devotions I preferred to read the word of the good Lord in French, I ordered a copy of Tyndale's New Testament in the vernacular to celebrate my accession as Henry's queen. At some considerable cost, I also commissioned Master Holbein to rebind the book in black velvet with brass corners, and upon its front to have emblazoned the king's arms impaling Anne's own.

Of course, it was against the law that I should own, let alone display, a copy of the English Bible in my chambers. However, during our reconciliation following our latest argument over Jane Seymour, Henry had assented graciously to my request. I look up to see the great joy shining from the faces of those reformers who had been gathered around me that morning. It was an historic moment that an English queen should openly, and without fear, encourage the true light of the word to shine from the heart of the king's court.

That day of all days was truly to be the most momentous I had yet experienced whilst walking in Anne's shoes. It was Saturday, 12 April 1533, and during this most holy week of Easter, I was to be presented to the court for the first time as Henry's lawful wife and Queen of England. In total contrast to my wedding nerves, on this occasion I felt perfectly serene; the hand of fate had alighted upon Anne Boleyn, and in the few weeks leading up to Easter, the preparations of my livery, the finalisation of my motto, coat of arms and badge, had been akin to a rite of passage. I felt the mystique of monarchy descend upon me and the metamorphosis which would set me above mere mortals begin to take shape. It was as if I were being blessed directly by the Holy Spirit, and the hand which now guided me left no room for fear, or uncertainty.

I broke away from my reverie and smiled at the faces of my household officers whom I had asked to gather that morning to instruct them in their duties. All the gentlemen whom I had appointed to the most senior administrative and religious positions within my household were present, as were the most senior ladies of the bedchamber including: Margery, mistress of the wardrobe; Lady Bridget, chief lady of the bedchamber, and Mistress Stonor, mother of the maids. Looking at the expectant faces around me, I addressed them,

'My lords, my ladies and gentlemen; this day is most auspicious, as you all well know. That I am here at all as your new queen is the Lord's doing.' I looked from face to face, knowing that many would share my belief that God had indeed chosen Anne Boleyn as His key instrument of change in the kingdom. 'We find ourselves in times of great change, and his most illustrious majesty, the king, in his eminent wisdom, has granted me the permission to display this new testament of Master Tyndale in my privy apartments for all to see.' I tapped my hand upon the book beneath it, to illustrate its presence and significance.

I reflected on a time gone by, when Cardinal Wolsey had set his spies about the court in England to cast out illegal and heretical books. Seized with Anne's courage, I was quick to retaliate when Wolsey stole my copy of *The Obedience a Christian Man*, skilfully turning the cardinal's own attack against him, striking another blow at the heart of his relationship with the king. Five years later, as I stood in my privy chambers as Queen of England, those events seemed a lifetime ago. I remember hearing my voice which was clear, strong and equally full of purpose and passion. 'I have summoned you here to instruct you in your duties. You are above all, the most senior and most trusted of my officers, and I ask that you bear this in mind in setting a goodly example at all times to those who look to you daily for guidance.' A number of gentlemen nodded their heads sagely, as I went on, 'I require from this day forth, and at all times, that every single member of this household shall prove to be honourable, discreet, just and thrifty in their conduct...' I paused for a moment, reflecting on the uncomfortable truth of what I had to say next. 'There are those who choose to speak falsely against me; those who seek to corrupt the holy state of sovereignty.' I looked solemnly from one individual to the next, 'I will accept not any stain upon this household, and I ask you,' I nodded my head slightly to emphasise my words, as I picked out first my vice-chamberlain, then my master of the horse, 'to set a godly spectacle to others, by attending mass daily, for I shall demand this of all junior members of this household, and everyone of you should display at all times a virtuous demeanour, which shall ever be beyond reproach.' My gaze alighted upon Margery, who smiled at me with encouragement. 'May it be upon your conscience never to quarrel in public, swear or...' I then turned my gaze back toward the young, male members of my court, as I went on, '...frequent evil, lewd and ungodly disposed brothels. For I swear to you my lords, ladies and gentlemen that upon my honour, should I hear of the like, you will be instantly dismissed from your post and perpetually banished from the court to your utter shame.' I then clasped my hands afore my swollen stomach and finished by saying, 'Now, tarry here no more, but go forth to your own departments and convey these words to those about you. You are—each and every one of you—my trusted ambassadors. Let us be beyond reproach, and do unto your queen an honourable service, such that in years to come, the household of Anne Boleyn will be remembered as a shining example of godliness and order.'

With the end of my speech, there were many nodding heads and many, 'Aye, Madame' heard from the little congregation. Each of them bowed or curtsied in turn, before dispersing to go about their various offices. I looked toward the entrance to my privy chamber to see my father sweeping into the room, acknowledging the gentlemen of my household, all of whom he knew well, as they, in turn, passed him to make their exit.

'My Lord,' I said as my father approached, taking my hand and kissing it in greeting.

'Your Majesty.' It was the first time my father had called me thus publicly, and a conspiratorial smile passed between us; a smile which spoke of our shared wonder that we Boleyns had finally arrived at a destination that for so long had seemed so utterly unobtainable. My father stood back, appraising my appearance, before he nodded his approval and said, 'You look truly radiant; I do believe majesty becomes you.' I smiled before breaking away from my father and resting my hand upon my visibly swollen belly, I caught Anne's reflection in the costly Venetian mirror on the wall of my privy chamber. I saw the truth of my father's statement; Anne was indeed a glittering spectacle of majesty, dressed in a gorgeous suit of tissue bejewelled with diamonds and many other precious stones. She was dressed perfectly for her official debut as queen.

A number of ladies began to re-enter my chamber, amongst them Lady Mary, who had brought some fabric samples to me so that I could choose the material for several new gowns. As I began to examine them, I cast a sideways glance at my father and asked,

'How do you find the king today, father?' The Earl of Wiltshire stepped forward, running his own hand across Tyndale's New Testament, no doubt enjoying the softness of the velvet beneath his fingertips, before he replied,

'His majesty is anxious to see you received as queen and yet...' my father cocked his head to one side, '...it is also true that his grace remains much offended that the Princess Dowager of Wales refuses to renounce her title of queen, or accept his grace's will that she should allow her case to be decided here in England.'

I continued to pick through the fabrics, running one hand across the costly materials, the other resting upon my belly, outwardly remaining impassive. However, at the mention of Katherine's name, I experienced a familiar flash of burning resentment and a fierce anger which tore through my body. I am ashamed to say it now, but I hated the bitch and cursed her stubborn refusal to fade into obscurity. As indifferently as I could, I said, 'Now that the Act of Appeals is passed through Parliament, she has no recourse to Rome.' I looked up at my father as I stated, somewhat rhetorically, 'Surely Katherine understands that?' My father raised an eyebrow and nodded his head sagely before replying,

'Indeed, but you know what an obstinate and disagreeable woman the princess dowager is.' My father continued, 'His grace has told her that from one month after Easter, he will no longer provide for her personal expenses, or the wages of her servants. The king has requested that she retire to some private house of her own, and there to live upon the small allowance assigned to her.' Without acknowledging my father's words, I turned to Lady Mary indicating with my hand and a nod which materials I had chosen. Mary Howard then curtsied and removed them, before I turned to face Sir Thomas, saying somewhat sarcastically,

'And I can well imagine what Katherine had to say about that!' I sighed reflecting upon how on such a great day of rejoicing for Anne, Katherine somehow managed to remain the ever present thorn in my side; even at a distance, the very thought of her existence—and that of her contumacious daughter—would always raise my hackles. I turned and indicated to my father that he should walk with me towards the great window, which looked out over the queen's privy gardens and Castle Hill beyond. At a distance from my ladies, and with my back turned to them to give us some privacy, I quietly enquired, 'What of ambassador Chapuys? What has he had to say about all this?'

Of course, to my modern day persona, the thirty-four-year-old Savoyard lawyer and his relationship to Anne Boleyn was infamous. He had been appointed imperial ambassador to Henry's court in 1529, when he was just thirty years of age; staunchly pro-Catholic, I knew full well of Eustace Chapuys' unmitigated hatred of Anne and his unceasing efforts to scandalise her reputation. I watched my father as he crossed his arms in front of his belly, bending one upwards so that he stroked his chin thoughtfully, before replying,

'The ambassador gained an audience with the king two days ago, on Maundy Thursday, I witnessed the exchange for myself,' Sir Thomas cast a glance in my direction, as he went on. 'His Excellency made a formal protest at the news of your marriage to the king and the moves made in Parliament to curb any future appeals to Rome. He questioned the king's conscience, and then dared to imply that his grace had no guarantee of a son from any present or future marriage.' My father gazed out of the window to watch the comings and goings of courtiers and merchants passing through the distant southern gate of the palace.

'And the king?' I enquired.

'The king was much aggrieved by matters that touched so closely upon his person. He became nearly incandescent with rage, he warned Chapuys that his master should mind his own affairs and interfere not in England's business, and that if the emperor held notions of waging war upon our nation, the English would soundly defeat him.' Whilst the fine detail of court politics and diplomatic wrangling between Henry and the imperial ambassador eluded me, I knew that no invasion of England was likely to take place. However, I also knew that this was not on account of any lack of trying on Chapuys' part. I was aware that behind the scenes, in his steady stream of dispatches to his master, the imperial ambassador ceaselessly sought to provoke a Spanish invasion to rescue Katherine, her daughter and the English nation.

My father hesitated, unsure whether to speak the rest. He relented when he saw that I had already read his mind, and that I knew that there was something more that I should hear. Somewhat reluctantly he spoke again. 'I heard tell that in private the ambassador accuses you of being the source of the king's cruelty toward the princess dowager and the Princess Mary; that you have perverted his naturally kind and generous nature and that now you have your 'foot in the stirrup', you will not relent in your persecution of Katherine until....' Sir Thomas' speech trailed away diplomatically, as he chose rather delicately not to speak of Katherine's permanent demise, which secretly, we both longed for. However, wishing for something was one thing, acting upon it, was entirely another. I laughed aloud at the ridiculousness of such a suggestion, catching the attention of many of my ladies, who spontaneously turned towards me with curiosity at my sudden outburst.

I suspect that those who had heard my laughter that day also heard the anxiety behind it. Although I thought the ramblings of the ambassador's fevered imagination to be both amusing and fantastical, I was irritated to be judged so harshly by one who had never met me, and, indeed, refused to meet me. Yes, I knew more than ever that Anne was no pawn in this game; she had at some point made a choice to wield the power of her intellect, grace and femininity to capture the heart of the king. But to lay the blame squarely at her feet was to frame the king— an icon of kingship, authority and masculinity—as a helpless victim, which was a ridiculous notion. I was about say as much to my father, when the arrival of the Dukes of Norfolk and Suffolk brought a swift end to our conversation. We turned to see the two noblemen enter the room, remove their bejewelled caps and sweep into a respectful bow as the Duke of Suffolk announced,

'Your Majesty' I stepped forward smiling warmly. Inwardly, I wondered how much it galled Charles Brandon to address me thus. 'The king's grace requests your presence in the chapel royal.' Charles was ever to keep his conversation with me to the point and flawlessly polite, a veneer of charming indifference concealing his true disdain for Anne, and all that she represented. Despite my knowledge of the duke's true sentiments, I thanked him for his pains, and with my father at my side, made toward my presence chamber, where my entire household had gathered, including the sixty ladies who were appointed to attend upon me and accompany their new queen to mass.

After our explosive quarrel over Mistress Jane Seymour, Henry and I had soon made amends. Both of us had been ashamed by our scolding behaviour, and sought consciously to atone for the hurt inflicted upon the other. It is not that I reconciled myself to Jane's presence in my household, but rather I determined instead to bide my time until the storm passed, and to seek a more discreet way of removing her from court. In the meantime, his majesty clucked around his pregnant wife, and I received the king's generous bounty with graciousness, sweet smiles and gentle caresses. It is true that our quarrels were violent, but our reconciliations were full of genuine intimacy and tenderness that for a long time confounded many, and bound us ever closer in a strange sort of emotional addiction that defied logic.

I knew full well that with the Act of Appeals upon the statute books, the king was emboldened to set forth the plans that he had been secretly making with Master Cromwell. I also knew from my father that on Good Friday, 11 April, the king received a letter from Archbishop Cranmer recommending that a court of goodly and learned gentlemen should set about trying the king's case in the matter of his marriage to Katherine, the Princess Dowager of Wales. On the same day, I was also instructed by Master Cromwell that upon the king's express command, I would, as Henry promised me at Whitehall, be presented to the court as his wife and queen the following day, Easter Eve. It would be his grace's pleasure that this would be accompanied by greater pomp and pageantry that had ever been bestowed upon Katherine. So it was on Black Saturday, the day during which Christ's body traditionally lay in its tomb, I prepared to go forth with a great train of sixty ladies, to pray and be prayed for as queen, in the chapel royal at Greenwich.

As I entered my presence chamber, accompanied by my father and the Dukes of Suffolk and Norfolk, all eyes turned toward me. Over 200 persons curtsied or bowed at my arrival. My favourite cousin, Lady Mary Howard, stepped forward, ready to carry the long train of my glittering gown, whilst the remaining sixty ladies arranged themselves in pairs to follow behind. Charles Brandon and my Uncle Norfolk led the way, escorting our regal procession through the queen's watching chamber, across the landing of the great stair, into the gallery leading to the king and queen's holy day closets.

I was not to meet with the king for he wished this day to be mine. Instead, I was instructed to first enter the queen's closet, then to a great fanfare of trumpets, to descend from the first floor into the body of the chapel. I can still see so clearly the modest-sized chapel packed to capacity; a great court of humanity fidgeting and straining to catch a glimpse of Anne Boleyn, a veritable sea of bewildered faces turned in awe as the royal household beheld the sight of their new queen. As I walked towards the high altar, my gaze transfixed upon the holy cross. I sensed the palpable, beating curiosity which pulsated through the thronging crowd. I heard the furtive whispers beneath the sound of soaring voices, both human and angelic, as the choir sang a *Te Deum* in celebration of the occasion. I was filled with a sense of the divine; Anne's fierce pride and my sheer wonderment sweeping me up in my own godly reverie. I felt Anne's body respond to this transcendental moment, moving with purpose, grace and regal dignity, as I knelt before the altar to pray for the life of the king, and for that of the child I carried. I humbly accepted the prayers of the dean of the chapel royal and the congregation for the long life of Anne, Queen of England and that of her unborn prince.

When the prayers were said, I rose, turning to see the entire court for the first time, including my mother, father and brother, who had hurried back from France just a few days earlier, as well as other leading nobles, each one bowing and curtsying upon my passing. I made my way back toward my holy day closet, acknowledging those who murmured their blessings and good wishes. I cast my eyes heavenwards, there to see Henry looking down proudly upon the scene from the king's closet, a satisfied smile upon his lips, and the slightest inclination of his head showed me his appreciation of my performance, before he disappeared from view.

I did not see the king again until after nightfall, when I held a celebratory banquet in my privy chamber at Greenwich. The guest of honour was the newly appointed French ambassador, Jean de Dinteville. It was a sumptuous and glittering affair attended by the king, my family and a number of Henry's most senior noblemen and women including: the Dukes of Norfolk and Suffolk; Henry Courtney, the Marquis of Exeter; the Dowager Duchess of Norfolk; Thomas Audley, the Lord Chancellor of England; Master Cromwell; Lady Rochford; Lady Mary Howard and her sister-in-law, Francis de Vere, Countess of Surrey. Also invited was twenty-four year old Georges de Selve, Bishop of Tarbes who had come to England at the beginning of March in order to visit his intimate friend.

When I overheard Monsieur de Dinteville speak of his friend, my interest was immediately piqued, the names of the two gentlemen from France seeming somehow familiar and important; my insatiable curiosity compelled me to bring the two together that evening for, as yet, an unknown purpose and so I had virtually insisted that he should present himself at court. In the end, it was the first and last time I would meet Georges de Selve, yet, his image would haunt me and remind me of Anne's day of triumph, centuries after the event had faded from living memory. I was yet to make the connection, or to be aware of how events were coming together and conspiring to produce one of the greatest pieces of Renaissance art known to the modern world.

My privy chamber was laid out for dinner. A large, ornately carved oak table was arranged with a great swathe of the finest, decorative gold plate available; whilst the most delicate and finely crafted Venetian glass caught the light from a multitude of beeswax candles, setting our party aglow against the dark night, which descended upon us. I adored the palace after nightfall when the flickering of tapers, candles and torches softly illuminated resplendent rooms, and dancing flames created a sense of greater intimacy; the wooden panelling, heavy tapestries and rich hangings sealing one into a warm cocoon, protected from the harsh realities of the world outside. After dark there is a particular nature to the light which causes the many precious metals and gem stones in the furnishings, and on the richly dressed courtiers, to sparkle more brilliantly, like delicate fairy lights illuminated against black shadows.

The mood around the table on that Easter Eve was festive on many accounts, and the king was in exceptional form. I remember the magic of that evening; how Henry had hardly taken his eyes from me, how he had been so tender and attentive to my every need, as if I were the most precious jewel in the world, priceless and utterly irreplaceable. Many a time, I turned to find him staring at me with the same wonderment that I had witnessed so often in the heady days of our early romance. Whilst Henry certainly held court that evening, commanding the conversation around the table, flirting outrageously with me and some of my younger ladies—to whom he directed most of his attention. How I enjoyed once more being the centre of his world. Although, I think not that this sentiment was shared by the likes of Suffolk, Norfolk, Exeter and Audley, who the king largely ignored—much to their chagrin.

Thankfully, his majesty paid court to the French ambassador and his guest, and both men warmed to his attentions. I liked Jean de Dinteville very much, and was very grateful that in January of that year, he had replaced Monsieur Montespat, a disagreeable character of conservative faith who made it quite clear that he was not supportive of the king's divorce. His stance had precipitated his early departure from English shores, and I quickly came to appreciate the newly appointed twenty-nine-year-old ambassador, a cultured man of significant wealth with French royal connections. He was one of the first foreign representatives to request an audience with me as queen, passing on his master's sincere felicitations on the news of my marriage, pregnancy and on my proclamation as Queen of England.

He was one of the characters that I would read about with great curiosity upon my return to the modern world. I knew very little about him, but retrospectively, I realised how well he had kept his counsel, like any skilled ambassador, always acting with apparent grace, diplomacy and tact. But beneath that mask, was the truth; Jean de Dinteville longed for his recall to France and suffered badly in the rather temperamental English climate. All this was unknown to me then, and amongst the banter and good humour that evening, I was curious to find out more about our French guests, particularly, the sudden arrival of Georges de Selve. So, I enquired of the gentleman,

'Your Excellency, Monsieur de Dinteville tells me that you are visiting him for just a short while. Pray tell me, is this just a personal visit or do you have some business at court?' I smiled a little mischievously, for in many ways my question was incredibly direct. If indeed the bishop was on a diplomatic errand, bringing new instructions to the French ambassador from King Francis in the light of my public elevation, it would not be a foregone conclusion that he would wish either Henry or me to know of it. With great aplomb and unflappable grace, the bishop replied,

'It is a personal visit Madame, for I have not seen my dear friend for a long time. Indeed, there is a possibility that in the coming months I will be appointed as ambassador to Venice for a second time, and methinks that then it will be some time before Monsieur de Dinteville and I will have chance to meet again.' As the Bishop of Lavaur was speaking, I picked up a nearby glass, indicating that it should be filled with wine by one of my pages, who waited in attendance. If his excellency carried new instructions in the light of the precipitous change in circumstances at the English court, as I suspected he did, he gave little away. Yet emboldened by the wine and the intoxicating atmosphere, I felt inclined to toy good-naturedly with the bishop, who I knew was a friend of reformist leanings.

'And yet if I were the French king,' I cocked my head coquettishly, as I spoke, 'I might wish to reissue instructions to my ambassador; for I would see that time runs ahead of his mission here in England.' It was clear that I was referring not only to Anne's sudden, apparent elevation at court, but also the passing of the Act of Appeals, which left the Pope's role in the *king's great matter* somewhat redundant. I knew that this must have changed the emphasis of de Dinteville's embassy at the English court. Georges de Selve smiled enigmatically, but was saved from answering by a sudden raucous peal of laughter coming from the king. After a few moments, during which a number of wry smiles were exchanged around the table, Henry exclaimed,

'Your Excellency, you must forgive my wife. Her grace is a woman of many talents, including the ability to extract from a man's heart that which he does not intend to reveal!' Then he directed his next comment to me. Clearly amused by my precocious probing of our French guest,

Henry proclaimed, 'Sweetheart, methinks you will never make a diplomat...' I raised an eyebrow, pursing my lips as if considering the king's words before, with idle mischief, I retorted,

'On the contrary, Your Majesty, I suggest that such a talent would make me the perfect ambassador, for what ambassador would not wish to extract the secrets of a man's heart?' With that the king, who had perhaps enjoyed a little too much wine, burst out laughing once more. At the same time, I noticed several of my ladies smile and giggle in appreciation at my boldness. That was the Henry I loved, the Henry who enjoyed my banter and good natured challenge, who revelled in my wit and company; a man who is now sadly lost to me forever.

As the king's laughter died away, I felt inclined to continue the conversation, albeit taking a different tack, and so I enquired,

'Your Excellency,' directing my question to Jean de Dinteville, 'I wonder with whom you have become acquainted since your arrival in England?' The ambassador put down his glass before replying,

'I have spent a considerable amount of time in the company of Francis Weston, who I find to be a most honourable and amiable gentleman, and who I believe Your Graces know well.' I nodded my affirmation, 'And then there is Master Nicolas Krantzer, a most fascinating man who has already taught me a good deal about astronomy. He has...' the ambassador continued to speak, but I was no longer listening. In a flash of insight, I saw clearly what had, up until that point, been but a vague intuition regarding the significance of the two Frenchmen who sat before me. I knew Master Kranzter well, for he had been at court for many years as the king's astronomer and clock-maker, and I had often witnessed his conversations with Henry. I recalled how, as I had sat for Master Holbein, he too had spoken a good deal about his friend, the very same Nicolas Kranzter. Finally, I connected the dots in a previously fragmented picture.

I was no great art historian in my modern life, but how could I forget *The Ambassadors,* acclaimed as one of Holbein's greatest triumphs. I remembered seeing this intriguing masterpiece hung in the National Portrait Gallery in London in the twenty-first century. It was a portrait of two friends, Jean de Dinteville and Georges de Selve, so full of symbolism, the true meaning of which had somewhat been lost in the sands of time. Of particular significance in the painting was the date and time shown on the pillar dial, one of the many scientific instruments occupying the centre ground of the portrait—Good Friday, 11 April 1533. It was clear that the portrait had been painted in the few short weeks that Georges de Selve was in England visiting his friend. A sense of urgency suddenly overtook me and rather rudely, I blurted out,

'What about Master Holbein? Have you met Master Holbein yet?' Monsieur de Dinteville shook his head thoughtfully,

'No Madame, although Master Kranzter has spoken a good deal about him.' I suspected as much and suddenly felt a strong sense of purpose take hold. I needed to ensure that the worlds of these three gentlemen did in fact collide, and so rather emphatically, leaving little room for argument, I suggested,

'Master Holbein is currently completing a portrait commissioned by his majesty; I can vouch that he is truly a genius.' I needed to convince the French ambassador of the merits of my next proposal. 'You must return to court tomorrow and I will also summon the gentleman in question. It would be most fitting if you take the opportunity to commission a portrait of the two of you, whilst you are both here in England. Master Holbein will soon be in strong demand, for I intend to support his work here at court.' The French ambassador inclined his head gracefully, accepting my invitation. There was little time to say more or think upon the possible consequences of my benevolent plotting, for as the evening drew to a close, the king stood up abruptly, offering me his hand. Along with everyone round the table, I too rose to my feet, as manners dictated. Henry then spoke,

'You should take heed of her grace's advice, your excellencies. Master Holbein is a rare talent indeed. Invest your money well for you are not likely to meet again one so masterful at his art.' I smiled. With the king's endorsement, I saw the light of genuine intrigue, which I had kindled, take hold in Monsieur de Dinteville's eyes. I knew that my job was done. The men would meet and a masterpiece would be created.

Henry then went on, 'My lords and ladies, you must excuse us for the hour is late, and my wife must not over-exert herself.' It was so strange to hear Henry refer to me so openly as his wife. However, the king's thoughtfulness in front of so many eminent courtiers made me glow with pride. At the same time, I had to conceal my surprise, for it was customary for the king and me to withdraw separately; if we were to spend the night together, we would do so privately using the privy gallery that connected the king and queen's sides, safely away from the public gaze. Yet, on that evening, Henry seemed unconcerned, and we took our leave of our dinner guests together.

Accompanied only by my sister and brother, the two of us slipped silently into the long, privy gallery, heading towards the king's apartments. I expected Henry to bid me good night at the door to my bedchamber, but the king seemed to need me by his side. As we walked slowly, my sweetheart placed his arm around my waist and drew me close to his warm, scented body. All evening I had seen a deep appreciation for me alight in Henry's eyes. I felt the heady mixture of his love and raw desire to sweep me up and consume me. Despite my pregnant state, my own desire for the king had not abated one jot. Indeed if anything, the new-found swell of my belly against my slender outline made me feel incredibly sexy. A frisson of sexual energy charged through my body as we walked along, side by side, the king with his arm around me. We had rarely slept together since the announcement of my pregnancy, and it is true that I desperately missed our sexual intimacy. I confess that I longed for Henry to peel away my clothes, to feel his breath upon my naked skin, the delicate touch of his fingertips run across the swell of my breasts and buttocks, to hear him gasp in sexual ecstasy, and to watch him lose himself, drowning in the sweet juices of our love.

Henry whispered lascivious comments in my ear, out of earshot of George and Mary, who were following discreetly behind us. We were once more like two star-struck lovers, and I giggled and flirted decadently with him in return. Henry teased me about my questioning of Georges de Selve and Jean de Dinteville; I playfully countered that I could outdo an ambassador at his own game any day. This was much to the king's continued titillation, as he puckishly mused on the merits of recalling his ambassador to the Spanish court and sending me there instead! As we entered the king's raying chamber, Henry halted and turned to face me and said quietly,

'Anne, I was so proud of you today. You were magnificent!' I backed my eyes demurely, smiling bashfully once more. In truth, it was rare indeed to receive praise from Henry Tudor. There was something in his psyche that prohibited him from praising others, lest it should serve to diminish his own self-concept or accomplishments. I can only pray to the good Lord that his majesty will be more generous with my Elizabeth when I am gone; for already she takes great delight in the attentions of her father.

Henry leaned in and kissed me on the tip of my nose, before he continued, 'I have a surprise for you, sweetheart. I thought to show you tomorrow, but somehow tonight seems more befitting.' The king then turned to George and Mary and commanded, 'Lord and Lady Rochford, you may leave us now.' With that my brother and sister bowed and curtsied, before taking their leave. Henry took me by the hand and led me across the threshold to his bedchamber. Before disappearing inside, I cast one last glimpse along the gallery, just as Mary turned her head and smiled at me enigmatically. Something was different about my English rose, yet I had not time to dwell upon it before the king pulled me inside the royal bedchamber. To my bemusement, we did not stop there, rather his majesty led me into the adjacent privy chamber.

I was not surprised to find the room rather eerily deserted, lit only by the glowing embers of the fire and several candles casting gentle pools of light around the room, keeping the darkness at bay; the rhythmic ticking of a rare and valuable mantle clock the only sound to break the silence. My attention was captivated by a full size painting, supported on a wooden stand and covered with a black velvet cloth, embroidered with the royal coat of arms. I knew immediately what it was. Master Holbein had completed his portrait of Anne, and this is what the king had been eager to show me. I was aware that my husband was watching my face, full, as it was, of excitement and anticipation. I looked from the painting to the king's grace and whispered breathlessly,

'Is it … Is it the painting? Has Master Holbein finished it?' Henry nodded, a satisfying grin spreading across his face. I must have looked as if I were a wide-eyed child witnessing the wonder of my first Christmas, as I rather excitedly asked, 'May I? Can I look at it, Henry?' The king nodded his assent as I gingerly stepped forward until I was standing in front of the covered portrait, a moment of the most exquisite anticipation. My whole life, I had wanted to behold a picture of Anne, and although now her true likeness is as familiar to me as my own, to see an original Holbein of her was beyond my wildest dreams. I reached up and allowed the tips of my fingers to run across the soft black velvet, before I grasped the fabric and pulled it away to reveal the masterpiece beneath, my gaze utterly transfixed by the majestic portrait of Anne Boleyn that towered in front of me.

Quite unusually for Master Holbein in those early days, it was a full length portrait that captured in the exquisite detail of the fabric and jewels which had adorned me on my wedding day. Yet what was so entrancing was the way in which the artist had captured the true essence of Anne's soul; such an effect was, of course, Holbein's signature. The painting was a *tour de force*, full of richness and subtlety; a piece of art with such depth and realism that it was entirely possible to believe that at any moment Anne might simply step out of the picture to greet me. For what seemed like an eternity, I studied the picture, drinking in thirstily every glorious detail before I whispered,

'Oh, Henry, Oh, it is truly exquisite. I simply adore it.' From behind, he circled his arms about me to embrace my swollen belly and planted a kiss on the side of my cheek and said,

'I shall hang this upon the wall of our privy chamber at Whitehall, and then all who shall request an audience with the King of England shall see my beautiful queen looking down on them from above.' At the time, I recall how I felt my breast swell with pride at the thought. It would only be later, when I returned to my modern day life, and lost myself once more in the details of Anne's life and the Tudor court, I would realise with tremendous sadness that after her fall, it was in that very same spot that Henry would commission Master Holbein to paint the great *Whitehall Mural,* the portrait of the genesis of the Tudor dynasty in which Mistress Seymour featured so prominently.

Such concerns, however, were temporarily brushed aside as the events of that historic summer continued to unfold at a pace. I was about to experience one of the most incredible experiences of my life thus far. I was to know first-hand what only a handful of people had ever known: what it was to be crowned and transcend this mortal realm; to be touched directly by the hand of God and be His own anointed upon this earth. In the eyes of the society in which Anne lived, I was about to become more divine than human, and Anne's metamorphosis to an immortal queen would finally be complete.

Chapter Seventeen

Greenwich Palace, Greenwich,
23 May 1533

I can see it so clearly in my mind's eye; the eighteen–year-old bride, Lady Frances Brandon, eldest daughter of Charles Brandon and Mary, Queen of France, being joined in union with Henry, son of the late Thomas Grey, Marquess of Dorset in the family chapel at Suffolk Place in Southwark. The king was to be guest of honour at the wedding of his niece and had left Greenwich that morning. I offered to stay behind for it was common knowledge that Henry's sister refused to accept his new wife, and so to avoid a scene, I tactfully suggested that I stay away, although I longed to meet the proud daughter of the Tudor dynasty. I would never have the chance again. I knew that shortly after the wedding, the former French queen would retire to the duke's country estate of Westhorpe Hall, in Suffolk, and would die just a few weeks later on 25 June. She was just thirty-seven years old.

I, more than anyone, knew of the significance of this historic match and these reflections were very much on my mind on that perfect day; however, such sombre thoughts threw themselves into sharp relief against the sheer vibrancy of the blossoming summer's afternoon. It was my favourite time of year. The palace gardens were a riot of colour, the sweet scent of blossom was heavy in the air, and while the weather was comfortably warm, there was rarely the oppressive heat of late July or August. To make the most of this most agreeable weather, the queen's party, which included: my sister; Jane Rochford, Lady Mary Howard, Nan, Bess Holland, Madge Shelton and the Countesses of Worcester and Surrey, had decamped to the gardens of Greenwich Palace, near the southern wall of the palace precinct, looking out toward Duke Humphrey's Tower.

Although my head teemed with recalcitrant thoughts, I was drawn by the sound of laughter and merry banter coming from a group of my friends, who were busy in competition, shooting at the butt in front of where I was sitting. Due to my condition, I was not allowed to join them; instead, a canopy of cloth of gold and silver tissue had been set up to provide welcome shade. Only the most gentle of breezes agitated the delicate white sarcenet that was draped in a luxurious swathe of fabric on either side of the entrance to our tent. I sat comfortably beneath it, reclining on a finely upholstered X-framed chair, my feet raised upon a stool. In a sea of cushions about my feet sat four of my ladies, Nan, Mary Howard, my sister and sister-in-law, Lady Jane. On either side of the entrance stood a yeoman of Henry's guard dressed in the royal livery, whilst a picnic was served by my pages, each one dressed in Anne's livery colours of purple and blue, and proudly displaying Anne's new falcon badge.

Several of the king's gentlemen also stayed behind and in the absence of their master, they gravitated to my chambers to dally awhile with their queen and her ladies. My brother, Francis Weston, Sir Henry Norris, Thomas Wyatt and Richard Page made up this gallant and good-natured band of virile, young courtiers. They entertained us with an earnest competition at the butt. Each lady backed a winner and cheered them on as a considerable amount of money changed hands, with a delighted Frances de Vere, Countess of Surrey, benefitting the most from the winnings. Later, Elizabeth, Countess of Worcester, Bess Holland and Madge Shelton were persuaded to join the gentlemen in a more genteel ladies competition.

As they began to take aim, I watched my brother instruct Elizabeth Worcester on the finer points of skilful play, and felt even more sadness wash over me. Maybe I even sighed unknowingly, or perhaps my sister simply sensed my melancholia and gently enquired,

'Are you well, Your Majesty?' I was roused from my thoughts to find Mary smiling at me reassuringly. I acknowledged her gesture with a rather feeble smile, before replying,

'His Majesty has informed me that he is to dispatch our brother and the Duke of Norfolk to France within the week.' Mary exclaimed,

'But that means that George will not be present at your coronation!' I sighed deeply again before replying,

'Indeed, it is so, sister and I am sorry for it.'

'Be of good cheer, Madame, for truly it will be the happiest day of your life. You will be his majesty's most beloved wife, England's anointed queen—and all this with a healthy child in your belly.' This time it was little Mary Howard who spoke, quite rightly pointing out my many blessings. In fact, despite my rather sombre mood that day, I truly was, *the moost happi*. Henry appeared to adore me evermore each day; I was in the most robust health, and having entered my fifth month of pregnancy found myself to be completely aglow. The tiredness that plagued me since the first trimester had evaporated; my skin was radiant, and my dark hair more lustrous than ever. Henry had even commented on it many a time saying that he had never seen a woman who blossomed so much on account of her expectant condition. Not only that, but never before, nor again, would I feel so confident. It was if I were untouchable, exuding a deadly feminine sexuality which many men, I knew, found utterly disarming.

I decided to honour the beauty of the day and sweep away my cares. Sometimes, I needed to remind myself who I really was, just plain Anne, caught up in the most unbelievable circumstances. Yet, I had become Anne the Queen, and it was easy to lose myself within her. I had to keep pinching myself to recall that in Anne's shoes, in just nine days, I would be anointed Queen of England in Westminster Abbey. I was not nervous; Anne's renowned courage, and my determination to savour every moment of this truly incredible privilege banished any such reaction. I still did not understand, 'why me?' but I was both awed and humbled by my good fortune. It was my dream, and I was in no rush for it to end.

My first time in Anne's world, I had remained there for a little over a year. Would the same happen this time? Would I see Anne's child delivered? Would Anne live to rewrite England's destiny? Eventually, I would come to know the answers, but I distracted myself from these rather profound thoughts by turning to Lady Mary and asking jovially,

'And what of you Lady Mary, are you not excited at the prospect of seeing your betrothed again?' I knew that as I spoke, Henry Fitzroy was on his way back from Paris, accompanied by his close companion, Henry Howard, Earl of Surrey. They were to attend Anne's coronation and the Whitsuntide celebrations. She blushed scarlet, which was ever her way when anyone spoke to her of her dashing husband to be, and a perfect cue for my ladies to tease her good-naturedly,

'Lady Mary, how you blush so!' said Nan gently goading our friend. 'Methinks that the king will soon announce your wedding date, and then you can enjoy your husband's attentions as much as you like!'

Lady Mary flushed an even deeper shade of scarlet at the intimation of physical intimacy betwixt the two young lovers, of which she was entirely innocent. I laughed aloud, whilst my sweet sister spoke up in Mary's defence,

'Nan, it is cruel of you to tease Lady Mary, just because you are enjoying so the pleasures of the marriage bed! Marry, it seems to me...' The two continued to banter for some time, but I confess that I tuned out, for my attention was drawn to the rather pinched face of Lady Rochford, who seemed oblivious to my ladies' exchange, and was sitting quietly watching the game of archery unfold before us. I followed her gaze and found myself watching George, standing behind the Countess of Worcester, his arms around her as he guided her right hand back to draw the bow. There was much laughter between them, and as Elizabeth released the arrow, she glanced over her shoulder, laughing heartily as she did so, to speak to my brother, flashing her blue eyes, which were alight with appreciation. Suddenly, I recalled a vague notion of seeing the two together dancing at the great Christmas Day celebrations. Something tugged at my sensibilities once more. I had not seen then what was suddenly obvious—and Lady Rochford saw it clearly as well. I wondered if anything had transpired between them, and was making a mental note to speak of it to my brother, when a messenger arrived from the king.

I was somewhat startled to see William Brereton appear, for I had expected no one. The gentleman was breathless, and I rightly surmised that there was some urgency to his mission. I drew myself up in my seat, just for the slightest moment a rivulet of panic flushing through my body. Master Brereton must have seen my concern. After sweeping low into a bow, he straightened himself and said,

'Fear not, Your Grace. I am sent forthwith from his majesty the king, who has commanded that I come to you with all haste.' I was aware that my forehead remained furrowed in confusion. William forged on, his face suddenly aglow. 'There is great news, Madame! Archbishop Cranmer and the court at Dunstable have found the king's marriage to the Princess Dowager of Wales to be unlawful and invalid.'

I rose to my feet as quickly as my swollen belly would allow, and through a haze of tears, I could think of nothing but eleven words of Psalm 118 which I spoke aloud, *A Dominum factum est illud, et est mirabile in oculis notris.* I heard myself say out loud in the unfamiliar Latin—for it was not a tongue in which Anne was fluent—and yet, I knew their meaning immediately. 'This is the Lord's doing and it is marvellous in our eyes.' It was a phrase that had gone down in history—not because it had been spoken by Anne, but by her daughter Elizabeth, upon hearing the news of her accession to the English throne. I have often wondered since, if many years from that day, one of my ladies, possibly Nan, had told the impressionable princess about her mother's story. Had she recounted this moment and the words of Anne Boleyn? Had Elizabeth thought of her mother as she was handed Mary's ring by Sir Nicolas Throckmorton, the man who had ridden in all haste from London to bear the glad tidings? I would never know, but I already sensed a connection to my unborn daughter that I knew would never be broken—not even by my death.

Chapter Eighteen

Greenwich Palace, Greenwich,
29 May 1533

Even from within the secluded sanctuary of my own privy closet, I could sense that there was nothing ordinary about that day. The court was a living, breathing creature, its pregnant expectation, and that of the entire city, seemed to be closing in upon me. I was immersed in a divine rite of passage from which I would ultimately emerge transformed from a mere mortal of this world into a anointed queen, one appointed by God to rule over the land at the side of one of the mightiest princes in Christendom. It was an estate that not even Henry could ever take away from Anne.

Since daybreak woke the land to a gloriously warm and still summer's morning, I had been enveloped by my family, friends and ladies, who were all caught up in the glittering excitement surrounding what portended to be the greatest pageantry, celebration and splendour that had been seen in the realm since the visit of Charles V in 1522. As the well-oiled machinery of the king's court sucked everyone and everything into the spectacle of coronation, I felt as if I were the profoundly still centre at the eye of this tornado of activity.

The palace and city were packed to capacity. Henry had commanded that all notable gentlemen must attend, and thus they came, descending from every quarter of the realm to pay homage to their new queen. Councillors worked tirelessly with the lord mayor, sheriffs and aldermen of the city to ensure that the next few days were flawlessly executed. For weeks, the craftsmen of London had been beavering away well into the night designing, constructing and assembling everything from rich gowns, new jewellery, tableaus and sets that would provide the stage for two major events; the coronation in Westminster Abbey, and the great banquet that would follow in nearby Westminster Hall.

At three o'clock in the afternoon, with the changing of the tide, I was due to set forth from Greenwich by barge, heading toward the Tower with Henry. The king had left the palace soon after attending mass that morning as he proclaimed that the occasion was to be Anne's, and that Henry would observe all that came to pass whilst remaining discreetly hidden from view. The king took with him a number of gentlemen of the privy chamber, and all the senior officers of the royal household, including Master Cromwell. This left the rest of the male nobility, and all of my ladies, to accompany me upstream amidst great pomp and ceremony.

Having bid farewell to Henry, I retired to the seclusion of my closet as I needed to find the stillness at the centre of my being, a place in which I could commune with God and my destiny. Thus, I remained for perhaps for two hours, alone and unaware of time as it slipped effortlessly by. I spent much of that time, despite my ever enlarging belly, kneeling in prayer and meditation, and was rewarded with a profound sense of peace that washed over me in waves. Then, at a little before half past two in the afternoon, my time alone came to an end. I felt profoundly ready for what lay ahead.

With my prayers completed, I was stealing the final few precious moments of solitude at the open window of my closet when there was a knock at the door, and I bid my messenger enter. I turned to see the very welcome face of my mother enter the room. Over the last few months, since our return from Calais, she had suffered two bouts of mild breathlessness and tightness in her chest which concerned me greatly; thankfully she made a swift recovery each time. On that day, Elizabeth Boleyn looked every inch the wealthy countess and mother of the new queen. A striking woman, she was dressed in the most gorgeous black, silk gown set off by pleated, russet fore-sleeves and a banding of russet and black chequer work that edged her traditional English hood. I admired the sleeves of her dress, which were trimmed with ermine, the white chemise of her under-gown visible through the slashing of the fore-sleeves that were, in turn, tied by aiglets of gold; about her waist was hung a double strand of beads of antique cameos, known as agates, whilst large tassels of fine gold thread work decorated the end of each strand.

My mother came forward, taking my hand in hers and asked,

'How are you, child?' I spoke the simple truth as I replied,

'I am very well. God has brought me to this day and I am ready.' My mother squeezed my hand and smiled, her eyes suddenly glistening with emotion. I put my hand on her arm, feeling the flesh and blood of the only mother I had ever truly known. With my new duties as queen, sadly we had seen less and less of each other. Sometimes, I longed for the simplicity and intimacy that we once shared during our time alone together at Hever. But I had left my carefree youth behind me, and such times of innocence and informality were rare indeed. As I alighted momentarily on these thoughts, Elizabeth Boleyn shook her head slowly as if in wonder, before she voiced the root cause of her emotion.

'Anne, I want you to know that I appreciate how hard it has been for you these past few years; that despite his majesty's great love for you, and you for him, the uncertainty of the *king's great matter,* and the ill-will of those who have blamed you for it all, must have been a great trial for you. In truth child, I am in awe of how you have kept your nerve. The Lord has protected you and brought you safely ashore, and I thank Him for the great blessing of this day.' My mother paused, gently cupping the palm of her hand against my cheek which I nuzzled into affectionately. She added, 'I am so very proud of you Anne, and England should be glad for they are about to crown a great queen.' My heart melted into an ocean of love and we fell into each other's arms. Aware of the impatience of time, the two of us parted, and my mother added in a more business-like fashion, 'Now child, my lord Suffolk and your father are waiting to escort you to your barge. A great flotilla, the likes of which will be incredible to your eyes, has arrived and waits to escort her majesty to the Tower.'

'Then we must tarry here no more, dearest mother,' was my reply. With a swish of her silken gown, Elizabeth Boleyn held open the door, and we shared one last private glance, before I stepped out into my chambers to face the world as Anna Regina, Queen of England.

Whilst Henry and I normally slipped unobtrusively in and out of the palace by the privy stair that led down from the king's private chambers to the jetty on the waterside, it was not so on that day. Anne Boleyn would be seen by as many people as possible, and so a grand procession, headed by the Duke of Suffolk and my father, made its way through all the public chambers at Greenwich. My ladies, and the principal noblewomen of the land, snaked behind me in a glittering human train, whilst those of the household who would not be accompanying their queen down the Thames toward the city, gathered to watch the spectacle—and to wish Anne well.

Leaving the queen's lodgings, our party descended from the royal apartments down the grand staircase and into the great hall, before turning into a shady inner courtyard. A short walk traversed this space and took us underneath one of the two gates on the northern facade of the palace. As we passed beneath it, I glanced upward to see the royal coat of arms carved at the centre of a decorative, fan-vaulted stone ceiling; the arms were painted with brilliant reds and vibrant blues, all gilded in gold leaf. I smiled inwardly at the sight of the cipher *HA* freshly carved into the stonework. Emerging from under the gateway, I was cast into the dazzling sunlight of a balmy summer afternoon; as my eyes adjusted to its glare, the sight that appeared before me was joyous. The river directly in front of the palace was full of some 300 vessels of various sizes, all dressed elaborately with colourful flags, bunting and gold foil. The movement of the boats upon the water caught the sun's rays causing a flash of brilliant light to dazzle the onlooker.

Fifty barges from the city's livery companies were part of this gathering, all having rowed in procession downstream to Greenwich to meet their new queen. Each one displayed along their length, pennants of arms that were beaten from fine gold, whilst from every vessel flew colourful standards depicting devices of the royal house of Tudor. At the same time, a fleet of private barges conveying great gentlemen, such as my father, the Duke of Suffolk, the Marquess of Dorset, the Earls of Arundel, Derby, Rutland, Worcester, Sussex, Oxford and Huntingdon were flying the arms of England's most noble families. A gentle breeze caused the streamers to flutter, agitating little gold bells that had been attached to the edges of the fabric, the scene was a riot of colour as well as sound, as the delicate tinkling of the bells was set against a marvellous sweet harmony of trumpets, shawms and diverse minstrels, all playing songs of joyful celebration. When we reached the foot of the jetty, I was greeted by my chamberlain, Thomas de Burgh and my vice chamberlain, Sir Edward Baynton. Both removed their caps and made a bow, before Sir Thomas straightened himself and said,

'Forgive me Your Majesty, I have taken it upon myself to appropriate the queen's barge, which is surely now yours by right. However, I must crave Your Grace's pardon, for until this morning the badges of the Dowager Princess of Wales were overlooked. Verily, Madame I have ripped them off with my own hands, and yet I am sorry to say that there has been no time to replace them with Your Majesty's own badge.' Lord Borough looked both irritated at the oversight and crestfallen that he should have let down his queen and thereby, the king, whose pleasure commanded the day. I was unconcerned about such trifles and determined that nothing of Katherine, not even the ghostly wisps of her memory, would derail Anne's happiness and said,

'Lord Borough, think nought of it, for it is my express desire that nothing shall spoil this day. Nevertheless, I thank you for your care.' I nodded my appreciation and made my way towards the queen's barge. There were some 120 large craft upon the river that day, each one approximately sixty or seventy feet in length with a shallow draft and a large, covered cabin for its passengers. These vessels were mostly powered by four to eight oars aside, however, a total of sixteen finely dressed, liveried oarsmen awaited my coming—just as it had been on the day, so many years ago, when I had journeyed with Katherine in the very same barge towards Richmond Palace. I took a moment to admire its truly sumptuous decoration. The craft was draped with cloth of gold and silver, with a fabulous tapestry of Anne's coat of arms was hung at the back of the cabin; soft velvet and silk cushions, all intricately embroidered, were festooned around the seating area for my comfort and that of the noblewomen who accompanied me. This included: Lady Mary Howard; Lady Jane Rochford; the Dowager Duchess of Norfolk; my mother; sister and a certain Margaret Wooton, Dowager Marchioness of Dorset. As ever, there were several notable absences: the king's sister and her daughter, the newly-wed Marchioness of Dorset; the Marchioness of Exeter, as well as the Duchess of Norfolk; all of whom continued to refuse to acknowledge Anne's supremacy and position as queen. Their snub was a proverbial fly in the ointment of an otherwise immaculately staged piece of Tudor propaganda, and I did not miss their company.

Our boat cast off from shore as the oarsmen sliced rhythmically into the water setting a goodly pace of seven knots. There was much excitement and chatter amongst us ladies, even great gasps of delight as one or other would point out an unbelievable spectacle that confounded the senses. First, there was the large mechanical dragon, which had been constructed in a light wherry ahead of us, and which carved its way down the Thames at the apex of the procession. To everyone's utter fascination, the dragon moved and belched out flames, whilst about it other models of monsters and huge, wild men uttered hideous cries, casting out fireworks that blazed across the Thames. This was meant to entice Londoners out of their homes and businesses to observe the spectacle of a new queen being honoured by all. And so they did, for along the banks of the Thames, thousands of excited spectators flocked to catch sight of Anne and all the great nobles of the land, who by their presence, signalled their implicit acceptance of the king's new wife.

My attention was drawn to another wherry that sailed alongside the lord mayor's craft, directly ahead of our own, that carried an enormous representation of Anne's white falcon badge, crowned and perched upon red and white roses that burst forth from a golden tree stump. Londoners could not fail to grasp its symbolism: Anne was to be crowned with the imperial crown, asserting England's new found independence from Rome. The falcon symbolises one who does not give up the quest until it had been won, then alighting upon the stump, which represented the Tudor dynasty, now fertile and bursting forth with the fruit of Anne's womb.

After much initial exhilaration at these many great sights and sounds, I settled back into my seat, allowing the steady rhythm of the boat to rock me, as it cleaved its way through the water. Heading westwards along the Thames, we were dazzled by the afternoon sunlight drawing us forward along its shimmering path. There was a strange mix of sweet smelling herbs that were being burnt in the barge to mask the odour of the water, and the traces of the gunpowder being fired from canons carried on the breeze across our bough.

Leaving Greenwich, we headed upstream navigating a huge *S* bend in the Thames, passing the royal dockyards at Deptford where huge sea-going vessels, the pride of Henry's navy, were under construction. A little further on, we passed the little villages of Limehouse and Radcliffe, both clinging to the northern bank of the Thames; these modest settlements proudly served England's navy with essential craftsmen. Finally, we entered the area known as the Pool of London, the point furthest inland on the Thames into which sea-going vessels could safely navigate. It was a vital area of trade, normally crowded with large vessels bringing in cargo from overseas, or busily loading up English exports destined for the continent. On that day, however, all such vessels were ordered to clear the main thoroughfare for the queen's procession with the effect that these great ships lined the processional route, forming a guard of honour, each one unleashing rounds of gunfire as we passed and which could be heard for miles around. Even Elizabeth, protected deep within my womb, wriggled as she sensed the vibration from the cannons' fierce roar. As my ladies gasped at this thunderous noise, the finest was yet to come. Rounding the last bend at Wapping, we came within sight of the Tower from where the final explosive round of shot rang out in welcome, alerting Henry and those who waited to receive me of my imminent arrival.

As the last sonorous echoes of that cannon fire died away, first the mayor's barge, and then my own, pulled up to the landing steps. I did not know what to expect; possibly that Anne was so unpopular that few would turn out to witness her arrival! If I ever thought as much, then I was greatly mistaken. Large crowds had, in fact, gathered on the wharf that day, in front of the mighty edifice of the Tower. As I stepped ashore, I cast my eyes upwards along the southernmost wall of the Tower's defences, my attention drawn by the great, White Tower that soared up behind the curtain walls, its golden weathervanes which surmounted each of its turrets glistened in the late afternoon sun and its famously white stone walls aglow in the bright, reflected light. No matter what one's relationship with the Tower of London, whether you saw its great, omnipotent beauty, or its dark, brooding menace, it was an ancient building, which commanded unconditional respect. A fanfare of trumpets, proclaimed the arrival of Anne, Queen of England, the most beloved wife of his sovereign majesty, Henry VIII of England. It was a majestic welcome. Master Kingston, Lord Lieutenant of the Tower, stepped forward to greet me on behalf of all.

'Your Grace, London welcomes you as her undoubted queen.' Master Kingston swept a bow, followed by other officers of the Tower, next to him. Sir William then added, 'If Your Grace would follow me?' We made our way across the wharf to a second reception party, the officers of the royal household, whose representative stepped forward to proclaim their combined honour and allegiance to Queen Anne. Having graciously thanked them for their kind words, we continued towards a wooden drawbridge that spanned the outer moat of the Tower where I was greeted by the great officers of state: the elderly Earl of Shrewsbury, lord steward; Thomas Audley, the king's chancellor; William Sandys, the king's long time friend and lord chamberlain, and finally my younger cousin, Henry Howard, who was standing in for his father, my Uncle Norfolk; the latter had left England on embassy with my brother just two days previously. With great solemnity, they welcomed me, and commended themselves unto the service of their new queen. With this ceremony, I was ready to be reunited with Henry.

Led by these noblemen, and followed by the other officers of the household, the mayor, aldermen of the city and my ladies, we crossed the moat heading toward the Postern Gate of the Byward Tower. There, by the waterside stood the king, feet astride, resplendent in cloth of gold. I had chosen a shimmering gown of the same fabric, adorned with rubies and seed pearls; both of us dripping in the finest of royal jewels. As the king embraced me, placing a kiss upon my mouth and laying a hand upon my swollen belly, we must have appeared otherworldly to the common citizens of London; a fabulous sight of opulent wealth, sparkling in the midsummer sun still sailing high in a deep blue sky.

'Trusty and well beloved in God, we greet you well.' I looked out over a sea of expectant faces, not only to the men and women of gentle birth and great citizens of the city who stood around the king, but also upon the distant wharf, where the common folk of London had gathered, drawn forth by their fertile curiosity. In that moment, I sensed how much Anne wanted to be accepted and loved as their undoubted queen and the king's true wife—how much I wanted London to love her. So with all the sincerity I could muster, I forged on, 'It hath pleased the goodness of Almighty God in his infinite mercy and grace, and that of the king's majesty, who is surely the wisest and best prince in Christendom...' I paused while shouts of 'Aye' and 'God save His Majesty', rang out spontaneously from the crowd, before I continued, '...to bring unto us such great honour and joy that I find here today. My sovereign lord has always shown me inestimable benevolence, such that we have cause to give high thanks, laude and praise unto our said Maker, as we do most lowly, humbly and with all the inward desire of our heart. We undoubtedly trust that this, our good fortune, is to your great pleasure, comfort and consolation and I thank you most heartily for the great pains you have all taken this day to welcome your new queen.' Finally, a smattering of 'God save Your Grace', greeted my words and I felt a surge of joy raise me up on its lofty wings. With renewed confidence, I proclaimed, 'On Whitsunday, I shall take the coronation oath in the great Cathedral of Westminster, and I pledge my troth unto you that I shall ever be faithful toward the people of this realm, and you will ever find me constant as a just and kind queen; and faithful to her lord as long as there is breath in her body. Therefore, desiring and heartily praying unto you to give with us unto Almighty God high thanks and to pray for the good health, prosperity of the King, your sovereign lord and mine.' Then the king kissed my hand to several more cries of 'good health' and 'long life to Your Grace' that soared up from the crowd, reaching across the moat to touch my heart in a way that those people will never know. The majority had remained stubbornly silent, making those who had called out to wish me well ever more precious in my eyes.

If Henry was concerned that more of the common people did not unreservedly welcome his new wife and queen, he did not show it. Taking my hand, he led me toward the inner most sanctum of the royal fortress, passing underneath the gateway of the Byward Tower, then known as Court Gate. The clinking of metal swords and the scuffing of feet upon the cobblestones reverberated around the confined space of the gateway. Such was my happiness that I did not then think upon the great sadness that history foretold would engulf Anne barely 1,000 days later, when in the same shadow of the Court Gate, she would be brought to the Tower as a prisoner. Overwhelmed by the bitterest sense of betrayal and blind terror, Anne would collapse upon the floor, begging those lords who had accompanied her to seek the king's mercy.

Oh, how different it had all been back then! I emerged from that gateway the king's most beloved wife and mother of the heir to the Tudor throne. The next four days were to be the most incredible of my life; I was walking in the footsteps of giants. Anne was the early summer queen, creating history that would last for an eternity.

The sultry, summer afternoon cast long shadows as Henry and I approached the massive Cold Harbour Gate guarding the entrance to the royal apartments. It was a formidable structure with two round towers dwarfing the central gateway. Normally austere and unforgiving in appearance, they looked much changed that day as two enormous brightly coloured banners hung from each turret, one bearing the king's coat of arms and the other Anne's white falcon badge. Despite my uneasiness at once again being firmly within the embrace of the Tower walls, I was somewhat giddy with excitement to see the rebuilt and remodelled apartments which lay within, for no one in my modern day life knew exactly what they had looked like in their glory days. When Henry and I had last seen them under construction, the inner ward had been hive of industry, strewn with paraphernalia of the workmen's trade, yet the sight that awaited us as we emerged from under the shadow of the great gate was very different and beautifully enchanting.

Hung from the walls of every building that faced the area known as the palace were cornucopias of flags bearing heraldic Tudor emblems, great swathes of colour fluttering gaily in the breeze, creating a joyful space full of pageantry and celebration. This palette was only added to by the striking red, black and gold uniforms of the yeoman warders, who had gathered to line the processional route to the great hall. I glanced at Henry, who smiled back, flushed with self-satisfaction at what he had created for his queen. Clearly everything was as he imagined, and I knew with one flash of Anne's beautiful black eyes that I conveyed my own heady mixture of exhilaration and gratitude. I hardly knew where to look first.

But these buildings that I stand in now, on the morning of my execution, had been borne out of a great love between a king and his lady. They symbolised the hope and faith which Henry had placed in me, and his determination that I would be accepted by the people of England as his lawfully begotten wife and queen. These walls have borne witness to Anne's greatest triumph and her pitiful tragedy. With Henry's attempts to erase the name of Anne Boleyn from history and from his conscience, after my death, these buildings, more than any other, will be tied inextricably with Anne's name and memory. In the weeks and months ahead, as my mortal body decays in the ground, so these apartments will stand as an empty monument to a love betrayed. The unbearable poignancy of Anne's life and death will be interwoven within the very fabric of this building, so much so, the king will never inhabit its rooms again.

Thus, when I paused briefly to take in the facade of the newly built queen's apartments, I noticed how pristine they looked, standing proud in the sunshine on the eastern side of the inner ward. Within 300 hundred years, all this will have disintegrated into dust and once again, I was consumed with mixed emotions; unbearable sadness for the future, yet wrestling with the exquisite joy of the present. The king was unaware of my inner turmoil and anxious to get inside, and so we entered the medieval great hall via the fine stone portico. Still at my husband's side, and in breathless anticipation, I stepped within the cool, shaded interior of Henry III's magnificent, thirteenth century hall.

Slightly longer than it was wide, the sixty feet of space was dominated by towering pillars fashioned from grey Purbeck marble; four pairs of columns supporting Gothic, stone arches, which led the eye upwards to a stunning vaulted ceiling that seemed to soar to the heavens. The heavy flagstone floor was already well worn with over 300 years of occupation, leaving polished but uneven stones.

Tired and desperately uncomfortable on account of Elizabeth, whose tiny body was pressing heavily on my bladder, I was relieved that Henry did not wish to tarry there and instead, we walked proudly in procession to the king's great watching chamber. Everywhere the palace was looking its fabulous best. The smell of fresh paint and the woody scent of newly hewn oak filled my nostrils as we passed from room to room. It was immediately clear why these lodgings had remained largely unused by Henry and his father. Contemporary living of the very wealthy had come to demand the space, privacy and access to pastimes that the Tower could no longer provide. In comparison to Henry's great houses, the rooms were cramped, with woefully little space to house the king's court and provide for its greedy appetite for leisure.

At the entrance to the king's watching chamber, Henry halted. Taking hold of my hand, he kissed it gallantly, saying,

'Madame, you no doubt need some rest and to make yourself comfortable. Master Kingston...' The king threw his words over his shoulder, bringing the constable of the Tower scuttling forward, '...show Her Grace to her apartments and see that she has all that she desires.' I watched as William Kingston nodded deferentially, whilst my husband turned his attention back to me. 'Sweetheart, I wish to parley with Master Cromwell. I want to ensure that all is ready for your procession through the city to Westminster on Saturday.' I was touched that Henry was so determined that I would be accorded every honour possible. He then kissed me softly upon the cheek, as he whispered, 'Fear not, for I will see you later, my love.' I could have interpreted Henry's words in many innocent ways, but with him standing so close, I felt an unexpected, yet familiar, frisson of sexual energy surge between us. But the king had been careful not to lie with me since I had first announced my pregnancy, terrified that he might cause me to lose the child. So with these enigmatic words, we parted company; my husband to his privy apartments beyond, and with a swish of skirts, I and my ladies followed the elderly Master Kingston to the brand new queen's apartments.

As it turned out, this room formed the first of six chambers, all of which were newly built for Anne's coronation. I was surprised at the sheer scale of the great watching chamber built in Anne's honour; it was about seventy feet by thirty feet, one-and-a-half times as long, and twice as wide, as the king's chamber. Such preference to the queen was unheard of in any of Henry's other houses. As I stood in those rooms, I realised that Henry had truly meant for his new queen to take centre stage during these celebrations. Like every great watching chamber though, there was precious little furniture to adorn it. Instead, as ever with these large, public rooms, it was the fabulous soft furnishings, the painted frieze running around the top third of the walls, and the elaborate moulded and painted fretwork of the ceiling that gave it its magnificence.

In short order, we passed two of Henry's bodyguards standing erect at the entrance to Anne's presence chamber. This room ran at right angles to the last. I remember how a blaze of golden sunlight had fallen in great shafts upon the black and white checkerboard floor from a large window positioned high above the dais, at the western end of the hall. Built at the same time that the great refurbishment of Whitehall was well underway, just a couple of miles away, it was unsurprising that the two interiors closely resembled one another. Despite my determination to maintain a dignified poise until I was within my privy chamber, in my excitement, I was compelled to pause, causing our party to halt suddenly in response.

Turning about, I lifted my face in awe to the pretty gabled roof, which made for a vaulted ceiling carved from great oak beams and decorated along its length with finely sculpted heraldic emblems and mythical beasts, all brightly painted with red, blue and gold. However, it was the brilliant and sophisticated decoration of the walls which stirred the senses and underlined the fabulous wealth and status of its mistress. Running along the north and south walls were a series of tapestries depicting *The Triumph of the Gods*; whilst at each end of the chamber, oak panelling had been carved into the most stunning and intricate designs. Life-sized classical figures, angels, beasts and garlands of flowers and fruit formed a backdrop to the canopy of state, situated at the west end of the hall. Anne's coat of arms and motto, *the moost happi* dominated the decoration at the east end.

Finally, I allowed Master Kingston to continue leading the way toward my privy chamber which turned out to be another sizable room of over fifty feet in length and approximately twenty feet wide. Once again, this ran in a north-south orientation. Once within it, I was greatly relieved, for I was able to dismiss the kindly constable of the Tower and gain a much needed moment of relative privacy with my ladies.

'Thank you kindly, Master Kingston. Please arrange for refreshments, some wine and ale perhaps, to be brought for my ladies and me. I fear the heat has parched us to the bone!' William Kingston nodded his understanding, as he said,

'Of course, Madame.' I remembered what would be expected of me. Turning back, I raised my hand in a gesture of command and declared,

'Oh, and Master Kingston, I shall sup in my presence chamber this evening, so that all may see their new queen.'

'As you wish, Your Grace. I will make arrangements immediately with Lord Burgh to ensure that everything is as you require.' I smiled and nodded my appreciation as Master Kingston added, '...and if there is anything else that you need, Madame, you have but to ask and I will see to it that all is arranged. The king has commanded it so.' I watched Master Kingston take his leave, shuffling off at the speed of a man much plagued by aches and pains.

Yes, back then, I needed only to click my fingers and the world would be delivered to me on a golden platter for the king 'commanded it so'. Anne was in the summer of her life, full of abundance and light, easy, sunny days in which I wanted for nothing. I had not yet felt the chill of the encroaching winter, nor known the icy tundra of the king's immutable displeasure—as I do now. It is bittersweet indeed to have tasted such bounty, honour and happiness; to hear all about me in these very same apartments that once lauded my great estate, ghostly echoes of laughter, chatter and melodies that once told of Anne's triumph—and which shall never be heard here again.

Barely three weeks away from mid-summer, the sun began to sink beneath the horizon at around half past nine in the evening. Standing in my privy closet, I watched the sky change colours as the light faded; a wash of gentle hues of pink, grey and orange rapidly morphing toward the night's inky blackness, pricked with a myriad of iridescent stars. My closet was at the northern end of the queen's apartments, adjoining my privy bedchamber, a part of the palace that abutted against the south-east corner of the White Tower and the eastern end of the Jewel House. A solitary window at first floor level allowed me to observe the comings and goings in the inner courtyard below. A number of lighted torches were already set into brackets at the entrance to the great hall, whilst its windows were pleasantly illuminated by the glow of candles and torches already lit within. I watched silently as shadowy figures, indistinct in the gathering gloom, came and went from the hall; some heading toward the Cold Harbour Gate, others who had been deemed of sufficient standing, returning to their lodgings on the western side of the precinct.

After Henry and I arrived at the Tower, the rest of the court followed us, and the tiny palace complex was soon abuzz with activity. To honour the occasion, I dined in public in my presence chamber, attended by the great ladies of the land including, the Countesses of Surrey, Derby and Worcester. Afterwards, there was music and dancing. However, I soon took my leave as I was only too aware of the great number of events which were planned for the morrow, and the need to conserve my strength.

The following day, at dinner, there was to be a great banquet held in my privy chamber for nineteen gentlemen, all of whom were to be created Knights of the Bath in an ancient ceremony that would begin that evening and conclude the following morning. Afterward, a further forty-six Knights of the Sword were to be created and was to finish shortly after midday on the Saturday, when I was to then go in solemn procession through the City of London to Westminster. Master Cromwell informed me that I would be received in great estate at Westminster Hall, before withdrawing to spend the evening with the king at Whitehall Palace in advance of Sunday, the day of Anne's coronation.

'Your Grace, I have the parchment and ink that you require.' It was Joan speaking. She had interrupted my thoughts and I turned to face her with a smile. Around me that evening, I had commanded the presence of Joan, Nan and Margery, the women I loved well and whose enduring love and loyalty for me finally allowed me to relax away from the insatiable curiosity of the court. In the privacy of my innermost chambers, with great relief, I shed my heavy gown, and was dressed in a fine nightshirt worn underneath a luxurious, full-length, grey, velvet nightgown, the sleeves much puffed at the shoulders and the collar turned and furred with sable. My hair hung loose about my shoulders. As I moved over to the desk, to write the letter that longed to be penned, I swept my hair to one side, so that it twisted about on itself and cascaded over my left breast in loose curls. Joan laid the paper and quill in front of me, curtsying as I said,

'Thank you, Joan.' I paused before enquiring, 'Are you attending on me tonight?'

'Yes, Madame, Nan and I are due to sleep in your chamber.' If I had not known Joan so well, if I had not spent so much time in her company, I would have easily missed the great well of sadness in her eyes. Since her return to court a month earlier, I had watched how deep, unbearable grief haunted her. Several weeks after giving birth to her first son, Arthur, in early February, the tiny infant had died suddenly, leaving her entirely bereft. I knew that Joan's belief in the will of God ran deep, and so she handed over the great weight of her loss into His hands. Although death was a more frequent visitor in Tudor England than in my modern day life, I still watched her struggle with her grief, acutely aware of how my goodly belly reminded my friend daily of her loss.

I reached over and took hold of Joan's hand, squeezing it and conveying silently how keenly I recognised her pain, as I replied,

'I am glad that you and Nan are with me tonight.' I paused before adding, 'Please prepare my bedchamber, for as soon as I have finished with this letter, I will sleep. I am truly exhausted.' Momentarily, I thought of Henry, and his earlier promise to come to my chambers. As he had not appeared, I assumed that business had kept him occupied elsewhere. In truth, my weariness mollified any irritation that I might have otherwise felt at the king's broken promise. Besides, I had other things on my mind. I was missing George terribly, although I spoke of it to no one. I knew that the king's command was law, and although I had argued for a delay in my brother's departure, I acquiesced to Henry's wishes with good grace. There had been great sense in it.

English intelligence had learned that a date had been set for a meeting between the King of France and the Pope. Henry was determined that English interests should be represented and consequently, a rather hasty departure of an English embassy was required. While he wished the premier nobleman in the land, my Uncle Norfolk, to convey the weight of the king's concern, my brother had also been picked out to accompany him. This was not surprising as George had already emerged as one of the most talented linguists and diplomats at court. Furthermore, being my much beloved brother, Henry trusted him implicitly to represent our interests. It also helped that the French king had grown fond of this most courteous and accomplished English nobleman, who happened to share Francis' taste in wine, women and high culture.

I had just lifted my quill to begin to write to my Lord Rochford, when the door to my chamber opened and Margery entered,

'Your Majesty, the king's grace is here to see you.' My friend stepped aside, holding the door open, whilst at the same time curtsying as Henry swept into the room. I rose to my feet, and Joan and I did likewise in honour of the king.

'Ladies.' Henry acknowledged both Joan and Margery with a nod of his head. I knew immediately that he was in an affable mood, for Henry was a man who wore his heart upon his sleeve in the presence of his subjects. 'You may leave us.' Both of my friends dipped a second curtsy before leaving the room, eyes downcast in silence, as the door closed gently behind them. Henry turned his attention to me, crossing the room to take me immediately in his arms, 'Are you well, my love?'

he asked softly, holding me close, my head buried into his broad chest.

'Very well, thank you, Your Grace,' I replied. With my cheek still pressed against the soft velvet of the king's jerkin, I felt my senses aroused by the familiar aroma of lavender and orange flower water that was used to scent Henry's clothes, and which by then, I automatically associated with our physical intimacy.

'I am worried that I have asked too much of you when you are already great with child. These next three days will demand great stamina—and I can see that you already look tired.' The king's voice was incredibly tender, full of concern. However, I was fiercely determined that I would not let Henry—or Anne—down. I lifted my head to look up into his eyes, stating defiantly,

'I am quite well, Your Grace; as is our child. You need not worry about us; although, I am most grateful for Your Majesty's care and concern.' As I spoke, Henry allowed his eyes to roam across my face, running his own hand through Anne's silken mane, twisting her curls somewhat absent-mindedly around his hand. I was unsure as to whether he was reflecting upon my words, or whether his mind had wandered elsewhere. Henry sighed, closing his eyes and leaning in, so that our bodies were as close as my swollen belly would allow. With his forehead resting gently against mine, he whispered,

'Oh God, Anne, I have missed you so!' I knew that the king referred to the sexual drought we had both experienced as a result of his self-imposed celibacy. Without further words, we began to kiss; delicate, hesitant brushes of our lips, one against the other at first, then yielding ourselves gradually to the well of passion that had simmered beneath the surface for the previous six months. Almost breathless, and in between kisses that were becoming progressively more searching, Henry panted, 'I need you Anne…I need you…but…I am so…afraid that…I will…harm…our child.' Then, he pulled away momentarily and declared with great solemnity, 'I would never forgive myself if you lost the child on account of my actions.'

Suddenly, I was no longer tired. Henry's expressed desire for me had unleashed a rush of my own hungry energy, and with a seductive tilt of my head and an alluring smile, I took the king's hands in mine; stepping slowly backwards, never taking my eyes from his, I drew him forth toward the bed chamber, and with breathless urgency whispered,

'Fear not my lord, for this child is safe within my belly.' I could see the king's mixed emotions play out their drama across his face, and in every sinew of his body. He so wanted to believe me, yet, his natural caution held him back. But Anne's sexual potency was as irresistible as any force of nature, and gradually Henry's remaining defences crumbled, as he yielded himself to me gladly.

My husband worshipped my pregnant body with more awe and reverence than I had yet experienced. Our love had indeed been tender and full of the greatest respect. This carried us through the night on a flight of silken wings, until the dawn heralded a new day of celebration and ancient ritual, with Anne—the icon of majesty—at the centre of it all.

Chapter Nineteen

The Tower of London,
30 May 1533

It was the most beguiling of spaces, incredibly romantic and beautiful in its simplicity. Located in the south-east corner, on the second floor of the 500 year old White Tower, the Norman chapel of St. John was without doubt a jewel in the Tower's crown. From the moment I stepped across its threshold, I was riveted by its charm; the walls that had seen so much history whispered to me of the great mystery of human life. On that Friday morning at eight o'clock, the court gathered in the place that once served as William the Conqueror's chapel for mass to give thanks to God for the long life and good health of the king and queen, and to prepare for the day's ritual purification of those gentlemen who were to be created Knights of the Bath.

As I listened to the dean of the chapel royal preach his sermon, my eyes roamed appreciatively taking in the elegant architecture of this Romanesque building. Built from white stone imported from France, it had a tunnel-vaulted nave with an eastern apse and groin-vaulted aisles. Twelve thick, round pillars supported unmoulded arches, with simple carvings of scallop and leaf designs around the top of each pillar providing the only decoration. I raised my eyes even further upwards; encircling the nave on the third floor level was a gallery formed by a secondary series of rounded arches once used by the ladies of the court to view the services below. In the centre of the east apse, an altar was decorated with the finest of Henry's gold plate and a large, bejewelled, golden cross.

I cast a glance across at Henry, who was listing intently to the preacher's words, before turning my attention to the play of light coming from the early morning sun which cast its final, bewitching spell over this sacred space, throwing the altar into shadowy relief, but setting ablaze the cloth of gold and the banners of chivalry that were hung about the chapel. I also remember being somewhat confounded by the fact that despite having visited the Tower on several occasions in my modern day life, I had paid scant attention to this treasure of immeasurable beauty.

Such thoughts naturally led me back to my modern day life; a life which was fast becoming somehow otherworldly, as if I had once acted in a drama that was not my own. I thought of Daniel and his last text, but they seemed so distant and unrelated to my everyday Tudor life that emotionally, I could find no footing in them. It was clear to me that whatever portal I had passed through to bring me into the sixteenth century remained firmly closed. I sensed nothing of a different paradigm reaching out its tentacles to draw me back across time. In truth, I was glad of it, as I was savouring Anne's life at the pinnacle of her triumph. Mesmerised by my own fairytale, I resolutely refused to face the realities of my own complex and difficult life. In a sense, I had borrowed Anne's life, as it seemed so much more compelling than my own; she had everything that I dreamed of, and I became lost in a fantasy whose sinister side would all too soon become apparent.

When mass ended, Henry and I processed out of the chapel and went our separate ways. I desired to take the air and explore the palace gardens, and so with several of my ladies in attendance, the rest of the morning was ours to enjoy before the formal celebrations commenced later that day. There was much chatter and light-hearted laughter as our colourful party emerged into the pleasant May sunshine. There was also much gossip about my chambers which was predominantly of the gallant gentlemen who were to be honoured that day with the second highest order of chivalry, after that of the famous Knights of the Garter. Many were married, but that did not preclude several of my maids swooning at the thought of such handsome young men being stripped and bathed in a ceremony of ritual purification. To heighten the sense of mystery further, there was the prospect of the solitary, and rather romantic all-night vigil, which was to be held by each man in his own specially prepared chamber in the White Tower. Only the advent of dawn would finally see them emerge transformed into a heroic knight of the realm.

In true form, Elizabeth, Countess of Worcester, had much to say on the matter; bawdy comments and lascivious gestures shared discreetly within our little band, made many of us laugh out loud; whilst Grace Parker, Madge Shelton and Lady Mary all giggled and blushed furiously at her outrageousness. There was much excitement to see two of these gentlemen, Francis Weston and Grace's young husband, Henry Parker, at leisure in the gardens, along with their companions, Master Thomas Wyatt and Sir Henry Norris. As we approached, I mused on how Tom Wyatt had been much about court of late, having been sworn to the Privy Council earlier that year. It seemed that the king had finally forgiven his former rival in love, and for his part, it became clear that Master Wyatt had exhausted his passionate pursuit of Anne. Much to my relief, he seemed content to fulfil the role of loyal courtier and friend.

'Ladies, it seems we have company.' I said brightly as we neared the gentlemen. All four had seen our coming and greeted my arrival with the removal of their caps and elegant bows. Master Wyatt spoke first,

'Your Majesty, ladies.' and then continued, 'Whilst Mother Nature staggers us with her exquisite beauty…' Thomas swept his arm open wide, pointing to the profusion of May blossom that had burst forth from every flower bed, '…she cannot compare to such beauty and grace as I surely see before me now.' I smiled, graciously accepting Thomas' poetic words of chivalry; somewhat abashed by the compliment, I heard Mistress Shelton giggle behind me.

Madge was a young girl of just seventeen, the youngest daughter of my Aunt Anne on my father's side. She was neither betrothed nor married. Appointed to my household just two months previously, she rapidly attracted considerable attention from various gentlemen at court. Indeed, Mistress Shelton was fast becoming famed as possessing considerable beauty. She was undoubtedly a fair damsel bursting forth into her first flush of womanhood. In appearance, Madge was of average height, slim with becoming curves, had a pretty dimpled face set against strawberry blond hair and stunning blue eyes. If these assets were insufficient to capture a man's heart, then her gentle countenance and soft speech won her many, additional plaudits. I looked over my shoulder, playfully winking at my charge. This set considerable mirth about my ladies, before I turned back to the gentlemen, playing with them somewhat flirtatiously, I retorted,

'Master Thomas, you are as gallant as ever, and we love you dearly for it.' I then indicated with a nod of my head toward the vellum-bound book in Tom's hand, enquiring, 'Pray tell me though, what are you doing?' Glancing at the notebook, as if noticing it for the first time, he replied, 'We…' Master Wyatt turned to his friends, and particularly toward Francis, who was holding in his hand a very fine lute, '…are endeavouring to put some of my poetry to music, Your Grace.'

'Then gentlemen it is indeed our good fortune that we should pass by, for there can be no more noble a pursuit to while away such a pleasant summer's day. Mayhap my ladies may help you?'

'It would be an honour, Madame.' I smiled to myself, for I understood well my role as match-maker for my young maids, and saw an opportunity to put my cousin, Madge, in front of the gentle Sir Henry, who had been a widower for some three years. I held out my hand, beckoning to Thomas to hand over his book of verse, as I said,

'Cousin Madge, come hither and help Sir Henry and Master Weston with their labours.' On this occasion, Master Wyatt handed over his prose without complaint. Several years had separated this moment from the first one, in which I had stolen Thomas's work from his very own hands in the orchard at Allington Castle. We had both grown up since then, and no longer cared for childish pranks. On this occasion though, I did not look at the contents of the book, but passed it straight to Madge, who stepped forward from amongst my ladies. 'My cousin has the sweetest singing voice; perhaps gentlemen, you could compose something for our pleasure at dinner this evening?' I then cast a glance at my other ladies, as I commanded, 'Ladies, you too must take part. You may remain here whilst I parley with Master Wyatt.' I turned my attention back to Tom, who looked surprised at my obvious desire to be alone with him. However, I sensed things had changed for Thomas, and I wanted to be sure that with the cooling of his ardour, he would be finally out of harm's way should, God forbid, anything happen to Anne.

Ever gallant, Thomas inclined his head and opened his arm, indicating that my will was his command, and that he would walk with me at my pleasure. Strolling idly side by side, Thomas and I soon left the little group behind us. We crunched our way along the wide central pathway toward the two-storey, red-bricked privy wardrobe, which formed the northern boundary of the garden. On either side of the path were low wooden railings painted in purple and blue, no doubt in honour of Anne's new livery colours. Great swathes of lavender, red and white roses made for a striking theatre of blossom.

Gradually, the chatter, laughter and sound of verses being tentatively set to the gentle music of the lute faded into the background as we walked. I glanced at Thomas, so handsome in the flattering black garments he wore, and which had set off his auburn hair and luminous blue eyes to great effect. Although I had a mind to speak, it was Tom who commanded the conversation by speaking first. As ever, in private, my old friend spoke without subtlety.

'Anne... ' I realised how much I enjoyed hearing Thomas speak my name, and I did not correct him. 'Are you happy?' I smiled, looking away out over the flower beds, always amused by the simplicity of this question, which never failed to cut through to the heart of any issue. It was easy for me to speak the truth, for I sensed Anne's overwhelming happiness daily. It was something even my own scepticism could not quell. I turned back and looked Thomas in the eye saying,

'Yes, I am happy.' Thomas stared into my face for a few moments, reading the truth within my words, before it was his turn to glance away, this time shaking his head and laughing aloud.

'My God, Anne, you really are a force of nature... but tell me, you knew back then didn't you?' I cocked my head, confused by the meaning of my friend's words. 'When we were in the garden at Allington all those years ago... You knew then you were going to be Henry's wife and Queen of England. Forsooth, I had all but teased you of the fact, but you, you never doubted it. How did you know? What is it that gives you such unshakeable belief in yourself?' For the briefest of moments, I considered telling Thomas the whole truth, that I knew the future because I was **of** the future. Yet, even though Master Wyatt was a true, honest friend and loyal servant, such revelations might be construed as meddling in the dark arts of witchcraft, and on no account could I think to endanger Anne's life with such careless banter. In any event, he would never believe me. So I simply spoke of an alternative truth,

'There is nothing mysterious about it, Tom. Prior to my visit to Allington, the king had told me of his determination to free his troubled conscience of his unholy union with Katherine, and in the gardens at Hever, he asked me to marry him.' Then I added, as an afterthought, 'His grace had sworn me to secrecy for he had not yet told Katherine of his intentions.' Tom had been watching me all the while I was speaking, weighing up my words, and making connections with past conversations. In the background, I heard Madge's angelic voice breathe life into Thomas's verse, the lute yielding its sweet notes in Master Weston's accomplished hands. I turned to look over my shoulder to see my cousin reading from the verse in Thomas' note book, whilst Sir Henry paid court attentively, and Francis skilfully accompanied her. I watched the scene for a few moments in silence, before Thomas interrupted, asking me,

'Madame, I must confess that I have been much troubled over the years about something you said that day at Allington.' I cocked my head quizzically once more.

'Pray tell me, Thomas, what bothers you so?' My friend's brow furrowed in concern. Thomas glanced back toward our friends, removing his cap from his head briefly and running his hand through his hair, as if grappling with his thoughts. Eventually, he said,

'You said that things might not always be so easy... that you and I would walk through the lion's den. What did you mean, Anne? What trouble do you foresee?' Thomas must have sensed a heavy weight descend upon my shoulders, as a vague sense of panic suddenly tugged at my sensibilities. For a fleeting moment, forgetting who I was, Thomas went to extend his arm and take hold of my hand to calm my obvious distress. Suddenly remembering himself, he withdrew it just as quickly, but not without whispering, 'What is it, Anne? What could you, with your courage of a lion, possibly fear?' I slowly raised my face to look at Thomas, our gaze meeting and speaking silently of the deepest, most searching honesty imaginable. I truly was not able to speak of the odds that I knew were stacked against Anne—and those men who loved her well. With as much veracity as I was able, I said,

'Thomas, you must pray for me, and pray that this child that I carry is a healthy son.' I could not say more, but to speak of such things in this place was to conjure the spectre of death before my very eyes. I knew by the look on Thomas' face that he understood me well enough and yet, I think my reaction unnerved him. Thomas and I were never to speak of the matter again until the day before my arrest. It would be the last time I would see my friend in this lifetime.

Chapter Twenty

The Tower of London,
31 May 1533

Anne was a shimmering vision of beauty the day of the procession through the City to Westminster. I can see her reflection now in the imperfect mirror that graced my privy bedchamber, a perfect vision of celestial grace clad from head to toe in white cloth of gold, her freshly-washed hair flowing loose about her shoulders, in stunning contrast to the deep, square-cut neckline displaying her sculpted collar bones and long neck to ravishing effect.

I stood patiently as my ladies made the final adjustments to my costume, whilst Margery stepped forward with a coif fashioned in the French style and made of white silk, cross-barred with gold cord and edged with passement. She placed it carefully over my loose hair, adjusting it into position, before turning to accept a coronet of gold from Lady Bridget. I watched the circlet being passed from one lady to the next, as each admired its beauty and the many rich inlaid stones. It was Henry's express wish that, with the exception of the great crown of St Edward, all the other circlets and crowns that I was to wear over the next two days would be designed and crafted specifically for Anne. With great reverence, Margery placed it upon my head, stepping back as she said,

'Your Grace, you look truly divine; surely the people of England will behold the sight of their new queen and know that it is God's will that this has come to pass.' Margery understood that I longed to be accepted; in so many ways, Anne's life depended upon it. Although she spoke to me, I did not take my eyes from Anne's reflection. I never wanted to forget the way she looked that day. I finally replied,

'I hope it is so, Margery.' Finally, I broke away from the spell which the queen's own unique brand of beauty had cast upon me, and asked, 'Do we know when the mayor will be ready to receive me?' So great was the procession that was to carry me to Westminster, that there were some delays in arraying the two and a half mile long train that would snake its way through the cramped streets of London in Anne's honour.

'Sir Edward Baynton informed Nan that all the great ladies, and many of your ladies of honour, have been asked to take their place in the procession. Your Majesty will be called forth shortly.' I was glad for the day had begun early and it promised to go on into the evening. Mass was celebrated at eight o'clock and shortly after, in a glittering ceremony held in the great hall, Henry and I received the knights-elect who had spent the night in solitary vigil; each one stepping forth to receive their golden spurs and gilded belt, before being dubbed by the king with a ceremonial sword. To a packed hall and a great fanfare of trumpets, a further forty-seven men of gentle birth came forth and were created Knights Bachelor. A celebratory lunch followed, served with all solemnity in my dining chamber, before a brief respite allowed me to change my gown and prepare for Anne's entry into the city.

I looked at Margery and Lady Bridget, who along with Nan, Joan, Anne Savage and Lady Mary Howard remained behind to help me make my final preparations. All my ladies were dressed similarly, in crimson velvet; the deep colours of their gowns in striking contrast to my own white cloth of gold. I was about to speak, when there was a knock at my door, and we all turned to see Lady Mary enter, dip a curtsy and announce,

'Lord Burgh is here Your Grace; all is ready for you.' I nodded and, with my ladies in attendance, followed my lord chamberlain down a short flight of steps that led directly from my privy chambers into the north-eastern corner of the palace ward. It was another perfect summer's day, with the late afternoon sun casting increasingly longer shadows upon the ground. I was grateful for the canopy of cloth of gold that would be carried over my head along the route as it provided much needed shade. I certainly felt for my ladies who, in their heavy, ceremonial, velvet gowns would feel the heat and enjoy no such luxury.

It was a short walk along the northern edge of the courtyard, in front the Jewel House and the main entrance to the White Tower, where we passed under the Cold Harbour Gate. The hubbub which I had heard from within my apartments grew louder as we approached the main exit gate leading from the innermost part of the palace. Emerging from underneath it, the sight that met my eyes was truly beyond belief. The inner ward of the Tower was a veritable melee of activity, and I could see why the entire procession had taken so long to assemble. There was barely a square foot of ground which remained unoccupied! All about me was packed with people, carriages and horses that were draped in an array of rich cloths. I made my entrance to yet another fanfare of trumpets, drawing attention from all quarters as shouts of 'God Save Your Grace' echoed round the Tower's inner ward. The crowds of Londoners swallowed their misgivings and showed every outward sign of acquiescence to the king's consort.

Directly in front of where we merged was the queen's litter, resplendent in white satin and white cloth of gold. The door was open, and a set of steps covered in white velvet was positioned in front of it, in order to allow me to board easily. The litter was a wooden carriage without wheels. It was borne by two heavy poles on either side, which fitted into the harnesses of two magnificent white palfreys; one positioned in front, the other behind, each one draped to the ground with white damask. The whole effect of Anne in her litter, resplendent in white cloth of gold, created a shimmering vision of divinity amongst the deep, rich colours of those mortals who attended upon her.

I had been briefed about the procession in some detail by my lord chamberlain and Master Cromwell. I knew that extending in front of my litter were 400 plus gentlemen, walking or riding, two by two, including servants of Jean de Dinteville, the French ambassador. The French had the great honour of heading the procession, thereby proclaiming to all Anne's strong alliance with its interests. Gentlemen of the royal household came next, followed by nine judges riding in scarlet gowns. The newly dubbed Knights of the Bath followed wearing their ceremonial robes of violet with hoods of miniver, followed by council members and eminent officers of the church. Barons, earls and marquesses, including my father, all mounted on horseback followed; and directly behind this group was Henry's chancellor, Thomas Audley, who rode alone. Behind him, Edward Lee, Archbishop of York travelled beside the Venetian ambassador, whilst Thomas Cranmer, Archbishop of Canterbury, was accompanied by Jean de Dinteville himself.

The next part of the procession was within view; two squires followed Thomas Cranmer and Monsieur de Dinteville. They were attired in old-fashioned dress as the Dukes of Normandy and Aquitaine, symbolising England's ancient claims to these French territories. They preceded the Mayor of London, Master Christopher Ascue, who bore in his arms the mayor's gilded ceremonial mace, a symbol meant to protect the royal person. Finally, and immediately in front of my litter, were the two fine and somewhat imposing figures of my twenty-three year old uncle, William Howard, standing in for his brother, the Duke of Norfolk, as Deputy Earl Marshall. By his side was Charles Brandon, acting as High Constable of England; both were mounted on horseback.

Without emotion, the duke lifted his cap and nodded cordially to acknowledge my presence. I reciprocated with equal refrain. His grace and I rarely spoke unless absolutely necessary. But the old order which had once been dominated by the likes of Charles Brandon and my Uncle Norfolk was being progressively eclipsed by Anne's all-consuming influence. Younger men, men with new ideas about faith, and England's imperialist ambitions, were fashioning the vision of a different future. It was a future in which the likes of Charles Brandon suddenly seemed almost obsolete. I knew that Charles had left his dying wife to attend these celebrations at the king's express command; no doubt he resented me sorely for it. But selfishly, I cared little for the duke's pains at the time. Looking back now, he must have felt that with the demise of his wife, familiar links with the past, and happier times, were all too rapidly dissolving.

Having acknowledged the duke and others close by, I stepped forward to climb up into the queen's litter when I noticed the lone, white palfrey following immediately behind it. The horse was being led by Master William Coffin, my master of the horse, and was fitted with a white, velvet side-saddle and trapped all in white cloth of tissue. It was my beloved Starlight, who I had scarce seen since the advent of my pregnancy precluded my riding her. I went over to her immediately, allowing her to sniff the familiar scent on the back of my hand, before running my hand down her strong neck and pressing my cheek close to hers. Starlight seemed as delighted as I to be re-united, and whinnied in appreciation, pushing her nose playfully against my body. I whispered in her ear,

'My dear friend, always loyal…I am so pleased to see you here.' Starlight lifted her soft, velvety muzzle up to my face and placing the most delicate of kisses upon it, I silently bid her to enjoy the day.

I returned to climb into my litter, however, my pregnant belly made me rather too ungainly to do so unaided, and so Margery and Lady

Bridget helped me ascend and settle myself safely into the carriage. They then made their exit, for I was to travel alone in solitary splendour. Once comfortably seated, the canopy of cloth of gold, borne above me by the four barons of the Cinque Ports, was moved into place. It was a beautiful thing, ornamented at each corner by four gilded statues and four silver bells, which made the gentlest of tinkling noises once the train pressed forth. The procession set off again from the Tower. Lord Burgh slipped his horse in between my litter and Starlight, whilst following my master of the horse were seven of the most noble ladies in the land, all of whom were riding on horseback including: Lady Mary Howard and the Countesses of Surrey, Sussex, Rutland, Derby and Worcester, as well as the young Lady Maltravers, wife of Lord Maltravers, the future Earl of Arundel.

Behind them, in a second litter, were the noble ladies of estate, including Anne's step-grandmother, the fifty-six year-old Agnes, Dowager Duchess of Norfolk, and the forty-seven year-old Margaret, Dowager Marchioness of Dorset, both dressed in crimson and ermine. A second, similar chariot carried my mother, sister and two of my aunts, including the hated Elizabeth Wood, Lady Boleyn. Despite a spirited argument with my father, I was unable to banish her from the day; with her was Ann Howard, Dowager Countess of Oxford.

Seven of my ladies-in-waiting followed behind them including: Nan, Joan, Margery, Anne Savage, Grace Parker, my cousin Madge and Mary Wyatt. Two more chariots, one furnished with white cloth, the other red, came behind bearing more of my ladies and maids of honour. A great train of thirty women, dressed in velvet and silk in the colours of those great ladies upon whom they attended, snaked behind; whilst bringing up the rear was the master of the guard and attendant constables, all in velvet and damask coats, white staves of office held proudly in their hands.

To a thunderous roar of canon fire, we passed along Water Lane, under the Tower Gate and across the bridge spanning its extensive moat. As the shot echoed about the Thames, I watched a pair of mute swans that had been gliding across the water take flight, startled by the sudden explosion of gunpowder. Anne was leaving the Tower in triumph, and, as we passed under Middle Tower and onto the final causeway that lead the procession into the city, I prayed to God that neither she—nor I—would ever see this place under the shadow of the sword.

We entered Tower Street, heading north-west toward Fenchurch in the heart of the city, where the first of many fine pageants arranged for Anne's pleasure and glorification awaited us. The procession took several hours, for we stopped often so that I could listen to the many verses sung and spoken in Anne's honour, and witness the many allegorical plays which spoke both of the new queen's imperial claim as Henry's rightful consort, as well as her blossoming fertility which, through the cut of my gown, was plain for all to see. How to put into words the overwhelming excitement and joy I felt that day at being so deeply honoured. The city had gone to considerable effort; even the usually bustling, dirty Tudor streets were newly cleaned and gritted against the queen's coming. Many of the brick and timber buildings that lined the route towered above the procession, being some three, or even four, stories high. All were festooned with arras, carpets, cloth of gold, silver and other rich fabrics and banners. Others, including monuments such as the Eleanor Cross in Cheapside, had either been repainted, or hung with coats of arms that glistened with gold and flashed against the richest azure blue in the bright afternoon sunshine.

Of course, it was the people who gathered in great curiosity to see their new queen that most fascinated me. Never had I witnessed the attention of so many ordinary Londoners, with their preconceived ideas, varying religious inclinations, and social prejudices; all of whom had come to be entertained by sweet harmonies, fabulous plays and the white and red wine that flowed freely from conduits situated at various points along the route. As I was borne along those streets, rocked by the gentle sway of the palfreys that carried my litter, I looked out across the sea of faces of the common folk of London that watched me with perhaps as much curiosity as I did them. From time to time, I dipped my head to see out from under the canopy above me, to those who had packed every single, open window along the route, even those who hung dangerously from rooftops to get above the seething mass of humanity that crowded the pavements below.

There were many cries of 'God Save Your Majesty' and 'God bless Your Grace' as I passed by. But for each one who cried out in celebration, another stony face met my gaze asking, 'Who is this woman who has stolen the heart of our mighty king? What right does she have to be our queen?' I wanted to cry out to them that I was not the whore they thought me to be; that it was not my fault that Henry had fallen out of love with Katherine; that she had never borne him the son that he so desperately craved. Whether they loved me or not, I looked at each man, woman and child with as much loving countenance, grace and dignity that God and Henry would expect of me.

I even felt the hand of Henry upon the pageantry itself. Although much of the design work had been completed by Master Holbein, and the verses written by Masters Nicolas Udall and John Leyland, when we arrived at St Paul's Gate, in front of the staggeringly beautiful, eponymously named Gothic cathedral, a virgin dressed in white held a gold tablet in her hand. Upon it, written in azure letters, was the phrase, *Veni amica coronaberis* – 'Come my love! Thou shalt be crowned!' I knew it was a message from Henry and oh, how I smiled, set aglow with the warmth of his very public adoration!

If I had needed any further shoring up of my resolve, it came in the form of Thomas Cranmer, whom I could see some way out in front of my litter. The sight of the archbishop brought to mind our first meeting, when Thomas had sunk to his knees in the gallery at Whitehall, and spoke of God's will that we should, in our own way, find ourselves treading this precarious and often difficult path. The tangible memory of my friend's deep faith stirred my own, each time resulting in a wave of serenity that rippled through my body. I was glad that it would be Thomas who would set the crown upon my head on the morrow. Those kind eyes would surely carry me through any trial or tribulation that I might face in the days ahead.

Finally, at Charing Cross, my litter turned left into King Street, and we made our way slowly down the broad avenue that bisected Whitehall Palace. I was mightily relieved to be approaching the old Palace of Westminster, which lay at the southern end of King Street, a distance of a little less than a mile. I was tired, my body ached, and my bladder was sore and felt fit to burst; nevertheless, I was exhilarated. Despite my fears of Anne's outright rejection from the crowd, many of those who had welcomed me, particularly the children who had sung Anne's praise, were real enough. In their innocence, I felt their love and affection for who I was, not who they imagined me to be. It was this memory that I chose to hold in my heart.

Thus, by the time we reached Whitehall it was early evening and London was pleasantly warm, with barely the slightest of breezes. Reaching the Holbein Gate, I looked out beyond the figures of my Uncle William and Charles Brandon, who were riding to the gentle sway of their horses. I wanted to see as much as I was able of the sheer beauty of one of Whitehall's newest and most glorious of buildings. Here, the wide thoroughfare narrowed to pass through the square gateway that symbolically announced entry into the royal enclave of Whitehall and Westminster. The gate was an undoubted triumph of Renaissance architecture, terracotta roundels of classical design set against the highly decorative chequerwork, fashioned from flint and stone. It was true to say that by then I was used to the elegant Tudor architecture that surrounded me daily. But the Holbein Gate was different, it demanded one's attention, and I admired her beauty with wide-eyed bewilderment.

I thought about how different was that cold day in January, when before dawn, Anne Savage, William Brereton and I had wound our way up one of its octagonal turrets so that Anne could be married to the king. In that moment, I wanted more than anything else to see Henry at the window of the upper chamber in which we had been wed. His Majesty had left the Tower by barge earlier that day, heading for Whitehall and leaving Anne to be the centre of attention. There, he was to await my arrival, but I just knew he would not be able to resist watching the procession come forth from the city. I sensed his gaze upon me, as one does when two souls are profoundly connected, and I strained forward to catch a glimpse of the window high above us. When I saw my love looking down upon me, our eyes met and my heart soared. It was a look of longing and love which I knew could, and would, never be dissolved. Sadly, the moment was all too brief. In short order, the canopy above my head eclipsed my view of Henry—the moment passed as I was conveyed beneath the gate. The spell was broken. I was thrown back to the lilting sway of my litter, surrounded by the clinking sound of the metal trappings worn by the many horses that carried us forth, and the scuffing of their hooves upon the roadway.

We continued south along King Street to Westminster, one of the most enchanting parts of Tudor London. It was effectively set on an island, as the River Tyburn and one of its tributaries flowed into the Thames on either side of the site. Thus, Westminster was connected to the mainland on the north, south and west by several bridges, encircled on three sides by open countryside; on the east side, the Palace abutted the Thames. Almost as ancient as London itself, the abbey and palace retained large, green spaces, wide thoroughfares and pretty ornamental gardens. Unlike the cramped streets of the city, the air was sweet and clean, so unlike the modern day Parliament Square, which stands on the same site and which I knew well from my other life. This square, which is England's modern day seat of government, is always a noisy, polluted place, besieged daily by traffic, demonstrators and tourists. I felt greatly saddened for the loss of this most dignified and tranquil of spaces.

Despite these fleeting thoughts, I was enraptured by the moment, holding my breath in anticipation as my litter was finally conveyed under the two-storey gate that opened up into the paved yard, in front of the old palace. It was already thronged with the great length of the procession that had come before me. Just as it was at the Tower, this outer ward was also a riot of colour and sound. My attention rested upon this for only a few moments as I was captivated by what lay beyond, by the ancient and majestic buildings of the abbey and palace which towered over us all.

The outer yard was, in essence, a huge courtyard which ran from the king's steps by the river on the east, to the great gateway through which I entered on the west. The whole area was enclosed by relatively modest, yet fine stone, brick, or wattle and daub buildings along its northern edge, whilst the magnificent facade of Westminster Palace ran along the south. I was facing an impressive range of stone buildings directly to my right. These were raised to two storeys and ran along at least half of the southern length of the yard. Like almost all of the palace, and the abbey alongside it, they were fashioned from fine, white stone, the roofs were pitched and crenellated in parts, chimneys and turrets rising into the sky. This particular range contained England's office of the Auditors of Foreign Accounts; at its centre, another beautiful gateway led through to the palace's inner ward, and the entrances to the privy palace apartments that lay beyond.

To the left of this range was the splendid, and probably the most impressive, building of the palace complex, Westminster Hall. Almost

242

rebuilt by King Richard II in the late fourteenth century, at 240 feet long, nearly 70 feet wide and just under 100 feet tall at the apex, the hall dwarfed many of the surrounding buildings. Like the abbey, it was a masterpiece of medieval architecture, a triumph and testament to man's ingenuity, creativity and spirit. I reflected upon how honoured I was to behold the sight of Tudor Westminster, this long lost jewel of England; the very cradle of the of the kingdom's civilisation, the seat of government, law and finance. I was grateful that Westminster Hall and the Abbey of St Peter stood indomitable, against even the blistering assault of the Luftwaffe during England's 'darkest hour' in the Second World War. They had been scarred, but not lost, and for this I said a prayer of thanks that day. Simply nothing could compare to seeing the glory of medieval Westminster with my own eyes. I truly thanked God for that blessing.

It had been a long road from the rose gardens at Hever, but finally, Anne had found her way to the very centre of England's power. As dusk began to settle over the land, I slipped out through the queen's apartments to make my way by barge to Whitehall. England prepared herself for the morrow and the most sacred anointing of its new queen.

Nan threw open the window to my bedchamber so that the joyful sound of the day's dawn chorus would rouse me from my sleep. I turned my face somewhat sleepily toward the light, the east-facing windows ablaze with the glory of the morning sun; it was to be the perfect day. I stretched out my arms languidly, filled with a sense of great serenity and expectation, yet I could not remember quite why I should feel so elated. Then, the wonder and excitement of what lay ahead of me exploded into my consciousness. I yawned amidst an enormous smile as I said to my friend,

'Oh, Nan, is it really true? Am I to be crowned this day? Nan came over to my bedside, bobbed a curtsy and replied,

'Indeed Madame, 'tis surely true; it is the king's will—and God's. His Grace will be so proud of you today!' I looked down toward my swollen belly, running my hand in smooth circular motions over its surface. Elizabeth was already sensing my excitement. I could feel her perfectly formed, healthy body kicking with her little feet in tune with my own stirring emotion. I suddenly felt overwhelmed, not just for the day, but for this little life that was already so inextricably intertwined with my own; a tear raced down my cheek. 'Oh, Your Grace is something wrong? Have I said something to upset you?' Nan was visibly alarmed by the tears that welled up in my eyes. Lifting myself up, half laughing I said,

'Nan, worry not, I think it is just my condition which makes me prone to cry at the slightest thing!' I then turned toward my friend, smiling and taking her hands in mine. Through my laughter, I said, 'Surely you will know it soon for yourself!' I knew that Nan would in time be the mother to a large family of twelve children. At the suggestion, she glowed demurely as I knew how much she already craved motherhood. Suddenly, the door to my bedchamber opened, and Margery and Lady Bridget entered with great purpose, bringing an end to our discussion. I knew there was to be no more tarrying. There was a great deal to do to prepare Anne for what was ahead and very little time in which to accomplish it all. I watched Margery's brow furrow in concern at my bloodshot eyes and tearstained cheeks. Before she had chance to say anything, I raised my hand anticipating the question.

'Do not concern yourself, Margery. All is well. This flood of emotion was merely a moment of great happiness, knowing that my sovereign lord is to honour me so highly today. You must forgive me,' I said as I placed a hand upon my belly. 'I was explaining to Nan how being with child heightens one's senses in the most peculiar way.' As an experienced mother, Margery smiled knowingly. 'But there is much to do, ladies. After I have eaten, I wish to bathe before I dress.' Margery nodded her acknowledgement, then turned to leave and supervise the bringing forth of a tun of hot water and linen to be arranged within my raying chamber in front of a well stoked fire. I then said, 'Lady Bridget, perhaps you could attend to my nails while I bathe and Nan, fetch my tweezers.' I had long since realised that Anne and her contemporaries placed considerable emphasis on grooming, enough to match the attention they paid to the elegance of their clothes. As Queen, Anne owned several particularly fine manicure sets made of bone and embellished with coloured enamel and gold; in addition, tweezers were used to maintain the fashionable arched eyebrows which are still in vogue in my modern day life. In such matters, I was entirely at home.

My ladies and I normally used these times of physical intimacy to chat and share gossip about all the latest comings and goings at court. However, the great solemnity of the day created an atmosphere of reverence in the queen's apartments, and my ladies worked efficiently in hushed whispers, with little fuss or chatter. Perhaps they had taken my lead, for I too found myself inclined to silence and inner reflection. As I sunk into the warm, scented bath, I laid my head back against the pillow balanced there for my comfort; the fire keeping me warm against any chill. I commanded that the window of my raying chamber be opened wide. I wished to soar on the sweet scent of summer that wafted gently in on the most delicate of breezes, and to be lulled by the great bells of Westminster Abbey, which had already begun their seemingly endless song of celebration in anticipation of the queen's coronation.

In my mind, I found myself floating between two planes: on the earthly plane, my concern was to rehearse all that would be expected of me that day. Master Cromwell, my Lord Chamberlain and indeed, Henry himself, had walked me through every painstaking element of the ceremony in which I would be expected to play my part. There had been no rehearsal in the abbey, instead an enchanting and entirely accurate miniature model of the abbey church and Westminster Hall had been fashioned, so that I could see how each element of the day would unfold. I knew Anne must be a vision of serene majesty, and I assiduously committed every detail to her sharp, incisive memory.

On a higher plane, in the realm of the Gods, the Good Lord was drawing me forth to take my place amongst those few souls anointed by His will to rule upon this Earth. I silently prayed that whatever may come to pass on either this day or beyond, that I would find the strength and courage to bear both this enormous privilege and burden with grace, wisdom and dignity. As I thought on these things, I became aware of Lady Bridget, who was kneeling at the side of my bath, massaging my hand, which was draped languidly over its edge. Bridget was so young and yet sadly, I alone knew from my knowledge of all that was to come that she had little time left in this world. Whilst a handful of ladies came and went from my chamber, I shared a solitary moment with Lady Bridget as I asked,

'Tell me, Bridget, are we after all perfect friends again?' The question took my friend by surprise, as she paused briefly, her eyes remaining downcast, before finally she raised them, her gaze meeting mine. She smiled sweetly enough and yet, from the merest moment of hesitation, I knew that the words which followed were not the truth.

'Of course, Your Majesty. Why should we not be?' My gaze lingered upon her face, but all too soon Bridget turned her attention back to her work, and I knew then that there was nothing that I could do to completely heal the rift between us. We would never speak of the matter again, and I would never hear of Bridget's displeasure until many, many months later when she would speak to me from beyond the grave, by those who would use her words against me.

It was a short journey by barge from the privy steps at Whitehall to the queen's stair, nearly half a mile upstream to the Palace of Westminster. Shortly after half past eight in the morning, accompanied by ten of my ladies-in-waiting, we alighted ashore, passing through the

queen's privy apartments toward Westminster Hall. The entire court and prominent gentlemen of the city had been assembling there since seven in the morning to await the queen's arrival.

As I approached the Hall via a gallery connecting it with the magnificent St Stephen's Chapel, I heard the hum of the expectant crowd grow louder. I paused just before the entrance, my right hand resting gently against the cool stone of the elaborate portico that led to the great chamber directly beyond. Momentarily, I needed to steady myself as adrenaline coursed through my body. From nowhere my heart began to thunder in my chest, and for the briefest of moments, I felt that my legs would be unable to carry me into the Hall. I laid my left hand gently upon my belly, there was something grounding about feeling my child as she squirmed inside me, so in tune with the nervous excitement that gripped every fibre of my being.

'Your Grace, are you well?' It was Lady Mary Howard who was concerned at my hesitation. I smiled reassuringly for I was quite well. I knew that what lay before me that day would test my endurance to the limit, but Anne had been preparing herself for this moment for six long years, and no earthly, transient discomfort would detract from her moment of triumph. So, I pulled myself up to my full height, and with a deep breath stepped forth into the hall to a fanfare of trumpets.

Even when I see the Hall stripped bare in my modern day life, it remains one of the most omnipotent of buildings, its majestic grandeur dwarfing even the enormous crowds that throng within it daily. Thankfully, the fine tapestries and rich fabrics, which were hung about its great stone walls, absorbed some of the sound from the trumpets which echoed loudly, filling the chamber with the announcement of my arrival. At the high end of the Hall, a dais that was raised high upon twelve steps, dominated the space. It was to be my stage, and from the moment I stepped upon it, Anne's performance was flawless.

I swept into the great chamber and approached the raised platform, lifting my skirts with both hands and ascended to the top so that I was visible to all who had gathered there that morning. As I stood under the canopy of estate, looking out over a court that had come forth to honour me, I remained a vision of regal splendour, my ladies arranging the long train of my coronation robes about me. These robes were as tradition dictated; a purple velvet gown, furred with ermine set against a kirtle fashioned from cloth of gold. My hair was left loose about my shoulders, and upon my head, I wore the same coif and coronet as I had done the day before. Agnes, the Dowager Duchess of Norfolk stepped forward and knelt at my feet as I offered her first my right foot and then my left, allowing the duchess to remove my purple velvet shoes, for I had insisted I would walk barefoot to the altar in an ancient act of reverence and humility.

I remained motionless as a great train of men from the King's Chapel, the monks of Westminster, and diverse bishops and abbots filed into the Hall in solemn procession. They had come from the Abbey to collect me and take me to my coronation. In their finely embroidered copes and mitres, carrying their golden crosses and crosiers, the gentlemen of the church swayed gently in unison toward me, treading reverently upon the blue carpet that brought them afore me.

When in place, the king's Officers-at-Arms commanded the procession to set forth to the Abbey; first came gentlemen, squires and knights, followed by the aldermen of the city, then the judges, all dressed in their scarlet robes. When they disappeared into New Palace Yard beyond the great northern doors of the Hall, barons and viscounts in their scarlet parliamentary robes followed, with England's nobility coming behind, walking in pairs; earls, marquesses and dukes in their crimson robes of estate, all furred with ermine and powdered according to their degrees.

In good order, the men of the king's chapel and the monks of Westminster began to process, following behind Henry's Lord Chancellor, Thomas Audley, each one chanting songs of God in my honour as they went. The last of the monks were followed outside by those abbots and bishops called forth to celebrate this day, amongst them, the Bishops of York, Bath, Lincoln and St Asaph. Of course, not all of the religious men present that day prayed for Anne and all she represented; John Stokesley, the Bishop of London and my old acquaintance from my days at Hever, Stephen Gardiner, by then the Bishop of Winchester, were both staunch Catholics and bowed reluctantly to the king's will. How perverse then that these two gentlemen, who hated and reviled me, were obliged to walk at my side, as custom required, as I entered the Abbey that day.

Finally, I was to take my place in the procession. I stepped down from the dais, my skirts raised so that Anne's delicate feet could feel their way safely to the ground. I took up my position beneath the same gold canopy of the Cinque Ports that had been carried over me the day before; John Stokesley and Stephen Gardiner stepped forward to take up their traditional positions as Bishops of London and Winchester on either side of their queen. Several metres in front of me, the newly married Henry Grey, Marquis of Dorset carried the Sceptre of Gold, whilst the twenty-one year old Earl of Arundel held the Sceptre of Ivory, topped with a dove to symbolise the Holy Spirit. Behind them, Charles Brandon suddenly appeared afore me, carrying St. Edward's Crown.

It was the first time that I had laid eyes upon this ancient crown, which was already five hundred years old and had reputedly sat upon the head of one of England's last Saxon kings. Inside, my cool reserved was fractured as I could not help but stare at such a thing of beauty; a thing which was so cruelly lost to the nation during the English Civil War when Oliver Cromwell had it melted down for money. My eyes lingered longingly upon its form, for I knew that after that day, I would never see it again.

I remember so clearly walking along, the soles of my feet sensitive to the fine texture of the silky carpet and every slight undulation of the stone pavement beneath them. It was cool within the Hall, yet as I approached the great north doors, which were swung wide open to receive me, I felt the warm air from outside brush gently against my cheek, as we emerged into bright light of New Palace Yard. The clock tower set almost directly opposite chimed the hour; it was nine o'clock in the morning and despite the early hour, the sun was already warming the Earth. Westminster looked resplendent in the sunshine, bedecked with colourful banners and flags, whilst above the sweet harmonies of the great bells of Westminster Abbey continued to ring out for Anne Boleyn whose time had finally come.

Set against the towering edifice of the Abbey that looked down upon us all, it had been impossible to prepare myself for how emotional I would feel that day. I had no choice but to keep my eyes focused forward and steel myself against the tsunami of emotion that constantly threatened to overwhelm me and choke me with tears of joy and pride.

The journey from Westminster Hall to the western entrance of the

Abbey took no more than five minutes, passing firstly beneath the shadow of the Great Gate at the southern end of King Street, before turning left and sweeping by the northern facade of the Abbey to reach its main, western entrance. With great reverence, we were drawn inside the womb of this most sacred of buildings by yet another great fanfare of trumpets, whilst sacred music called to God himself to bear witness to my arrival at the heart of his church, already packed to capacity with the great and good of the kingdom. Of course, I had been inside this most treasured building upon many occasions in my modern day life; yet nothing had prepared me for how beautiful the Abbey looked that day; how small and yet how blessed I felt. I was just one mortal woman about to kneel at the feet of God and be anointed with immortality.

Moving in solemn procession, I entered the Abbey passing through the quire where the voices of the boys and gentlemen of the King's Chapel and the monks of Westminster suddenly rang out in soaring harmony, an exaltation of 'Anna Regina'. I swallowed hard against the tears that stung at the back of my eyes. Directly in front of me was the high altar at the heart of the sacrarium, and afore this was erected a scaffold covered in arras. At its centre stood the two hundred-year-old wooden coronation chair of King Edward I, a chair which was already steeped in the mystique of the English monarchy. With the Bishops of Winchester and London at my side, I mounted the steps of the scaffold assisted by two of my ladies, to take my place where a lineage of kings had been anointed and crowned before God.

In front of me, the high altar was resplendent in shimmering gold. To the north of the altar were three, fine medieval tombs of knights in repose, whilst to the south were the traditional sedilia where several of the officiating priests had already seated themselves. Beyond the high altar, I could see part of the tomb of St Edward the Confessor surrounded by seven great Gothic arches of the eastern apse. Once more, my eyes were drawn skywards, this time to the decorated gallery that ran around the apse above the vaulted arches. Over the central arch, the elaborate open window had been in-filled with gilded latticework. I could not see beyond, but I knew that Henry was looking down upon me, his love and his queen. As ever, he was observing all from behind the scenes, this time in the company of the French and Venetian ambassadors.

My attention returned to Thomas Cranmer, who was completing the very first part of the ceremony. I knew my cues by heart, even though the entire service was conducted in Latin. With Cranmer's closing words of prayer, I rose to my feet and walked forward to the altar, still barefoot, like a penitent child before a merciful father. A cushion had been laid upon the floor and I sank to my knees before the golden cross that was standing upon the high altar. On account of my swollen belly, I was unable to lay myself entirely prostrate and face down upon the floor, as tradition required. Instead, I stretched my arms and fingers out in front of me upon the ground, reaching forward as far as I was physically able, my forehead touching the cold stone of the sanctuary's floor. I could not believe I was experiencing this most sacred and mystical of moments and felt truly touched by the Holy Spirit. With such emotion coursing through me, a single tear welled up, before it ran down my cheek and splashed upon the ancient Cosmati pavement below me. I was glad that my good friend, the Archbishop of Canterbury, continued to say prayers evoking the Grace of God over me for some time before eventually, and once again in control of my emotions, I rose to my feet. Two of my ladies stepped forward and unfastened the purple surcoat that had hung about my shoulders, slipped my shoes back upon my feet and removed my coronet and coif from my head. About my body was tied the plain, white anointing gown, before I took my place once again in King Edward's Chair.

I knew that we were upon the most sacred part of the ceremony as Thomas Cranmer stepped forward accompanied by William Boston, the Abbot of Westminster. In his left hand he carried the golden, eagle-shaped ampulla containing the sacred oil which would anoint me, while in his right was the golden spoon into which the oil would be poured. It was a moment of great intimacy between us. I looked into his eyes and saw there the greatest love and admiration a sovereign could wish for. For a fleeting moment there was the faintest of smiles playing upon his lips, before he extended his right hand, pouring the oil from the spoon first upon my hands, then my forehead and finally, my breast. This so done, Thomas handed the ampulla and spoon to the Abbot of Westminster, before he raised his right hand above me, and made the sign of the cross, blessing me as England's newly anointed Queen.

As Thomas stepped aside, I rose again to my feet. My ladies also moved forward, this time removing the anointing robe and dressing me first in a white undergarment of fine linen over which was placed a long coat of gold silk trimmed with gold lace and fashioned with wide, flowing sleeves; it was a sumptuous piece, lined with rose-coloured silk and richly embroidered on its exterior with various heraldic emblems. These gowns were heavy enough, but there was more to come. I was then invested with the royal robe, an outer garment fashioned as a four-square mantle; it was lined in crimson silk and decorated with silver coronets, heraldic emblems and silver imperial eagles in each of the four corners. This done, I sat down again and was presented, each in turn, by all the great symbols of sovereignty; golden spurs denoting chivalry, the orb symbolising Christ's rule over the world, and a ring which was placed upon my finger to signify my marriage to England.

All the time, I remained outwardly impassive, yet inside the fluttering of my stomach set my baby wriggling in my womb. I silently blessed my unborn child, and the life which awaited him. Yes, I confess that some part of me still foolishly clung onto the hope that I carried the King's son. I asked God to protect him and make him a mighty sovereign, and prayed for Anne, for her life and for a happy ending.

Lost in my own reverie, I returned abruptly to the present moment. Before me, Thomas Cranmer was already holding the Crown of St. Edward between his hands and I saw its brilliance flash right before my eyes. I kept those eyes firmly fixed ahead, as Thomas raised the crown high above me for all to see, before lowering it reverently to place it snugly upon my loosely flowing hair. Then, one after the other, the Sceptre of Gold was delivered into my right hand, the rod of ivory with the dove into my left. It was done; Anne was anointed and crowned as queen, and the choir came alive singing a *Te Deum* in thanks to God. Oh, how beautiful it had been but oh, how heavy the crown had felt upon my head! I admit that with the *Te Deum* over, I was greatly relieved when Thomas stepped forward and removed it, replacing it with a glittering, but smaller and lighter, crown that Henry had commissioned for me alone.

A Solemn Mass was then celebrated with the liturgy sung in Latin and during which, on two occasions, I stepped forth in all regal splendour to kneel before the high altar; first to make an offering and the second, to receive the sacrament from the Archbishop of

Canterbury. All told, the service went on for several hours, and I admit that under the many layers of my clothing and in the packed and stuffy, church, I became increasingly hot and desperate for the jakes. It was to my great relief that the time eventually came for me to pass out of public view. And so with my ladies in attendance, with abbots and bishops at my side, I made my way behind the great altar, to the Shrine of St Edward the Confessor. There I knelt in prayer, and once more silently begged the Saint for the safe delivery of healthy son.

I had tried to prepare myself for the sheer physical exhaustion that I knew the day would bring but in spite of this, I was tired, hot and thirsty and so was greatly relieved that with all this complete, it was time for me to take my leave of all but four of my ladies. These included: my grandmother, the Dowager Duchess of Norfolk; her daughter Ann Howard, the Dowager Countess of Oxford; Lady Mary Howard, and Margery, officiating as mistress of the wardrobe. Together, the Abbot of Westminster showed us to a room which had been set aside for my private use on one side of the quire. When the heavy wooden door closed behind us, shutting out the world for a few precious minutes, I felt the tension begin to drain my body. An enormous sense of the most profound relief washed over me. I stood in the centre of the room, my eyes closed momentarily as my ladies fussed around me, trying simply just to take in the enormity of everything that I had just experienced. When I opened them again, it was Margery's face that greeted me with the most radiant and loving countenance,

'Your Grace, food and wine have been provided for your sustenance.' Margery indicated towards a table set with gold plate and a goodly array of food and wine, before she added, '...and your closed stool is next door for your comfort which I suspect by now you sorely need!' For the briefest of moments there was silence between us, Margery raising an eyebrow indicating that she knew all too well of the very practical predicament that was surely troubling me, being so great with child as I was that day. Suddenly, I found myself laughing out loud, clutching onto my friend's hand as she had joined me in my mirth. Our laughter was such a blessed relief and in truth, we sniggered more than the occasion demanded. Our somewhat childish humour cut through any remaining sinews of tension and I was deeply grateful for it. Margery dried the tears from her eyes, as I did the same, when suddenly

253

she looked at me once more and added softly, 'It is done, Your Grace... you can relax now and enjoy the rest this day, for surely Madame, you deserve it.' I felt Anne's familiar insecurity bubble to the surface, and in doing so I tentatively asked,

'Yes, it is done. But tell me, Margery, did I do everything that was required of me? Do you... do you think they will love me as they loved Katherine?' I briefly cast my eyes to the side to see the elderly Dowager Duchess frowned in disapproval. No doubt, she felt that as a Howard girl and as queen, I should not entertain such silly notions. Margery followed my eye line, before turning her attention back towards me. As ever, I could rely on my friend to tell me the truth,

'Anne' she spoke my name in almost a whisper, causing yet more disapproving stares from my grandmother, 'You did everything right. It was just perfect. As for people, they will be fickle as they always are. There will be some who will never forgive you for stealing the king's heart, but in truth, it speaks more of their own fears than it touches upon your person. You must not let these matters concern you anymore, for you are the king's beloved wife and anointed queen. It is your destiny alone that speaks to you now. You answer only to God and the king's grace.' I nodded, appreciating my friend's words. In her honesty, I would always find the strength and courage I needed to stay the course and veer not from my purpose; even though now I stand on the brink of paying for it with my life.

The Palace of Whitehall had finally fallen silent. The great pageant of the day eventually exhausted everyone until, by degrees, the household sank into a peaceful slumber. Yet for me, much needed sleep remained stubbornly elusive. I was tired to the bone, and every sinew of my body ached for rest. But my head remained full the sights and sounds of the day, and I could not, for the life of me, bid them to settle. In fact, I was beyond tired, so that every molecule of my body seemed to be vibrating, humming even with nervous exhaustion. However, I was grateful that the little one inside my belly must have drifted off to sleep when I could not, for she had eventually given up kicking the wall of my abdomen to both my great relief and comfort.

I looked at the great oak, four-poster bed and the dishevelled mound of silken sheets which were half covering Henry's body. I could hear by the deep and rhythmic pattern of his breathing that my husband was sound asleep. I was glad that I had not woken him as I slipped out of the bed that we had shared together that night and went over to sit in the window seat of my bed chamber, looking out across the Thames. A pristine night had followed a perfect day, and the full moon cast its own silvery light across the surface of the river below. I rested my head against the stone moulding of the window frame, drawing my fur-lined dressing gown around me to ward off any unwelcome chill. Although, in truth, the heat of the day had ushered in a warm night, and so I had propped open the window, luxuriating in the blessed silence that only comes at such a late hour.

Over on the south bank, solitary lights flickered in various buildings and I watched a flock of geese swim into the path of the moonlight, bobbing upon the surface of the water for a couple of minutes before disappearing into the shadows beyond. I watched, but I did not see. In my mind's eye, I was reliving every moment of the most glorious day of my life. In the stillness of the night, thoughts rushed in, jostling with each other to steal away my attention. I saw again how Thomas Cranmer had knelt at my feet in Westminster Abbey, declaring on behalf of all the clergy to be faithful and true according to the law; how he had then been replaced by Charles Brandon as one of England's leading nobleman who, as tradition dictated, had knelt upon one knee and taking both his hands between my own, had declared before all that in God's name he was Anne's 'liege man of life and limb', and of earthly worship, faith and truth; that he would bear unto me, to live and die against all manner of folks should they challenge my right to be queen. He had spoken all this, and yet I saw all too vividly the emptiness of his words.

My mind fast forwarded, as I recalled the face of my father leading me from the Abbey; how we had stepped, side by side, from the muted shade of the sanctuary into the dazzling light of the midday sun; how he had supported me by holding my right hand in his, whilst on the other side, the young Lord Talbot, the Earl of Shrewsbury's son and heir, had done the same. In the presence of so many, my father had said little, but his smile showed both his great pride, appreciation and even awe at the achievements of his youngest daughter; a daughter in whom he had come to invest all his hopes for a glorious Boleyn future.

This scene dissolved as my mind wandered once more, only to be replaced by another; the vision of magnificence that was Westminster Hall, where I had taken my place below a canopy of estate and saw before me a sea of faces. The sight of the long and empty table at which I had dined alone, save for the Archbishop of Canterbury who sat away to my right. I recalled his kindly face, how he had nodded his encouragement from time to time, and how I had been careful to return his good graces for truly, I loved him dearly. All too soon, yet again another montage of images and sounds broke through the last. This time it was the echoes of giggling that floated in and out of my consciousness, filling the silent room in which I sat. It was the quiet laughter of my dear friends, Joan and Nan who had sat at my feet under the table during the entire banquet, serving my most personal needs. They were responding to the occasional jibe that I made under my breath at the expense of one or more of the many guests. In truth, I pitied their plight, being hidden from view with no food, and little to drink, for hours at a time, and so I had done my best to amuse them and alleviate their boredom.

Then a great clatter of hooves washed away the sound of their voices. As if from a fairytale, and out of the mists of my imagination, the valiant figures of the Duke of Suffolk and Lord William Howard had emerged, both mounted upon horseback. The Duke had indeed cut a fine figure, his doublet and jacket dripping with pearls, his white charger draped in crimson velvet. Together, they rode up and down the Hall, escorting in the courses of the feast which followed, a vision of chivalry and honour. Finally, I heard my own words ring out loud and clear in my mind, as I had stood to take my leave of the feast, 'I thank you all for the honour ye have done to me this day...'

'Sweetheart, are you well?' It was the king's voice, and in an instant the thoughts that had filled my head vanished into nothing. I turned my head away from the window to see Henry propped up on one elbow. Something had roused him from his slumber and he was clearly concerned that I was not sleeping peacefully by his side.

'I couldn't sleep; too many thoughts filling my mind,' I shrugged and smiled, indicating my inability to tame my unruly mind. Henry smiled and nodded his understanding in return. Stretching out his arm toward me, he beckoned me forth saying,

'Come hither, my love.' I obligingly slid off the window seat, allowing my dressing gown to drop to the floor to reveal my underlying smock, as Henry lifted the silk bedcovers so that I could slip in close to his own warm body. At first, Henry stretched out on his back, his left arm behind his head, his right stroking my loose hair as I lay on my side in the crook of his shoulder, as close to my husband as my swollen belly would allow. Henry spoke again, whispering quietly into the night, 'Tell me sweetheart, did you enjoy the day?'

'Oh yes, it was more than I ever imagined!' That surely was the truth. I lifted my head, studying Henry's face, half cast in shadow, before he turned toward me, saying,

'And you, my love, looked every inch my queen…' Henry paused for a moment, staring at the ceiling then, concerned as ever with how things would be seen abroad, he added, '…and I think that the French and Venetian ambassadors will report that all was well done by you, that you are now accepted as England's true queen. You will see, Anne, that when our son is born, a new age of glory will descend upon this realm.' With that he smiled and kissed me gently upon my forehead.

I think to that point, I had been so focused on getting rid of Katherine, and being recognised as Henry's wife and queen, that to a great extent I had been able to deny the stark reality of my pregnancy and the brutal fact that everything, absolutely everything depended upon the sex of the child that I carried. Of course, the spectre of my failure to bear the king a son stalked me daily, but valiantly I continued to hope against all hope that I would give birth—that Anne would give birth—to a healthy, male child. I completely failed to appreciate that while I had sailed through the first six months of my pregnancy without complications, the last trimester would see me scarcely escape with my own life—let alone that of my darling Elizabeth.

Chapter Twenty-Two

Greenwich Palace, London,
28 June 1533

For a time, the summer continued innocently enough. The skies were as clear and untroubled as my leisurely existence as England's new queen, each glorious day rolling seamlessly into the next, a time of carefree pleasures. A great tournament, banquets and unending dancing had followed on from the coronation, with the court soon moving from Whitehall to Greenwich, where festivities continued, albeit on a slightly smaller scale.

I looked down at the parchment in my hands, slightly crumpled after its long journey from France. It was a letter from my brother, the page filled with his spidery, yet decidedly flamboyant, handwriting; so like the man I knew—and loved. I re-read the note. My brother began by greeting me well, sending his hearty congratulations on the success of the coronation festivities, before setting about berating me in a rather tongue-in-cheek way for the merry pastime in my chambers, which he said, according to my Lord Chamberlain, had 'never been more'. I must have smiled enigmatically. I could only think of my brother's jealousy at missing out on all the fun! However, with a much more befitting and serious countenance, I looked up at the two gentlemen standing before me in my presence chamber, their arrival happily coinciding with that of the letter from Paris. Sometime before, George had been presented on my behalf with a magnificent litter and three mules as a wedding present from King Francis, and consequently, the French ambassador, Monsieur de Dinteville and a certain Master St. Jullien had come forth to Greenwich to formerly present it to Anne.

'Your Excellency, May I convey my great joy and hearty thanks at your master's kindness and generosity. He is a faithful friend and I beseech you to tell King Francis of the great honour he does me and the love I bear for him in my heart.' I sensed Anne's happiness at yet another obvious gesture of the French king's acceptance of her legitimate position as Henry's wife and queen. I was in high spirits that day, and there had been much carefree banter and laughter about my privy chambers. However, when the ambassador's arrival was announced, I had broken away, choosing to receive Francis' wedding gift in my presence chamber and therefore, in public. I wanted as many people as possible to witness the great esteem in which Anne was held by the French king and court.

I tapped the letter against my breast thoughtfully, seized as I was by a sudden desire to see King Francis' gift for myself. Thus, I asked, 'Pray tell me, Your Excellency, is the gift here? May see it?'

'Indeed, Your Majesty. In anticipation that you may wish to inspect it, I have had it prepared for Your Grace and it awaits your pleasure in the inner court.' Jean de Dinteville smiled graciously, clearly pleased with himself for anticipating my desires and committing himself further into my good graces.

'*Alors, c'est magnifique, Monsieur L'Ambassador. On y va, toute de suite!*' With that, I swept down from under the canopy of estate, pausing in front of the French ambassador and offering him my right hand. Always the gracious gentleman, he swept into a bow, taking my hand lightly in his and kissing the ring upon my finger in an act of reverence. He was a handsome, young gentlemen and I found my natural flirtatiousness, cultivated at the French court, was awoken once more by the cultured finesse of this fine, French nobleman. I could not help it; I cocked my head playfully, backed my eyes behind my long and thick, dark lashes and smiled alluringly. I nearly giggled aloud, for even despite the ambassador's polished veneer, I had seen his maleness stir, just for a moment, before I broke away coquettishly, turning to hand George's letter to Lady Mary Howard, and then indicating that my ladies and Monsieur de Dinteville should follow me.

The entrance to the privy stair, which led down directly to the large inner courtyard of the palace, was wedged between my presence and privy chambers. Just as I turned to make toward it, the Earl of Wiltshire was announced at the door of my chamber, so I paused, allowing my father to come forward and greet me.

'Your Majesty,' he greeted me ebulliently, taking off his cap and inclining his head in respect of my status.

'Good 'morrow, my Lord! You should join us father, for I am just about to go and inspect my wedding present from his most gracious majesty, the King of France.' Thomas Boleyn glanced at the French ambassador, and although my father said nothing, he did smile, acknowledging his gratitude on my family's behalf. Then, with a sweeping gesture, my father indicated that he acceded to my wishes. Walking side-by side, Sir Thomas gallantly offered me his arm for support. Behind us, and at a discreet distance, we were followed by the French ambassador, his guest, and a train of my ladies. In Anne's non-pregnant state, I had become accustomed to her light, lithe body, which moved swiftly and with grace. However, I was slowed down on account of my burgeoning belly; I was nearly seven months pregnant and had lately started to waddle in order to compensate for the swell of my abdomen. Leaning close to my father, we were able to speak with a degree of privacy, out of earshot of those who followed in our wake. I spoke first.

'I have heard from George. He seems well. Has he written to you?' Sir Thomas nodded in the affirmative saying simply,

'Yes, he has.' With little more forthcoming, I continued my probing.

'He mentions little of his embassy in France with Uncle Norfolk; how goes it? Have they had an audience with the Pope?' Many questions began to tumble forth, all demanding an answer.

'It seems that King Francis is in good spirits, and that he continues to be a friend of the Boleyns.' The latter he added softly, almost under his breath. My father avoided answering my question regarding the Bishop of Rome, so, I pressed the issue again, determined that I would have an answer. Instinctively, I sensed something was amiss.

'And what of the Pope and his meeting with the French king? Have we heard anything of that?' Just for a moment my father looked away, hesitating briefly, before replying,

'Everything appears to be going smoothly. I do not think that Pope Clement can damage us now.' For a second, I recognised a flicker of disingenuousness in my father's response; it was so hard to put a finger on why, but as his daughter, I knew that he was lying to me. I stopped suddenly locking my gaze with his and challenged,

'What is it? What are you not telling me?' Sir Thomas patted my hand, trying to reassure me, before cleverly avoiding further interrogation by swiftly changing the subject to something even more compelling.

'Have you heard the news?' My father's face betrayed a happy, self-satisfaction as he added,

'Mary Tudor, the Duchess of Suffolk died at Westhorpe Hall this Tuesday last.' Realising that it was indiscreet to speak meanly of the king's once beloved sister, he said quietly, 'It is indeed a happy day for us; one less viper in the nest!' I raised an eyebrow, not out of any great sentimentality toward the woman whose beauty had once been renowned amongst the courts of Europe, but rather, I was surprised that my father still considered her a threat. Surely there were two other women in England who eclipsed all others in the harm that they sought to do to me and my unborn child. I replied,

'I care not for Mary Tudor; however, she is not in a position to harm us. No, father, if you want to protect your daughter and grand-child, you should turn your attention to Katherine and that arrogant daughter of hers, for surely they deserve the brunt of the king's displeasure.' We were almost at the lobby, which opened out underneath the southern gateway of the inner court. I faced Sir Thomas; this time it was my turn to lean in and whisper under my breath. 'Katherine still refuses to style herself as anything but queen.' Even as I spoke, I could feel the long-standing, burning resentment against this woman, who simply would not go away, begin to grip me within my chest. It was true that whenever I thought about Katherine and her vainglorious daughter, the ferment that simmered within me always managed to sweep away the joy of any sunny day in an instant. Thus, out of pure frustration, I almost hissed the following words, '…and Mary will recognise no other queen than her mother!'

'Anne please, calm yourself! You should not disturb either yourself or your child. You know it is the king's command.' My father started to speak, unwittingly taunting me with something that he had said a hundred times or more, that everything would change once a healthy son was born. I wanted to scream at him that I knew what was required of me and that I wished not to hear it again! Yet, I could not. I was acutely aware that I was being watched closely by the French ambassador, and that any discord witnessed between us would be about the courts of Europe in a blink of an eye. So, with a carefree smile upon my face, I took my father by surprise, leaning in to kiss him on the cheek that faced away from our audience, so that my lips could not be seen or read. In doing so, I whispered in his ear,

'Their intransigence is an act of treason against the king and against me. I will not allow anyone to threaten the safety of my child. I will see to it that the king acts decisively against them.' I had never felt as fiercely protective of anyone, or anything, in my life as I did about Elizabeth, even before she had been born. I was shocked by the depth of my ruthless determination to shelter her from harm. For the first time, I truly empathised with wild beasts that were driven by pure instinct to fight to the death for their offspring.

Still smiling, I looked into the courtyard, purposefully ending the conversation. There in the sun was the most splendid litter, draped in cloth of gold and white satin, three fine mules in attendance. In an ostentatious display of gratitude, I insisted that two of my ladies should accompany me on a three mile ride. This was only a ruse but I had felt an overwhelming need to escape the palace, and get away from those who seek to do me harm when I was most vulnerable.

I could not easily shake off the conversation that I had shared with my father earlier in the day. By late afternoon, I began to feel a little unwell with a slight headache. So, I took to my bed, dismissing my ladies to the next chamber in order that I might doze undisturbed. At the time, I put it down to sheer exhaustion, however, I found it impossible to keep from turning thoughts of Katherine and Mary over and over in my mind and I became unwittingly lost in a drama of my own making. I fantasised about how I wanted to lash out and tear them both down to size, in the way one does when one is hurt or wounded by another. I am not proud of it. Now, I see with different, compassionate eyes; eyes which were not mine to see with back then; a time when so much still hung in the balance and Anne's very survival was at stake. I suppose it was a war of sorts. While our husbands donned armour and rode on their chargers upon a very physical battlefield, ladies had different weapons of warfare; our words, courage, stubbornness and pride. We could not strike out, but we could refuse to yield, and I was determined that I could match Katherine and her daughter every step of the way.

Thus, that June afternoon, I lay curled up on my side, gently wafting in and out of a sleep, my temples pricked with an insistent throbbing. A sweet and pleasant breeze brushed like silk against my cheek, whilst outside my window I could hear the occasional screeching of a distant

262

peacock in the palace gardens, or the scrunching of feet on the gravel paths running alongside and beneath the windows of my apartments. As I slipped out of my gown and took refuge under the covers, I noticed the first signs of slightly swollen ankles, easy to see on Anne's slim body. At the time, I merely dismissed the symptom as being of no significance; just part of a normal pregnancy. I was there not ten minutes when a gentle knock at the door roused my senses. Margery entered, dipped a curtsy and said,

'Your Grace, the king's highness has sent forth a messenger inviting you to join him for supper this evening in his privy chamber. He awaits your reply.' I knew immediately that I did not have the strength to attend, and so had shaken my head saying,

'Margery, please convey to the king my hearty and most humble thanks, but also to crave his majesty's forgiveness, for I feel a little unwell and think it best that perhaps I rest this evening.' My friend, of course, looked concerned.

'Anne, would you like me to send for your physician?' I shook my head as I frowned, dismissing her concern by saying,

'No, no, no, I am just exhausted. I am sure that it is nothing that a little rest cannot cure.' I must admit that Margery did not look convinced. Being at heart a modern-day woman, I feared Tudor doctors and their interventions, as kind hearted and as well meaning as they might be. Indeed, daily I thanked God for Anne's usual robust constitution, which meant I had, until that point, largely avoided their attentions. Margery somewhat reluctantly accepted my protestations, curtsied and left, leaving me to drift off into a fitful slumber...

...I found myself walking in bare feet into the queen's presence chamber at Greenwich, dressed only in my linen nightgown, my hair loose about my shoulders. It was empty, save for me and Katherine, who was seated imperiously upon the chair of state before me at the far end of the room, her daughter standing haughtily at her side; Katherine's fool sat on the steps of the dais, next to a large mirror. I hated the look of smug, self-satisfaction pasted across Katherine's imperious face and remember suddenly being engulfed by anger. My subconscious mind had no compunction about releasing the full force of its suppressed fury as I slept and so, in my dream, I began to scream at her, 'Get out, you bitch! Don't you know it is over! He doesn't even love

263

you...' I surged forward in a torrent of white hot fury, determined to be rid of them once and for all. Continuing to rant, I felt blood coursing through my veins, throbbing at my temples as I cried, '...In fact, not only does he not love you, he hates you and wishes you were dead! Now get out of this palace, you are nothing anymore, nothing! Do you not understand?' I heard my own plaintive frustrations pour forth whilst Katherine continued to smile at me impassively, apparently undisturbed by my cursing. Suddenly, Katherine's fool burst into cackling laughter. Through her laughter, the fool did not speak, but beckoned me over, indicating that I should look at myself in the mirror. Despite myself, I felt compelled to do so, and moved slowly forward, step by small step, before I found myself facing my reflection.

I was horrified to see my bloated figure; my delicate ankles swollen to twice their size, with great, distorted puffy hands, eyes and an enormous belly. Anne was hardly recognisable and I felt like a monster. Katherine's fool was still rolling around on the floor, her hideous laughter tormenting me as my own scream torn through the palace...

'Sweetheart, sweetheart, Anne, wake up, wake up! It is just a dream.' My eyes flashed open feverishly, to see Henry sitting on the edge of my bed, his hand lightly shaking me on the shoulder and a look of considerable concern etched deeply upon his face. For a moment, I was disorientated, caught between my 'real' world and the hinterland of my nightmare. I propped myself up only to feel the throbbing pain sear through my head and collapsed back onto the pillow, rubbing my temples. I realised that Henry must have hurried to my bedside upon hearing I was unwell. 'Margery tells me you are unwell. What troubles you?' he said, searching my face. I waved my hand in the air, desperate to avert a visit from my physician as I mumbled,

'It is nothing, my Lord. Nothing at all, I am just exhausted. I have not been sleeping so well recently. It is getting evermore uncomfortable as the child grows.' Of course, Henry was no fool either. Clearly seeing my discomfort was greater than I was admitting to, he pressed me again for the truth. 'I think not Anne, you look unwell. Tell me the truth, what vexes you? Are you unwell?' Really without thinking, I sighed, rubbing my hand across my face as if to wipe the sleep from my eyes. Rather carelessly, and perhaps somewhat irritably on account of my exhaustion and the pain which gripped my head like a vice, I snapped,

'She bothers me!' Henry naturally frowned and recoiled, somewhat bewildered. He was quite unaware of the events of the day that had affected me so, and therefore, he was left struggling to understand to whom I referred. I was even more irritated that the king could not read my mind and know the cause of my vexation. Groaning in frustration, I answered his silent question rather impatiently, 'Katherine, of course! She bothers me! I'm sick and tired of her constant interference in our lives.' Meeting Henry's gaze directly, I pressed on fearlessly, 'Katherine and Mary are virtually the only subjects in this land that refuse to accept that I am your wife and the queen of this realm. Is that not treason, My Lord?' Then I delivered the final cutting blow, 'I thought by now to be rid of her. Yet as ever, I see that when there is an argument, she is always sure to have the upper hand with you.' My tirade at an end, I closed my eyes dismissively, rubbing my temples once more, foolishly unconcerned at Henry's wounded pride.

Anne's temper could cut with the sharpest blade at the best of times. However, looking back now, I understand that in those last few months of that pregnancy, I had been incomparably volatile and often deeply irrational. If I have any excuse, it must be that not only did my pregnancy destabilise my emotions, as might be expected, I was also becoming ill, but did not yet know it. In time, I would recognise that my illness was a syndrome that in my modern day life was known as pre-eclampsia; a dangerous condition of raised blood pressure brought on in the later stages of pregnancy—and one which was potentially life threatening to both mother and child. Of course, the simple tests that in the twenty-first century could confirm or refute this diagnosis in minutes were not available in Anne's world. And so, I would never know for sure, but the probability seemed inescapable. It would become clear to me what was happening, although the Tudor doctors sent to treat me recognised only the symptoms. Through experience though, they knew, as I did, that only the delivery of the child could affect a cure. It certainly would make those last few weeks increasingly difficult to bear—and fraught with tension.

In the midst of Henry's interrogation, though, none of this was in my mind; yet, I had his attention. He was terrified of losing the child, and I am ashamed to say that I saw the opportunity to manipulate the king into turning the screws upon Katherine and her daughter. In my modern day life, I had nothing to compare with how Anne's very life and security, and that of her child, was threatened by the mere existence of another. I had never known, until that moment, what it was to face the truth of a simple matter of survival; it was me or her. If I did not destroy Katherine and Mary first, then Anne's life would perpetually hang in the balance. I realised that if I had ever condemned Anne for her treatment of Katherine and Mary, then I had no right to judge, for I had never walked in such dangerous shoes. Deliberately, I added a comment that Henry could not ignore.

'Yes, Your Majesty, I do feel unwell and if you want to know why, then I fear it is on account of the great distress that Katherine and Mary's intransigence causes me daily.' I could not hide my contempt for Henry's inability to deal with his daughter and her mother. I think now that my outburst deserved less kindness and understanding than the king showed me that day. Despite my intemperance, he took my hand and gently kissed it, brushing a lock of hair from my forehead, before he said what I knew he would.

'I will deal with Katherine and Mary and make plain my great displeasure in this matter. You must not worry yourself Anne, for the safety of this child—of our child—is what should concern you now.' He spoke so earnestly, I could not tell if he was angry at me, or whether, with rare insight, he saw beyond my words to my genuine discomfort. He had perceived what I could not, that it was the illness which was taking hold of my body that was largely responsible for my insolence and irritability. 'In the meantime, Margery will call for your physician, for it is clear to me you are not entirely well, Madame. You must rest in bed until you are seen.' With that, the king turned towards Margery indicating that she should carry out his wishes. When Margery had left the room, Henry bent down and kissed me on the forehead, before sweeping out of the room, leaving me alone with my troubled thoughts and a throbbing headache that portended imminent disaster.

Chapter Twenty-Three

Windsor Castle,
28 July 1533

Once more, I found myself looking down from the great oriel window of the queen's presence chamber at Windsor Castle onto the courtyard below. There was ever the same great flurry of activity that accompanied the king's coming or going from the castle. Yet this time, there seemed to be more urgency than usual. Everything had been called together in a matter of hours, and this added to my already considerable anxiety. I looked on silently with a heavy heart, for the first time, I was not to accompany his majesty on what would amount to a mini progress along the Thames Valley. I watched several gentlemen of the king's privy chamber mount their horses, the king striding out from the privy stair of Henry VII's Tower, speaking briefly with Cromwell, who was busy slipping his finely embroidered, leather riding gloves onto his bear-like hands.

As I watched my husband, I thought back to our meeting that morning; how Henry explained that he was leaving me at Windsor for my comfort and safety, while he headed further afield for the chase and mayhap, to visit some of those courtiers who had been less than supportive of the seismic events that had rocked the kingdom over the previous few months. I protested vehemently. I suddenly felt scared— at being left alone as my pregnancy became increasingly difficult, and scared that the source of Henry's high spirits were not due to the love he bore me or our child, but rather a budding affection for an unknown *inamorata*, whom he wished to meet in secret, away from the castle.

Looking back, no doubt the stress of my condition, and the illness which was beginning to steadily take hold of my body, was starting to take its toll. Not only was I increasingly volatile and irritable, as my belly grew ever larger, I felt increasingly like a beached whale; the swelling of my girth being matched by a growing, irrational paranoia that the king was seeking solace elsewhere. Had I not known of Henry's reputation from my modern day life, had I not known that Anne's downfall lay with another, perhaps I would not have seen competing lovers round every corner, or lurking in every shadow. As the weeks wore on, I was snapping at everyone; Henry, my father, my beloved mother and even my dearest friends. It little surprises me that from time to time, the king's temper also wore thin. Although, much to his credit, I often saw him biting his lip, determined to remember that my life, and the life of his heir, hung in the balance; remembering that God willing, this pregnancy would soon come to a happy ending and we could put these difficult few weeks behind us.

I am ashamed to say that I argued and fought, and refused to accept with any grace, my Lord's wishes. Thus, we parted on difficult terms. As I stood at the window, watching the king's leaving, I regretted my actions. It would be over two weeks before I would see Henry again. Two weeks before we would have a chance to mend bridges, and use our physical presence and intimacy as the balm to heal the wounds arising from our tempestuous disagreements.

I did not know, nor had I remembered at the time, the truth of the matter; that Henry had received news from Rome that the Pope threatened excommunication of both the king and Thomas Cranmer if Henry did not repudiate our marriage and take Katherine back as his wife. I did not know that my brother had ridden all haste from Paris under orders from my Uncle Norfolk to convey the news to the king; that George had sent ahead a relay of riders from Dover, so that the message would reach Henry more quickly. I was ignorant of how, the previous evening, the king had commanded George to rendezvous with his majesty and the Privy Council at Guildford in Surrey, part way between Windsor and the port of Dover. Henry had not been seeking the warm embraces of another; rather, he wished to conceal from me this most disagreeable intelligence from Rome. He was greatly concerned for the precarious state of my health, and had ordered that no one should tell me of this turn of events. Tragically, I sensed only that something was amiss, and the vacuum created by a desire to protect me, I filled with paranoid delusions of the king's infidelity.

With great longing, I looked upon the impressive figure of the king as he settled himself in his chocolate brown, velvet saddle. His back was turned to me as he shared a joke with Sir Henry Norris, who was mounted on his own, feisty stallion. I so wanted Henry to turn round and look up so that he might see my face and know that despite my outburst and protestations, I loved him with all my heart. I willed him to do so, but our discord had fractured the connection between us. With a raised arm, I watched the king lead the party through the Norman Gate and out of sight. He departed without a backward glance, entirely oblivious to my futile attempts to communicate my love for him.

'Your Majesty, Lady Mary Rochford is here to see you.' It was the sweet voice of Madge Shelton that cut through my misery and self-pity. I was delighted to see the face of my English rose, as ever radiant and seemingly happy to see me. I had not seen my sister for nearly six weeks as, after the coronation festivities, I had granted her leave to return to her home at Rochford Hall. Mary sank into a graceful curtsy before we embraced with warm sisterly affection. It was so good to see her, a chance to take my mind off Henry's departure. Mary had seen the preparation for the king's leaving and enquired innocently enough,

'I hear that the king will be gone some two weeks.' I knew that Mary was curious to understand what was afoot. Henry and I had not been out of each other's sight for any length of time since the build up to the Blackfriars trial in 1528, and that his departure signalled an unusual turn of events. Before answering, I indicated that we should link arms and walk together towards my presence chamber.

The symptoms of my illness had been occurring since late June. I suffered daily with some moderate swelling of the ankles and feet, along with the occasional headache that waxed and waned without obvious cause. My physicians urged bed rest which I was happy to accede to as I often felt exhausted and welcomed sleep. I was forbidden to move further than my chambers lest I place too great a demand upon my body. As a result, I had spent almost the entire time since my arrival at Windsor in my rooms, away from the prying eyes of the court, and visited regularly by the king at the end of a long day's hunting. I cannot deny that after being used to such a vigorous outdoor life, my confinement was tantamount to torture. I found it difficult not to resent Henry's glorious freedom, whilst I remained cooped up day after day. With the king gone from the castle, along with the entire Privy Council, the palace had become rapidly deserted. Only my household of around two hundred, and a skeleton staff to support us, remained behind. In order to protect my privacy and provide me with as little disturbance as possible, Henry had also strongly discouraged all unnecessary visitors.

Thus, on that morning, with my sister walking at my side, I decided to make the most of the virtually empty presence chamber in order to stretch my legs and enjoy a different perspective out of the seven enormous windows that looked due south onto the inner ward of the castle. As usual, several of my ladies including: Lady Mary Howard, Madge Shelton, Grace Parker, Jane Rochford, Nan and Joan, all followed in our wake. As we strolled along, I indicated to Mark Smeaton to entertain us with sweet music and serenade us with song. I hoped that the delicate harmonies would fill the cavernous space of my apartments with beauty and life, for they seemed eerily empty. It also provided some privacy for my sister and me to parley about certain sensitive issues. As Mark struck up a gentle ballad upon his lute, I answered my sister as well as I was able.

'His majesty said that he is following the chase and that he wishes to visit those subjects who have become *disaffected* during recent months.' I said, 'disaffected' rather pointedly and with a degree of resentment, for I knew that they blamed me for the great ills they perceived had fallen upon the kingdom. Perhaps my bitterness from my earlier altercation with Henry crept into my voice, as Mary asked tentatively,

'Do you not believe him, sister?' I let go of my sister's arm and wandered over to the nearby window, staring out toward the enormous crenellated range of lodgings running directly across from my presence chamber, and answered bluntly,

'No, I do not believe him. I think he has taken another to his bed.' I turned to look at Mary, whose face was etched in shock and confusion.

'No, sister you are mistaken!' I nodded towards my ladies, indicating that they should drop back further, allowing Mary and me to converse alone. Once they had done so, I exclaimed in a whisper,

'Why not? Surely you, of all people, know what the king is like! I mean, just look at me, Mary!' I indicated with a gesture of my hand that she should take note of the size of my pregnant belly. Lifting my skirts slightly, I showed her the swelling of my ankles. 'Do you think this pleases his grace? Oh Mary, I feel so utterly hideous. I have not lain with the king since afore my coronation, and my temper has been both bitter and disagreeable…I fear that his majesty seeks solace elsewhere.'

'No, sister. I do not believe it! The king adores you, and I have heard many say that he has never been as merry as he is now.' Mary took hold of both my hands, squeezing them tightly to emphasise the truth of her words. She spoke with great conviction and a rare authority, 'Anne, you must listen to me; I know how hard this is for you. Most women in this realm can give birth in a barn, and be the child alive or dead, there would be little consequence. But you have the eyes of England upon you. In truth sister, I cannot begin to imagine what pressure you must feel. It is not enough that you must deal with being pregnant, which can be difficult at the best of times, but all Christendom waits for news from the English court. What is more…I hear from a good source that you have been ill. Is it not surprising that you do not feel at your best?' I looked down toward the ground, shrugging my shoulders as if to signal my reluctant agreement, before my sister forged on. 'But look at you, look how far you have come and what you have achieved! All the great astrologers and learned men in this realm have said that this child you carry is a new prince. You have but six, short weeks to wait until he is born, God willing. In the meantime, what you think to be true is only the result of demons of a fevered imagination. It is the king's great joy to see you thus.' My sister indicated toward my swollen abdomen. 'Do not take that joy away from him. Do not turn him away with the sharpness of your tongue.'

I confess, at that moment, it was exactly what I needed to hear. I needed to snap out of my deluded self-pity. Her heartfelt words allowed me to release my fears about Henry's infidelity, at least for the time being. So, I nodded my acquiescence, flicking my eyes up to meet my sister's gaze, sharing my understanding and appreciation of her honesty and support. We both knew that there was little more to say on the matter, so Mary abruptly changed the subject to something which she knew lay close to my heart.

'I hear from our lady mother that the king has taken further action against Katherine and the Lady Mary's refusal to accept their new status?' I nodded once more, and began to amble forth along the length of the queen's presence chamber.

'It is true.' I sighed, thinking upon how I had had to plant the seed of discontent in Henry's mind, before he sought to move against the princess dowager and his wayward daughter.

'She also said that the king has sent orders to senior members of

Katherine's household stating that only Katherine's arrogance, selfishness or inordinate vainglory would lead her to believe she could still use the title of queen; that you and he are married, and you have lately been crowned queen at Westminster.' I smiled for a second time, on this occasion with a certain degree of self-satisfaction.

'And did you hear the rest?' I asked. It was Mary's turn to look over at me, a frown of confusion pinching at her brow, urging me to continue.

'That his grace also said that she was sadly mistaken if she thought that he could, as long as he lived, ever go back to her and that he would never do so on any consideration!' There were a few moments silence between us, as my sister then asked tentatively,

'And what if Katherine will not stop styling herself as queen? What then?' It was a question which vexed me constantly, for at the heart of it lay the question behind the question; would I do anything to get rid of Katherine? Would I urge the king to spill her blood? Did I want her dead at any cost? I admit that there had been many, many times when I felt that I would have done anything to see the back of her. But these times were transient, and as much as I wished that death from natural causes might carry her away, I was no Lady Macbeth and did not seek to have her blood on my hands. I knew this to be true, but I was reluctant to talk of this to Mary, and so I said something that I knew would end the conversation.

'She will stop when my son is born.' Mary nodded in agreement. The enchanting sound of Mark's lute provided a gentle lullaby to accompany our conversation, but I wanted to change the subject and the mood, so I adopted a bright countenance and warm smile, and asked,

'But tell me sister, how art thou?' Then with a degree of playfulness and a wry smile, I probed, 'What have you been doing with yourself whilst you've been shut away in the countryside?' I noticed how at my impish enquiry my sister blushed. Yet, she answered boldly enough,

'Oh Anne, you know how much I enjoy the sweet country air. I walked out every day to delight in the summer meadows around Rochford Hall. They were idyllic, so peaceful, and full of summer flowers and butterflies; quite a tonic I confess after the hurly-burly of the city and your coronation!' As she spoke, I felt a prick of nostalgia, remembering that for the longest time I had not known the peace and solitude that I once tasted at Hever. Oh, how I missed it so! Once more, I felt suffocated by the golden fetters that bound me to the court with all its complex pleasures and vices. My sister continued unaware of my heavy sadness. 'I managed the estate and even welcomed Sir John and Lady Frances on several occasions; they kindly visited me knowing I was home.' I was aware that after her husband's death, my father had allowed Mary to use one of his properties, Rochford Hall in Essex, as her principle residence. In return, my sister acted as chatelaine. It was a role which suited her, for although my English rose enjoyed the court well enough, she was a contented woman at heart, and one who could take pleasure from the very simplest of things in life. It was easy to see that the country life of a noblewoman, without the cut and thrust of a ruthless and ambitious court, suited her kind and gentle manner.

I began to feel tired, with my legs and back aching, I walked back toward my privy chambers; my sister taking my lead and once again looping her arm through mine. In her absence, and with a great deal of time on my hands, I had been thinking about the rather difficult conversation that I had had with Mary at Greenwich over Christmas. As the new head of the Boleyn family, I had a duty to see that she was suitably married. I was determined to prevent the fate that history foretold awaited her—that my sister stood to lose all her family by taking an unsuitable husband, whose lowly status would threaten to undermine all that the Boleyns had achieved. Feeling rather pleased with myself I whispered, 'I have been thinking about a match for you, sister. The Countess of Surrey has spoken of her father's desire to remarry; as you well know, he has been a widower for some five years.' I thought that the gallant and knighted John de Vere, 15th Earl of Oxford, some nine years older than Mary, could be the perfect suitor.

'The Earl of Oxford?' Rather than the intrigue I expected, I heard only a note of panic in Mary's voice. I fear that I disregarded my intuition and pushed on blithely, insensitive to my sister's reaction.

'Yes. Lord de Vere. You have always spoken favourably of him. He is most beloved of the king and importantly, shares our views on religion,' then added brightly, 'Would it suit my sister to be a countess?' In truth, I did not know how Lord de Vere might react to taking on an ex-mistress of the king, but I was willing to try. After all, her sister was now the Queen of England and such a match could well bring the earl great wealth, status and numerous other rewards. When I looked at her face, to my great surprise, I saw tears welling up in her eyes; shaking her head, she whispered breathlessly and with a good deal of panic,

'No, no, I cannot! I cannot take him as my husband!' Mary was thrown into turmoil by my gentle questioning, but the vehemence of her reaction took me completely by surprise. Suddenly, I was gripped with panic. I knew what lay behind my sister's distress.

A sense of urgency seized our conversation. I needed to hear the truth from Mary directly and indicated that she should follow me immediately into my privy closet. Closing the door, I turned to my sister as she stood before me, her hands clasped in front of her belly, her eyes downcast in shame. I watched a fat tear spill down her cheek, as she fought to swallow the emotions which threatened to engulf her.

I was so determined to save Mary from herself, and to protect Anne and the Boleyn name, that I thought little of her happiness. Before I walked in Anne's shoes, I could never understand why the Boleyn family had so cruelly cast Mary out when she wed the lowly William Stafford, without seeking her sister's permission. But I had come to realise how easy it was to judge them from a position some 500 years in the future, where everything about social hierarchy, status and etiquette was entirely different to the unspoken—and sometimes spoken—laws which governed Tudor England.

The Boleyn family had been catapulted into the stratosphere by the stellar rise of their youngest daughter; Anne had rewritten the rulebook. Through the king's great love for her, she had displaced a queen of impeccable lineage and thereby had fatally undermined the stability of her own position as Henry's queen. Without a son, she would ever be vulnerable, falling prey to the sharks that circled her endlessly at court. In all this, I had come to realise that Mary's passionate flight of fancy to follow her heart could never be allowed. For to do so would be like spilling blood into the water, tempting the sharks into a fatal feeding frenzy that could seriously undermine the reputation of the Boleyns— and of Anne. Thus, I pressed on, 'Whatever it is you conceal within your heart, you must speak to me now of the truth. I command it as your mistress and queen.' My words sent Mary tumbling into a pit of despair, collapsing to the floor in front of me upon her knees, her skirts billowing around her as she cried with great racking sobs.

274

'I am in love with another and I cannot face to be parted from him.' I stood my ground. I could not afford to be sucked into Mary's plaintive distress. I needed to keep a clear head. So, a little more softly, I asked the question, to which I already knew the answer.

'Who do you love, Mary? Who have you foolishly given your heart to?' Mary looked up at me, her tearstained face full of despair, and the words delivered in great anguish-laden gulps of air.

'His name...his name is William Stafford. He serves his majesty as a soldier...and I met him ...whilst we were in Calais. Oh Anne, he is not a nobleman, but he has a good family.' Then steeling herself, she managed to say in one go, 'What is more, despite everything that I am, he truly loves me and treats me with great kindness. It is as if I am the centre of his world.' She delivered her last words defiantly, and they were filled with a joy and pride that I had rarely seen in her. I think I realised in that moment how little Mary thought of herself; I saw that she too had bought into the myth of being the 'great and infamous whore'. She expected to be used and cast aside by men as a trifle. I suspect that she had never dreamt that she would ever meet a man like William, who would love her only for who she was, and not for what she could do for him. Yet her fierce defiance was momentary, and soon melted away to be replaced by even greater, tormented sobs that grieved for a love which she feared to lose.

I walked over to my sister and awkwardly sunk to my own knees, taking her hands in mine and asking with all solemnity,

'Mary, have you given yourself to this man; are you betrothed?' Still crying, she shook her head and groaned simply,

'No, no...no, I have not.'

'Then as your queen and head of this household, I command you for your good and that of this family to leave him.' Mary knew what I was about to say, yet my words sent her into great convulsions. I did not let go of her hands, but allowed her to wring herself dry of tears for several minutes before I repeated my command. 'Do you understand me, sister? You must write William Stafford and tell him that your relationship is over. If you commit yourself to him, you will be thrown out of this family forever, do you not see that?' Mary looked up at me with her bloodshot eyes, her creamy complexion mottled with great, red blotches bearing testament to her anguish, as she protested,

'Why is it that you alone are allowed happiness in this family, Your Majesty?' The words, 'Your Majesty' were virtually spat at me with a disdain that I had never heard from my sister before. I saw the anger in her face, and flinched involuntarily at her accusation. 'I have done everything that our father has asked of me. I gave myself to the king when I was commanded. I accepted William Carey, who was virtually bribed to take me as his wife when no one else would touch me, and you... Have I ever denied you your happiness? Have I ever sought to cause you pain? Why is your heart so set in stone against me? Why can you not just do this one thing and allow me my own happiness?'

I can still see so clearly the angelic face of my sister, so contorted with desolate pain and burning resentment. I knew that in the short term I would break her heart, but I hoped sincerely that with the passage of time she would find love again and forgive me. Thus, I ignored my sister's words. Moving over to the richly bound Bible on a nearby table, I turned to face my sister, laying my left hand upon it as I said,

'Mary, I am sorry for your pain, but one day you will understand that what I ask is for the good of us all, including you. You must promise me that you will forsake him. Place your hand upon this Bible and swear to God that you will do this. And in return, I swear to you that I will speak to no one of this, neither to the king, nor to our father.'

Reluctantly, Mary stepped toward the Bible and rested her right palm upon the words of the Good Lord. In a whisper, I repeated my command, 'Swear upon the damnation of your soul that you will leave this man.' Mary looked at the Bible, as she whispered,

'I swear that I shall so do.' Then she added, 'So help me God.'

I was certain that to swear upon the damnation of her soul was to make a pledge she would not break. I could never speak to her of the fate of which she was entirely ignorant; a fate of banishment, social isolation and poverty. It is truly a testament to my beloved sister that she would risk the great displeasure of the king and write to me here in the Tower, casting aside all the hurt that had been done to her, speaking to me only of her heartbreak that George and I were thus imprisoned; that above all else, she would always love me most dearly—both in this world and the next. I pray silently in my heart for her forgiveness.

Chapter Twenty-Four

Greenwich Palace,
7 September 1533

It was the dead of night, the stillness of the room disturbed only by the rhythmical sound of the breathing of two of my ladies who slept soundly on pallet beds nearby. I lay on my side, curled up, my hands tucked beneath my cheek as a pillow, the pain in my head a constant bedfellow. To minimise my discomfort, I remained perfectly still, watching only the flicker of light cast out by a solitary candle burning at the side of my bed. Beyond it, the hand of the lantern clock, given to me by Henry as one of my many wedding presents, approached four o'clock in the morning. The elaborate copper gilt case glistened in the candlelight and in my mind's eye, I allowed myself to trace its outline, admiring the fearsome lion which surmounted it, holding within its paws the coat of arms of England, whilst two weights hung down beneath the case, each engraved with the initials 'H' and 'A' entwined with true lover's knots.

I was lost for a moment, recalling the events that had led to this night. In my mind I was suddenly in my presence chamber at Greenwich. I saw the faces of courtiers who had gathered there, parting to allow me to pass; falling away with the ease of autumn leaves which, as winter approaches, finally surrender their claim to the branches that once nurtured them. Faces filled with intense curiosity and expectation followed my every delicate step. I was walking toward the entrance to my privy chamber and my confinement until the birth of England's new Tudor rose. I recall how the fiery, summer sun of that August afternoon streamed through its south facing windows, capturing every vivid detail etched into the faces of those noblemen and women that surrounded me; how the light illuminated their eyes—the windows to their souls— and the truth written across their hearts; that for every person that prayed fervently for Anne's safe delivery, another wished that death would take her and Henry's Boleyn heir, without mercy, in childbed.

As the last melted away, the door which divided the very public outside world from the inner secluded one loomed in front of me. Once

I passed through it, I would be sealed off from the court, living within an entirely female domain until my child was born. I halted. The liveried guards on either side of the doorway awaited my command. During the few moments in which I paused there, I was besieged by a multitude of conflicting thoughts and emotions. On one level, I was sure that Anne would live, but I was terrified at the ordeal which lay ahead of me. This was Anne's first child, and she was no longer in the first flush of youth. I wondered how her body would physically cope with labour, or how I would cope without access to any kind of pain relief. As I entered into my eight month of pregnancy in this unbearably hot summer, I began to long for this baby to be born, to relieve myself of the discomfort that grew daily. I was utterly exhausted, not just because of the countless sleepless nights I endured as Elizabeth kicked and stretched her tiny body in my womb, nor indeed on account of the fact that the sheer size of my belly made it increasingly difficult to breathe when I tried to lie down, but because I had felt ever more unwell since Henry had left me alone at Windsor.

The altercation with my sister had troubled me sorely; nevertheless, as I promised, I spoke of it to no one—not even Margery. Perhaps it was a coincidence, but by nightfall on that very same day, I took to my bed with one of my usual headaches which I attributed to the stress of our emotional exchange. However, this time the headache did not abate within a few hours as it had done before, but persisted for several long and increasingly uncomfortable days. To begin with, I was aggrieved that the king should leave me so nigh, whilst he made merry chasing deer—and in my own fevered imagination—pretty women, up and down the Thames Valley. However, by the time Henry returned, I had become too ill to care. The headaches, which had been unpleasant but tolerable to begin with, were becoming increasingly severe. The swelling that had been confined to my feet and ankles had begun to spread up my legs to my shins.

I tried to remain calm, but the fear I saw mirrored in the faces of my mother, those ladies who attended me, and my doctors, reflected only what was becoming increasingly clear to me. Something was terribly wrong and that daily, my life and that of the child I carried, hung evermore in the balance. Although the Tudor doctors knew not the cause of my peril, they certainly recognised the symptoms—the effects of high blood pressure, which was potentially life-threatening to both mother and child in the later stages of pregnancy. Perversely, in some ways, I was thankful that they had little more in their medical toolbox than prayers and amulets. I feared any more invasive intervention might do more harm than good. Occasionally, I submitted myself to leeches prescribed to balance my humours, which according to my doctors had clearly gone awry. Of course, I knew all this was fruitless, and within a few short weeks, was indeed living daily in fear for my life. I was reminded what it was to feel entirely in God's hands with nothing, absolutely nothing I could do but pray for divine intervention and the Lord's grace to save us both.

Henry had been informed of my deteriorating condition and hastened back to my bedside, arriving at Windsor on 12 August. I remember opening my eyes to see my husband over by the window recess in my bedchamber, discussing my condition with my physician, Richard Bartlett. The two men spoke in hushed whispers, thinking I was asleep. However, in the quiet stillness of the afternoon, I overheard their exchange quite clearly. Dr Bartlett spoke first,

'I fear that as the child grows, he is weakening her grace's constitution.' Still nobody dared touch on the possibility that I might be carrying a new princess of the realm. Henry was standing half cast in shadow as I saw him stroke his cropped beard before speaking with a hint of irritation,

'What are you saying, man? Is the queen's life in peril?' Through the throbbing pain in my head, I barley opened my eyes, but it was enough to see my physician nod in affirmation, before adding,

'Your Grace, the longer the pregnancy continues, the greater the danger to her Grace's life...and indeed that of the child.' I watched Henry turn aside and begin to pace in front of the window. For a moment he paused, running his hand over the back of his head in desperate agitation. I could not think straight, but even in my half-conscious state, I remember feeling happy to see Henry again and somehow consoled that he seemed so genuinely distressed at my suffering. Suddenly, the king halted; turning about on his heels, he approached Dr. Bartlett once more, asking,

'What can be done? She must not die, I could not face...' Henry's words trailed away. For a moment, I heard the vulnerability and fear of a child in his voice, and was flooded with a sense of peace. With these words, I knew that Henry loved me as he ever did.

'I suggest that we bleed her majesty again and see if we can stabilise her condition. I do not think it wise to remove the queen to Greenwich while she is afflicted with such severe pain in the head.'

'Are you saying that we must delay her grace's lying in?' Again Dr. Bartlett nodded slowly, as he replied,

'Yes, Your Majesty that is exactly what I am saying. Until her grace is a little stronger, I think it would be most unwise to attempt the journey.' Henry leaned in even closer and in a menacing voice hissed, '*We* will do as you suggest, but you had better make sure that the queen is brought to bed safely—for the sake of this realm—and yours!'

Henry's words echoed briefly in my mind. Once more in my mind, I saw the great, gilded oak doors, and above them my falcon badge. I turned to look over my shoulder. Beyond the train of ladies who had processed with me to the doors of my privy chambers, I could see Henry. He was surrounded by his nobles, including my father, with Master Cromwell at his side. I wanted to see the king's face for one last time. Indeed, I wondered if I would ever see him again.

I knew many women did not survive childbirth. But even if history continued to stubbornly unfold as it should, and Anne survive, for the first time in many months, I felt precariously balanced between her world and my own twenty-first century life. In fact, I had begun to wonder if the trigger that opened up the portal between this world and the other was illness. As I grew more unwell, I was sure that I began to hear ghostly voices that spoke to me in modern parlance—even sometimes calling out my name. Yet, whenever I turned about, there was no one there. It reminded me of the time that I had heard the distant echoes of Mary's voice on the spiral staircase at Hever Castle, just before I had crossed over into Anne's world for the very first time. Then I had fallen ill with a ruptured aneurysm, and I wondered, as Anne fell ever more gravely ill, if the tentacles of my modern day life were beginning to reach out and encircle me; whether, when Anne emerged through that doorway to re-join the court, I would be long gone, sucked back to the twenty-first century for good.

As I reflected on all of this, I saw that Henry hardly moved, his eyes meeting mine. A faint smile of remembrance played upon his lips which spoke of his great love and faith in me; that he longed for my return to his arms, and to place a new prince in the nursery. In that moment, I saw every struggle and hope of the past six years encapsulated in one brief glance. I swallowed hard at the sheer suffocating weight of expectation. I could not bear it anymore and looked away. Summoning every molecule of courage and strength available to me, I turned to face the door, indicating that it should be opened. With a train of ladies in attendance, I stepped forward, taking my leave of the male world, walking ahead to meet my fate—and Anne's.

The interior of my privy chamber was a startling contrast to the presence chamber that I had just left behind me. I immediately felt claustrophobic. Gone were the light, bright, airy rooms that I had become so accustomed to. Instead, they were replaced by a series of gloomy chambers devoid of any light, save for the flicker of candles and flames licking at the coal-fuelled fires that burnt in every room. I knew what to expect, although I had dreaded this moment of confinement. The stuffy, darkened conditions that I must endure for the next few weeks were entirely at odds with Anne's love of open spaces and fresh air.

I had no choice. According to the rules set out some years earlier by the indomitable Margaret Beaufort, Henry's grandmother, the suite of rooms that I was to occupy must be sealed against any drafts that might cause a chill or allow in evil spirits to steal the baby's soul. They were to be made warm and 'cosy' by keeping the curtains drawn at all times—except at one small window—and by fires that were kept burning day and night, regardless of the outside temperature. As I stepped inside, I halted for a few moments, allowing my eyes to adjust to the darkness. A wave of heat was the first intense sensation to hit me. It was not made any more tolerable on account of the fact that I was still quite unwell. Indeed, it had been a considerable accomplishment that had brought me from Windsor Castle to Greenwich at all; although it had taken more than the two days that had been originally anticipated in Cromwell's meticulous plans.

Some three weeks before, in early August, carpenters and other workmen had set about preparing the queen's chambers for my confinement at Greenwich. However, the date for the ceremonial entry into those chambers was calculated according to my delivery dates, the

16 August—which came and went as I still lay in my sickbed at Windsor. In the meantime, I continued to insist to both Henry and Master Cromwell that the difficulties I was experiencing in these late stages of pregnancy should be kept, as much as possible, from reaching outside ears. I did not wish information spreading abroad that could in any way be construed and used by my enemies against me. As a result, Cromwell continued to issue statements that everything was progressing well, that the king and queen were merry and in good health. I, in turn, ensured an Oscar-winning performance when I finally emerged to face the court, transferring first to Whitehall and then, after a few days' rest, to Greenwich.

With considerable relief to both the king and my physicians, we eventually arrived at Greenwich. With all due haste, a mass was sung in the chapel royal, before I made my way at the king's side to my chambers. The solemn ceremony of 'taking to my chambers' had taken its toll though. I was feeling increasingly unwell once more as exhaustion and a familiar pain began to grip my head like a vice, tightening with every passing moment. I made toward my bedchamber, for I needed to lie down.

My bedchamber had been transformed into a cocooned, inner sanctum in which I would finally give birth to my darling Elizabeth. Once again, it was cast in gloomy darkness, as if it were already night-time. The curtains were tightly drawn across every window, while about the walls, some of Henry's most expensive carpets and tapestries were hung to exclude unnecessary drafts. In the many hours that I was to spend confined to my bed, I would become intimately acquainted with those tapestries. They told the story of St Ursula and the 11,000 virgins—a myriad of ancient faces—led by St Ursula herself, a martyred English princess, who stared down upon me hour after hour, with a fitting blend of piety, compassion and sadness etched upon her young face. And so, accompanied by my ladies, I was finally hidden away from the outside world, about to face the most dangerous ten days of my life thus far.

My recollections were interrupted as the handle of the door to my bedchamber made the lightest of noises, giving away the arrival of two shadowy figures that slipped inside my room from the privy chamber beyond. Wincing against the pain, I turned my head, lifting myself up on one elbow. I watched as the two ladies picked their way carefully toward me, guarding their silence jealously. As they came close to my bedside, the willowy light of the nearby candle illuminated their faces, revealing my sister, Mary and the woman I had chosen some weeks earlier as my midwife, a certain Margaret Symons.

Thankfully, the king had allowed me to select the woman who would attend me during my confinement. Thus, in good time, I had interviewed several midwives, knowing the qualities and attitudes that I needed in them. Of course, they had to be of good standing and reputation. Yet, I also knew that if I did suffer from pre-eclampsia, as I strongly suspected, a time may come when I would need that midwife to hasten my labour to save Anne's life, and that of her child. In such a scenario, I would need her to be discreet, and obey my instructions, for I knew many of Anne's contemporaries frowned upon such practice, ignorant of the fact that in this case, it might be the only thing that would allow us both to survive. I could not speak of what I knew to be true as I was terrified that such a tendency to premonition could so easily be used as an indictment for witchcraft by careless tongues.

In the end, I chose a good-natured young woman with enough experience to give her credibility, yet not of sufficient age to make her opinions brittle and inflexible. Her main focus appeared to be on comforting and cheering the women in her care, encouraging other women present to say prayers and do the same. I had heard terrifying stories of midwives intent on pushing down upon the belly from above, of forcing the child to be born, or of manipulating a woman's parts with their hands, ahead of the woman's readiness to deliver. I wished for no such intervention, and Margaret, it seemed, also held no such aspirations. It was the perfect match. Arriving at my bedside, both ladies curtsied, before my sister leaned forward and whispered,

'Your Majesty, I have brought forth Mistress Symons as you have commanded.' I silently nodded my thanks to my sister, and indicated with the beckoning motion of my hand that Margaret should come in close. I too needed to speak in hushed tones. I did not yet want to disturb Nan or my sister-in-law, Lady Jane, both of whom still slept peacefully in attendance at the foot of my bed.

'Mistress Symons, it is yet a week until my child is due, and yet as you know, daily I feel ever weaker and fear that if this child does not come soon, neither of us will survive this ordeal.' Since my confinement, I made it my business to meet with Margaret regularly, appraising her of my state of health and I confess, gently and rather manipulatively, sowing the seeds in her mind that I then set forth to reap. 'I think you would do the king and me a great service if you would bring on my labour this night.' I watched as Mistress Symons frowned and d my sister drew breath. In panic, Mary made to speak,

'Anne, you cannot...' I raised my hand, commanding her to silence. I did not even look at Mary; instead, my gaze remained fixed upon my midwife as I feared that in that moment, she would deny me. But I had selected well, and the trust and loyalty I had painstakingly built then bore the fruit I desired. Slowly, Margaret's frown melted from her brow and she had nodded almost imperceptibly, adding,

'You wish me to break your water, your Majesty?' Her voice was calm and even, and her words merely those of clarification. I replied,

'Yes, Margaret that is exactly what I'm requesting. Will you do as I command?' Mistress Symonds nodded in affirmation, and thus I added, 'Then I ask that you wash your hands thoroughly, and Mary...' I then turned to my sister, and with urgency requested, '...fetch some strong spirit so that Mistress Symonds can clean the instrument she needs to use.' I knew that my request sounded strange in a time when there was no understanding of the role of bacteria in creating infection and illness. Yet I did not care, for I could not take the chance that the risky procedure that I requested would be complicated by lethal infection. Then I added, 'I need both of you to swear to me upon your honour and life that you will speak to no one of what we have done here this night,' I looked earnestly from one to the other, making plain the gravity of my request. Both women nodded their assent before I continued, '...and until it is done, you must progress without disturbing anyone.' Again Mistress Symons and my sister acknowledged their understanding and slipped away silently to make preparations.

As the midwife slipped her hand inside me, it was done as I felt the warm rush of water between my thighs and the embryonic sac that had nurtured my child for so long was broken. Covering myself once again, I drew myself up with some considerable effort, sitting up straight in the bed as Mistress Symons whispered,

'Now, Your Majesty, I suggest that you break your fast and eat well while you can, for once the pains come on strongly, there will be little chance to take food...and you will need all the strength you can get in the coming hours.' I suddenly felt afraid, even vulnerable, and so it was my turn to nod my understanding, silently and wide-eyed with fear. Margaret must have seen my distress. Brushing aside all the normal rules of etiquette in Tudor society, she reached over and squeezed my hand. In the intimacy of my bedchamber, before dawn cast itself upon the land, she added with calm reassurance, 'There is nothing to fear Your Grace. You are held in the love of God and will not be forsaken, and by the end of this day you will be delivered of your child.' I knew these were only words but, oh, how her certainty, her calm decisiveness—which had so often been my own but had now inconveniently deserted me—was just what I needed to hear.

Thus, at my command, my sister raised Nan and Lady Jane from their quiet slumber. As first light crept over the horizon on that Sunday morning, Mary, Margaret and I kept our shared secret, knowing that my pains were soon to come. As the queen's apartments stirred into life, I ate well, before making my way to my privy closet and the oratory to pray for my safe delivery and that of my child. In the quiet of the only space that I could call my own, I knelt before the altar, hands clasped in prayer before my breast, my eyes lightly shut, and my eyelids flickering as adrenaline coursed through my body. It was just like when I had set out from Greenwich afore my coronation, I had to gather in my energy, to calm myself in silent meditation, and to prepare myself for what I must endure. In a whisper, barely audible even to myself, my lips moved in exhortation of the Good Lord as I prayed.

'Dear God, whatever happens this day, give me the strength to face my duty with courage, dignity and calm.' I hesitated for a moment, before asking again for the thousandth time, 'please God, let this child come forth safely into this world, I ask not for me, but for Anne...let this child be a boy. Just let me do this for her, then, if you must, take me back to my other life, to whatever fate awaits me.'

It was increasingly rare that I saw myself as separate from my heroine; her body had become mine and her life absorbed me completely. Yet that morning, I felt the two of us precariously balanced, our souls slipping in and out of the other. I was sure that at some point, I would leave Anne's body and my sixteenth century life behind, possibly forever. All I had wanted was a happy ending for her, and I was determined to play my part.

Suddenly, whilst contemplating these thoughts, a dull ache gripped me around my belly. It was as if someone had tightened a belt strongly around my waist. The suddenness of it made me gasp, one hand involuntarily reaching down to embrace my swollen abdomen. I knew immediately that it was Anne's time. My labour had begun. It was the beginning of the day that changed my life in a way I had simply never conceived was possible. I had been so focused on the need to give Henry his male heir that I had never accounted for the fact that I would fall so utterly in love with my darling Elizabeth; that I would know a love that was so fierce and utterly unconditional that I would be hopelessly swept away in her innocent vulnerability and forever bound to protect her at all costs against her enemies—and mine.

For a number of hours, the contractions remained quite far apart, allowing me time to rest in between, while my ladies chatted to keep my spirits high, occasionally offering me cordials made from alcohol. I soon realised that these were the sixteenth century equivalent of pain relief. The delightful glow brought on by the sweet liquid flushed through my body, initially taking the edge off the pain in my belly and my head, helping me relax into the moment. As the laughter and banter of my ladies filled my bedchamber, I thought of Henry in another part of the palace. On my orders, he was informed that my labour was underway. I was sure that with a mixture of both excitement and trepidation, he prayed fervently for our safe delivery.

Of course, as the morning progressed, the pains became considerably more intense, each contraction coming closer to the next and with ever greater force. By the time the clock on my wall was striking midday, each one felt as if red hot pokers were being forced through my abdomen and down my inner thighs. The pain was searing and I cried out for the love of God to save me; and there were times when I was sure that I would die, and that what was being asked of my body was utterly impossible. By and by, I became overwhelmingly tired, and during the brief respite between contractions, all I had wanted to do was lay my head upon the pillow and sleep for all eternity.

Yet, the worst was to come. Shortly after two o'clock in the afternoon, eight hours after my pains commenced, I felt the strangest snapping sensation in my spine, as if I was being broken apart. I was abruptly engulfed with an overwhelming desire to bear down, and in this way, the second stage of my labour began.

As well as my midwife, my sister was by my side, kneeling on the right hand side of my pallet bed and gripping my hand as surely as I gripped hers. On my left, was the sweet little Mary Howard. I saw a mixture of awe, excitement and fear in her young eyes. Despite being consumed with exhaustion and fiery pain, I was touched that yet again this young woman was once more loyally at my side. My indomitable friend, Margery, a mother many times over herself, assisted my midwife calmly, whilst Lady Jane Rochford, Nan and Joan busied themselves fetching and carrying nourishment, linen and other such items requested by Mistress Symons. Several times, I heard myself cry out plaintively, 'I cannot do it! I cannot do it!' and as I did so, either my sister or Margery would lean in and sweep a lock of hair away from my fevered brow, smiling calmly and reassuring me that all was well.

With every contraction, I pushed harder, garnering every ounce of strength that I had until suddenly, a fiery burning tore through my perineum as my baby's head was delivered to great cries of joy from the ladies surrounding me. Finally, with the next contraction, the shoulders slipped out effortlessly followed by the rest of its tiny body. In the rush and confusion, I saw a flash of my baby lifted into the air, the midwife wrapping it in linen and rubbing at the infant until a small but determined cry rang out from its newly inflated lungs. I was exhausted but utterly elated, forgetting for the briefest moment about the Sword of Damocles which hung above my head. I was so utterly relieved that it was over, and that the child was alive, that for a few short seconds, I failed to notice the hush that had descended upon the room. However, when I looked up at Margery, I saw despair in her face and I noticed that as Mistress Symons attended to the child, she too, like everyone else in the room, would not look me in the eye.

'Margery, what is it?' Suddenly, I was consumed with a blinding panic, and the blissful moment of ignorance, which I had all too briefly enjoyed, was instantly swept aside. Margery finally turned to look at me. I watched as she summoned the bravest of smiles and said,

'Your Majesty, you have given birth to a very beautiful and healthy baby girl.' It was as if I had been hit by the hardest blow to my chest. Everything that I had hoped and prayed for lay smashed around me. How can you describe the overwhelming maternal love and joy that I felt for my child, against the desolate sense of failure which suddenly engulfed me? I had been ill for weeks, and had just endured a labour that felt as if it had physically torn my body in two. But what I feared more than anything was that I would have to face Henry's bitter disappointment; and whether our precious love would be irreparably rent apart by my failure to give the king his longed for son and heir. I was inconsolable. Great racking sobs poured forth and wrung every remaining ounce of energy from my body. I howled in despair, turning my face to God and crying out over and over,

'Why God? Why? Why? Why have you deserted me?' Of course, my ladies tried to console me. My sister sweeping me up in her arms, as I sunk headlong into her lap crying a seemingly endless torrent of bitter tears, until after perhaps ten or fifteen minutes, Margery approached me, holding in her arms a tiny bundle of swaddled cloth. She leaned over, lowering my daughter so that I might see her face. There she was, my Elizabeth, my own flesh and blood, my own beating heart; a tiny nose and mouth so perfect, so delicate, and a shock of red hair declaring to all that she was indeed the cub of the great lion of England.

'Come, Your Grace, she is beautiful. Why don't you hold her?' Until that moment, I had been so devastated by my failure to bear the king a son that I had not thought to see her again, nor did I want to hold her in my arms. I will be forever grateful to Margery, who gently insisted that I did so; Elizabeth, the most precious consolation to me in this life.

I wiped the tears from my eyes, before taking Elizabeth tentatively in my arms. Right there and then, I fell so deeply in love, it was unfathomable. Her tiny eyes struggled to flicker open, bemused and bewildered as she fought to focus upon my face. My instinct took over and I immediately put her to my breast, utterly beguiled by the miracle of her existence. It was 3.10 pm on Sunday, 7 September, 1533, and I knew that I held within my arms the future Elizabeth I, one of the greatest sovereigns who would ever sit upon the throne of England. She had been born into a violent and treacherous world, but in that moment, as I gazed into the depths of her deep brown eyes, I vowed that nobody would harm her so long as there was breath in my body.

I was free. For thirty days following the birth of Elizabeth, I remained secluded from the outside world. Despite the difficulties I encountered during the final weeks of my pregnancy, in the end, my daughter had been delivered easily enough. Henry, of course, was devastated that I had not given him his longed for son and heir. Although our reconciliation would be bumpy, he seemed as relieved as I that within a matter of a few short days, the persistent headaches and the swelling in my legs had begun to recede quickly. Daily, I regained my former strength and oh, what a blessed relief to feel the lightness in my body return! The weight that I gained during pregnancy miraculously melted away, and Anne's famous lithe body was soon recognisable once more.

Of course, my breasts remained swollen with milk, and much to the shock and consternation of several senior noblewomen who visited me in my chambers, I was to be found breastfeeding my child, quite contrary to accepted practice. Word of this soon reached Henry, and although he indulged me by allowing me to keep Elizabeth close by my side, he forbade me to nurse her. No doubt, he was eager that I would shortly fall pregnant again—this time with the son he so desired.

I will never forget though the ordeal of seeing my husband for the first time after Elizabeth was born. He came in to my chamber the very afternoon when I was sitting in bed, holding Elizabeth in my arms, surrounded by my ladies. He entered the room, stood at the foot of the bed and stared down at our daughter. I was not able to look him in the eye to begin with, for I did not want to face what I might see there. Eventually, I raised my gaze to acknowledge the presence of my sovereign lord. I remember seeing a tempest of emotion in those piercing, unforgiving, blue eyes of Henry's. I saw his anger, disappointment and bitterness at what I was sure he perceived as my betrayal. I desperately searched those eyes for a shard of love or pride in our beautiful daughter, and I confess that when I saw none, I was heartbroken, afraid and angry that he might easily cast her out. Eventually, he raised his gaze to meet mine. There was the longest silence between us, a silence filled with the prickly energy of contempt and resentment. Finally in a strained voice, Henry said,

'Is the child healthy?' I nodded silently, hardly able to speak myself, before Henry continued, 'You and I are both young, and by God's grace, boys will follow.' In a whisper, I replied rather feebly,

'Yes, next time we will have a son, Your Grace. I am sure of it.' I watched Henry's jaw clench, and I knew that in private, away from my ladies, I would have to bear a storm of discontent that in that moment, the king struggled to contain. Henry did not move to kiss me, or give me his blessing. I could not feel the king's love for Anne, as I had always done before. As a result, an ominous panic took hold that chilled me to the bone. In a feeble attempt to reach out to my love, and heal the rift between us, I said with a heart full of sorrow,

'I'm so sorry... Please forgive me.' Around me, I was aware that Nan, Lady Mary and my sister-in-law, Jane, hung their heads, surely suffering the palpable tension between Henry and me. They were no doubt desperate to melt away from the explosive outburst they feared would surely come from the king. Yet Henry said nothing—which was perhaps worse. Instead, it was my husband's turn to nod his head in acknowledgement of my apology. However, it was not a gesture that spoke of understanding and forgiveness, but one filled with tension, humiliation and rage. Henry then turned upon his heals and swept from the room, leaving in his wake a palpable air of discontent.

He visited me and Elizabeth several times thereafter over the next few weeks while I remained patiently cooped up in my continued confinement. Then, on the morning of 7 October, much to my own wonderment, I stepped out of the queen's chambers at Greenwich, my foothold in Anne's world becoming ever more secure following the birth of my child. The ghostly voices that wafted across darkened corners of the palace suddenly vanished, and it seemed that my adventure in the sixteenth century was far from over. I left my apartments and confinement behind, carrying a lighted taper in my hand with a veil of black lace, edged with black damask, draped over my head. My time of seclusion was had come to an end. I was to be 'churched' in the chapel royal as custom dictated, before my re-entry into court society—and Henry's bed.

Looking back, I remember how, in the few weeks leading up to Elizabeth's birth, when I was ill and afraid of failure, I began to dream of release; how I had wanted to return to my twenty-first century life. Although far from perfect, it carried nowhere near the heavy weight of expectation that daily haunted me as I walked in the shoes of a Tudor queen. Yet after Elizabeth was born, a whole new light was cast upon my world. She was Anne's child, but I had borne her, and in my heart, she was also mine. I had never loved with such a frightening intensity. It was a love which seemed to know no bounds, and overnight, I became terrified of being snatched away from her. I could not bear the thought that I might never again feel her warm, tiny body pressed close to mine. With Elizabeth in my arms, even my relationship with Daniel paled into insignificance. I quickly recognised that my karmic duty lay with my daughter and in my mind, I resolved to keep hold of my sixteenth century life, no matter what the cost.

Following mass, I received a message that the king wished to speak with me alone. With a certain amount of trepidation, I made my way to the king's privy apartments. I dreaded the time that I would be truly alone with Henry, when there would be no pretence for the sake of appearances, and when I would see, in grisly detail, the true extent of the damage that had been done in the wake of Elizabeth's birth.

So I processed in full regal splendour from my holy day closet, through Henry's presence chamber to the inner sanctum of his privy apartments. I was escorted to the entrance of the three-storey donjon that contained the king's most private of rooms by one of the king's gentlemen, Sir Richard Page. Once within the donjon, I did not pass straight along the short gallery that led into the king's bedchamber, as I had done on the night that Elizabeth was conceived. This time, I was to meet with Henry in his library located on the second floor. Sir Richard indicated that I should proceed alone. I took my first steps up the narrow, spiral staircase, my left hand running against the rough surface of brick, whilst my right lifted the hem of my gown. Beyond me, just a couple of turns of the staircase away was the King of England, who awaited me with accusations of failure and betrayal, of that I was sure.

At the top of the staircase, a heavy oak door fitted with an elaborate golden lock was already partially ajar. Knowing his majesty's will, I entered alone. The king's library occupied the same footprint as the bedchamber directly below it. These most privy of Henry's chambers was intimate, covering only approximately twenty-five feet by fifteen feet. Like the bedchamber below, it was also embellished with two octagonal towers that protruded over the water's edge, giving fine views up and down the Thames. As in every royal library, the books contained within were so precious and expensive that they were not packed together tightly on shelves with their spines outermost. Rather, the most expensive ones were laid out on sloping shelves set around the room, displayed so that the front cover was visible to all.

When I first entered the room, to my surprise, I could not see the king. So instead, I took a moment to forget my cares and look around me, to admire the many fine illuminated manuscripts and printed books that were on display. I was familiar with the layout of all the king's principal libraries at Greenwich, Hampton Court and Westminster; libraries which had all recently been refitted and modernised to accommodate the increased numbers of books that were acquired by Henry to provide academic and divine justification for his divorce from Katherine. The library at Greenwich contained, all told, seven desks, combined lecterns and bookshelves. Over 300 books were arranged, for the most part, by colour.

Many of the books hidden within, or under the desks, were of less value and bound simply with embossed leather. However, the more costly amongst them were on display, each and every one bound in rich velvet of purple, crimson, blue, green or black, the corners protected with elaborate gold mountings, the edges of every page gilded, and finally, each book fastened with two similarly ornate gold clasps that were bejewelled with precious stones. I took a couple of steps closer to the nearest shelves to my left, running my fingertips across the bindings of one such book. Like all its companions, it was ornately decorated with delicate embroidery of coloured silks, gold and silver thread, in this case detailing the coat of arms of Henry's father, Henry VII, for whom it had once been commissioned or gifted. Such a great collection of books was rare indeed, and beneath my fingertips, I felt the subtle vibration carried by each one, an imprint of the individual king, queen or nobleman who had most loyally thumbed its pages in times past. I was aware that even in the sixteenth century, some of these manuscripts were already many hundreds of years old. Held within their pages was not only a wealth of knowledge, but traits of the greatest attributes of mankind, as well as the seeds of its worst excesses. I would come to take many things for granted in my Tudor life, but I would be forever awed in the presence of these priceless gems.

Enjoying a moment during which I thought that I was alone, I continued to trail my finger idly along one shelf, until I turned my attention toward one of the tables positioned in the centre of the room. Upon it, and next to an astrolabe and an ornate ink well, lay an open manuscript. Even from a distance, the vivid illumination of its pages, glistening with gold and set against vibrant reds, blues and greens, caught my eye and drew me in like a magpie. I walked towards it, but before I had chance to inspect the book, I suddenly became aware of the king, his broad back turned towards me, arms folded, standing inside the north-west octagonal tower and looking out from one of the windows set within its wall.

It was a clear, frosty morning, as the first breath of winter cast itself upon the land. I saw easily beyond his silhouette, through the window and toward the sight of several galleons under construction, perhaps half a mile upstream at the Port of Deptford. Engrossed in watching his navy being built, Henry had not heard my coming. For a moment, I wanted to turn on my tiptoes, and leave the room silently, but of course, I knew that I must face him. So, I finally broke the silence.

'Your Majesty.' The king turned his head quickly, looking over his shoulder. I had taken him by surprise. I dipped into a humble and submissive curtsy. After a few seconds, I raised my eyes and then myself, whilst Henry turned about to face me, taking several steps forward to the centre of the room where I was standing. I watched him study me, as if he had never seen me before, as if I were alien to him and he wished to see into my heart; was I a friend or foe? After what seemed like an eternity, my husband spoke ominously.

'You promised me a son.' I waited for more, but nothing came. Indeed, I wished it had, as this simple, piercing accusation cut through me like a knife. There was nowhere to hide. In the silence I nodded, feeling the tension build in my neck and shoulders, as I replied in barely a whisper,

'Yes, Your Majesty.' Then my emotion burst through the veneer of my defiance, and I rushed forth, making to throw my arms about Henry. We had not touched since Elizabeth had been born and I longed for our physical reunion. As I did so, I cried out plaintively, 'Please forgive me, Henry…I am so, so sorry.' I would have said anything to make things right again between us. 'It was not my fault. I didn't do anything wrong!' Henry's response was vitriolic, brushing me aside with his hand, unable to receive my affection. Thus, he stepped away, pacing the room, his face hardened with fiery fury.

'It is your fault, Anne! Have I not born a son with Elizabeth Blount and your sister? Am I not like any other man? You promised me a son and you did not deliver. I gave you everything, and what do I have in return? Nothing. I look like a fool afore the whole of Christendom!' The ferocity of Henry's attack seemed all too unfair. I had come wanting to apologise. I wanted to show him my love and my loyalty and yet, in that moment, the gross injustice—that all the blame should be laid at my door—triggered an outpouring of my own reckless anger. Somewhere in the logic of my mind, I knew the truth; neither of us was to 'blame'. Of course, I was unable to attack the ridiculous Tudor superstitions that surrounded conception and birth, superstitions that lay so much of the blame for any such mishap firmly at the woman's door. In my frustration, I directed my attack toward the obvious continued cause of my discontent—Katherine and Mary.

'Perhaps if you had managed to get yourself a divorce from Katherine earlier, there would be no question of the validity of our marriage. Perhaps, God is angry that it took so long for you to get out of that unholy union. Perhaps, if I hadn't been so distressed for months, no years, wondering if we would ever be together, then all would be well and we would have a son by now, in fact many sons.' I knew that everything I was saying was illogical and irrational, but Anne's intemperance was no bedfellow of logic, as I was swept up once more in a primitive desire to both lash out at Henry, and defend our new-born daughter. Thus, I forged on, 'You have no idea how great your daughter could be, but I have seen it in your eyes; you do not even love her— and yet you love Mary, your bastard child.' My voice was full of resentment, as I spat out the word 'bastard' with venom. 'You refuse to bring either Katherine or Mary to heel, and in the meantime, what am I supposed to think? How do you think that makes me feel?'

When Henry replied, he did so with a steely authority that was often more intimidating than his outright anger. Brooding within his words were laced the most dangerous of tones.

'Madame, it seems you forget yourself—yet again.' Henry moved back around the table, across from where I was standing. Leaning forward upon both sets of knuckles, the king lowered his head, before raising his eyes to meet mine. Speaking softly at first, he said, 'You are my wife and my queen...' and then suddenly rising to a frightening and thunderous crescendo, he shouted, '...and I will not tolerate your insolence!' His fist smashed down on the table, spilling a pot of ink that rushed forth, engulfing all that lay within its path. Thankfully, the precious manuscript lay untouched and out of reach. After Henry's explosion, there was utter silence, during which I followed the rivulet of black fluid with my eyes, as it raced to reach the edge of the table and began to drip down onto the tiled floor below. Henry glowered at me, his face congested, his veins bulging as a flash of red exploded across his forehead, cheeks and neck; the intensity of his attack finally bringing me to my senses. Anne was quick to temper and easily enraged by injustice, but she was also smart. I recognised that in this instance, I had pushed it too far, and so collecting myself, I rather meekly nodded my head in understanding and apologised quietly.

'I'm sorry, Your Majesty. I should not have spoken thus. Please forgive me, Henry.' My husband stared at me for what seemed like several minutes, before finally, his anger begin to drain from his body. For all our fight and fury, for all our burning disappointment, I was still the love of his life, and sometimes I think that whilst he wanted to be angry with me, he could not sustain his rage. Thus it had been that day; he had wanted to hate me back then but I knew that having been 'churched' we could once again lie together, and I saw that beneath Henry's deeply wounded pride, he wanted me as fiercely as ever. All I needed to do was to surrender myself to his will, allow his ego to conquer me once more. With the cooling of my temper, I saw how I needed to deal with Henry, and made my silent commitment to rebuild his bruised pride and bring him back to my bed.

Suddenly, there was a knock at the door. The king adjusted his head, stretching his neck first his way then that, as if to release any final shards of tension that lay embedded there, before he called out,

'Enter.' With a gentle click of the latch, the door opened and my brother, George, stepped into the room. George had returned with the Duke of Norfolk from his embassy to Paris just in time for Elizabeth's christening, and our reunion was an emotional one. He held me knowingly within his strong, protective arms, kissing the top of my head and stroking my hair. George said nothing to me which spoke of disappointment, nor had he turned away from Elizabeth. Instead, I saw a side to my younger brother that I had not witnessed before. He took Elizabeth and unwrapped her from her swaddling clothes, lifting her above his head, her little arms and legs punching the air, clearly thrilled at being elevated so high. My brother cooed and gurgled with the same delight as my infant daughter, and in my heart, I loved him even more for his easy acceptance of her. In front of us that day, however, my brother bowed formally, no trace of that carefree, easy manner evident. Sweeping his cap from his head, he addressed the king directly,

'Your Majesty, Ambassador Chapuys has sought out his grace, the Duke of Norfolk and Master Cromwell and complains bitterly of what he perceives to be the unfair treatment of the princess dowager and the Lady Mary. In particular, he fears that with the proclamation of your legitimate daughter as Princess of Wales, the rights of the Lady Mary might be impaired, depriving her of her lawful succession to the throne. His grace felt that you might wish to intervene.' I felt my own temper flare; the lioness stirring to protect her cub. However, if I had offended the king that morning, then all memory of it had vanished. For if there was one thing that Henry could not abide, was that his will should be questioned, and even worse, by a mere foreigner. Immediately the king asserted,

'Go straight back to Norfolk and Cromwell. Tell them that I wish to meet with my councillors immediately. I will then speak with his grace and Master Cromwell alone in my privy chamber, to get them away from Chapuys' claws.' George swept a bow, and turned to make haste with the king's message. For a moment, Henry looked at me once more. This time, I took the initiative and curtsied again, before proffering,

'Your Majesty, it would honour me greatly if you would sup with me this evening, for I am holding a banquet for my family and our friends in celebration of my churching.' I was still as angry with my husband as he was with me, but I was determined to make amends for

Elizabeth sake, if not my own. Thus for once, I played the role of grateful and submissive wife. It was not an easy one. Nevertheless, I sensed it was the balm that Henry needed to begin to heal the wounds that he perceived I had afflicted upon him. It was the beginning of our reconciliation. Henry accepted my invitation, nodding rather curtly, before following George from the room.

I was alone inside the library as I heard the king's voice issuing orders, receding into the distance as the door to his privy chamber was closed behind him. The weight of my conversation with Henry pressed heavily upon me, and suddenly I felt exhausted. However, I was disinclined to return to my chambers, for the quiet intimacy of the library afforded me some precious moments during which I might gather my composure. It had been a difficult conversation, and one which I had much feared. Yet, by the time Henry had left the room, I sensed the tender roots of the king's love, and even forgiveness, beginning to take hold. It would just be a matter of time before we were merry once more. As I contemplated all this, I cast my eyes upon the manuscript, which remained untouched upon the table. My curiosity aroused, I walked around the table until I stood before it.

In the time that I had been in Anne's world, I had spent hour upon hour perusing the precious books collected within the king's libraries. Yet this particular one I had not seen before. The manuscript lay open at its frontispiece. On the left, was a full-page heraldic composition, depicting a shield bearing the royal coat of arms of England, which hung down from a branch of a crowned hawthorn bush: the arms were supported by two beasts: the red dragon of Cadwaladr, and the white greyhound of Henry VII's Lancastrian ancestors. Below these beasts was the inscription *Vive le Noble Roy Henry*—long live the noble King Henry. On the right-hand page, at the top, a scene illustrated in vivid colours of red, blue, green, gold, black and pink of a queen accepting this very same book from its author. In the background hung a mirror, metaphorically evoking the title of the manuscript, the famous, *Miroir des Dames*, or, Mirror of Women. Written in French, I knew that it had been composed for Joan of Navarre, a French queen, who was, no doubt, the lady pictured in the illustration.

The book was a well-known medieval manual of moral instruction specifically for women. In this respect, it was rare as far more such texts were written for men, for princes and kings. This one detailed the ideals of the spiritual and moral life of a woman; virtues such as piety, humility and moderation, all deigned to reflect the royal dignity of the queen, and therefore representing the feminine image of perfection. My mother had spoken of it many times. I traced my finger across the rough surface of the vellum, feeling beneath it the raised gold lettering, admiring its intricate beauty. I knew that Henry had placed it there so that I might see it and consider the wisdom that it contained. In my curiosity, I scooped up my skirts and sat down upon the chair in front of it, delicately turning the crisp pages and absorbing the book's instructions on moral edification.

I had been reading for five or ten minutes, when the door to the library opened once more and my brother reappeared having completed his errand. Closing the door gently, he came toward me, whilst I looked at him and smiled warmly. No matter what my mood, a light was always lit within my heart when George entered the room. He raised an eyebrow, as if inviting me to recount what had just passed between Henry and me. I did not want to speak of it, and instead was seized by the sudden desire to break free from the palace walls. After all, it had been nine, long months since I had been allowed my freedom, since I had been allowed to ride with the wind. Suddenly, there was nothing in the world that I desired more. Thus, I rose to my feet and said,

'I know what is in your mind, but I do not want to speak of it.' I wagged my finger from side to side to indicate that I had no intention of dissecting my altercation with Henry and then added plaintively, 'George, get me out of this place, for if I spend one more moment within these walls, I shall go mad!' Considering our options, I continued with some excitement, 'Let's go riding! Or hawking! I want the freshness of the air to flood my lungs and feel the warmth of the sun on my face. Will you? Will you take me?' My brother simply stood before me, listening to my bubbling enthusiasm, his arms folded, shaking his head and chuckling in amusement.

'And if I don't? What then? You have only just been churched, Anne!'

'Then I shall go anyway—on my own if I have to!' I was defiant, and suddenly the strength of my indomitable spirit resurfaced once more. George laughed out loud, extending his arm wide as if inviting me to snuggle myself within it, as he exclaimed,

'Now, why did I know you were going to say that? Come sister, let us go hawking and take our friends with us. For whilst I've no doubt that I shall be yet again in trouble with our parents for allowing you to ride out so early after your churching, methinks that it is indeed exactly what you need.' I came close to my brother, accepting his extended arm, which he put affectionately about my shoulder, as I slipped my arm about his waist. He added playfully, 'Perhaps then you will not be so utterly insufferable and finally stop snapping at everybody!'

'George!' I swiped my hand at him as he dodged my retaliatory gesture. With much laughter and banter at each other's expense, we left the room. At last, I was to feel the thrill of being free once more, and for the first time in several months, I felt my spirits soar.

It took barely an hour to assemble the hawking party. Along with my brother and me, I was attended by several of my younger ladies including: Madge Shelton, Grace Parker, Lady Mary Howard, my sister-in-law Jane, and a new lady at court, Nan Cobham. Nan had been introduced to me by letter of recommendation from my brother while he had been away in France. Her name was immediately familiar although I admit that at the time, the role she would play in Anne's life remained stubbornly elusive. Had it not, I would not have accepted her so easily into my household. Yet, back then, I saw only a good-looking, polite and intelligent woman of strong character, and on George's recommendation, she was appointed as one of my ladies. As a friend of my brother, Mistress Cobham fitted easily into our intimate circle.

To add to the pastime of our day, my brother brought along with him Sir Henry Norris, Sir Richard Page, Thomas Wyatt, William Brereton and the newly knighted Sir Francis Weston. Together, we rode out that morning from the Royal Palace of Greenwich, a merry band of brothers. My energy and enthusiasm was infectious, and as our party set out through the southern gate of the palace, heading uphill towards Duke Humphrey's Tower, there was much chatter, laughter and gallant flirtation. Accompanied by a number of Henry's bodyguard, I led our little group, with my brother at my side, the royal standard fluttering above our heads. Each of my ladies was partnered with a gentleman, whilst following up the rear were a number servants travelling on foot, some of whom led dogs that would be used to flush out our prey from the undergrowth; others were hawkers, who would handle our birds, and finally, the cadgers bearing the wooden frame upon their shoulders that carried our hawks into the field.

As winter began to assert her dominance over the landscape, it was cold outside. The harsh frost, evident at first light, was already melting in the wintry sunshine as Mother Nature laid on a stunning display of her winter jewels. Many of the trees were bedecked with a myriad of sparkling drops of water refracting the sun's rays, glistening like polished diamonds, as the ice thawed out along their branches.

I was wrapped up warmly against the morning chill, wearing a warm, English gown of patterned damask, fashioned from black velvet; the sleeves were fitted to allow for the practicalities of hawking, whilst the cuffs were edged with sable and the inside of the gown lined with the same. My hair was tied up beneath a white coif, whilst this in turn was worn under a black velvet cap embroidered with gold thread, studded with jewels and pearls, and finished off with a white ostrich plume, itself decorated with gold thread. Beside me, my brother looked devilishly handsome, seated easily upon his black stallion. In appreciation of his efforts in France, the king had presented him with a doublet, jacket and hose of black velvet cut on cloth of gold, as well as a riding coat of green velvet lined with coney; all of which he wore with great panache. As we started our ascent through the parkland, up Castle Hill and toward the turreted tower that stood at its summit, George looked particularly pleased with himself, and so I enquired,

'How now, my Lord, what delights you so?' There was a moment of silence, whilst my brother clearly considered his answer; the sound of our horses' hooves scuffing the earth, and the clink of their tack being the backdrop to his silence. Then, he smiled, turning his head and raising an eyebrow, as he said playfully,

'Other than the fact that I am riding out on such a fine morning with the fairest queen in Christendom!' I sensed that he was teasing me, and so I smiled graciously, inclining my head as I played his game, but urging him to continue. I knew that there was indeed more to tell. '…then perhaps it is because I have sent forth this day my servants to make ready my manor at Beaulieu for I wish to inspect it before Christmas.' George grinned at me. He knew he was telling me something that I was not aware of, and quite rightly anticipated my shock and surprise.

'Beaulieu! What...? I thought that the Lady Mary...'

'The Lady Mary has been moved to Hertford Castle on the king's orders and I...' George paused; I suspected for dramatic effect, '...have been granted the Palace of Beaulieu instead.'

'The Lady Mary...moved by the king...but why?' I frowned, shaking my head in some disbelief. How had all this happened without my knowing? George replied matter-of-factly,

'Because of her downright arrogance and disobedience to her father and sovereign lord, I should imagine. She should be glad she is not being moved to the Tower!' I was shocked and wholly confused by this turn of events. I knew that the king had declared Elizabeth, our beloved daughter, to be the rightful Princess of Wales, and as such, had sent the Earls of Oxford, Essex and Sussex, as well as Dr Sampson, to inform Mary that she was to henceforth abstain from using the title. Mary had characteristically refused outright to obey her father. Why had I not heard of these other developments earlier from Henry or my own father? Seeing my bewilderment, George kindly continued to answer the many questions that were bubbling up in my mind. 'Well what else should his majesty do with a daughter who refuses to do as she is told? Punishment for her intransigence is a natural consequence.' He hesitated before adding nonchalantly, 'The palace has been granted to me for my lifetime, and so it is now back within our family; just think, the place where we once played as children is ours again...I have already made arrangements for furnishings to be moved in.' I watched my brother as he spoke, still trying to take in all the ramifications of this latest piece of news. As George continued to describe his plans for the refurbishment of Beaulieu, I felt somewhat sickened that I had that very morning poured disdain over Henry for not taking action against the Lady Mary when in fact, probably in an effort to please me, he had already done so. To my shame, and in my intemperance, I had not given him an opportunity to speak of it. I felt irritated with myself, and redoubled my commitment to make amends over the coming weeks.

There is no doubt that I was slightly disoriented by this turn of events. However, as the knowledge of this further shift in power toward the Boleyns integrated itself within my psyche, I felt uplifted by

Henry's show of loyalty toward our marriage and our daughter. I turned my attention to the magnificence of the natural beauty that surrounded me, appreciating as if for the first time, the omnipotence of Mother Nature in all her wondrous perfection. I wanted to fly on the wind, to be carried by the natural strength and grace of my beloved Starlight, who I was riding for the first time in many months. Suddenly, I caught my brother's eye. With a look of wickedness and mischief, I urged my horse forward, with a loud, 'Ha!' until we were all racing up Castle Hill, across the Dover Road and deep into the woodland that stretched southwards from the palace.

We slowed down as we reached our intended destination, allowing those on foot to catch up with us. I was breathless but exhilarated by the danger of riding a horse side-saddle, at full gallop. It occurred to me, with some amusement, how my recklessness on Starlight was a metaphor for how Anne approached everything in her life. It seemed to me that there are two types of people; those who choose a cautious path, well-trodden and safe, but the price is obscurity. Anne was among those who chose to burn brightly, with fierce intensity, like a meteor hurtling through the heavens, forging through uncharted territory. It was a dangerous way to live, but the reward is immortality.

In the place we came to rest, the wood thinned, giving itself up to open ground. Our horses breathed hard plumes of hot air, spewed forth against the chill. At my command, a falconer stepped forward carrying one of my birds upon his gloved hand. I slipped on my fine hawking glove and took the merlin upon my arm, whilst beaters with hounds began their work of flushing out prey from the undergrowth. Within a few minutes, a rabbit darted out from its cover and I slipped the bird from my hand, timing its flight precisely, as it took to the air, swooping down upon its prey with deadly accuracy. The creature screeched as the merlin's claws crushed its skull in an instant. My comrades applauded my skill, as the falconer rushed forward to extract the dead rabbit from the bird.

'Bravo Madame!' Sir Henry had called above the rest. I turned upon my horse, flashing my friend a flirtatious smile, before I replied,

'Well, thank you, Sir Henry!' I could not resist teasing him by adding, 'I wonder if you have been practising your hawking in my absence, my Lord?' It was well known that while Sir Henry was

302

extremely gifted in so many ways, he had, on one famous outing, failed to capture a single item of prey, whilst everyone else had filled the larder with bounty. This, of course, had been much to the hilarity of the other gentlemen present. It was one of those moments that Sir Henry had never been allowed to live down, and with Anne's mischievous flirtatiousness, I wickedly decided to remind him of this once more. Several of the other gentlemen and ladies present laughed good-naturedly, understanding well the butt of the joke. Sir Henry took it in good heart, as I invited him, 'Please, my Lord, perhaps you could fly your bird next? I am sure Madge could lend you her favours if that would help.' Of course, the practice of giving favours was reserved for the tiltyard and thus, with my gentle jibe, I made to tease my friend even further. It was cruel of me I know, but like our entire inner circle, we were assured of the genuine friendship and loyalty which existed between us, and such playfulness and gentle taunting was accepted practice—and no offence was ever taken.

Whilst Sir Henry graciously took up my offer, the other gentlemen and several of my ladies followed George's charismatic lead, tracking the hunt a little distance along the edge of the woodland, whilst I indicated that for a time I was happy to watch from a gently raised ridge, accompanied by Lady Mary and Jane Rochford. We ladies watched for a while, appreciating the efforts of our comrades. I applauded and called out to acknowledge Sir Henry's swift success at making a kill, whilst Lady Mary clapped her hands together, giving encouragement and taking similar delight in the hunt. After a short while, I turned toward her and said,

'So cousin, tell me, how is it to have your future husband returned from France?' The fourteen-year-old Duke of Richmond had very recently come back to English shores with Henry Howard, Earl of Surrey, his long-time boon companion, their year-long French sojourn finally at an end. With the news of Henry's excommunication, and the refusal of Francis to refrain from meeting the Pope, Norfolk and his party, which included my brother, the Duke of Richmond and the Earl of Surrey, had been immediately recalled to England. As the duke had just celebrated his fourteenth birthday, which was the accepted marriageable age for a man, plans were in motion for the union between the premier nobleman in the land and the young Lady Mary.

Despite her early enthusiasm for Henry Fitzroy, there was a degree of caution in her dealings with the opposite sex. Perhaps her keen young mind had been watching the way the king had treated me since the birth of our daughter. And despite her tender age, she had already seen the harsh treatment of her mother by her father, the Duke of Norfolk. Through her experiences and innate nature, Mary was emerging as a realist, intelligent and wise beyond her years, not likely to be sucked into the fantasy of happy-ever-afters. I never underestimated the astuteness of the young girl who would come to lead an extraordinary life.

In becoming the Duchess of Richmond and Somerset, Mary knew that she would not only be fulfilling the role expected of every Tudor woman, that of a wife and mother, but she would also become one of the most senior noblewomen in the land. With Katherine and Mary effectively banned from court, as the new Duchess of Richmond, she would take precedence above all other ladies, with the exception of Anne herself, the new-born Princess Elizabeth and the king's niece, Margaret Douglas, who was fast becoming one of Mary's closest friends. Whilst still bound to her husband and the king, this elevation would give her the closest thing to independence and freedom that a woman of her age was ever likely experience. It was much in keeping with her spirited nature, and something that I knew she quietly coveted. In reply to my question, Mary beamed a somewhat proud smile.

'Indeed, Your Majesty. His grace came by to speak with me just this morning. I do not see much of him, after all his majesty is grooming the duke to take up his responsibilities at the king's side and in Parliament.' There was no sadness in her voice as she relayed this news because Lady Mary knew no different than that which her society had taught her. Indeed, as was expected of a woman of her breeding, she understood that both she and her future husband had their roles to perform and accepted this without question. She was also aware that given their tender age, the newly-weds would not be living together as man and wife for some time to come. The king was adamant about this. In line with contemporary thinking, he feared that the rigours of sexual activity before the body was fully developed were dangerous to the health of both parties. It was clear that Henry would never take such a risk with his son, even if he was illegitimate.

After a few moments consideration, I smiled warmly, lifting my chin high in order to take in a deep, clear breath of fresh air as I stated,

'Well, now that I have been churched, methinks it is time that we made ready a new gown for your wedding. I will ask Margery to arrange for the keeper of the king's wardrobe to bring some fabrics so that we might choose something suitable; it will be part of my wedding present to you.' Mary broke into an enormous grin. Like much of Anne's circle, she had a keen appreciation for fashion, luxurious fabrics and jewels. Although blushing slightly at my generosity, she accepted my offer graciously, thanking me heartily for my kindness. I then turned my attention to my sister-in-law who was listening quietly to our conversation. She seemed somewhat distracted as hers was not a countenance of a woman who was happy with life.

Much like Mary, Jane had been at my side almost constantly since my household was appointed earlier that year, and I had come to know her well. I was convinced that she was not the harridan that history painted her to be, although her natural character inclined her to be reserved and prickly. Over time, our personal relationship had become warm, and with genuine affection, particularly since our intimate conversation in Calais. However, Lady Rochford was the kind of person who always seemed compelled to withhold part of herself from any relationship; as if she were forever weighing up the pros and cons, judging if it were safe to give of herself to the situation. But it was evident to those who knew her well that underneath that harshness was a fragile vulnerability that kept Jane Rochford at war with the world. So, as a tonic that day, I sought to engage her with the same infectious enthusiasm as I had Lady Mary.

'Jane, you must be delighted with your new property, for Beaulieu is a grand house indeed!' I admit that I expected nothing short of excitement on my sister-in-law's part. So, I was surprised to see a mixture of sadness—or was that anger—that played upon her face. I watched as Jane's expression hardened. Finally, she replied petulantly,

'Perhaps Madame, I might feel this way if my husband would find the time to involve me in any of the plans for its refurbishment. However, I fear that his attention is too much taken elsewhere.' Entirely confused, I tried desperately to decode the meaning of my sister-in-law's dissatisfaction. Jane saw my bewilderment, and flaring her nostrils in indignation, she continued, 'Your Majesty, it seems that the news of the king's gift to his lordship is not the only secret that Lord Rochford chooses to keep from you.' For a second time that morning, I was lost for words. I glanced at Lady Mary, who lowered her pretty eyelids and looked away, clearly not wanting to meet my gaze. Looking back at Jane, I saw her rather deliberately look over my shoulder toward the hunting party in the distance. I twisted about, following her gaze and watched George reach up to help Mistress Cobham dismount. The lady virtually fell into his arms and I couldn't help but feel it was not an accident that caused Nan to press her body a little too closely and provocatively against my brother's chest as he steadied her to the ground. Indeed, there was much laughter as she righted her skirts, flashing a look at him that I read instantly; this was an exchange of passionate intimacy, and I knew immediately that the two were lovers. Even more disturbing was that vulnerable, jealous and potentially dangerous Jane knew it too.

Chapter Twenty-Six

Hampton Court Palace,
26 November 1533

It did not take me long to confront my brother in private. George denied everything, stating that his fondness for Mistress Cobham was within the context of a relationship defined strictly by the rules of courtly love. I pressed him hard to speak the truth for I knew how much our lives depended upon it. If George had found a mistress in Nan, at that time, I was not to know of it. My brother admitted to the neglect of his wife, Lady Jane, because he found himself drawn into the witty and vivacious company of friends, male and female, who formed our inner circle at court—this did not include Jane. I urged him, nay commanded him, to pay more attention to his wife, and to try for all our sakes, to be discreet and sober in his behaviour as any rumours of his recklessness would reflect on the good name of his sister, the queen, and the entire Boleyn faction. George understood my warning as he stood before me, sheepishly accepting my admonishment, but it was hard to stay cross with him for long. Yes, he made mistakes in his life, but it was never born from vindictive cruelty, rather an overwhelming *joie de vivre* that led him down several dark alleys, where sadly enemies lurked, ready to take advantage of his temerarious passion.

I reassured my initially sceptical sister-in-law of George's continued love and respect for her. I encouraged her to understand my brother's natural ebullience, and that Mistress Cobham posed her no threat. Once more, George dutifully responded to my earnest request, and over the next few weeks, I watched Jane's frostiness begin to thaw for a second time, as my brother paid her court. Thereafter, she demonstrated her thanks and loyalty to me; and never would this be more apparent than in the enormously trying months that lay ahead.

Such stormy seas were as yet out of sight, and on that icy, cold and foggy November morning, I felt only genuine happiness for the young woman seated next to me in the queen's barge. For later that afternoon, Lady Mary Howard would finally relinquish her modest title and become the Duchess of Richmond and Somerset, and Countess of Nottingham, in an intimate wedding ceremony that was to be conducted at Hampton Court Palace; the king and I were the guests of honour. Henry, his household, and the young Henry Fitzroy, Duke of Richmond left Greenwich Palace by barge at first light. A little while later, my ladies and I followed, in order to catch the tide before it turned, the fourteen-year-old Mary Howard taking her place at my right hand side.

It was one of those terribly English winter mornings, overcast and miserably grey, with the damp cold penetrating through to the bone. As we carved our way up the Thames, the freezing fog that hung heavily over the river was sent swirling in eddies about our boat. Only occasionally did any of the great sites of the City of London and Westminster reveal themselves to us through the thick mist as we passed by. I mused that it must have sounded strange indeed to anyone on the shore, to hear the playing of a lute and the sweet singing of the minstrels who serenaded our progress upstream—like disembodied and ghostly voices emerging eerily from the foggy shroud that had descended upon London and the river that day.

Nevertheless, this did not dampen our spirits. There was great anticipation at the wedding of the beautiful Lady Mary to one of the wealthiest men in the land. All the songs that accompanied our travel were songs of love, and several times, I had to calm the giddy elation of some of my younger maids, whose chatter was full of speculation and excitement about romance, gallant young gentlemen, and the thought of dancing into the night in the arms of some handsome young courtier.

As all this was going on, Lady Mary remained poised and dignified, undisturbed by the significance of the moment. I glanced in her direction, studying her profile as she listened intently to Madge who was in conversation with Lady Rochford. Over the months that I had come to know her, Mary had become nothing short of my protégé. She was like Anne in so many ways; her beauty, intellect, wit and sharp tongue were amongst her natural gifts from God. However, since she had been in my care, those gifts had been rounded off and polished by learning from Anne: how to dress to catch the eye, how to carry oneself with grace and poise, and how to use every movement of her body to charm and dazzle. She had fine-tuned her social graces at the centre of a glittering renaissance court, and much to the chagrin of her father, shared countless hours reading and debating religion with her mistress. In doing so, Mary had become firmly established in the reformed faith, thus following in the footsteps of her prestigious mentor. Indeed over time, she became like a daughter to me, and I recognised that the love that we shared was strong, deep and eternal.

I mused on all this as our barge, and those carrying the remainder of the queen's household, slipped away from the city as the fog began to thin, affording us the occasional glimpse of watery light. By late morning, the alchemy of the sun's rays finally began to work magic upon the day, progressively melting away the low lying cloud and opening up an ever greater expanse of blue sky. The last of the fog cleared as we neared Hampton Court which nestled snugly on the northern bank of the Thames, close to a bend in the river where it snaked its way through the gravel terraces below the Surrey Hills. It was surrounded by open countryside and a vast expanse of deciduous woodland where the king and court found such fine hunting.

I often reflected that in my modern day life, the palace was somewhat lost amongst the rubble of suburbia. But in Anne's time, it soared above all else around it, an utterly exquisite masterpiece of Renaissance architecture, crafted by the vision of the king's late, first minister, Cardinal Wolsey. At that time, it was still essentially Wolsey's Palace. Although it was already a great house, perhaps one of the largest in all England, it had not yet metamorphosed into the extraordinarily beautiful and extensive palace that Henry would finally leave behind upon his death in 1547.

In all the time that I spent in my sixteenth century life, I never failed to be moved by its regal presence, despite that fact that each time I saw it, the palace looked more like a building site than a royal residence. For when the king took possession of it 1529, he began an extensive programme of building, remodelling and refurbishing with Anne at his side. The aim was to create a stunning palace, befitting Henry's magnificence at the head of a glittering court. It would incorporate all the latest design trends in a project that would last nearly a decade. Most of this building survived largely intact into the twenty-first century, and so to come to Hampton Court was like coming home.

I sat back in the barge that day to appreciate it once more in all its resplendent glory. Approaching by water from the east, the first feature to greet the visitor was the great red-brick wall that surrounded the palace, beyond which was the impressive 200 foot-long gallery which extended in a south-easterly direction from our approach along the Thames. Wolsey's great gallery would sadly not survive even Henry's reign. In the last decade of his life, that very same gallery would be incorporated into a new set of secret lodgings reserved for the everyday use of the king. These apartments would provide him much needed privacy, out of reach from his expanding court which, like a malignant growth, gradually and relentlessly invaded Henry's private space, always greedy, always wanting more of the man who had the power to give, or take away, everything. I silently reflected on how ironic it was that such apartments would look out over the gardens, which a decade earlier, the two of us had planned together at the height of our romance. I often wondered if Anne's spirit had haunted him in the blossom which came forth year after year, reminding Henry of a love which would not die, a love which he could not hide from.

By 1533, the gallery had already been elegantly refurbished. Over the next few years, the remainder of the building work would see completed a sumptuous set of new lodgings, originally intended for Anne, as well as galleries connecting the sides for the king and queen, the king's privy stair which led down to the formal gardens, and the remodelling of the chapel. Henry also added an upper gallery running above Wolsey's existing two-storey building, completed in November 1533. It looked magnificent with great towers soaring up at its eastern end, each beautifully fenestrated and surmounted by gilded, onion-shaped domes which shone brilliantly in the midday sun. Beyond this structure, the pitched roofs of the great hall and chapel towered above all else, while the roof tops which outlined the palace were pricked with tall, barley-twist chimneys. On that icy morning, comforting plumes of smoke escaped into the sky from many of those chimney stacks, while octagonal towers and a plethora of golden capped turrets created a magnificent grandeur befitting one of Henry's most favoured residences.

After a couple of hours, our oarsmen at last pulled in towards the Water Gate, which was the only river frontage access to the palace complex. Built from individually fired red bricks, the main entrance projected out over the northern bank of the Thames. It was to be two stories high, guarded at each corner by fine octagonal staircase towers which, like the rest of the roof, would in time be crenellated above the string course. Only partially complete, an ornately decorated bay window jutted out above the main entrance to the Water Gate. I lost the view as we slipped inside the gatehouse itself, our barge coming to rest next to a fine stone staircase, leading up into the heart of the building.

I led the way in a sumptuous gown especially made for the wedding which consisted of a mantle of brocaded purple cloth of gold, bordered with pearls and diamonds of great size, and contrasted against an underskirt of white satin embroidered with silver. The sleeves were turned back with ermine, and the long train lined with the same. To complement the gown, I chose a French hood in black velvet, surmounted by a double row of large diamonds, interspersed with seed pearls, a stunning masterpiece of glittering, sartorial elegance that truly honoured the occasion.

Then came the bride, Lady Mary, followed in turn by my ladies-in-waiting, walking in pairs, including: the Countesses of Worcester and Surrey, my stalwart friend, Margery, who accompanied Lady Jane Rochford, and Lady Bridget Tyrwhitt, who walked alongside Mistress Jane Seymour. Nan Gainsford was partnered next to Joan, and completing the train were Madge Shelton and Grace Parker. Other officials and servants snaked their way behind us as the barges of the queen's flotilla moored, one by one, against the riverbank.

After dining together in the queen's apartments, I gave Lady Mary my blessing and took my leave of her, processing to the chapel royal to take my place as guest of honour alongside the king. Entering the chapel at my husband's side, we descended via the privy stair, leading down from the holy day closet on the first floor. It was enormously exciting to see this space in all its sixteenth century glory, untouched by the monstrous eighteenth century reredos, which had latterly come to dominate the modern day chapel at its east end. Whilst it was true that some refurbishment had yet to be completed, much of the work commissioned by Henry to embellish Wolsey's original chapel, dating from the late 1520s, was already done. The beauty of the original, great double window stood gloriously intact before me. It filled my heart with joy to see it there. There was no doubt that Wolsey's chapel was the epitome of divine splendour, sculpted and ornamented to the glory of God. At double height, the northern and southern walls were punctuated with large windows on the first floor level. These were largely inset with clear glass, with the exception of various painted heraldic devices, which pricked them with colour thereabouts, whilst the huge eastern window was entirely decorated with coloured glass, including figures of the crucified Christ in the centre, and those of the king and queen in prayer on either side. As I looked upon these figures, it was clear that the king was Henry, and that the queen who prayed at his side was Anne. If Katherine had once filled this space, like the cardinal, no trace of her presence remained.

I cast my eyes heavenwards to the beautiful vaulted ceiling which was not yet the richly ornamented, carved oak ceiling which Henry had fitted in 1536, and which I had breathlessly admired on so many of my modern day visits to Hampton Court. That was still to come. Unfortunately, like so many alterations to be made at Hampton Court, I feared that destiny would prevent Anne from ever seeing them.

The chapel was full on that November morning, happy to witness the union of the king's only natural son to the Duke of Norfolk's youngest daughter. The assembled congregation curtsied and bowed low as Henry led me by the hand to take up our position at the front of the chapel. Before the altar, the Dean of the Chapel Royal and a somewhat nervous looking Duke of Richmond, attended by my cousin, the Earl of Surrey, awaited the arrival of his bride-to-be. It was just as well that Henry had claimed his illegitimate son as his own, for he was the spitting image of his father. With the same the pale complexion, bright blue eyes and rich auburn hair, it would have been difficult to deny his paternity. Like his father, Henry Fitzroy was also tall, although his rather lanky silhouette was that of a young teenage boy who was still to fill out with the musculature of his manhood.

Since arriving back in Anne's world for the second time, it was clear that the marriage between Henry Fitzroy and Lady Mary was largely due to Anne's influence. By the autumn of 1532, much of the work had already been done by the woman in whose shoes I walked daily. Listening to comments made by my own family and ladies, it seemed that Anne had planted the first seeds as far back as 1529. However, I often wondered about Anne's motives. I had fallen for the youthful charms of Mary Howard almost as soon as we had met and wished only the best match possible for Thomas Howard's youngest daughter. But I sensed that Anne knew that until she gave the king a son, Henry

Fitzroy, would always be preferable as a successor to any daughter they might have together. I knew from gossip that such ideas were spread about the court, undermining the position of my Elizabeth. In time, I appreciated the importance of keeping the young duke within the family fold. It had taken some considerable persuasion to prise Lady Mary away from the match that had already been muted between her and the future Earl of Derby; a match preferred by the Duke and Duchess of Norfolk who greatly resented Anne's interference. But while Anne may have pulled the strings, it was the king himself who commanded their betrothal and with that, the die was cast.

With soaring voices carrying the love of God upon angel's wings, Lady Mary Howard entered the chapel, walking forth with a grace and maturity on the arm of her father, Thomas Howard. Both paused to acknowledge our presence with a respective curtsy and bow before moving toward the altar, taking up her position at the side of her husband-to-be. Mary looked ravishingly beautiful as she stood by the side of her betrothed, illuminated from the heavens by celestial shafts of light that poured through the southern windows of the chapel. The dress we had designed together was perfect: a cream damask gown embroidered with gold, a profusion of seed pearls sewn into the bodice, with the sleeves turned back with ermine and the generous train lined with the same. As a symbol of her virginity, Mary wore her dark auburn hair loose about her shoulders, and a simple coronet of gold, which I had lent her, upon her head. Next to her, Henry Fitzroy wore a white satin doublet and hose with a short crimson velvet gown furred with sable. In the light, the pair appeared almost iridescent. I was moved deeply by the purity of their youthful innocence, blissfully unaware, as they surely were, of the tumultuous events yet to come.

The wedding service continued as the Dean of the Chapel Royal proclaimed that all had gathered to join in the marriage of Henry Fitzroy, Duke of Richmond and Somerset, and Earl of Nottingham to the Lady Mary; that if anyone knew any impediment thereto he should declare it. Thankfully, none spoke, for who would dare! The licence for the marriage was duly produced, and the Dean put the question to the Duke, who with cheerful countenance replied 'Yea'. In a clear voice, Lady Mary replied that it was her wish to be joined with this man. The young Duke took her right hand, repeating after the Dean the words,

'I, Henry, take thee, Mary, to my wedded wife, to have and to hold from this day forward, for better, for worse, for richer, for poorer, in sickness and in health, till death us depart, and thereto, I plight thee my troth.' Then, releasing and again clasping hands, without fault or waver, Lady Mary likewise recited,

'I, Mary, take thee Henry to my wedded husband, to have and to hold from this day forward, for better, for worse, for richer, for poorer, in sickness and in health, to be bonny and buxom in bed and at board, till death us depart, and thereto, I plight unto thee my troth.' With their vows complete, there was silence in the chapel as the newlyweds exchanged rings of gold, before the Dean offered up a prayer and pronounced a benediction, making the sign of a cross above their heads. It was done. The diminutive Mary Howard, whose petite frame belied a core of steely strength and fiery will, had become one of the premier ladies in the land.

By arranging the marriage, Anne unwittingly set Mary on a course that would bring her protégé dangerously close to intrigue that would have the potency to undo her. But I remembered something of Mary's fate from my reading of history and that despite all the ups and downs that life would throw at her, I knew she would be safe. Nevertheless, I thanked God that despite brushing perilously near to the throne, and the thunder which Thomas Wyatt so eloquently stated rolled around it, my dear, sweet Mary would survive it all.

Henry commanded that in honour of the day, Wolsey's original great watching chamber was to be used for the wedding breakfast, and for the revels to follow. Sadly, the great hall was in the midst of its reconstruction, being raised from the ground floor to a more fashionable first floor level. Thus, the great watching chamber was the largest available chamber in the palace at that time. On that pleasant evening, the hall reverberated with the affable chatter of a multitude of polyphonic voices, pricked with resonant laughter, as an entire court gathered to celebrate the good fortune of the newlyweds. Great, long tables were arranged in a typical U-shaped design; the most prestigious guests seated on the dais at the top table, alongside the king and queen. These included: the bride and groom, as well as the Duke and Duchess of Norfolk; the Duke of Suffolk and his new wife, the young and intellectual Katherine Willoughby; the Earl and Countess of Surrey; the stunningly beautiful Margaret Douglas; as well as my own dear mother, father and brother. However, my sister was not with us as, by that time, Mary had been absent from court for four weeks, returning to her estates in the country once my churching was complete. She craved my pardon, and promised to return for the Christmas festivities. Thankful for her support during the last, few difficult weeks of my pregnancy, I gladly gave her my blessing, and by mid-October she was gone.

It was both a pleasant surprise and a blessed relief to find Henry in good spirits once more. It seemed that the happiness of the occasion had worked its magic. For the first time since the birth of Elizabeth, I watched the king in profile as he chatted and laughed heartily with Richmond and my father, seated on his left. My husband looked genuinely relaxed and truly merry and oh, how I hoped that the tide of discontent between us had finally turned! Whilst minstrels serenaded us from the low end of the hall, jugglers and other entertainers courted us with their antics, eliciting applause—and sometimes gasps—from an appreciative audience. We were served with several courses offered up on the king's finest silver-gilt plate including numerous meat dishes of roast quail, turtledoves, partridge, venison, boar and peacock, followed by other courses such as; cheeses, walnuts, candied fruits, ale-flavoured bread, tarts, custards, and preserves were all washed down with increasingly copious quantities of spicy mulled wine. As the celebrations bubbled on around me, I swirled the rich, dark nectar that smelt of cloves and cinnamon underneath my nose, allowing myself to sink into its warm embraces. Taking a sip, I was assaulted by a flush of comforting warmth, as the alcohol rushed through my body. I smiled inwardly at the irony of how something as straightforward as wine was so often the perfect companion. It soothed one's anxiety, emboldened one's desires, relieved a person of stifling inhibitions and uplifted the spirits. Yes, in its wake, the room began to take on a welcoming aura, full of the potential for lascivious pleasure, and for the first time since I had given birth, I felt my sexuality begin to stir.

Suddenly, I was aware that Henry had broken away from his conversation with my father and Henry Fitzroy, with the duke rising on the king's command, in order to lead his new wife to the dance floor. A pavane commenced the evening's dancing, and as the music began, Henry turned toward me and enquired,

'Anne, sweetheart, how art thou? Is it not a happy day indeed?' Henry's affection quite took me by surprise. His eyes flashed with an appreciation that I had not seen for some time, and I wondered whether the devilish spirit of the wine had also begun to cast its spell over my capricious husband. However, I cared not for the reason for his warmth toward me, I merely delighted in Henry's attention. I sensed that the day was for celebration and reconciliation, and so seizing on the moment, I replied somewhat flirtatiously,

'I am well, Your Grace. Thank you.' I lifted my glass to toast the king. Henry smiled appreciatively in response, picking up his own crystal glass and returning my gesture with an inclination of his head, before sitting back in his chair and adding thoughtfully,

'I have been thinking that it is time that our daughter takes up her own household. I have spoken to Cromwell of it, and put plans in place to establish her as Princess of Wales at our Palace of Hatfield. She will move there at the beginning of December.' There was a moment's pause as the king looked out over the court, swilling his own wine mindlessly around the inside of his glass before adding, '…and in the light of my other daughter's ungodly disobedience, I have decided to send the Lady Mary to attend upon her. I hope that it will teach her the humility that she has been so sorely lacking of late.'

It took every ounce of determination to maintain my composure and merry countenance. Henry's words had winded me, no less than if I had been struck directly in the belly from a blow that I did not see coming. Had I been so caught up in the one thing that I loved without question, Elizabeth, that I had forgotten that I was the Queen of England and she, the new Princess of Wales? In the cold light of day, I would come to understand that Henry had suggested nothing less than that which her honour deserved. Yet, in the moment that Henry spoke those words, I was consumed only by my love as a mother, and my natural instinct to keep my daughter close to my side. I knew that in Hatfield, I would see little of her, and that had broken my heart. An unbearable pain of grief descended upon me in an instant, and I made to object.

'But…' Henry quickly held up the index finger of his left hand to silence me as he cut through my plea, before I was able to make it.

'No! It is my word... Do not think to spoil this evening, Anne. That would be such a pity.' If I had lulled myself into believing for one moment that nothing had changed between us; that deep down, our consuming love had not been seriously wounded by the blow of Elizabeth's birth, then I was fooling myself. Once again, danger lurked behind Henry's words and thankfully, this time, I was wise enough to see how injudicious it would be to press the matter further. Thus, I mustered every ounce of dignity and refrain that I was able, smiling bravely and thanking his majesty for the great pain and consideration he was taking with regards to our daughter. Inside, I could hardly breathe. I urgently needed to get away from Henry. Amid my sadness was resentment that he should take such a decision without consulting me. Even worse, that Master Cromwell had known the king's mind before I had been aware of the plans being made for the future of my daughter. Therefore, I craved his majesty's pardon on the pretence of sharing the good news with my mother, who had left the top table and was standing in discussion with George. Henry smiled and nodded, granting my leave. As soon as I turned my back on Henry, I felt tears begin to sting at the back of my eyes, the room began to blur as I fought to contain my emotion. Arriving at the side of my brother and mother, they immediately saw my distress and reacted with predictable concern.

'Anne, what on earth is the matter?' Keeping my back turned to the king and the rest of the court, I took a few moments to try and compose myself, gulping back the tears, determined that Henry would not see my distress. Finally, I managed to say,

'The king is to send Elizabeth away. She is to have her own household at Hatfield Palace.' Elizabeth Boleyn, who had looked dreadfully concerned until that moment, suddenly broke out into a delighted smile. I watched the tension drain from her body as she laughed, gently reaching out to take my hand, as she said softly,

'But Anne, this is to be expected. She is after all the heir to the throne! It is nothing less than her status requires.' I knew she was right, yet this did little to assuage the pain that I felt at the thought of being separated from my daughter. Closing my eyes, willing the tears to subside, my mother brightly proffered, 'George, take your sister at once onto the dance floor and make merry so that she has no more time to think on this.' Turning to me, she beseeched me, 'Anne you must

317

remember that you are the Queen of England now. You must accept that this is the greatest honour that his grace can do your daughter.' I nodded feebly indicating that I understood and with the brightest of smiles upon my face, I accepted my brother's hand as he led me to the dance floor.

It was a brilliant performance, and I played my part with exceptional finesse—*the most happy*—queen at the head of a brilliant court, but inside I was dying. Hurt, grief and anger continued to tug gently at my consciousness. Despite all that I understood about sixteenth century convention, I was still mad at Henry. I confess that for the rest of the evening I carelessly flirted and paid court to those gentlemen who honoured and served me; all the time appearing to innocently ignore the king. Reckless perhaps, but I wanted him to be jealous. I wanted to hurt him in retribution in the only way I knew how. I danced with those men in turn, teasing them with my playful flirtatiousness, and yes, I was sinking gratefully into the never-ending flow of wine that George dutifully made sure was poured continually into my glass. I lost myself in a blur of colour, laughter and chivalry.

As I was twirled around the room, I noticed Henry watching me with a smouldering intensity that spoke of desire. My indifference seemed to have aroused the king's lust, and it reminded me once more that ours was a passion not easily derailed, not even by the most testing of times. As I danced the night away, no matter which way I turned, or how often I was lifted high into the air, I sensed Henry's presence as he moved about the room. We were connected by a ferocious intensity, acutely aware of the other's magnetic presence, circling each other, full of simmering passion. In my slightly inebriated state, my awareness must have been broken, for suddenly as I turned about, I unexpectedly came face-to-face with my husband. No words were spoken between us as Sir Francis Weston who was my partner, bowed and stepped aside, leaving the king to take his place. The music of a volta struck up as the king pulled my body close to his and we began a dance of passion, paying scant attention to those around us. It was, as on that very first day at Hever, when I found myself in Anne's world dancing in the king's arms, the centre of Henry's world. He did not take his eyes from mine, and I felt every delicious sinew of his masculinity respond to my feminine softness, grace and welcoming sexuality.

As the dance dictated, our bodies brushed close, one against the other, first on one side, then the next. The familiar scent of the man that, despite everything, I still adored, stirring my most primitive instincts. As a natural response, I drew Henry in with Anne's beautiful black eyes that spoke of unfathomable depths of sensuality and seduction. We danced within a vortex of passion and potency, weaving a web of intimacy that would bind us once more in hope that England would soon have its male heir.

When the dancing was over, I took my leave of the king and court. Cast in flickering shadows, I ascended the great, stone staircase at the centre of Wolsey's old palace to reach the queen's apartments on the second floor, my ladies following behind. I asked that Elizabeth be brought to me immediately from the royal nursery. The exhilaration of being once more within the arms of the king had done little to assuage the pain I felt thinking of the removal of our daughter from court. I ached to see her, even at that late hour.

I returned to the queen's privy chamber which was tucked away on the top floor of what would, in time, become the old privy lodgings in the south east corner of clock court. I desired privacy and so dismissed many of my ladies, with the exception of my aunt, the sixty-five-year-old Lady Bryan—who would soon be officially appointed as the lady mistress of Elizabeth's household—Margery and Nan. While I waited for Elizabeth to be brought to me from the royal nursery, I was undressed by my ladies, wearing only my chemise, and over this a crimson satin nightgown, that was lined with coney for extra warmth. Finally, in front of a gentle fire, which was well settled into the grate of a splendid, stone-carved fireplace, I knelt on a rich carpet strewn with velvet cushions and held a jubilant Elizabeth up in the air, her face alight with joy at the attention and adoration being lavished upon her, her little legs gleefully kicking the air. The mellow light thrown out by the fire, flushed her cherubic features with a rosy glow, whilst the auburn hair she shared with her father and half-brother, Henry Fitzroy, shone with an even deeper intensity of fiery red, flecked with gold. I drew her into my body, nestling my face close to the side of hers and smelling the scent of her baby skin. Whispering my words of eternal love into her ear, my daughter gurgled her obvious delight. For the millionth time, I marvelled at how I was spellbound and completely devoted to this tiny being, who in her utter vulnerability wielded an unfathomable power to which I had surrendered myself willingly.

Thoughts of Henry, the court, and even the increasingly trying circumstances in which I found myself, simply ceased to exist in such moments. However, on that night, as we played, my mind wandered to the king's apartments on the floor beneath my own. I imagined Henry retiring into the privacy of his rooms, as he had done every night since my churching. In the beginning, I was quite relieved not to be on the receiving end of the king's attentions. The difficult pregnancy I endured had taken its toll, and I did not relish finding myself in that state again. However, as days turned into weeks, I began to miss the warmth of Henry's bed and wondered again if another had taken my place. Such thoughts usually pricked me with rabid jealousy, but when I was with my daughter, I could forget even this, and be filled only with love for her tiny presence. Given Henry's continued absence, as I knelt in front of the fire and played with my daughter that evening, I was startled when Margery suddenly announced,

'The King's Grace is here to see you, Madame.' I turned my head just in time to see Henry sweep into the room behind Margery, my friend stepping aside to let his Majesty past, whilst all three ladies sank into deep curtsies, their eyes downcast to the floor in humble respect. I made to rise, though Henry immediately indicated with his hand, and a shake of his head, that I was to remain kneeling. Instead, he walked over to me, reaching out his arms to take Elizabeth within his bearlike grasp. He swung her up in the air, both their faces a picture of happiness, as the Lion of England toyed with his cub, showing toward her a gentle affection that belied his omnipotent strength. I was consumed with such enormous pride; whatever Henry felt about my failure to give him the son he desired, he doted on Elizabeth, just as he did upon all his children. Henry turned towards Lady Bryan and said,

'Lady Bryan, it is late and time that the princess was in bed. Please take her back to the nursery.' Lady Bryan stepped forward, taking Elizabeth into her arms. Clearly resentful of being torn from her father, Elizabeth's face crumpled in distress, and as she was carried away, her sorrowful cries disappearing pitifully into the night. The king then turned to Margery and Nan. 'Ladies, you may leave us.' Both curtsied and retreated from the room, closing the door behind them. With a gentle click of the latch, Henry and I were alone.

My husband towered above me, for I was still kneeling on the floor in front of the fire. I saw that he too had been divested of his doublet and hose, and wore only a smock and outer nightgown. The king was clearly ready for bed, and I wondered whose. He looked slightly dishevelled, handsomely so, and quite in spite of myself, I felt my body respond to his presence, hoping that he would stay. Suddenly, I wanted him to touch me, that through that touch, I would know soon enough if he loved me still. As if the king sensed my stirring, Henry sunk to the ground, sitting casually in front of me, one leg drawn up with an arm hooked around his bent knee. For several minutes there was silence between us, as he stared thoughtfully into the fire. In the silence, I studied his face, illuminated just as Elizabeth's had been moments earlier. It was one of the rare times that Henry could be just a man and not a king. When he turned to look at me, I was surprised and moved to see tears welling up in his eyes, and I sensed Henry's deep yearning to meld with me once more. And so I rose up, and moving over to him upon my knees, we threw our arms around each other's body, Henry's face pressed against my torso. I ran my hands through the same rich, auburn hair that I had touched on Elizabeth's delicate head, and buried my face within it. It was the familiar scent of my friend, my companion, my lover, my husband and my sovereign lord. As we rested there in silence, our bodies communicating through our intimacy all that we needed to say, Henry looked at me and whispered plaintively,

'Anne, give me a son. Please God, give me a son!' In those few words were held the most exquisite pain and longing I had yet known from my husband. I understood then how his vision of his own kingship was absolute; that the notion of his success was as potent as life and death itself and within that success was Henry's duty to provide a male heir for England's future. I saw the unreasonableness and futility of it all and yet, I could never explain this to a Tudor king. My modern day persona would never understand the all-consuming desire to fulfil this need, for it was a concept that had lost all meaning in my twenty-first century life. I also understood that Henry's desire and love for Anne was almost as potent. In his plea to me that night, he conveyed his desperation that he loved and wanted Anne as fiercely as he had wanted anything in his life, except a son. His tears foretold the future of which he was as yet unaware; that Anne's fate hung in the balance and only a son could salvage Henry's fractured faith in his wife.

I wiped away the tear before reaching down to kiss Henry upon his lips. I remember feeling his body yield to mine, as I whispered,

'Then let me make love to you.' With that, our kisses gradually deepened, becoming more greedy and passionate as we remembered the sweetness of our love. I felt no resistance from the king as I knew it is what Henry had wanted from me the moment he set foot inside the room. At first there was a tenderness and ease in our movement, as if we were savouring the return of grace. Henry stretched out his legs, lifting up my nightgown and shirt so that I could straddle his body. Our kisses were insistent, my hair tumbling down upon his chest as I opened his nightgown, pulling the open necked-shirt to the side and flicking my tongue across his nipple. I heard Henry groan in a familiar response, as together the king and I grappled to lift what clothing kept him from sinking himself inside of me. For a moment, I felt the exquisite anticipation of union and we were joined. I moved rhythmically astride him, the king tearing at my nightgown to reveal the breasts that he adored. He ran his hands across them, and I saw deep appreciation in his eyes and I exalted in feeling like Venus once more, the King of England worshipping at my altar.

Henry suddenly raised me up, taking me in his arms, and in one swift movement which spoke of his strength and dominance, flipped me over so that he controlled our love-making. I watched Henry sink deeper into an ocean of erotic hunger, as he moved with ever greater ferocity, biology and instinct driving him to the peak of his sexual pleasure. In my own desire, I grasped the king's buttocks, sinking my nails hard into his skin, as I knew he liked me to do, until Henry cried out loudly, half in pain, half in exquisite pleasure. I watched the veins in his neck bulge, his eyes fixed ahead as he arched his back in a final thrust which unleashed his semen within me.

As the clock struck midnight, a new day was heralded and a new dawn in my relationship with Henry. Within a very short space of time, I would know that once more I was carrying Henry's child, and this time it would indeed be a son.

Chapter Twenty-Seven

Greenwich Palace,
1 January 1534

New Year's morn presented herself magnificently, shrouded in her finest mantle of pure, white, virgin snow. All of us had awoken bleary-eyed to find Greenwich Palace, the surrounding gardens and park covered in a thick blanket of precipitation some several inches deep. It was an enchanting sight to behold through the window of my bedchamber; everything as far as the eye could see was heavily bedecked with snow that glistened in the sun, from the rooftops of the palace, to every single branch of every single tree. Greenwich looked as pretty as a picture, and I yearned to be amongst it, despite the cold. Thus, shortly after mass and dinner, just after 10 o'clock, I made my way with several of my ladies down from the queen's lodgings and toward the gardens on the south side of the palace.

I adored going outside to taste the stillness that is utterly unique to the morning after a heavy snowfall. In those few short hours when the snow lies untouched, even the birds seemed to fall silent, adding an even greater depth of serenity to the wintery scene. Only occasionally did we catch sight of the flash of a red robin's breast as it hopped from branch to branch in search of food, leaving a gentle flurry of snow to fall to the ground in its wake. Wrapped up in our richest furs to ward off the worst of the chill, we nevertheless welcomed the frosty morning air that flushed our cheeks and nipped at our fingers and toes. I savoured the sound of snow softly crunching beneath our booted feet, as we left behind us a trail of dainty footprints to give clue to our passing.

There was a good deal of giggling amongst us ladies, as we lifted our skirts to pick our way precariously towards the gardens beyond. I was in a truly ebullient mood, for I held within my breast the happiest of secrets, one that I had shared with the king the previous evening. I was pregnant again, and my spirits were immeasurably buoyed by the memory of Henry's great joy, as he had swept me up in his arms and cried out for the love of God that he was the happiest man alive. I felt that 1534 would be a truly happy year.

I know it is odd to have these thoughts with such certainty when I, the woman from the twenty-first century, knew that tragedy lay ahead. However, a strange thing began to happen to me in those months after returning to the sixteenth century for the second time. The deeper I sank into Anne's life, the more inextricably merged we became, and the fine details of what history had determined would come to pass were less clear. Sometimes, it felt as though a mild amnesia of sorts was descending upon me. Truly, I could not tell if this was simply because I had not had access to any of my history books in well over a year, or whether it was something more profound. Was I losing my grip as the true nature of my 'reality' became increasingly less clear? Though I remember with clarity that Anne's second pregnancy ended in miscarriage, I could not remember the exact details. I held a vague notion that somewhere in the first few months the baby had been lost, and I was so anxious that this would be her fate again. Despite all of this, perhaps for the last time, I faced the future with optimism—that all that had passed before was just a test, and that history would set itself on a different course, that the coming year would finally be Anne's uncontested moment of triumph.

Leading my ladies with a vigorous spring in my step—Lady Jane Rochford, Lady Bridget Tyrwhitt, Nan Gainsford, Madge Shelton, Nan Cobham, the Countesses of Worcester and Surrey, as well as the new Duchess of Richmond—we made our way to the great orchard that lay immediately south of the queen's privy apartments. A sturdy six-foot red brick wall ran around its perimeter. That morning, it was adorned along its top with perhaps four or five inches of snow, whilst along its face, a delicate frosting of snowflakes were left clinging there by wind that had whistled around the pathways of the palace the night before.

As we approached the entrance, we heard men's voices calling out to one another on the other side, laughing and taunting opponents in a rather puerile, but clearly lusty, snowball fight. I recognised the voices immediately. Many were part of the young, cosmopolitan faction at court which had become synonymous with the Boleyns; my brother, the Earl of Surrey, the Duke of Richmond, Sir Francis Weston, William Brereton, Sir Richard Page, Tom Wyatt and his close friend, Sir Thomas Clere. I turned to my ladies playfully raising a finger to my lips to usher in their silence, whilst indicating that they should follow me toward the stone archway that stood sentinel at the entrance to the orchard. We did not need to tip-toe for the newly fallen snow was a willing accomplice to our mischief, muffling the sound of our furtive advances. A set of tracks leading into the garden from the opposite direction foretold of the band of brothers that had passed this way before us. Poking my head round the corner, I was met by a joyful scene that filled me with delight.

In the centre of the orchard, there were seven great men of the land playing with the same innocent delight as children. Despite their fine clothes, every one of them was covered head to toe in snow. Snowballs flew back and forth, finding their targets with deadly accuracy, eliciting cries of triumph from the thrower, or cries of foul from the receiver. Mary Howard appeared at my side to behold the scene, her rosy face alight with the same carefree joy that filled my breast. We smiled at each other conspiratorially, sharing a look which spoke clearly of our genuine affection for the men who daily shared our lives and who we had caught out behaving like children. I decided to make our presence known and lifting my skirts, picked my way through the gateway until I stood before the scene, my ladies gathering behind me.

They were blissfully unaware of our arrival until Sir Francis Weston glanced over aware that he was being watched. As a result, he desisted from throwing the next snowball, and was about to bow in acknowledgement of our presence when the young Duke of Richmond capitalised on Sir Francis' momentary lapse of engagement. Unaware that we were watching, Henry Fitzroy launched an opportunistic attack, sending a snowball ricocheting off Sir Francis' cap, momentarily causing a plume of powdery snow to explode all over him. Whilst Richmond collapsed in gales of laughter, one by one, the other men present sensed that they too had company. In turn, they stopped their game and swept into a courtly bow. Eventually, Richmond realised that he was laughing alone, and took his cap from his head to greet my arrival with all due courtesy. I stood in silence for a moment, my hands clasped before my stomach, my head held high, as a faint smile toyed at the corner of my mouth. In fact, I wanted to laugh heartily, but decided rather mischievously to make the most of the opportunity to tease these great noblemen. And so I declared loudly to my ladies,

'Why ladies, is it not comforting to think that his most gracious

325

majesty is so wisely advised…' the word, 'wisely' I said in a rather deep and emphatic tone to emphasise the irony of what I was about to say, '…by men of such great maturity?' Of course, every person present knew that my words were said with a gentle playfulness, and I heard good-natured giggling coming from a number of my ladies. I turned to look at them and was about to say something more when suddenly, I was struck by a snowball on my upper arm. I spun about only to see my brother grinning defiantly. George was glowing with exertion; he had lost his cap in the snow such that his hair was already wet and tousled. In that moment, time stood still. I saw in front of me a child looking exactly thus. In the grounds at Hever, the three of us, Mary George and I, had fought many a snowball fight. It was a happy memory which my brother was silently sharing with me in his shining eyes and devilish grin. I was not cross in the slightest, but decided to play the game for all it was worth. Folding my arms in front of me, I raised an eyebrow imperiously, as if demanding an explanation. George swept into a magnanimous gesture of humility, before rising and saying,

'Your Majesty must surely forgive me. I meant to throw that snowball at young Tom here,' indicating towards Thomas Clere, who was clearly in the opposite direction to me. 'It seems I am a terrible shot!' I bit my lip to prevent myself laughing. Instead, with apparent seriousness and much gravity, I replied,

'Indeed it seems so, my Lord Rochford. Yet, all here will bear witness that you, and the gentlemen you represent, have dishonoured the Queen of England and for this you will surely pay the price!' With that, I said under my breath to those ladies behind me, 'Ladies, arm yourselves!' None of those present needed any further encouragement. I was the first to quickly scoop up a ball of snow, which I hurled towards my brother within a few short seconds. George was ever quick and seeing it coming, he dived to the side, my snowball just missing the side of his torso. With my act of war, the whole orchard exploded into a riotous crossfire of snowballs. For a few moments, all notion of status was lost, and I was as much a target as anyone else there. Along with my ladies, I fought valiantly against the gentlemen of the court. There were shrieks and laughter, and I confess that we ladies came off somewhat worse, for the gentlemen were practised in the art of war and their aim was maddeningly accurate. However, the *coup de grâce* came after several minutes, when rather unexpectedly, a snowball thrown at my brother from his wife, Lady Jane, hit him directly between the eyes. It did not hurt him for the snow was soft, but in staggering backwards, he must have tripped, for George fell into a deep drift of snow piled up against the garden wall, landing in a great, unceremonious heap. Perhaps it was the sight of George flailing around in the snow, himself taken aback but laughing heartily at his own misfortune, or perhaps it was just the sheer relief of tension which built-up so easily in the stifling environment of the court, that caused us all to collapse into gales of unbridled laughter. I was bent double clutching on to Lady Bridget as tears streamed down both our faces, until I became aware that Lady Bridget's laughter had turned to deep and racking coughs which made it hard for her to breathe. Concerned, I righted myself without making any undue fuss and said,

'Enough! Enough, I can't take any more, and dear Lady Bridget here will cough herself into her grave if we don't stop laughing.' I smiled at Bridget, placing an arm around her shoulder. I had no idea then that my friend was not well. I thought her symptoms nothing more than a troublesome tickle in the throat, which would subside when we were back inside, a cup of posset to warm us up. Thus, I commanded, 'It seems we are all soaked to the skin and frozen to the core. We need to get Lady Bridget inside immediately and make sure that none of us catches our death of cold.' As I spoke, I shook away the excess snow that had stuck to the hem of my skirts, before taking Lady Bridget's arm in mine, as we made our way back inside the palace.

It was a wonderful feeling to be cosy and warm again in front of the fire; my fingers and toes tingling as the blood rushed once more to defrost those extremities that were chilled to the bone. It was exhilarating to play in the frosty morning air, and yet so comforting to find oneself cosseted by the warm luxury of the sumptuous apartments that I had come to call my own. As soon as we arrived back in my privy chamber, I urged my sister-in-law to make sure that Lady Bridget was dried well and given some spiced wine to warm her from the inside. My sister Mary, who had returned to court for the Christmas festivities just two weeks earlier, and my beloved Margery, began to help me change in front of a roaring fire that had been laid in the grate of my raying chamber. There was a good deal of hearty laughter between us, as we chatted about all the comings and goings at court. I asked them about developments with their respective children, and Mary speculated excitedly about what the king would give me as his New Year's gift.

The act of gift giving at New Year was without doubt one of the highlights of the Twelve Days of Christmas. It was a time when the great and wealthy of England could demonstrate their appreciation and commitment to their monarch. I had seen the aristocratic classes jostling to present the king with the most costly, beautiful, ingenious and flattering gift that their creative flair could conceive—and that money could buy. Then there was the agonising moment to wait to hear if one's gift had been accepted by his majesty, for rejection was a clear indication that a courtier had fallen from grace and could no longer expect the generous bounty of their sovereign lord. I felt assured that the king would once more lavish upon Anne the same magnificent array of fabulously expensive gifts as he had done the year before, including such costly items as: materials for gowns, curtains, carpets, glittering items of jewellery and above all gold and silver-gilt plate. As I thought on such things, Margery and Mary delicately stripped me of my clothes, until I stood naked in front of the fire.

I glanced down to admire Anne's still youthful body. With the exception of her breasts, which were now a little fuller than they had once been, the nipples darkened in colour rather than rosy pink, her shape was once more slender and unblemished by the trials of the previous pregnancy. Staring into the flames, I thought only of the tiny embryo that was yet to stir in my belly. It was but six weeks old, and yet I sensed its life force, which relentlessly impelled my child to take his form, to grow healthy and strong within my womb. While my mind rested in the sense of peace which this thought engendered in me, Mary continued to chatter, telling me about the finely embroidered linen shirts that she had worked as her gift for Henry. As she went over to pick up my kirtle, Margery stepped forward with the linen smock that formed the first layer of my clothing. I had just slipped it over my head, when there was a knock at the door.

Frances de Vere, Countess of Surrey, announced the arrival of my mother. I was anxious to see Elizabeth Boleyn, for I had not yet wished her the happiest of New Years. The Countess of Wiltshire halted momentarily, just inside the doorway, and dipped a curtsy as I had become accustomed, before I stretched out my arm, keen for her to come forth so that I might kiss her good 'morrow.

'Mother, I'm so glad to see you. Happy New Year!' My ladies halted their activities for a moment in order to allow my mother and me to embrace. I kissed Elizabeth Boleyn on each cheek as she wished me the same glad tidings, before Mary followed suit. Over the previous few months, along with Margery, my mother had been my rock, an indefatigable source of strength. I worried about her increasingly though, for evermore I saw lines etched into her face, and at times she looked noticeably pale and drawn. Although Lady Boleyn would never admit it, I feared that she worried constantly about me and the king's capricious moods. I thought to send her away from court where she would not be so exposed to the corruption, greed and envy that constantly threatened our safety. I felt guilty that she surely suffered on my account, and perhaps, just perhaps, I thought to save her if she could lose herself in Hever's isolated tranquillity. I had even gone so far as to suggest such a notion on several occasions, but Elizabeth Boleyn was adamant, she would not under any circumstances leave me or George. In the end, I understood that to be banished to Hever, and disconnected from what was happening, would have been even more unbearable than to walk with us towards our fate. In truth, I was relieved that she refused to go. I had grown to love her with all my heart and soul. Indeed, it had become difficult to think of my life without her, and every time I saw her, quite illogically perhaps, I felt safe.

However, that day was not for such sober reflection. I had regained the love of the king, the man I adored. I had his child within my belly, and was surrounded by those whom I loved most in the world. Thus, when my kirtle was fastened around me, I moved away from the fireplace to examine the three gowns that were displayed on the 'babies' in my raying chamber. Watched by my mother, sister and Margery, I moved from one to the other, admiring each in its composition; one of crimson velvet, another of cloth of silver damask and the third, fashioned from purple cloth of gold. My mood was light and carefree, as my sister explained to our mother,

'We were just talking about New Year gifts.' With a certain degree of childish exuberance, she added, 'I was asking Anne what she thought his grace would present to her this year.' As she spoke, I stood back from the gown of crimson velvet, admiring the billament comprising of clusters of rubies, pearls and diamonds which had been laid alongside it for my inspection. My mother then replied,

'I see, and what does her grace think?' As my mother spoke, I moved casually along to the next gown, the one made of silver damask, running my fingers first across the raised pile of its rich fabric, and then sinking them into the soft fur of sable that had been used to turn back the sleeves. Looking up at her, I beamed the happiest of smiles, and replied somewhat mischievously,

'I know not what the king will give me, but I know that with my gift, his majesty will surely be the happiest prince in Christendom!' I knew that I was teasing them, barely able to keep to myself any longer the news which had caused my spirits to soar. I was conscious that with the flash of my eyes, and the way I cocked my head playfully to accompany my reply, my mother, sister and friend would immediately see a hidden meaning in my words. Elizabeth Boleyn moved towards me somewhat breathlessly, her eyes suddenly alight with excitement, as I broke into the broadest of smiles, exclaiming, 'I'm with child again!' My mother scooped me up in her arms and gave me her unconditional blessing, followed in turn by Mary and Margery.

Thus, in the heart of the queen's apartments at Greenwich Palace, we all held and hugged one another, tears of joy in our eyes. It was if a light had been lit in the world, and a new hope for the brightest future burned once more in the breast of the Boleyn family.

Almost as soon as it had begun, my joy turned to an immeasurable sadness, for barely one week later, just after Twelfth Night, I found myself standing silently at the foot of Lady Bridget's bed, her body laid out peacefully before me, lifeless but still flushed by the fierce fever which had ravaged through her, ultimately taking her from us. She looked so at peace, her hands holding a golden crucifix placed there by the priest who had been called to administer the last rites.

As I stood motionless afore her corpse, I replayed the events which had, unbelievably, brought Bridget's life to a swift and unexpected end. It soon became clear that the cough that I witnessed during our New

Year's outing into the gardens at Greenwich was nowhere near as innocent as I had at first believed. The very next day, Bridget had become progressively unwell; a slight chill, and that very same cough, quickly turning ominously into a high fever, breathlessness and pain that seared through her lungs with every laboured breath. I sent Richard Bartlett, my own physician, to attend upon her. With a grave countenance, he quickly diagnosed pneumonia. For the next few days, her life hung precariously in the balance. Increasingly delirious on account of her fevered brain, weakened and unable to take in the fluids she needed, my friend gradually fell into unconsciousness as the deadly infection consumed her and the bacteria spread into her blood. We watched hopelessly as, one by one, her vital organs gradually shut down. There were no antibiotics to save her, and our prayers for her deliverance were futile. Although I sat by Lady Bridget's bed for several hours at a time, I was awoken that morning with the news that she had finally succumbed to death's haunting spectre. Thus in solemn procession, I arrived at her bed chamber just a few moments earlier, in order to pay my last respects.

When I entered her comfortable, modest lodgings on the ground floor of the palace, the fire was still glowing in the grate and in front of it lay a half-finished embroidery, which Bridget had been working on and which, with a heavy heart, I knew would never see completion. The main feature dominating the room was the oak, four-poster bed upon which my friend spent her final days, its head-board pushed against the wall opposite the fireplace. Three of Lady Bridget's ten children, her husband and two of my ladies, who all had become close friends with her since her return to court, were already in attendance. I was unnerved to see that one of those friends was Mistress Jane Seymour.

Since the day I was forced by Henry to accept Jane into my household, I had disliked her intensely. I knew what a snide and conniving bitch she had the potential to be, her sweet and demure ways made me sick, and I loathed her lack of authenticity. Perhaps a wiser woman than I would have treated her more kindly, tried to win her into my friendship, but I could not hide my disdain, and it was clear that just as with Katherine and me, no love was ever lost between us.

Standing at the end of the bed, I raised my eyes from my friend's body to find Mistress Seymour staring at me with her own particular brand of contumacious defiance. Suddenly, I saw within those eyes a flicker of accusation. I was momentarily confused, slightly unnerved by my intuition which told me that despite my status, I was not a welcome guest. My eyes swung around to behold the sight of Sir Robert, Lady Bridget's husband, standing opposite. I knew well that he was my enemy, and his dark eyes stared back at me with something akin to hatred. I sensed that I was being blamed for her death, perhaps by my reckless outing into the cold, January morning. I felt my stomach tighten and wanted to flee from the room, from the overwhelming stench of death, contempt and anger that threatened to suffocate me. However, Anne's legendary courage and sense of grace gave me the strength to lift my head high and say in an even voice,

'Sir Robert, I am deeply sorry for your loss. I considered Lady Bridget to be a dear friend and I will miss her greatly.' The man who had never shown love towards me, stared back for some moments, before he inclined his head slowly to indicate his respectful acceptance of my words. It was an empty gesture. But what I had entirely failed to remember, or realise, was that the malice toward me was not simply that I was being held—at least partly—responsible for Bridget's death, but as I would one day find out, in her final hours, Lady Bridget had spoken ill of me. Fatefully, Jane Seymour had heard the deathbed 'confession' that disparaged my good name and defiled my honour. Another woman, friendlier to my cause, might have dismissed the ramblings of Lady Bridget's fevered mind. However, Mistress Seymour was not a friend and I see now that it was the first time that fate played directly into the hands of my enemies. Of all this, I was entirely ignorant. As I walked away from my friend's bedchamber, I knew that I would never see her again. I thought only of the sadness in my heart that we had never completely reconciled our differences following our altercation at Stone Castle, barely fourteen months earlier. However, I had no idea just how deadly my failure to truly make amends with my friend would ultimately be—to Anne and to me.

Chapter Twenty-Eight

Whitehall Palace,
20 January 1534

The sadness surrounding Lady Bridget's death was difficult to shake off. I carried the heavy burden of remorse around in my heart for some weeks afterwards, compounded by the grief that I felt over Elizabeth's departure to Hatfield. I became reconciled that I could, and should, expect no less an honour for my beloved daughter. But this acceptance had done nothing to alleviate the constant aching I felt in her absence. To fill the void that Elizabeth's absence had left, I found myself writing to Lady Bryan virtually every day, and spending many hours choosing fine fabrics, and discussing designs for my daughter's dresses. I knew of Elizabeth's greatness, even in those first few precious months of her life, and I was determined that everything about the estate in which she was held would mark her out as a great princess of England.

By that time, the child I was nurturing within my belly was barely eight weeks old, yet my maternal instincts that had been awakened by my daughter's birth, were already binding me to this tiny soul, my longed for son. New Year 1534 saw a melting pot of emotion: enormous grief and sadness, mixed with tremendous happiness, and the excitement that the prospect of new beginnings often brings. I was not alone in the advent of my pregnancy. Just the day before, my dear friend, Nan Gainsford, confided that she too was with child, the first of many. She had conceived her future son just two weeks after I fell pregnant. It was a joy to think that the two of us would share the trials and tribulations of pregnancy together.

After having dinner in my privy chamber, I decided to take exercise in Nan's company, and walk together along the queen's long gallery, which overlooked the Thames at Whitehall Palace. With the exception of the privy bridge, which provided the main royal waterfront entrance to the palace at its most northerly end, the queen's gallery was largely unaltered from its construction in the early 1520s, and stood on exactly the same footprint as Wolsey's original gallery. It was regarded as one of the finest and most opulent examples of Renaissance architecture of its day. I heard tell that the rather self-contained Sir Thomas More was so impressed with the finished structure that he had told Wolsey of his distinct preference for it, over its counterpart at Hampton Court.

History would have it that Sir Thomas and Anne agreed on very little, but on this, I could see his point. Like all great, royal galleries it was a magnificent space of some 150 feet in length, occupying the entire first floor. Through a total of fourteen transomed and mullioned windows set into its long western and eastern walls, the queen's gallery afforded spectacular views of the Thames on one side, and a delightful panorama of the privy gardens on the other. Therefore, despite the fact that it was a rather dull morning with heavy rain driving vertically downwards from leaden grey skies, the gallery remained as light and airy as ever, warmed comfortably by fires burning within the grates of three, large fireplaces, spaced out along the length of the western wall.

As I stepped through the doorway with Nan, my eyes swept along the length of the chamber, taking in its grandeur and beauty. The ceiling was marvellously wrought in stone, highlighted throughout with gold, such that the chamber shimmered in reflected light. The walls were covered in wainscot panelling, intricately carved, with around one thousand beautiful figures of grotesque design. They were decorated with Wolsey's enormous tapestries, including twenty-one pieces telling the story of Jacob and Joseph that had been specifically commissioned by the Cardinal to adorn the space. Here and there were hangings of cloth of gold and silver with rush matting laid beneath our feet for comfort and durability; a few large pieces of oak furniture were pushed against the walls, displaying plate of gold and silver-gilt, much of which had once belonged to the king's disgraced first minister. It truly was a breathtaking sight.

The gallery had been partially redecorated as part of a complex of sumptuous apartments being refurbished for Anne at the king's command. Access to the queen's gallery was from the queen's privy closet, which I used often when the court resided at Westminster. Sometimes, I would bump into various members of the king's Privy Council making their way busily to or from the council chamber, which was situated directly off the gallery at its most northern end. However, that day we were undisturbed, as the king had taken to his chamber with a pain in his head. I was not unduly concerned as I had been informed by Sir Henry Norris that the king's discomfort was not severe, but enough to keep his majesty away from court. Perhaps a little ungenerously, I mused that like all men I had ever known, illness and incapacity unduly tormented my husband. He did not tolerate infirmity with good grace, after all, he was the alpha male of England and in his youth, he saw himself as utterly invincible. It must have been very difficult for him when he first fell seriously ill in 1528. At that time, he had been unsettled by the leg ulcer that would trouble him for the rest of his life. By early 1534, these bouts of suppuration and pain were still occurring intermittently although in between these short spates of ill health, the king was little afflicted and remained, for the most part, in good spirits. Through Sir Henry, I sent my husband my most hearty commendations for his good health and speedy recovery.

In the meantime, due to my own 'delicate' condition, I was once more banned from partaking in any vigorous pursuits. I admit that of all the things related to the news of my second pregnancy; this was the one thing I found most difficult to bear. When my confinement ended in October of the previous year, I was able to take to the saddle, hunting and hawking without care, and dancing with gay abandon until I was refreshed and reinvigorated. For just two short months, I felt my health return to its former resilience and I was free of any physical restraint, which suited not only my body, but my spirits well. However, for the sake of my child, I struggled valiantly to comply with what was expected of me. So that day, I walked rather sedately down the length of the queen's privy gallery at Whitehall, Nan at my side and several of my ladies following in attendance, pausing at one window or another, to watch vessels of all shapes and sizes navigate their way up and down the silent highway of the Thames. Eventually, we went over to one of the great, stone fireplaces carved into the western wall of the chamber. I scooped up my skirts and train and seated myself down on a crimson, velvet clad, X-framed chair that was fringed with Venice gold and embroidered with Anne's falcon badge. Across from me, I indicated with a gesture of my hand that Nan should sit down upon one of two stools placed there. As I did so, I reached over and picked up my lute, which was propped up next to the chair upon which I was seated.

I had long ago become familiar with Anne's mastery of the lute. So, I took the instrument on my lap, and with an easy familiarity, Anne's long, slender fingers ran across its taught strings, impatient to pick out its sweet harmonies. Suddenly, Nan spoke.

'What do you think to play, Your Grace?' I looked to the ceiling, musing upon her question as if seeking divine inspiration and closed my eyes briefly. Instantly, my mind was filled with a swarm of happy memories that called out to me across time; some of which were my own, and some of which I recognised as Anne's—memories that I could by then access at will. At first, I saw myself at Hever, in the library, the long gallery and in the parkland surrounding the castle. My body was instantly flushed with warmth and gratitude for one of the most precious times in my life and the memory of the happy days that I had spent there! Then, quite unexpectedly, I left my own recollections and was seeing Anne's memories. I found myself thinking of the king, and I saw how during the earliest and very heady days of his romance with Anne, he had once taken a lute like mine and sang a love song to her, one of unrequited love that reflected his circumstances. When it was over, I saw the plaintive look in Henry's eyes, as he explained to Anne that it was his own composition, and that it was his own heart which was breaking without the woman he loved by his side. He had beseeched her once more to give herself to him. I heard Anne decline the offer, but the words and the melodies poured into my mind, through my body and into my fingertips. It was a song I knew well, for it was still celebrated at court. My fingers moved of their own accord, plucking at the strings to release their uniquely Tudor sound. At the same time, I began to sing the words in old French, a language which Henry had once used to serenade Anne so romantically;

> Helas madame, celle que j'ayme tant:
> souffrez que soye vostre humble servant;
> vostre humble servant je seray a toujours
> et tant que je viv'ray ault' n'aymeray que vous.

Rather than the jaunty melody normally played at court, my hands moved more slowly producing a rhythm that was more haunting than joyful. By remembering happier times, I had inadvertently thrown into stark contrast only that so much had already changed; that the lightness and innocence of my carefree youth had long since departed. As my hands came to rest, I stared into the fire, lost in the sad realisation that I would never again taste the singular pleasure of falling in love with Henry, or of being the centre of his world. Thankfully, my self-pity was cut short by George Zouche, my equerry, who appeared by our side.

'Your Grace, Archbishop Cranmer and Dr William Butts request an audience.' Without hesitation I replied,

'Please, show them in.' As I watched Master Zouche head off back down the gallery, I pondered upon the possible nature of their visit. Of course, it was commonplace for me to see Dr Butts about the court where we would exchange words of friendship, and often discuss developments which touched upon our shared love of the gospel, and those who were active in the cause of spreading the word of the good Lord, in England and overseas. I knew well that William Butts had many evangelical contacts at home and abroad, and since Anne's ascendancy, he had established himself as a conduit between her and those reformers who sought the queen's support. Despite Anne's failure to yet bear Henry his son, she remained a wealthy, powerful and influential figure, a *femme sole*, which allowed her to act independently, although Henry's patronage and support often remained pivotal.

I saw Thomas Cranmer less frequently. Naturally, given his position, he was busy with church business and often away from court. Whenever time did allow, my friend would always go out of his way to visit me in my privy apartments. In many ways, at just twelve years older than Anne, he was like a much older brother to me, always there when I needed him, always ready with words of sanity and wisdom. Indeed, like my mother, Thomas Cranmer had been one of my most stalwart of supporters in the difficult days following Elizabeth's birth. Not only had he spent many hours reassuring me that I was truly blessed by God and that I should not give up my faith and hope in His holy mercy, but he also spoke with the king on several occasions. Whilst the good Archbishop never broke confidence about the discussions he shared with the king, I knew they were of a similar nature. I owed Thomas Cranmer a debt of gratitude. I was sure then, as I am to this day, that he played a significant role in healing the enmity that Henry held towards me in the autumn of 1533.

Thus, I was delighted to see the two men walk together down the length of the gallery towards where Nan and I were seated. Naturally, Nan stood up and gave way to the gentlemen, who I indicated should step forward, allowing them to greet me with all due courtesy. As was ever the way, both men first bowed then, they came over to kiss the ring that Thomas Cranmer had placed upon my hand at my coronation. I smiled warmly, as I said,

'Gentlemen, take a seat. It pleases me greatly to see you both.' Thomas spoke first,

'Dr Butts tells me that there is great cause for celebration, Your Grace.' I suspect that I smiled rather coyly, yet no doubt my eyes flashed with pride, as I replied,

'It is indeed true, Your Grace.' I laid one hand upon my still very flat stomach, as I went on, 'I am with child once again. You were right, Thomas. God in his infinite mercy has seen fit to bless the king's majesty and me with another child, and we feel sure that this time it will be a prince.' Both men smiled and nodded. I heard myself speak so confidently but in truth, I had no idea where this certainty came from. On that January morning I sensed there was more to their visit than the conveyance of hearty congratulations, so I enquired, 'Gentlemen, please tell me, how I may help you, for I sense that there is another purpose to your visit?' Lowering his voice, clearly wishing to maintain a degree of privacy to our conversation, Dr Butts replied.

'Indeed Madame, we have come on a rather sensitive matter.' Almost in a whisper, he went on, 'We have a friend abroad who needs our help.' Immediately, I knew that the king's physician referred to an evangelical who was in trouble, and most probably persecuted by Catholic authorities. It was indeed a matter of some delicacy, and surrounded by my ladies, I stood up and said,

'Gentlemen, perhaps you would walk with me,' I indicated towards a doorway leading from the gallery, 'Methinks that the view of the Thames from the gilt chamber is particularly fine at this time of the day. Would you care to accompany me?' Both men smiled, appreciating my respect for discretion. In the said chamber, we could talk more privately, away from those whose inclinations lay more naturally with the conservative faction at court and abroad. I indicated to my ladies that they should remain at leisure within the gallery, whilst I led Archbishop Cranmer and Dr Butts inside the chamber.

The gilt chamber was most aptly named. Its origins lay with the original owner of the palace, Cardinal Wolsey. The room was of a modest size, and, as in Wolsey's day, it was still used as a small private study, jutting out from the eastern side of the queen's long gallery, on the western bank of the Thames. Therefore, it had unprecedented views up the river toward the City of London and downwards, to Lambeth Palace. If any room, in any palace, had once shone with gold then it was this one; for when Wolsey fell from grace in 1529, those servants that the king sent to inspect his goods had found this room stuffed with gilt, mostly laid out on a large trestle table in the centre of the room. Henry himself once reminded me of the great cupboard beneath the window, furnished only with plate of solid gold, many items enriched with pearls and other precious stones. Over the years, the majority of pieces had been redistributed, or moved to the Jewel House at the Tower. Yet, several items remained to give continuity to its history, all which had been gifted to Anne by the King.

I crossed to the window and gazed out over the Thames, as I asked,

'Gentlemen, which friend needs our help?' Dr Butts spoke first.

'His name is Nicolas Bourbon and lives in Paris. He has been outspoken lately, attacking the 'popish' cult of sainthood in his church.' Then Thomas Cranmer added,

'As Your Majesty is aware, the King of France is increasingly intolerant of those who love well the true word of the gospel, and unfortunately, Master Bourbon finds himself stripped of all his worldly goods and honour, and has been thrown into a Paris jail.' After a few moments of silence, I replied,

'Tell me Dr Butts, can you vouch for his good character?' William Butts stepped forward, his hands clasped lightly in front of his slightly rotund belly, as he answered without hesitation,

'Indeed Madame. On both accounts, and in the sight of God, I can answer you 'yea'. Master Bourbon is not only a man of God but a gifted poet and scholar. We have corresponded for some time, and I am sure that in gratitude for Your Grace's intervention, he would gladly serve you well and bring you much honour.' I nodded my head thoughtfully, turning over the gentleman's name in my mind. It was once again frustratingly familiar to me. I knew that this 'Nicolas Bourbon' was a character set to play his part upon Anne Boleyn's glittering stage; yet was he friend or foe? I simply could not remember, and it vexed me to the core. I slowly paced back and forth in front of the window, one arm folded across my chest, the other elbow resting upon it, as my fingers toyed thoughtfully with my lower lip. I did not want to help another predator build a nest close to Anne's throne and yet, I knew that it was in Anne's gift to help those persecuted in the name of the reformed religion. I reminded myself again of the sense that I had been given this gift by God himself, and that it was my duty—Anne's duty—to assist the spread of the true word of the good Lord in England and beyond. I knew what I must do. I trusted the two men who stood before me, men who I knew would never betray me. They had asked for my help, knowing that Anne alone was in a position to provide a safe haven for our friend. Thus, I turned to Archbishop Cranmer and William Butts and nodded my head before saying,

'Of course, I will do all that I can to secure Master Bourbon's release and pay for his safe passage to England and his boarding whilst here. However, if I do...' I looked first to Thomas Cranmer, and then toward his sagacious companion, as I added, '...will you provide our friend with a safe house and comfortable lodgings?' William Butts was perhaps best placed to answer, and this he did with a simple,

'Aye, Madame. It will be an honour.' With that our business was concluded. I asked Thomas simply to say a prayer for our friend's safety, and give us the Lord's blessing, before I led them both back to the gilt chamber and the gallery beyond where both gentlemen bowed and kissed the ring upon my hand, and took their leave of me.

I watched them walk down the gallery, their black, loose gowns billowing behind them, when the figure of Sir Francis Bryan emerged at its entrance. Stopping briefly before the good Archbishop and Dr Butts, the three men acknowledged each other cordially, before Sir Francis continued to swagger his way toward me, a young lady, whom I did not know, following in his wake.

By 1534, along with Sir Henry Norris, my cousin, Sir Francis, was well established as one of my husband's closest friends. Our relationship had been a little rockier since my outburst over Mistress Jane Seymour's appointment to my household; however, in the cold light of day, I had seen the rashness of my behaviour—despite my dislike of the said lady—and had gone out of my way to humbly make amends. The appointment of Margaret, Lady Bryan, as the lady mistress to Elizabeth's household was part of this strategy. As Lady Bryan was Francis' mother, and the half sister of my own dear mother, I had lent on family ties, showing great favour toward Sir Francis's family in an effort to heal the rift. Both of us made an effort and, over time, we reached an uneasy truce of sorts. However, I can confess that I liked him not. Despite his rather superficial charms, I believed at heart he was a rake and a libertine, but his social accomplishments, courage and ruthlessness had long ago won him the admiration of the king and for Anne's sake, I tried to be always gracious in his company.

As he approached, I saw that he held a compact little dog with a domed head, a pug nose and large, dark eyes. Its black and tan coat was long, soft and wavy, and large, hairy ears hung down to the level of its shoulder. I recognised that the little creature was an English toy spaniel, much loved by noble ladies at court for their gentle, playful and loving temperaments. Like Anne, I adored animals, particularly dogs, and was enchanted by its innocent and inquisitive expression. Breaking into an enormous smile, I threw my arms out wide in front of me, insisting that I take the dog from Sir Francis before either he, or the lady who accompanied him, had a proper chance to greet me. I had already taken my new companion in my arms, stroking its little head and staring deeply into his big brown, beguiling eyes.

'Why, Sir Francis, who is this little fellow? He is absolutely gorgeous! Where have you been hiding him?' I looked up to find Sir Francis grinning at me, full of masculine charm as he replied,

'Your Majesty, it is a gift from Lady Lisle who sends you her most hearty commendations. He has just arrived here from Calais. '

'Oh, but he is simply adorable! And look at his little face...' Just as I said this, the little creature cocked its head to one side, as if trying to comprehend the meaning of my words. '... He seems to be trying to understand me. He is an intelligent little chap.' Sir Francis replied,

'And thus he is aptly named, Your Grace.' I looked again at Sir Francis, raising my eyebrows, silently beseeching him to tell me more. 'His name is Purkoy.' Purkoy was a gift from Lady Lisle via Sir Francis; a gift that Anne had loved at first sight, 'stealing' him immediately from the arms of her cousin and claiming him as her own.

Pourquoi? Yes, of course, I see it! His little expression is asking 'why?' Loyalty was a commodity that I had come to value highly, and there were no such creatures more loyal than companion dogs. In a heartbeat, I fell in love with his happy innocence, and it seemed our love affair was mutual, for little Purkoy suddenly stretched forward his neck and licked me on the end of my nose as I held him close. It was clear that we were not to be parted. When I put him down and seated myself back in front of the open fire, my new friend jumped up on my lap, curling himself up, content to be close to my person.

'It seems that he has chosen his mistress, Your Grace.' I smiled at Sir Francis, running my hand across the silky smooth coat of the little dog, which over the next few months, would follow me faithfully wherever I went. Once more, as history ordained, another line was written across the page of Anne's life, just as it had been foretold from the start. After a few moments of silence, my cousin cleared his throat, clearly wishing to change the emphasis of our conversation.

'Your Majesty, may I present to you Mistress Elizabeth Harvey, the niece of the late Sir Nicolas Harvey.' Remembering the presence of the young lady who had accompanied Sir Francis into the gallery, I looked up to see a very beautiful young woman who curtsied before me with an uncommon grace. I sat back in my chair to appraise the maid who stood before me. She was of middling stature, of slim build, dressed in a blue satin gown of the latest French fashion with a French hood upon her head revealing hair the colour of spun gold tucked neatly away beneath it. Her face was of delicate proportions but I remember her most striking feature was her flawless, porcelain skin, set against the most magnetic grey, blue eyes I had ever seen. Those eyes remained downcast in deference, raising them only when I addressed her directly.

'Mistress Harvey, you are new here at court, are you not?' Elizabeth slowly raised her eyes to meet mine, as she replied,

'Yes Your Majesty. Indeed I am.' Sir Francis interjected, explaining her presence on Elizabeth's behalf.

'Mistress Harvey has just turned eighteen and has long been a friend of our family. Since her father is sadly no longer with us, I have taken it upon myself to have a care for her well-being. She is a woman of great virtue, piety and grace. I am also aware that following the tragic death of Lady Bridget, Your Grace has a vacancy for a new lady within your household. Perhaps it is bold of me, Your Majesty, but I think that you will find Bess' accomplishments to your liking, for she sings, dances and plays the lute...' Sir Francis indicated with his hand towards my lute, '...with as much skill and grace as I have ever seen in one so young.' I watched Mistress Harvey blush at the compliments being bestowed upon her, before I spoke again to the lady in question.

'Perhaps you would care to play and sing for me?' I took the lute within my hands and held it out, indicating with a nod of my head that she should take the seat opposite and play for our entertainment. To her credit, Bess did not falter, but accepted my offer without hesitation. She was self-assured and I admired her courage. I watched her take the instrument within her delicate hands, caressing it with the same easy intimacy that I myself had done a little while earlier. After a moment's pause, she sang another love song of Henry's composition, 'Whoso that will all feats obtain', in a voice that was as sweet and clear as pure spring water. I was deeply moved, not only by the purity of her voice, but by the emotion with which she spoke about the joy of love and the suffering of disdain. Lost as she was in her act of creation, as Sir Francis suggested, I was indeed not only impressed with her accomplishments, but beguiled by this talented young woman who was unafraid to show me her heart. Once more, I wondered if she would be loyal to Anne Boleyn. For the sake of building further bridges with my cousin, and that she was the niece of a man who Anne Boleyn had once much favoured, I decided to accept her into my household without further question. I asked Nan to take Bess away and instruct the newest member of the queen's household in her duties.

The following day she was to stand before me, a hand upon the Bible, swearing her loyalty and allegiance to her new mistress. Never had such a sweet creature hidden within her breast such a sinister capacity for dissimulation. On that unassuming day in January, I agreed to bring a man—who would indeed be a light unto the world—into the English court; I also inadvertently admitted a woman who would soon wreak havoc within my marriage and threaten Anne's very safety, at what would turn out to be one of the most vulnerable times in her life.

There is no doubt that I was tense through those first three months of 1534. In the back of my mind was the nagging threat that Anne was fated to miscarry her second child, and each day I prayed to thank God that my son remained safe within my womb. By the end of March, I was nearly four months pregnant. For a second year in a row, with the advancing spring weather, my ladies began to let out the laces of my gowns. Of course, I was exceptionally careful to ensure that I was well rested and never exerted myself unduly as I again found that I tired easily in those early weeks of my pregnancy, Otherwise, I was in truly excellent health. In fact, knowing that with every week that went by, a miscarriage was increasingly unlikely, I finally began to relax and enjoy my happy state as the great court celebrations of Easter approached.

Indeed, I could hardly believe that a year had slipped through my fingers already. So much had happened in barely just over twelve months. I had become a wife, a queen and a mother with her second child well on its way. And I sensed that in that time, Anne too had changed, shaped by the monumental events which had crashed through her life, one after the other. On the one hand, Anne's elevation to Queen of England, ordained by God himself, had seemed to bring an assuredness of purpose and an unstoppable conviction in all matters of business and religion. On the other, however, I knew that regardless of how one looked at it, Anne had let Henry down with the birth of a mere daughter. We had ostensibly rebuilt our relationship from amongst the wreckage of broken pledges, but I knew that deep down, the ground upon which Anne walked was no longer stable. As his wife, the heady days of their romance began to wane, and while Anne still had the capacity to enthral him, the magic of the allure that once held Henry spellbound, had become just a little jaded, had lost just a little of its potency. I had tasted what it was like for Anne to glow in the light of Henry's all-consuming love. When he held her up as a goddess above all women, she radiated an inner confidence that was truly unassailable.

However, by March 1534, I sensed a fracture in her self-confidence as it related to matters of the heart. Seeping through that fracture were glimpses of the worst of Anne's personality traits: anxiety, rash intemperance, haughtiness and jealousy, which in those terrible days of 1536 would finally and utterly consume her and me.

On that March morning, I was caught up in the excited buzz palpable in every corridor and room of the palace. It was well known that any day the Parliament, which had been in session since 15 January, was due to ratify the Act of Succession, placing the heirs of Anne's body above all other claimants to the throne. So whilst the great men of the land, our husbands, fathers and brothers had been called to sit in the 'house' barely quarter of a mile away in Westminster, I took my ladies into the great garden of Whitehall Palace to wage a competition at the butt.

Beyond the palace walls, the bustling sounds of London continued unabated whilst within the sanctuary of the great garden, we were held in a haven of tranquillity. I was accompanied on that fine, warm day by my sister and Lady Elizabeth, Countess of Worcester, both of whom wagered themselves in competition against me, whilst we were observed by Lady Rochford, Mary, Duchess of Richmond and her close companions, Madge Shelton and Margaret Douglas, the king's niece, who had been assigned the honorary title of Lady Paramount for the duration of the tournament.

The archery butt was positioned at the far end of the garden, in the middle of the wide, central walkway that ran up and down its length. To the north-east of the garden was Henry's low gallery with its mullioned windows stretched along its length, until it met the privy gallery range running perpendicular to it from east to west. This beautiful timber-framed building, the panels in-filled with painted and gilded grotesque design, had at the far end of it, Holbein's fabulous new gate which towered over King Street. The rest of the garden was surrounded by a high, red-brick wall, keeping away from the hoi polloi of London.

As far as our competition was concerned, my friends were in fine form, Lady Elizabeth hitting the target face exceedingly close to the centre on several occasions. I was less fortunate. My first few arrows swung wide, piercing the outer rim of the target, which was unusual for Anne was an archer of considerable skill. I was clearly unsettled for some reason, and sensed that it was not my day to win money from my friends. As Lady Elizabeth completed her end of shots, I spoke my thoughts aloud.

'You shoot well today, Lady Elizabeth. I fear that between you and my sister, I will be all the poorer for it!' The Countess smiled and inclined her head gracefully, accepting my compliment. She added graciously,

'It is but the child in your belly which unsettles you, Your Grace. ' I smiled wryly in response, accepting an arrow from a page that stood nearby. Taking up my stance, I knocked the arrow on the string, paused before drawing that self-same silk string smoothly back until it and my index finger rested momentarily on the anchor point, close to my upper lip. I lined up to sight the target, feeling the tension held within the bow, and an unsettling vibration of my energy that caused an uncommon wavering in my preparation. When I released my hold, I watched the arrow sail toward the target, the wind singing in its fletching, as it cut through the air, and eventually came to land, piercing the butt way to the right of centre.

I was just about to exclaim my frustration when I saw Master Cromwell walking towards us. He was a burly man, his rolling gait reflecting his size. Moving as quickly as his bulk allowed, I watched him approach from the path running down the eastern side of the garden, sensibly well out of the line of sight of our arrows. Clasped in front of his chest was a brown, leather folio. In truth, I rarely saw Thomas Cromwell without state papers about his person; he was an industrious man and worked tirelessly to ensure the king's majesty obtained all that he desired—not without benefit to Master Cromwell himself, of course. As he came closer, I greeted Thomas brightly and with good cheer, whilst indicating that my sister and Lady Elizabeth should continue the game.

'Master Cromwell, good morrow. Have you come to join us at the butts?' With the approach of the man who was virtually always at Henry's side, I knew that he had come to convey a weighty message from the king. Knowing this, I felt a frisson of anticipation pass through me. As Cromwell came before me, he removed his cap and swept into a bow, before righting himself and replying,

'Sadly no, Your Majesty. However the king's grace has bid me to find Your Majesty and convey the hearty news.' I cocked my head and raised an eyebrow, a slight flutter taking hold in anticipation of what glad tidings Thomas Cromwell had been gifted to deliver. 'This very morning, Parliament has passed the Act of Succession. From this day forth, Madame, all lords of this land, both spiritual and temporal, as well as the Commons, have declared that his Majesty's former marriage to the Lady Katherine took place against the laws of Almighty God, and it is thus declared null and void. Furthermore, that the matrimony betwixt his majesty and yourself, his most entirely beloved wife, is deemed beyond doubt to be true, sincere and perfect ever hereafter.' I listened avidly to Master Cromwell, digesting his words. As I did so, I watched my sister take aim, loosing several arrows with great skill at the butt. Master Cromwell continued, 'The Lady Mary is now declared a bastard, and only children begotten between Your Grace and his majesty stand to inherit the kingdom.' I turned my head back towards Master Cromwell, interjecting with incisive enquiry,

'And Elizabeth?' Cromwell took a moment to clear his throat before, with the faintest of smiles, he replied,

'The Princess Elizabeth will inherit the kingdom should you have no sons by the king's body. It is also the case that should the king die before your children come of age, you will rule England as regent.' Of course, I knew of the Act of Succession from my modern day life, but like so much that had gone before, the details eluded me. I did not realise that Henry had gone so far as to entrust his kingdom to Anne should he die before their children reached eighteen years of age; it was an enormous act of trust that literally took my breath away. I suspect Master Cromwell saw enormous pride and satisfaction swell up from within my breast. As I remained speechless, Thomas took the opportunity to finish the message he had been entrusted to deliver. 'In addition, his majesty has instructed me to inform you that from 1 May, all subjects of this realm will be required to sign an oath confirming their adherence to the Act. Should anybody refuse to do so, they may be found guilty of high treason. Such will also be the case for those found speaking against your marriage to the king, or slandering in any way either yourself or your heirs. They will be imprisoned, stripped of their lands, titles and properties, and tried as traitors as the king pleases.'

I confess that the word, 'traitor' always sent a shiver down my spine.

My twenty-first century life was far from perfect, and there were many undesirable aspects of the society in which I lived. Yet, in England at least, the death penalty no longer existed, and I had to struggle to reconcile myself to the ruthless brutality of Anne's world. Upon Master Cromwell's words, I thought immediately of two men whose distaste and opposition to the king's divorce, the break with Rome, and of Anne herself, was notorious—Bishop John Fisher and Sir Thomas More. Finally, I let go of my necklace, and passing the bow to one of my pages, I turned back towards Thomas and asked,

'Do you think that there will be those who will not sign?' Cromwell pursed his lips in thought for a few seconds, before answering.

'It is unclear as yet as to whether the Lady Katherine or the Lady Mary will put their names to the Act. Of course, there is both Fisher and More to consider; the first is outwardly condemnatory of the king's actions and I think he seeks martyrdom for the cause.' Thomas stroked his chin thoughtfully, then raising his eyes to meet mine, as he added, '...and as for More... he dissembles well, and I suspect he will be like a slippery eel with the Commission entrusted to enact the oath and collect his signature.' I knew that history had already condemned the two men to death, but I was curious to seek Master Cromwell's opinion on the matter regardless.

'Do you think they will die on account of it?'

'Madame, if they do not sign the oath and swear their unconditional surrender to his majesty's will, then they will deserve to die a traitor's death.' Suddenly, at the thought of what might await them, I wished to change the subject. I found it was my turn at the butt once more and in an effort to free my mind of gruesome images of death, I smiled at Master Cromwell and said,

'Master Cromwell, I find that I'm out of sorts today and am losing sorely in this competition. If Lady Mary and Lady Elizabeth allow, perhaps you would care to take the final shot on my behalf. Sadly, I think not that it will salvage the outcome, but it may restore some of my honour.' Thomas graciously accepted my invitation and stepped forward. He handed his leather pouch to my page, in exchange for a fine bow made of yew, waving away the leather bracer designed to protect his left arm from the fierce backlash of the bowstring. I knew that the king's wily servant was as skilled an archer as any man, and had no need of it, knowing exactly how much to flex his arm to ensure the bowstring remained clear of his flesh.

I had learned much about Thomas Cromwell and his early days as a mercenary fighting with the French army in Italy, since first meeting him in the autumn of 1532. While I witnessed his considerable administrative capabilities and his intellectual flair daily, I saw much less frequently his talents in the field of sport and leisure. With assured ease, Thomas drew the bow with his right hand, his strong, muscular arms making easy work of his instrument. I watched his laser-like focus take aim, and with unflappable calm, he released the bow string, sending the arrow hurtling toward the target, slicing the centre mark with deadly accuracy. My ladies broke out into a ripple of appreciative applause, before I remarked somewhat pointedly,

'Master Cromwell, I see that you make it your business to never miss your target.' My words, laced with double entendre, did not elude Thomas. With a shrewd smile, he replied,

'I try not to, Your Grace.' There was a moment of unspoken knowing between us, perhaps even of mutual admiration. Then I added,

'Then my honour is greatly restored, but sadly I have lost the match.' I summoned my page to my side, commanding, 'See to it that Master Taylor pays my debt to Lady Elizabeth and Lady Mary from the privy purse.' Turning back to Cromwell, I added, 'Perhaps you would care to walk back to the palace with me?' The invitation of a king or queen was rarely declined at court, and the request that I made that day was no exception. As we began to walk, Thomas proffered,

'If Your Majesty may allow me...' I cast my eyes sideways to see an enquiring look upon Master Cromwell's face, no doubt silently requesting my permission to tread on sensitive ground. I nodded my assent, and so he continued, 'We have also received news this morning from Rome.'

'Oh.' I remained silent, thus encouraging Thomas to continue.

'We have heard that the Pope has finally pronounced the sentence of excommunication upon his majesty.' I continued to look ahead of me, my hands clasped in front of my belly, silently digesting the information. I thought of Henry, the great defender of the faith, entitled thus by the Pope himself, cast out from the bosom of the Holy Roman Catholic Church. There would have been a time when such a thing was utterly inconceivable, even to Henry himself. But stone by stone, the Pope and the Catholic Church had, in effect, dismantled its own power and influence in the kingdom—and I feared not for its imminent downfall. I knew that if nothing else, Henry was utterly convinced that God had set him upon this Earth as divine ruler of his kingdom, and no one, ultimately not even the Pope, could challenge that conviction without dire consequences. I could not help feel that the sheer arrogance of the church had been responsible for its own demise.

'And what say you, Master Cromwell?' As I spoke, I paused briefly, kneeling down to pick up little Purkoy who, like my ladies, was following dutifully in my wake.

'I say that all-round it is a marvellous day for the Kingdom of England, Your Majesty.' A wry and self-satisfied smile played upon Thomas' lips, and I sensed the harmony that flowed between Anne and Henry's astute clerk. I knew that it was not that she and Thomas were the closest of friends, or that they deferred to each other in every decision, but they were working toward a common aim. Their shared goal—to see the reformed religion established in England—made them natural allies, which for Anne's sake, I intended to maintain so long as I walked in her shoes. I then decided to change the subject and said,

'The king is very pleased with your diligence and appreciative of your... talents.' I paused again for a moment, standing still as I stroked Purkoy and kissed the top of his delicate head before adding, 'In fact, his grace asked me at supper just the other day how I thought he might repay you for your loyalty and service.' Thomas Cromwell remained silent, merely inclining his head and smiling appreciatively in an act of humble submission. I continued, 'I said to his Majesty that I thought that an official recognition of the job which his loyal subject fulfils daily would surely be an excellent commendation for your service.' I then knelt down and placed my little dog back upon the ground, before righting myself and adding, 'After all, as I said to the king, Stephen Gardiner has hardly shown himself to be loyal to his majesty in recent times, and I cannot see how he deserves the title of the king's principal secretary.' I referred to Gardiner's revolt over the question of Henry's divorce. The wily courtier had saved his neck by realising his mistake just in time, and in his unprecedented, grovelling submission, after the event. However, I knew that Henry never fully trusted him thereafter.

350

Cromwell, as ever, remained largely impassive, although I knew he understood well the meaning of my words. By that time, we had walked almost the entire length of the garden and were approaching the main privy gallery at its northern end. I stopped, raising my head and inhaling deeply the sweet, fresh air of that glorious spring day. When I looked back at Thomas, he finally responded by saying,

'I most humbly thank Your Grace for recommending me unto the king.' I was acutely aware of Anne's sharp, political acumen, and my own driving desire to keep Cromwell close within the Boleyn fold. Thus, I replied in words pregnant with meaning and expectation,

'There is much to be gained by our mutual high standing with his majesty, Thomas.' I had not openly stated that I expected Cromwell's unswerving loyalty, but I knew that, as a shrewd man of politics, Thomas would clearly understand my intimation. 'Now, I will go and find my Lady Mother and tell her the good news.' Then, deliberately, and to underline my point, I spoke to Thomas Cromwell using the title which through my influence, the king would shortly bestow upon him. 'You are dismissed 'Master Secretary', and I thank you for your pains.' I saw a glint of greed alight in Thomas' eyes, no doubt his imagination already hummed at the thought of what power such recognition would bring. Once more, he took his cap from his head and bowed, walking backwards for several steps, before finally turning and disappearing into the main body of the palace.

My Lord Father and Lady Mother were lodged in one of the several ground floor apartments that occupied the space beneath the king's own privy chambers within the long gallery at Whitehall. Thomas Boleyn had been granted lodgings there on account of his close association to the queen, and because of his position as his majesty's lord privy seal. Adjacent to the chamber, my brother George also held lodgings, along with a number of my husband's closest intimates including, Sir Henry Norris, Sir Francis Bryan and Henry Courtenay, Marquess of Exeter.

It was easy for me to visit my parents in their apartment on the way back to the queen's side. I would often use the privy gallery to return to my own lodgings after taking the air in the great garden. Thus, I left behind me the bright sunny morning, and accompanied by my ladies, entered into the shaded privy gallery next to the great 'Adam and Eve' staircase that led up to the king's privy apartments on the first floor, and just a short walk to the entrance of my parent's lodgings. As my status dictated, I allowed my page to step forward and knock upon the heavy oak door. My father's page answered and announced the arrival of the queen's grace to those within. I turned briefly to indicate to my ladies that they should wait for me outside the room. I entered the chamber to find not only Thomas and Elizabeth Boleyn, but also my brother, George. Immediately, I sensed that all was not well and was grateful that I had asked my ladies to wait in the gallery.

Due to their status, my parents were allocated two chambers of comfortable size. The larger of the two was the outer chamber which had two mullioned windows opposite the entrance and afforded pleasant views over the great garden from whence I had just come. The room was clad, like much of the privy gallery, in linen-fold panelling, and was hung with two fine tapestries, no doubt from Thomas's own private collection. Carved into the left wall, a large fireplace lay empty, in acknowledgment of the warmer weather that had arrived with the coming of spring; in front of this, two finely embroidered stools stood like sentinels on either side of the hearth, while in the centre of the room, a heavy, oak trestle table served as the focal point for dining, socialising and transacting business.

However, I was barely concerned about the accoutrements of the chamber, for it was the heavy atmosphere that was most noticeable, almost suffocating. Clearly, something was very wrong as I looked from one to the other. The first was my mother, who when I appeared in the doorway, had stood up and dipped a curtsy. Only when she raised her eyes to meet mine did I see that they were pricked with tears. My father had been pacing up and down in front of the window, and when he looked at me, his face was set hard, clearly angered by whatever had come to pass. Finally, I turned toward George, who was standing to my left, looking terribly sheepish, and I knew immediately that whatever had caused such consternation, it involved Lord Rochford.

In a brusque manner, I began pulling the soft leather archery glove off my right hand, as I asked nobody in particular,

'What's wrong?' Unsurprisingly, my father spoke first. Like Anne, Thomas' temper was legendary, and I suspect that before I arrived, my brother had felt the heat of my father's displeasure for whatever transgression he had committed. Sir Thomas answered me in clipped tones that were still simmering with anger.

'Your brother here has managed to get one of your ladies *enceinte*.' I turned toward George, who seemed unable to look me in the eye. There were several moments of deathly silence, whilst I silently recalled my brother's pledge to keep away from Mistress Cobham. I did not know if my brother had lied to me from the outset, or whether he had simply been unable to live up to his promise, but I just knew that this adulterous pregnancy involved the said lady. I felt my own fury begin to take hold of my body, as I lashed out with some sarcasm.

'I suspect dear brother that our Father is not referring to your own, long-suffering wife is he?' Laced with shame, George raised his gaze to meet mine; he did not speak, his silence said all that I needed to know. I was ever aware of the ladies outside the lodgings, and wondered sometimes if even the walls at court had ears. Although the words that I spoke next were full of disdain and fury, I kept my voice low, firing my artillery of attack in barely more than a whisper. 'Of course not! That would be too much to ask wouldn't it?'

As God is my witness, I have ever loved my brother as dearly as life itself, and soon I will gladly accompany him in death. But on that day, I was furious. Perhaps it was not even so much what he had done, which was bad enough given the circumstances, but worse was that he had misled me, possibly even lied to me. Thus, my tolerance snapped as a brittle twig, and my reaction a primitive one. Brimming with hurt and frustration, I went over to my brother and swiped him across the face with my glove. I saw George flinch, but he did not move; but I had not finished with him. 'Is it her? Well, is it?' We both knew that I was referring to Nan Cobham. Averting his gaze in shame once more, my brother nodded his head, and said in barely a whisper,

'Yes.' With that one, innocuous word, all my fears were confirmed, and unleashed an outpouring of anger that came from the pain of deceit.

'George, how dare you lie to me?'

'I didn't lie, I...' My brother tried to speak but I was in no mood for excuses. I swiftly brought both my palms up to face him, shaking my head to keep out the perfect reasons for his lies and his infidelity. I silenced him with my gesture and forged on, incandescent with rage.

'No, don't even try to worm your way out of this one. I won't have it! I asked you outright if you were having an affair and you said no. You even promised me faithfully that you would be good to your wife!' I could see my brother's shame etched all over his handsome face.

'Did you know about this, Anne?' My father interjected, interrupting my accusations. I snapped my head back to look at my father, before lowering my tone even further and explaining,

'Jane suspected something last year. She told me of it, and I asked my carpet-knight brother here, if it were true. He assured me nothing was going on.' Turning back to George and boiling over with frustration, I hissed, 'I really don't know what is worse; that you have deceived me, or that your wife is standing outside my door and living cheek by jowl with the woman you are swiving! At this, George turned a deathly shade of white, followed by a flush of scarlet embarrassment that raced across his cheeks and neck, matching the colour of his scarlet doublet. My father bent his knuckles upon the table, sighing deeply; his head hung forward, sore-hearted and weary from my brother's foolish actions. We watched him in silence as he addressed my brother.

'If you were not the age you are, I swear I would beat you until I knocked some sense into you.' Shaking his head slowly from side to side, Thomas Boleyn added with ominous quietness, 'Do you not understand the precariousness of our position? Do you not understand that everything depends on the safe delivery of the child that your sister is carrying? Do you not realise that this selfish inability to keep within your marriage bed might dishonour Anne…' then in an explosion of anger, during which the earl's own face burned with fury, he brought his fist crashing down onto the table, and shouted, '…who happens to be the Queen of England!' My mother rushed forward, ever level-headed, ever the peace-maker; putting her arm about my father's shoulders, she said calmly,

'Everyone, let us be at peace. No more shouting Thomas, it is neither good for your health, nor helpful.' I saw her look somewhat anxiously toward the door, only too aware that whilst those outside would not have heard most of the conversation, but with my father's last outburst, they surely knew that all was not well. The earl stood up running his hands through his hair as if to clear the fog of fury which had momentarily blinded him. I knew that there was little more to say. Like my mother, I saw that what was called for was a remedy to our predicament and so, with a similarly even tone, I said,

'Father, you need to orchestrate Mistress Cobham's removal from court before her condition becomes evident, and Jane's suspicions are aroused.' I looked from my father to my brother, as if to emphasise my next words. 'She must not know of this pregnancy, under any circumstances, do you understand?'

'What if Nan tells Jane upon her return? Or if she sees her children at court?' For the first time my brother spoke up, finding his voice from within the wreckage of his condemnation. However, Thomas Boleyn's ruthless determination to protect his family finally surfaced. Speaking without a moment's hesitation he replied,

'I will arrange it so that Mistress Cobham will leave court immediately, and will never speak of this again. In the meantime, we cannot have any suggestion of illegitimate children that might be linked back to this family. We are too vulnerable to those who wish us harm. I will also see to it that the children are taken away at birth; perhaps even sent to a branch of the family in Ireland, where they will be well out of the way but cared for.' I shivered at the thought. I knew first-hand the pain of separation from a beloved child. I could not even begin to envisage the thought of never seeing my daughter again, just as I surely knew that this was the fate that faced George's paramour.

The following day, Nan was gone from court, ostensibly called back to care for her mother who had been suddenly, and unexpectedly, taken ill. Initially, I thought often about the woman who had been banished to the country to face the prospect of losing her child as soon as she was brought to bed. I felt her pain keenly; but as the days stretched into weeks, disturbing events much closer to home would overtake me and consume me completely.

Chapter Thirty

Eltham Palace, London,
1 April 1534

'Master Holbein, this is indeed a work of genius. I simply adore it.' I
looked up from the parchment stretched out beneath my hands to meet
the shining eyes of the man whose creative flair and mastery of his art
would leave behind priceless relics of the Renaissance. Hans Holbein
smiled in simple gratitude, inclining his head humbly to accept my
words of commendation. I turned to gaze at the drawing sketched out so
delicately on the rough parchment held beneath my fingertips that of
Holbein's design for a silver cradle of estate, commissioned by Henry
and me against the coming of the new prince. I delighted in the sight of
several pillars adorned with Tudor roses, subtle shading depicting the
many colourful, precious stones which were to be set in a gold border
around its rim, whilst gold figures of Adam and Eve were crafted to
look over my expectant son as he slept. Entirely satisfied, I clasped my
hands afore my visibly swollen belly, and said, 'You have truly outdone
yourself, Master Holbein. The king and I are delighted with your work.
I will see to it that Master Hayes is instructed to bring your creation to
life and that you are recompensed well for your pains.' With that, the
most gifted and most humble man at court turned about the velvet cap
in his hands, as he inclined his head once more, replying simply,

'Thank you, Your Grace.' I nodded indicating that our audience was
over and watched Master Holbein take several steps backwards before
he turned and disappeared from my privy chamber. I walked over to
one of the great angular bay windows, the predominant feature of the
privy apartments that formed the western range of Eltham Palace. It
was not my first visit Eltham Palace, indeed, I had only glorious
memories of the time Henry and I visited it on our way back from
Calais in November 1532. It was a time of carefree romance, and
decadent pleasures of the flesh, as we first explored the warm delights
of a shared bed. More recently, Elizabeth had spent time in the
refurbished nursery at Eltham, and I had visited my daughter at the
palace only two months before, at the beginning of Lent.

Eltham was one of five 'great houses' owned by the king, and despite its size, it was charming and utterly enchanting. In its glory days, this most royal residence witnessed so much of England's history, and had been treasured by its royal owners as a place of pleasure, nestled amongst some of the finest hunting ground in the country. Although at the time it remained one of Henry's premier residences, able to accommodate the entire court of near 1,000 people, the nearby Palace of Greenwich was assuming far greater importance. As a consequence, Eltham was increasingly being used as a nursery for royal children, a place of entertainment for important visitors, or as a simple hunting lodge.

From out of my window, I watched the sun set on the western horizon, revealing by degrees the night sky in a final blaze of vibrant oranges and pinks. The palace stood proud atop of some of the highest ground in the neighbourhood, excepting nearby Shooter's Hill. Thus, I looked down across a broad and beautiful landscape that stretched out for more than a mile below me. In the foreground, the odd tree, not yet quite in leaf, stood in silhouette against nature's dusky pallet. While two miles away appeared the bold and finely wooded outline of Greenwich Park. Still further in the distance, I could trace the spire of the Gothic Cathedral of St Paul's and the lofty roof of Westminster Abbey, both pricked out against the London skyline. It was a scene of great peace and incomparable beauty. Yet I was saddened to think that there I was, witnessing the beginning of the end of this great, historic building, just as surely as I was witnessing the end of another day in Anne's world.

We arrived at Eltham on the Wednesday before Easter, and I was overjoyed that the court would be spending a few days where my darling Elizabeth was being cared for in the royal nursery. Just to think of seeing her always filled me with such happiness. Upon my arrival at Eltham, it took me little time to make my way through its many corridors and rooms to find my daughter and take her in my arms.

Elizabeth was almost seven months old, and when I held her, I felt her small body bursting with vitality. I spent so little time with her that I was ever afraid that she would turn from me when we were reunited. However, her senses were sharp and instinctive, and my welcome was always one of rapturous delight in which my baby girl would gurgle her happiest of smiles and stretch out her chubby arms to touch my face and tell me, in her own way, of her continued and unconditional love. I spent much of that day in her company, playing in the sunny privy garden, walking with her in my arms under the arch of an interlaced alley of plum and cherry trees, teaching her about the form and texture of the natural world that surrounded her, or speaking to her, often in French, of how much I missed and loved her as dearly as life itself. She was bright, and filled with an insatiable curiosity for everything that I put before her. It was easy to see, even then, the foundations of the formidable intellect for which she would later become famous, and which would one day save her life.

Henry joined us that morning, delighting in his daughter's company as much as I. And when he left an hour or so later, in order to meet with the Privy Council, I gave him little further thought. I knew that he would most likely go out hunting afterward, but in my pregnant state, I was forbidden to join him. Yet, I cared not, for during those few precious days that we were to spend holding court at Eltham, I had a mind to spend every waking minute possible in Elizabeth's company.

'It is a beautiful view, is it not, Your Grace?' Suddenly, my isolated reverie was interrupted by the sound of Joan's voice, as my friend came up silently behind me. I saw the glowing reflection of her face in the glass in front of me first, painted in hues reflecting the colour of the sky; then, twisting my head round to look over my right shoulder, I smiled at her in acknowledgement.

'It is indeed, Joan' Turning about fully, I slipped my arm through hers with familiar affection, and enquired, 'But tell me, how are you feeling?' In the last couple of weeks, like Nan Gainsford and I, my friend had proudly announced that she too was pregnant once more, this time with her fifth child. I was so pleased for her, for she had accepted the infant death of little Arthur so gracefully the year before, and I prayed that this time all would be well. However, we all knew that Joan suffered notoriously from severe morning sickness, and the expected new arrival was proving to be no exception. Thus, she raised her eyes to the ceiling, and with a slight smile that belied the true nature of the discomfort that her condition caused her, she stoically replied,

'I am feeling better this evening, Your Majesty. At the moment, my wretchedness is confined mainly to the mornings.' I nodded my understanding and squeezed her hand in support, before speaking my mind to all of the ladies who were in attendance upon me that afternoon. 'Ladies, I wish to thank the good Lord for this day and show gratitude for our good fortune. Let us go to the chapel and say our prayers.' It was a short walk as we made our way along a first floor gallery that led directly to a square lobby and the entrance to the chapel's holy day closet and the royal pew, which looked down upon the body of the church below. The light was fading fast and torches were being lit around the perimeter of the great court below. I made my way directly to the royal pew, picked up the skirts of my black damask gown and sank to my knees upon the prie-dieu leaning my elbows upon the arm rest; I clasped my hands in prayer, closing my eyes, as I inhaled deeply the scent of incense that filled the chapel, and felt the divine stillness of this most holy place. In my own private world, I remembered how, just twelve months ago, Anne had first been presented as queen in a glittering ceremony of pomp and majesty on Easter Sunday. I had yet to give Henry his son and heir, but I prayed to God that day in earnest, thanking him for his mercy and for the continued well-being of the man-child that I carried within my belly.

When my devotions were over, I made my way down one of the two the stone, vice-staircases that were built into identical turrets positioned at both the northern and southern corners of the holy day closet, into the main body of the church where several members of the royal household were in the midst of their own private prayers. As ever, I was attended by several of my ladies, including Lady Rochford—who thankfully was none the wiser of her husband's indiscretions. Much to my chagrin, my aunt, Elizabeth Wood, Lady Boleyn, had managed to inveigle her way back into my household. She had pressed my father, her brother, to regain the place of honour that she felt was her due. Under considerable pressure from my father, I acquiesced to his wishes thinking, foolishly as it turned out, that the generosity of my action would bring forth a degree of gratitude and humility in her overbearing and haughty character. She was accompanied by the lady I hated most at court, Jane Seymour. It occurred to me, with some irony, that since scorpions lurked beneath the honey coated image that Mistress Seymour presented to the world, the two were, in temperament, quite well suited.

Night had almost fallen and the chapel's interior, bedecked with gilded grotesque work and ornately carved oak panelling, was lit by a myriad of flickering candles. I made my way toward the altar and as I did so, I recognised the solitary figure of a young noblewoman kneeling in the front pew of the church, consumed entirely in her private devotions; it was the Lady Mary. I had seen Katherine's daughter at court little since I walked in Anne's shoes, for she had long since been banished for her disobedience and intransigence against the king's wishes. It was only since Mary had been sent to attend upon my own beloved daughter that our paths began to cross more frequently.

The king's bastard was now eighteen years of age, a young woman in her own right, certainly no longer a child. She was also utterly impossible to reconcile oneself with. Her pride and stubbornness ran as deep as the ocean itself, and I saw only too clearly how her brittle inflexibility would ultimately heap upon her a tremendous amount of self-inflicted suffering. Indeed, as I passed her on my way toward the high altar, I saw her face in profile, just as I had seemingly a lifetime ago, when I first beheld the young princess in the Church of the Observant Friars at Greenwich. She had truly been in the first flush of youth back then, her mind untroubled by worldly cares, her body undisturbed by the deleterious effect that the stress of her parent's matrimonial difficulties would come to exert upon her health. However, that evening, in the willowy candlelight, her face looked drawn; her brow furrowed and pinched in concentration, whilst her complexion appeared translucent, almost ghostly, set as it was against her rich auburn hair and gown of russet damask. If she was aware of my presence, she showed no sign of it, for the Lady Mary remained still, her eyes closed, her hands intertwined in prayer; a gold crucifix attached to a rosary that she held clasped within those hands. I turned my head away wishing no confrontation in public as I was still painfully aware of the outcome of our last encounter. I sank to my knees afore the high altar, my mind immediately flooded with memories of my last 'meeting' with Mary some six weeks earlier when I was visiting Elizabeth during Lent. Yet, with a son safely conceived, I felt generous and determined to make amends. In my heart, I knew that she was an innocent victim of the love between Henry and me, a love which had torn her parents—and her life—apart. I even felt guilty. In the aftermath of Elizabeth's birth, when I had been so unsure of my footing with the king and fiercely protective of my new-born daughter,

I had commanded Lady Shelton to slap Mary for her disobedience and obstinacy as befitted her status as the cursed bastard that she was.

Oh, I have asked God's forgiveness for my actions many times over since I have been incarcerated here in the Tower. And I pray that in His mercy, I am truly forgiven for my sins. My only defence is that fear soured the milk of my human kindness. It was on account of this realisation that I was determined to offer Mary the hand of friendship and goodwill, providing that she accepted Anne as queen.

However, when my message was delivered, Mary had repudiated the offer with the greatest rudeness, saying that she knew of no queen but her mother—but if I, the king's mistress, would intercede with her father, she would be grateful. I recognised the words as soon as I heard them. Their potency echoed clearly across time. I was not only furious with the great offensiveness of her remarks, but wildly frustrated that there was absolutely nothing that I could to do to change any of the events passing through Anne's life. I tried once more before I left my daughter's household thinking that surely there was a heart within this young woman, and that I would be able to warm it toward her new stepmother. I could not have been more mistaken. Mary remained intransigent, and her arrogant impudence left me with even greater venom flowing through my veins. I see now that it was in childish retribution that I once more urged my Aunt Anne, Lady Shelton, to beat her as she justly deserved.

Eventually, I released myself from events of the past, calming my mind to complete its prayers. Finally, making the sign of the cross afore me, I raised myself to my feet. However, when I turned about, the Lady Mary was gone. I expected little more. I suspected that seeing that I was also present within the chapel, she had made a hasty departure, unwilling to pay court to the heretic who, in her mind, was also the king's mistress and whore. When I returned to my privy chamber, one of my ladies was relating some malicious tittle-tattle that would begin a sequence of events that I could not have foretold; events that would leave me under no illusion that I occupied a singular place of affection within the king's heart.

It seemed that whilst I had been deep in prayer in front of the high altar in the chapel, the Lady Mary had curtsied toward me, before taking her leave. My desire for reconciliation ensured that I responded with reckless enthusiasm, and immediately despatched a lady of honour with a message of apology for not noticing her gesture, and conveying the fact that the love of no other would be dearer, nor more respected than hers, and that I would embrace it with the kindness of a true friend. Thus, standing in my raying chamber, I nervously awaited the response. I hardly dared believe that at last the king's eldest daughter might be thawing in her affections for Anne. As I waited, my mind swirled with 'what ifs'; at the same time, my two friends efficiently stripped me of my jewels, my hood was lifted delicately from my head, and Nan began the task of unlacing the bodice of my gown. With my outer garments removed, Joan began to work on unlacing my pair of bodies, and as she did, I laid my hand upon my pregnant belly, running my palm over its firm and insistent swell. I had not yet felt the child move, but at almost five months gone, I knew it would not be long until I did so.

Interrupting these thoughts, there was a knock at the door. Joan opened the door just a crack and exchanged whispered words with the invisible messenger. I could just make out Joan's face in profile, she seemed disturbed, her brow furrowed as she listened intently. When she closed the door, her face was ashen white as she turned toward me, and the hopeful expectation of a rapprochement with the Lady Mary disintegrated into dust before my very eyes as I asked,

'What is it? What did she say?' In a rather choked voice, she relayed the message hesitantly.

'The Lady Mary answered Your Grace's message by saying that 'the queen could not have possibly sent it; nor is it fit that she should, nor can it be so sudden, her majesty being so far from this place' and that 'your messenger should have said that the Lady Anne Boleyn had sent it for she could acknowledge no other queen but her mother, nor esteem them her friends who are not hers.' Neither Joan, nor Nan could meet my eyes: they were ashamed to hear such offensiveness, as much as I was furious to receive it. After a few moments, when I sensed that there was more, Joan finally raised her eyes slowly to meet mine, and added, 'Apparently, the Lady Mary made a curtsy to the altar, in her words, 'only to your Majesty's maker and hers alone, and that you have been deceived to think otherwise.' There was a deadly silence in the room, as a familiar flash of anger tore through my body. Perhaps my pregnancy left me more emotional and vulnerable than I might otherwise have been, but whilst I knew well that Joan had been innocent in relaying her message, I sensed that it came from ladies within my chambers who loved me not, and who had maliciously set me up to be humiliated. On that occasion, Mary's repeated insolence proved to be the final straw in my efforts to build bridges with her.

'Nan, give me my nightgown.' I beckoned impatiently for her to pass the garment to me, just as a sickening tightness began to take hold within my throat. My anger constricted itself around my chest like a vice being tightened by an unseen hand. I was rapidly becoming blinded by a familiar fury and determined that, this time, the Lady Mary would be made to pay for her downright rudeness. 'I simply will not accept such vulgar impudence for one moment longer. I shall find the king this very evening, and put an end to her haughty pride once and for all.' Perhaps with my declaration of war, my friends privately questioned the wisdom of my hasty temerity, but in the uncomfortable silence, they said nothing. Instead, Nan did as I had requested, helping me dress in my black, taffeta dressing gown, trimmed with sable furs.

The hour was late and the palace beginning to fall silent as courtiers returned to their lodgings. I wanted no contact with those who might read much into my late-night venture toward the king's apartments, so I knew exactly where I must head. With my long gown tied around my expanded waist, I walked quickly, first from my raying chamber into my privy chamber beyond, then toward the turreted staircase in the far south-westerly corner of the room. This led down to a private, lower floor gallery connecting the king's apartments with my own. With my anger boiling over with indignation, my prickly energy was palpable to those ladies who were in attendance in my privy chamber. Several of them had been working on intricate embroidery, or reading from the Bible in front of the fire when I burst into the room. I was vaguely aware that each of them made to stand in respect of my presence. They were undoubtedly taken by surprise as I tore, like a tornado of unstoppable energy, across the room, Joan and Nan, following in my wake. At the top of the staircase, I turned, holding up the palm of my hand, abruptly halting their progress. Snapping somewhat unfairly, I commanded 'No, I wish to speak to the king alone. You will all remain here.' I saw the look of concern etched into each and every one of their faces. Yet like a hunter locked onto its prey, I cared not for such distractions, only that Henry would finally take action against his contumacious daughter. That night I wanted to bring her down once and for all. If events had not intervened otherwise, I admit, with shame that my intention was to use the full force of my influence with the king to do whatever was necessary to curtail her stubborn, Spanish pride.

Leaving my ladies behind, four turns of this staircase brought me down from the second floor of my lodgings and out into the northern end of a truly magnificent 100 foot-long gallery. During daylight hours, this chamber afforded the most extraordinarily beautiful views out across the skyline of London, to the west of the palace. However, it was utterly deserted that night, lit mainly by the silvery light of a full moon that cast its reflected glow in ghostly pools upon the chamber's walls and floor. I made my way in all haste toward its southernmost end, where a similar stone staircase rose up in another corner turret, leading to the heart of the four-storey, king's privy chambers. But for the swishing made by my taffeta gown and the occasional chime of a clock from inside one room or another, I was surrounded by an expansive stillness, passing only the occasional guard of the king's body, who stood motionless outside shadowy doorways. The peculiar nature of my solitary journey even caused one to step forward, not recognising me at first, as I emerged from the shadows. However, he quickly made out my identity, and humbly craved my pardon, allowing me to pass on my quest unimpeded. If they thought it odd to see the Queen of England moving alone around the king's apartments at such a late hour, the burly men of the king's guard did not show any sign of their surprise.

Eventually, I found and entered the king's withdrawing room. With the exception of a couple of lowly pages, who were busy cleaning the room and relaying the fire, nobody was to be seen. I admit that the vigorous exertion of my journey had taken a little of the heat out of my tempestuous anger. While I hesitated for a moment to consider my next move, my brother unexpectedly emerged from the chamber beyond.

'Anne, what on earth are you doing here?' I could see that George was deeply perplexed by my presence, and somehow, strangely, he seemed a little agitated. If the wind was momentarily taken out of my sails by my exertion, my brother's questioning just as quickly swelled my chest with defiance once more. I felt slighted by the world that day, and was determined that I would not be intimidated by anybody. Thus, I did not directly answer my brother's question. Rather, I lifted my chin defiantly and enquired directly,

'Where is the king? I need to see him now.' I watched George's brow furrow in concern as he hesitated for a moment, before asking,

'What is the matter, sweet sister? What has happened that you are so sorely troubled?'

'Brother, I neither have the time, nor the inclination, to discuss the matter with anybody but the king. Now, where is he?' At first, I was irritated by his reluctance to answer me, thinking perhaps that he was playing one of his usual impish, but good-natured games. Yet when he finally replied, I saw no mischievousness us his eyes, rather a growing disquiet that aroused my own instinctive sense of danger.

'Anne, I do not think it wise to disturb his majesty, he is… busy.' There were several moments of silence between us, as George first turned his head away and then, when his gaze finally met mine, I saw that he was imploring me to heed his words. I frowned, my eyes narrowing as I fought to make sense of what my brother was saying, and just as crucially, what he was not saying. Within the blink of an eye, the most horrific feeling of panic began to burn its way up through my belly. In an explosion of movement, I suddenly brushed past my brother, heading straight through the doorway that led to the chambers beyond. Behind me, I heard George call my name plaintively, beseeching me not to press the matter further. But, I was like a woman possessed. All thoughts of the Lady Mary had dissolved from my mind, and all I could smell was the stench of betrayal.

The room beyond was the king's state bedchamber, which lay empty and undisturbed. I looked around before deciding to take a passage to two of the king's most secret chambers—his library and study. I approached the door to the former, my heart thundering in my chest, the sound of the blood pounding in my ears, like a symphony of my own fear. I could hardly breathe as I tentatively reached out my left hand and pushed against the door which swung open, silently before me, I stepped across the threshold.

I was standing in Henry's library, surrounded by shelves displaying richly bound manuscripts, the walls decorated with elaborately carved Renaissance panelling, and over to my right, a stone fireplace aglow with a roaring fire filling the room with warmth. Yet, I felt no heat, just the cold, ruthless hand of perfidy, which had frozen my body to the core. Standing in front of the fireplace, was the young and beautiful Lady Elizabeth Harvey held in the tender embrace of my husband who, unaware of my presence, was kissing her passionately, one hand about her waist, pulling the lady toward him, the other running across the swell of her breasts that were heaving breathlessly beneath her tightly laced gown. Perhaps I let out a moan of despair, but suddenly the two looked in my direction, their faces frozen in guilty shame, and for just a few moments the three of us hung there, suspended in time, as if everything was passing before my eyes in the very slowest of motion.

At some point, probably within a few short seconds, I must have found my voice, and I remember hearing myself wailing with the guttural pain of a wounded animal.

'No, no, no, no!' Each word louder than the last, as the very centre of my heart was ripped apart. Tears streamed down my face, I could not believe that the man who had pursued me to distraction, who had torn his kingdom apart to have me at his side, who had looked into my eyes and sworn on the damnation his soul that he would rather lose his kingdom than lose me, had betrayed our love. Henry collected his senses, and breaking free of Lady Harvey, commanded her gently,

'Leave us, Elizabeth.'

Perhaps it was hearing the man whom I loved with all my heart speak to another with an intimacy and tenderness that had once been mine alone, but as Bess Harvey curtsied and scurried from the room, my fury was venomously unleashed. There was only one exit from the chamber, and as she made to pass me, I suddenly lashed out, first drawing blood with my fingernails as I scratched at her flawless face, then hailing down upon her head with a series of vicious blows of revenge. Of course, I was her mistress and queen, and so she had not fought back, but instead, wounding my pride even further, Henry lunged forward in her defence and grabbed me from behind, clutching me close into his body so that my arms were pinned to my side.

'Lady Harvey, please leave, now!' Bess took no further persuading, and quickly disappeared from sight, whilst Henry tried to calm me, reminding me to be still so that I should not harm the baby. As he held me tightly, I cried with great racking sobs,

'How could you? How could you do this to us? You told me you loved me! 'In my tirade, I wanted him to let go of me. I could not bear the fact that he was touching my body when he had so carelessly given his away to another. All I could think about was that surely it must all have been an elaborate deceit from the very beginning, and that I had been mad to think that it was ever going to be anything else than it was. I hated Henry for his unfeeling selfishness, and I hated myself for being such a fool, and for believing any of the lies which had masqueraded before me in the place of genuine love. I felt dirty and sullied by it all. 'Get off me!' I pulled away from my husband, as he finally released me. Swinging around, I faced the man who without care, or remorse, had sought to tear my life—and that of my daughter's—apart.

In his eyes, I saw a strange confusion of anger, shame, fear and guilt. He was the King of England, and furious that I would challenge his behaviour when my role as his wife was to be played with submissive acceptance. Yet I knew that in his heart Anne Boleyn was the only woman he had ever truly loved, and he feared to lose her still. I was unable to hold back the true force of my venom as I spat at him,

'I will never, never forgive you for what you have done, Henry Tudor. I cannot comprehend how you, who have lured me by so many fine promises of your inestimable love, have since repented your purpose so blithely.' Suddenly, I was suffocated by the deepest, black weight of sadness born from the memory of happier times. With my face still wet with tears, more dolefully but with cutting accusation, I added, 'I acknowledge Sire, that I have put much confidence in your promises and in which I now find myself sorely deceived.' There were a few moments of dreadful silence as I absorbed the pain of knowing that the foundations of our love had just been irrevocably torn apart. Trust had departed and it would never again grace our relationship with its presence, and for a moment, I yearned to forget that which I could never again ignore. In that moment, I knew that Henry could betray me in cold blood, as he had done others before me. This thought worked to provoke both fear and dismay, and as a result, I felt Anne regain her balance, finding her footing in her pride and insoluble courage. Nobody, not even the King of England would ever crush her spirit. Thus, my anger spilled over once more, as I began to hurl accusations at my husband; ones that I knew would wound his sense of chivalry.

'Whilst my belly does it duty, I see you think to cavort with any whore you please. Well, my Lord if the Lady Harvey pleases you so much, then so be it! You may take my body, for I am your wife and have no choice in the matter, but whilst that bitch lies in your bed, you will never have my heart.' We stood facing one another, our bodies taut in verbal combat, our eyes locked in challenging defiance. It was true that Anne almost always held the upper hand in their private quarrels, for she knew well how to handle the king. Yet, on this occasion, the fight had not yet gone out of Henry, who retorted with disdain,

'Madame, you should think to avert your eyes as your betters have done afore you.' It was a weapon that had meant to disarm me and cow me into submission through guilt. But I was having none of it. I was in no mood to be compared directly with Katherine, who had been the sole cause of so much of the turbulence within our relationship. With even greater ferocity, I exclaimed,

'Oh no… no!' I held up my hand, wagging my finger in abject refusal to accept the king's words. 'Do not think to use that against me, for I am not like Katherine, nor any of the others!' Then with heavy sarcasm, I added, 'If you recall, that is why you hunted me down in the first place, Henry Tudor. Do not think that you can have me change the very fabric of my being, of the very woman that you fell in love with!' I had had enough, sickened by the sight of my lover's treachery, I had made to turn; then, snapping back around quickly, I added, 'If anything happens to this child, it will be your fault Henry, for the wrong you have done me has caused me very great sorrow, but I feel infinitely more in seeing myself betrayed by a man who pretended to enter into my interest only to discover the secrets of my heart.' The blow was final. Without courtesy, I turned upon my heels and swept mutinously from the room, leaving Henry alone to consider the damage he had done to me, and, perhaps more importantly, our unborn prince.

When I left the king's apartments, luckily for her, Lady Harvey was nowhere in sight, and I wondered when she would have the nerve to show her face to me again. I gathered my composure as best as I was able. In truth, all that I wanted to do was to get back to my privy bed chamber as quickly as possible, where I could bury my face in my pillow and cry myself to sleep. Thankfully, as I retraced my steps through the king's lodgings, I met only the same handful of guards as I had on the way in. In fact, I met nobody else, even my brother seemed to have disappeared. Those guards must have seen my blood-shot eyes and blotchy cheeks, but if they did, their expressions remained immutable, as I fought to keep another tide of emotion back from completely overwhelming me and drowning me in anger, sadness and the self-pity of my wounded pride and shattered dreams.

Moving as fast as I could, I was determined that I would not succumb to the pain that was renting me apart, yet I suddenly found myself hardly able to breathe. The crushing grief of everything that I had lost, and my fear that I had failed Anne miserably, begot an unstoppable tumult of emotion that forced its way up through my belly and poured out in great, pitiful sobs. I reached out with my right hand to steady myself against the wall, finally collapsing against the wood panelling, my tears flowing into the cloth of gold that was hung there. Utterly bereft, no longer able to maintain any self-control, I sank by degree to my knees, sliding slowly down the wall until I lay curled in a ball, half slumped against it in a silvery pool of light.

'Dear God, please help me! In your mercy, please help me for I know not what to do.' I turned my face toward the window, as if looking to find God directly in the heavens above the palace. In that moment, I felt so utterly, completely alone. Through my tears, I saw only the solitary moon, which bore silent witness to my agony. I realised that I was tired and afraid, and I wished only for the floor beneath me to open up and swallow me whole so that I would no longer know such blinding pain. Suddenly, a hand was laid on my shoulder, and I turned my head around to find my brother kneeling over me.

When I had seen him in the king's chambers, I was angry that he had surely been an accomplice to Henry's duplicity. Yet, when I looked into his face, I saw it too was contorted in grief, born of unconditional love for me and the deepest compassion for my plight. I had meant to tackle him furiously when I next laid eyes on him, but when I saw the tears welling within his eyes, that he was feeling my pain as his own, I knew that if my brother had concealed this secret from me for any length of time, it had torn him apart to see me thus betrayed. In that moment, any ill-will that I bore towards him dissolved away. I twisted my body about to throw my arms around his neck and bury my face in his chest.

'Why, George? Why has he done this to us? I love him so much...'
My voice trailed away rather pitifully into another round of
uncontrolled sobs. George held me tightly against him, as if to protect
me from the evils of the world. As I cried, he stroked my hair and
kissed my forehead soothingly, saying over and over,

'I know, I know,' rocking me gently in his arms as he did so.

Perhaps we stayed there for five minutes, or fifteen, until my brother
simply scooped me up in his arms as if I were as light as a feather, and
carried me back to my chambers. Through half closed eyes—for my
face was still buried against my brother's chest—I saw only the worried
faces of Nan and Joan, who dutifully awaited my return. As my brother
carried me into my bedchamber, he turned to kick the door shut with his
foot. As he did so, I caught a glimpse of Lady Rochford and the
Countess of Worcester. The Countess looked concerned and confused at
this, and whilst Jane shared her concern, I saw something else pass
fleetingly across her expression. It was hurt of a kind, a jealousy that
her husband was shutting her out from the bosom of our family once
again, as if she was an outsider, a woman who could not be trusted.

At the time, I was far too upset and exhausted to attach any great
significance to anything other than the thoughts of Henry's betrayal,
which would haunt me that night and for many weeks to come. In the
privacy of my bedchamber, my brother simply laid me on the bed and
pulled the covers about me. Much like we had done when we were
children, when one of us had been distressed or unwell, George loyally
knelt by my bedside and stroked my forehead, until I drifted off into the
tormented land of a fitful sleep. Perhaps I should have seen it and
known better, as I alone was guardian of the future, but I did not think
that my brother's attempts to protect me that night would lead me into
even greater ruin than I already found myself. Minds able to pervert the
most innocent of gestures had borne witness to my brother leading me
into my bedchamber alone. The clock had begun its countdown to
Anne's annihilation; it was just a matter of time until those who wished
to destroy me, and my family, would use that incident with such deadly
force against us.

Chapter Thirty-One

Hampton Court Palace,
30 June 1534

The unbearable, searing pain of my labour tore through my body with the same ferocity as when I had brought forth Elizabeth into the world, just ten months earlier. Yet, on this occasion, there was no flutter of expectant joy breaking through my intermittent agony. In my heart, I knew that something was dreadfully wrong. My mother and some of my closest friends had tried to reassure me that all would be well, but my maternal instinct whispered faithfully to me only of impending tragedy. Indeed, if I look back now to those two fraught days of uncertainty following the accident, I can tell you that whilst my child still appeared to move within my belly, something had changed. No more did I feel the lively stretching and squirming of my boy in my abdomen, as he adamantly communicated his determined will to be known. Rather, the movement somehow lacked animation and later I would realise that it had only been the weight of his lifeless body being turned by gravity that had given a false sense of his stirring in a womb that could no longer sustain his fragile life.

Cocooned from the public glare of the court, I was brought to bed before my time, in the queen's privy apartments, on the second floor of Wolsey's original privy lodgings at Hampton Court Palace. However, on that fateful day in June, few knew of the impending tragedy in the royal household. Many of those still residing at court over the summer had been summarily dismissed by the king, sent home to their country estates on the pretext that he would shortly set out on a belated, and rather brief, summer progress, while I would stay behind at Hampton Court, keeping about me only those who I knew loved me well. And as my body ruthlessly fought to expel the child it could no longer nourish, downriver, life continued on as normal. The queen's apartments at Greenwich were once again being prepared against the coming of England's new heir. Henry and I were due to leave Hampton Court Palace just two weeks hence, to progress by barge via Westminster to Greenwich, where I was to take to my chambers in mid-July, there to await the birth of our child the following month.

It was utterly inconceivable that this was happening to me. After so many months during my early pregnancy where I fretted daily that this precious child that I carried might be lost, in the later months, I was increasingly certain that all was well. I suffered from none of the complications of pregnancy that I experienced the previous year. My health, and that of my unborn child, seemed excellent and robust throughout. I could not believe that I was just over seven months pregnant and that my son was dead. As my labour progressed and I entered its final stage, I prayed for a miracle; that somehow I had made a dreadful mistake, and that the good Lord in his infinite mercy had protected my son and would bring forth from my body a healthy prince.

I was both utterly distraught and completely exhausted by the events that consumed me, and by the outcome which I thought would destroy my marriage once and for all. I remember well every detail of that room from that ominous day; the flecks of dust caught dancing in the shafts of the afternoon sunlight as it poured though my west-facing windows; the oppressive heat of a sweltering midsummer's day that was augmented by a roaring fire—the only preparation possible given the unexpected onset of my labour; the smell of the wooden panelling that clad the walls of my room, and above all, the haunting silence. For in between the ferocious contractions, when I cried out to God to help me, I remember only a deafening silence. Not a word was said, nor was any laughter to be heard from my friends or the midwife who attended me. It was as if they had finally accepted what I already knew in my heart; that the child was dead and that I found myself close to ruin.

Once again, my dearest friends remained faithful and loyal in their constancy: Margery assisted my midwife who had been summoned under cover of darkness to the palace; Nan and Joan, both visibly pregnant themselves, each holding one hand of mine as I gripped onto them for dear life; and the Duchess of Richmond, who had also refused to leave my side, looking pale and drawn. I suspected that every fibre of her young body was tuned into the stickiness of my black fear.

Oh, how different had it all been just a few days before! How cruel is Madame Fate who toyed with my emotions and deceived me into thinking that finally, the tide was turning in Anne's favour. After the vicious argument between Henry and me at Eltham in the spring,

372

through our own veil of deception, we carried on as if all was well, deceiving the court that we were merry. But behind the veil, for those who looked carefully, our marriage was breaking down. Anne was ever the proud and courageous woman, and my modern day sensibilities only poured fuel on the fire of her haughty pride. I refused to be cowed or apologise for a betrayal that was not of my doing. Thus, for two weeks, I withdrew physically and emotionally from the king, and pointedly paid court to those men who served me loyally in friendship. I deliberately flaunted all of Anne's most flattering accomplishments before Henry's eyes, whilst keeping them well out of his reach. 'Noli me tangere' was truly Anne's motto, but it was the king who was denied access to my heart. It was wrong and foolish of me to do so. In my hurt, I placed innocent men—my friends—in the path of extreme danger. However, at the time, I did not consider the future, even though I, of all people, should have known better. I wanted revenge, and my carefully crafted ploy eventually had the desired effect.

Slowly, the king's wrath was defused, as I played on his fears for the safety of his unborn child. By mid-April, Bess Harvey had been removed quietly from court. About the same time, on the 14th of the month, my brother was dispatched to France to arrange a grand meeting between the king and his royal brother, King Francis, near Calais, to take place later that year. It was to be a repeat of the triumph of 1532, and I was to be at the king's side, his most beloved wife and mother of England's true heir. It was Henry's way of apologising to me, as he was too proud to admit directly that he had been wrong. So, as the weeks rolled on into summer, and my belly continued to swell, affectionate warmth retuned to our relationship and the king and I once again started to spend an increasing amount of time in each other's company. The truth of the matter was that Anne had not yet been discarded. However, a deep fracture had appeared in the foundations of our love, and I suspect that in my heart, I knew that it would never be truly mended.

By the time the court arrived at Hampton Court from Richmond, at the end of May, the king and I were indeed in good cheer, idling away the long summer days in carefree pastimes; enjoying banquets, masques and mummer plays in the evenings, and picnics shaded by leafy bowers during the day. Sometimes, the king rode out to hunt, or otherwise played tennis in the open play adjoining the main palace buildings when I would watch the heat of fierce competition with my ladies and other gentlemen of the king's privy chamber at my side. I would cheer my husband on, and exchange large amounts of money in wagers with my friends. Other times, I would spend time alone, reading religious texts that I imported from France, or writing to friends, or those who craved the queen's indulgence. Sometimes, Henry and I would review the progress of the building works that were underway to construct the new, east-facing, queen's apartments, commissioned especially for Anne. By the summer of 1534, it was over two thirds complete. We would watch the great windows being lifted into place, or discuss the next stage of development with the king's master builder over great platts laid out in the king's study. Yes, all had looked rosy as midsummer arrived at Hampton Court. Then tragedy struck.

It is crystal clear in my mind, even now. The last day of June 1534 was the most perfect summer's day. Shortly after mass, I was informed that the king had already departed on a day's hunting with a select party of close companions including: my brother who had lately returned from France having secured a meeting with the French king toward the end of the summer; the thirty-eight year old Henry Courtenay, Marquis of Exeter, who was the king's cousin—staunchly Catholic and no friend of Anne's; Sir Francis Bryan, who, since my attack on Bess Harvey and her subsequent dismissal by the king, had severed all pretence of support for the Boleyn faction; and finally, Sir Nicolas Carew, who was Sir Francis' close friend and also my long-term, sworn enemy.

I was a little unnerved when the king surrounded himself with gentlemen who loved me not. But my brother was there, so I knew that Anne would come to no harm. In the company of my dear, beloved mother, I was relaxed and happy, as we had made our way from the queen's apartments, through both the king's privy library on the top floor of the newly constructed Bayne Tower, which joined the king's most secret rooms with the upper gallery on the south side the palace. On account of the south-facing aspect of the gallery, the 200 foot-long chamber made for a simply delightful place in which to pass the time. It had splendid views across the gentle contours of the Surrey hills to the south, and the privy garden as it stretched down toward the river.

As well as my mother, who walked slowly by my side, I was

accompanied by several of my ladies. I soon asked Mary Howard to set herself down and play upon the lute, and indicated that my cousin, Madge, should accompany her playing with her own sweet, angelic singing voice. My mother and I meandered along the length of the gallery, arm in arm. I wanted to give her some extra support, for it was clear that whatever ailed her was of a chronic disposition. She was not yet greatly unwell, but as age advanced upon her, Elizabeth Boleyn was clearly no longer in the most robust of health. Intermittent episodes of excessive tiredness, mild breathlessness and the occasional pain in her chest caused her to look pale and drawn and to take to her chamber to rest. Pausing from time to time to enjoy the uplifting views looking out toward the river, my mother spoke.

'You look well, Anne.' I laid my hands on my very swollen belly. Breaking into the broadest of smiles, I replied,

'Indeed, I am. This time pregnancy seems to suit me well, and this little one kicks more by the day!'

'And his majesty? How are things between you?' My mother cocked her head to the side, studying my face intently as the subject was the cause of much tension within the Boleyn household over the previous few months. I unlinked my arm and stepped toward the window. Outside, a trail of white, mute swans flew over the palace garden. Through the open window nearby, I heard the sound of the wind whistling eerily through their feathers in-flight, as they manoeuvred themselves this way and that before making their final, graceful descent upon the river. It was a question that played upon my mind constantly. This time, I was grateful to be able to answer truthfully, in a way that I knew would ease her mind. I smiled once more and replied,

'His Grace shows me daily ever more affection, and George continues to assure me that the king remains loyal and has taken no mistress to his bed.' Much to my relief, this was the blessed the truth. I watched my mother nod and smile, undoubtedly relieved to know that her child seemed safe in the king's good graces. She touched my cheek delicately, conveying the great depths of her motherly love and concern, before I slipped my arm back through hers and we continued to amble toward the end of the gallery.

Suddenly, outside one of the windows, I caught sight of the familiar figure of Thomas Cranmer emerging from one of the galleries that led from the water gate by the river. He was walking briskly toward the palace, his gown billowing about him in the usual fashion, his Canterbury cap upon his head. As the weather was fine, he walked through the garden, rather than using one of the covered walkways which sheltered important visitors arriving at Hampton Court from the most inclement of weather. I peered out of the nearest window at our approaching guest and said,

'Look, it is Archbishop Cranmer! I wonder why he is here?' I was not concerned for Thomas Cranmer came and went from court regularly with various items of business concerning the king. Delighted to see my old friend, I paused, releasing my arm from my mother's once more, as I moved towards the partially opened window. I knew that with the king out hunting, Thomas and I would have time to parlay alone, whilst my mother retired to her chambers to rest. Thus, seeking to intercept the good archbishop, I opened the window wide and leaned out of it in order to call out his name and attract Thomas' attention.

'Good Morrow, Your Excellency!' I called out loudly as Thomas was but half way along the wide, gravelled walkway that cleaved its way down the centre of the garden. My friend heard my greeting and paused to remove his cap and swept into a low bow. 'Wait, Your Excellency! I will come down and join you in the garden.' How silly of me to forget my heavily pregnant state. Without thinking, I rashly picked up the skirts of my gown, and with my mother and ladies in my wake, made quickly toward the east end of the gallery where the king's newly built privy stair led down to the garden below. Reaching the top of the staircase, my mother who was several paces behind me, called out in warning,

'Anne, do not hurry so! I cannot keep up with you and you must take great care.' I was full of childish enthusiasm, as I always found such joy and comfort in Thomas's company. Yet, I had made to heed my mother's warning, turning half about as I replied,

'Do not worry, mother. I will...' I did not have the chance to say anything more. In the blink of an eye, I misjudged my footing at the head of the stair, my foot slipping away from beneath me, and the heavy weight of my enlarged belly causing me to lose my balance easily as I began to tumble backwards down the flight of stairs. Margery was closest to me when I slipped. As I fell, I saw her face looking utterly horrified, as she desperately reached out her hand to grab my flailing arm. For an instant, my hand brushed against hers, but our timing was imperfect, and in slow motion I saw myself helplessly slip away from the hand that would save me—and my son. I seemed to be falling forever, crashing down first on my back, before turning head over heels to come to rest in a mangled heap at the foot of the stairs.

As I fell, there was a great cacophony of noise; firstly, cries of abject alarm from my ladies and mother as they watched me helplessly tumble to the ground; secondly, the noise that came from the sound of my own body tossed this way and that as it came in contact with the hard, unforgiving, oak staircase. And then, when I came to rest, for the briefest of moments there was silence. In the silence, I heard myself breathing. I heard the sound of my heart, which was pounding wildly in my chest, before my body was thrown into shock and I began to tremble, a deafening ringing reverberating in my ears. I started to fade in and out of consciousness.

For the shortest period of time, I had this peculiar sensation of floating up above my body, wondering idly whether this was my time to leave Anne's world once and for all; of seeing my mother and my ladies pick up their skirts and fly down the length of the staircase to gather around me with the greatest of concern. I saw Anne lying there, semiconscious and curled up almost into a ball. Then suddenly, I was back in my body. I think I heard myself moaning, although there was no sharp pain anywhere that I could feel. Instead, I was gripped by a dull ache in my lower abdomen, and the sensation of warm, sticky fluid escaping from my body between my legs. I think for a moment I might have passed out, for I saw myself again from above, this time alone and lying in a pool of blood. As I came to, I heard Thomas Cranmer's voice close to my side and Mary Howard being commanded to run and fetch my physician. I was certain that my baby son was dying inside me and there was nothing, absolutely nothing that I could do to change it.

And so began, two days of waiting during which I recovered my senses fully following the concussion sustained during the fall. The bleeding was moderate but soon stopped, and I was left feeling battered and bruised for many days afterward. But nothing seemed to have been seriously damaged or broken, except the life of my unborn child, whose death would haunt me for the rest of my short life. Of course, there was no modern equipment that could tell me that my baby's heartbeat had fallen silent. Although, in my own heart I knew it had, for I guessed what had happened. Everything told me that the fall had brought about a placental abruption, where the placenta is torn away, at least in part, from the lining of the womb. As nature worked her magic to shut off the bleeding, a clot formed, which gradually cut of my baby's oxygen supply. I felt sure that he had suffocated to death inside my belly. Whilst Henry paced the palace like a caged tiger, teetering precariously between anxiety, hope, despair and a fierce anger aimed solely at me for my rash carelessness, my doctors hesitated to proclaim whether the limited bleeding foretold of inevitable disaster in the royal nursery.

I was confined to bed rest during this time. Those who knew of the calamity that had befallen the queen were sworn to secrecy. Everybody was aware of how much—and who—Henry had sacrificed to put Anne on the throne. The king's uncompromising stance all centred on the validity of his second marriage, which would be confirmed in the eyes of God by the bestowing of sons upon the king. If this child were a boy born dead, I knew Henry feared to be the laughing stock of Europe. Thus, only my parents and brother, Archbishop Cranmer; Thomas Cromwell, my Uncle Norfolk, the Lord Chancellor, Thomas Audley, Anne's Lord Chamberlain, Edward Baynton and those ladies who had witnessed my fall, knew that so much hung in the balance. All unnecessary hangers on at court were dismissed and those who remained and were aware of matters unfolding in the queen's bedchamber, held their breath. For two-and-a-half days, it was as if the entire palace had forgotten to exhale.

Finally, at just after 3am on 30 June, my contractions started. I sobbed almost continuously for the first few hours as any hope of my child's survival ebbed away. My ladies knew that the only comfort they could give me was their loving presence, but I was utterly inconsolable as a cavernous hole opened up within my heart. My husband was woken with the news that I had gone into an early labour and swiftly left the palace, taking only Sir Henry Norris and Sir Francis Bryan with him. He, like everyone else around me, knew that the birth of a child almost seven weeks early, and following loss of blood some days earlier, did not bode well for a happy outcome. Along with my escalating grief, my fear reminded how I was about to fail my husband for a second time. I imagined, accurately as it turned out, that Henry was so utterly dismayed and furious with me that he could not bear to be anywhere near my person. Attended by my ladies and a midwife, I was left to get on with my labour alone.

Eventually, at just after two o'clock in the afternoon, my baby was delivered. Momentarily, I rested my head back on the pillow, as an enormous wave of relief swept over me that finally, the ordeal was over. Just as quickly, I was seized by an overwhelming panic. Clinging desperately to the final shards of hope that my baby was alive, I longed to see his tiny limbs punch the air with vigorous life, to hear his furious screams as he was wrenched from the warmth and safety of my womb. Yet I heard nothing, except a muffled sob coming from the Duchess of Richmond who stood motionless at the foot of my bed. Even though the most desolate grief verged on the edge of utterly consuming me, panic and fear heightened my senses. I quickly lifted myself up, only in time to see the still hand of my baby peeking out from beneath the white linen shroud that had been quickly wrapped around his lifeless form. It all happened so terribly quickly. The midwife, unable to look me in the eye, scooped him up to take him away, when I was gripped by a mother's overwhelming desire to see her child—be he dead or no. Cutting through the deathly silence, I cried out,

'Don't take him away from me. I want to hold my baby.' I saw the faces of my friends stare at me in horror, frozen in their own overwhelming sense of shock and suffocating sadness. My midwife turned about slowly, her face hesitant, perhaps even confused that I did not understand what had happened to my child. Falteringly, she said,

'But, Your Majesty, the baby is …' I could not bear to hear the word. Struggling to maintain any modicum of composure and authority, I cut across her defiantly, in a voice choked with misery,

'I know…but I want to hold my child. Give him to me!' I did not take my eyes from my midwife. Instead, I sat forward, holding out my arms, as tears welled up once more from within my eyes.

'Your Majesty ... Anne, are you sure…?' Margery spoke softly, her voice laced with concern for my well-being and sanity. I turned toward her, my face contorted with grief. Gulping back the tears, I nodded nervously, knowing in my heart that I needed more than anything in the world to see my baby; to know for the briefest time that he had been mine, that he had been real. Seeing my response, Margery silently indicated to my midwife that she should hand me the child. Slowly, my midwife walked over to the bed and passed my son into my outstretched, aching arms. In that moment, the world melted away. I uncovered his naked body. Tears of the most unspeakable sadness rolled down my face and landed on his tiny, lifeless form. I can see him so well in my mind's eye. His skin was mottled and discoloured, for he had clearly been dead, as I had thought, for over two days. Oh, but in every other way he was a perfect little boy; his eyes tightly shut as if he were asleep, a shock of Tudor red hair making clear his paternity. Speaking to him, as if he could hear his mother's voice, I whispered,

'Look at you; you are so perfect, so beautiful in every way. What a handsome prince...' my words suddenly stuck in my throat as the emotion I struggled so valiantly to contain began to bubble over, and enormous, fat tears streamed down my face, splashing with increasing frequency upon the body I held within my arms. Through choking sobs, hardly able to speak, I continued with my words of love, 'Your father...would have been...so proud of you. I know...you would have made...a great king...' With that, I finally lost all control over my emotions, which suddenly burst forth in an overwhelming torrent of abject despair and desolation. Around me, my ladies watched silently, unable to move, hardly able to breathe, as their own tears flowed freely at the sight of their mistress, queen and friend, holding her dead son close to her chest, rocking back and forth and howling in pitiable grief.

There would be no banquets, bonfires or jousts waiting to welcome my son into the world. However, I commanded that our baby be taken to the king and showed to him upon his return to the palace. I wanted Henry to see that he was perfect in every way, and that Anne Boleyn had not given birth to a monster, that somehow from this tragedy I could show the world that if it were not for a freak accident, the king's wife would have borne him a healthy son. But a perfect, dead child was no use to Henry. In the midst of my desolation he visited me in my bedchamber that evening, tearing into me, accusing me of false promises, lies and deceit. I had killed his baby boy, and, as if the pain I felt was not unbearable enough, before he swept from the room with great venom and spitting fury, he hurled at me the fact that he wished he had never laid eyes on Anne Boleyn, that he loved me not and that if he were to have his time over again, he would surely not raise me as high as he had seen fit to do before. He stormed from the room, leaving behind no words of consolation, or affection, to ease my utter despair.

I did not see or hear from my husband again for nearly four weeks. He left Hampton Court the very next day in disgust, commanding me to remain there, while he headed toward The More in Hertfordshire. Here he was sought refuge and collected the broken pieces of his shattered dreams. Later, I was to find out from my father that Henry had summoned both my Uncle Norfolk and Cromwell to join him there on Sunday, 5 July. Urgent discussions were held regarding the implications of this latest disaster, particularly what should be done about the Calais trip that had been set for the end of August. In the end, Henry was not able to bear the prospect of meeting with Francis, who already had three healthy sons in the royal nursery. His pride was too deeply bruised, and he had no intention of rubbing salt into his bleeding wounds. As a result, by Tuesday, 7 July, my brother was dispatched once more to France, in order to seek an audience with King Francis; this time his mission had been to secure a postponement of the meeting until the following spring. Many lies were told to save face during those weeks, as well as to reassure the French king that the change of plan augured no ill-will on Henry's part.

In the meantime, I stayed behind at Hampton Court, attempting to recover from the traumatic events that had befallen me. The physical wounds healed quickly enough, but the psychological ones opened up into the deepest chasm from which I thought never to emerge. After two weeks, there were no scars on my body, but if you could have seen inside me, you would have beheld a bloody gash through my heart that would never be entirely healed. Only a skeleton staff remained behind to serve me, but I needed little from them. While life carried on, cruelly indifferent to my pain, my own small, cosseted world stopped entirely. For the most part, I remained in self-imposed confinement in my privy chambers, eating little and seeing no one, except those who made me feel safe—my closest friends, my mother and Thomas Cranmer, who visited me often from his Palace of Lambeth in London. We spent many hours together in quiet conversation, I poured out my grief, he attempted to console me and reconcile my fury with God.

For several weeks, I watched the world continue to turn. But in my grief, I no longer felt a part of any of it. I was merely a detached observer, sometimes aware of the utter futility of it all, sometimes angry that people could carry on with the pathetic minutiae of life; seemingly oblivious to the fact that I had lost my son and my world would never be the same again—ever. I hated myself first and foremost, blaming myself entirely for my son's death. I hated Henry for his infinite selfishness and utter preoccupation with his own wounded ego. I hated God for betraying me and snatching away my child and I was angry at my son for leaving me. However, the worst of it was that I could not bear to have either Nan or Joan in my company. They loved me dearly, but to look upon their goodly bellies was just too much to bear. At almost seven months and five months pregnant respectively, their very presence mocked me, reminding me not only of the child that I had lost, but of my growing sense that I was a complete and utter failure. Oh yes, I could not escape from myself no matter which way I turned. In those dark days, I was increasingly haunted by the growing conviction that I had failed my son; that I had failed Henry and perhaps even worse, I had failed Anne and those of the reformed faith who prayed to their God daily that she would bring forth a protestant heir.

Finally, after nearly four weeks, a letter arrived from the king toward the end of July. It was brief, with all the relevant courtesies that counted for nothing. It summoned me to meet with his majesty at Guildford in Surrey, on twenty-eight day of that same month. The king was to travel westwards from Eltham Palace, where he had been visiting Elizabeth and I would come from the east, travelling from Hampton Court. However, if I had thought the summons signalled a melting of the king's heart, then I was to be sadly mistaken. The wheel of Anne's fate was beginning to turn with ever greater velocity. When the king left me behind at Hampton Court, I had been plunged into a chasm of sorrow, loss and resentment. Yet, the misery was not quite over; two more tumultuous events would tear into Anne's life before I would finally be snatched from her world in the most dramatic of circumstances.

Chapter Thirty-Two

The Old Manor of Langley, Oxfordshire
15 September 1534

Dutifully, I obeyed my sovereign lord, and was reunited with the king at the Dominican Friary in the heart of the Surrey town of Guildford at the end of July. In public, I was received with affection and all due solemnity, however in private, the king's reception was both cool and muted, and throughout August and September, he remained distant, spending little carefree pastime in my company. To augment my misery, it soon became clear that Henry had found solace in the arms of Lady Harvey once more. Although the king retained only a small household during this time, I was utterly dismayed to find the said lady on my arrival at Guildford. Once again, she had been placed into my service, this time by the king himself.

I was in no position to remonstrate with Henry, although Lord knows, I rallied against her presence. My father wisely counselled my silence and acceptance of my position. This I had uncharacteristically done as grief had shaken my confidence to the core and drained my usual vibrant energy. I had nothing left to fight with in the summer of 1534, and so whilst jealousy seethed deep within my breast, I outwardly looked the other way. Yet, I confess that to the lady herself, I was less kind. In the grip of such a tumult of emotion, my natural intemperance was stretched to the limit. It took little for me to snap in the privacy of my chambers, and often I would take out my suppressed anger on Lady Harvey, slapping or scratching her at the slightest of provocation. God forgive me, I made her life an utter misery.

By the beginning of September, the court progressed north, and was well lodged at the Old Palace of Woodstock in Oxfordshire. My husband continued to brood upon his misfortunes, and being in no mood to face his nobles, soon retired to the old, medieval Manor of Langley, which lay about ten miles to the west, deep in the heart of the ancient Forest of Wychwood. It was a remote place that afforded much privacy away from the prying eyes of the court, with good hunting to distract my husband from his cares. As usual, Henry took along but a few close friends and key courtiers of his household, including: Master Secretary Cromwell, my father as Lord Privy Seal, Sir William Fitzwilliam as Treasurer of the king's household, Sir William Paulet as Comptroller of the king's household. Sir William Kingston, and my old friend and staunch supporter, Dr. Edward Fox; Sir Francis Bryan, Sir Henry Norris, Sir Francis Weston and my brother were also selected to accompany Henry in the hunt. I wondered whether, in my disgrace, I would be left behind at Woodstock, but as I was to find out, the king needed access to Lady Harvey, thus, I was ordered to accompany Henry on his sojourn to Langley Palace.

We arrived at Langley several days earlier, approaching from the east along a forest track that was protected by pleasant, dappled shade. Autumn was just beginning to bewitch the landscape as the leaves, touched with the first flush of autumnal colour and a cool freshness to the early morning air, foretold of the coming winter. In time, the dense woodland opened up to reveal a jewel of medieval kingship—The Old Palace of Langley. The building was largely remodelled and updated by Henry's father after he had acquired it from the powerful Neville family in 1478. In anybody's book, it was a charming two storey retreat, built from mellow, honey-coloured Cotswold stone, with fine moulded windows, elaborate carvings and a stone tiled roof. Fashioned in typical Tudor style, its ranges were built around a central courtyard.

It was truly an idyllic hideaway, except there was nowhere that I could hide from what tormented me day and night. Waves of shock, disbelief and the most profound grief continued to pound me, sweeping me away in its wake as if I were mere flotsam carried helplessly upon a torrent of Anne's destiny. It had been two months since the death of my son, and whilst my position required that I valiantly struggled to present an air of normality to the outside world, inside a part of me had died. Daily, I struggled to reconcile myself with how my heart could go on beating, how I would manage to draw my next breath. My days had lost their shining vitality, and I longed for the happy innocence I had once known, but which would never be mine to hold again.

During the following two months, I suffered from strange psychological and physical symptoms that plagued me from the moment of my waking, until I retired exhausted to sleep every night. Perhaps most strange of all was a pervasive sense of fear that haunted my every waking hour. It's odd, nobody ever warned me that grief could feel so like fear; but there it was, stalking me day and night, a constant companion. I was persistently tired, yet paradoxically, my mind was restless, pining for what had been lost, racing this way and that, desperately searching for a part of me which I seemed to have misplaced and could no longer find. As a result, most of the time, I felt so sick that I could not eat, becoming painfully thin in a few short weeks. In fact, sometimes, I could have sworn I was going mad. My innocence was lost, and it was a humbling experience.

I confess that I knew little of what was in Henry's mind during those two months. Communication between us was minimal, and we largely executed our affairs independently of one another. I know that he continued to be furious with me, and that in his own way, he was also suffering acutely and in deep pain. Whilst I yearned to find solace with the man I loved, I realised sadly that my presence only reopened the wounds which Henry was struggling to heal. And so, he avoided me where possible, indulging instead in delights that distracted him and which soothed his stricken mind. And so, on a sunny Tuesday morning in mid-September, my husband headed off hunting for the day, taking with him four gentlemen of the privy chamber and three of my ladies.

There had been some changes in my household since the stillbirth of my son. Nan and Joan had meekly requested to take leave from court. They soon realised that their advanced state of pregnancy was causing me unspeakable distress. In their love for me, they removed themselves quietly from the royal household. Although I missed my friends and their loyal company, I was also incredibly relieved that I no longer had to face them and watch their bellies continue to swell with the healthy babies they carried. By the time I left Hampton Court, I had with me just Margery, Lady Rochford, Mary Howard, Madge Shelton and Grace Parker and of course, we were now joined by Bess Harvey at Guilford. I still had little appetite for carefree pastimes, and so, on that particular day, I gave leave for Lady Rochford and my two maids, Madge and Grace, to accompany his majesty in the hunt. Whilst at the same time, Bess had been commanded by the king himself to join the royal party.

I hated it all. On this occasion, Henry took no care to conceal his affair with Lady Harvey. This was his retribution; to openly flaunt his affection for the lady, knowing that with every tender gesture, he would drive the knife deeper into my heart. What great cruelty we are capable of towards those we say we love the most! And thus it was, a fierce jealousy constricting my heart, as I watched the hunting party head out from the palace, soon melting from sight beneath the forest canopy.

'Come away from the window, Anne. Do not think to torture yourself so. Bide your time. When he has done with his hurting, he will return to you. I know in his heart he loves you still.' It was my mother's reassuring voice who interrupted my self-pity and drew me away from the window, so that I might warm myself in front of the fire. I scooped up the skirts of my gown and seated myself down opposite Elizabeth Boleyn, who was working some delicate embroidery of blackwork on one of my father's shirts. 'Damn!' I looked up briefly to see my mother suck upon her thumb, pricked by the needle in her right hand. 'My eyesight is not as good as it used to be. I can hardly see what I'm doing!' It was a throwaway comment, not meant to address either me, or my father, who had joined us a little earlier in my privy chamber. Only Mary Howard, Duchess of Richmond, was in attendance, doggedly determined never to leave my side. Just like little Purkoy, she had become one of my most faithful companions. I remember being grateful that with so few people around, I could relax and allow myself to feel my sorrow without pretence.

'Nevertheless,' my father suddenly spoke up, addressing my mother's previous comment, 'It is important that you seek to regain the good graces of his majesty at the earliest opportunity. I...' Interrupting my father, my mother set down her embroidery indignantly. With a sigh and clearly some irritation, she retorted,

'Oh Thomas, can you not see this child's pain? You may be but a man, and such matters mere trifles to you, but your daughter has lost her son and is steeped in her grief. Now the heaven's sake my lord, have some pity on her!' Then more softly she added, 'We must all do what we can, but these things take time to heal.' Then she added more poignantly, 'As you well remember from our own misfortune.' I glanced fleetingly at my mother to see a shadow of the agony associated with the loss of three of her own children many years earlier, still etched upon her face. Picking up her embroidery once more, she added brusquely, 'Indeed, if anything is to be done husband, then it is to remove Lady Harvey from court. It is difficult to mend a marriage when there are three people in it.' I was staring into the fire, but looked sideways toward my mother to find her staring knowingly at Thomas Boleyn. I wondered what had passed between them over the years—for who knows what secrets lie within a marriage.

My father was about to reply when the door to my privy chamber opened and Margery entered. Immediately, I saw upon her face a mild panic of sorts which I could not fathom, and which caused a frisson of fear to grip my body. Looking in my direction she said,

'Your Majesty, Lady Mary Rochford is here to see you.' Margery was trying to warn me of something with her eyes, but I did not understand and frowned. I was not expecting my sister back at court. I had not seen Mary since Eastertide when the king and I were lodged at Eltham Palace. She had not written to forewarn me of her coming, as would be customary. Margery stepped aside, and through the doorway emerged my English rose, quite clearly in the full bloom of pregnancy.

At first I made to greet her, and then my eyes fell upon her goodly belly, which foretold that my sister was probably at least six months with child. In truth, she looked simply beautiful. Both Mary's children had been born before I had entered Anne's world, and so I had never seen her pregnant before, but I saw how much the condition suited her. She was radiant; her skin clear but slightly flushed, her eyes sparkling and alive. She sank into a curtsy, whilst I stood utterly transfixed and disbelieving of her condition. Mary spoke, breaking the shocked silence that descended upon us.

'Your Majesty,' then turning toward Thomas and Elizabeth Boleyn inclining her head respectfully, she acknowledged them, saying simply, 'My Lord Father, my Lady Mother.' I did not see the faces of my parents, for I was desperately trying to recover my balance. The unexpected appearance of my sister in such an obvious state was just as if I had been stabbed through the heart. I suddenly felt the blood pounding in my head, as I realised I could barely breathe. Since the death of my son, I had shut myself away and banished from my sight any trace of motherhood. I was even fearful of seeing my own darling Elizabeth, and so purposely did not even attempt to accompany the king to Eltham, prior to our meeting at Guildford. I had carefully arranged my world to keep me safe, so that I might pretend that there was not a single baby left anywhere in the world to torment me. Yet, here was my very own, beloved sister flaunting her fecundity before my very eyes. I was left reeling with shock and unable to speak. Barely able to contain his anger, my father enquired,

'Mary, what is this?' He pointed to my sister's swollen abdomen as he spoke. I watched my sister intently. From the very moment I laid eyes on her, I had wanted to scream, scream at her to get out of my sight. I felt sick to the core, transfixed, barely able to comprehend what was unfolding before me. Mary fidgeted nervously with a pair of fine, brown leather riding gloves; her breathing shallow and agitated, and I knew exactly what she was about to disclose.

'I have married, father and as you can see,' she laid her hands upon her pregnant belly, the light of motherly love already playing in her innocent, wide eyes. '…I am with child and have come to ask for the blessing of her majesty and my beloved parents.' Her proud declaration was met with utter silence. I was dazed, and yet I knew well the identity of her new husband from my knowledge of history. As she spoke, my mother rose from her seat and came to stand next to me. She, like me, sensed the perfect storm brewing, a powder keg of volatile emotions about to be ignited by my sister's precipitous timing. Rather ominously, the Earl of Wiltshire took a step toward Mary, replying with barely disguised contempt,

'I see. And who might you have married?' My sister took a deep breath, sensing that the words she would utter would blow our family apart. But the die was cast and deeply stricken with my own grief, I remained silent until she finally found her courage and blurted out,

'William Stafford. He is soldier in the service of his majesty. He has distant connections with the Stafford family and so is of noble blood by descent.' I had still not said a word. The shock I felt upon seeing my sister in her pregnant state was rapidly turning into my own powerful tempest of rage. However, my father erupted first. With a dangerously calm voice, itself pregnant with the coming storm, he spat out,

'You stupid, selfish, ungrateful child! Then thunderously, he tore mercilessly into his eldest daughter. 'Do you mean to tell me that you have married a mere commoner? Did you just simply forget that your sister happens to be the Queen of England?' Thomas Boleyn was utterly incandescent with rage, his faced flushed red, and his eyes bulging in a firestorm of anger. 'You cannot marry anybody you feel like. You have a duty to your queen, and to this family, to marry according to your status. This…' he faltered for a moment, waving his hand dismissively in the air, as he snarled at my sister, '…union not only degrades you, but it degrades our family and your sister. What you have done is utterly unforgivable.' At the end of his tirade, Thomas Boleyn made to turn away—or so I had thought. Suddenly, unable to contain his outraged emotion, he swiftly turned back toward Mary and struck her across her cheek with the back of his hand. The powerful blow caught Mary entirely off guard and she was sent reeling to the side, crying out in her own shock.

'Thomas, no!' my mother cried out, taking a step forward to take hold of her husband's arm and prevent a further assault, which threatened to rain down on my cowering sister. My father shook off Elizabeth Boleyn's hand, and thinking better of it, he merely tutted in disgust, finally turning his back on Mary and stalking over to the nearby window. Despite her heavy belly, Mary launched herself at me, falling to her knees and grasping the hem of my skirts. She looked up at me, silently imploring her sister with her tear-filled eyes, her face contorted with its own deep sadness. With tears streaming from down her cheeks, she begged,

'Please, Your Majesty, take pity on me! I love William so much and he is such a good man, so kind, so generous and he loves me so. I am sorry that I have wronged you; that I married without Your Majesty's express permission. Please forgive me sister, but I love him so much. I would rather die a thousand deaths than to be without him…' Her words trailed away as she buried her face in my skirts and sobbed uncontrollably. For a few moments, I stared down at her before finally, in a steely voice laden with poisonous recrimination, I replied,

'Mary, you swore upon the damnation of your soul that you would leave this man alone. You have not only lied to me but you have lied to God, and I think you will surely suffer hell and damnation for what you have done.' Upon hearing my words, my sister had only sobbed louder, finally releasing her face from my skirts, she cried pitifully,

'Please, Your Majesty…Anne.' In my grief, I could not locate my forgiveness, or the warmth of my heart. I continued without mercy.

'Not only have you sinned against God, I marvel at how you of all people could think to do this to me?' For a moment Mary seemed confused, unsure as to my unspoken meaning. I knew in my heart that her actions had not been malicious, and yet her sheer thoughtlessness had stirred me to even greater anger. As I spoke, my voice was thick with resentment and my own incredulity at Mary's insensitivity to my plight, as I forged on, 'Sister, have you not noticed that my own son died just eight weeks ago; that the heir that his majesty craved, and which I solemnly promised him...' I heard my own voice beginning to crack as I finally began to shout at my sister in scorn; the truth of the words that followed driving yet another stake through my heart '...is dead and buried in a cold unmarked grave? How do you think it makes me feel to see my own beloved sister flounce in to my rooms with a healthy, sweet babe in her body? Do you think to mock me? Do you think to make the king, who can barely stand the sight of me as it is, turn from me entirely?

At this, I tore my gown away from my sister's hands. Turning my back on her, as tears streamed down my own cheeks, I buried my face in my hands and finished my tirade by crying, 'Mary you are banished from court. I do not wish to see you in my sight again. For what you have done to me, your own sister, is truly unforgivable. I do not want to see you, and I do not want to see or hear of your child again.'

'No, no! Please Your Majesty, please forgive me, please have mercy upon me!' The pain in my sister's voice rings loud and clear to this day. She wanted my understanding, my love and my forgiveness. But my own grief had turned my heart to stone and I was numb to all suffering except my own. I had nothing to give her, and so with my back still turned towards her, I simply raised my hand to indicate that I had heard enough. At this point, my father spoke, driving the final nail into the coffin of Mary Boleyn's relationship with her proud family.

'You will obey her majesty and leave court immediately. What is more, you are disowned by this family. You have brought great shame upon us. You have made your own bed, Mary; now go and lie in it!'

I did not turn around. I could hear my sister's muffled sobs and the sound of her skirts as she picked herself up slowly from the floor and left the room. I did not see her wretched, sorrowful face as she was thrown out of the bosom of her family to make her way alone in the world. I did not turn around; and to my great sorrow, I never saw my English rose again—ever.

All I had wanted to do was to get drunk. The agony of my private grief, of Henry's rejection, and of my sister's banishment was too overwhelming to bear. I had utterly failed everyone. I could no longer tolerate to be with myself, or with the abject misery that caused my body to ache in despair. When my tears were sprung and spent, I called my ladies about me and ordered two musicians of the king's chamber to come to my privy lodgings to provide merry disport for our dancing. For a short while, all I was resolved to do was to sink gladly into a place where all my sorrows could be temporarily submerged by an elixir of sweet, full-bodied wine. Word of the revels soon spread to my brother, Sir Francis and Sir Henry Norris, all of whom soon joined the feasting and dancing in my privy chamber. They were not needed by his majesty as I knew well that my husband had closeted himself away for the evening with Lady Harvey, surely the sweetest assassin that a mistress ever had the misfortune to know.

By the time night fell, my privy chamber was lit only by flickering candlelight and an established fire that glimmered in the substantial grate, adding to our cosy seclusion, while radiating warmth and light as it cast hues of orange and gold upon the faces of those friends who had gathered around me. The room was filled with merry music accompanied by laughter and the sound of dancing as slippered feet kept time to the beat of the music, along with the swishing of my ladies' skirts, as they were turned about by their gallant dancing partners.

Whilst Henry plunged himself deep inside the body of another woman, I gave myself up entirely to the virile god of wine, allowing him to caress me with the greatest intimacy. His welcome kindness and generosity washed away my cares and my sins, as I discovered again, for the briefest, sweetest time, the carefree pleasures of my youth. I danced gaily with all the gentlemen present, throwing my head back in laughter, crying out with joy, as I was lifted into the air and passed from partner to partner in a blur of vibrant colour and happy smiles.

I suspect my friends welcomed the joyous release as much as I. The tension between Henry and Anne had been palpable within the royal household for several weeks. However, that evening, I was determined to celebrate, watching each and every one of my friends sink into the free-flowing wine. Oh, how I wish I could have frozen that moment in time, surrounded as I was by some of my most loyal and faithful companions! I did not know then that it would be the last time that we would all be together.

At the end of one particularly strenuous dance, I curtsied with an elegant flourish to my brother, who had partnered me, before I turned around to pick up another goblet of wine, finding myself at the side of my sister-in-law, Lady Jane. Even in my drunken state, I discerned that I rather enjoyed my sister when she had had too much alcohol—it melted her stiff reserve and smoothed away the prickliness in her nature. She smiled much more, and how there was even a hint of brash flirtatiousness peeking through her usual fortified defences.

'Jane, you look well and happy. How was the day's hunting with his majesty?' The moment I thought of Henry, my stomach constricted into the tightest of knots. As a salve, I took another hearty swig of the blood red, claret wine from within my goblet, feeling its warmth rush through my body as I did so, happily melting away my bitter jealousy.

'It was an excellent day's hunting indeed, Madame. The king brought down two mighty stags and was in a fine mood on account of it.' I'm not sure whether she was aware of how her words cut through me—that Henry could be merry without me by his side. I think not, for she smiled innocently enough and took another sip of her wine, letting out a drunken giggle as she did so. I rather sarcastically replied,

'The king is always merry when he is hunting, do you not find?' A smile of irony played upon my lips, but my meaning was lost on the drunken Lady Jane. Thus, I changed the subject as I wanted to speak to my sister-in-law regarding matters which touched upon the future of Lady Harvey in my household. Whilst the wine temporarily numbed my pain, it also left me feeling bold and reckless in my desire to rid myself of Bess once and for all. I realised that my mother was right, that her presence continued to be a thorn in the side of my relationship with my husband. Goodness knows how she was poisoning him against Anne when she lay within his arms, her legs wrapped around his body. That afternoon, I resolved to pull myself out of my despair, and at least take action against my traitorous lady-in-waiting.

As I pondered such things, I looked idly into my goblet, to find with some surprise that the wine had already been drained away. I remember clearly thinking, with some amusement, that I must have been drinking more quickly than I thought. I looked up and beckoned over a page of my chamber that made his way over toward me and filled my cup up to the brim once more. At the same time, I lent in closer to my sister-in-law and spoke conspiratorially, 'Jane, you and I are sisters.' Jane smiled at me, clearly happy to hear me speak thus; I continued, 'Lady Harvey is no friend of the Boleyn's, and I hear tell that she has smuggled secret messages to the Lady Mary and Ambassador Chapuys saying that soon the Lady Mary's troubles will be over.' Jane listened intently, her eyes widening at the implication of the treasonous speech that I shared with her—and which had lately fallen upon my own ears. 'Sadly, the king continues to blame me for the death of our son, but I cannot heal the rift with his majesty while she undoubtedly pours poison into his ears.' Before I was able to say any more, Jane spoke up, obviously drunk but clearly indignant at the presumptuous behaviour of the said lady.

'Your Majesty, you know I am no friend of Lady Harvey.' Then more sorrowfully, she turned her face away, staring into nothingness as she reflected, 'Lord knows, I know what it is to have another in one's marriage.' She then turned back to me, saying in earnest and with some apology, 'Madame, I know I speak of your brother and I do not mean to be of offence, but it is true that I understand your plight and I condone not her wanton behaviour. You have been a kind and gentle sister to me, and if I can serve Your Grace in this matter, you need but ask, and I will willingly carry out your command.' With one hand still holding my goblet of wine, I placed the other on my sister's shoulder and lowered my voice and said,

'Then I ask this of you, Jane; you must take an item of my jewellery and place it in Lady Harvey's possession, where it may be found. In due course, I will see to it that is she is accused of theft from the queen's person.' I cast my eyes around the room to see if anyone had overheard our exchange. However, all those present were preoccupied in only their own gay pastime. So I continued, 'His majesty will not be able to ignore such action, and I'm sure that it is on these grounds that we will be able to have her removed from court—forever.' Jane nodded slowly, raising her own goblet of wine to toast our daring conspiracy. I could see in her eyes that she relished being taken in confidence into the tightly-knit, Boleyn fold.

Just as our exchange was completed, the door to my privy chamber was suddenly thrown open, causing all present to look toward the entrance to the room. There standing within its frame was Henry himself, dressed casually in hose and boots, a frilled, loose-fitting open-neck smock covering his broad, muscular chest. I admit that I was surprised, for I thought the king to be deep in fleshy pleasures elsewhere in the palace. But Lady Harvey was nowhere to be seen, and I wondered what had drawn Henry to my chambers at such a late hour.

Whilst my husband stood still, surveying the room with his typical majestic presence, all of us dipped a curtsy, or bowed to greet his arrival. I straightened myself first, swaying slightly in my deep sense of inebriation. I noticed how the room was moving just ever so slightly, and as a result of the large volume of wine I had consumed, an unpalatable sense of nausea had begun to sweep over me. However, in my drunkenness, I somehow found myself again sensing Anne's bold courage; her magnetic sexuality, aloof grace, and provocative allure began to take hold in my body. I stared defiantly at Henry, locking with his piercing, blue eyes. For a moment, we held each other's gaze silently, before the king commanded,

'You may leave us. The dancing is over.' All those present had once more shown humble reverence, before scurrying quickly from the room. My brother was the last to leave, casting a glimpse in my direction that told me of his love for me, before he too closed the door quietly behind him. Precipitously, I spoke first, raising my goblet towards the king, as I greeted him somewhat sarcastically,

'How now, my Lord? I am deeply honoured that you should think to join me. I understood that Your Grace was plunged...' the last word I emphasised with a cutting tone and irreverent smile, '...deep into matters of state elsewhere within the palace; matters that have much preoccupied Your Majesty's time of late.' Every word that I spoke was laden with double entendre and heavy sarcasm. And whilst I soon realised that my husband had perhaps been drinking as heavily as I, he understood my meaning well enough. Henry walked over to a nearby sideboard, taking a silver gilt goblet within his hand and pouring his own wine from an elaborate ewer standing next to it. Taking a hearty swig, he then walked towards me with his usual arrogant swagger. I once loved that walk, full of virile masculinity, now I hated it, despising its conceited pomposity. He stopped short of where I was standing, fully aware that in his presence, I was radiating the full force of my feminine sexuality. Henry watched me carefully enough, but did not deign to reply, and so quietly, I asked in a voice laden with sadness, 'Do you love her?' Shrugging indifferently, my husband replied,

'She pleases me well enough.' I saw then that Lady Harvey meant nothing to Henry. She was, as I suspected, a diversion from his pain and a means to torment me. Like most lovers, we knew intimately the vulnerabilities of each other's soul, and exactly how to exploit them. She was a meaningless nothing, and so I cast her aside in my mind, and was seized instead by a burning need to know the truth of the past seven years. It was a question that plagued my mind.

'Why?' My voice was soft, sincere and desiring to know the secrets of Henry's heart. The king frowned, unsure of my meaning. While I felt increasingly unwell, the alcohol evermore taking hold of my starved body, I pressed the matter again. 'Why did you hunt me down?'

'You...promised...me...sons.' As Henry spoke, he raised the hand in which he held the goblet of wine, extending his index finger as he pointed it accusingly in my direction, emphasising each word with a jab as he spoke. Oh, I knew deep in my heart that his reply was borne of his puerile need to taunt me, and it spoke not of the truth. Nevertheless, it unleashed a torrent of recklessness on my part, as I raised my voice in growing anger,

'Was that all I was to you? Was I just your brood mare?' I spat out the words, sweeping my left hand through the air, as I brushed away his comments with cutting disdain, daring him to confirm it. When he did not, and I saw the yearning for me in his eyes, I brushed his first answer aside, determined to flush out the real truth. I cried out angrily, demanding to know the answer to the questions that poured forth in my mind. 'Why? Why me? Surely there were other, more worthy persons than Anne Boleyn to be a suitor for Your Majesty's heart? Tell me, was it all just to game to you?' Then, extending my arm to point toward the forest, I went on, 'Was I just like that poor creature that you hunted down today?' My arm collapsed back to my side with weighty despair, as I said more poignantly, 'Did it please Your Grace to possess me— and does it now equally please you to destroy me? Are you here only to gloat over your victory?' Henry shook his head slowly. I could see that buried in amongst his grief was the great love which he had once been so keen to show me. Yes, for a moment, I saw again the tenderness that had once been mine to behold. Reaching out to seize the moment, I whispered, 'Do you still love me?'

There was the longest silence, whilst the king turned his head away. I could see that he wanted to say 'yes' but that his pride and the viciousness of my surprise attack had been bold beyond words. Perhaps, I should have held my tongue and remained silent for longer, allowed Henry to find his voice. However, intemperate as ever, I lost my temper. 'Where is your courage, my Lord? Why do you not speak your mind?' My face was contorted in anger, as I dared to question firstly not only the King of England's integrity, but now his valour. I saw Henry's infamous anger flash dangerously within his eyes, as he turned his head back to glower at me. It was a step too far. Yet, as I watched the king's face—the dance of the light and shade cast by the flames of the fire—I realised that quite contrary to his intention, Henry had been drawn to me that evening like a moth to the light. Yes, he loved me, as if I was of his own flesh. Yet he hated me for the way in which he perceived that I had betrayed him. I sensed that Henry knew in his heart that he was addicted to Anne, and whilst he wanted to hurt me, he had also come to find solace in my arms. I saw it play out across his face just as clear as day, his confusion, weakness and self-loathing for even being there in my presence, silently begging me to take him in his arms and heal him of the pain that had passed between us.

As I saw all this, and the tragic irony of it all, I began to laugh hysterically, throwing my head back, one hand resting upon my belly, the other swaying with the goblet still in my hand. Once more, I gestured toward my husband, his own growing anger mixed with confusion at my obvious, and slightly unhinged, madness. After several seconds, I began to speak my mind, hardly able to do so though, on account of my wild, unbridled laughter.

'I see it now. Poor Henry Tudor hates me yet, he can't live without me!' As my hysteria subsided, I slurred drunkenly taunting the king with my own prophecy. 'You never thought that anyone could control your heart, or get under your skin as much as Anne Boleyn has, did you, my Lord? Let me tell you Henry Tudor, no matter where you run, no matter how many women you sleep with, you will never get me out of your heart.' I took another indelicate swig of my wine, carelessly spilling a few drops over my rich gown as I pressed on, cutting right to the truth. 'You want to love me but you don't know the real meaning of the word, and so you hate me. You want to control me but you can't; you can't command my body to give you what you want, and I will never be the meek, dull wife that part of you needs me to be, so you want to destroy me instead.' I took a few daring steps forward, my eyes narrowed, and lost in my own brazen world of utter defiance, I raised my goblet close to my face and extended my own index finger toward Henry, in a mirror of his previous gesture. I began to sway quite badly, my head beginning to pound. I felt hot and light-headed, but no force on earth could stop me saying what I had a mind to speak. 'So, Henry Tudor, destroy me…and believe me, you will!' I had never spoken of the future before, but I was barely in control of what poured from my mouth, 'But let me remind you, you made a pledge to love me forever and when you destroy me, it will eat you up from the inside out. For you will never be able to break that promise—never!'

I was standing almost in front of the king, watching the fury build within his eyes. Oh, but the desire and the passion that also stirred within him! My brazen words and defiant stance had inflamed him in more ways than one; he was disgusted yet excited by me—as he always had been, and still was. Suddenly, Henry threw his goblet aside and lunged down upon Anne's tiny frame, sending my own cup crashing upon the ground, bouncing loudly across the wooden floor. His strong arms gripped my body, turning me about and sending me colliding with an oak sideboard that was positioned close by. I knew he wanted to take me, and to begin with I fought hard, as he jammed my feet apart and tore at my clothes. Yet, I was not afraid; my mind and body were utterly numb. Most bizarrely, I suddenly began to laugh wildly once more, seeing the perversity of it all.

'Go on, my Lord, rape me. I won't feel it anyway. I am already dead inside! Show me what a mighty and powerful man you are, Henry Tudor!' I do not know what stopped Henry in his tracks. Perhaps, beneath his narcissistic personality, he despised himself as much as I hated myself. Whatever it was, he cried out in frustration, pulling away and crashing his fist against a nearby wall. It was clear that all that I had said was true, and that somehow the truth had both infuriated my husband and jolted him out of his own self-pity.

'Let me tell you this Anne Boleyn; you have a stout heart, but you sail far too close to the wind, Madame. Whatever you are in my heart, you are also my wife and my subject. Do not think to push me beyond my limit...for I will not tolerate such impudence from anyone! Henry jabbed his finger in my face, as he towered over me. I found myself clinging onto the sideboard, for the room had begun to swim violently before my eyes. Whilst Henry continued his tirade, I was sure that I was about to be sick. A raging heat tore through my body. I knew that I had drunk excessively on a stomach that had eaten little in weeks, and I was surely paying the price. In a panic, I realised that the sensation was familiar. Suddenly, I thought of Hever Castle, and the very first time I had crossed the portal of time that had thrust me into Anne's beguiling, but dangerous, world. The edges of my consciousness began to blur, as I watched Henry's furious face begin to melt into concern,

'Anne, Anne...are you...' I suspect the king, my husband, had finished those words, but the deafening ringing in my ears precluded my hearing them. I remember Henry's scent as he must have tried to prop me up in his arms, close to his own body. Then, Anne's world began once again to implode, and within seconds I was falling into oblivion.

Part V

Chapter Thirty-Three

University College Hospital, London
21 April 2009

For several seconds, I had absolutely no idea where I was, or indeed, who I was. All I knew was that I was surrounded by brilliant, white light, and in my drowsy confusion, I was incapable of placing any verifiable coordinates upon my new reality. Gone was the cosy darkness of my privy chamber, illuminated as it had been by the soft light of numerous flickering candles. Gone was the musky scent of Henry's skin next to my own, and gone was the welcome taste of claret which had played so deliciously upon my lips. Instead, glaring light blinded my eyes, and a slightly nauseating smell of disinfectant and body fluids filled my nostrils. It was a sharp and shocking contrast to the intimate warmth of the surroundings which had made up my last memories; memories that clung to me tenaciously, despite my rather befuddled state of my mind.

I fought to focus my eyes and my consciousness, struggling valiantly to orientate myself. By degrees, I began to find my first, tentative foothold in my new surroundings only to realise that I was lying half propped up on some kind of trolley. Faded beige curtains were pulled around me, sealing me into a small, austere and rather notional cubicle, whose walls were as flimsy as my own grip on reality. Beyond those curtains, I began to tune into the sound of the comings and goings of faceless strangers, some of whom stopped to speak to one another as they walked by. Above their voices, the incessant sound of polyphonic bleeping provided a wholly monotonous accompaniment to the hum of life beyond my curtained walls.

I felt something upon my finger, and so lifting my hand before my face, I blinked my eyes several times until I focused in on a grey, plastic clip which had been placed over the tip of my middle digit. A red light which shone from the device illuminated my nail and the pad of my fingertip. Next to where I lay, a bleep—which appeared to be responsive to my own vital signs—proclaimed loudly that I was still alive. Suddenly, the curtain was drawn back and an attractive woman of

Asian descent approached me. She was dressed in medical 'greens'; a stethoscope, which was worn like a badge of honour, was slung casually around her neck, and a set of notes was tucked under her arm. I presumed these to be my own. I was familiar with the attire she wore, and knew immediately that she was a medic. I admit it had been a welcome sight to see her broad, relaxed smile.

'How are you doing?' I heard her words clearly enough, but it was as if the circuitry of my brain had been grossly rewired, for I could only stare at her blankly and deconstruct her meaning, word by word, forcing myself to assimilate a coherent reply.

'What happened?' It was the first thing that I could think to say and even that seemed to take an inordinate amount of effort. Despite my disorientation, it was clear that I was in the twenty-first century and still very much alive. I was surprised, but unlike the first time that I had been drawn back from my heroine's world, I was not immediately consumed by grief or sorrow, but instead, I felt only a sense of blessed relief. Yet, it was a sentiment that would come to haunt me and fill me with guilt, as in my release and the safe obscurity that it brought, I failed to take into account that I had left behind my beloved Elizabeth. In my postdromal state, however, such emotional intricacies were too complex for me to grasp. Instead, I watched the young woman intently as she went about her work. My eyes followed her as she checked the various instruments above my head, before finally reaching above me to press a button which temporarily caused the bleeping to desist. Having done so, she turned her attention back to me once more. Leaning against the trolley, the young woman folded her arms in front of her, this time clutching the notes tightly to her chest, as she replied,

'It seems you had an epileptic seizure that caused you to lose consciousness. You're in the Accident and Emergency Department at University College Hospital in London; my name is Dr George; I am the SHO on call here tonight.' Once again, I was slow to respond. 'Epileptic seizure'; 'lose consciousness'…these were words which floated around in a sea of hazy consciousness for a few indistinct moments, until gradually more of my story began to reveal itself. In my mind's eye, I saw Greenwich and the river trip…the strange auras of familiar smells which had overtaken me—and there was something about Daniel. It seemed important, but frustratingly, I couldn't quite put my finger on what it was.

'Daniel' was all that I had managed to say, screwing up my forehead in some confusion, bizarrely hoping that this woman called Dr George, who had never met me before in her life, would hold the answers to my unspoken questions.

'Is that the guy who has been texting you?' I didn't answer; I just kept staring at her hopefully. Clearly, she was used to dealing with disorientated people, and my vagueness did not seem to faze her. So she continued, undeterred by my silence. 'Don't worry, one of the ambulance crew who brought you in picked up your phone and noticed someone was texting you. You must have been holding it at the time you lost consciousness because it was lying on the floor, a few feet away from where you collapsed.' I lifted my hand to sweep away a lock of hair that had fallen into my face while she had been speaking, only to wince with pain. As I pressed against my forehead, the skin there suddenly felt raw and deeply bruised. Dr George smiled sympathetically, anticipating my question and explaining in turn, 'You must have hit your head when you fell; you have a nasty bump on your forehead.' Then opening the notes, she scanned quickly down the page, pursing her lips this way and that, as she reviewed all that had been written about my previous medical history.

'I see you are under the care of Mr Harris. You had a ruptured cerebral aneurysm about eighteen months ago. Is that right?' I nodded my reply. Then, unexpectedly, she closed the notes once more and went on. 'What do you remember of what happened today?' 'Today?' I wanted to tell her about Henry going out hunting with his mistress, about Mary turning up at the Old Manor of Langley heavily pregnant, of her banishment and of my drunken argument with my husband, the king...Oh, and then the pain hit me with a savage force! Through her question, Dr George had caused me to reflect on the raw emotion of the last twenty-four hours, all set against the backdrop of the dead child that I was still grieving—and I knew then that I was still grieving. I did not know if the death of Anne's second child had been her loss or mine, but the pain I felt was my own—and exceedingly real. I realised the young medic in front of me was not asking me about my sixteenth century life, though, so I struggled to push its heavy weight aside and think of what I recalled of the last time I had been in my own body.

'I remember that I was at Greenwich, in the park; and there was a river trip but…I don't remember where I was going.' My last memory had been getting off the boat at Westminster; then the images dissolved, leaving only a void which jealously guarded the secrets of my last half hour of consciousness.

'You were picked up at the British Library. Do you remember going there?' It was as if she had picked the bubble with her words, one which had sought to conceal my fragmented memories. Suddenly, they all came rushing in; the text from Daniel, the one that had, in a single sentence, turned my world upside down. I began by slowly nodding my head, reluctant to discuss this turn of events, which seemed wholly irrelevant to my current predicament. In a rather parched voice, I replied,

'Yes, I do. I do remember going there.' Then, realising just how dry my throat was I asked, 'May I have a drink?'

'Of course.' Dr George turned about, pouring a tumbler of water from a plastic jug that stood on a nearby trolley table. Propping myself up, I sipped the sweet nectar, licking my lips before asking what surely was beginning to prey on my mind,

'Did I have another bleed? I don't remember having a headache like I did last time.' The young medic shook her head.

'No, it seems from the scan that it was just a seizure, which can happen in cases like yours. I see that you were placed on anti-epilepsy drugs early on, but they were stopped about a year ago.' I nodded my head in affirmation of her assumption. 'I guess they warned you that this could happen, but I must say that it is unusual that it should do so, so long after the initial bleeding.' As she was speaking, I realised that I had already been in the MRI scanner. I was surprised, for I didn't remember anything about it. Thus, I asked rather incredulously,

'Have you already scanned me? How long have I been unconscious' I wondered just how much time had slipped by. There were no windows in my cubicle, and I had no idea of whether it was night or day.

'You weren't unconscious for long but it is not unusual to be really groggy after a seizure. I suspect that your memory of the last few hours will be a little patchy.' She glanced at her watch and said, 'It's 3:30 in the afternoon, and you've been here for about three hours.'

'Oh,' was all that I managed to say. I certainly remembered nothing of being brought into hospital, or of having any kind of scan. Gathering my thoughts, I enquired, 'So if I have not had a bleed, then what happens next?'

'We have called a friend of yours, Kate?' Once more, I nodded my understanding. I knew well that Kate's details were kept in my purse as my next of kin. I realised that the hospital staff must have looked through my belongings and found her name scrawled across a piece of card that I carried with me at all times. Dear, dear Kate; what would I do without her? She was my rock. As I reflected on my gratitude for my friend, Dr George continued, 'In the meantime, we need to keep you overnight for observation. You are still quite drowsy and we can't let you go home like this.' I must have raised my eyebrows as I wanted to go home, curl up and recover in the comfort of familiar surroundings. I thought to protest, when, just as she finished speaking, as if on cue, the curtain where I lay parted and Kate's face appeared in the gap

'Can I come in?' She nodded towards me, and explained, 'I'm Anne's friend, Kate.' Dr George beckoned to her to enter, saying,

'Yes, perfect timing!' Then she added, 'We will get you up to the ward soon, and hopefully in the morning Mr Harris, or one of his team, will have chance to come and review you before you go home. I suspect they'll want to start you on some medication to make sure that this does not happen again.' With that, she smiled and touched my arm lightly. It was a simple gesture of human kindness which was profoundly reassuring. As Dr George swept out of the cubicle, Kate approached, smiling, as I shrugged my shoulders in resignation, as if apologising for bringing my friend to my rescue once more. She shook her head playfully as if to say, 'can I not leave you alone for one minute!'

'I know, I know! I'm sorry to drag you out here again. You are truly my angel of mercy.' She leaned over and put her arm around me, kissing me lightly on the cheek, as I fondly did the same in return.

'So what happened? Did you have another bleed?' As I explained what I had just heard from Dr George, Kate said. 'Then it's a good job that I brought this, isn't it?' With that, Kate lifted up an overnight bag that she had been carrying, before laying it down next to me upon my trolley.' I smiled and said gratefully,

'What would I do without you?' She began to unzip the bag to fetch

404

something she thought I might need, when I suddenly blurted out, 'He's left her, Kate.' Immediately, Kate froze, her hands poised, half inside the case delving into its unknown contents. She snapped her head about to look at me incredulously.

'You are kidding me! Daniel has left Rose?' I nodded my head almost imperceptibly, as I watched my friend's eyebrow rise in shocked surprise. 'When? How? I mean, how do you know? Have you seen him?' A flurry of questions fluttered in my direction like a rabble of butterflies. Once more, I found myself shrugging, and even shaking my head in my own disbelief. After seven years of interminable waiting, it was almost incredible to think that this moment had finally arrived. Kate gave up her quest to retrieve something from the bag and turned to face me. It was her turn to shake her head, as she said in a voice laced with equal disbelief,

'I can't believe it! He's actually left her.' This time it was a statement and not a question. 'So have you seen him?' I pushed myself upright, fighting with the various wires that kept me tethered to the trolley.

'No. I was heading to the British Library when I got a text from him out of the blue. He said that he just couldn't stand it anymore and that he was leaving her. Then about half an hour later, literally just before I collapsed, I got a second text.' I couldn't remember exactly what it had said, and so I asked Kate to look for my phone in my bag. Locating it, she handed it to me, and pressing the 'messages' button on the screen, up came a series of texts, all from Daniel. There were three waiting to be read. The first two were laced with a sense of a desperate need to connect with me, to know that I was there in the moment that Daniel had finally gone over the top of the trenches—that I had not deserted him. Clearly, somebody from the hospital had then contacted him and told him something of my situation. They had been trying to find out more of my medical background and my next of kin. It read:

'Hospital has called. Told me that you are in A&E. They won't tell me what's wrong with you. R U okay? I'm driving back from Devon. Will be in London soon. Text me, please.'

My knight in shining armour was coming to rescue me. Rose was the one being left behind this time, just as Henry had once left Katherine behind at Windsor. At last, I would know what it was like to have somebody put their arms around me and tell me that everything was going to be okay, that I did not have to face the future alone. It is the truth when I say that I did not particularly want Rose to be hurt, but neither did I care much for her pain. For this negligence, I do truly repent and from my doleful prison, I have beseeched the good Lord to show me forgiveness for this unkindness. Just then Kate cut through my thoughts by asking,

'What is it? What does he say?' I handed her the phone so that she could read the messages for herself. As she did so, I lay back on the trolley, raising my eyes heavenwards, daring to dream of the future. After Kate had absorbed the full implication of Daniel's texts, she spoke cautiously. 'Do you think he is for real?' I had already asked myself the same question. I had been through such unspeakable agony in the name of love for Daniel, but my lover and friend had dithered interminably about our future, and with each hesitation had cut an invisible wound through my heart. Now, within my grasp, lay everything that I so desperately wanted; his commitment and his undivided love, and above all, a friend with whom I could share the rest of my life.

I knew behind Kate's tentative question was the same fear which had already begun to stalk me. If I once more opened my heart to him, what would happen to me if Daniel were to change his mind and walk away again? What if he found that he had made a mistake and returned to Rose almost as soon as he had left her? I was excited and terrified at what was about to unfold. I was also hugely optimistic and oh so, utterly foolish. In Anne's world, the prize that had been so hard-won was done so only by paying the ultimate price. So, I too, would soon drink from the same bitter cup of betrayal. For both of us, time was rapidly beginning to run out.

Chapter Thirty-Four

University College Hospital, London
22 April 2009

The following day felt nothing short of a new beginning. I brushed aside the cares and concerns which had begun to plague me the previous afternoon. It was as if a whole incredible chapter in my life had dawned alongside a brand-new beginning, the early morning sunshine streaming into my private hospital room, heralding a bright new future. Whilst I awoke to find that parts of my memory from the previous day remained stubbornly elusive, the heavy grogginess that had clouded my mind had been swept away effortlessly. My awareness felt clear and sharp, no doubt honed by the delicious excitement I felt at being reunited with Daniel after what, in my other world, had amounted to two extraordinary years walking in the footsteps of Anne Boleyn.

I was also aware that I was not the woman he had once known. It is a truth, is it not, that it is our suffering which most transforms us. And the last two months in Anne's shoes had done just that—irrevocably destroying my innocence and forging a sadness in my heart which I knew would never heal. It was becoming evident that the death of my son—Anne's son—would never leave me. And whether Anne and I were two separate souls caught up in a freakish time slip, or whether we were indeed one and the same soul, living its time over, I knew that we had become bound in an intimate sisterhood of shared adversity, which not even death could destroy. So, whilst I found myself back in my modern day life, I carried with me the profound pain of an old loss. I yearned to hold my Elizabeth in my arms, and felt a desolate pining for my dead son, whose tiny skeleton, I knew, lay buried beneath the floor of the chapel royal at Hampton Court Palace. His death had come 500 years earlier, but my grieving for him remained fresh as if it were yesterday.

Of course, Daniel knew nothing of this, and for some reason I felt either disinclined, or unable, to tell him. Perhaps I was afraid of dragging it all back up, when I would do anything to forget my misery, or perhaps I feared that this time he would truly think I was gripped by some kind of madness. Perhaps worse, that he might dismiss it all as just a flight of fancy. Whichever was the truth, I resolved to tell no one of my adventures in my other, long-lost world. I felt immeasurably old, and I did not know how these traumatic events, which had so sorely touched my life, would influence our relationship. Would Daniel notice the change in me? Would my heavy heart constantly interfere with my intentions to create a fresh start? I knew that I would soon find out.

I had been expecting Daniel to pick me up at the hospital within the hour. On the previous day, he had driven back from holiday in a hired car, first to clear out and pack some of his things from his home, before staying overnight with one of his close friends, Peter, who like most of Daniel's friends, I knew only by name. I was aware that Daniel had always kept our relationship entirely to himself. I was the 'other' woman kept hidden in the shadows, and I wondered how his friends would react when they finally found out about my existence. After my exchange with Kate, I had managed to steal a quick call with my lover, briefly explaining that I was fine but tired, that I was being kept in hospital overnight, and insisting that he get some sleep before collecting me in the morning.

Shortly after breakfast the next day, my consultant appeared at my bedside, bringing with him his usual, affable manner. Mr Harris proceeded to question and then examine me before confirming what I had already been told, that I had had a general seizure. The aneurysm was still there, but on this occasion, the very good news was that there was no bleed. As a consequence, I was restarted on medication in order to try and prevent further fits, and finally given the all clear to go home. Thus in short order, I was divested of all the mechanical tubes and wiring, and jumped into the shower where the steamy, hot water could wash away not only the dirt, but the resentment that had built up over the years of being rejected, and coming last on Daniel's list of priorities. I was happy to find that it was easy to let go of the hurt, and eager to make up for lost time, I wanted to press 'play' on a life that, despite my best efforts, had been on 'pause' for far too long. I dressed quickly in black jeans, a crisp white fitted shirt and a feminine, black cardigan which was cropped at the sleeves. It felt fabulous to put on fresh clothes, make-up and tie up my hair loosely, pinning in place my usual soft curls. I was glad to be going home.

Suddenly, there was a knock at the door, before it opened hesitantly and Daniel's face appeared round the corner. After everything I had been through, he was a sight for sore eyes! It had been easy during the halcyon days of walking in Anne's footsteps to set my twenty-first century life aside, and revel in the adoration of a mighty prince. But as her world started to crumble, and fear became my constant companion, my thoughts often turned to the simple and welcome obscurity of my modern day life. I thought more often of Daniel, and despite our troubles, I had appreciated all the more keenly everything that I had taken so very much for granted, including my very survival.

Inevitably, with my relief came the guilt. I had made a pledge always to be there to protect Elizabeth, and I felt that I had deserted her, even though the circumstances which had brought that separation about were entirely out of my control. But given the chance, I would return for her in an instant, and to live again Anne's precarious sixteenth century existence. I admit, however, that I was also glad that I did not have to witness Henry's great love for his lady turn evermore to hate, nor know for myself the terror that Anne must have felt sensing her enemies close in around her.

Sweeping all of these concerns aside for the sake of the moment, I rushed forward as Daniel closed the door softly behind him and we fell gratefully into each other's arms, clinging to each other as we so often did when we found ourselves first reunited. But on this occasion, there was a deep poignancy; so much was said silently in that moment. Our eyes craved forgiveness for the hurt that we had surely inflicted upon one another in our struggle to be together, and through our kisses came sweet relief mixed with smouldering passion.

'Is it true? Have you really left her?' I was the first to speak, and I couldn't help but voice my insecurity, and my incomprehension that finally the waiting was over. If I hadn't wanted Daniel so very much, I might not have been so blind; perhaps I would have seen the faintest flicker of hesitation, the seeds of regret and remorse which were already taking hold. I would have sensed his own guilt at leaving Jemima begin to consume our happiness through its pervasive and relentless growth. Once more, my optimism was unseeing of all of this, and I sensed only the surface of his emotion, which welcomed me into his arms. With a broad smile, Daniel nodded his head in reply, and taking my face in both his hands, he drew me forward to kiss me tenderly, melting away all my fears.

'Are you okay?' I watched his forehead crumple into a frown of concern, as he searched my eyes from the truth. It was my turn to nod, and with a smile, I replied in all sincerity,

'Yes, I am okay. I had a seizure but no bleed. They started me on some tablets and fingers crossed, it won't happen again'

'And the aneurysm?'

'It's still there. It's always going to be there, unless...' My voice trailed off. I did not like to think of what might happen if it were to rupture. Daniel let go of my face, and took both my hands in his. Lifting them up, he placed a gentle kiss upon the back of them. It was a gesture of love meant to sweep away my cares, and I melted inside, for unless one has known what it is to be starved of a love you have lost, it is impossible to appreciate the true beauty of its rediscovery. Eager to know more of what had happened to him in the last twenty-four hours, I took Daniel by the hand and led him into the room. Seating myself down upon the bed, I patted the mattress, to indicate that he should sit down beside me. I needed to hear exactly what had brought about this seismic shift between him and Rose. Searching Daniel's face earnestly, I asked as much. He briefly looked away, shaking his head. I could imagine only too well that Rose would have not taken whatever had transpired between them lightly, that it would be a scene in his memory that he would rather erase. Finally, through obvious pain, he replied,

'I watched them on the beach together, Rose playing with Jemima, building sandcastles that had no firmer foundation than the relationship that Rose and I have tolerated over the past ten years. I saw them laughing, and suddenly realised that I no longer felt a part of it, of their intimate little world.' Daniel sighed and looked down at his hands. He was playing subconsciously with the wedding ring that he had always worn on his left hand—even in our most intimate of moments. I mused idly that there were times when I had hated that ring. It seemed to mock me constantly, as if it had a voice of its own, whispering that I was a fool, and more so, that I could not see it. I was distracted for a moment by my own thoughts, but turned my attention once more upon Daniel as I knew that there was much he needed to say, and so I kept my counsel. I watched the man that I loved attentively, as he slipped into his own private reverie, barely aware of my presence as he continued to speak. 'I spent the whole first two days of the holiday somewhere else entirely. In my mind, I was with you everywhere I went.' Finally, he looked up at me, smiling warmly, clearly moved to happiness at the tender swell of love that washed up on our shore. 'I saw us walking along the beach together, and I wanted so much just to watch the sun catch against your tanned skin, run my hands through your hair, watch as the sea breeze whipped strands of it across your face. I wanted to kiss your salty lips and just be together, unfettered by the cares of the world.' It was a beautiful speech of longing, and one which I had shared too many times to count. However, I watched just as quickly as storm clouds suddenly passed across his face, a mirror to the turbulence rising within as he went on, 'Sitting there on the sand dune, I knew that I couldn't stand it anymore, the 'happy families' and the never ending pretence toward a love that had become as dry and barren as the grains of sand between my toes.' Finally, I blurted out,

'What did you do?' Daniel cast a sideways glance at me as he replied,

'Actually, I didn't have to do anything. Rose must have known something was up. I guess I must have been downright surly for the rest of the day. Everything she did, every movement she made, irritated me. I was going to say something... but she beat me to it. After Jemima was in bed, Rose cornered me; accused me... said it was as if I didn't want to be there.' Daniel laughed ironically, falling silent for a few moments before adding, 'When I didn't reply...well, I guess my silence spoke volumes ...she went mental, demanding to know if I loved her and if there was somebody else ... that she had suspected so for a long time.'

I said nothing. Indeed, I could hardly breathe. I was terrified that like Peter, the apostle, Daniel may have ultimately denied me. But I was also afraid that he had finally admitted to our relationship to his wife. Each action held ingrained within it, its own particular flavour of consequence. No matter how Daniel might plead, to deny my existence and our love would be an implicit act of betrayal that I feared might fester, gnawing away at the foundations of our life together. I knew that to admit that he loved someone else would unleash a torrent of vicious recriminations from Rose, with repercussions that would roll around us for months, if not years to come. I needed to know which way the wind was to blow.

'Did you tell her about us? Did you tell Rose about me?' Everything else fell away in that moment. I forgot temporarily where I was and the circumstances that had brought us together that morning. I fixed my attention only upon the man who sat before me. I watched as Daniel nodded his head, saying in reply,

'Yes, I told her about you and that I love you.' Daniel looked into my eyes. It was a look which had spoken of an eternity of longing and searching. A jolt of electricity shot through my body, and I found myself feeling slightly nauseous, even though it was a moment that I had been waiting for, and for what had seemed like forever. With these feelings, I was unexpectedly swept up in memories from my other, sixteenth century life. At first I saw Henry in my mind's eye, kneeling at my feet and pledging his eternal love for Anne in the private intimacy of my apartments at Calais, then just as quickly, the king's face was replaced by Katherine's and her imperious disdain of my presence. And I was sick of it, sick of feeling guilty and apologising to God for my existence. Suddenly, something of Anne's spirit took hold of my body, as I sensed her stout heart beating its own defiant rhythm. Like Anne, I realised that I would not be held responsible for a marriage that had died long, long ago. Daniel was still watching me quizzically, and so I stretched out my hands, indicating that he should put his in mine. I was no longer just plain Anne, but Anne the Queen—afraid of no one. Tentatively, he accepted my invitation and I drew him to his feet, declaring boldly,

'Good. I'm glad of it. Finally, we can put aside all these years of creeping shamefully around in the shadows.' I squeezed his hands, as if I might convey my own courage through my action. Somehow, I must have sensed Daniel's hesitation and so with conviction, I entreated him with my own passionate words, 'Look, it is the lying that has been so heavy and weighty to bear. It is the deceit which has eaten away at you, and I promise you that whilst this path will not be easy...' then I added somewhat wryly, '...for I have no doubt that Rose will play the victim for all she's worth—whatever we have to face, we will face it together, and eventually it will end—everything does. Believe me, Rose will accept what has happened and eventually move on. We just have to be strong and steer a steady course.' I hoped that my words would shore up my lover's courage, fortify his resilience, and reassure him that it would be our determination and perseverance which would see us through to our own happy ending. I knew that with Henry, Anne once had to play Lady Macbeth and 'screw her courage to the sticking place' when her man vacillated in the face of Rome's might—and the Pope's disapproval of Henry's desire to set aside his wife.

As I had made my own 'Churchillian' speech that day, I prayed to God that Rose would not strike too deeply at Daniel's Achilles heel; his deep and overwhelming love for his daughter. I hoped that she loved her daughter with maturity enough to prevent her using Jemima as a weapon against her father in the weeks and months to come. I hoped that she would pragmatically accept the truth of the matter; that to be in a marriage with someone who did not love you must surely be greater torture than to have to carve out a life that one might proudly call one's own. Yes, I hoped beyond all hope that I was dealing with a woman who had enough insight and dignity to let Daniel go.

And so, as we headed out of the hospital that day, walking arm in arm, full of hope for the future, I was unaware of the perfect storm that was racing toward me. It was a storm which would tear through my already fragile existence, wrecking without mercy, both a love which I had so desperately clung to the past seven years, and the life which I now see is so temporary, so precious and, despite all the pain and sorrow that I have known in both my lives, remains so incredibly beautiful.

413

Chapter Thirty-Five

Hampton Court Palace,
29 April 2009

Just one week had passed since I left hospital. Daniel had taken me back to my flat where we began to take the first tentative steps of our life together. If I held any aspiration that the tender shoots of our fledgling relationship would be given room to breathe, then I was sadly mistaken. My naive hope that Rose would react to the situation with dignity was crushed within just a few short days. Daniel found himself bombarded by a barrage of increasingly hysterical phone calls. I overheard some of them, coming as they did night and day, and every time it was the same: accusations, abuse, and emotional blackmail. I heard myself being called a 'whore' more times than I care to remember, but having walked in Anne's shoes, I was used to it. In truth, I felt sorry for Rose, that she could not see the futility of trying to hold on to a love which had long since taken flight.

More dangerous by far was the fact that Rose immediately began to threaten Daniel with preventing him from seeing his child, if he did not return to the family home. My own heart was impervious to her threats, however, I watched helplessly as Daniel got sucked deeper into the drama of it all. Of course, it was easier for me. I was not so emotionally shackled so I could see that although it might take time, the shock would heal, and with patience and tolerance, the very worst of the storm would eventually blow over. In the meantime though, the peaceful tranquillity of my little abode was rudely shattered by a seemingly never-ending stream of one-sided arguments and bitter recriminations. And when those calls were over, Daniel would emerge, his jaw set hard, tense and agitated by the tempest which raged around their disintegrating relationship.

And then there was his daughter. Jemima had quickly withdrawn into her own bereft world. Her reluctance to see her father broke Daniel's heart and threw him into an ever more despondent state of self-pity and loathing. It became quickly evident that to make matters worse, Rose readily poured fuel on the fire of Jemima's distress, making it quite clear to her daughter that she laid the blame squarely at her husband's door—and mine—for the predicament that had befallen them both. Oh, how like Katherine she was—forever the victim! I could not believe that I was reliving the situation over again. Daily, I watched Daniel's spirit crumble as despair over his daughter's reaction increased. All too soon he began to lash out at me, holding me predominantly accountable for his misery. With frightening speed everything began to revolve around Daniel and Jemima—as I now see it had always done. Yet I was unable to find respite. When Daniel was not with his daughter or at the office, he sulked around the house that we had come to share, sometimes even withholding his affection in retribution for his pain. I was determined to give him all the time and space he needed to lick his inevitable wounds. Indeed, I had braced myself for this moment, and the rough waters in which I knew we would all be tossed. But by the end of the first week, I was exhausted and needed to escape; to find solitude and have a chance to digest all that had happened to me. I also needed to find a place for my own hollow misery, to be able to set time aside to grieve for my dead son.

Therefore, when Daniel set out that morning to take Jemima to school, I scrawled a brief, hand-written note explaining that I had gone out to visit a friend and would be back after lunch. I felt a little guilty for it was not entirely the truth, yet I could not face explaining where I was heading, or why. Slipping on my oversized sunglasses and slinging my faded, leather bag over my shoulder, I headed out in a plain white, fitted tee-shirt and my usual denim blue jeans. There was only one place where I could ground myself and be near that which I had so treasured, and had so tragically lost—Hampton Court.

Since returning to my twenty-first century world, I had harboured a desperate longing to be close once more to the body of my son, who I alone knew lay buried beneath the chapel floor of Henry's magnificent Tudor palace. And so it was, that on an exceptionally crystal clear, warm spring day, I walked alone down the long, tarmac drive, toward what was left of Wolsey's original five-storey gatehouse. I arrived early, just five minutes before the palace was due to open. Eager tourists were gathering in front of the gnarled oak doors that guarded the entrance into Base Court. Although the front of the west-facing palace was cast in shadow, the warmth of the narrow red bricks, the familiar sight of moulded stone arches, the crenellated rooftops and barley twist chimneys filled me with a comforting sense that I was returning home.

Approaching the stone bridge, which spanned a dry moat in front of the gatehouse, I heard the delicate chime of the bell perched above Anne Boleyn's gateway, deep inside the palace. The bell was in fact older than the palace itself, dating from the time when the site was occupied by the Knights Hospitallers. Chiming eleven o'clock, the palace was about to open as I heard the clinking of keys brought forth by an invisible hand on the other side of the doorway, and mused that there had been a time when that bell had marked all the important occasions in my day. The customary sound of its unfaltering presence stirred something within me, sending me hurtling head-long into a life which I had so recently left behind.

As the double fronted gates swung inwards, the palace opened itself up to me once more, with the sound of a hundred voices—all whispering my name—rushing forth, as if carried on an ethereal breeze. My breath caught momentarily for the strength of Henry's presence seemed to be everywhere. It was the first time that I had returned to Hampton Court since I was last in Anne's shoes, and whilst I had visited this place many times in my modern day life, on that occasion everything felt different. It was as if the great courtyard in front of me was exactly as it had been when I had last passed through it as queen. As Henry's consort, I was not accustomed to frequenting this part of the palace. But on my visit to Hampton Court for the marriage of Mary Howard to Henry Fitzroy in November 1533, I had often galloped through it at the king's side, as we returned from one of the regular hunting forays in the vast forest that lay beyond. Thankfully, it remained untouched by the gaudy hand of Baroque grandeur, thus the energy of the Henrician court remained imprinted in the fabric of the building, undisturbed by its later inhabitants.

For a moment, I stopped to look about me, shading my eyes from the reflected glare of the sun. Out of the corner of my eye, I was sure that I kept catching glimpses of familiar ghostly faces, caught momentarily in the dancing light that glinted off leaded windows. Turning my head, I swear that I saw the train of a gown disappearing through a Tudor archway into the cool shade of the enclosed corridors which ran round the courtyard. I truly sensed that part of me remained in Anne's world, and that the veneer which separated this one from the other was as flimsy as the wisps of smoke that had once escaped the palace's many chimneys.

As a gush of tourists began to spread out across the courtyard, going this way and that to various exhibitions, I felt drawn deeper into the inner sanctum of the palace, toward the old Tudor royal apartments. With every step on the uneven cobblestone, more memories of the great pleasure and pain that I had known whilst living within the palace's walls came knocking, insistent that I should pay them homage once again. Lost in my own world, I had walked across the length of Base Court and found myself beneath Anne Boleyn's gateway. I glanced briefly skyward to see a rather romantic Victorian replica of the cipher 'H' and 'A' carved into the stone-vaulted archway above my head. In front of me, the fabric of the three-storey apartments that Wolsey had once built to accommodate his sovereign lord, Queen Katherine and their daughter Mary, still towered majestically over Clock Court. It was sad for I knew that these rooms had long ago been robbed of their interior splendour, and were no longer open to the public. Nevertheless, my gaze was drawn to a window high up on the third floor, on the right hand side of the range, the window which had once looked out from the queen's bedchamber. It was here I had been brought to bed of my dead son. The poignancy of the memory was fresh and raw causing my throat to constrict, and a sting of tears to prick at the back of my eyes. Determined to maintain my composure, I turned away. I feared that if I did not place my attention elsewhere, I would surely collapse in a heap of festering grief, unable to contain the emotion which continually threatened to overwhelm me.

To my left was the great stair which swept grandly upwards, leading toward the first floor and the great hall of Hampton Court Palace. In my mind's eye, Henry's guard stood silently at the summit, keeping an eternal watch over the king's residence. My feet scuffed across the worn stone steps as I mounted the stair, jostling with a thousand courtiers who had passed this way before me. Many had been my friends, even more my enemies, but I remembered them all. Finally, I pushed open the enormously weighty door that ushered me inside the room—a room which had been and remained, one of the most breath-taking sights in Tudor England.

During my time in the sixteenth century, the great hall at Hampton Court was nearing the end of an extensive rebuilding programme enthusiastically commissioned by Henry. Yes, I had glimpsed its burgeoning grandeur which could never be disguised, not even by the mess created by workmen who toiled tirelessly upon its fabric. I had not remained in Anne's world long enough to see the final result, although, in my modern day life, I had visited on many occasions. Usually crowded with curious tourists, happily on that day, I swiftly reached the hall ahead of the hordes and found myself alone, save for a guide who loitered unobtrusively toward its lower end, beneath the minstrel's gallery. I stood at its heart, awed by the regal splendour that had endured for nearly 500 years. The hall was roughly 120 feet in length by 60 feet wide and craning my neck, I could admire the magnificent roof, which pitched to a height of roughly 90 feet, and supported by an exquisitely beautiful hammer-beam structure. Whilst not strictly architecturally necessary, the design echoed that of Westminster Hall, and I knew that Henry had conceived it deliberately in order to symbolise royalty, antiquity and chivalry; values which had always been close to my husband's heart. Like all great medieval halls, a stone hearth had once stood in the centre of the space, directly in front of the dais. These fires heated the room as the smoke was vented through a shuttered louvre high in the vaulted ceiling. I mused that in all my time at Henry's palaces, I had never once seen any such fire laid. It seemed that even then, the great halls, which had been the centre of medieval life for centuries, were virtually obsolete as the monarch retreated evermore deeply into his privy chambers. My eyes traced their way downward, coming to rest upon the enormous faded tapestries that were once part of Henry's fabulous, and extremely expensive, personal collection. The years had taken their toll. I closed my eyes and saw again the glittering brilliance of the arras in their heyday; the vibrant colours, and the gold and silver thread shimmering with life in the glow of a myriad of candles set about the great chamber. I smiled remembering how the images depicted were so vivid that it always seemed that they might step out from the walls and walk among the living.

If anywhere on earth still epitomised Henry's omnipotence and power, it had to be within the walls of that building. As I made my way toward a trestle table laid out across the dais at the high end of the hall, upon which a few pewter plates and goblets were displayed afore two velvet-clad X-framed chairs, I glanced over my shoulder to find that I was still alone and so I walked round the edge of the table, my finger idly trailing across the starchy, white linen cloth and sat down, once again taking my imaginary place at Henry's right hand side.

Tears welled up within me. I was catapulted into retracing the most unbelievable and breathtaking journey of my life; how against all imagining, a simple girl such as I had been swept up in one of the greatest love stories of English history. Once upon a time, I had commanded Henry's heart with the same unquestionable dominance with which he had ruled his kingdom. Despite everything that had happened between them, I was sure Anne Boleyn had gone to the scaffold still loving Henry—angry, bitter and full of resentment, but still somewhere in her heart yearning to know once more the sweet and tender love of her sovereign lord, the king. My heart could not have been more weighed down with the burden of so great a love lost. Henry had slipped through my fingers, my Tudor friends and family were once more in their cold graves, and my baby son, who as far as the world was concerned I had never known, was dead and gone. And then there was Daniel.

If I admit the truth to myself, then I already knew that we were lost before we had even begun. I thought again about Henry's pledge to love me forever, for whilst I was sure that Daniel loved me well enough, if the two of us were indeed Henry and Anne living their love over and over again, then did our predestined fate ensure that we too would suffer the same unhappy ending? Despite what I knew in my heart, stubbornly, doggedly even, I clung to a piece of driftwood in an ocean of shattered dreams. On that day, when it was so close to the end, I was unable to bear the truth which was this; that Daniel was held hostage emotionally to Jemima, and was being sucked back into a relationship from which he had barely escaped.

I thought on all this and my misfortune to be cast into relationships that always seemed so terribly complicated. As I did so, my eyes swept round the room; I found my vision becoming increasingly blurred as salty tears brimmed over with sorrow for us all. Despite that overwhelming sadness, I allowed myself to hear instead the echoes of music and laughter, sounds of great merry-making which had so often filled spaces such as this, chambers in which we had dined in sumptuous splendour. It was a gentle moment where benevolent memories allowed me to preside over a merry court with a king who had adored me sitting at my side. Such happiness, in amongst such pain, was filled with beauty and poignancy; like poppies that flower in the summer sun, whose delicate, papery petals cast their final flash of glory before falling, all too soon, to the ground. And so it seemed that my happiness was to be as fleeting.

A group of visitors descended into the hall from the great stair, and the spell was broken. I pushed my chair back and took one final glance at the great hall before I turned and headed towards the chapel royal.

Like all visitors to Hampton Court, I approached the chapel royal via the main entrance on the ground floor. It was strange for me to do so as it was at odds with what I had become accustomed to in my Tudor life. I had always watched mass from the privacy of the queen's holy day closet which looked directly down upon the body of the church. If I needed to enter the chapel itself, as was necessary only during great court occasions, I would accompany the king via the privy stair, which led directly down from the first floor. The memory of it was so fresh in my mind, and yet my time at Hampton Court as Henry's queen could not have felt more lost to me as it did that day.

I paused outside the chapel entrance to see who was around, but I was still well ahead of the growing crowds, so I pushed hard against the door and with a creek, it gave way to permit me entrance to its inner sanctum. It was quiet inside, the atmosphere enshrined by the usual reverent hush, typical of a holy place. I was disappointed to see a young couple had arrived ahead of me, and were poring over some document displayed in a cabinet at the back of the chapel. I ignored them; the entrance delivering me straight into the central isle where the 'click, click, click' of my heels could be heard striking against the black and white tiled floor. The only other person present was a guide who stood close to the altar, his hands clasped in front of him. As I approached the front pew, he smiled, acknowledging my arrival. It was a gesture of politeness that I returned in kind. If the truth be known, I was crushed to see him there as I desperately wanted time alone at the side of my son's grave. Hoping that he would move away, I decided to bide my time and seated myself quietly on a pew in the front row as if I were simply taking a moment to admire the beauty of the place.

However, the chapel seemed far from beautiful. Having seen its full Tudor magnificence, the Baroque interior had stripped away its former elegance leaving the chapel feeling dark and oppressive. Gone was the great east window that had so elegantly allowed natural light to stream down upon the nave, only to be replaced by a monstrous, carved reredos made from a red wood that I assumed was mahogany. Matching panelling, quire stalls, and pews only added to the heavy austerity of the space. Despite my distaste for the eighteenth century changes, I smiled momentarily seeing the ghostly image of my beloved Mary Howard standing at the altar. She had been a dazzling sight in the bright morning sunshine of November 1533. Eventually, I lowered my gaze to look upon the tiles beneath her imaginary feet. The smile melted away as I remembered one of the most dreadful days of my life.

After I had given birth to my dead son, I begged Henry for him to be buried within the church. I could not bear to think of his little body flung upon some fire, or into some pit as would be customary, and despite Henry's fury, he finally agreed. It was to be done without ceremony, under cover of darkness when the palace was otherwise asleep. As I had not officially taken to my chambers, I did not need to be churched to leave my rooms and so on that very same evening, and with only two of my ladies to accompany me, we tiptoed through the darkened corridors and into the stillness of the chapel. Eventually, we found ourselves at the side of a shallow grave that had been dug in the centre of the nave, just afore the altar. My ladies stood on either side of me, holding my arms to give me support as without them, I would have sunk to the floor in weakness and sorrow. I was exhausted and heartbroken, and wanted nothing more than to curl up in the grave next to my son and sleep for all eternity. By the light of just a handful of flickering candles, my chaplain, William Betts, had said mass before my son's tiny body was interred in the sacred ground. The next morning, the green and yellow tiles had been replaced immaculately, as if the ground had never been disturbed. All who were present, from the gravedigger to my ladies and chaplain, were sworn to utter secrecy. And so it came to pass, that the memory of that sombre night was suffocated in my failure and shame, never to be spoken of again.

Suddenly, my mind came back to the present. The young couple spoke up from behind me, asking the guide for some information about the chapel and the artefacts on display. It was as if by a miracle that the guide finally moved away from the altar as he responded to their request. He walked passed me, making his way toward the back of the church before falling into deep discussion with the two eager tourists. I wanted to make sure my way was clear and looked over my shoulder in their direction. The guide fortunately had his back toward me as he followed the young woman toward the rear of the chapel where the trio huddled over the glass cabinet, clearly discussing whatever was displayed within.

'Thank you, Anne.' I whispered beneath my breath, as I stood up and walked quickly toward the spot where I knew that my son lay buried. I knelt down and without hesitation lifted my bag from over my shoulder, placed it on the ground, and opened it. Within it was a single white rose that I had bought from a florist on my way from Greenwich. Taking it within my hand, I laid it directly over where I knew that his tiny skeleton lay. Closing my eyes, I spoke to him of how much I missed him, telling him that I had not forgotten him and that I loved him with all my heart and for all eternity. As I did so, a single tear splashed down upon the floor.

I was suddenly very aware of my public grieving and desperate not to be challenged over what I was doing, I wiped my eyes, gathered up my things and made a hasty exit past the couple and the chapel guide. I did not want them to see my tears, or that my heart was breaking.

Chapter Thirty-Six

The Old Royal Naval College, Greenwich
1 May 2009

I intended my visit to Hampton Court to be one of cathartic healing; one through which I might lay my son and the memory of Anne Boleyn to rest. I wanted to move on with my life and celebrate a fresh start with Daniel. Naively, I underestimated my ability to walk away from a woman whose soul and destiny seemed so much entwined with my own. Instead of my suffering softening me and opening me up to the difficulties of Daniel's predicament with his wife and daughter, it unexpectedly served to create a harsher brittleness, in which I struggled daily to find the energy and empathy to steer us into calmer waters.

Over the next two days, my own prickly grief stirred up the firmament of our emotion, so that Daniel and I began to snap at each other at the slightest provocation. I look back now at the craziness of what we were trying to achieve: two people deeply hurt and wounded for their own reasons struggling to take full responsibility for their actions. At some level, to blame each other was so much easier than facing the reality of our own deep imperfections.

Until that point, I had played the role of pacifier, trying to soothe and comfort Daniel's disquiet, absorbing his anger and fear like a sponge. But something snapped in me after that day at Hampton Court. I became furious at life. I was sick and tired of constantly fighting for someone who seemed incapable of fighting for me—for us. In my own grief, I began to lash out at him, just as I had done with Henry. It was if I had taken on some of Anne's intemperance and began to rail against my predicament, accusing Daniel of lacking the courage to stick up for himself against Rose. Daniel was in no position to deal with my grief, which he did not even know existed, nor had he the resources to cope with my sudden turn of temper.

It was Friday, 1 May. I awoke thinking of Anne, as I always do on that day, the day that Henry stormed off and left her at the May Day joust in Greenwich, never to see her again. The cold betrayal of a woman he once loved so completely was always so difficult to accept. My mood was sombre. To make up for the difficulties of the last three weeks, Daniel took the day off work, and we were due to head off into the countryside for a long walk, to talk about the future and just enjoy each other's company. I was looking forward to it immensely as it would give us a chance to put Rose and Jemima behind us, just for one glorious day. In the end, we did not even make it out of the house before everything blew apart with a force that I had not seen coming.

Having eaten breakfast and dressed, I was in the bedroom, just sweeping a final coat of cherry-red lip gloss across my lips, when I heard the phone ring in the living room. Daniel was closer, so I assumed he would answer it. As it rang, I was looking outside my bedroom window, watching menacing grey clouds, heavy with rain, push and jostle the pristine blue sky away to the north; another day's squally showers and blustery winds to contend with. I sighed and began to search around in one of the cupboards for my umbrella, as I heard Daniel pick up the phone.

'Hello, Daniel speaking.' At first, I was only vaguely aware of the conversation pricking my consciousness. I concentrated, instead, on taming my hair by sweeping it up into an elegant ponytail. As I did so, I watched the neighbour's tortoiseshell cat pick her way delicately, and with an assured grace, along the top of the fence that separated our gardens. As a few drops of rain began to fall, she quickly dropped out of sight over the fence, no doubt heading home to take shelter from the inclement weather. As her tail disappeared from view, I became more aware of Daniel's voice. He was troubled, hesitant even; the brightness in his voice replaced by harsh intensity which I associated only with one person—Rose.

'Rose you can't just drop this on me out of the blue... of course I want to see her but...' I felt my stomach tighten involuntarily, a flash of adrenaline instantly coursing through my body. I closed my eyes, taking a deep breath as I tried to steady the anger that began to constrict my chest. It was not the first time that Rose had called precipitously, demanding that Daniel go over immediately to take care of Jemima, whilst she went out to fulfil whatever supposedly pressing appointment awaited her. It was Rose's way of not only keeping tabs on Daniel, but of causing as much disruption and discord in our relationship as she was able. Her timing was always perfect—to coincide with any engagement that we had pre-planned. Putting down the umbrella that I was holding, I leaned against the doorway whilst Daniel concluded his conversation with Rose.

'Yes, yes, okay... I'll be there in an hour.' He did not hear me come into the room, and if I had not been so caught up in every painful twist and turn of the drama, I would have seen the weight of the world bear down on his shoulders. Clearly, he was considering how he would break the news that once more our plans were being thwarted. Perhaps a wiser person than I would have walked away, however, like my namesake, such equanimity was not mine to command. My face must have reflected my irritation and anger, and so anticipating my reaction, Daniel shook his head saying, 'I'm sorry, Anne but I have to go.'

'Have to?' I think those were the words, those two little words, which were the final straw. I voiced my thoughts aloud.

'Have to? Have to? Daniel, you don't have to do anything!' I stretched out my arms plaintively, palms upturned before dropping them to my sides in disgust. 'We arranged all this over a week ago. Don't you see how important this is to us—to me?'

'Rose has to go out unexpectedly, and there's no one to take care of Jemima.'

'Argh!' I cried out as I buried my face in my hands. I wanted to weep in frustration as I could no longer contain the poisonous mixture of anger and dangerous resentment that brewed inside me. 'Do you not see how she plays you, what she's doing here?' Daniel looked momentarily bewildered, as if he had never anticipated there could be an ulterior motive. 'It is her way of keeping you involved with her, of controlling you; and by the way, of undermining our relationship in the process!' Daniel ran his hands through his hair. He looked increasingly agitated and trapped, no doubt torn by the two great loves in his life— Jemima and me. But I could not leave it there. Instead, I foolishly issued an ultimatum. 'We agreed that we would spend the day together. You can't just break your agreement—it's just not fair! Call Rose back and tell you can't come.' I watched something snap in Daniel, his face suddenly suffused with anger.

'No, I won't just tell her I can't come!' Jesus Christ, Anne! Who the hell do you think you are, telling me what I should and shouldn't do? You really are unbelievable!' Daniel's fury crashed down on me as hard as if it were a physical blow. I found myself reeling from the acerbity of his words which sliced right through my heart. Everything changed in that moment; the words of such disrespect floated above an undercurrent of growing acrimony. Daniel had not finished. 'You simply have no idea what I have put on the line for you. Let's get this straight, right here and right now... Jemima is, and always will be, the most important thing or person in my life. I would give my life for her; and if she needs me, I'm always going to be there for her.'

I confess that I was too hurt by the implicit accusation that I did not care, nor was even mindful of Daniel's relationship with his daughter, to reply with any coherence. I stood still, utterly stunned and still trying to process the full ramifications of his words as he snatched up his jacket, car keys and wallet and strode past me, saying brusquely,

'I have to go. We'll talk about this later.' I reached out to touch him, but my love was too angry to accept any olive branch of peace.

'Dan, I...'

'Later, Anne!' There was little warmth in his voice, and it chilled me to the bone. It seemed like only yesterday I had heard the warm tones in Henry's familiar voice turn frosty; and I had just heard the same change in Daniel. I stood hurt and bewildered as he stalked off down the hallway, closing the door behind him with considerable force. There was a second or more in which all the glass in the apartment reverberated angrily before I was left standing alone, utterly deafened by the silence of my abandonment. All the emotions which had rushed forth to hijack me just a few minutes before abruptly found themselves redundant, kicking and scuffing their feet as they reluctantly dragged themselves from the battlefield in the quiet aftermath of our heated exchange.

I felt entirely defeated, hopelessly caught up in a morass of sticky emotions that left me bound to two men who had once so adored me, but now appeared to resent me with ever greater ferocity. I could hear the throaty growl of Daniel's Aston Martin trailing off into the distance. I had no desire to remain alone, confined by walls that seemed to be closing in on me, so grabbing my fitted coat made of pure, English wool, I buttoned it up snugly against the cool breeze before heading out with only a few pounds in one pocket and the keys to the flat in the other. I wanted to travel light. I was weighed down enough with ponderous cares.

Making my way through the bustling streets of Greenwich, I crossed into the park as a gentle breeze that so often chased down Castle Hill was whipping itself up into gusts of ever increasing force as the heavens grew ever angrier. People who had been walking their dog, or simply strolling in the park, were clearly thinking better of remaining outdoors; the falling temperatures and gusty winds portended the coming storm, driving people back towards their homes, or the many coffee houses on the High Street where they sought shelter.

I was indifferent to the distant rumbling thunder, which seemed some considerable distance away to the south, gnashing its teeth over suburban Surrey. I began to walk along the path that ran roughly where the most southerly boundary of Greenwich Palace had once stood. Strolling along the open palisade, constructed as part of the Royal Naval College in the eighteenth century, I headed towards Queen Anne's house. The conversation with Daniel churned over and over in my mind. Had I been so unreasonable to request that we keep just one solitary promise to one another? I paused to contemplate this, looking out over what had once been the great garden at Greenwich. In front of me, I imagined the disguising and banqueting houses which were so often the settings for the most intoxicating pleasures I had ever known.

My daydreams were interrupted by the sound of thunder approaching far more rapidly than I had anticipated. Pulling the collar of my coat up for extra warmth, I continued to walk eastwards along the palisade, and with every step, a sense of foreboding pressing down upon me. Our exchange had finally shown me the truth in Daniel's heart and although I was still not ready to see it, I touched upon the wisdom that our time was almost over. Thoughts of Daniel and memories of Henry were washing up, one after the other, on the shore of my shattered dreams. Two lives, two men, whom I had loved with all my heart and who I believed would never forsake me.

I finally stepped onto what had once been the tiltyard at Greenwich Palace. I could see it all so clearly: the magnificent tiltyard towers that had dominated this part of the palace precinct, the lists lying in front of me, where I had applauded the many fine gentlemen who jousted in my honour. Henry, as ever, by my side. But it had all been lost long ago, and I found myself standing in the middle of a car park as fat drops of rain began to splash down upon me, sporadically at first, then in a deluge of water that was soon running down my face and soaking me to the skin. The time was fast approaching. It was as if the earth felt our pain and wept inconsolably as both Anne Boleyn and I danced on the edge of oblivion.

Returning from my walk in Greenwich Park, my clothes soaked through from the storm, I spent the rest of that day alone. Daniel did not come home until later that evening when it was clear that a gulf of animosity had already opened up between us. Sadly it would be one which would prove impossible to bridge in the following days. I suspect that too much hurt had passed between us over the years for us to ever entirely trust each other again, the latest argument serving as a tipping point which was inevitable. And so the seed of our future relationship together was plucked abruptly from the ground, uprooted by the inability for either of us to see beyond our selfish needs.

After that day, we never again achieved the innocence we had once known. Daniel began to do his usual thing and withdrew defensively behind his own carefully constructed curtain wall, whilst I found it increasingly difficult to respond without irritation at what I saw as his lack of commitment toward our future. I still do not know exactly what happened to finally end it. Did Jemima threaten to cut off her father if he didn't come back? Had Rose and Daniel's friends persuaded him that he was merely having a midlife crisis, and that he should return to the family home? Or did Daniel simply realise he did not love me? This perhaps would have been the most crushing of all. Yet, I have no idea of the answers to these questions, for I never had the chance to ask him. My time had run out. I was about to find myself alone as the central protagonist in the final act of our drama.

Chapter Thirty-Seven

The Tower of London,
19 May 2009

It seems that a lifetime has passed since the day Daniel left. And in many ways it has. I still remember the desolate pain, although it no longer pricks me through the heart as it did on that black Monday. I have accepted that what happened between us was inevitable; that from the very first day we fell in love over that glass of champagne, I had been playing my part in carving out my fate. But I was not the sole contributor to our unhappiness. When Henry had pledged to love Anne for all eternity, he set our souls upon a path of shared destiny, which assured the two of us that we were always going to meet again; we were always going to fall in love under the same impossible circumstances.

On the last day I saw my love, it was a particularly frantic day at work. My diary was full with meetings that took me from one end of London to the other. For several days, the city basked in unseasonably warm weather, leaving its busy streets to bake in the sultry sunshine. And whilst above the ground the heat of the early summer was uncomfortable enough, but it was almost unbearable, underground, on the Tube. The nauseating smell of overheated bodies and stale sweat was alleviated only momentarily by the intermittent blasts of air heralding the arrival of an oncoming train. By the end of the day, I was desperate to get home and take a cool shower, to wash away the grime and the usual difficulties of an ordinary day.

I arrived home around 6.30 pm, uncomfortably sticky under my tailored suit, my tired feet feeling as if I had been walking on blades all day. The front door clicked shut behind me and I immediately kicked off my stiletto shoes, groaning in relief as I hobbled my first few tentative steps without them, allowing the bones in my feet to adjust once more to their natural state. I bent down to pick up a handful of letters that lay unattended on the doormat, then paused to listen for the sound of Daniel cooking in the kitchen, or messing about in the bedroom. But the flat was unusually quiet, and I realised that I had not seen his car parked outside on the driveway. Strange! I knew he'd been working at home all day.

'Dan!' Silence returned my greeting. I walked toward the sitting room, checking to see if he was there, but it was empty, everything tidy and untouched, just as I had last left it earlier in the day. 'Daniel, are you home?' I popped my head into the bedroom thinking he may have snatched a quick nap before I got home. But it was deserted. I was perplexed, even a little irritated at the thought that maybe Rose had called again and he had jumped at her command. I wandered into the kitchen. I was starving and ready to raid the cupboards to throw something together for dinner. Then I saw it on the kitchen table. I knew immediately what it was; scribbled on a scrap of paper were the words that finally ended our sorry saga;

I'm sorry. I can't do it. I've gone back home to Rose. I will always love you, but I just can't leave Jemima. I can't believe I have done this to you. Please forgive me. Let's find a way to talk at the weekend.
I need to explain.   Daniel x

I picked up the note, reading it over and over, feeling suddenly panic-stricken. Even despite our many problems, Daniel and I had been to hell and back to be together. He was not only my lover, but also my friend. He was the future that I had invested in so heavily, but which in the end had never really arrived. And now everything we had enjoyed in the name of love was gone. Daniel was gone. I was hardly able to breathe as I doubled over with a wrenching pain that tore at my heart. Then the tears came, furious and unrelenting. I must have screwed up the note into a crumpled ball before it fell from my hand, tumbling to the ground and rolling away from me, along with my dreams. At the same time, I slowly curled up into my own ball of misery, lost entirely in grief and despair, calling out his name and saying, 'No!' over and over. I could not believe that I had allowed myself to be lured once more by his promises of happy endings. Oh, what an utter fool I had been! As I lay on my kitchen floor feeling utterly abandoned, I hated him and grieved him in equal measure.

When eventually I got to my feet some considerable time later, I called Daniel on his mobile. It was switched off, and I knew that I could not face calling his family home. So instead, I called Kate. Of course, she came round like any true friend, laden with two bottles of chilled

Chablis. We talked and I cried a lot. Eventually exhausted and somewhat numb from the alcohol, I said good night and collapsed into a joyless sleep.

Despite my own sorry predicament, when I woke the following morning, the significance of the day did not escape me. It was Tuesday, 19 May; the anniversary of Anne's execution. By the time I lifted my head off the pillow to look at the clock, she was already dead. It was 8.30 am. I must have lain there for nearly an hour, my thoughts a montage of, 'what ifs' from both our shattered lives. So much pain and so many regrets! I phoned work and thankfully managed to take a day's holiday; my conscience now clear to lead me where it would.

Over breakfast, I logged onto Facebook, listlessly flicking through the endless messages of support and condolences for Anne from those who, nearly 500 years on, were still inspired and moved by her story. I slumped back in my chair, a cup of my usual lemon, ginger and honey tea resting in my hand. I had said 'goodbye' to my dead son at Hampton Court just a few weeks ago, and although he would never truly leave me, somewhere from the depths of my fractured life, I felt the overwhelming need to start again. Daniel had finally left me, and stoically, through the heartache, a sliver of common sense nudged my conscience with the notion that, in time, I would see that it was for the best. Even through the sorrow, I was determined that there would be no reprise. I would not put myself through one iota more of suffering on his account.

Nor did I want any more of Anne's life—of that I had been sure for some time. I had tasted enough of her misery and drunk my fill from that poisoned chalice. Under no circumstances did I want to walk in her shoes to the scaffold, even the idea was terrifying. Each life I had known had held so much promise, but somewhere along the way it had all gone so terribly wrong. I knew it was finally time to say goodbye to it all; 'goodbye' to Daniel and 'goodbye' to Anne and Henry. I determined that I would stop chasing rainbows of fancy and give myself over to rebuilding something of substance and meaning in my messy, confused existence. As I stared at the computer screen, looking at one particular post in homage to Anne—one which featured the basket of red roses laid annually upon her grave—I knew what I must do and where I must go. Anne was calling to me, and for one final time, I would go to her and say our final farewells.

Shortly after 11am, I emerged from Tower Hill tube station onto the busy pedestrian concourse that leads down to the Thames and the entrance to London's iconic medieval fortress. I was immediately assaulted by memories of happier times: of my Tudor family, my mother, brother and I making our way toward the Palace of Beaulieu. We had ridden our horses along the roughly hewn track that once cut across Tower Green to the north west of the Tower itself. I had thought of Anne's demise back then, in those early days, when it had seemed impossible to comprehend that Henry could ever abandon her. Such thoughts reminded me of the reason for my visit as I looked down at the basket of yellow roses I was carrying, luminous in the bright morning sunshine. I had picked them up from my local florist in Greenwich, adamant that they be yellow, knowing that this was Anne's favourite colour. I paused to look out on the sprawling magnificence of the place that stood as an indomitable witness to over 1,000 years of English history. And somewhere in amongst those years, it had been Anne's palace—my palace; one that had feted the coming of England's new queen. Back then, the prevailing sounds were of cannons roaring, bells tinkling, and music playing. I held it all joyously in my mind before the memories gradually dissolved, and the delicate sounds of times gone by were washed away by the throaty drone of the modern motorcar.

My ultimate destination was the little chapel of St Peter ad Vincula, within the Tower walls, but beforehand, I had another destination in mind. Turning away from the vast swathe of eager tourists who had come to drink their fill of London's most iconic of landmarks, I made my way to the right, heading toward Trinity Square Gardens and a relatively deserted but a well-manicured spot that stood on what was once known as Tower Hill. The site of the scaffold was demarcated by a series of small stone obelisks with flowerbeds surrounding the central, paved area, which were in full bloom—a living memorial to over 125 men who died bravely there, despite the grave injustice that was done to their mostly, innocent souls. I stepped forward to read the names of some of the victims of society's brutality, saddened to see that neither my brother's name, nor the names of any of those who died with him, was recorded on the tarnished copper plaques that surrounded the site.

I sank down onto my haunches, brushing my hand across the plaque upon which was engraved the names of, amongst others, John Fisher and Sir Thomas More. 'Sir Thomas More – 1535...' I read the name aloud, before tracing my finger down to the one recorded directly below that of Anne's implacable enemy: Thomas D'Arcy, Lord Darcy of Templehurst, KG, 1537. Just like Anne, the five men who had been unjustly killed, had been erased from history. Whoever had chosen which names to record upon the memorial clearly thought that those who died with a condemned adulteress did not merit recognition, certainly not next to lofty martyrs like Fisher and More. Still raw from the deep cut of Daniel's departure, it took little for a single tear to escape from my reluctant eyes. I brushed it away quickly, determined not to make a public spectacle of myself, which I was recently doing with increasing, and embarrassing, regularity. Collecting myself, I plucked a single rose from my basket and laid it with love upon the ground in front of the plaque, as I whispered, 'I miss you, George. I am so sorry that you were dragged into that mess. Sweet brother you did not deserve to die so horribly. Please forgive me.' As I uttered the words, suddenly George's handsome face appeared within my mind. I remembered all too well how he always sought to protect me, and in my head, I swear that I heard his voice as clear as if he were next to me.

'Do not worry, sweet sister. All will be well, you will see.' I know it was my imagination, but he sounded so happy and peaceful that I smiled, heartened to be able, by whatever means, to touch my brother's essence.

Leaving my blessing behind, I turned and began to make my way toward the main entrance to the Tower. As I did so, an odd sensation swept over me. It was impossible to put my finger on what made me feel so out of sorts. I had certainly slept fitfully and felt utterly wretched from the emotional tempest of the previous day. The several glasses of wine that I so readily consumed the evening before did not help matters either. I took a deep breath. I was determined to press on and made a covenant with myself that once I had laid the flowers on Anne's grave, I would skulk off home and lose myself under my duvet for the rest of the day.

Normally when visiting the Tower of London, I time my arrival towards late afternoon, when families begin to head home to rest and feed tired and fractious children. Only the most tenacious of tourists hang on doggedly to witness the ancient Ceremony of the Keys, which takes place within the confines of the Tower every day at dusk. On that Tuesday, though, I arrived in the middle of the day when the Tower was at its busiest and swarming with people of every conceivable nationality. Thankfully, my annual pass allowed me to circumvent the long queues snaking their way toward the ticket kiosks, but as I approached the main entrance, I was engulfed by a mass of humanity. Weaving my way through the crowds, I was just another ordinary tourist, unremarkable in every way. Yet I knew that I was literally walking in the footsteps of the long dead queen who remained as alive to me as if I had spoken to her only yesterday.

The entrance to the modern day Tower is a little different to the Tudor fortress that I had so recently known. The old Bulwark Gate that once led out towards Tower Hill was long since demolished, as were the smattering of buildings that had faced the Tower's principal entrance, running southward to a further gateway that opened up onto Tower wharf. Having queued patiently to have my bag searched, I slung it back over my shoulder and passed immediately under the ancient Middle Tower; a moving montage of faces flooding relentlessly toward me. My dislike of crowds had intensified since becoming accustomed to a time when the whole population of England equalled the number that now tried to squeeze into London's sprawling metropolis. I felt as if I were drowning in a sea of anonymity as I wove through the crowds, being buffeted now and again by an errant rucksack or elbow. I wondered what secrets each person carried within their heart. Were they living in their own private paradise, or like me, were they watching the fabric of their lives crumble around them, living their lives like automatons, barely able to function through the pain.

These thoughts carried me forward until I was under the shadow of the Byward Tower. As Anne, I knew it as the Tower by the Gate. The joyful reception of the king's most beloved wife filled my mind as I thought of my triumphant arrival from Greenwich amongst a flotilla of vibrant river pageantry. I was being lauded as Henry's queen-in-waiting; visibly pregnant with the next generation of Tudor kings. Everything seemed perfect, utterly perfect; it was a day that I could truly have lived over and over, leaving no room for unhappy times to smuggle their way into Anne's life. Under the lugubrious shade of the Byward Gate, I paused, as hordes of visitors streamed around me in each direction. Unexpectedly, those happy memories were wrenched from me, and out of nowhere I found myself recalling something that was unfamiliar—something that I had not yet experienced. With shocking clarity that shook me to the core, I witnessed a melange of images in which I was lying on the uneven cobbled stones in front of where I was standing. And with those images came feelings of terror; sheer, unadulterated blind panic and unspeakable sorrow. I was not alone. Suddenly, I was looking up at a man who I recognised, from my stay at the Tower in 1533, its Lieutenant, Sir Edmund Walsingham. He was staring down at me with a mixture of disdain and bewilderment evident upon his stern face. I knew that I was crying and calling out to God for help. And was Anne saying something about her innocence? As quickly as they had appeared, the images were gone.

Next to me, a woman who had been busy taking photographs stepped backwards, bumping into me with considerable force. She turned about, holding up her hands in a physical gesture of apology, as she said what I assumed meant, 'sorry' in a language that came from some distant corner of the world. I smiled and nodded my acceptance. But honestly, I hardly noticed, for I was stupefied, left struggling to understand what exactly I had just witnessed. Slowly, I moved away from the Byward Gate, deeper into the heart of the Tower complex. I was lost in the potential ramifications of what had just happened, and also aware that I was feeling increasingly unwell with every step. Although my body was growing heavy, I continued walking along the lane that was sandwiched between the inner and outer curtain walls as I was determined that I would deliver my flowers to Anne's grave, say my farewells, and leave.

Up ahead, I saw a huge group of visitors huddled around one of the Tower's famous Beefeaters. The portly gentleman, sporting a gingery beard and moustache, stood on a small box, which served to raise him slightly above the eager crowd. They were gathered right next to the flight of slimy steps that led down to the infamously named Traitor's Gate. At first, all I could make out was the tone of his booming voice above the crowd, but as I approached, I heard the story he was regaling to his enthralled audience. Clearly a showman through and through, he mesmerised the crowd with his tales of traitors conveyed to the Tower through the famous gate, there to await a grisly end. As I turned away to make my way up hill, under the Bloody Tower, I heard him speak of Anne collapsing on the steps as she was conveyed to her prison. Even in my sorry state, the myth propagated in the name of entertainment irritated me. Like so many myths about Anne—her sixth finger, the goitre in her neck, her adulterous and incestuous affairs—struck me as being infuriatingly akin to trick candles on a birthday cake—impossible to extinguish.

Emerging from under the Bloody Tower, I surveyed all that was around me, a good deal of which had changed since I last saw inside the Tower during Anne's coronation festivities of 1533. The imposing Cold Harbour Gate, which stood guard over the royal apartments in the Tower's inner ward, was all but gone; just a few ragged stone fragments of the ancient sentinel remained. The medieval great hall, the king and queen's lodgings were also entirely lost, only the occasional outline of a wall paid testimony to the network of fine buildings that had once witnessed a momentous time in England's history. I saw them all in my mind's eye soaring up from the ground where only others saw grass and stone and paving slabs. In my head, I said 'goodbye' to the palace that Henry had built for me—for Anne. On account of my queasiness, I did not linger but quickly pressed on with my task, mounting the steep flight of stairs that led up to large, open area to the north of the White Tower. To my left, I was well aware of the site commemorating those of noble birth, including Anne, who were executed within these walls, but I paid no attention to it. The story that the spot marked the site of the scaffold was another myth, propagated by the Victorians, and sealed by a twentieth century monument that had subsequently been erected to honour those who had lost their lives there. At the head of the stairs I paused again, just to catch my breath and steady myself. I felt slightly nauseous and hot, too hot, as if an internal fire had been lit that was baking me from within. What was the matter with me? Surely my hangover could not be getting worse?

My intention had been to go straight to the chapel and charm my way inside. All I wanted to do was lay my flowers on the tiled floor which marked Anne's final resting place, to give her my love, and then go home. But quite inexplicably, I was drawn to walk in the opposite direction, toward the entrance to Waterloo Barracks. And then it happened.

Once more, I was catapulted headlong into a memory. The modern day Tower dissolved around me, and suddenly in its place, the Tudor fortress that I had known in my sixteenth century lifetime appeared, but I was not alone. I was surrounded by an enormous escort of guards all bearing fearsome looking halberds. Gone was the midday heat, instead the day was bright but cool against my skin, the early morning chill warded off by the fine mantle trimmed with ermine that I was wearing about my shoulders. The crowds that just seconds before were criss-crossing the parade ground in front of the barracks melted away. Instead hordes of men and women dressed in familiar sixteenth century garb were pushing and pressing to catch sight of me, but kept back by yeoman warders. Occasionally, an arm stretched out from the seething crowd, trying to touch me, whilst many voices called out, 'God Save Your Grace' and 'God be with you!' I turned to see my dear four ladies following me: Margery and Anne Wyatt, Nan Gainsford and Madge Shelton, each one looking deeply distressed. Emerging above the crowd was the sight of a high scaffold draped in sombre black. My heart almost stopped. I was nearly upon it. I could barely breathe as pain suddenly tore through my head.

In an instant, all of it was gone, and I was once more in my modern day body. I would have tried to make sense of it, but the pain I felt was not in my imagination. In blinding agony, I dropped to my knees right in front of the place where Anne had died. I felt the flowers fall away from my hand and from nowhere, several concerned passers by hurried over. Hands were touching me. I heard their concerned voices asking if I was all right. But I could not reply. My world was rapidly closing in around me. The last thing I felt was pain searing through my neck and head, and the sight of the bright Caen stone of the White Tower being replaced by inky blackness. And with that my life in the twenty-first century was over.

Chapter Thirty-Eight

Greenwich Palace,
Sunday, 30 April 1536

Ghostly voices echoed in my mind, weaving their way seamlessly through a series of vivid images that flooded my stricken brain. In my fevered imagination, I was pleading my innocence to anyone who would listen, running this way and that, beseeching anyone who would believe me to take up my cause; but countless faceless strangers I met remained coldly unmoved by my plight. Then suddenly, the disembodied voice which had hitherto echoed faintly in the deepest recesses of my mind finally cut through my wild imaginings with its own insistent urgency,

'Your Majesty, Your Majesty,' I became aware of a hand shaking my shoulder, and of a warm, hard surface pressed unyielding against the side of my face. Once more, I heard the voice call my name, 'Anne, Anne … are you all right?' My eyes gently flickered open. Taking a moment to focus, I found that I couldn't move, I was confused and could remember only the blinding pain which had ripped through my skull in the seconds before I lost consciousness at the Tower. Yes, yes, I remembered. Then I saw it all with painful clarity. I remembered Daniel's final, cruel betrayal, and with that memory came shackled a cavernous emptiness that once more opened up within my heart. I recalled my lonely pilgrimage to the site of Anne's execution on the anniversary of her death. However, I was no longer at the Tower.

It took me very little time to understand what had happened as by then, I was familiar with my inexplicable propensity to travel across time, and I immediately recognised the sights and smells of my other world. I was sure from the pain that I experienced exploding in my head just before I passed out, that the aneurysm, which I knew one day might rupture, had finally done so, and I was once more catapulted back in time, into the body of Anne Boleyn.

'Your Grace!' Again, the hand shook my shoulder, and I heard the familiar voice say, 'Thank the Good Lord, her majesty is coming round.' As the ringing in my ears began to abate, I was seized by a haunting sense of impending disaster. It surged up from my belly, galloping with the speed of the Four Horsemen of the Apocalypse to grip my chest and throat. I was so very hot, overcome by the desire to flee from the unknown spectre that tormented me so. Yet, when I looked around, I found myself in the most familiar of surroundings; I had woken up in the queen's privy chamber at Greenwich. How could I not know it? I had spent so much time there, even given birth to my darling Elizabeth within its very walls.

I could hear the ticking of a clock, the gift that Henry gave me on my wedding day—Anne's wedding day. It told me that it was approaching quarter to eleven in the morning. I did not know then that in only a few short hours, Anne's marriage to Henry would be completely destroyed. It is painful to admit that in the end it would be my actions that precipitated the crisis that Master Secretary Cromwell had been waiting for. Anne's shrewd political acumen would momentarily desert her, and in my own blind terror, I would play right into the hands of those who had waited patiently to ensnare the queen. Dear God forgive me for letting Anne down; that I, of all people, who have loved her so entirely, could be responsible for tipping the balance of power against her.

I turned away from the clock and looked instead toward the two ladies who knelt close by. Studying me intently were the faces of two of my most dear and loyal friends; Margery Wyatt and Nan Gainsford. I was aware of their genuine concern and their frowns of consternation. I suspect that I looked terrified, for I could still not shake the feeling that I was being hunted; but by whom, I did not yet know.

In my twenty-first century life, it had been but four weeks since I last walked in Anne's shoes, and seen the sweet faces of my friends and beloved family. Though I was so happy to see Margery and Nan again, this time I knew immediately that something was dreadfully wrong. I needed urgently to understand why I had awoken with such an awful sense of impending doom. Thus, I focused first on Margery, her face graven with concern. Anne had clearly fainted. I decided to make the most of her temporary illness and feign confusion, which of course was not far from the truth.

'What happened? I must have passed out.' I said hoping for an explanation from my friends.

'You did indeed, Your Grace.' Margery's face crumpled with

disquiet as she went on, 'I am dreadfully sorry, Madame for I should not have told you about Mark.' I raised my hand to my forehead, rubbing briefly at my temple, and wincing against the pain, as I must have knocked my head when I collapsed. My brow furrowed in confusion as I asked quizzically,

'Mark? I'm sorry. I don't remember.' I let my words trail away inviting my friend's response. I watched Margery hesitate, turning to glance over at Nan. 'Margery, please … you must tell me what you know.' It was enough to entice the words reluctantly from my friend.

'I heard tell from my husband that, under the greatest secrecy, Master Smeaton is being interrogated by Master Secretary Cromwell. I know this only on account of the fact that my lord husband accidently overheard a conversation betwixt Sir William Fitzwilliam and the king's Secretary early this morning. It was not a conversation he was meant to hear, but they did not see him as they passed by.'

What were they saying? I knew that the two men Margery spoke of would be steeped in the thick of Anne's downfall.

'Master Secretary was explaining that he was leaving for his house in Stepney. He had invited Mark Smeaton to go thither for his dinner as his guest, but that there he would make to investigate the abominable accusations that had been laid before him.' In all the time that I had known Margery, she had always been unflappable and little moved by idle gossip and wagging tongues. Yet I saw disquiet in her eyes that surely mirrored my own. She could not know what was really afoot, but with her words, all my most sinister suspicions were confirmed. I knew with terrifying certainty that I had been flung headlong into the gathering storm that would tear the Boleyn faction apart. I knew that I stood in Anne's shoes on the cusp of that fateful month of May, 1536.

'No, no, no, no…'I looked away from Margery, shaking my head, 'This cannot be happening to me!' Whilst I had relished walking in the shoes of my heroine during the heady days of Anne's romance with Henry, I could never face the fact that I might find myself thrust onto the stage of her life at the very moment that a *coup d'état* was about to sweep Anne off the face of the earth. I felt trapped and utterly terrified. I suddenly understood why I sensed Anne's desire to flee although she could not have known exactly what lay ahead—as I did—that her relationship with Henry was about to come to its dramatic climax. My ladies were distressed at the vehemence of my response and did not understand my words. Margery tried to soothe my frayed nerves.

'Please, Your Majesty … Anne, try to be at ease, surely this does not touch upon Your Grace's person, for Mark is just a musician of the king's chamber.' Margery reached out and uncommonly grasped my hand, squeezing it tightly to reassure me. I was becoming almost hysterical, tears spilling over my eyelids as they raced one after the other down my cheeks. I tried to wipe them away, as I moaned,

'No, no, don't you see!' I seized both of Margery's hands in mine. My eyes must have been wide with fear, for Margery looked taken aback by my sudden, uncontrolled and frightful ranting. 'It has started; Henry wants to get rid of me!'

'No, no!' Nan added quickly, 'His majesty would never seek to harm you, for you are the queen.' I let go of Margery's hands, throwing my head back in hysterical laughter at the naivety of Nan's words.

I could no longer contain the surging restlessness in my body. I got to my feet and, in Anne's typical fashion, began to pace the room, casting my arms about; great sweeping, frantic gestures cutting through the air as I spoke in a diatribe of a troubled, fevered mind. 'Do you not see that I am but his majesty's lowly servant and wife? I have no powerful family abroad who could fight for me; no … the king got rid of Katherine for her failure to bear a son, and now I too have failed in the one thing that I promised him; two dead sons, and a daughter that in his eyes amounts to nothing. Nothing!' Placing one hand on my hip, I raised the palm of my other hand to my forehead as if to rub away the knotty tension which had gathered there, I cried plaintively, '… how can I conceive again when the king barely shares my bed!'

I noticed how I spoke easily of Anne's 'sons', of my assuredness that Anne's marriage bed lay cold. Unlike my previous sojourns into Anne's world, where it had taken some time to become one with Anne, on this occasion, I found her thoughts, feelings, and memories flood through me without restraint. I buried my face in my hands, the tears stopping as quickly as they had started. My fear was too overwhelming to allow me the privilege of crying. I wiped away the last moisture from my cheeks, and as I drew my hands down my face, raised my eyes to find myself staring into a mirror which hung upon the wall of my chamber. I nearly gasped aloud. Anne looked drawn and pale, and those eyes which had once invited sparkling and witty conversation with their vibrant sexuality and self-confidence, now spoke only of self-doubt and haunted uncertainty.

I knew that a little over a year and a half had elapsed since Henry and I had argued violently at the Palace of Langley—and since I had my sister, Mary, banished from court. I was aware that the intervening months had not been easy for Anne. Theirs had continued to be a relationship of uncommon passion for a royal couple. Storms had followed sunshine and around her, political and court factions continued to shift like quicksand, with figures like John Fisher, Bishop of Rochester and Sir Thomas More, swallowed whole as a result of their opposition to the king's will. Perhaps even more tragically, after the extended and apparently merry summer progress of 1535 resulted in another longed for pregnancy, that, too, had tragically ended when Anne miscarried of a male foetus at around fifteen weeks gestation, in January, 1536. I knew well of the great, immutable pain that she must have carried in her heart following the death of her second child. From 500 years in the future, I had often looked back and wondered about the psychological impact of the death of the child which Chapuys had prophetically called, 'her saviour'. The blow must have been devastating. The child was dead, and not only did she have to cope with the grief of her loss, but with the heavy burden of her failure to deliver on the one thing that mattered—a live, healthy, male heir. And whilst their marriage had been far from over, Anne must have felt the king's love and protection slowly slipping away from her. Oh, the pain to watch the man that had once to so worshipped her, so adored her, evermore turn his attentions to another.

As I stood in the queen's apartments at Greenwich, I was thus subsumed by conflicting emotions: bitterness, sadness, grief, anger— and above all fear. I sensed that in those unbelievably challenging months that followed Anne's last miscarriage, fear had stalked her daily, cruelly stealing from her the one thing that might have saved Anne's life—her political acumen. In retrospect, as I stand here in the Tower waiting for Master Kingston's word that they are ready for me at the scaffold, I can see how everything changed on that Sunday. Transported into Anne's body and overwhelmed with fear, I was unable to command Anne's intemperate nature; frightened, angry and dangerously impulsive, I was led by my heart into the most treacherous of territories. Staring at Anne's reflection in the mirror, I asked the question which had begun to plague me, and although I already knew the answer, I felt strangely compelled to enquire,

'And what of the Mistress Seymour?' I watched my hand in the mirror rise up and touch the 'B' carcanet that once again hung around Anne's slender neck. It was a subconscious desire perhaps to gain strength from that which I had always considered my talisman. Tracing the gold 'B' with my finger, I found myself adding vindictively, 'Is the insipid, conniving bitch here?' There was silence from my friends as Margery shook her head and replied,

'No, Madame, I believe she is lodged well at Carew Manor in Beddington Park, as a guest of Sir Nicolas.'

'At the king's expense and command, I presume?' I spoke curtly, my temper quickened with jealousy. Suddenly, there was a knock at the door, serving to hold my anger in abeyance. 'Enter!' was all that I said. Anne's cousin, Madge Shelton, appeared in the doorway. It was good to see her pretty face again, but I could see immediately that Madge's face was besmirched with signs of her own distress. Her eyes were reddened, her cheeks moistened with tears.

'Sir Henry Norris is here to see you, Your Grace.' I watched as Madge kept her face downcast, ashamed to show her emotion. Anne's own fond affection and loyalty toward her young cousin caused me to forget my own troubles and seek out the cause of her obvious upset.

'What is it Madge? What has distressed you so?' I lifted her chin with my hand, finding a smile from somewhere to reassure her of my good intentions. Struggling to maintain her composure, Madge shook her head silently as her face crumpled, fresh tears spilling over her generous lashes. 'Come now, Madge. Perhaps I can help.' Through great gulps of air, Anne's young cousin finally spoke.

'I have just argued with Sir Henry. I don't even know how it happened.' Beleaguered and confused, Madge shook her head as if embattled by her own inner turmoil. She forged on to speak of what had transpired between them. 'Sir Henry arrived to see you … and for a moment we fell into idle dalliance, sweet words passing between us as ever is our way.' Madge then looked me straight in the eye, as she confessed through her tears, 'I do love him so very much, but I sense that he thinks not to marry me as he has promised! Through her sobs she said, 'Oh, I know I should not have said anything, but I found myself asking when we should be wed …. and … and…' there was a great pause before she had blurted out, 'I felt him draw away from me. Oh, he tried well to conceal it, my lady but I saw it in his eyes…he does not want me, I know it…he thinks that I am a whore!'

'Whore!' the word sparked a dangerous fury within me. I may have just arrived back in Anne's precarious and sinister world, but it had taken me no time at all to be entirely at one with her mind. I knew immediately to what my cousin referred. Anne's memories spilled easily into my consciousness showing me that Madge had indeed been Henry's lover, manoeuvred into his path by Anne and the Boleyn faction in order to distract the king from a more dangerous liaison with an imperialist sympathiser. The ploy was successful, but Madge's reputation at court lay in tatters. Sir Henry was caught between not wanting to offend the queen who had encouraged the match, but reluctant to take the lover of another man as his wife, even if that lover was the king. I sensed Anne's guilt for enticing the girl into something she herself had once rejected with disdain. Perhaps it was this guilt which had truly ignited the fuse that was to blow apart everything that Anne had so carefully built around her. Perhaps it was that I was so heartily sick of seeing women, like myself, being used and manipulated by men who seemed to attend only to their own, so very selfish needs. Suddenly a deadly cocktail of circumstance— anger, fear and guilt— erupted into a cataclysmic explosion of fury, made worse only by Madge's final revelation, which was infused with further pitiable tears,

'Some ladies at court even laugh at me behind my back. They say that Sir Henry comes not to court me, but to see you; that he has given his heart into Your Majesty's hands … that he pretends to like me to win Your Grace's favour.' There was an audible gasp from Nan, for she knew that in the tense atmosphere that had pervaded the court over the previous few months, if it were true, then it was a dangerous game indeed that the king's groom of the stool was playing.

Now that I have reconciled myself with my fate, and my friends and brother already lie dead within the walls of the Tower, it is easy to see that Sir Henry's love for me was only one of courtly love, borne out of his deep esteem for his mistress and queen. But on that day, everything seemed infused with sinister meaning. I became ensnared in Anne's paranoia; she was unbalanced and fighting for her life—thus, what happened next should never have happened. With a fiery fury and a swish of my own purple taffeta gown, I stormed past Madge and my friends, out of my bedchamber toward my privy chamber. Guards on either side of the entrance opened the doors, and once inside, I immediately stalked toward the fine figure of Sir Henry, who waited casually in a nearby window embrasure overlooking the south-facing gardens. He was talking idly with the young Lady Parker.

'Sir Henry!' My greeting cut with a hostile edge. Nevertheless, Sir Henry bowed briefly to the lady he had been speaking with. She withdrew graciously and he immediately turned to face me, acknowledging me with all due deference and good manners. My friend had been smiling, but faced with my obvious displeasure, I watched his own expression collapse into a troubled mix of confusion and concern as I approached him. Sir Henry had no notion of the tempest which was about to rain down on him, and I regret that I failed to show my friend even the briefest courtesy. 'I see you have come-a-courting Mistress Madge again?' Sir Henry made to reply, but in my intemperance, I was in no mood to listen. I forged on, cutting straight to the chase. 'But pray tell me, my lord, why dost thou not make your marriage with my cousin, for she is a fair maid is she not? In front of me, I watched the handsome Sir Henry begin to bluster in his reply.

'Your Majesty, I...I...' Of course, the ever affable and polite Sir Henry had not been expecting such directness, but in his hesitancy, I read only the truth of Madge's words and felt my temper quicken even further. Under normal circumstances, we may have made light of Sir Henry's reluctance, or I may have used Anne's considerable charms to persuade my friend toward the marriage bed. But that was no ordinary day. Anne was blind, struggling for survival and the future of her daughter. Then quite without care, I spoke oh so foolishly. Indeed now, I see how tragically those little inconspicuous words had sealed Anne's fate—and mine—on the scaffold.

'You look for dead man's shoes, Sir Henry, for if ought were to come to the king but good, you would look to have me!' Such innocuous words, are they not, when each is taken individually? But vented as I had, they turned instantly into winged messengers of Anne's doom. I watched Sir Henry's face drain of all colour. The look in his eyes was torn between disbelief and horror that I should have spoken thus. There was something in those eyes that jolted me, had awoken me forcibly from my temporary insanity. It was a moment of recognition between us that what I had said was treason—and worse, I had spoken the words in public. I so wanted was to run after those words, catching up each one within my hands and smuggling them away so that they might never be heard again. Instead, Sir Henry attempted to protect us both by speaking emphatically in his defence.

'Madame, it is not true. Verily, if I were to have any such thought then I would my head were cut off!' Unlike Sir Henry, who had been facing into the room, I was turned toward the window and had failed to recognise that we were not alone. I watched my friend's gaze cast itself over my shoulder. Feeling sick, I hardly dared to turn around. When I did so, not only were we in the presence of Lady Parker, but also two of my ladies who stood near the doorway, both clearly aghast at what they had just overheard. Whilst one of those ladies was Mary Howard, who was ever deeply protective toward me—and who I knew upon pain of death would never speak against my honour—I was horrified to lay eyes upon someone who would not hesitate to make use of my indiscretion. It was the woman who George had once made pregnant and who had been cast from the court by my family, Nan Cobham.

For several moments, a stony silence descended upon the room as everyone, including Nan, Margery and Madge, who had all followed me from my privy bedchamber, stared at me in stunned disbelief. Deeply panic stricken, I reacted precipitously, and made my second, fatal mistake. I turned back to face Sir Henry, barely able to contain my own crushing sense of hysteria. Moving urgently forward until I stood immediately afore my friend, I whispered with pressing necessity,

'Sir Henry, I command that you go forthwith and find my almoner, John Skip, and swear to him upon the sacrament that I am a good woman, clear of all stain on suspicion.' Sir Henry hesitated, still shocked at my most brazen and treasonable behaviour. I wanted to reach out and touch him, to urge him physically to go and find Master Skip without delay. But I dare not make physical contact, something that might be construed as further evidence of an unholy and treasonable intimacy. Thus, I beseeched him with my eyes and begged

446

him plaintively, 'Please, Sir Henry, swear that that you will do so!' Sir Henry nodded his assent and bowed awkwardly, before sweeping from the room to carry out my command.

I would see my loyal friend that evening, and again at the May Day joust the following day, but it would be the last time that we would speak together. One by one, without really knowing it, I was saying my final 'goodbyes' to those who have ever loved and served me well. From inside my bedchamber, I heard the clock chime eleven.

With Sir Henry's departure, I was in shock, petrified at what I had done. I was impelled to seek out a love that I sensed had sustained Anne in her darkest of hours—Elizabeth, always my Elizabeth. Through Margery, I quickly located her whereabouts in the royal nursery, on the west side of the palace courtyard, close to my own privy chambers. Attended by Margery, Nan, Madge and another of Anne's young maids, I moved swiftly back along the queen's privy gallery and into Elizabeth's lodgings. At the entrance to the nursery, I paused, overwhelmed with a pure and blinding love for the bright-eyed, red-haired child that sat in the centre of the room, playing with one of her wooden dolls. The two maids in attendance immediately rose from the floor, where they had been playing with the infant princess, dipping into deep curtsies in deference to my presence. It is strange, I know, that in amongst such sinister events, I felt so overjoyed in that moment to see that one of those maids was Kat Champernowe, the woman, who it seemed a lifetime ago, I had begged to serve a child that had yet to be born. Somehow, Kat had kept her promise, and I was immeasurably thankful for it. Elizabeth, who was now over two-and-a-half years old, finally looked up and upon seeing me, she extended her chubby little arms and I rushed forward in a rustle of skirts, collapsing to my knees and scooping her up into my hungry embrace. She had grown so much, and whilst I silently grieved for the precious moments that I had missed, I melted with joy to hold her close once more. I covered her in a thousand kisses, all the while stroking her hair and telling her over and over how much I loved her. Elizabeth chuckled and planted big, wet kisses on my lips and cheeks in return. For a few precious moments, we were entirely consumed by the infinite love we shared, its beauty and innocence sealing out all that was predatory and which sought to tear us asunder.

However, I could not keep my reality at bay any longer. I thought of Elizabeth on the brink of losing the mother she so adored, rejected by a father who would always see Anne Boleyn in those precociously intelligent and sparkling eyes; of the painful legacy of her mother's disgrace that she alone would have to bear, and how her precious, fragile innocence would all too soon be destroyed. Tears welled up in my eyes; still holding Elizabeth's squirming, lively body close to my own, I lifted up my eyes, and with as much composure as I could muster, dismissed all my ladies except Kat. When they had left the room, I turned my attention toward Mistress Champernowe and spoke in most solemn tones, 'I must speak plainly to you of things that I should, in truth, not speak of...but I believe you love Elizabeth more than your own life.' I hesitated, guessing from my knowledge of Kat's life-long, unswerving service to my daughter that I had spoken the truth, and that I was on safe ground. Without a moment's hesitation, the thirty-four-year-old Kat nodded her head vigorously, saying,

'Oh yes, Your Majesty. I would die for her. I swear upon the damnation of my soul that what I say is true.' I, nodded, indicating that I believed her without question, before forging on.

'Kat, I cannot speak much of the grave matters that churn around me and my family, but I fear that mine sworn enemies are bent upon my destruction.' Kat's eyes widened in fear, however, I sought not to spare her, for I needed Mistress Champernowe to be prepared for what might come, for Elizabeth's sake. I continued in barely a whisper as I had already spoken far too indiscreetly once that day. 'Something is dreadfully wrong, and I fear that my life is in danger...'

'Madame, surely not...'I held my finger up to indicate that time was of the essence, and that she must listen carefully. Kat dutifully fell silent as I went on, 'If anything should happen to me, I beg of you to do whatever you can to protect and care for my daughter. She will be at great risk from those who are not of our faith.' Kat gravely nodded her understanding, before I added, 'You are not alone, for I have already spoken in greatest secrecy with my chaplain, Matthew Parker, and requested the same.' I knew it was true, not only because I had often read of it in my history books, but because I could see the scene in my mind's eye. Just a few days before, Anne had sought out her chaplain after her private mass, grabbing his hand and beseeching him on her knees to have a care for her daughter, should ought come to her. I went on, 'He is a good man of influence and means...and of the reformed faith...he will be able to help you.' Elizabeth summarily plonked herself down next to me, continuing to play happily, and reaching round my neck, I removed Anne's iconic 'B' carcanet, with the pearls and gold still warm from lying against my skin. Pressing it into her palm, I spoke earnestly. 'Keep it safe for her, and if I do not have chance to speak again with Master Parker, and you need to prove to him that we have spoken, show him this, I ...'

I wanted to thank her for all that she would do for my daughter when there was an insistent knock at the door, and before I had chance to collect myself and speak, it opened quickly and my brother George entered the room, looking greatly agitated and much perplexed. My heart skipped a beat at the ever welcome sight of my sweet, sweet brother. But my joy was short-lived, for he swept toward me and rather indelicately grabbed me by the elbow, dragged me to my feet saying,

'Your Majesty, may I have a word?' It was not a question but a command. George spoke with chilling urgency, as I said to Kat,

'Mistress Champernowe, please mind Elizabeth for a moment.' She knelt down next to Elizabeth who, seeing her much beloved uncle arrive, called out George's name, stretching out her arms, asking to be lifted high above his head, which to her great delight, he so often did when he greeted his little niece. With weighty matters bearing down upon him, my brother had no time to play that day, and in ignoring her, Elizabeth's tiny face crumpled in distress. She finally began to cry, kicking her little feet as Kat held onto her trying to give George and me some privacy.

My brother led me over to a fine oriel window, which looked out westwards towards the Church of the Observant Friars and the City of London that lay beyond. The window was open that morning, allowing the sweet scent of summer to waft gently in from the garden below. It was a sign of the dangerous times in which we lived, but the first thing he did was close it, so that we could not be overheard by anyone who inadvertently happened to be passing beneath the princess's lodgings on the footpath below. He turned towards me and with great urgency whispered,

'What on earth have you done, Anne?' I knew exactly to what my brother referred. George was clearly deeply troubled. I sensed his growing disquiet, which only served to stir up my own into a greater frenzy. I shook my head and was barely able to speak. To admit what had passed between Sir Henry and me was almost to accept that I had indeed spoke treasonably.

'Did Sir Henry tell you?' I needed to know if it had come from another source, for I was aghast that already George had heard about the events of that morning. My brother merely nodded his head. It seemed that the gossip had not yet spread too far, and I knew that Sir Henry himself would not be tempted to speak indiscreetly.

'What were you thinking? Did anyone overhear you?' I bit my lip, casting my eyes down, ashamed at my carelessness. George could read me like a book, and confirming his worst suspicions, whispered, 'Who?' Rubbing my throbbing temple as if to wipe away the shame from my face, I admitted the horrible truth,

'Mary Howard—who I know would never speak against me … and Nan Cobham.' It was as if I had struck George with my words as the heavy weight of the truth cast him deeper into despair. But ever the gentleman and always my protector, just as quickly, I watched him muster his courage and wit and reply decisively.

'Then I will speak with father. We must intercept Mistress Cobham and persuade her to remain silent before she is tempted to speak to those who would seek to turn the king against us.'

The king! Of course, I had to speak with Henry. In my overwhelming desire to see Elizabeth, had I forgotten everything that I had learned about how to handle Anne's husband? I knew well that Henry was highly suggestible, and that on account of this, I had to speak with my husband before the likes of Cromwell could seek to influence him against me. I knew that I must act decisively. I must reach the king with all haste. I laid the tips of my fingers upon my brother's chest, nodding vehemently in agreement as I replied,

'Yes, yes, you must go to father. Tell him what has happened, and tell him I have gone to speak with the king myself.' I watched George's brow crumple in concern as he protested,

'Anne, are you sure? I have been with his grace this very morning, and I pledge my troth that he is in a black mood indeed.' However, I

450

was consumed with a conviction that I must see Henry at once. Thus, I made to hurry from the room. Scooping up a tearful Elizabeth in my arms as I went, I half turned, pausing momentarily and catching his eye, as I said,

'George, it is our only hope.' Then, I looked at Kat before turning my attention back to my brother and adding softly and with great sadness, 'I beg you both to pray for me.' With that I swept out of the room, an ever more distressed Elizabeth balanced upon my hip as I tore through the palace in search of Henry, the one man who still had the power to protect us all against the coming storm.

I followed the same route to Henry's privy chamber that I had walked with my brother on the night that I conceived Elizabeth, back in the winter of 1532. It was just over three and a half short years earlier. A snow storm had raged outside the palace, and oh how very different had things been back then! Greenwich had been my home, a place of pleasure and merry disport. Anne was untouchable; loved and adored by a generous prince. But on that fateful Sunday, in my paranoia, I saw only predatory stares in everyone that I saw. It felt as if the guards, who had once fiercely protected me, were fast turning into my gaolers, and that the walls of the palace were no longer my playground, but were becoming my prison.

I was rushing toward Henry to plead for my survival and for the future of our little girl. I knew it would have to be the performance of Anne's life, and for the first time, I felt afraid at the prospect of seeing the king again. As I retraced my steps of that wintry night, I awkwardly shifted Elizabeth from one hip to the other. She was not the small babe she had been when I last held her in my arms. Her weight was considerable, thus slowing down my determined progress. I am not ashamed to say that as I hurried northwards along the privy gallery, I prayed to the God to have mercy upon me, and to give me the courage and wisdom to persuade the mighty King Henry VIII that I was guiltless and without stain of suspicion. In truth, I did not even know if Henry had already turned against me in his heart, or whether, I would be refused entry to his presence. After a short wait, I was thankfully admitted into his majesty's privy chamber.

I found Henry standing alone inside the embrasure of an enormous bay window, staring down onto the great courtyard of Greenwich Palace below. The towering, stone-carved window framed my husband's magnificent stature. With my heart thundering in my chest, I lifted my eyes to be dazzled by the sun, which apparently was unconcerned by my distress, as it continued to stream in joyfully through the south facing window. Even Henry's 6ft 2" frame was dwarfed by its enormity, despite the fact that his broad shoulders were made broader still by a cloak of sables lined with black damask. Standing behind him, I could make out that beyond his rich cloak, white hose and slippers, Henry was wearing his usual bejewelled, black velvet cap, adorned with a white ostrich feather, as well as a great collar of gold, inset with rubies, emeralds and sapphires. My eye traced the king's silhouette down, until I was staring at Henry's chubby right hand which was gripping the silver handle of a mahogany walking stick upon which the king appeared to be leaning his bulky frame, in some discomfort. For a moment, it took me by surprise. I had never seen him thus. Henry had clearly gained considerable weight since I last saw him, and appeared to be suffering with some significant infirmity. Even without seeing his face, I sensed that he was a man much changed.

I was caught off guard, forgetting that Henry had suffered a serious jousting accident just days before Anne had miscarried of her son in January 1536. I had been too wrapped up in my own, sorry predicament to give it any forethought. But seeing him thus reminded me how the king had lain unconscious, teetering precariously between this world and the next for over two hours following the accident, many of his contemporaries being amazed that the king had survived at all when his fully armoured horse fell upon him, crushing Henry beneath its own great weight. Lesser men would surely have died right there and then. Whilst Henry recovered, the accident reopened an old wound in his thigh which would plague the king with excruciating bouts of pain and fever for the rest of his life. Anne had blamed the subsequent loss of her child on the shock of the accident. But despite her pleas for understanding, in the final analysis, she had failed her husband and sovereign lord once more and so, by degree, events began to conspire to turn the tide against her.

My husband did not speak, the silence broken only by the everyday sounds of court life going on outside the window, and Elizabeth's occasional snuffling, and of the clock fixed upon the wall, which continued to count away the last hours of my precious freedom. Finally, Henry spoke gruffly, with not one iota of warmth or tenderness in his voice. 'What do you want, Anne?' A sickening knot tightened in my stomach, but I knew that I could not show any fear. The king was a predator, and if I did so, I would be lost.

'I have heard rumours Your Majesty; vile and abominable things, which stain the good name and honour of your wife and queen. I have come thither to beg Your Majesty, in your bountiful wisdom, to root out such evil and punish those who think to defile me and sever me from Your Majesty's good graces.' The king remained unmoved. It was unnerving not to see my husband's face, and although I sensed that Henry was angry with me, I did not know for sure which way the wind was blowing—whether I had come too late with too little, or whether his mind had already been bent against Anne. Indeed, I feared Henry's silence more than his outright anger; for I had seen his dissimulation hide many treacherous secrets from those he later destroyed. Thus, with some desperation, I stepped forward, heaving Elizabeth up high on my hip, until she was pressed close to my body. She was hot, and I could sense her increasing agitation. Anne's daughter was a child of uncanny intelligence, and I suspect that she could feel her mother's growing distress and consequently, she began to whimper in my arms, clinging to what she could of my gown. I was about to speak again when finally, Henry growled menacingly,

'Pray tell, what is it that these evil men accuse you of?' He was playing games with me, that much was clear. Henry knew something, but was far from ready to share the information, which undoubtedly had so far been laid against me. I knew it would be fatal to hesitate or falter in my reply, and despite the danger, I spoke resolutely in a clear voice; a voice which I hoped would convey the conviction of my innocence.

'I hear tell from my ladies that there are those about court, and close to Your Majesty's person, who claim that I have behaved improperly with certain gentlemen of Your Majesty's privy chamber. I assure Your Grace that these are evil lies brought against me by my sworn enemies.' I pressed forward once more, until I stood just behind the king, imploring him, 'I beg you, Sire, to cast out such vile and slanderous gossip, and clear my name of all suspicion. I swear to you before God that I am your true and loyal wife and subject.' I moved forward again, until I stood within clear sight of the window at his majesty's side. I think perhaps that I was not able to bear Henry's silence for one moment more, and leaning forward, I extended my arm and cried, 'Your Majesty... Henry... Say it will be so!'

Standing at my husband's side, I watched his face in profile, his small, piercing, blue eyes narrow—almost imperceptibly. Finally my husband turned his face toward me in angry rebuke.

'Madame, verily it is a fine thing indeed when a woman thinks to command her husband and king on what he should do!'

'But it is not so, my lord. Please, Henry...' In truth, I did not know whether to speak the rest or no, but I had a mind to address what I feared was Anne's greatest vulnerability—the lack of a male heir. 'My Lord, I know that I have not always borne you the humility that I should have, that I have reacted angrily and with great jealousy to see your affections heaped upon another, but it is only because of the great love that I bear you—and have always borne you.' With my impassioned words, I moved in close to my husband, coming in front of him and reaching out to place my hand lightly upon his chest, my eyes beseeching Henry to see into my soul and to know with all my heart that I spoke the truth. 'My Lord, I have borne you a healthy daughter...'With that I nodded towards Elizabeth, who by now had begun to cry in my arms, '...and although two sons were taken from us, were it not for a strange accident, we would have a son right now. Please, please...I am still young and healthy. My Lord, for the great love that you have known for me, I beg you to let us try again, let me give you a son...and I ask you most humbly—not as a command, but as a most humble request—to cast out those vipers that would seek to tear you from your wife and daughter.'

Henry finally turned to look at me, eyeing me warily. Anger still smouldered dangerously in his eyes. But what hurt most, what tore my heart from my breast, was to finally see the full extent of my husband's disdain for me. In that moment, I saw that his own heart was cold, and that his passion for Anne had been entirely extinguished. Suddenly, the king turned about, and leaning heavily upon his walking stick, he limped across the room saying quite unexpectedly,

'You have spoken well, Madame, and if indeed you are free of all suspicion as you so speak, then you have nothing to fear from me. Go back to your chambers, Anne, for there is a great banquet and masque tonight as you well know. We will be merry as ever we were.' It was more than I could have hoped for. I thought the king to be unmoved, and that my desperate pleas, and the protestations of my innocence had gone entirely unheeded. Yet, there it was—a glimmer of hope. Looking back now, I realise that I was too eager to believe it. I had missed one vital thing; when Henry had spoken these words, his back had been turned towards me. It was easy to lie to the woman he had once so adored when he did not have to look into her eyes and show her the treachery in his heart.

Of this, I was at the time ignorant. I knew that there was nothing more I could say, and humbly took my leave of the king. Stroking Elizabeth's fine hair and burying my own face within it, I walked slowly back toward my privy apartments, holding her close to my body and hushing her to be still. I was still afraid and utterly exhausted, still uncertain as to what the next few days would bring. As I made my way back toward the queen's side, I soothed Elizabeth's disquiet with my sweet kisses, and promised her repeatedly that everything was going to be all right. Yet, I feared that my promises were hollow. Somewhere just north of the river, I wondered what they were doing to Mark, and I prayed that the young man of barely twenty years old would find courage to uphold my honour and his innocence. Outside the privy gallery, the courtyard clock chimed midday.

I arrived back at the royal nursery entirely despondent, clinging on to the merest glimmer of hope that Henry would not forsake me, and that by some miracle, we would all be saved. I handed a somewhat fretful Elizabeth back to Kat, who had waited dutifully for my return, along with the rest of my ladies. She took my daughter in her arms. I was touched as through her eyes, I saw how deeply moved she was by my plight. Before I turned to leave, I gently stroked Elizabeth's silky, soft red curls and lay a kiss that was filled with a mother's love upon her forehead. Hesitating for a moment, I stared deeply into her eyes, as if I were trying to implant in her memory the picture of her mother, and the knowledge of how much she was loved. Eventually, I knew I could tarry there no longer. Turning towards Kat, I whispered simply,

'Remember,' Then I turned my back and finally, left the room.

With Elizabeth safely returned to Kat's tender care, there was only one person who I wanted to see above all others, my beloved mother. Just as I had taken my daughter in my arms and reassured her that all would be well, I too yearned for the same comfort. I knew from my previous time at Greenwich that Elizabeth Boleyn's apartments were directly beneath my own privy chamber, fine double fronted accommodation with pleasant, west facing views over a pretty privy garden and the Church of the Observant Friars. A privy, vice-stair took me down to the ground floor. Several of my ladies followed me to the entrance of the queen mother's lodgings. There was none of the usual chatter and laughter that normally accompanied our progress through Henry's palaces, something had changed that morning. A sinister, creeping threat was slowly engulfing the court, an invisible enemy whose presence was becoming increasingly palpable in every nook and cranny of the palace. We all thought that if we spoke nought of it, then the calamitous events which threatened to engulf us all, would dissipate on the breeze, just as easily as they had arrived.

I waited silently as Margery summoned my mother's page by knocking on the door to her chamber. It was duly opened and I stepped inside. I turned to my ladies and my mother's attendants and bade them leave us. For a moment, I stood silently afore her in the parlour, shocked to see the robust and handsome woman that I had once known looking so much older. Lines hewn by the difficulties of recent years were etched more deeply into her face than I last remembered. Her face, no longer full and flushed with vitality, looked drawn—not unlike her daughter's. Protracted fear and ill-health had chiselled away at Elizabeth Boleyn's famous good looks to leave behind a sculpted, angular visage of far less beauty. I suspected also that the illness which had been evident when we visited Calais in 1532, had marched along its own inevitable path, sapping my mother's strength, gradually leaving behind a shadow of her former self.

Elizabeth Boleyn made to curtsy with some difficulty. However, I moved forward, grasping her hands in mine and making it clear that she should not trouble herself so, as I said with great concern,

'Oh, my dear mother, are you unwell?' Despite my own troubles, I saw clearly that my mother was in some considerable discomfort, her brow pinched, her breathing laboured.

'Oh, do not worry, my child. I have a little difficulty with my breathing today and a slight pain in my chest. But with a little rest and the good Lord's graces, I will soon be on the mend.' Then wanting to change the subject and not trouble me further with the suffering she bore so nobly, my mother enquired, 'But you look troubled, Anne. Is something the matter?' Clearly, the countess had not yet spoken to my brother or father, and I so wanted to spare her the pain of knowing my great peril! I loved her so very much and if, as it seemed, Master Secretary was on the brink achieving what no one else had yet done—to wrench Anne away from Henry—then I knew that along with my daughter, it would be my mother who would suffer the most for it. Suddenly, I felt as if my heart would break for her. I hated Henry for his lies and callous cruelty, but I hated myself more for so carelessly giving myself over to earthly pleasure. My great love for Henry had caused me—and Anne—to pursue a path leading to the pinnacle of Tudor society. But in the end, it had brought me into greater calamity than ever afore I was queen. Much worse, it would bring such immeasurable pain to those who loved me most. Consumed with grief and terror, I dropped to my knees, still gripping my mother's hands, I bowed my head in shame, as tears began to stream down my face.

'Dearest mother, please forgive me. I think to have brought this family to ruin, and I fear that in my sinful wretchedness, I will surely break your heart!' Having shored up my courage to face the enormity of confronting Henry in such precarious circumstances, I finally succumbed entirely to the great jeopardy which faced me, my daughter and my family. Great, racking sobs consumed Anne's tiny body. Letting go of Elizabeth's hands, I gradually sank to the ground, until I was curled over on the stone floor, clutching the hem of her gown and crying over and over through my tears, 'I am sorry, so very, very sorry.' Within moments, my mother was next to me, trying to scoop me up, pressing my cheek close to her breast, as she cradled me in her arms. She tried to question me, to understand why I was so distraught, but each time I went to answer, a fresh gale of tears washed away my words. And so it was, when several minutes later the door to the lodgings was opened and my father and brother appeared, Elizabeth Boleyn had still been none the wiser about the cause of my evident

457

distress. Whilst I heard the door open and close, I was beyond caring who might see me thus. I was alerted only to Sir Thomas and George's arrival through my mother's words.

'Thomas, come hither immediately and help me with Anne! Something is dreadfully wrong but I can't make…'

'Anne, get up … now!' My father's voice cut across the Countess. Clearly, he was in no mood for pleasantries. Just as George had done, I found myself wrenched from my mother's soothing embrace and hauled onto my feet by my elbow. 'George, help your mother up off the floor and then order the servants to bring us some wine…Anne sit down.' It had been a long time since Sir Thomas had commanded me so, and yet, at that moment I felt like a small child again, lost and biddable to do my father's will without question.

'Will someone please tell me what on earth has happened?' George helped my mother to her feet as she scooped up her generous skirts to sit opposite me, her face deeply etched with concern. I knew that in a million years, whatever great calamity she feared had happened, it would never come close to the reality of the tragedy that was about to befall her family. I watched my brother briefly leave the room in order to call forth a page who might fetch us some wine. At the same time, my father recounted the events of the morning to my increasingly panic-stricken mother.

'Oh, Thomas! But what does this all mean? Husband, you must do something!' My father paused as my brother re-entered the parlour, bringing in his wake a page of the chamber who began to pour out a rich burgundy wine into four glasses. When the young man left, closing the door behind him, Sir Thomas stood silently for several moments, swirling his drink rhythmically in his glass, staring into its vortex with such intensity that I wondered for a moment if he expected to find the answer to our troubles within its sweet nectar. 'Thomas?' My mother's deeply troubled voice pressed the matter again.

My tears dried, and although I was utterly exhausted, the hysteria which would overtake me on many occasions over the following days, temporarily melted into abeyance. I watched my father pull at his collar, stretching his neck this way and that, as if to gain release from the invisible noose of his ambition, which had slowly, but surely, begun to strangle him. For the first time since seeing him again, I appreciated that unlike Anne, her mother and Henry, Sir Thomas had outwardly changed little. Always a gaunt looking man, there was little flesh to lose from his slender frame. But when I looked beyond external appearances, I saw that he was not unscathed. The polished veneer of Sir Thomas's self-assurance had been chipped away by fate, revealing a tarnished interior of suspicion and nervousness. The Earl of Wiltshire then spoke decisively; he was not yet done fighting for his family.

'George, you will go forth again and find Mistress Cobham—and when you do, bring her to me.' Clearly, they had not yet located the lady whom I feared might speak against me. 'And whilst you are at it, get that troublesome wife of yours under control.' Sir Thomas extended the arm, which was holding his glass, outward, pointing a finger at George for emphasis as he added disdainfully, 'We do not want that wretched woman deciding to use so inopportune a moment to set her tongue a-wagging in the ears of our enemies.' George, whose ever handsome features were set hard in his desire to protect me, nodded brusquely and made toward the door. I watched my father drain the last of his wine, before he turned about, placing his empty glass upon a nearby table. 'I must find Master Secretary Cromwell and speak to him of this perfidy. He has the king's ear and...'

'He is not here.' In a voice devoid of emotion, I cut across my father with the brutal truth. In front of me, I stared down at my bejewelled hands, holding within them the twisted stem of the Venetian glass that cradled my untouched wine. There was silence in the room for a few, brief seconds, before my father said,

'Who's not here ... Cromwell?' I raised my head to find my family staring at me, perplexed as to the assuredness of my statement. Steeling myself against the ominous news that I must lay at their door, I replied,

'Indeed. I understand that Master Secretary is at his house in Stepney, working tirelessly,' I placed a heavy, resentful emphasis on the last word, 'on behalf of the king.' I tipped back the glass of wine myself, consuming it all in several, great gulps. I closed my eyes briefly, enjoying the simple and easy sensation which my body welcomed before I added, 'Lady Lee's husband...' I referred to Margery's formal title, 'overheard something this morning that was not meant for his ears ... that Mark Smeaton has been taken to Cromwell's house for interrogation by Master Secretary himself.'

'Mark?' George stepped back from the door, letting go of the handle as he did so. He was clearly shocked at this latest revelation.

'Why Mark? What is he being accused of?' My mother addressed me, clearly wanting to know more. Of course, I knew all too well of Master Secretary's plans, but I could not disclose them—to anyone. I feared that even my family, who loved me well, might question Anne's innocence if I spoke of such things before they were public knowledge. Thus, I simply bowed my head in sorrow, as I thought of Cromwell and his thugs, just a couple of miles north of where we sat, setting out to extract whatever they desired from a guiltless man who had no powerful family to protect him. Cromwell hunted like a wily old fox, picking out the weak and the vulnerable, cleaving them off from the court and the protection of those who might have save them from their own sinful lies. I replied simply,

'I fear that great treachery is afoot and that Cromwell means to destroy us.' I put the empty glass on a nearby table; the wine, consumed far too quickly, had already begun to cast its wicked charms, blunting my senses and causing me to misjudge its placement. Everything suddenly slowed down as I became numb, the potency of my father's burgundy lifting me out of my sharp and bitter reality, gently transporting me into another worldly state which seemed somehow kinder and more yielding. I watched the glass teeter on the edge for the briefest of moments. I seemed to watch the unfolding drama for a whole eternity—an eternity which was caught in that one moment. I mused on how the Boleyns also teetered on the precipice with the court watching, waiting, speculating upon which way the die would be cast. Alas gravity won the day, its powerful force drawing the object into its own freefall toward its end, as it smashed into a myriad of irretrievable pieces on the stone floor below. In just three weeks' time, the Camelot that Anne had created would lie similarly destroyed through a brilliant act of ruthless political manoeuvring by Master Secretary Cromwell.

On the wall opposite, a clock, which had been a gift to my parents from the king, struck one o'clock in the afternoon.

That evening the whole court gathered for a great masque and banquet, held as usual in honour of the May Day celebrations. I saw them all, those who had been my friends, and those who had hated

460

me—the latter on account of my religion, others because of my intemperance; others because I took away their influence with the king, and many more through sheer jealousy of my ability to beguile men with my eyes, my grace and my French ways, ways that had made so many women feel so incredibly dull in my presence.

But it mattered not who was there, for it was those who were not present that mattered, and which most preoccupied my mind. There was the prolonged and sinister absence of Thomas Cromwell, who worked into the night; Mistress Seymour, who the king had recently removed from court and from the queen's service, lodged just ten miles away as a guest of Anne's arch enemy, Sir Nicolas Carew. Undoubtedly, she was already being feted by some as a queen-in-waiting—just as Anne had once been, gathering power and influence from those who evermore flocked to pay their respects to the court's new, rising star.

Thus, the court went on that glittering evening as it had done for countless generations. Dancing, feasting and merry-making, whilst seething under the surface was a bed of lies and deceit and impending tragedy. The gossip about the queen's argument with Sir Henry, and subsequently the king, was rife at court, as beneath the masks, curious spectators waited for the drama to unfold, while those of us who unwillingly took centre stage, played our parts. As I sat up on the dais, seeing all my friends dance together, I swear that I watched the dark spectre of death pass between the revellers, laying his cold hand upon the shoulders of those he had marked as his victims.

As the solitary bell above the Church of the Observant Friars rang out midnight, I knew that Anne had just presided over her last full day as Henry's most entirely beloved queen. I felt chilled to the core at what lay ahead of me, tomorrow, the 1st of May, 1536.

Chapter Thirty-Nine

Greenwich Palace,
May Day 1536

It was the fairest of May days. A great profusion of blossom filled
the gardens at Greenwich with a sweet and heady perfume, whilst the
sun climbed undisturbed in a sky, unfettered by even the merest hint of
a cloud. Not even the gentlest of breezes ruffled the luxuriant pastures
of Henry's green England, nor sought to unfurl the flags and banners
which decorated the tiltyard at Greenwich. The first day of May
traditionally heralded the beginning of summer and was a time of joyful
merry-making across the country. At court, the sumptuous celebrations
were renowned; courtiers flocked to Greenwich from their estates to
enjoy traditional pagan celebrations such as May Pole dancing,
alongside feasting, masques, dancing and the great centrepiece of
chivalric ideals—the feted, annual May Day joust.

Every window of the queen's apartments was cast open that day, yet
not a breath of air had the strength to reach inside. I could hear the
activity of an entire court coming to life with excited expectation at the
revels which lay ahead. Everything beyond the walls of my rooms
spoke to me of new beginnings, new life, and new hope; but inside, I
sensed the chill of death's icy grip steadily separating me from a life
that I was not yet ready to relinquish. I stood in the centre of my raying
chamber, whilst the young Duchess of Richmond and the Countess of
Surrey worked silently about me, lacing me into an opulent gown of
cloth of silver. The great weight of matters that touched me deeply
meant that I cared not for idle chatter. My friends worked deftly but in
sombre silence, undoubtedly reflecting the dark mood of their mistress.

It was clear from idle gossip that I picked up the previous day, that
the twenty-year-old Countess of Surrey had recently re-entered Anne's
service. She had been churched following the birth of her first son,
Thomas Howard, the future 4th Duke of Norfolk, in March of that year.
For a moment, I considered the fate of her child; a child who would
lose his father to the headsman in the dying days of Henry's reign, and
who would later plot treason against my own daughter, Elizabeth. Like

Anne, he would come to pay the ultimate price on the scaffold. How strangely the wheel of fate turned! I do not deny that I was terrified at what surely lay ahead of me on that bright May morning, and yet for a time, the strangest sense of calm, borne from resignation and unfathomable sadness, settled itself within my breast following the tumultuous events of the day before.

As I felt the bodice of my gown pulled ever tighter, gripping my still slim figure into an even tinier frame, I reflected gravely on the final, disturbing events of the previous evening. Shortly after midnight, accompanied by several of my ladies, I had made my way along the ground-floor gallery connecting the banqueting house to the queen's privy apartments. About me, torches had sent flickering pools of light across our path, casting our reflection in the many blackened windows which ordinarily provided fine views over the tiltyard to the east, and the great orchard to the west. I was about to mount the staircase that led up to the first floor of the queen's apartments when my father suddenly stepped out of the shadows, causing me to start with fright. His absence at the banquet had not escaped my attention. Furthermore, it was clear that a number of other key gentlemen of the court including Sir William Fitzwilliam, Sir William Paget, Lord Chancellor Audley, Sir John Russell and my Uncle Norfolk, were also nowhere to be seen. I had even approached my brother and in a hushed tone asked of our father's whereabouts. Feigning a lack of concern regarding Lord Rochford's reply, I continued to scan the room, whilst George whispered quietly in my ear that he understood the Privy Council were meeting at the king's behest. It was yet another portentous sign that sent a shiver down my spine. The council was rarely in session until such a late hour, unless it was to discuss a matter of great concern.

Lest we be overheard, Thomas Boleyn took me by the arm, leading me aside from my ladies, before he poured words of poison into my ear—words which caused me to sink toward the ground in despair; only the strong arms of my father preventing my complete collapse, as I gasped for air in a frantic attempt to control my rising panic. The Privy Council had concluded with the unexpected announcement that the forthcoming trip to Calais, due to commence just two days later on 3 May, had summarily been cancelled until further notice. My father made no further comment, nor sought to interpret its meaning, but he was deeply perturbed, and not yet done with the day's business. In my desperate state, Sir Thomas commanded that I return to my chambers and speak to no one of matters unfolding, urging me to keep my counsel. I feared for Anne that such advice was already far, far too late.

With first light, I had awoken from a tormented sleep; shattered fragments of my nightmares flashing briefly through my mind. I was exhausted and gripped with nausea as the reality of the previous day inveigled itself into my memory. My ladies continued to dress me, adorning their queen with costly fabrics, which spoke only of majesty. One by one, I stretched out each arm in turn so that my false sleeves could be tied into place above my elbow; the luxurious velvet of the flared sleeve then being turned back and pinned in place on my upper arm. I closed my eyes, hearing outside my window the delightful warbling of a wren that flitted lightly amongst the blush of roses that scrambled up the walls of the palace. The air was gloriously warm and divinely still. I was filled with the sense that despite everything, there was a world of boundless peace and incredible beauty just beyond my reach; as if it were no longer mine to enjoy. I was already subconsciously passing into another, ethereal world that required me to surrender all earthly pleasures. Although I could watch life continue on about me, the future was no longer mine to command. The feeling was momentary, but it would come ever more to haunt me, as day by day, Cromwell, the King and those who wished to see me destroyed, put in place the process of justice that sought to take my life.

Mary Howard had just begun to place a number of magnificent rings upon my fingers, when there was a knock at the door. I bid the stranger enter. Jane Rochford appeared in the doorway, curtsying momentarily as she addressed me,

'Your Majesty, Lord Rochford is here to see you.' I did not reply but stared at her in silence, willing her to raise her eyes from the ground. Since my return to Anne's world, she seemed uneasy, barely able to look me in the eye. In the time that I had spent in Anne's shoes, I had tried so hard to build ties of loyalty with her sister-in-law. However, after I had been torn from Anne's world in the summer of 1534, Jane had found herself exiled from court somewhat unfairly and with dire consequences. Through Anne's memories, I had seen the blazing rows with Henry that continued through the final months of that fateful summer; painful recollections of defeat and humiliation as the king retained his mistress by his side, lashing out with dangerous anger at his wife's interference. I felt Anne's shame, for I saw that in attempting to protect herself and her daughter, she had reacted precipitously, laying the blame for trying to get rid of Henry's mistress squarely at her sister-in-law's door. Consequently, Lady Rochford had been rusticated from court, her name blackened and her honour besmirched. Anne had felt guilty, but the damage was done. Jane's lack of confidence meant that her character was all too fragile and easily wounded. She had taken the betrayal as a deep personal affront, more evidence of how she was a mere chattel to be used and abused by her powerful Boleyn relatives. It was all too easy for her to divert her loyalties to the Lady Mary, who had long been staunchly supported by her conservative family.

Lost amongst such thoughts, I stubbornly maintained my silence, and eventually Jane was forced to raise her eyes to meet those of her mistress and queen. I felt my breathing steady and calm, my breast rising rhythmically, pressing against the low cut, square neckline that flattered my décolletage. In the quiet, I stared into her soul and saw her fear—and her guilt. Part of me wanted to scream and defile her with my words, rape her with my questions about how she had been able to betray me and her husband so carelessly. Yet, my anger would not come. Instead, I found myself touching the golden cross which hung from the string of pearls that Frances de Vere had so recently placed about my neck. I knew that George and I had been forsaken by our kinswoman, and although I tried to draw strength from my faith, to find the same compassion that the good Lord had done when betrayed by Judas, I could not locate such forgiveness. Although I did not speak of it, my eyes conveyed that I knew what she had done and that I despised her. Finally, I spoke to her in clipped tones.

'Let Lord Rochford come forth.' Jane stepped aside, relieved that I had released her from my penetrating stare. As my brother swept into my chamber, paying deference to his sister, the queen and the two noblewomen who stood on either side of me, I could not help but notice that George did so with the same dashing presence that always followed in his wake. But, I could see all too clearly how recent events had stolen from my sweet brother his carefree joy and playful innocence. The Boleyn world was crumbling fast around us, the wolves were closing in, and the halcyon days were over. We were a hunted species, teetering on the brink of extinction.

I dismissed Lady Rochford and the Countess of Surrey, indicating that Mary Howard should remain behind. I was mindful of how dangerous it was to be closeted alone with my own brother, and sought to keep Mary present as witness to our innocence. I knew with my life that her position and strength of character meant that Cromwell would not dare touch, or question her; and if he did, she would not be swayed by Master Secretary's bullying tactics. Once the two ladies had withdrawn from the room, and Mary had stepped back a distance, I stood facing George, as I asked plainly, 'What news, brother? How is the king this day, and has anyone heard anymore of Master Secretary Cromwell?' My brother hung his head momentarily, before raising his doleful eyes to meet mine. He was afraid; I had never seen him so moved before. After a few moments, in which he clearly gathered himself to speak of what he must, my brother said,

'The king keeps his counsel and is not merry... as for Cromwell... we have heard nothing.' I placed my hand upon my brother's arm, as if to reassure him, gladly sharing what little courage was left to me.

'And Nan Cobham?' My brother shook his head for a second time, his eyes filled with pitiable grief. I sensed the deepest remorse that he had not been of more use to his beloved sister.

'We cannot find her anywhere. I fear you are right sister, she has fallen into the hands of those who would seek to harm us.' I looked away for a moment as I tried to control the panic that was once more threatening to engulf me. When I looked back at my brother, an ocean of love poured between us—it was poignant and beautiful. I watched George fighting to control his emotions, before the two of us collapsed into each other's arms, gripping onto each other as if our embrace would shelter us from the world and the cruel vicissitudes of fate which sought to tear us apart. 'Oh Anne, what will become of us? Where will this all end? I'm so afraid for you.' Then, as if realising the burden he had put upon my shoulders, he continued quickly, 'I'm sorry, I'm so sorry. I should not speak thus. I know everything will be fine...' I knew they were empty words meant to ease my pain. My face pressed against the soft velvet of my brother's doublet. I could not look him in the eye, as my own silent tears finally broke through my defences and began to run, one after the other, down my cheeks. Yes, I cried for myself in my own self-pity but more, I cried for my brother, who selflessly cared only that I should be safe.

I knew only too well that events were about to overtake us both at an alarming pace, and that our time together was fast running out. My brother was to take part in the joust that morning, but I did not want him to leave me. I did not want to shatter a moment of perfect peace in which we would share, for the very last time, a sweet and delicate intimacy that had been ours alone—and which was about to be turned so violently and shamefully against us.

The message which I had been expecting all morning finally arrived from the king. It commanded that I should come forth and preside as queen over the May Day tournament. Thus, I processed with all due solemnity from my privy apartments, through the queen's presence chamber and down toward the gallery which connected the main palace complex with the two, mighty tiltyard towers. That day, I gathered about me all of my friends, for in truth, I needed to draw upon their strength to face what lay ahead. To the entire world, it would appear as if I was, as ever, the king's most beloved wife. Indeed, beyond hope, I prayed fervently that there would be a last-minute reprieve for Anne; that Mark would hold out against Cromwell's threats; that no message would arrive for my husband. I beseeched God to give me strength and faith that *He* would keep me safe, and that all of this had been but a test from which I would arise triumphant, the falcon reborn.

As ever, the queen's entourage cast a glittering spectacle. A vibrant palette of rich, dark colours set against soft velvet, shimmering silks, fabulous damask and a vast array of glittering jewels. I was deeply afraid, and yet determined that I would not let Anne down. Thus, I held my head high, as I headed the queen's party down staircases and along sunlit corridors, a rustle of bristling taffeta accompanying our steady progress. Amongst those ladies attending me that day were my dear friends; Nan, Margery and Joan who was once again pregnant with her fifth child. Also present was Elizabeth, Countess of Worcester.

Unlike my sister-in-law, Jane, the Countess had seemed her usual, larger than life self since I returned to Anne's world. Yet, I was aware that it was my Lady of Worcester who had apparently first laid claim against Anne's indiscretions and inappropriate behaviour. However, if she set out to maliciously slander me, I saw no evidence of it. There was neither guilt or shame in her eyes. Instead her soul seemed at peace, genuinely concerned with both the curious events unfolding at court and the babe she carried within her swollen belly. It occurred to me that Elizabeth's 'accusations' had, as far as she was concerned, been made only as passing comments, of no great significance, to her brother, Sir Anthony Browne. Indeed, she had oft' complained to me of Sir Anthony's priggish behaviour and his tendency to reprimand her for her warm, natural sexuality. Theirs was not a close relationship, holding within it a brittle tension between two characters sculpted from very different clay. I suspected that sadly, during one such incident, and with her usual thoughtless recklessness, the countess had retorted to her brother's admonition that she was no worse than Anne for her flirtatious behaviour. Yes, over the last days of my life, I am sure that Elizabeth never meant to bring into question the queen's chastity. I suspect that she was never even questioned. Others less close to Anne—and more willing to speak against her—had been picked off by Cromwell and his cronies for more searching exploration of 'the truth'. I can tell you as I stand here in the Tower that my Lady of Worcester's accusations were never laid against me at trial. It seems that Cromwell made maximum use of my friend's impulsive, but genuinely innocent words, to catalyse his witch-hunt against me. May God forgive him.

As we made our way along the gallery, I was followed by five noblewomen: Mary Howard, Duchess of Richmond; Frances de Vere, Countess of Surrey; Elizabeth Brown, Countess of Worcester and my aunts; the pregnant Countess of Derby and Eleanor, Countess of Rutland. Then followed my maids of honour and ladies of lesser rank, including my most stalwart friend, Margery Wyatt. My eyes momentarily met with hers. It was to Margery, who was ever the mother figure to me that I had confessed all that I knew, as well as my deepest fears. Stoic to the last, I saw in her eyes only fierce reassurance and undying loyalty, and I silently thanked my friend for it, before turning my head again and pressing forward to meet my fate.

At the end of the 250 foot-long gallery, lay the grand entrance to the tiltyard towers, the disguising and banqueting houses. However, on this occasion, rather than continuing directly ahead into the great disguising house, I turned left, gathering my skirts in my hands to climb the stone staircase, which led up to the first floor. I knew it well. Henry had once insisted that I lodge here with my mother when measles had broken out at the palace, afflicting amongst others, the then Princess Mary. How different things had been back then! We were in the midst of the most glorious days of our romance, and Henry was ever Anne's most humble and devoted servant. Today, in the rooms above, the man whose heart had become cold toward me awaited my arrival.

The king, his friends and nobles gathered to observe the jousting from the first floor viewing gallery, which ran between the two towers. Before I entered, I paused momentarily to gather my courage. I felt physically sick, and I feared that Anne's stout heart might desert her. Far from unaware of my predicament, I suddenly felt Mary Howard take hold of my right hand, which had dropped down by my side. Mature well beyond her years, deeply intelligent and fiercely protective of me, the duchess sensed my hesitancy, squeezing my hand discreetly in reassurance that I was not alone. I knew not who faced me in the room beyond but I imagined many of them would be gentlemen who had allied themselves with the Seymour faction and therefore were no friend of Anne's. Even though every cell in my body, every inkling of my intuition urged me to run and hide, I knew in my heart that there was no escape. I squeezed Mary's hand in reply, silently thanking her for her gesture, before clasping my hands in front of my belly, raising myself up until I was standing tall, and finally swept into the room.

With the announcement of my arrival, all present turned in my direction. It is true that I read into the faces of many of those who stared at me, a myriad of sinister thoughts. In the vivid fantasies of my mind, it seemed that behind the flimsiest of veneers a goodly number of the gentlemen were barely able to contain their happiness at Anne's imminent and great misfortune. As I walked forward toward Henry, I noted them all: the Seymour Brothers, my turncoat cousin, Sir Francis Bryan, Sir William Fitzwilliam, Sir John Russell, Sir William Paulet, Henry Courtenay, Marquess of Exeter, my long-term enemy, Charles Brandon, Duke of Suffolk, and of course, perhaps the man who had come to hate me most, my uncle, the Duke of Norfolk.

It was difficult to walk, perhaps even more difficult than the walk that awaits to take me to the scaffold. Sticky, black animosity poured itself in my direction. I took solace in the few men present who were still my friends and allies, including: my father; Sir Thomas Wyatt, Sir John Wallop and Sir Richard Page. Yet, I knew that many of the gallant young gentlemen who had always served me loyally were to joust in the tournament, and so absent from the king's company. With sweeping majesty, I approached my husband and fell into a deep and elegant curtsy, hardly daring to raise my gaze to bear witness to the cold calculating betrayal which played out behind those piercing, blue eyes. I eventually did so and watched as Henry indicated with a gesture of his hand that I should rise. I see him so clearly in my mind's eye. It was the last time I was to lay my eyes on Henry; the two of us standing face-to-face before God; *He* who surely knows the secrets of our heart. Eventually, through a lump in my throat, I managed to speak.

'Your Majesty.' I could not help but notice a faltering uncertainty in the usual warm, rich tones of Anne's voice. I sensed that she seemed to have lost all confidence in herself as uncharacteristically, I demurely awaited my sovereign lord to indicate his pleasure. It was difficult to hold Henry's gaze in those moments. Although to others, he showed no outward discourtesy toward me, I knew Henry's emotional landscape as well as I knew every thicket and trail that wound its way through the forest surrounding Hever. Henry, who had once dismantled his kingdom to have me, now despised me. I saw it plainly in his eyes. I saw all too clearly how he waited, waited to see if he would be handed the reason to rid himself of Anne Boleyn.

'Madame, let us be seated.' His words were emotionless, practical even, as Henry took my hand within his, and indicated with the other that we should take our seats to view the tournament below. The gallery itself had been designed specifically for such purpose. The first floor was windowless, and upon a raised dais, chairs of state for Henry and I were positioned in full view of the lists below. Stools were arranged behind us in rows, where Henry's nobles took their places according to their rank. In the tiltyard below, large stands full of spectators rose to their feet, as the king and I stepped into view.

Our arrival was accompanied by a fanfare of trumpets, as I sat down next to my husband. I suspect that I looked unruffled, calmly surveying the scene below me, whilst the king merrily engaged in blustering conversation with my Uncle Norfolk, who sat at his majesty's left hand side. Those who would write about the day would later comment that all had seemed well betwixt the king and queen. How well they were deceived! How could anyone know that the king was on the verge of committing judicial murder with his very own wife? Henry was proud of his ability to 'dissemble', and I hid my troubles deep within a body that was already sickened to the core. What could I say? Who could I ask for help? No one. The Sword of Damocles hung invisibly above my head, and whilst my mind raced on elsewhere, the shell of my body remained impassive as I watched events unfold before me.

In Greenwich that day, the tiltyard had been arranged in the usual manner. Directly opposite the tiltyard towers, stands had been erected for the use of the wider court, officials and aldermen of London, as well as members of the public who could afford to pay for a seat. It was ablaze with colour; the stands festooned with flags and banners, as were the brightly coloured tents positioned at each end of the lists. As the morning progressed, only the very slightest of south-westerly breezes had begun to chase down the hillside from Duke Humphrey's Tower, barely stirring the cloth of gold, silver and other brightly coloured fabrics which were hung about the yard below us. Of course, this lack of breeze left the tiltyard baking in the late morning sun. I must admit, that despite my own difficulties, I felt sorry for the gallant gentlemen, bedecked in heavy armour, who were to joust beneath the midday heat.

Suddenly, the king broke away from his conversation with Thomas Howard, raised a bejewelled hand and indicated to the constable on the tiltyard below us that the tournaments should begin. In response, the constable's guard of eight men-at-arms entered the lists and took up their positions. Within moments, as was customary, there followed a thunderous knocking at the gate at the northern end of the list, and in reply, the rather formidable looking master of revels boomed in a resonant voice, so that all might plainly hear his asking,

'What is your purpose, Sir?' Above the hushed whispers of the crowd came the defiant reply,

'My name is Lord Rochford and I am come to accomplish a deed of arms with Sir Henry Norris. I demand entrance into the lists to do my *devoir*!' With all ceremony, the constable turned toward the king, who as tradition demanded, indicated by his gesture that permission had indeed been granted. To a fanfare of trumpets, and a crescendo of cries from the delighted crowd, the gate heaved inwards as, in a great burst of colour, my brother led the 'challengers' into the tiltyard. Bedecked in polished armour that reflected flashes of brilliant light off its shiny surface, each of the eleven men was mounted proudly upon the most majestic horses. Lord Rochford himself riding a fine, grey charger called Braveheart, in homage to the horse's renowned fearlessness. Like the rest of the challengers, George's horse was caparisoned in black velvet, the sumptuous fabric covered with branches of honeysuckle, wrought from fine, flat gold of damask. I watched as the men commanded their spirited mounts, each and every sinew and muscle alive with anticipation, as the creatures pranced expectantly about the lists, their noble riders acknowledging the crowd as they passed by. Once in front of the royal gallery, all the knights lined up and bowed gallantly toward their royal master and mistress. George's eyes met mine, as he righted himself. I knew even from a distance, he was watching over me. I lamented that even the fierce depth of a brother's love could not protect his sister from the approaching tempest.

With the briefest of acknowledgements from me in return, George retired to his pavilion on the southern side of the field, in order to make way for the 'answerers' led by Sir Henry Norris. The ceremonial entry was repeated in similar fashion. This time, my long-term friend headed a further group of ten men, whose horses were trapped in blue velvet and fringed about with gold. To a great cacophony of rapturous noise— cheers, trumpets, and the rhythmic beat of the dronslade, the knights paraded proudly around the ground until they too had paid homage to their sovereign lord and queen. I could not help but notice that Sir Henry kept his eyes averted from mine. Beneath the unruffled outer veneer, I saw only too clearly how the king's closest confident was deeply disturbed by the undercurrents of tension that eddied dangerously beneath the merry pastime of the day. I was sure that of all people, it was Sir Henry who most keenly felt the creeping sense of doom which encroached evermore upon the court. Reluctantly, he found himself at the centre of a tense drama, caught up in a maelstrom, which he had never wittingly courted.

Eventually, the king's groom of the stool turned his horse about, and retired with his men towards the tents, which were pitched at the northern end of the tiltyard. Here several grooms waited to take away horses which were not immediately needed, whilst pages flitted industriously about their masters, helping make final preparations for the tournament ahead. It took only a little time for those competitors enlisted to fight in the first tourney to be readied for combat. Eventually, the pleasant music which had entertained us as we waited was drowned out by a further herald of trumpets. It was a call to arms, and a great roar was let out from either team as two small groups of men were instantly dispatched at a gallop, hurtling towards one another to fight with the sword on horseback.

The horses charged forward, their manes whipped up in flight, nostrils flared, eyes wide with wild anticipation. I watched as their ears flicked nervously back and forth, a great thunder of hooves accompanying the charge. The fine cloth in which they were draped was caught by the wind and billowed about their flanks. The headlong charge ended in a clash of furious battle, one knight set doggedly against the other. About the tiltyard echoed a crescendo of battle cries and cheers from the crowd, intermingled with the sound of iron slicing upon iron. The knights manoeuvred their horses deftly, turning this way and that as they undercut one strike from below, before wielding their mighty swords to block another from above. Even in my desperate state, it was a thrilling spectacle to watch, the battlefield recreated with all its raw aggression and pulsing adrenaline.

After some time of furious engagement, my brother's team emerged as the victors, raising their swords to salute the crowd, as the defeated withdrew honourably from the field—as was expected by the code of chivalry. At the same time, my brother and his team came forth graciously to accept their acclaim from the royal party. Thus, it continued for some time; individual tourneys, with one knight fighting another on foot and later, young knights such as Henry Fitzroy, Duke of Richmond running at the ring in a display of their promising jousting skills. The crowd clearly delighted in the day, filling the lists with their cries of appreciation for a battle won, or a task successfully accomplished, whilst drawing in their collective breath when a man fell to the ground, or took a near miss to his body. It was difficult not to be drawn into the intensity of masculine aggression on display and of the courage and noble chivalry that unfolded before me. On several occasions, I applauded with delight at some great feat of courage, or smiled appreciatively toward the gallant knight who offered humble submission towards his mistress and queen—until I became aware of my dangerous folly. Shrinking back nervously into my seat, I cast my eyes furtively this way and that, to see if I was being watched by those close to the king, men who prayed daily for my undoing.

On one such occasion, I found my gaze meeting that of Thomas Wyatt, who was seated next to his sister to my right, at the far end of the front row. His face was full of questions, but mostly concern and fear. I had not spoken to Thomas directly since I returned to Anne's world for the final time. I knew that he had sat with Council 'late into the night on the previous day; and if not from there, then surely from his sister, he would know of the great calamity that approached me and my family. A desperate sense of helplessness passed between us. His eyes full of warning for the terrible danger that I was in, and mine silently beseeching his forgiveness for the bloody days ahead, which Thomas himself would later claim had broken his heart and stolen his fleeting youth. Only too aware that any man I was seeing dallying with was put in the gravest of perils, I consciously turned away to look back over the lists, as another fanfare of trumpets heralded the pinnacle of the day's competition—the joust.

Leading the answerers, Sir Henry was first to take part in the lists, jousting against his counter-part, my brother, George. Bedecked in his full suit of tailor-made armour, I watched Sir Henry reach down to accept his shield in his right hand from one of his pages. However, his favourite horse, a huge chestnut destrier, Neptune, seemed unusually unnerved, prancing restlessly about as Sir Henry struggled to steady his mount. In his other arm, my most loyal of friends made to take his lance. Although he managed to do so, a groom and page were sent scuttling for cover in the process, as Neptune reared and kicked out with his front hooves. My friend then attempted to position his horse for the career, but Neptune steadfastly refused the request, constantly backing away or shying up against an invisible force, which seemed to have frightened this most mighty of beasts. I suspected that the horse sensed his master's growing disquiet, and showed only what several of us that day had struggled to conceal—naked fear. Next to me, I watched the king lean forward awkwardly, clearly still in some considerable pain from the wound festering in his thigh. Henry's eyes narrowed, as he surveyed the belligerent refusal of his friend's mount to engage in the joust. As a result, his majesty beckoned to a nearby page, leaning forward on his walking stick, he commanded,

'Lend Sir Henry one of my horses.' The page scurried in all haste down toward the tiltyard. Henry cast a glance at me, and I, in return, smiled, appreciating the king's gesture. Finally, finding something of little consequence, and of no controversy, I spoke to Henry for the first time since taking my seat at his side.

'It was kind of you, my lord.' Henry smiled the faintest of smiles which could have spoken of many things, but I chose to hope that it was the first olive branch of peace to pass between us that day, thus breaking the coldness that had hung in the air since my arrival in the gallery. A few stilted pleasantries were then shared between us, as we waited for the king's horse to be made ready. All the while, I desperately wanted to ask Henry if I had truly been forgiven, if he had heeded my pleas from the previous day. And I tried, oh how I tried to form the words, questions that would just not come. It was strange, as I had only ever known a fearless ease and familiarity in our conversation and yet, I suddenly felt tongue-tied, as if everything had been said between us; as if we had literally exhausted our words. With a start, I realised that there seemed to be nothing more to say. Was Henry bored of me? I remember wondering if it had all been that simple. Did Henry ravage and devour Anne, searching in every nook and cranny until he unravelled her—the enigma that was Anne Boleyn? Did he gorge himself so indulgently in his fantasy, until the sweetness of their passion fermented and sickened him to the core? Whilst Henry looked the other way, speaking easily with Charles Brandon and my Uncle Norfolk, I stared at him as such thoughts taunted me, and I wondered with all solemnity how it had ever come to this.

It took some time for his majesty's own horse to be brought from the stables and made ready for the joust, but eventually all was set. With the onset being sounded by the trumpeters, each man placed their lances at rest, and charged toward one another in a thundering blur of colour and sound. I swear my heart always stopped beating during those moments, as the two men met in the middle; for although the lances were blunted, gallant knights had been seriously injured, and even died in the heat of mock battle. I remained outwardly impassive, but inwardly I was unable to breathe. I closed my eyes momentarily, as if by shielding my sight, I might avert any disaster.

Perhaps disadvantaged by the change of horse, Sir Henry received the first blow with force enough to cause him to reel back in the saddle, just managing to retain hold of his lance and shield in the process. A great gasp rose collectively from the crowd, as horses were reeled in, and in a cloud of dust, swiftly turned about at the far end of the list, only to race once more at full tilt against the other. This time, Sir Henry delivered the *coup de grâce*, a blow which caused his lance to shatter and send fragments of wood exploding in a cloud-burst of pieces, ricocheting off his opponents shield. A huge roar erupted from the crowd, the king himself crying,

'Huzzah!' and breaking into thunderous applause. I was increasingly heartened by Henry's apparent merry engagement, and found myself eventually starting to relax by degree, as my husband seemed in turn more attentive to my presence, even at one point calling for wine to refresh and replenish his beloved wife.

And so the jousting continued, challengers and answerers in impassioned combat under the sweltering afternoon sun. To my enormous relief, as minutes turned to hours, nothing untoward transpired. No message arrived for the king, and Henry still remained at my side. I had little idea of the time, but by the length of the shadows upon the ground, I suspected the hour approached three of the clock. I knew that the competition had but one more round before the tournament would draw to its grand, ceremonial close. I suspect that I had finally begun to breathe easily, daring to believe that as yet, all might be well. On the lists, Sir Francis Weston, who was fighting on my brother's team, had just won a resounding victory over the Earl of Surrey. With magnificent pride, he manoeuvred his white charger in front of the royal gallery, handing his lance to a page, who scurried to his side in order to assist his master. The crowd were enraptured by his performance, and cheers accompanied his parade in front of his majesty and the queen. Lifting off his helmet, Sir Francis bowed to pay his homage to his sovereign lord and lady, his horse lifting his hooves in turn, as if dancing gracefully with equal gratification.

As he raised his head, I saw how the heat and dirt of the afternoon had taken its toll. Sir Francis's face was glowing with sweat and smattered with dust. Without thinking, I withdrew a lace handkerchief from within my sleeve and stood up. Leaning over the balcony, I tossed it into my friend's waiting hand. Sir Francis urged his horse forward, catching it with ease, right in front of where the king was seated. The crowd enjoyed the gesture of simple chivalry, and gratefully, Sir Francis kissed the handkerchief to yet more cheers, before bowing again and wiping away the grime and sweat from his brow. It was the most spontaneous and innocent of gestures, entirely in line with the code of chivalry, so well-known and valued at Henry's court. It was a moment in which Anne was just herself, forgetful of those who watched her, and whose twisted minds and malevolent intents would seek to construe her flirtatious spontaneity into covert acts of depravity and concealed lust. Indeed, I laughed for the first time that day, and smiling, I turned to remark to Henry about how valiantly and skilfully his knights had fought.

As I did so, I found I could not breathe. It was if I had received the most vicious of blows. There, in front of me, sat the king, reading a note scrawled on parchment which had been handed to him by a young man I recognised as Master Secretary's nephew, Richard Cromwell. Henry's eyes slowly rose up to meet my own terrified gaze. I knew what words of poison had just been poured into the king's mind. I knew that it was the note from Cromwell that I had feared all day—and which I thought I had cheated. It was the note that carried the tale of Mark's confession—that he and I had committed unholy adultery. My hand reached up involuntarily, touching lightly upon my stomach. Part of me wanted to be sick, and yet part of me wanted to fall to the ground and beg Henry to turn away from the sinful lies that were surely being cast against me. And yet I could not move. In Henry's eyes I saw only pure, unadulterated hatred. I saw his accusations of my callous unfaithfulness and my cruel, mocking deceit. And I saw him wash his hands of me— of Anne Boleyn. Oh dear God, I swear that I tried to speak, but my mouth was suddenly so parched that the words would not come forth. Indeed, with enormous dread, I realised that in the light of Mark's confession, all that I had spoken of with the king on the previous day would be seen as yet more evidence of treachery and guilt in trying to cover up my faithlessness.

Then, it was as if everything happened in slow motion. I watched the king crumple the note within his bear-like hand, slowly and deliberately, all the while never failing to take his eyes from mine. I knew, oh yes, I knew that without words Henry was telling me that he would crush me with the same ease—and without mercy. With his hand still clutching the parchment, Henry abruptly rose to his feet, snapping his gaze away from mine and stormed off in a hailstorm of fury. As I watched his towering frame disappear from sight, all I remember in my terror was hearing the 'tap, tap, tap' of his walking stick on the gallery floor, marking the deathly rhythm of the king's hasty and furious exit.

'Henry!' Barely a whisper escaped from my lips. And just like that he was gone. It was over. The last days of Anne's life were set before me.

The gentleman who knelt on the ground in front me, reached forward to kiss the ring upon my hand. It was an act of homage, and as he raised his head so that his eyes met mine, I saw them brimming with tears of regret. 'Your Majesty, I kneel before you to most humbly crave your pardon for my most sinful wretchedness, although Lord knows, I fear that I do not deserve such kindness.' John Skip, my almoner, released my hand and bowed his head in shame, before adding mournfully; 'I fear that I have brought you into great calamity, Madame. I have sinned against you; you who has ever been a kind and loving mistress unto me. And in my wretchedness, I prostrate myself afore you willingly and beg for your understanding and forgiveness.'

I stared down at the gentleman silently, as I recalled for the thousandth time Henry's abrupt departure from the tiltyard. All eyes had rested upon me as the king was heard making his way down the staircase, followed by several of his nobles, commanding that his horse should be brought forth immediately, his voice trailing away as he left. Eventually, everything had fallen silent. I stood still, staring transfixed upon the doorway through which my husband had departed. I was so afraid that for what seemed like minutes, I was unable to move, until the gentle voice of Thomas Wyatt enquired with a mixture of concern and anxiety about what would be my pleasure. Would I wish the tournament to continue? I had snapped my head around, gazing upon him as if I had never seen him before. I was no longer in my body—just a witness, cast out from a mind which was slowly crumbling in terror.

When Thomas had pressed the matter again, I shook my head, in barely a whisper, I replied that the time for 'Maying' was done; that it was over. In my words, he understood my deeper meaning, that all we had built around us, our fairytale without end, was no more. With that, I too turned and swept from the gallery.

With my ladies in attendance, I returned to the queen's apartments, entirely bereft and engulfed in a howling despair. I was in fear of my life, and desperate for the safety of those I loved. In my presence chamber, I was met by my almoner, who looked almost as tormented and desolate as I felt. Opened up by the rawness of my own sorrow, I took pity on the young man who I knew well, and who Anne had long since patronised and promoted at court—John Skip. He requested an audience, and I had nodded indicating that he should follow me into my privy closet where, before my place of private devotion, the reformist cleric had fallen abruptly to the ground in a heap of sorrow. I turned my attention back to the present moment and looked down upon my trusted friend, for I had only ever known his loyalty. Thus, I was confused as to what he might have to confess which could be of such consequence. Looking back, I see now how something indistinct had tugged at my consciousness, something that I felt I should already know. But plunged suddenly into Anne's body and the calamitous events unfolding around her, I had little time to collect myself or rise above the heavy weight under which Anne had laboured since the tragic miscarriage of her son just four months earlier. I clasped my hands before my stomach, cocking my head to the side, as I enquired softly,

'What have you done? What is it that you feel you must confess?' Master Skip hesitated, shaking his head, no doubt in disbelief of what he must say. Finally, he courageously met with my own enquiring gaze, and began his explanation of the events as they had unfolded.

'After the sermon on Passion Sunday, I was approached by Master Secretary Cromwell, who made his displeasure clear.' I knew immediately that John Skip referred to the sermon that Anne had asked her almoner to preach on 2 April, just four weeks earlier. The sermon had been clearly meant to attack men such as Cromwell, who increasingly had the king's ear, and who Anne believed were advising him wrongly over the matter of reform in England's monasteries; advice that I sensed she felt was fed purely by personal gain. In commanding such a public assault, Anne had unequivocally condemned the king's first minister, throwing the gauntlet to the ground and challenging Cromwell to a metaphorical duel from which there could only emerge one victor. It would be a bloody battle; one Anne would lose. Master Skip continued, 'Madame, Master Secretary spoke to me in barely veiled threats; that I should consider where the balance of power increasingly lay...that it was clear that the king...forgive me, Your Majesty for what I must say...' I saw the great discomfort of the cleric's unspoken words caused him to flush with shame,

'Go on.' I commanded evenly.

'...that his majesty was evermore tiring of Your Grace and seeking to take another wife to beget him an heir; that if such a thing were to transpire, my words and present loyalty would surely bring me into considerable difficulties...that I might consider my great folly and look to make amends...that such a show of loyalty to his majesty, the king, might in time save me from the most wretched of ends.' I watched Anne's almoner stare at the ground, the heavy weight of his sorrow upon his broad shoulders, as he finally confessed his deed, '...and so, when Sir Henry came to me declaring your innocence, my weak and feeble mind was beset by the work of the devil, and I went forthwith to Sir Edward Baynton. I fear in doing so, I have delivered through the back door information which will be used against your person in the most foul and abdominal ways.' With the end of his speech, I watched him slump forward upon himself, in disgust of his betrayal.

Fresh to the misery of suffering, and acutely aware of the frailty of the human condition, I could not bear to turn away such a heartfelt request for forgiveness. I saw in Master Skip's eyes his deep misery, and how he truly repented his actions against me. In my longing to be forgiven myself, I could not deny the moment an opportunity for compassion, and was about to say as much and take away my almoner's burden of guilt, when my attention was caught by a great commotion in my privy chamber. I looked toward the door, hearing the sound of raised voices growing louder, one of them my brother's, another that of the young Madge Shelton—clearly in a state of some altercation. George was obviously looking for me, and Madge was resisting his request, explaining plaintively that I was holding a private audience with my chaplain. Despite her protestations, the door to my closet was abruptly wrenched open and there, framed in the doorway, appeared the youngest of the Boleyn children.

For a moment, there was silence between us as George looked first at me, and then towards Master Skip, who remained kneeling at my feet, his head turned, no doubt startled by George's precipitous and somewhat inelegant entrance. It was clear that my brother was deeply disturbed, and in a state of considerable agitation. I doubted not that he had changed quickly from his armour, for his dark curls were moistened with sweat, his elegant clothes noticeably dishevelled, as if he had dressed in a hurry. He had been the first to break the silence.

'Your Majesty...sister... I need to speak with you on a matter of some urgency.' I noticed how his gaze shifted again toward my almoner, as if indicating the need for us to be alone. However, I could not countenance placing either of us in a situation which could so easily be used against us. I alone knew the depth of our plight. Despite John Skip's confessions, I trusted him as ever I did. Thus, extending my hand so that my palm faced outwards in a gesture of authority, I said,

'Whatever it is you must say, brother, you may speak of it here, for I have nothing to hide.' As I spoke, I also indicated to my almoner that he should rise and bear witness to the events unfolding. George hesitated, unsure of himself, but I held his gaze defiantly, willing him to speak his mind, whilst in my heart, I knew full well the news that he was about to lay at my door. Accepting my authority, my brother spoke, his voice full of nervousness, his attention flitting here and there as he asked,

'What happened, sister? We saw the king leave and then, shortly afterwards, a guard arrived commanding that Sir Henry accompany his majesty to Westminster. Yet it seemed that there was much displeasure in the command, almost as if he was under arrest.' I cast my eyes to the ground, the great weight of heavy resignation assaulting once more my beleaguered heart. At that moment, I was not afraid, but quietly reconciled to my fate. Indeed, it was to be ever thus over the next three weeks; cast betwixt feverish terror and calm resignation, with little control over which way my emotions were tossed—until by God's grace I would eventually find my peace and deliverance from the weighty cares of this cruel world. Thus I answered my brother,

'The king received a note via Master Richard Cromwell.' I paused for a moment raising my eyes to meet with my brother's. I knew with my words and the deliberate nature of my gesture that George would understand my meaning and the connection between Richard Cromwell and his illustrious uncle. 'I fear that there are those who spread salacious and wicked lies about me to save their own skins.' I thought about how Cromwell and Anne had been locked in a ruthless struggle for supremacy, before adding reluctantly. 'And I also fear that Sir Henry has been unwittingly and innocently snared in a web of treachery that has been cast about us by those who love me not.' Ever impetuous, and eager to defend my honour, my brother retorted boldly,

'Then I must ride in all haste to Westminster and explain to the king how he has been deceived!' George sensed the terrible danger which faced us but he was innocently unaware of the unprecedented scale of the coup that had been set in motion by our enemies. Placing my hands upon his shoulders, I beseeched him,

'No! You must not go... I command it!' My brother recoiled at the vehemence of my reaction. He had expected me to give him my blessing to ride with all haste to the king and plead my case before his majesty. For without the king's command, I was stranded at Greenwich, separated from Henry and unable to influence him. George seemed torn between the duty to his queen and his deep, instinctive love for his sister. I watched him shake his head as he replied,

'I cannot in all conscience leave my friend alone against those who would seek to do him harm. Just as I could no more stand by and watch the sister whom I love as dearly as life itself be slandered by evil men who are moved only by jealousy and pride.' Then George took my hands, raising them to place a heartfelt kiss upon the ring of my coronation, as he went on, 'Forgive me, Your Grace, but my honour requires that I do battle for my friend, my sister and mistress.' I tried to be brave but knew that there was no force on earth that would stop my brother in his quest. I was so afraid for him as I realised that I was about to say goodbye to the only brother I had ever known; to the man I had come to love so deeply. I knew that I could not stop him, and yet still I begged him not to leave me as without him, I would truly be alone. But I felt so entirely lost, and knew not how to stop the wheel of fate which was ruthlessly gathering momentum. As we stood facing each other, on the brink of our final goodbye, I wanted to tell him how much I loved him, but I dared not, in case my words of sisterly affection were misinterpreted.

I wish I had spoken for my silence ultimately made no difference. They are all dead and gone, and I wait patiently to join them in heaven. I remember those last few seconds; George's beautifully chiselled face, his sweet brown eyes full of brotherly love. He had managed a smile— a smile that had filled me with joy so many times. It was his last selfless gift to me; the memory of his smile and of his eternal love etched forever in my heart. With a stroke of his hand lightly across my cheek, he turned and walked courageously toward his fate.

When George was gone, I collapsed to my knees entirely bereft. I knew I would never see him again. My ladies gathered round me, trying to soothe me with their words, but they could no longer help. I was alone with only God to watch over me. I was inconsolable. The sound of my wretched sobs and howling grief echoed through the rooms of a palace that was rapidly becoming deserted. For with the departure of the king, Henry's Lord Steward, the Earl of Shrewsbury and his Lord Chamberlain, William Sandys quickly set about organising the transfer the entire king's household to Westminster. It was like watching rats flee from a sinking ship as courtiers scurried like vermin out of Greenwich, making their way on horseback or by barge upstream towards Whitehall. Even my ladies seemed to fritter away, some following their husbands, others making their way to Beddington Park to pay their respects to Mistress Seymour.

Just as I was wrung dry of tears, my father entered my chambers and brusquely commanded me to my feet. The Earl of Wiltshire was not a sentimental man, and although I saw his deep concern for our plight, I do not know how much of that anger was directed at Anne's reckless flirtatiousness and failure to bring forth a healthy son, or whether Thomas Boleyn was furious with himself for failing to protect his family and the honour of the Boleyn name. I will never know for our time together in my chambers that day was fleeting. I did not need to explain to my father what had happened, he had been present in the gallery when the king received the note from Cromwell. Nor did he need me to explain its likely contents and ramifications. The earl had witnessed enough first-hand to guess what might be afoot. Instead, he helped me to my feet, and asked with some urgency,

483

'Where is George?' Wiping my eyes dry with my lace handkerchief, I recounted to my father my recent exchange with my brother. Sir Thomas turned his head and stared out of the window, the feverish stream of his anguished thoughts was as clear as if he had spoken them aloud. He was calculating his next move. I had not expected what he then said. 'It will be difficult to intervene. The king has commanded that I do not seek to meddle in his affairs.' I don't know why I recoiled at his words. Perhaps it was the starkness of my father's evident banishment from the king's grace which brought home the full extent of his majesty's displeasure toward the Boleyns. I was left with nowhere to turn. The utter futility of our struggle crashed down upon me and I could only think of protecting those who I loved. Finally, as my father continued to gaze out over the orchard below, I laid a hand gently upon his arm. It was if I had suddenly tapped into the well of my strength once more, and with a clear and steady purpose I commanded,

'Father, there is nothing more to be done with the king. I fear we are in the hands of God now.' Sir Thomas turned his head to look upon me, perhaps surprised by the calm conviction of my words. 'There is one thing that you can do here though.' My father frowned as I went on, 'I ask that you make sure that my Lady Mother repairs with all haste back to Hever, away from all…this.' I circled my hand around to indicate my disgust with the cesspit of human nature in which I found myself drowning. Then, I added the truth, 'I cannot bear to think of her here; spurned on account of the king's great displeasure toward me—the cause of which she is entirely innocent.' I could not say that I did not want her in London where she would hear the obscene gossip about her children spread like wildfire through the taverns, streets and great houses of the city; where she might be tempted to stand witness to Anne and George's executions, a sight that would surely haunt her every waking hour thereafter; or if not that, hear the roar of the Tower's cannons signifying their demise. I thought of Hever and its peaceful tranquillity. I knew that Elizabeth Boleyn would never be spared the heartbreak that would follow on from her children's death, but perhaps at a distance she could imagine that it was not real, that the two of us would one day ride home again to sweep her up in our loving embrace.

After the longest of silences passed between us, the earl nodded his head slowly, and turned to go. Suddenly, I reached out my hand, stopping him as I rested my fingertips forcefully upon his chest, our faces but a hair's breath away, as I whispered, 'Do not let my Lady Mother come to see me, make any excuse, for I fear if she were to come here, I could not bear to let her go.' I knew well enough that Anne's mother would not want to leave her children to face their fate alone. Her love was a mother's love, and I knew if she could, she would gladly die to save us. So, I added a white lie. 'Tell her, it will all be righted soon enough and then I will summon her back to court.' Thomas Boleyn continued to stare at me, as if fathoming for himself what I might know that caused me to speak with such finality. He clearly recognised that my final words were meant as a sweetener to help my mother swallow the bitter pill of her departure. 'Please father...will you do as I ask?' It was a plea, to which the Earl consented. I watched Thomas Boleyn leave the room, carrying with him the heaviness of a broken man. Just as he was about to disappear, I spoke up for one final time, 'Father!' Sir Thomas turned slowly toward me, as I added more softly, 'I love you both very much.' I watched as he made to speak, as if he wanted to tell me the same. Indeed, I willed him to tell me the same, but the words would not come. Instead, I watched him nod his head, unable to deal elegantly with his tattered, conflicting emotions, before he turned his back toward me and disappeared from my life.

Two hours later, from the windows of my privy chamber, I watched as the mounted figures of my mother and father headed out from the palace toward its southern gatehouse, followed in turn by a trail of precariously-laden carts, carrying their belongings and their shattered dreams back to Hever. I leaned my forehead against the cool glass, my fingertips resting lightly on the window pane, as the sad train trundled its way up hill, *en route* toward Dover Road. To my left, I noticed the merry banners and flags that had bedecked the tiltyard being taken down in the lustrous glow of the late afternoon sunlight, whilst through the nearby opened window, the lazy buzz of a bumble bee foraging for pollen momentarily took me back to Anne's childhood home. I recalled the same sound in the rose garden at Hever that fateful day when I had first woken to find myself in Anne's shoes. It was the day I first met Henry, and he asked Anne to be his queen. The events of our time together poured one after the other through my mind, followed by immeasurable sadness and furious anger at my betrayal. Yes, I hated Henry that evening, livid that I was being discarded as if I had never meant anything to him. But my thoughts were broken by the pain I felt at losing my mother, as I watched the train of carts reach the brow of the hill. It was almost unbearable. However, there was one more twist that I had not considered.

As my parent's party halted at the summit, I saw my father bid his wife goodbye before turning his horse north-west and headed directly for Henry's Palace of Whitehall. My beleaguered spirit was gratefully uplifted at the sight of Anne's father heading toward the eye of the storm. I thought my father had washed his hands of me. Yet his hasty ride back toward court gave me hope that it had been otherwise. In all honesty, I do not know exactly what happened after he rode out of sight, toward Westminster. I choose not to think that he willingly abandoned me, but that rather like me, upon his arrival at Henry's court, he found that there was nowhere to turn. Henry had determined to destroy me, and the king's will was absolute.

With my father gone, I watched my mother head off in the opposite direction, riding toward the idyllic county of Kent. Slowly, the train passed over the ridge of the hill and out of sight. I prayed silently for my father and brother. They were all that stood between me and the tsunami of destruction which hurtled in my direction. But, in my heart, I knew that they would be utterly powerless against the ruthless might of the king who had already set his heart upon another, and bent his will toward my destruction.

Chapter Forty

Greenwich Palace,
Tuesday, 2 May 1536

I will be forever grateful for those most loyal friends who remained staunchly and defiantly at my side during the last twenty-four hours of my freedom, especially Margery, Nan and Joan. Then there was my beloved Mary, Duchess of Richmond, who flatly refused to yield to her young husband's request to visit Beddington Park and pay her respects to Mistress Seymour. Even then, the tragic events unfolding around the duchess were shaping her seventeen-year-old character and forging a steel core that would henceforth never bend to the will of any man.

I kept my own counsel on the matter, but from my knowledge of history, I knew that Henry Fitzroy had barely as long to live as Anne. Indeed, it had lately become clear to one and all that Henry's great hope for his bastard son to be legitimised as his future heir was fast dissolving. The Duke of Richmond had been blighted for several months by a pernicious cough that evermore tore through his slender body. Mary saw, as well as anyone, how the spectre of death clung evermore to his person. The duchess was disgusted by her husband's readiness to embrace the king's wench. Jane had long been Anne's implacable enemy—but Mary could not forgive her for acting so treacherously against her mistress. She despised his lack of moral fibre, and I was certain that she would not grieve his passing. Alongside the duchess were her close friends: Frances, Countess of Surrey; Madge Shelton, as well as Elizabeth, Countess of Worcester; and two of my mother's sisters, the Countesses of Derby and Rutland.

And so began my last day of freedom. I awoke with the dawn chorus at around four o'clock in the morning on 2 May. I lay curled up on my side, motionless, watching flecks of dust shining momentarily as they floated across a shaft of sunlight that cut through a gap in the curtains. I watched and yet I was not there. Exhausted from a fitful sleep, I was entirely lost in the frantic chatter that filled my mind.

It was only forty-eight hours since I had found myself once more in Anne's body, but it felt like a lifetime of suffering and agony had passed before me. In my despair at Anne's plight, I had thought little of what had become of me in my modern day world. In the vacuum of that solitary night during which I felt so incredibly alone, images of Daniel and Henry flitted interchangeably through my mind, both of whom I had loved with a fierce passion, and yet all I had known in return was cold-hearted, callous betrayal. As I tossed and turned my way through that night, I sensed that in my modern day life, I was dead, and that there was no going back. I was stuck in Anne's world, fated to follow her story to the end. Greatly disturbed by these thoughts, I lay unmoved for several hours until Nan and Joan stirred on the pallets at the end of my bed, as Margery entered my bedchamber, throwing back the curtains and allowing a glorious summer's morning to flood into the room. Several times she tried to persuade me to rise, and I turned her away each time until I was eventually lured from my self-pity by the arrival of my almoner, who had been summoned to comfort me and say mass in my privy closet.

When finally I rose, I allowed my ladies to dress me in a fabulous gown of crimson velvet, with a rich cloth of gold kirtle and matching sleeves. The square-cut neckline raised the outline of my breast, and set against it, was a trim embellished with pearls, rubies and diamonds; all of which matched the billament of my hood; an elaborate carcanet draped about my neck, and an expensive girdle was hung from my waist. A heavy, sombre atmosphere clung to my chambers. After hearing mass, and praying to God to help me, I summoned Lady Bryan to bring Elizabeth from the nursery. As ever, my daughter greeted me with a profusion of kisses, before settling to play happily on the floor of my privy chamber, while I broke my fast. As I dined, I watched Elizabeth pick up a wooden doll in her increasingly dextrous hands, and then turning towards me she held it out, with a joyful smile radiant upon her angelic face. Elizabeth was completely unaware that in a few short hours she would never see Anne again, and I had no idea how she would ever manage to reconcile the fact that her father had murdered her beloved mother.

Once I had eaten, I found that I could not bear for Elizabeth to be taken back to the nursery. So, in the company of my ladies, I left the queen's lodgings with my daughter holding my hand. I noticed from the clock in my privy chamber that it was shortly after ten o'clock in the morning. We made our way outside to take the air in the garden. In truth, I did it only for her. As Elizabeth laughed, giggled and played, I wanted to fill my daughter's growing and impressionable mind with as many happy, heartfelt memories of Anne as possible. And so, I determined that we would walk and play in the gardens at Greenwich, basking in the warm sunlight of another glorious, May morning.

With Elizabeth dictating the pace, we meandered idly towards the south-west corner of the palace precinct. It was an area defined to the north by the Church of the Observant Friars, and to the south by the closed tennis play, in which I had previously whiled away many happy hours watching Henry, my brother and friends contest their masculine prowess. With the king and court upstream at Westminster, and Anne clearly *persona non grata,* there was strangely nowhere I had to go, no important ambassadors or dignitaries to meet, no audience to play to, except my ladies. Thus, we were unhurried, unfettered by the stuffy formality of court as the palace fell into silence with only a skeleton staff remaining behind to support a disgraced queen.

The gardens overflowed with an abundance of colour, scent and foraging wildlife. I stopped often, kneeling down to put my arms around Elizabeth, to share in her delight at the sight of a magnificent peacock in full display, or to accept a daisy that she had plucked from the grass to proudly present to me, as if it was the most precious jewel in the kingdom. Eventually, on the other side of the gravelled perimeter of the garden, we came close to the entrance of the open tennis play. Much to my surprise, the sound of heated competition was clearly underway within. The noise of masculine voices, cries of glory, hails of defeat, and the familiar thwack of the ball against the heavy and unforgiving racket, floated out from inside. With the king gone, I was intrigued to know who had remained behind, and of course Elizabeth's keen and bright mind was at once captured, her insatiable curiosity causing her to dash forward through the opened doorway. Despite my heavy heart, I could not help but smile at her exuberance, and followed her quickly inside.

Plunged into the cool shadows of the viewing gallery that overlooked the playing court, much to my surprise, I found Sir Francis Weston deep in the heat of battle with William Brereton's younger brother, Urian. Both gentlemen made to stop and acknowledge my presence. In turn, I thanked them well, smiling from behind the netted grill, before leading Elizabeth and my ladies toward the far end of the tennis play, and into the dedans, where we could sit awhile and enjoy the game. It was hard to believe that in this oasis of peace and pleasure that surrounded us, elsewhere those who had drawn their plans against me were moving in for their moment of triumph. It was if everyday life was continuing as normal when absolutely nothing was normal. My friends did their best to hide their fear, a fear which left me sickened to the core.

Elizabeth clambered upon my knee immediately I seated myself under the canopy of estate. It was a picture of perfect love and innocence, as I put my arms around her and drew her in close, bending my neck to bury my face in her soft reddish curls. We watched the two men battle for a while; Urian Brereton declaring himself my champion and playing with fierce commitment, so fierce that I lamented to my ladies that I had not placed a bet upon the game.

Suddenly, at a distance, I heard the insistent, angry marching of footsteps upon the gravel path outside. My head snapped round to look across the court toward the doorway through which we had entered. I could not breathe and began to feel my heart thundering in my chest. I was not alone. My ladies heard the same commotion that was growing ever louder, ever more threatening. Suddenly, I turned my head toward Margery, and leaving no room for protest or complaint, I begged her,

'Margery, take Elizabeth…now…get her away from here!' Margery hesitated. I saw her blind fear, the words of disbelief that she wanted to share but would not come. Momentarily, the sound changed as it became more present, more resonant as a contingent of six men lead by the constable of the king's guard appeared at the doorway and made toward me. I was aware that both players had stopped the game of tennis; the service ball, running down the penthouses without anyone to care for its presence. Urian and Sir Francis watched the men approaching, curious and unsettled as to what was unfolding before them. Time was of the essence, I could not bear Elizabeth to see her mother's arrest. I did not want that to be the last thing she remembered of Anne. I stood up abruptly and thrust my daughter into my friend's arms, commanding her, 'Go now!' With one final kiss planted upon my daughter's suddenly flushed cheeks, Margery snapped out of her state of shock and turned swiftly. Elizabeth, of course, did not understand why the sweet time with her mother had been so rudely snatched away from her. Ever the head-strong child, she began to squirm and kick, crying out for me as my friend ignored the child's pleas and disappeared from sight through a different doorway, one which led out of the other side of the building. I stared at that doorway with such desperate longing—how to say goodbye to your child, your own flesh and blood, knowing that I would never see her in this world again? I swear that I felt a part of my heart ripped out from my chest, trailing its blood in her wake. Yet, there was precious little time for such thoughts, for the yeoman of the king's guard was fast bearing down upon me. I sensed Nan draw in close on one side of me, Mary Howard on the other, as if they were bravely trying to shield me from harm. I turned to face the constable and his men, drawing myself up to my full height and digging deep to find the courage which I knew I needed for what lay ahead. He halted a few feet in front of me, bowing briefly, before righting himself and saying,

'Your Majesty, the king has ordered that you come forthwith immediately and present yourself to members of the Privy Council, who as we speak, await your presence in the council chamber.'

'On what grounds?' I retorted.

''Tis not for me to say Madame, but the king commands it.'

'And my ladies?' My tone was curt. Anne was fiercely proud, and I refused to give any man the satisfaction of seeing me flinch at words meant to intimidate me.

'Your ladies are to return to your apartments to await further instructions, Your Grace.'

'No, we must…'It was Mary Howard who had spoken up from a collective gasp of anguish arising from my ladies. I held up a hand before she had chance to say more. I wanted none of my ladies cast into the line of king's anger. Turning my head over my shoulder, I said,

'My Lady of Richmond, it is the king's command, and we should not forget that we are his majesty's true and loyal subjects. You will do as Master Constable commands. Return to my privy chambers. I will see the council and come to you thereafter.' I then turned my head back toward the constable, staring defiantly at him for a moment, before softening my gaze and inclining my head in a gesture of submission to the king's will. There would be time yet for goodbyes, for I remembered that the tide on the Thames turned in my favour, and if I was to end this day at the Tower, as I feared and dreaded, then the constable would have to wait until later in the afternoon before he could convey me by barge into her waiting arms.

It had been so long since I had walked unaccompanied by my ladies in Anne's shoes. As queen she had been attended everywhere. But that day I walked alone, following Master Constable who strode along purposefully, his physical invincibility betrayed only by the slightest of limps, no doubt collected during his time serving as a soldier in the king's army. In my wake came not my ladies, but the six burly men-at-arms, three pairs walking side by side, all carrying gruesome looking halberds, as they escorted me towards the council chamber, which at Greenwich, was in the north-west corner of the royal apartments.

As a woman from the future, I knew what accusations awaited Anne. For the last twenty-four hours, I had known that this moment would arrive, and had been planning her defence, rehearsing how she would command her heart and emotions in the face of her private terror. As we walked, I reminded myself that my conscience was without stain, and asked Christ, my Redeemer and Saviour, who had also been cruelly and unjustly accused, to fortify my faith and courage. I needed a clear head to face my accusers, and that it would be my own hysteria that would defeat me.

As Master Constable led our party back through the queen's privy apartments and along the western privy gallery, we met several members of the queen's household, lower ranking nobles and servants, who would normally have melted away at the first inkling of my presence, and who stood confused, barely able to know what they should do. They were caught between court etiquette and burning curiosity as it was obvious that their queen was no longer at liberty. I knew that the news of her arrest would spread like wild fire along the banks of the Thames from Greenwich to Westminster. Thus, within a couple of hours, crowds would gather along the river to watch the unprecedented sight of a queen being conveyed to the Tower under arrest for the most abominable of crimes.

I stood facing the doors of the council chamber, the constable stepping aside as they were opened and my arrival announced. Keeping my head held high and my eyes fixed afore me, I stepped inside to face those sent by the king to accuse me.

The council chamber was a room of average size, about thirty feet by twenty-five feet; an octagonal tower built into its north-west corner with several mullioned windows facing out over the Thames. The chamber was entirely clad in wainscoted panelling, a couple of tapestries hung upon the walls; and a large, half portrait of Henry that glared down on the long table in the centre of the room. I had never been there before, as only men were allowed to take part in council meetings, so I was unaware of the protocol. On that day, three men were seated on one side of the polished oak table with their backs to a north-facing window. A single chair was arranged on the opposite side—clearly this was meant for me.

I moved forward, standing opposite the men who remained unmoved. I said nothing, yet conveyed everything I needed to as I waited for them to stand for their queen, as custom and courtesy required. I would never be intimidated by them, nor give an inch of ground that was mine by right of my innocence. Reluctantly the men scraped their chairs back and rose to their feet. Accepting their submission, I then swept up my skirts before seating myself with all due dignity, and took a moment to appraise the men dispatched to do the king's work.

First amongst the three was my uncle, the Duke of Norfolk. Beneath his cold exterior, I saw the warm fires of his self-satisfaction glowing at my calamitous misfortune. Thomas Howard and Anne Boleyn had only ever tolerated each other, but even those days were long behind them. I was sure that Norfolk was at the centre of Cromwell's plot to overthrow Anne. The premier nobleman in the land had seen little of the personal power or glory that he had expected to follow in the wake of his niece's stellar rise at court. Even worse, she had been instrumental in catalysing the burgeoning reformation in England, something that was repugnant to his Catholic faith. As I watched him flick through his papers, I remembered only too well Norfolk's threat that he would gladly see Anne thrown to the wolves, and when it came, he would do nought to help her. And so my uncle had been the first to stand as my accuser. No doubt he had spent the last twenty-four hours grovelling at the king's feet, casting aspersions upon my good name and frantically trying to inveigle himself into Henry's good graces. There he sat in front of me, full of this own grandiose pomposity; and from the safety of dry land, smugly watching the Boleyn ship slowly sink beneath the waves.

Sitting on my uncle's right hand side was the second of Henry's enforcers; Sir William Fitzwilliam, a forty-six year old brutish looking knight, whose coarse features and tongue betrayed the origins of his northern roots. His ruthlessness and stern demeanour was hewn from the hard granite of Yorkshire, and firmly chiselled into his face, which was hard set, penetrating and unforgiving. He was a lifelong friend of my husband's, having been chosen as a companion to Henry when he was still Prince of Wales and William was only ten years old. Once Henry had succeeded his father, Fitzwilliam worked tirelessly in his majesty's service, rising steadily at court until Wolsey had spotted his potential as a diplomat. His diligence and impressive acquittal of his tasks, as well as his mastery of French, meant that by 1525, Sir William had advanced still further, becoming treasurer of the king's household.

Sir William's eyes slowly rose to meet mine as I pondered on such things. For a moment, we were locked in silent contempt for one another. For whilst Master Treasurer had toiled without question to bring to pass the king's wish for a divorce from his first wife, it was not on account of any love he bore Anne Boleyn. His steely blue eyes conveyed only his distaste for everything that I stood for, and for my part in the destruction of his much loved, one-time master, Cardinal Wolsey. Not only that, but I knew that Sir William's ties to the conservative faction at court ran deep. He had once been an advocate of Thomas More and was considered a 'very good servant' of the Lady Mary. He also happened to be the step-brother to Sir Anthony Browne, who, in my opinion, has been the catalyst of the whole affair against me. I suspect that being politically shrewd and cunning, like my Uncle Norfolk, he had seized upon the opportunity laid before him to exact his revenge upon a woman who he had long since despised.

With the faintest sneer, he broke with my gaze and turned his head toward Norfolk, clearly waiting for my uncle to speak. As he did, my gaze travelled to the right, to take in the appearance of the third gentleman of the council—Sir William Paulet, who sat as my interrogator on my uncle's left hand side. Of course, like all the gentlemen at court, I knew Sir William Paulet well; he had accompanied Henry and me to Calais in 1532. At fifty-one years of age, Sir William still had an abundance of sandy coloured hair and a close-cropped, rather pointed beard and moustache. I think his dark blue eyes had been the only ones to look upon me with any kindness that day. From my earliest acquaintance with him, I was intrigued by this knight who seemed to have few enemies, a feat so rare at court that it could not help but catch my attention. As a result, I had studied his manner carefully, and found him always calm, courteous and amiable to all. Yet, when I was back in my modern day world and had the chance to forage through my history books and learn more on this enigmatic character, I finally understood the secret to his success. As it turned out, Sir William Paulet would live to the grand old age of ninety-seven. Indeed, I was shocked to read that he would die whilst still in office to my very own daughter, having survived the great twists and turns of religious reform in the intervening years. In all, Sir William Paulet would change his religious inclinations five times and declare proudly that he had survived on the account of 'being a willow and not an oak.' Yes, the future first Marquis of Winchester was a pragmatist first and foremost, allowing matters of conscience to be a handmaiden of necessity. I knew that Mr Comptroller, as Sir William had been known since his appointment in 1532, was the only one present who harboured no personal motive to see my destruction.

Suddenly, my Uncle Norfolk spoke. His voice was silky smooth, as if he were savouring every moment of being the harbinger of such bad tidings. I noticed that he did not deign to even look at me, raising his eyes to meet mine, only with his final question.

'Madame, we have been sent on command of the king. You have been charged with the most evil behaviour and we are duty bound to formally charge you with committing the most ungodly crime of adultery against his majesty's person. You are accused along with Sir Henry Norris, Master Mark Smeaton and one man more. Furthermore, both the former of your co-accused have confessed to the treachery of your crimes against the king. How do you plead?' Thomas Howard sat back in his chair, folding his hands across his belly, savouring the sweet taste of revenge. I, however, was determined not to betray any notion of the fear which gripped my body, nor to give him the satisfaction of seeing how close I was to the edge of hysteria. I teetered precariously, holding on to sanity by my fingernails, whilst peering down into a firmament of madness. Somehow, and I have no idea how, when I spoke it was with a calm conviction of my innocence, the tone of my voice asserting my incredulity and steely resolve to be cleared of the lies which had been laid at my door. Of course, all hope that somehow the course of history would change, and that Anne would be saved was fading fast, but strangely it was still not entirely lost. My belief that the king could never turn entirely from a love which had been so beautiful remained tethered delicately to me by a silken thread. The time had still not yet come when all hope would forever be extinguished. And so, as I did at my trial, I engaged in my defence with a passionate rebuke.

'Then if it is so, Your Grace—and indeed such words are truly strange unto my ears—I think that their confessions have been extracted by foul means, for I am, and ever have been, the king's most true and loyal wife, and that no man but my husband has ever touched my person.' Norfolk absorbed my words, before he began to slowly shake his head three or four times, saying,

'Tut, tut, tut…Madame. Not only do you think to commit such heinous crimes against his majesty, but you have the temerity to deny your depravity in the light of two confessions most soundly acquired. For Mr Treasurer here, he heard Sir Henry Norris speak against you at Westminster not twenty-four hours ago.' Norfolk nodded toward Sir William Fitzwilliam, at whom I glowered defiantly. I admit that perhaps I should have remembered every little detail of the events unfolding, but my overheated mind could grasp only the broad brush-strokes of the story; the fine detail dropping away and resurfacing again only when prompted. But with my Uncle Norfolk's words, I recalled Master Treasurer's role in extracting what Sir Henry would later claim was a false confession by devious means. I had no doubt that Sir William was a man of great cunning. I would never find out what Sir Henry had purportedly confessed to, or how Fitzwilliam had achieved such a feat as, from that point forth, my gaolers would strictly control the flow of information that would reach my ears. As for Mark, the statement that his confession was freely given made me laugh out loud, as I retorted,

'Sound means?' I threw my head back, an overtone of panic

creeping into my voice, before I gathered myself again and fixed my uncle defiantly once more. 'You know as well as I do, Uncle, that these accusations are false and have been most cruelly laid before the king by certain men at court.' I glowered first at Sir William, making my wrath at what I believed to be foul tactics plain upon my face, before turning once more to the duke. 'Certain men, who knowing well my great displeasure with their actions, and who, for their own ends, have sought to turn the king against me.'

It was strange that in that moment, for the first time in a long time, I should think of Katherine. As I sat there, almost daring them to go further, I recalled Katherine's impassioned speech to Henry at the Blackfriars hearing back in 1528, the hearing which had meant to bring about a resolution of *the king's great matter*. How, having pleaded with the king, she had then walked out of the court and refused to take part in the trial whose authority she flatly refused to accept. I was in a much more dangerous situation than Katherine ever was, and I did not have Henry to appeal to. Yet, I was inspired by her feisty defiance and the dignity she always placed in her role of queen. Yes, for the first time, I found myself empathising with the woman who I had displaced and who, for so long, I had so bitterly resented. I realised that I had stated my innocence and had, as their sovereign queen, nothing more to defend. As if through my actions I might make a more powerful statement than with my words alone, I stood up abruptly. The men were taken by surprise. They hesitated for a moment, my Uncle Norfolk frowning with great displeasure. Sir William Paulet was the first amongst them to stand in respect, saying as he did,

'Your Majesty, we are here on the king's command, and have questions that we must ask you about your conduct. Please Madame, take your seat.' Master Comptroller spoke kindly, indicating with an outstretched arm toward the seat behind me. I noted he was the only one of the three men to speak to me as if I were not yet convicted of my crimes. However, I was furious at being so cruelly handled by my Uncle Norfolk and Master Treasurer, and so I replied with equal civility, but determined authority,

'My Lord Norfolk...gentlemen...I have stated my case of innocence. I have not offended the king with my body, or even in my thoughts, and I marvel at such accusations, whereof I know nothing. I am clear from the company of any man, and have no stain of guilt upon my conscience. It is clear that the king has taken it in his head to rid himself of me for a reason that now resides some ten miles hence at Beddington Park. What is more, I fear my lords that ought I might say will make little difference. He who has thought up and plotted this affair has done so with great diligence, setting his majesty's mind to be filled with pernicious doubt about my faithfulness toward my sovereign lord.' I referred to Master Secretary Cromwell, and knew full well that each of the gentlemen present would also understand where I pointed the finger of blame. 'I will pray to God to forgive his wickedness—and yours.' I directed my last comment squarely at my Uncle Norfolk, for I was enraged that he could act in such a way that would clear break his own sister's heart. I hated him. Norfolk rose to his feet, followed by his lapdog, Sir William Fitzwilliam, as he said gravely,

'Then Madame, it is my duty to inform you that according to the king's command, you are henceforth under arrest. You will return to your chambers and be placed under guard. You may not leave your chambers at any time.' Although, I knew it had been coming, his words set my heart pounding, my knees almost giving way beneath me. I swallowed hard, willing myself to retain my composure. I felt every muscle in my body tighten as I braced against the fear that was overwhelming me. I thought of Katherine and her proud Spanish defiance which I was determined to copy. Drawing myself up to my full height, I inclined my head as I submitted to the will of my husband, saying,

'If that is the king's pleasure, then so be it. I will go willingly and with a humble heart. Good day, my lords.' I turned and swept out of the room. I was desperate to get away from the atmosphere that had been suffocating me. With every ounce of self restraint, I stopped myself running back to my privy chambers, there to fall into the arms of my beloved friends.

Once back on the queen's side, the doors to my privy chamber were closed behind me by the guards who had been placed there, not to protect me, but to keep me prisoner. I watched over my shoulder as the doors clicked shut, before turning my attention toward my ladies. They had been waiting for my return in a high state of anxiety. For several seconds, we stared at one another. I saw their faces full of questions, and yet in deference to my position, they waited for me to speak first and explain what had transpired. I did so plainly.

'I have been arrested for adultery against the king's highness, along with Sir Henry Norris, Mark Smeaton and one man more—who they will not name.' Several of my ladies gasped aloud, their hands reaching up to their faces to cover their mouths in horror, whilst Nan and the Countess of Worcester, who were always more freely expressive with their emotion than the others, began to cry openly. In all honesty, part of me felt as if I could dissolve into an ocean of tears. But suddenly, seeing my ladies so distraught at my predicament, I felt overwhelmed by the need to protect them. I did not know if once the tide turned, I would ever see any of them again. I could not bear to think that after all the times that we had shared together that they would remember me—Anne Boleyn—as a woman destroyed by fear and drowning in a well of self-pity. Thus, I once more fought to retain my composure on foundations that were fast crumbling under the rising tide. Elizabeth spoke first through great sobs of sorrow.

'Your Majesty, I cannot bear to think of you so cruelly accused. How could such charges be laid against you, when it is plain for all to see that you are never left on your own?' I could not bear to speak of how her careless words had been scooped up and moulded into a ball of vicious lies; a ball which had gathered its own momentum before crashing down upon me. I suspected that eventually she would find out, but I could not bear it to be yet. I knew how anxious she was for me and for her unborn child. And so, I took her in my arms and shushing her to quieten her grief, I dabbed away her tears and said,

'My Lady Elizabeth, you must calm yourself, as you have your babe to think of. Do you hear me?' Through tearstained eyes, Elizabeth gathered herself and nodded her understanding. I knew of course, what they did not, that in just a few hours, in all probability, I would be taken away from Greenwich to my imprisonment in the Tower. I had little time left to me. Every second suddenly became more precious than every jewel I owned. There was much I wanted to say, and so I began, 'You all must promise me this…' I took Lady Elizabeth's hand in mine, before turning to face the others and added, '…whatever rumours you might hear about how this affair came about, I want you to be sure that

I know in my heart that no person here has acted with any ill-will toward me. You must remember that there are men about the king who are bent upon my destruction, and would use any titbit of gossip, any innocent exchange to serve their purpose of my undoing.' Then I added more quietly, 'I fear that I may have only a little more time in your company...' I paused for a moment knowing that what I must say next, explaining the stark brutality of the current situation, would cause a good deal more distress amongst those who loved me well, '...and in truth I do not know whether I will see any of you again.' As my words sent a new wave of horror sweeping amongst my ladies, I forged on. 'We must remember that the good Lord was wrongly accused, and we must take heed of how the Lord's disciples quarrelled amongst themselves when their master was gone, accusing one another of his undoing. I beseech you to take comfort in my surety of your everlasting friendship, to be of good cheer and to support one another in the days that come.' I looked around the room: Madge hung her head, clearly fighting back her own tears, whilst the indomitable Mary Howard, and my dearest friend Margery, nodded with all the composure and solemnity that they could muster. Despite their inner turmoil, they were determined to be strong for me, and I was indeed most grateful for it.

Then I turned my attention to the errands that I needed my ladies to run. I sent the Countesses of Rutland and Derby to prepare some clothes and personal jewels from my wardrobe in case I needed to have such items at my disposal. Joan, I despatched to the nursery on the pretext of officially informing Lady Bryan of the king's command, and passing on my love to the Princess—instructing her to secretly deliver a letter to her cousin, Kat Champernowe, on my daughter's behalf. It was one of three letters which I had penned in the quiet of the night before, spending several hours alone in my closet. By flickering candlelight, I had scrawled down the story of Anne Boleyn for her daughter, making clear Anne's innocence and everlasting love for her only child. I was determined that Elizabeth should know the truth about her mother first-hand, and not through stories construed by men with their own agendas. Joan hid the letter inside her stays, and I watched her slip outside, thankfully unmolested by the guards at my door.

I left Elizabeth, Countess of Surrey, to be comforted by Frances de Vere, whilst commanding Mary Howard to organise dinner to be brought to my chambers. I was not hungry, but I wanted to keep my ladies busy to distract them from their despair, and allow me time alone with the two women who had been my dearest companions from the beginning of my incredible journey in Anne's shoes. Indicating that I wished Margery and Nan to follow me, I retired into my privy closet. When the door was closed and we were alone, I was suddenly overwhelmed with the deepest sense of appreciation. I saw with a poignant and painful clarity how precious such friends were, and I addressed them with deep sincerity.

'My dear friends, I fear that our time together is nearly over.' Nan swallowed hard, whilst Margery went to interrupt, but I held up my hand, indicating that I needed to speak. 'You have both been my true and loyal companions, which I now see is one of the greatest blessings which can be bestowed upon a person. My only regret is that I have, even for one moment, taken this friendship for granted. But in most humble wise that a heart can think, I lay myself open to you and declare my great love for you both—and Joan and Mary, whose love and faithfulness shall in turn be rewarded in heaven.' I breathed deeply, gathering myself to go on, 'I ask that whatever happens, hold firm the memory of my innocence and always think the best of me. For none of what they will bring against me is true.' Both ladies nodded vehemently. It was hard for me to speak of what I had next to say, 'I fear that—as we have known for some time—the king seeks to replace me with another mistress.' Then, I addressed Nan specifically, for I knew this touched her most keenly. Her beautiful blue eyes were wide with fear and unbearable sadness. 'I realise, Nan that your husband is at court, and that in your devotion to him, you may wish to remain close. You must not out of loyalty to me withdraw from court. You have my blessing to stay and serve Mistress Seymour. I wish you only to be happy and no doubt you will soon have a growing family of your own, and many things, other than the pretty baubles of court life, to keep your interest.'

I reached for the two further letters off my ornate writing desk, which I had penned the night before and with the heaviest of hearts, I met Margery's gaze and asked, 'Margery, take these letters and deliver them. One to my sister, Mary, whom I fear I have deeply wronged.' I knew by then that Mary had moved to Calais with her husband William, who was stationed there as a soldier in the king's garrison. 'If you get the chance, tell her that I am so sorry for what happened between us, but that I am glad she is safely away from court. Tell her she must not try to intervene for me, for I fear that the king in his anger will lash out at her. Ask her to forgive my parents for their pride, and beseech her to comfort our dear mother for she will be heart-broken for what I fear will come to pass. Then go to the Countess of Wiltshire, my most dear and beloved mother. Give her this second letter, and please tell her that I am innocent of all the charges that they will bring against me.' I wanted to say that George was also innocent, but of course, I was acutely aware that the news of Lord Rochford's arrest was not common knowledge and therefore dared not mention it.

'Of course, Your Majesty…Anne.' I smiled as Margery used my Christian name, as we usually did in private and it reminded me of our long and easy intimacy. Unable to hold back our tears any longer, the three of us collapsed into each other's arms, overwhelmed by the pain of our parting, and our terror at what lay ahead.

I dined in silence, seated for the last time under the great canopy of estate in my presence chamber at Greenwich. As I looked out across the room, I recalled the courtiers who had once flocked there to get a glimpse of Henry's new queen. However, on that afternoon, my chambers were virtually deserted. My friends had gone about their duties diligently, serving their mistress both reverently and solemnly. Just as the cloth upon my table was being cleared, the door to my presence chamber opened and in swept the unwelcome sight of a number of the king's Privy Council headed by my Uncle Norfolk. He was followed by several council members, all of whom I suspected had congregated at Greenwich for this moment, including: Lord Chancellor Audley, John de Vere, 15th Earl of Oxford, Sir William Paulet, Thomas Cromwell, Lord Sandys and Sir Francis Bryan, who Cromwell referred to as the 'Vicar of Hell'. As they came before me, I rose slowly to my feet, assured of the miserable journey which lay ahead of me. Nevertheless, I bravely enquired,

'My Lords, why do you come thus?' I could not help but gaze down at the scroll of parchment in Norfolk's hands. With my words, he began to unravel it, adjusting the parchment to a distance where his ailing eyes might readily focus, my Uncle Norfolk began to read aloud.

'Anne, Queen of England, at the king's command, you are hereby arrested for the crime of adultery against the king's majesty and we have come forth to conduct you to the Tower, there to abide during his majesty's pleasure.' Barely concealing his pleasure, he added, 'I must also inform you that there will be no time for packing, your ladies will not be following you, and nor are you permitted to see the Princess Elizabeth. Appropriate attire will follow you to the Tower in due course; the king, in his graciousness, will provide money for your upkeep.' Whilst he had been talking, several gasps erupted from my ladies. Although I kept my eyes fixed on my uncle, I heard muffled sobs break the tense silence, as the reality of their mistress's predicament was finally brought well and truly home. I stared at him for a moment. Even though I had been prepared for what was coming, my panic was beginning to set in. I was determined that I would not forget who I was. Anne was a queen, ordained so by God, and silently, I beseeched Anne to help me to find the courage to walk bravely, without shame, to the barge that awaited me at the privy stair. After the briefest of moments, I collected myself and nodded before answering,

'If it be his majesty's pleasure, I am ready to obey.' Norfolk then indicated that I should step down from the dais, as he instructed,

'Follow me, Madame.' I wanted to be sick, but swallowed hard to suppress my rising nausea. I remember passing some of my ladies, who had been close by in attendance, their ashen faces and eyes brimming with tears as each one dipped into the deepest of curtsies, before raising their stricken faces to meet my own bewildered gaze. Thus, we said our final goodbyes silently, beyond the ears of men. Far too soon, I was following the duke from the chamber; the other gentlemen and members of the Privy Council falling in step behind us, while a troop of guards escorted us sombrely through the corridors of the palace. All my friends and family were gone, I was utterly alone, and despite my veneer of collected calm and dignity, I was terrified.

On some level, I was the woman from the future who had known of Anne's fate from the very first day that I had stepped into her shoes. I now realise what capacity we humans have to deceive ourselves. If I ever allowed my mind to alight on such a horrific eventuality, I had never thought to witness it. I convinced myself that my adventure in the sixteenth century would be long behind me and that I would grieve Anne from a safe distance of 500 years in the future. I had always secretly hoped, even up to the very end, that somehow I had found myself in Anne's shoes to change the course of history. But fate was cruel, tormenting me with seemingly endless possibilities to do so, and then ruthlessly seizing them away again, just when I thought I might win the day. But more than this, I could not believe that Henry had deserted me so entirely. It no longer mattered what I knew from my knowledge of history, only what I was experiencing, as I was marched toward my waiting prison. Images came crashing through my mind: sweet kisses, warm embraces, moments of profound intimacy and promises, hollow and empty as it turns out, to love me forever. Betrayal of trust is the cruellest to endure, and in my mind, I began to watch the changing tide of Henry's unstable emotions begin its final assault, washing away everything that I held dear.

When we emerged from the privy staircase, it was approximately two o'clock in the afternoon on another dry and warm summer's day. I cast my eyes along the sunny embankment in front of the palace and toward the village of Greenwich where crowds of spectators had flocked, undoubtedly drawn by the rumours of unprecedented events unfolding at the palace. Even in her innocence, I felt Anne's humiliation. She had not even been afforded the usual grace of being conducted to the Tower under cover of darkness. I remember that my mind was filled with thoughts of Henry. I wondered if the lion had been licking his wounds of self-inflicted pity, lashing out in his anger, declaring that my deceit and wickedness should be paraded for all of London to see. No doubt his intention was to inflict the greatest shame upon me that a queen of England ever had to endure. But I was determined that I would not be bullied into submission, to shrink into ignominy. I would have none of their cruel and spiteful games, but would hold my head high, for I was innocent of all accusations.

Norfolk led the way down the steps and onto the royal barge. As I followed, I once more looked upon the magnificent heraldic beasts which sat on gilded poles and kept guard over the stair, silently watching this final journey of a disgraced queen. Lifting my skirts to assist my transfer into the barge, my uncle offered me a hand of assistance. I stared at that extended hand in disgust as I raised my eyes to meet his and said,

'Do not think to touch me Your Grace, for I see that you already have blood on your hands—as well you know it.' With that, I managed to step into the barge unaided, sweeping past him to take my place under its covered canopy. When the members of the Privy Council including Norfolk, Audley, Sandys, Oxford and Cromwell had also seated themselves on board, we cast off from Greenwich Palace, the place I had most come to call home, soon slipping out of sight forever.

We travelled in silence. From time to time, I sensed my Uncle Norfolk look upon me and shake his head saying over and over, 'tut, tut' in tones meant to patronise and humiliate me. But if he wished to goad me into obvious despair, then he must have been disappointed, for I had nothing to say to him and ignored him completely. Only once did my eyes stray from the vast expanse of shimmering water, whose tidal ebb and flow jostled with the oarsmen, powering us up river toward the City of London. On that occasion, my gaze shifted deliberately to look upon Master Secretary Cromwell, whom I noticed had hitherto kept his line of sight averted from mine. I stared at him defiantly, daring him to look me in the eye. While I did not wish to speak to him, I knew that Anne's expressive eyes would make plain her belief in his guilt. I suspect that after a few moments, the comforting bubble of denial which Thomas Cromwell had placed about himself was pricked by my silent accusations. No doubt sensing that he was being watched, Master Secretary's eyes flicked up to meet mine where I held him for several seconds. Eyes that had once 'invited conversation' stood only in cold condemnation. I wanted to tell him to take that smug look off his face-that those men who had rallied about him to bring about my downfall would, in just over four years, ensure that it was Thomas' head upon the block. In that moment, a certain irony occurred to me; that if Thomas Cromwell had not torn Anne from the king and remained loyal to his mistress, he might not have strayed into the debacle of the disastrous Cleves' marriage, which would leave him vulnerable to his enemies. But I dared not speak of any of this. It all lay in the future. What was more, I feared that to begin to speak thus would unleash a torrent of pitiable ranting, pouring forth from a mind already stretched to the point of breaking. Thomas could not hold my gaze for long. Like my sister-in-law, Lady Rochford, the guilty are those that must turn their face away from the innocent, lest they see their own darkness reflected.

In their eagerness to convey me to the Tower, our party had set out too precipitously from Greenwich. Someone had made a rare error misjudging the tide which had not yet turned in our favour. I was sure that whoever it was would soon bear the brunt of my Lord of Norfolk's displeasure. The team of fourteen oarsmen had to struggle valiantly against its mighty currents, considerably delaying progress in our journey. It was as if Mother Nature alone had been left to fight for me.

To distract myself from the horror that awaited me at the Tower, I turned my attention to nature. As I did so, something miraculous occurred. On the river bank ahead was a meadow flushed with a proliferation of poppies that cast a swathe of bright, vibrant, red across the landscape, whilst more of the same wild flowers ran down to the edge of the river, making it look like the very land itself was crying tears of blood in sorrow for my plight. I realised that I would never see such immeasurable beauty again; it was if I had been jolted awake, as if I were really seeing them for the first time. It was an awakening that would ultimately bring about my deliverance from earthly suffering, and allow me to face death with peace in my heart. The moment passed almost as quickly as it came and I did not yet understand its significance. As the City of London and the Tower came into view, my oasis of harmony was wrenched away, and would not return for many days. Life was about to break me apart irrevocably.

Water lapped insistently against the slimy, stone stairs of the privy entrance to the Tower, referred to as Court Gate. Nearly three years earlier, I had alighted there to be greeted by huge crowds gathered to celebrate the coronation of a new queen. On that day, there were no celebrations, and the sombre party retraced my steps that had been cold for something close to 1,000 days. As I was escorted across the wooden bridge, ahead of me, where Henry had once stood to greet my arrival, was Sir Edmund Walsingham, the Deputy Lieutenant of the Tower. A notoriously unforgiving man, and by all accounts cruel, I began to really panic at the sight of him as I suddenly felt that my freedom and my life were ready to depart, along with the lords who had accompanied me to my prison. The reality of my betrayal, my isolation, and my likely fate suddenly crashed down upon me with a thunderous force, as my sanity began to break down.

Sir Edmund bowed in reverence to our arrival, before indicating perfunctorily that we should follow him through a substantial oak door and into a narrow stone corridor that led under the gate onto Water Lane. I followed without question, but with every step, I seemed increasingly unable to bear the weightiness of my predicament. Swept up in the tragedy unfolding, I quite suddenly collapsed on the cobblestones beneath the gate's shadowy interior, my crimson velvet gown flowing away like rivulets of blood around me. Crying out to the heavens, I heard Anne's voice echoing round the cramped interior.

'Dear God, I beseech you to help me, as I swear upon my soul that I am not guilty of my accusement.' Tears streamed down my face, as I sobbed loudly. The Deputy Lieutenant stopped to look back at me, confused as to what appropriate action he might take. After a few moments, Lord Chancellor Audley stepped forward and offered his hand which, with much pitiable sorrow, I accepted. Finally, righting myself upon my feet, I found myself pleading with Henry's Privy Councillors in a state of mild hysteria. 'My lords, please, I desire that you ask the king's grace to be good unto me.' My wretched request had been borne of desperation and fear, but my uncle did not reply. Instead he addressed Sir Edmund Walsingham, stating coldly,

'By the king's command, we have come forth to commit the queen to the Tower as your prisoner. Her grace is to remain so, at his majesty's pleasure.' The Duke of Norfolk made the appropriate reverence to me, before turning to stride out of sight, followed by the other lords of the Privy Council. As the last disappeared from view, a sonorous roar of cannon fire thundered from the wharf. Across London, gossip raged like a firestorm through the taverns of the City. The firing of the cannons signalled that a person of high rank had been committed to the Tower. With a wretched heart, I finally said goodbye to the outside world, and to the freedom which I seemed to have so carelessly frittered away.

Chapter Forty-One

The Tower of London,
Thursday, 4 May 1536

From the window of the queen's privy chamber in the Tower, I watched the slightly stooped figure of Sir William Kingston walk as quickly as his aging bones would allow, down from Cold Harbour Gate and toward the entrance to the great hall. He paused briefly to speak to a man I did not recognise, I could just make them out behind the leaves and branches of the flowering cherry tree which cast its magnificent, blossom-laden bower across a part of the Tower's inner ward. As they chatted, sharing words I could not hear, I recalled how Master Kingston had been one of the few men who had treated me with kindness when I was first thrown into my prison. He had spoken gently to me and assured me that I would not be cast into a dungeon as I had feared. Instead, the constable informed me that I was to be lodged within the royal apartments that had been built specifically for Anne three years earlier. I have become exceptionally grateful for such small acts of kindness, for Master Kingston's unshakeable humanity and determination to treat me with every courtesy and dignity.

I watched the two men make their reverence to each other, their conversation clearly complete, before they went their separate ways. I was physically exhausted from the previous four days as the unimaginable strain of my perilous predicament had stretched my sanity to breaking point. Looking back, I can see that in the first four days of my captivity, I was on the brink of a complete nervous collapse, half crazed, every nerve frayed. I felt chaotic and virtually incoherent.

I looked at my hands. In one, I held a velvet-bound book of hours; the other I stretched out in front of me, fingers splayed as I watched the tremor that had lately caused my hand to shake violently against my will. Feeling sick and virtually unable to bear my weight, I sat down in the window seat, one leg bent up and tucked beneath the other. I rested my head against the leaded glass, my hands in my lap. Within them, I carried the book that had been constantly at my side but which I was too disturbed to read, for I had lost all concentration. In the centre of my chest, I felt the heavy weight of a burdened heart—a heart so afflicted with sorrow and which would never again be able to piece together all its shattered fragments. For the brief time I rested there, I reflected upon the last two days which had been nothing short of a living nightmare.

After Norfolk and the other lords of the Privy Council had left me in Master Kingston's care, great swathes of my defences summarily collapsed casting me into a sort of incoherent instability from which I was just beginning to emerge. This, I am afraid, is my only excuse for what happened next. I should have known better, how to protect Anne and those men condemned with her. But my temporary madness disabled all rational thought, all ability to control Anne's famously indiscreet tongue. And so, out of control, and to my shame, I had thought little but spoken much during my first two days of incarceration. In those first forty-eight hours, the voice in my mind had been crazed, turning everything upside down and inside out, running around an endless labyrinth of 'what ifs', from which there was no escape. As a consequence, my fevered brain had spoken carelessly of dangerous, but innocent liaisons, whilst a wiser person than I would have maintained silence. In between, I wept inconsolably for hours, my ladies much perplexed by the great laughing which would quite suddenly and irrationally break forth from the same sorrow. They did not understand that only I saw the painful irony of how I had been deceived into believing I was truly loved by not one, but two men, who 500 years apart, had abandoned me to die alone.

By the third day of my imprisonment, my initial shock began to subside so that there were times of greater lucidity. During those times, I was increasingly beset with dread regarding things that I had uttered with the sole intention of defending myself, but which in retrospect, I feared would be used against me and my co-accused. Fragments of conversations with Mark Smeaton, Sir Francis Weston and Sir Henry Norris, to which I rapaciously filled in the gaps with my own perilous ramblings. My only defence is that in my fragile state, memories flooded into my mind with a pressure that had been difficult to contain. Clever Cromwell capitalised on my unstable state, deliberately releasing only the merest slivers of information, tempting me to taste a morsel of their deception, carefully ensuring that they never gave me enough that I knew their suspicions. Of course, none of it would have mattered if I had been surrounded by the ladies of my chamber, friends of unquestionable loyalty. But here Cromwell had dealt Anne another decisive blow. As I thought on it, I turned my head to look toward the four women so cruelly placed by Cromwell who sat nearby, three of them busily working their embroidery, the third reading from a prayer book. I deeply resented them all.

The eldest of these was my namesake and aunt, Anne Boleyn, Lady Shelton, my father's elder sister. At sixty-one years of age, she remained a vigorous woman, who had for some time been in charge of the Lady Mary's household. My father had first suggested Aunt Anne's appointment shortly after my daughter was given her own household in December, 1533. I could never warm to my aunt's sombre character and austere nature, but my parents reassured me that she was a strong disciplinarian who would put Mary firmly in her place, thus protecting my daughter's interests during my long absences. At the time, I had just conceived the son I would lose the following summer, and despite my happy estate, I still feared that my daughter's future was far from safe. So, I welcomed Lady Shelton's loyalty and rigorous application of Elizabeth's primacy. Along with my Uncle Norfolk and my brother, I even encouraged my Aunt Anne's antipathy toward her charge, and to my shame, her denigration and the mistreatment of Mary if she continued to defy the king's will to accept me as lawful Queen of England. Words and actions I would truly come to regret. But on that day, I merely studied Lady Shelton as she embroidered blackwork on a linen shirt in her lap, her English hood hiding her greyed hair, the delicate lines upon her face giving tell to her advancing years.

I wondered if she resented me for the pressure that the Boleyns had placed upon her to mistreat the king's bastard daughter, or indeed, if she despised Anne because of what the queen had done to her own daughter, Madge. Dear, sweet Madge, her pretty face flashed through my mind. I knew that in the spring of 1535, the Boleyns had deliberately placed the young girl as a tasty morsel before the king. It was a deliberate ploy to divert Henry's affection away from Lady Elizabeth Harvey, whose religious inclinations and sympathy toward the Lady Mary had made her a thorn in Anne's side. I did not command it myself, for at the time, I had been plucked back into my modern day life. But I saw it all clearly enough in my mind's eye, accessed through Anne's own memories. My cousin's famed beauty and pretty charms quickly lured Henry. All the Boleyns had to do was steer her into his path at exactly the right time. Once his majesty commenced the hunt, such a sweet and innocent child was hopelessly overwhelmed, unable to defend her honour against the overbearing omnipotence of her sovereign lord. So he had plucked the sweet, fleshy fruit of her maidenhood, devouring her until he sucked the nectar of her innocence dry, before discarding her six months later.

Next to Lady Shelton, seated on a stool to her right, was Margaret Dymock, the forty-six year old wife of my master of the horse, Sir William Coffin, appointed by the king in 1533. Both Margaret and her husband had been at court during the early years of the king's reign; Sir William proving himself to be trustworthy and diligent as a household administrator, his wife having served Katherine since the Field of the Cloth of Gold in 1519. Neither of them cared anything for Anne Boleyn as their loyalties were with the king first, and with Katherine's death, her daughter, Mary.

Margaret was also engrossed in her embroidery. Sensing the icy chill of my stare, she briefly looked up to meet my gaze. Like all the women present, I knew her from about the court and had long ago formed the opinion that Margaret Dymock was as thin and pasty in her face as she was in her spirit—at least toward Anne, whom she served reluctantly. She relished her new-found role as my tormentor, jibing relentlessly at my supposed indiscretions, or refusing to answer with any kindness my heartfelt enquiries about the health and wellbeing of my mother, or those who were imprisoned on my account. In her antipathy toward me, she had soon fallen into step with the woman opposite her, a woman with whom I was sadly well acquainted, Elizabeth Wood, Lady Boleyn, wife of my uncle, Sir James.

Of course, I had had many brushes with Lady Boleyn. And despite my mother's warning to treat her well and with kindness, unfortunately, I never found the generosity of spirit to do so—and I now pay the price for my negligence. Years of simmering resentment toward her much vaunted niece were unleashed without reserve. She took every opportunity to place a thousand cuts upon me, her sneering disdain and salacious accusations stinging me like a swarm of angry hornets. I watched her revenge shore up her own fragile personality, and in those early days of my imprisonment, I truly hated her for it.

I reacted to their mean-spiritedness by fighting their cruelty in kind, lashing out with my own angry tongue; at other times begging them to show mercy and to give me news of my family and friends. To their shame, my obvious suffering seemed only to fuel their wickedness and determination to inflict ever greater misery upon me. Seized with a conviction to give these two women no further satisfaction from their toils, I played the only card I saw left in my hand. Anne was still their queen, and the strict rules of Tudor society deemed that without my implicit consent, they could not speak to me unless they were spoken to first. And so, I withdrew my favour, refusing to address them and making clear my own contempt for their rudeness and ill-will. I smiled inwardly to myself just thinking on it. It was churlish to be so pleased by their obvious frustration at having their merry disport curtailed. Perhaps to my shame, I had, with great satisfaction, rubbed salt into their wounds by making a point of only addressing Lady Shelton and the last of my four ladies-in-waiting, Mary Scrope, Lady Kingston.

Lady Kingston was, of course, Sir William's wife. I knew well enough from my history books that she, like all the others, had been commanded to report my every word to the constable of the Tower. She was a firm supporter of the Lady Mary, and showed no great gentleness toward me, however, she remained ever courteous and took no obvious pleasure from my misfortune. It seemed that Master Kingston's humanity had rubbed off on his wife. Of the four women, it was Lady Kingston who read from religious texts, wearing a set of spectacles upon the end of her delicate, little nose. Like the other ladies, she was around sixty years of age. Her English hood covered the blonde hair of her youth, which had long since become coarse and flecked with grey.

My troubled thoughts were suddenly interrupted as the door to my privy chamber was opened and the supper which I had recently called for was announced. The room in which I was to dine remained virtually untouched since I last saw it in May 1533. The chamber was exquisitely decorated in the height of Renaissance style; the walls panelled with wainscot, inlaid with elaborate antique work. Sandwiched between the great presence chamber and my privy bedchamber, the unusually large space was meant to also serve as a grand dining chamber. Once I had presided in that very room with the king at my side; a sumptuous feast for many of the noblest men of the land had been served in my honour: dukes, earls, lords and knights had sat alongside an archbishop, and other clerics who had become amongst my most favoured of reformist bishops. But I feared that few of them would speak up for me, their loyalty was as fragile and transient as a snowflake falling upon warm skin—melting away into nothing, as if it had never existed.

The table, which dominated the centre of the room, was laid with my own silver-gilt plate. I stood to take my seat with a swishing of skirts, my ladies rising with me, as courtesy dictated. Taking my place at the head of an empty table, I arranged myself, placing a white, linen napkin across my right shoulder, as I spoke to Lady Kingston,

'Madame, have you heard from your husband regarding the sacrament that I requested be put into my closet?' It was one of the first requests that I made to my gaoler, yet still it has failed to arrive. Anne's faith was unswerving and in truth, it had been my only comfort since my return to her world, as it seemed all but God had deserted her. Lady Kingston replied bluntly,

'Nay, Your Grace. He has not spoken of it.' For a moment, I felt tears sting at the back of my eyes. It seemed as though the extent of the king's callousness toward me was without depth. Yet, as had become commonplace, my self-pity was suddenly swept aside and replaced with a black humour that saw only the utter absurdity that I had been so comprehensively deceived in love, I was entranced by kind words and pretty baubles. Quite without warning, gentle laughter bubbled to the surface, before breaking into a great belly laugh. I lifted my hand to cover my mouth, unable for a moment to quieten myself. When I looked back at my ladies, they were staring at me, perplexed once again by my erratic, illogical behaviour. As my laughter finally died away, I addressed myself to Lady Kingston.

'Tell me Madame, what of your husband? I marvel that I have seen him not today.' As I spoke, Lady Boleyn and Margaret Dymock came forward, the first carrying an elaborate silver gilt ewer, and the other a matching bowl. I placed my hands over the bowl, as my aunt poured warm water over them, so that I could wash before I began to eat. As I did so, Lady Kingston replied,

'My Lord husband has been busy this day, Your Grace. As I have been attending Your Majesty, I have no knowledge of what matters have occupied him.' Drying my hands on a cloth, I turned to look Lady Kingston in the eye. I knew she was lying, but I was growing used to it, for they only told me what they wanted me to know. Seeing that I would get little from her, I commanded,

'I should be grateful, Lady Kingston, if you would ask your lord husband to attend upon me presently, for I wish to speak with him.' After a moment's hesitation, Lady Kingston dipped a curtsy before retreating from the room to convey my request to her beleaguered husband. As I waited, I turned to gaze out of the open window. I sensed no breeze, but the pretty, warbling song of a blackbird as it heralded the onset of dusk upon the City of London. For about the thousandth time, I cast my mind beyond my prison walls and thought on those who I had loved and loathed, and where they would lay their heads that night; whether they celebrated, or mourned my downfall; whether there was anyone left in this world to fight for the life of Anne Boleyn.

It was a good hour after supper before Master Kingston finally appeared in my chambers. In the time it took my gaoler to arrive, I had swung from merry conversation with Lady Shelton into the depths of despair. After my table was cleared, I went alone to my privy closet, which I used as an oratory. Clutching my book of hours in one hand, I knelt in a pitiable state before the golden cross. No chaplain of mine had been assigned to my chambers, so I was unable to hear mass, hence I avidly sank into my private devotions. Since my imprisonment, I had spent many an hour in that room; for it was only there that I could escape the unwelcome company of those who loved me not.

I began to pray to God, begging the good Lord to have mercy upon me, a miserable and wretched sinner. I pleaded with my Father in heaven for a miracle, beseeching Him to bend his majesty's mind against those who had accused me so falsely. I begged the good Lord to deliver me, and those men who had been enslaved on my account, from the jaws of death. I prayed fervently for my brother. Even though they had not said as much, I was sure that he was imprisoned no more than 200 yards from where I knelt in prayer. I thought of my mother, and how the news of my imprisonment must surely have reached her ears and cast her into the greatest calamity. I prayed to God to give her strength, to let her know how much I loved her, and to keep the truth within her heart that her daughter was innocent.

I looked down upon the book that I clutched in my hand and tried to read some words of comfort. But the tears came all too soon! By degree, I sank to the floor, wrenched apart by guttural sobs. I lay there for some time, tormented by my sorrows before my tears were finally spent. I began to gather myself up when in the distance, I heard two men talking. One I recognised immediately as Master Kingston, clearly finally responding to my summons. The other sounded like Sir William Fitzwilliam, and I wondered what business he had with me. I pulled myself up from the floor, straightened my skirts and dabbed my eyes with a handkerchief. Having mustered some degree of composure, I opened the door of my closet and stepped into the presence chamber surprised to find Master Kingston alone. Whoever owned the masculine voice had clearly disappeared. Instead, on the far side of the room on the other side of the raised dais, Sir William was deep in conference with his wife, Lady Kingston. Lady Boleyn and Margaret Dymock stood close by in attendance. As I emerged, all looked in my direction. Lord knows what a sight I was! My tearstained face reflecting the weighty cares of the world. Sir William took the black velvet cap from his head and swept into a deep bow. I acknowledged his reverence with a slight inclination of my head, before saying,

'Where have you been this day, Sir William, for I have not seen you since yesterday?' Master Kingston righted himself, placing his cap back upon his head before replying,

'Forgive me for my negligence of you, Your Grace I have been busy with prisoners.' I turned to look back down the length of the queen's presence chamber, toward the entrance from the great hall, and from where I was sure that I had heard Sir William Fitzwilliam's voice.

'I thought I heard Master Treasurer.' Sir William shook his head,

'Nay, Madame. By my troth, I can assure you that he is not here.' My gaze lingered upon the lower end of the chamber as I weighed up the veracity of Master Kingston's words. The mention of Sir William Fitzwilliam sent a frisson of irritation surging up from my belly. I thought of his obvious contempt and arrogance towards me when he had interrogated me at Greenwich. Much aggrieved by these recollections, I could not help making my displeasure known. In the absence of Master Treasurer himself, I heaped my anger upon Master Kingston as I chided,

'More's the pity, for if he were here, I would admonish him most severely for his disrespect and unkindness!' Master Kingston raised an eyebrow, as if to enquire upon the meaning of my words. 'Sir William, I was shown great unkindness and little respect when I was arrested at Greenwich by the king's council; my Uncle Norfolk even saying tut-tut! And as for Master Treasurer, he was in the Forest of Windsor!' I looked away for a moment shaking my head three or four times, still burning with indignation at the great slight upon my honour, as I lamented, 'but I, a queen, so cruelly handled as was never seen.' I looked back to my gaoler and added, 'Yet, I do swear Master Controller to be a very gentleman. He alone remembered his good manners!'

I turned away from my audience and picking up the hem of my skirts mounted the carpeted dais and approached the empty seat of majesty that I had once so proudly occupied. I ran my finger across one of its velvet arms, lost for a moment in my thoughts of Henry and all that had passed between us. It was difficult to believe that he had entirely abandoned me. Such a notion fruited upon my lips as I said quietly, almost to myself, 'But I think the king does it test me.' I did not wait for an answer. Instead, I slumped languidly upon the throne, as I once more saw the futility of the illusion I had created to prevent myself from spiralling into an unbearable terror. Indeed, it had been the only thing which stood between me and the acceptance that my life was over. Suddenly, I began laughing at it all once more, not only at my predicament, but my pathetic attempts to shield myself from the truth of what was unfolding. Those who looked upon me did so with curious eyes and impassive stares, and sought to understand my peculiar brand of madness. As my laughter died away, I sat forward in my throne engaging Master Kingston as I declared, 'But I shall have justice!'

'Have no doubt therein, Madame.' I stared at him for a moment. I knew he spoke of the king's justice, which would be but an empty, laughable charade. I spoke of something more profound; a justice from which no man could escape—karmic justice. Those mere mortals, who had exacted their revenge upon innocents, would have to answer to their conscience, to their God, upon judgment day. Just a few days ago, such a thought had given me great comfort, but now I feel only great sorrow for those who have cast their souls into the greatest of tragedies. However, I decided to leave Master Kingston alone with his misunderstanding as I stated solemnly,

'If any man accuses me, I can say but 'nay' and they can bring no witness.' I slumped back in my seat, staring at the floor before turning my attention again to the men who suffered alongside me. I glanced up, this time addressing Lady Kingston, 'Madame, you yourself told me that on the day of my arrest, Mark was brought to the Tower.' Lady Kingston replied,

'Yea, Your Grace, I spoke the truth,' before her husband added,

'Indeed he was, and was well lodged by ten o'clock that night.'

'And Sir Henry was brought here on the following day.' Master Kingston inclined his head, nodding his agreement. 'I know of such things, and yet I fall accused with one man more—and nobody will speak anything of it. With whom else am I accused, Sir William?' In my heart, I knew well the answer; that my brother had also been committed as prisoner on the same day that I had been conveyed to the Tower. I had singularly failed to carve out an alternative ending for Anne Boleyn, and I saw no reason why the other men—whose names I already knew—had not followed their queen into her dolorous prison. I thought again of George, and wondered why they had not laid his unhappy fate at my feet. I could only guess that Cromwell hoped that in my incoherent ramblings, I would implicate my brother in acts of unholy debauchery and incest. Master Secretary would be disappointed, for there was not a drop of sin to taint our fraternal love.

My question was answered by resounding silence, and I saw that my pressing the matter would bring me no further satisfaction. Suddenly, I felt agitated and rose quickly to my feet, beginning to pace back and forth in front of Sir William and Lady Kingston. Once more angry, I lashed out, determined to defend my innocence.

'If I could lay my case before the Council, as is surely my right, then I would win the day...' I spun about to face my witnesses, '... for as God is my witness, I am innocent of these charges!' Stretching out my arms in an open gesture and crying to the realms of heavenly angels, who surely witnessed my torment, I lamented, 'I would to God I had my bishops, for they would all go to the king for me.' As I said it, I knew full well that whilst they might wish to in their hearts, no one, not even Cranmer, dared cross the king so directly. I placed my hand upon my brow, increasingly vexed and fearful of my fate, I began to grasp at straws, falling helplessly into a blithering rant. 'For I think most of England prays for me and if I die...' I paused, then broke into laughter, which spoke of the fact that I was barely able to comprehend such an eventuality, before I continued, '...you shall see the greatest punishment for me within these seven years which ever came to England!' Then rather more earnestly, I added, 'But then I shall be in heaven, for I have done many good deeds in my day.' I was still for a moment before taking a few paces towards Master Kingston, and fixing him with my eyes, I rather pointedly complained,

'But I think it much unkindness in the king to put such about me as I never loved.' I deliberately flicked my eyes across toward Lady Boleyn and Margaret Dymock, making it plain where my disgust lay.

'Madame, I can only say that the king takes them all to be honest and good women.'

'That may be so Sir William, but I would have ladies of my own privy chamber which I favour most. Although Master Kingston would never be cruel to me, I saw that he was unmoved by my remonstrations. He was the king's man, a soldier, through and through. Thus, for the time being, my requests for small comforts: for the sacrament to be placed in my oratory, for my almoner to say mass, and for those ladies whom I loved well to attend me, would fall upon barren ground. I would have to wait for many more days before I would finally taste even a dusting of the king's mercy.

Chapter Forty-Two

The Tower of London,
Saturday, 6 May 1536

The nib of the quill hovered over the crisp, clean parchment as I recalled the first letter that I wrote to Henry. I had been cocooned in the quiet, sun-lit sanctuary of Hever's library, flushed with excitement that was stirred up through love's sweet nectar, intoxicated with wonder at finding myself in the shoes of Anne Boleyn, a woman on the brink of an historic love affair with the mighty King Henry VIII. Life was the sweetest symphony, its notes played with an easy grace back then. It was inconceivable to me then that his majesty's love was anything but inexhaustible, and I felt sure that Anne would be adored forever. In the quiet stillness of that balmy, summer's night, such a song was but a distant memory, the words unclear, and the melody long since forgotten.

The hour was approaching midnight; I was exhausted but sleep had forsaken me, my mind would not settle. Since receiving confirmation from Master Kingston of the names of those seven men who languished within the confines of the Tower alongside me, the hysteria which had plagued me over the previous four days gave way to anger. I looked up from my desk as I was suddenly distracted by the sound of Lady Boleyn as she turned over on her pallet at the side of my bed. Both my ladies stirred when I had got up not half an hour earlier. I reassured them that I needed nothing from them, that I would sit awhile and read, whilst giving them both leave to slip back into their slumber. This they had done, and I was left to sit alone at my writing desk, the pale, silvery light of the moon casting is muted glow through my windows.

I opened the curtains to look down upon the privy gardens, propping opening the window so that I could get closer to the quiet stillness of the night. The sky was clear, and looking up, I found myself transfixed by the sheer, unfathomable vastness of the universe which stretched away before me. But I turned away too soon to find the real solace that I searched for. My mind was too preoccupied by thoughts that smothered me with their busyness. I sought my peace instead by trying to understand how it had ever come to this, by trying to work out my next move in this deadly game.

I turned once more to my letter to Henry, which I steeled myself to write. Whilst my fear paralysed me, the anger within my breast drove me with a new energy of indignation. I reached over to a letter from Henry that had been delivered that afternoon by Sir William Fitzwilliam. I placed the parchment upon the desk in front of me, and smoothing out the creases therein, as I began to read over again.

Madame,

The bearer of this letter is to advertise to you the great displeasure of your Sovereign Lord, who has borne with the heaviest of hearts, the most afflicting news that could have arrived. It has grieved me sorely to hear of such vile wickedness, such ungodly demeanour in one whom I have loved well and raised to so high an estate, believing, would to God it were true, that you have ever loved and honoured me, solely, discreetly and in all faithfulness; and I assure you, all the greatness of this world could not counterpoise for my satisfaction, the knowledge and certainty thereof.

Yet, I fear that I have put much confidence in your promises, in which I now find myself deceived. The wrong you have done me has caused me much sorrow; but I feel immeasurably more aggrieved in seeing myself betrayed by a woman who beguiled me with her charms only to discover the secrets of my heart. Madame, you cannot avoid being censured by everybody for having drawn yourself the hatred of a king who raised you to the highest of degree to which the greatest ambition of a person could aspire. I acknowledge that, believing you sincere, I have been too precipitate in my confidence and the love I have borne you; but it has induced, and still induces me, to keep more moderation in avenging myself, not forgetting that I have been 'your humble servant'. Wherefore, I urge you not to clog your conscience, and confess your sins to the bearer of this letter, or else the Council, who I have commanded will visit you on the morrow. If you shall do this, then you will know the mercy of your husband, King and Sovereign Lord, who will inflict not the most extreme of punishments worthy of one who has committed these most heinous of crimes.

Westminster, 6th May,

H.R

I read it through several more times, each time feeling more indignant than the last. I despised Henry's capacity for self-pity and his ability to deceive himself of the righteousness of his cause should it fit his purpose, of which I knew well enough! A certain Mistress Seymour, and the empty cradle which waited to carry Henry's longed for son. Henry Tudor was a man who had honed the art of self-deception to assuage his conscience. I could only reflect on the irony of how that mastery had once served me so well, allowing the king to sweep Katherine aside without regret or remorse. I recognised that I must suffer the same. I turned my head to look out of my window into the night, as I whispered under my breath,

'Forgive me, Katherine—I was blind.' I lingered only momentarily upon her unhappiness, as the empty parchment upon my desk waited to be written upon. Dipping the nib in the ink once more, I began to scrawl across its scratchy surface.

Sir,

Your Grace's displeasure, and my imprisonment are things so strange to me, as what to write, what to excuse, I'm altogether ignorant; whereas to send unto me (willing me to confess the truth and so obtain your favour) by such a one, who you know to be my ancient and professed enemy; I no sooner received the message by him, and I rightly conceived your meaning; and if, as you say, confessing truth indeed may procure my safety, I shall with all willingness and duty perform your command.

I paused for a moment, watching the ink dry in front of me. I remembered Fitzwilliam's sneer as he handed me the king's letter, and when I had finished reading it, how he had repeated his majesty's offer to see me safely housed within a nunnery, if I would agree to confess my guilt. I admit that while the devil danced upon my shoulder, I had been tempted to find refuge in a life of quiet prayer and devotion. Yet, I knew to do so would be to perjure my soul before God, and that having done so, even a lifetime of prayer could never be my salvation. In such circumstances, I would surely die an ignominious death, a self-confessed adulteress, who had committed incest with her brother, with no shred of dignity left to uphold my good name. And then, there was my Elizabeth. I could not bear that my Elizabeth might despise me as a liar; an untrustworthy mother who had poured forth sweet words of innocence in my letter to her, and yet within the week, had confessed my adulterous sins to the world. I could not leave as a legacy such a cross for her to bear. And so I took a much shorter path which would lead me to the scaffold. With the courage of my convictions, and my mind made up, I wrote,

But let not Your Grace ever imagine that your poor wife will ever be brought to acknowledge a fault, when not so much of thought thereof proceeded. And to speak the truth, never Prince had a wife more loyal in all duty, and in all true affection, then you have found in Anne Boleyn, with which name and place could willingly have contented myself, as if God, and Your Grace's pleasure had been so pleased. Neither did I at any time so far forge myself in my exultation, or received Queenship, but that I always looked for such an alteration as now I find; for the ground of my preferment being on no surer foundation than Your Grace's fancy, the least alteration, I knew, was fit and sufficient to draw that fancy to some of the subject.

The anger poured thick and fast from my quill. I was furious with Henry for betraying me, but even more furious with myself for being such a fool to have ever believed in him so entirely. If I was to die, then I wanted Henry to know that the eye of my conscience saw right through his self-pity, and that the innocent blood which stained his hands would never be washed out. My troubled mind emptied my spiteful thoughts upon the paper as I dipped the nib of my quill in the black ink once more. I wanted to give Henry one more chance to redeem himself.

You have chosen me, from a low estate, to be your Queen and companion, far beyond my desert or desire. If then you found me worthy of such honour, good Your Grace, let not any light fancy, or bad counsel of mine enemies, withdraw your princely favour from me; neither let that stain, that unworthy stain of the disloyal heart toward your good grace, ever cast so foul blot on your most dutiful wife and infant princess your daughter.

Try me, Good King, but let me have a lawful trial, and let not my sworn enemies sit as my accusers and judges; yes, let me receive an open trial, for my truth shall fear no open shame; then shall you see either my innocency cleared, your suspicion and conscience satisfied, the ignominy and slander of the world stopped, or my guilt openly declared. So that whatsoever God or you may determine of me, Your Grace may be freed from an open censure; and mine offence being so lawfully proved, Your Grace is at liberty, both before God and man, not only to execute worthy punishment on me as an unlawful wife, but to follow your affection already settled on that party, for whose sake I am now as I am, whose name I could some good while since have pointed unto: Your Grace being not ignorant of my suspicion therein.

Jane Seymour: I could not bear to write her name, but knowing well Henry's inordinate self-righteousness and vanity, I knew the only thing that would truly move him would not be his fear of Anne Boleyn's judgement—but God's. Henry was a devout Catholic, and above all, he feared the wrath of God. Try as he might to hide from the truth, it would always be there in his heart for God to see. Thus, I drew my letter to a close by writing,

But if you have already determined me, and that not only my death, but an infamous slander must bring you the enjoying of your desired happiness; then I desire of God, that he will pardon your great sin therein, and likewise mine enemies, the instruments thereof; that he will not call you to a strict account for your princely and cruel usage me, at his general judgement-seat, where both you and myself, must shortly appear, and in whose judgement, I doubt not (whatsoever the world may think of me) my innocency shall be openly known, and sufficiently cleared.

My last and only request shall be, that myself may only bear the burden of Your Grace's displeasure, and that it may not touch the innocent souls of those poor gentlemen, who (as I understand) are in straight imprisonment for my sake. If ever I have found favour in your sight; if ever the name of Anne Boleyn hath been pleasing to your ears, then let me obtain this request; and I will so leave to trouble Your Grace any further, with mine earnest prayers to the Trinity to have Your Grace in his good keeping, and to direct you in all your actions.

Your most loyal and ever faithful wife, Anne Boleyn

From my doleful prison the Tower, this 6th May.

I put down the quill and sat back in my chair. There was nothing more to say.

Chapter Forty-Three

The Tower of London,
Sunday, 7 May 1536

I took the long stem of the rose delicately between my thumb and fore-finger, burying my nose amidst its pale pink petals, striped through with deep, rich crimson. A heavy, sweet perfume of unfathomable beauty emanated from its vibrant yellow centre. Intoxicated from the scent, I nodded to the usher to arrange a bunch of my favourite *Rosa Mundi* roses to be cut and placed within my lodgings. Still holding the rose within my hand, I turned away to walk deeper into the garden.

I was granted the privilege of taking daily exercise in the gardens, although my predicament was never far from my mind. Tower guards, positioned strategically as living statues about the perimeter wall, reminded me that I was no longer at liberty to enjoy all that had once been at my command. With some amusement, I wondered who they thought would attempt to rescue me, and where might the Queen of England seek to hide, if I were to somehow make it over the walls in all my finery. I had joked as much with Master Kingston; although my black humour singularly failed to stir a jocular response.

Making it clear that I wished those ladies who waited upon me to remain at a discreet distance, I sat alone on a gritty grey-stone bench in front of the fountain, in the centre of the garden. It faced north toward the great wardrobe beyond which was the Martin Tower, where I knew my brother was imprisoned. I had hoped to catch a glimpse of him from one of the upper windows, but there were too many other, loftier buildings obscuring my view. So instead, I merely imagined that he could hear the silent words of love that I spoke to him in my mind. No sooner had I settled myself, I heard the sound of scurrying footsteps on the gravel path behind me. I turned to see my angel of mercy moving hastily toward our little group; it was Mary Orchard. Sweet, sweet Mary, how I thanked God daily for her presence, for she alone saved my sanity during the first few days of my captivity.

I knew Mrs Mary Orchard well. She had served as a nurse to Mary, Anne and George when they were children, then later as one of Elizabeth Boleyn's maids. By the time that I arrived back in Anne's world in September, 1532, Mary was already in Anne's service. I sensed the love that Anne bore her; she would always enquire about her and the health of her husband and children. On the day of my arrest, I had been too distraught to even think about who awaited me in the Tower, but when I saw her face, it took every ounce of my determination to not just fall weeping into her arms, as Anne had done so often when she had fallen over, or been scolded, as a child. Over those first few days, she became my lifeline. She had always been close to my mother, and so I felt that in Mary's presence a part of my mother was always by my side. I drew tremendous strength from this.

The eagle-eyed Lady Kingston supervised her closely ensuring that we were kept at a safe distance from one another. She knew where Mary Orchard's loyalties lay, and I suspect she had been ordered to make sure that no uncensored messages were smuggled either into, or out of, the Tower. It was a mission in which she was almost entirely successful—but not quite. There were two occasions during the first week of my confinement in which the moment presented itself for Mary and me to steal the briefest of moments away from prying eyes. She did not dare carry letters about her person, but on both occasions, she whispered a message to me as she passed close by.

On the first occasion, I was quite startled by her quiet words, not expecting any kind missive from outside my prison to reach me. But there it was—a message from my sister that all was forgiven and that she prayed for me daily, and she hoped that the king would be delivered from his wicked council. Mrs Orchard was unable to say more, as Lady Kingston re-entered the room. Mary dipped a curtsy before scuttling from the chamber, with Lady Kingston's suspicious eyes following her. The second message came two days later when Mrs Orchard had been clearing up the ashes from the grate. Lady Boleyn had been doing her embroidery opposite me, and got up to take a message at the door. Mary took her chance and without looking up, she whispered,

'The countess knows of your innocence, Your Grace. She begs God to give you courage and strength, and bids me to tell you of her eternal love for you.' Tears immediately stung at my eyes, for these were the words that I had so desperately wanted to hear, and which brought me immeasurable comfort. I could bear the weight of England's accusations upon my innocent shoulders, but I could not have met my death with any shred of composure if my mother held me guilty of my accusement. I was immensely grateful for Mary's presence; I do not know what had moved the king to show me this one kindness. I watched Mary approaching; it was clear that she had something important to say. As was customary, she made toward Lady Kingston, who would then convey the message to me. Yet, I would rather have one Mary to a thousand Lady Kingstons, and far preferred to hear her sweet, noble voice. As she drew close, I commanded,

'Mrs Orchard, if you bear a message for the queen then approach me directly, for I have a mind to hear it from your tongue.' I knew it was a slight against my ladies of higher rank, but I relished every opportunity to cause them some discomfort. More than happy to obey my command, Mary dipped a deep curtsy, before she announced,

'Your Majesty, his grace, the Duke of Norfolk requests Your Grace's pleasure in your presence chamber.'

'Is my Lord of Norfolk alone?' Mary shook her head replying,

'No Madame, accompanying his grace is Master Secretary Cromwell, Lord Chancellor Audley and the Archbishop of Canterbury.' I knew from Henry's letter of the previous day that a delegation of the Privy Council was due to arrive to extract my confession. I had expected the first three, but the presence of Thomas Cranmer saddened and angered me in equal measure, for if there were any of Henry's Councillors whom I trusted with my life, it was my old friend, Thomas. As the request was but a veiled command, I nodded and rose, sweeping my skirts about me before striding fearlessly toward my chambers.

It was a considerable walk back to the queen's lodgings. With every footstep, I recalled fragments of past conversations, of deep rooted rivalries and resentments that brought forth bitter fruits of revenge—of dishonour and shame being heaped upon Anne's good name and upon her family. I became increasingly furious with Henry; furious that to save his conscience, he wanted me to carry the burden of his shame. Well, it was not going to happen, and having stirred all this up in my mind, by the time I swept into the queen's presence chamber where the four men awaited me, I was in no mood to take prisoners.

The lords of the Council were in discussion at the high end of the hall, awaiting my arrival. Cromwell, as ever, was clutching a portfolio of papers close to his chest and as he saw me enter the chamber, he murmured something to his companions before nodding in my direction and sweeping into the customary reverence; Norfolk, Audley and Cranmer all followed suit. I swept past them, audaciously mounting the dais to make a very deliberate and provocative statement of Anne's greatness. Once under the canopy of state, I swung about in my taffeta skirts glowering at them as if they were filth dragged in off the street. My disdain and pride made perfect bedfellows; I showed them no humility. To my surprise, it was not my Uncle Norfolk who stepped forward to speak first, as I had expected, it was Thomas Cranmer. Had I looked carefully into his eyes, I would have seen his silent plea for forgiveness for what he must do. Only later would I come to accept the impossibility of my friend's predicament, and how in his heart he had been glad of the stern rebuke which rained down upon the king's delegation. Later, Thomas and I would have our time alone, and I would understand his transgression against me.

On that day, though, my fury ensured that I saw very little of how things really were, indeed, little of anything more than my determination to cling onto my innocency. As per my right and rank, I addressed the good Archbishop first.

'Your Grace, say what it is you have a mind to say.'

'Madame, there is no one in the realm, after my lord the king, who is more distressed at your bad conduct as I am, for all these gentlemen,' he indicated with an outstretched arm toward the rest of his group, 'know I owe my dignity to your goodwill, and...' I sensed that I was about to receive a lecture on my wickedness and great dishonour to the king. Unable to bear one more word of their hypocrisy, I held up my hand in interrupting Archbishop Cranmer without apology.

'My Lord Bishop, I know what is your errand, for the King has advertised to me your coming.' With fearsome contempt, I spat out my next words in a voice pricked with impatience. 'Waste no more time. I have never wronged my sovereign lord.' Lowering my tone, I huffed in contempt, before adding, 'But I know well that he is tired of me, as he was before of the good Lady Katherine.'

'Say no such thing, Madame, for your evil courses are clear for all to see in Mark Smeaton's confession.' Cranmer indicated to Cromwell to pass me the parchment upon which were written the treacherous lies. Suddenly, Anne's intemperance erupted, and I roared at the man who so arrogantly wore his newly turned coat.

'Go to!' I flung my arm out toward the door, emphasizing my desire to see them gone. I watched Cromwell flinch momentarily; Lord Chancellor Audley raised an eyebrow, surprised at the ferocity of my attack. They had expected to meet a woman cowed into submission by fear, and it gave me some satisfaction to disabuse them of their expectation. Indeed, had they not always underestimated Anne, every single one of the men who dominated her life? Henry, Suffolk, Wolsey, Cromwell; Anne may have lost the war, but never would their memories burn as brightly as Anne Boleyn's star. I raised my eyes to meet Cranmer's and added, 'It has all been done as I say because the king has fallen in love, as I know, with Jane Seymour, and does not know how to get rid of me. Well, let him do as he likes, he will get nothing more out of me and any confession that has been made is false.' I watched a rather nonplussed Archbishop cast a glance over at Norfolk, who could not resist one parting shot.

'Madame, if it be true that your brother has shared your guilt, a great punishment indeed should be yours and his as well.' At the mention of my brother's name, I swear that I could have torn his heart out with my bare hands. With simmering fury, I retorted,

'My brother is blameless, and if he has been in my chamber to speak with me, surely he might do so without suspicion, he is my brother; you cannot accuse him for that. No, the truth is that the king had him arrested so that there should be none left to take my part.' My eyes flicked over to Cromwell making it clear that I knew full well that he too was steeped in innocent blood and would soon enough drown in a morass of his own making. 'Now my lords, I pray you to be gone, for you will find out no more.' There was an uncomfortable silence, before Norfolk swept a bow, turned and stalked off towards the great hall. One by one, the others followed. The last to depart was Thomas, who cast me one final look before reluctantly taking his leave. The room fell silent. I moved over to the window to watch them leave the palace complex through the Cold Harbour Gate and wondered how Henry would take my defiance. I sensed that if there had ever been an alternative to death for me—for Anne—then through my steely defiance and bold words, I had just closed the door forever on the possibility of the king's mercy.

Chapter Forty-Four

The Tower of London, Monday,
15 May 1536

My ladies bustled around me, going about their work quietly with barely baited breath, leaving the atmosphere in my bedchamber pregnant with tension. Layer by layer, I was carefully dressed whilst I stared impassively straight ahead, lifting or stretching my arms above my head, or out from my body, to accommodate the many petticoats, the kirtle and gown, which were being laced and pinned into place around me. I tried to remember what Anne had worn for her trial but only one thing stuck in my head, and that was that she had worn a cap, decorated with a jaunty black and white feather. I could never forget it. It seemed so elegant and glamorous, as if Anne had deliberately set out to show that she was not cowed one iota by the might of the State. Yes, I sensed it keenly, Anne's dramatic flair and determination that in amongst those 2,000 souls, she would be distinctive—and so unforgettably Anne.

Seeing no threat in a lady's petticoats, Cromwell had allowed several of my dresses, hoods, and jewels to follow me from Greenwich at my request. I set about selecting the gown that I would wear for my trial the evening before, perusing several soft velvets, rough damasks, smooth silks and bristling taffeta, until I felt drawn toward a black velvet English gown and a petticoat of crimson damask; crimson the colour of martyrdom. I smiled to myself, for in amongst those items sent from the queen's wardrobe was a black velvet cap and a black and white feather—it seemed that the mistress of destiny had chosen for me. My costume was set for the charade in which I would shortly take centre stage. I began to gather myself into a state of profound serenity and unwavering focus. I would need every ounce of my wit about me if I were ever to out-manoeuvre Cromwell.

I glanced toward the window, my attention caught by the increasing hubbub of commotion coming from the crowds pouring through the Cold Harbour Gate and into the great hall. The hour of Anne's trial was approaching, as hundreds of men and women, eager to witness history in the making, were jostling to get prime seats. At the same time, I was being drawn backwards, as Lady Boleyn pulled tightly at the laces of my kirtle. I had lost weight over the previous weeks, and I felt the looseness of the bodice, where it had once fitted snugly about my slender frame.

'Tighter!' I spoke firmly. 'It still feels loose and it must not.' I needed the physical tightness of the gown to help hold me together emotionally.

'You have lost weight, Madame.' Elizabeth said, unflustered by my command. I threw her a glance over my shoulder, and replied,

'It seems that being falsely accused of adultery and treason by one's husband has its benefits, Lady Boleyn.' Whilst my aunt continued to pull at my laces, when I looked at her again, her eyes flicked up to meet mine and the faintest of smiles played on her lips. Elizabeth Wood had hated me from the very first moment that I met her. How ironic, then, that just when we were about to say goodbye, we had come to a truce of sorts. A reluctant respect and admiration for her niece had begun to take hold of Lady Boleyn, and through the slimmest of cracks, she began to show me a warmth and regard that I had never seen before.

As Elizabeth continued her work, I thought back on what most recently had transpired. It had been exhausting; for a full five days, the sound of the sawing of wood and hammering of nails continued virtually unabated from dawn to dusk. The relentless noise came from the army of workmen who had arrived at the Tower on 9 May. Although Master Kingston had come to my chambers to explain what was afoot, I already knew the nature of their work. Lord Rochford and I were to be tried in the king's hall within the precinct of the Tower, and a great platform, benches and stands were to be erected to accommodate the estimated 2,000 spectators who were expected to throng to witness the first trial of a queen in England.

As the hall stood just across the inner ward, the sound inveigled its way into my rooms, gnawing away at what little peace I had. After my altercation with members of the king's Council, I had received no other visitors but Sir William Kingston, and whilst the machinery of state continued to turn and build its case against me, I was no longer pressed to confess my guilt. To my relief, the spiteful torment of not only Lady Boleyn, but of my other ladies, had also begun to abate. It seemed that they had tired of their game. They saw me as a condemned woman, although I had not yet been tried; the die was cast and there was nothing further to be gained from taunting someone who teetered on the edge of eternity. In fact, I often caught them looking at me, trying to make out the enigma that was Anne Boleyn. They had expected my utter collapse, of that I am sure. Although I was yet to be completely transformed by the incredible events that would shortly overtake me, if anything, I was progressively strengthened by the steadfast knowledge of my innocence, unshakeable in my defiance of the injustice against me, my sweet brother and my friends.

A deep sense of calm momentarily found a home within my breast, and despite the continued absence of my almoner and the sacrament in my oratory, I immersed myself in prayer and quiet reflection. As it turned out, such tranquillity, such assuredness that all would be well, would soon be rent apart. As I look back at those middling days of my imprisonment, I think my serenity was borne more from a deep sense of denial, rather than an acceptance of my imminent demise. For who can comprehend the moment of their own death, particularly when faced with such a violent end? But my ladies were beginning to respect Anne's courage and her strength of character, which seemed to be maturing under the enormously trying circumstances.

In the end, Henry granted my request for an open trial. But I did not flatter myself that this was assuredly on my account. As ever, it served the king's purpose; for to murder a queen without staining the king's reputation required a delicate dance of law and state procedure. I knew Tudor society well enough by then to be under no illusion that the law existed to defend the state—and king—first and foremost. It mattered little that the evidence presented was either missing or deeply flawed. Having been accused, Anne already carried the burden of guilt, and must seek to establish her innocence without knowing in advance the charges against her, what evidence might be presented, or if any witnesses would be called. I had thought on it a thousand times in trying to prepare myself for the ordeal ahead; I thought of finding myself alone in the centre of the cavernous great hall with no one, not even counsel, to defend me.

I knew the charges that would be put to the court, though I could not remember the dates already etched on the indictments that would soon be read aloud; but I did remember from my history books that Anne was either pregnant or being churched when most of the offences were allegedly committed. I was prepared. Nothing that they would say to me that day could surprise or ambush me. As God is my witness, it is not that I expected that my wit would clear me of the charges. Even if I had not known Anne's' fate, an acquittal was extraordinarily rare in the sixteenth century, so I did not expect salvation. What I set out to do that day, I did for Elizabeth. I wanted my daughter to be proud of her mother, to draw upon this moment in years to come; when she would need a role model to find the strength and courage to guide her through her own hour of darkness.

I was roused from my endless machinations as Lady Boleyn came in front of me to fasten the loose English gown from its flared collar to my waist, where the front of the dress split to reveal the crimson damask petticoat underneath, and about my middle, my aunt clipped an elaborate gold girdle. Over the white linen coif already fitted snugly over my plaited hair, my velvet cap was pinned in place, along with the soft, dancing feather, which was attached to its brim. Finally, with a gold and ruby carcanet placed about my neck, and many fine rings slipped onto my long, elegant, Boleyn fingers, I was ready to make my first public appearance since my incarceration nearly two weeks earlier.

I glanced at the clock; it was half past eight in the morning. I knew Master Kingston would arrive at my chambers at nine in order to conduct me into the courtroom. I exhaled deeply, determined to contain the anxiety that pushed its way up from my belly. Extending my hand toward Lady Boleyn, I opened my palm indicating that she should pass me my book of hours for I wished to spend the next half hour in prayer, beseeching the merciful Lord to give me strength. Elizabeth placed the soft, velvet-bound cover into my hand. I thanked my ladies kindly, before sweeping off toward my oratory, there to wait my calling forth, and to write yet another page in the tragedy of Anne's life.

'Madame the court is ready for you.' I was kneeling before the altar in my privy closet, when Master Kingston's gravelly voice cut through the silence. With my hands still clasped in prayer, I turned my head to see Sir William standing at the door of my little sanctuary. I crossed myself, before rising to my feet, the soft folds of my petticoats arranging themselves around me as I did so. I could already hear the indistinct rumble of 2,000 expectant voices in the direction of the king's great hall. I felt my body tense as the adrenaline that flowed through me primed my senses such that my awareness was sharp and clear.

Once outside my closet, I fell in step behind Sir William. Following me was the Lieutenant of the Tower, Sir Edmund Walsingham, who, thankfully, I had seen very little of since my imprisonment. Lady Kingston and my Aunt Elizabeth followed; my other ladies were given leave to join the crowds that would stand witness to my trial.

Anne's destiny seemed impatient for her to arrive. We progressed at an all too brisk pace, heading along the length of the queen's presence chamber, before turning right to pass through the king's. Guards lined the route, more in ceremony than necessity, until, within a minute, our little party approached the entrance to the great hall.

When the double doors were opened by two burly yeoman warders, a wall of deafening sound hit me—as if it had a tangible presence— momentarily crushing Anne's tiny frame under it enormous weight. Yet, I did not want anyone to see me flinch. I was stepping onto the grandest stage on which the eyes of Europe would scour my every gesture, every word and intonation for meaning, for a sign of the queen's guilt. I would rather die than give them that satisfaction. I was determined that foreign dignitaries and merchants would be writing accounts back home that the Queen of England surely stood more accused than convicted.

And so, I boldly stepped across the threshold and was delivered into the heart of a seething mass of humanity, all held within the crucible of the king's great hall. Despite the warmth of the May morning, and the fervour of the closely packed crowds, the hall remained cool with a sense of spaciousness ennobled by its thick, stone walls, vaulted ceiling and soaring pillars of cold, Purbeck marble. The medieval masons had carved out a space in which even the softest whisper was magnified tenfold, and so the cacophony of sound that greeted my entrance was almost deafening in scale. I hardened myself to it, instead focusing on every footstep, as I followed Master Kingston. Over and over, I reminded myself that I was still the Queen of England, and that through their false accusations and my innocence, I had already been elevated by God to a loftier position of grace and honour than heretofore.

I entered the hall through the doors in its south-east corner. In front of me, two outer aisles were formed by great banks of seats hastily arranged to accommodate the enormous level of public curiosity in the trial and condemnation of England's 'goggle eyed whore'. The sheer aura of the queen's presence subjugated each one, as faces turned toward her and voices fell silent. When Master Kingston reached the raised platform, draped in black cloth, in the centre of the chamber, he halted, stepped aside and indicated that I should take my place before the bar, upon a seat placed there in honour of my status. Lifting my skirts, I mounted the steps confidently before turning to face my Uncle Norfolk who, occupying the temporary office of High Steward of England, awaited my entrance.

The duke was seated upon a raised platform for all to see, while above his head stretched a rich cloth of estate, finely wrought from silken thread, glistening with gold, and emblazoned with the royal coat of arms. Its presence was symbolic of Henry's majesty; it was against the Crown that I had purportedly sinned, and it was to the Crown that I would answer. My uncle was dressed in his finest robes: a doublet of orange satin, worn beneath a gown of black velvet, lined and trimmed with the softest ermine; a closely fitted, black, velvet cap came down around his ears; in his hand rested the white staff of his office. Sitting at his feet was his son, the nineteen-year-old Earl of Surrey. As Earl Marshall of England, he also held a golden staff of office in his hand, the role playing all too well to Henry Howard's vain imperiousness.

I glanced to Norfolk's right to see the only other lord to have already taken his place, Lord Chancellor Audley, who I understood to be charged with ensuring that that the trial was conducted in accordance with the law. Like the other two men I faced, Lord Chancellor Audley rose to his feet at my entrance, adjusting his gown before sweeping into the usual deep bow. I understood that he was but a conscientious instrument of the king's business, a man who wasted no extraneous emotion on undue kindness or cruelty. I dipped a curtsy, inclining my head in polite recognition of their reverence. I then seated myself with graceful elegance followed by Norfolk, Surrey and Audley. No sooner had I done so than a thin, miserly looking man stood to speak at Norfolk's direction. I had never seen this man before, but it seemed to me that his lined face was etched from a lifetime of punctilious application to his work. Everything about him—his clothes, his demeanour and even the tone of his voice—spoke of a joyless existence, which I imagined was fulfilled as some kind legal administrator. He picked up a sheet of parchment from the desk in front of him and began to read aloud, calling out the names of twenty-six peers, requesting each one to answer their names, and to take their places in accordance with their rank on either side of the Lord High Steward. My heart thundered in my chest as I watched a procession of Anne's most intractable enemies take their places, chief amongst them was Charles Brandon, Duke of Suffolk, who sat next to Norfolk.

I suspected that the two men, who had long been my enemies, gloated with a sense of satisfaction that they had lived to see the day when the 'night crow' would be destroyed. I remained inscrutable, never taking my eyes from theirs, until finally the court was brought to order and my uncle began to speak, addressing me directly.

'Anne Boleyn, Queen of England, this court has been assembled to try you on charges of high treason, adultery and incest against His Most Sovereign Majesty, King Henry VIII of England, Ireland and France. Through His Majesty's express command, these lords who sit before you have been summoned under the powers granted to me, as Lord High Steward of England, to both hear the evidence against you, and forthwith to make their judgment as to your innocence or guilt in those matters shortly to be presented to the court.' Norfolk sat forward in his seat, furrowing his brow as if locking onto his prey, adding sombrely, 'Madame, I must press you most earnestly to answer without fear, for you will be heard patiently; be assured that justice will be done.'

Justice! I wanted to spit at him that this court mocked justice, for how could George and I ever be acquitted when four men had already been publicly convicted of being my lovers just three days earlier in Westminster Hall? But instead, I focused on the feel of the soft, velvet-clad arms of the chair beneath my palms. I was determined to draw my attention away from my anger. I knew much worse was to follow and could not risk my intemperance. It would win me no glory. My uncle explained, 'It is my duty to apprise you of what will occur here today. In a moment, the indictments against Your Grace will be read for all to hear. I will then request the prosecution to press its case, before you will be given leave to defend yourself in clear and unmolested speech. And when all this is done, I will grant the lords here assembled to prudently consider their verdict before passing judgement.' I knew not if my uncle expected me to reply. Instead I continued to breathe, slowly, deeply, mindfully. As I did so, I saw the muscle in his jaw twitch involuntarily, as it always did when his grace was unduly disturbed. It was such a small victory, but I knew my steadfastness and majestic dignity had just pricked my Lord of Norfolk's noble self-assurance. I wondered if it had suddenly occurred to him what might happen if I were to be found 'not guilty', as Lord Dacre of the North had so sensationally been declared by a similar court only the year before. My uncle had also sat as High Steward at that trial, and I knew how furious Henry was at the outcome. But the king's anger would be nothing compared to firestorm that would sweep right through Norfolk's house if he were to fail to bring in a guilty verdict against me.

After a few moments silence, Norfolk assumed my understanding, and nodded once more to the Clerk of the Crown, who pushed his chair back for a second time, and rose slowly to his feet. Stretching the parchment open within his two hands, the man with a long, pointed nose and small, piercing eyes began to read. As he did so, I did not take my eyes away from him, my face set in fearless self-righteousness throughout.

'Indictment found at Westminster on Wednesday next after three weeks of Easter…' I listened carefully as names of the members of the jury were read out, before the clerk continued to the substance of the accusations laid against me, 'Whereas Queen Anne has been the wife of Henry VIII for three years and more, she, despising her marriage, and entertaining malice against the king, and following daily her frail and carnal lust, did falsely and traitorously procure by base conversations and kisses, touchings, gifts, and other infamous in citations, divers of the king's daily and familiar servants to be her adulterers and concubines, so that several of the king's servants yielded to her vile provocations; viz., on 6 Oct. 25 Hen. VIII, at Westminster, and divers days before and after, she procured, by sweet words, kisses, touches and otherwise, Henry Norris, of Westminster, gentlemen of the privy chamber, to violate her, by reason whereof he did so at Westminster on 12 Oct. 25 Hen. VIII, and they had illicit intercourse at various other times, both before and after, sometimes by his procurement, and sometimes by that of the queen.'

I listened impassively, as one after the other of the vile and despicable lies were read aloud, dragging Anne's good name, dignity and honour through the filth of England's streets. With each sensational claim of depravity, the crowd murmured their horror which was not surprising. For two weeks, the whole of England, London in particular, seethed with salacious gossip from the stews of Lambeth to the noblest dining chambers of England's aristocracy. During that time, only the smallest number of people really knew the truth of what would be laid before the court. But the time had come for the torrent of carefully crafted slander, meant to permanently dismantle the queen's reputation, to be spewed forth and lapped up greedily by the common folk of London.

I was furious, but I had expected all this and so remained unmoved. In fact, as I listened to the seemingly never-ending list of dates and places in which Anne had purportedly woven her carnal web of debauchery and treason, I felt the greatest weight of sadness in my breast, a sadness borne from the fact that she had been so utterly forsaken, a sadness that would surely last for all eternity. '... further the said queen and these other traitors, 31 Oct. 27 Hen. VIII, at Westminster, conspired to the death and destruction of the king, the queen often saying she would marry one of them as soon as the king died, affirming that she would never love the king in her heart. And the king having a short time since become aware of the said abominable crimes and treason against himself, took such inward displeasure and heaviness, especially from his said queen's malice and adultery that certain harms and perils have befallen his royal body. And thus the said queen and the other traitors aforesaid have committed their treason in contempt of the Crown and of the issues and heirs of the said king and queen.'

With the completion of the Middlesex indictment, a great uproar burst forth within the court, as men and women turned to their neighbours, exclaiming their shocked disbelief at such heinous crimes. Some in the crowd had cried out 'Traitor!' others, 'Whore!' Yet, I drew strength for amongst those defamatory voices were those who shouted, 'God save the Queen!' and 'Lies!' Such was the commotion that the Duke of Norfolk had to hammer upon the table before him, crying out for order and restraint in the court. Eventually, as silence gradually descended, the Clerk of the Crown continued reading, this time from the Kent indictment. The gathered crowds heard the same again; this time offences committed at Greenwich and Eltham were detailed. And if such dates could not be proved specifically, then with some inward disdain, I noted that the added term 'divers days before and since' would generously cover the prosecution's failings to deliver the irrefutable evidence of my crimes. With the completion of his task, the clerk placed the parchment back upon the table in front of him, and raised his eyes to meet mine, asking,

'Anne Boleyn, Queen of England, how do you plead to these charges: guilty or not guilty?' I lifted my hand, as I spoke for the first time in the court, Anne's clear, strong voice replying,

'Not guilty.' Another rumble of discontent echoed about the court, as Norfolk then turned to one side and then the other, addressing those peers who were to try me.

'My Lords, you have been brought forth to most soberly consider all the evidence which will be laid before you, and conclude with your judgment in the case betwixt her majesty and the king.' I noted how my Uncle Norfolk did not fail to miss the opportunity to remind them exactly who was waiting but a short distance up river to hear the jury's verdict. 'It is my duty to remind you that you should try the accused indifferently and according to the evidence only.' I looked up and down the jury, appraising the characters that had been brought forth to condemn Anne to die, and realised full well that such a request was nothing short of another pretty pantomime. Amongst the lords supposedly considering the evidence 'indifferently' were Henry Courtenay, Marquess of Exeter who, next to Charles Brandon, was one of the leading figures in the Aragonese faction and had always openly hated me; Lord Morley, Jane Rochford's father and a staunch conservative, who was strongly allied to the Lady Mary's cause; Edward Grey and Thomas Stanley, both sons-in-law to my Lord of Suffolk; Edward Clinton, stepfather to the Duke of Richmond; Lord William Sandys, a life-long supporter and friend of Katherine, and Lord Wentworth, Jane Seymour's cousin, who had everything to gain from my destruction.

After much nodding of their collective understanding, Norfolk turned to a man I knew well, Sir Christopher Hales, the king's Attorney

General. Supported by a nervous looking Thomas Cromwell, Sir Christopher was to lead the prosecution for the Crown. Of course, I could not help but remember a much happier time when we were on our way to Calais, and the king, Lord Sandys, Cromwell and I, dined at Sir Christopher's house in Canterbury. How convivial it had been; a time when Anne was untouchable, a time full of so much promise! But the memories dissolved before my eyes as Sir Christopher rose to speak. Referring only intermittently to the papers laid on the table in front of him, he spoke soberly to the jury. And as one might expect of a lawyer at the pinnacle of his profession, his slick, velvet tongue eloquently wove a story of despicable deceit and depravity, delivering the full force of the shock intended to raise men's judgement against me.

Still unmoved, I sat patiently at the centre the maelstrom of lies. From the stony silence emerged Sir Christopher's catalogue of accusations, punctuated intermittently with a great outcry of shocked disbelief from the court. As I had expected, it was delivered only as a damning statement of my guilt; no witnesses were brought into court, merely a miscellany of testimony, gossip and hearsay was laid before me. In his own theatrical tone of exaggerated amazement, the court heard from Sir Christopher how Anne had discussed marriage with Norris at Greenwich on that fateful Sunday when I had so foolishly allowed anger and fear to blind me; that it was clear to any learned man that by implication, the queen must have wanted to marry him, and therefore, must have wished the king dead. The court was reminded how such words were undoubtedly treasonous, not only under the 1352 statute, but also on account of the one ratified by Parliament only two years earlier. Under the former statute, it was argued vehemently that through my proclivity for illicit sex, I had also been a willing accomplice to the act of treason, and thus equally guilty as those men who had defiled me. If this were not enough, I had entreated Henry Norris with gifts, and Sir Francis Weston with money, only in order to lure them into depraved acts of lechery. Of course, the prosecution showed no shame in describing in some graphic detail the sexual intimacy between Anne and her co-accused; that I had put my tongue into my brother's mouth, and his into mine, and that I had lain with the men in a shocking and wanton display of insatiable lust, mocking the king and degrading the honour of my estate. Numerous ladies from my chambers had come forward—apparently—to testify to my wickedness that was so foul and incontinent that they could no longer conceal it from the king or his councillors. To a great uproar in the hall, Sir Christopher Hales announced that chief among these accusers was the queen's very own sister-in-law, Lady Jane Rochford, who had sworn under oath that the queen and Lord Rochford were guilty of incest.

But they were not quite done. It seemed that they could not even leave the dead to rest in peace, as Sir Christopher turned to the testimony of a woman who had died over two years earlier. That woman was Lady Bridget Tyrwhitt. Oh Bridget, how they used your words against me! From beyond the grave, the woman who had once been Anne's friend turned into her accuser. I showed nothing of it in my face, but remembered all that had passed between us. How we had rowed during my visit to Stone Castle as the king and I made our way from Greenwich to Calais, and despite my need to make amends, we had never quite healed the wounds. And so the court heard how it had come to pass that upon Lady Bridget's deathbed, she had confessed that prior to Anne's involvement with the king, the queen had been guilty of sexual misconduct. No specifics were brought forward, but the information and innuendo was relied upon heavily by Council, who used the confession of a dying woman as evidence for Anne's most base and common nature to support its case.

At the end of his forty minute speech, Sir Christopher indicated toward the Lord High Steward that he was done with the prosecution's case for the Crown, then added that he wished to call no witnesses into court. The crowd erupted once more, but this time with a tense murmur of discontent that bubbled its way around the hall. I sensed a seed of disquiet planted amongst those gathered, as in such a serious case, it was usual to bring witnesses to court to swear to the wrong-doing of the accused. I realised that in the Tudor court, the absence of such witnesses spoke volumes to those who looked on, and I sensed the tide of popular opinion, which had been so wholeheartedly in favour of the Crown, suddenly begin to falter and turn in Anne's favour.

Then my moment came. It would be Anne's only opportunity to speak and convince the world of her innocence. I was not afraid, for my right was the sword that I would yield in battle. Free from guilt or shame, I would ride into the fray to die in a blaze of glory; ride triumphant on the back of a spirited defence of my honour. When my Uncle Norfolk addressed me, I was formidable in my readiness to reply.

'Madame, you have heard the case for the prosecution. You now have the right to defend yourself against those accusations laid against you.' I nodded my acknowledgment, deliberately surveying every lord present, before I began to speak.

'My Lords,' Anne's voice was even and filled the hall; no shred of hesitancy could attach itself to her words. 'I come willingly before you as your queen, for I seek justice, which is mine by the divine right of my innocency. I will speak openly and without fear, as my Lord of Norfolk urges…' I inclined my head toward Norfolk, who sat with the tips of his fingers pressed together, listening attentively to my every word. '…for indeed, I have nothing to hide and my conscience is without stain. All the charges that have been laid against me are false, and whosoever accuses me I can say but 'nay', without I should open up my body and my guiltless soul be there revealed.' I paused momentarily, feeling the eyes of the world upon me. Yet, I was sure-footed in my crusade, as I forged on, 'Never has a king found so loyal and true a wife has he has done in Anne Boleyn. I have always been, and remain, his majesty's most devoted servant, bound to his grace, next to God alone, as his most assured subject and wife. And my Lords,' I looked deep into the eyes of those who watched me intently, as I added with great gravity, 'I swear upon the damnation of my soul that I have never transgressed against his grace in thought, word or deed.' A great murmur rushed through the court room, for such a declaration in Anne's world carried considerable weight, and could not be dismissed lightly. I allowed my words to sink in before continuing, 'As the world is aware, I indeed know all those men accused with me, but have only ever treated them properly, in accordance with their status of their birth. Yes, I have given some of them gifts on occasion, and yes, I have given Sir Francis money.' A sonorous tumult of noise erupted at my 'confession'. Whilst the commotion erupted, I remained impassive like a parent who waited for her naughty children to settle. I then added soberly, '…just as any master or mistress has a right to do for those that serve them with friendship and loyalty. Indeed, do not many of you here today, sit comfortably upon your houses and titles, only upon the account of the great love that his majesty bears you?' I raised an eyebrow with a wry smile, as I could not resist but point out the hypocrisy of such ludicrous accusations. Accompanying my words had been many jeers, and much taunting laughter from the common folk of London, who clearly appreciated my sense of irony. Then with renewed seriousness, I went on, 'As for those who allegedly have spoken against me, I marvel that they have not been brought forth as witnesses. My Lords if these 'confessions' were properly and legally begotten, then why do these witnesses not come here to court, where all may hear them freely swear to my guilt—as you so claim they would? Surely, they have nothing to fear from one woman when the might of the Crown and good graces of a king stand behind them? I say they do not come, for it is clear that Sir Christopher brings not evidence to this court, merely tittle-tattle and gossip woven into a case fabricated for the purposes of seeing an innocent woman, and those who might speak up for her, utterly destroyed...' I paused again to look carefully at each person who sat before me. 'I stand accused on the evidence of Lady Rochford alone. For other than Lady Bridget, whose evidence is mere hearsay, a woman delirious with fever and on the edge of death, you have spoken of no other names. And if indeed, my lords, Lady Rochford passed on treasonous words that I have supposedly uttered, to her husband Lord Rochford, then why does she not also stand accused? For to know of treason, but to report it so belatedly, is an offence in itself, is it not? I say yet again that it is because no such treason existed!' I drew in my breath. I knew I was coming to the end of my speech and steadied myself for the final surgical incision which I was to make consciously and deliberately, slicing fearlessly through the heart of the real truth of my predicament. 'Nay, my lords, you bring no evidence of my guilt because, in truth, there is none to bring. It is clear that, as I have said before, the king simply grows tired of his poor wife. Mistress Seymour now takes his fancy, and as he does not know how to get rid of me, he has allowed himself to be led into accepting false and wicked counsel from those who would find it more convenient to their own prosperity if I and my brother were destroyed.' I stared defiantly at Cromwell, as the king's hall, which had held its collective breath listening to the entirety of the queen's defence against her accusers, finally exploded into a tumult of rowdy disorder. My words unleashed the truth I had so desperately wanted the world to hear. With it, came more cries than ever of 'not guilty!' and 'God save your Grace!' Anne may be doomed, of that I was sure, but I had planted seeds of serious doubt, and began to turn the crowd in her favour. I felt exonerated. I had exposed how Anne was an innocent victim of one man's capricious moods, and the court's insatiable desire for power. So riotous was the response to my speech that it took nearly five minutes to quieten the court, before Norfolk spoke again.

'Madame, the constable will escort you back to your chambers for a time, whilst the lords here present will consider all the evidence before them. You will be recalled when there is a verdict.' I was slightly surprised, for I did not remember any accounts of the queen's withdrawal. Nevertheless, I did as requested. Rising from my seat, I curtsied, and retired to the queen's lodgings along with my two ladies.

For a short time, I teetered in the hinterland between the living and the dead, wholly accused, not yet condemned. It is hard to believe that I clung to the mere wisp of hope that somehow Anne would be delivered from the jaws of death. I could not accept that in less than four days, I would have to face Anne's execution and make it my own.

One after the other they came. I was prepared knowing that there could be no other outcome. Still, as each lord declared his verdict of 'guilty', I felt as if I were drowning under the weight of a hundred stones being laid upon my chest. As the most senior peer passing judgment upon Anne, Suffolk delivered the *coup de grâce* with barely concealed relish. With a unanimous conviction, I watched tears run down my uncle's gaunt face, as I remembered they would. I found it difficult to believe that the emotion that flowed so openly spoke of anything other than his relief that he had secured the verdict demanded by the king. Perhaps it was self-pity, for Anne had totally dismantled his vision for the glory of the house of Norfolk. Then followed the words which I had long dreaded, and never thought to hear:

'Because thou hast offended our Sovereign the King's Grace in committing treason against his person and here are attained of the same, the law of the realm is this, that thou hast deserved death, and my judgement is this: that thou shalt be burnt here within the Tower of London, on the green, elsewhere to have thy head smitten off, as the king's pleasure shall be further known of the same.' As he finished speaking, from amongst the deafening roar of mixed emotion that washed down over me from the stands on either side of the hall, I heard the familiar voice of Mary Orchard, as she shrieked out in anguish. It was a gut-wrenching, primitive sound, which spoke of a lifetime of love and devotion to one who had been raised as if she were her own. I did not flinch or turn my head. All that I had achieved that day could have been thrown away in an instant if I allowed fear to steal away with my composure—and I feared that if I saw her face, I would be lost. I maintained my silence as the court came to heel, and Norfolk sat forward in his chair. We had walked a long path together, Norfolk and I, and it seemed our act was all but over. Did I see a flicker of something coming close to regret pass across his face, as he asked me, 'Is there anything that you wish to say, Madame?'

'Yes, my Lord, there is.' The words came quickly and easily, and I knew not who spoke them; perhaps they were Anne's, perhaps they were mine, but they came from our heart. 'My Lords, I will not say your sentence is unjust, nor presume that my reasons can prevail against your convictions. I'm willing to believe that you have sufficient reasons for what you have done, but they must be other than those which have been produced in this court, for I am clear of all the offences which you then laid to my charge. I have ever been a faithful wife to the king, though I do not say I have always shown him the humility which his goodness to me and the honour to which he raised me merited. I confess I have had jealous fancies and suspicions of him, which I had not discretion or wisdom enough to conceal at all times. But God knows, and is my witness, that I have not sinned against him in any other way.' I paused, my eyes flicking down to the coronation ring that I still wore upon my finger. I was defeated but I was determined to uphold Anne's enormous bravery and dignity to the end. 'Think not I say this to prolong my life. God has taught me how to die and will strengthen my faith. Think not that I am so bewildered in my mind as not to lay the honour of my chastity to heart now in my extremity, when I have maintained it all my life long, much as ever a queen did. I know these my last words will avail me nothing but for the justification of my chastity and honour. As for my brother, and those others who are unjustly condemned. I would willingly suffer many deaths to deliver them, but since I see it pleases the king, I shall willingly accompany them in death, with this assurance,' I paused once more this time consciously and for effect. With my voice steady and strong, I stared into the hearts of each of the men afore me, and added, '...that I shall lead an endless life with them in peace.' And so it was done. Anne was judged and condemned, and I feared that together we would walk the loneliest of paths to the scaffold. With nothing more to say, and in amongst a great hubbub of sound, I stood to my feet and curtsied to the lords afore me, and swept from the chamber without a backward glance. My life in this world was over, and all that was left for me was to prepare to die. I had no idea that one, final dramatic turn of events awaited me that would be both my undoing and my salvation.

Chapter Forty-Five

The Tower of London,
Tuesday 16 May, 1536

I watched her playing in the garden below the window of my privy apartments at Greenwich. She looked so beautiful in her tiny gown spun from cloth of gold, the morning sunlight setting her hair alight with shimmering reds and gold. Elizabeth, my Elizabeth; my heart soared to see her, and I pressed my palms against the cool window, tapping on the glass with my forefinger to catch her attention. I could not understand why she was alone, but she looked so happy chasing after two dancing butterflies, her face alight with radiant joy. I called Elizabeth's name aloud, but she could not hear me. I tapped harder on the glass, this time with my knuckles, until she stopped and turned her head about searching with some confusion for the source of the sound which had caught her attention. As I rapped on the glass again, she finally located me, raising her eyes to meet mine. I was overjoyed to see her again and wanted to sweep her up in my arms and cover her in kisses—but I knew I could not. I called her name and she smiled at me, reaching out her small, delicate hand, opening and closing her fingers in a childish, carefree gesture of greeting.

My joy suddenly turned to horror as a man swept into view dressed head to foot in black, a long, woollen cloak billowing behind him, as he strode forward heading towards my daughter. I could not see his face as it was covered by a hood that hung forward over his head. He was dark and menacing. I was gripped by fear. I knew my daughter was in danger, so I hammered hard on the glass, trying desperately to work the windows open, shaking the handles violently so that I could warn her to run and hide. But they were sealed and the latches would not move. Elizabeth did not see him. She stood smiling and waving at me. I was frantic and ran from window to window, banging hard against the glass, calling out for somebody to help her. Tears streamed down my face. I remember so well the sense of overwhelming impotence, of failing her so entirely because I just could not reach her. Horrified, I watched as the man grabbed her and she began to kick and scream,

546

screaming out my name, calling for her mother to help her...

'Elizabeth!' I cried out aloud, waking myself up, as I sat bolt upright in bed, my face wet with the tears. In the silence of my bedchamber, all I could hear was blood pounding through my temples, driven by the adrenaline which surged through my veins. I had been lost in a nightmare, and then remembered that I was living under my own horrific spectre of death. The events of the day before rushed in as the words of condemnation replayed over and over in my mind; as did the news that George, too, awaited a traitor's death, having been condemned to death in a trial which had immediately followed my own.

A thousand times, I turned my mind away from the imagined stench of burning flesh and the spectre of white hot flames dissolving my clothes, and melting my body to its charred remains. I took solace from what I knew should be Anne's fate, but had little time to gather myself further before the door to my bedchamber opened. Like a vision that was no less welcome to me than if I had seen the Virgin Mary herself, the faces of two women that I thought I would surely never see again appeared in the door frame. Coming toward me were Margery Wyatt and Nan Gainsford with expressions of unspeakable pain and of great concern for my welfare, mixed with the greatest joy possible that we were to be briefly re-united. I could not believe my eyes. I had begged for my friends to be allowed to attend upon me, to provide me with some shred of solace and comfort amongst the ruins of a life dismantled. But each time Master Kingston promised that my request would be passed on to Master Secretary Cromwell, I was met with stony-faced denial. I surmised that with my condemnation, Cromwell now had no further need for his spies, and what would best serve both the king, and himself, would be the sight of the queen accorded all due courtesy and respect—despite her heinous depravity. How gracious would the king's majesty be in showing such kindness to a woman who had traitorously deceived her sovereign lord!

But I did not care why they were here, just that we were together once more. Thus, I swung my legs about, and without any care for my rank, or the usual reverence that would pass between us, I hurled myself at both of them, sweeping them up in my arms, each one of us hardly able to speak for the emotion that choked us. We clung to each other; tears of joy, tinged with fearful anguish at what lay ahead,

547

streaming down our faces. Barely able to find my words I spoke,

'What...how...are you really here? Where is Lady Kingston, Lady Boleyn...Can it be true?' Unable to let go of each other, Margery replied,

'Lady Kingston remains in attendance to supervise us all; the others have been dismissed and we are here now, and I swear we will not leave your side. They have said that we can attend you until...' My friend looked away, her eyes brimming over with tears, unable to speak of the fate that awaited me. I brushed it aside caring only for their presence, to hear the sound of their kindly voices, and to be held again, touched with the soothing balm of human kindness. I was desperate to hear news first and foremost of my family, who had never been far from my thoughts. I took them both by the hands and pulled them toward the bed, indicating that they should sit down by my side.

'I cannot tell you how much it means to have you here with me...and oh, how awful it has been to have those about me who never loved me!' Both of them smiled at me sympathetically, Nan linking her arm around mine, intuitively understanding my need for physical contact, as was always her gift. She then added,

'Madge Shelton and Margery's sister, Anne, have also come with us. So rest assured, Your Grace, you are only surrounded now by those who love you.' I smiled at her, conveying my enormous relief, touching her cheek with my hand in appreciation of her words. Then she continued, 'I have also been bound upon my life to speak for her grace, the Duchess of Richmond.' I thought of Mary Howard and felt my heart ache for the young woman that I loved almost as much as if she was my own child. 'Mary wanted me to tell you how much she desired to come and serve Your Grace in the Tower, but sadly, the duke and his majesty strictly forbade it.' I raised an eyebrow, imagining only too well what the seventeen-year-old duchess had had to say about the harsh realities of being subject to the will of the men who dominated her life. Margery confirmed my suspicions, as she added,

'I heard from Mary herself that she rowed fiercely with his grace about the matter. Only the direct intervention of the king finally ended the argument.' I knew only too well how much Mary longed to see me, as I did her. But for a royal duchess and daughter-in-law of the king to attend upon a traitor was surely unthinkable and would never be sanctioned. I could not contain my curiosity any longer.

'What of my family, my mother, father and sister? I heard tell that George acquitted himself admirably at his trial, so much so that many thought he would be found not guilty. Have you heard anything more of him?' Margery took a deep breath before launching into her account of all that had passed since I had been cast into the Tower, and how the machinery of Tudor society had churned on, seeking to devour the Boleyns and those who stood in honourable service of our family.

'After you were taken from Greenwich, I travelled straight to Hever, as you asked, to your mother who fell into much weeping and great sorrow at the news of your arrest.' In anguish for the love I bore Elizabeth Boleyn, I sighed heavily, shaking my head as I exclaimed,

'Oh my poor mother, she will surely die of sorrow!' I imagined her face, and momentarily longed to be held her in my arms. Margery however went on, sweeping my vision temporarily aside.

'I gave her your letter, which she read with tears in her eyes before kissing it and holding it to her breast.' In that letter, I had told the countess what I feared would unfold; of my suspicions of Cromwell and the king's desire for Mistress Seymour. I had sworn again upon the damnation of my soul that I had never sinned against the king, nor besmirched my chastity or honour. I had begged her forgiveness for my pride and intemperance, which I feared had driven the king into the arms of another. A whispered message from Mrs Orchard had already assured me that my mother knew me guiltless, and that her love had never wavered for her youngest daughter, but I was thirsty to hear more. I was sure that Mary Orchard had somehow received this part message from Margery, who alone held within her breast the entirety of my mother's last words to me. Margery shifted herself round to face me more fully taking my hand in hers as she went on. 'She is angry Anne, but not at you. I swear that having read your words and fully digested their meaning, she ranted with a ferocity that I had never seen in your most noble and serene mother.'

'What did she say, please speak of it all?'

'She was furious with his grace the Duke of Norfolk, her brother, and your father, using the most opprobrious language for their failure to protect you, or beg the king for mercy. Yet...' Margery then lowered her voice and looked around, indicating to Nan that she should get up and close the door to my bedchamber. Nan swiftly slipped off the bed and did so before returning to our side, perching once more on the edge of the bed next to her two friends. When she was settled, Margery continued her story in hushed tones, '...the worst of her invective though was reserved for his majesty who she cursed for his faithlessness and cruelty. Madame, I had to calm her for I feared that she might be overheard!' I covered my mouth with my hand as if I could hold back her words of treason. 'In the end, your mother fell into my arms and wept for the longest time. But eventually, she calmed herself, and urged me to find a way to send you her message.' Margery squeezed my hand in all earnestness as she repeated the words of comfort that bound me in love to a woman who had shown me a mother's unconditional love and who, even in my deepest gratitude, I could never repay. 'Anne, your mother begged me to tell you that she knows that you are without stain, and as surely as God knows the truth in men's hearts, whatever comes to pass, you can be assured that the Good Lord will not forsake you, just as your mother wished me to tell you that her love for you is without end. Indeed, she asked your father permission to return to London to plead for herself with the king and Master Secretary Cromwell, but he has steadfastly refused to allow your mother to travel.'

I thought on all that Margery said. My father had clearly kept his pledge to me, to keep my mother away from the wreckage of our young lives. However, I also realised that when my letter was delivered by Margery, my mother did not yet know of George's arrest, or that we, along with four other men, were to shortly die. Anxiously, I asked,

'Is my mother still at Hever? Does she now know that George and I are shortly to die?' I saw in my friend's face that she loathed being the harbinger of such difficult news, but out of her friendship to me, she was determined to at least honour me with the truth.

'Yes, she remains at Hever, and we are in constant correspondence. Unable to be in London herself, she asked me plainly to inform her of how events were unfolding. Of course, I wrote to her of George's arrest, and of the other men who also languish here in the Tower.' Then Margery paused, looking down at her hands in sorrowful reflection, before adding, 'I also honoured my pledge to your mother by writing to her of your conviction—and George's. Although, they were words that my pen scrawled reluctantly upon the parchment, for they were weighty words indeed, words which no mother should be forced to read.' I crossed myself, imagining the messenger arriving at Hever, probably sometime later that day and my poor, dear mother, receiving the news all alone. I was utterly heart-broken and a tear spilled down my cheek in sorrow for her, but I wiped it away, determined that I would be brave for my friends. Margery then added quietly, 'Anne, you should also know that she begged to be allowed to attend upon you, but your father has forbidden it.' I admit I was both deeply touched and shocked that Elizabeth Boleyn had fought so hard to be close to me. I was sure that she was terrified for her children, but I was also certain that the same maternal emotions that had accompanied Anne Boleyn's arrival into this world had driven her mother's need to be at her daughter's side at the end. Yet I was relieved that this had been denied. How could I have faced my mother's grief when I struggled daily to contain my own? In this, I was grateful for my father's intransigence.

'And what of George, and my father?' I asked again.

'Of your brother I have heard very little other than all about London, people are remarking on how well he spoke at his trial. On account of this, and the lack of witnesses brought to court, increasing numbers whisper of his innocence—and yours.' Then Nan interjected,

'Yes, it is so. I think that evermore the people of London have sympathy for Your Grace, Lord Rochford and those other poor gentlemen. His majesty has been seen virtually every night aboard his barge on his way to visit Mistress Seymour. Many are now saying that it is indeed as you proclaimed at your trial.' I wondered if my two friends had been somewhere within the midst of the crowds in the king's hall, just the day before. Nan continued, '…that the king's lust for Mistress Seymour drives him to seek a convenient way to dispatch of his true wife!' I knew from history that many assumed Anne's guilt once she had been arrested. And while I wondered if my friends over-exaggerated for my sake, there was a level of disquiet and suspicion against the Crown that possibly there was something in what they said. I was proud that my brother and I had planted the seeds of doubt that would, over the years, take root in the ground of our innocence. Margery continued,

'I have seen little of my Lord Wiltshire. If gossip and hearsay hold a kernel of truth then I understand that he did indeed make every effort to reach the king's majesty on the day George rode after his grace to Whitehall, and indeed for several days thereafter. Yet his majesty has been little seen at court, with only very few of the king's most favoured gentlemen allowed access to his privy chambers. It is said that Master Secretary Cromwell now controls access to the king entirely, and that not even the Archbishop of Canterbury has been granted an audience with his grace.' I nodded again adding soberly,

'Master Secretary does not wish anyone to speak on my behalf; he is a man afraid of his own shadow.' There was a moment's silence whilst I suspect we three all pondered upon how savagely Cromwell had turned on the family who had done much to enable his meteoric rise at court. Finally, I added softly, 'and my sister? What of Mary?' Margery answered.

'Mary remains in Calais, as you instructed.' I knew then that Mary must have relayed to Margery at least some of the contents of my letter. Not only had I begged Mary's forgiveness and understanding for my transgression and harshness toward her, I had also beseeched her to remember her pledge to me—the one she had made in Calais in 1532, to remain away from court if anything were to happen to her sister. Clearly, Mary honoured her word, and I was glad for it. At least I knew she would be safe away from the simmering intrigue. Suddenly, there was a knock at the door.

'Enter!' I spoke up, all three of us turning to see who announced themselves. When the door opened, Madge Shelton appeared. In truth, I was a little surprised that the Sheltons allowed my cousin to serve me, but Madge and I had an affectionate relationship and perhaps Lady Shelton, too, had been ultimately moved by Anne's courage and protestations of innocence. Both Margery and Nan rose to their feet as I beckoned the child forward. Madge curtsied before I welcomed her into my arms as she was overcome with emotion at the sight of her erstwhile mistress. Having composed herself, my young cousin stepped back and announced,

'Your Majesty, the Archbishop of Canterbury is here to see you.' Of course, how could I forget! Thomas Cranmer would visit Anne in those final days. I wondered what news Thomas would bring from the king. Something tugged at my memory, something significant, I was sure.

But my mind was so agitated that I often found it difficult to think of anything but the horrors of the execution that awaited me; all my energies were directed at maintaining my dignity and composure as best as I was able. I replied,

'Then ladies, you must help make me ready. Madge, please tell his grace that I will be with him presently.' Madge curtsied and withdrew closing the door behind her. I was keen to meet with Thomas alone and perhaps I would find out the truth. Had Thomas deserted his patron, or had his majesty been moved to clemency toward the woman he had once so cherished and adored?

From the dais in my presence chamber, I looked down on Thomas Cranmer, the man whom I had long entrusted with my well-being, and with all matters that touched upon my conscience. However, on this occasion, the usual delight I felt at seeing my friend was tinged with anger. Thomas' appearance some eight days earlier, alongside my Lord Norfolk, Lord Chancellor Audley and Master Cromwell, had eroded the trust which existed between us. Had Thomas betrayed me like so many others? Despite everything he knew of me, had he so readily accepted my guilt as a wanton harlot and traitor against the king, or had his speech that day only been for show, for a reason as yet unknown to me? On account of the great love I had always borne him, I gave my old friend the benefit of the doubt. Nevertheless, I felt my body tense and my defences sharpened. I was weary of the world, and had seen too much betrayal in my short life to allow myself the grace of innocence. Dressed in his usual clerical garb, Thomas took off his Canterbury cap in deference to the woman who, despite everything, remained his queen. He looked a man much troubled by life due no doubt to weighty matters of state placed upon his shoulders by the king and Cromwell. I saw the light in his eyes flicker precariously, as if the slightest breeze might have extinguished it forever. Finally, I spoke in a calm and relaxed voice while keeping an emotional distance.

'My Lord Archbishop pray tell, why have you come before me? Is it on the king's business?

'Your Grace, there are indeed matters of some delicacy which touch his majesty's conscience and which I have been instructed to discuss with you. But I have also been charged with the honour of delivering to you the sacrament this day, and hearing your confession, as I believe Your Grace has requested.' I felt Anne's soul soar, finally to receive the spiritual solace which she had longed for since being committed to her prison! With an outstretched arm, I indicated that the Archbishop should walk with me to my oratory so that we might speak in private. I sensed that Thomas craved forgiveness almost as much as I craved to have a priest absolve me of my sins. I led the way indicating to my ladies that they should remain outside of my closet in attendance.

Finally, Thomas and I were alone, the door of my oratory clicking shut behind us. Dressed soberly in my French gown of black velvet, I turned about to face my friend, who to my surprise, abruptly sank to his knees before me taking my hand, he kissed the coronation ring that still remained upon my finger, whispering fiercely and with all solemnity,

'Madame, I beg you to forgive my transgressions against you for I fear that after all your goodness, I have failed you utterly.' He raised his doleful eyes to meet mine, but I remained silent allowing Thomas Cranmer to say all that he had a mind to say. Understanding that my silence was my implicit permission to continue, Thomas went on with his story. 'When I was summoned from Knole and first heard of the accusations made against Your Grace, I set myself down with all haste to write to the king. I was mindful not to offend our sovereign lord, but I beg you to believe that my only intention was to move his grace to see your innocence without further incurring his majesty's wrath, which would have been of little help to you or those who find themselves equally nigh.' I was acutely aware of the tense energy of his tortured soul as he continued, 'As I was writing, a messenger arrived summoning me without delay to the Star Chamber to meet with Lord Chancellor Audley and other sundry lords of the king's Privy Council. They laid before me Master Smeaton's confession and that of Sir Henry. Forgive me Madame, but it was with the heaviest heart that I saw how those around the king were bent to move against you.' Shaking his head, he recalled with great sadness the moment that he realised that all was lost. 'I thought perhaps the only way that I might steer his grace away from this course of evil destruction was through an audience, and so I pressed Cromwell to grant me access to the king, for as you well know, he has often taken it upon himself to confide in me certain matters which have pressed greatly upon his mind.' Indeed, I did. I remembered vividly how Thomas Cranmer had intervened to soothe the king after the disappointment of Elizabeth's birth. 'Yet, despite my requests to Master Secretary Cromwell, I was turned away and I fear that those who advise his grace presently have cast the king's soul into the greatest of perils.' Thomas spoke those words softly for they were dangerous words indeed. 'Madame, I...' Thomas found it impossible to voice his dilemma which was evident for me to see. Moved with pity for the man who had clearly been rent apart by the impossible choices forced upon him, I sank down onto a chair positioned immediately next to where I was standing. With Thomas still kneeling before me, I spoke aloud to ease his troubled mind.

'My Lord Archbishop...Thomas...you were right to do what you did. I see that you have never truly forsaken me, nor judged me guilty in your heart. Whilst we are loyal subjects of the king, we are first and foremost servants of God.' Thomas raised his eyes to meet mine and I smiled at him with resignation, placing a comforting hand upon his shoulder as I went on, 'You and I have been chosen by the good Lord to set the king's soul alight with the true word of God; to free England from the evil vices and abuses presently at work within the Roman Catholic Church. This is the work we have begun, but it is not complete. I am grateful for what you have tried to do for me, and for those men falsely accused alongside me, but God in His almighty wisdom has determined that we must die, and you were right to see that our cause was lost.'

My hand fell away from my friend's shoulder as I stood once more, turning away from Thomas, and taking a few steps towards the altar upon which rested the figure of the crucified Christ. In the intimate confines of my privy closet, we were illuminated by the morning sun that poured in through the small, stained glass window facing eastwards over the privy garden. With my back still turned toward my friend, I studied the forlorn figure, betrayed and abandoned by all but God. Never had I been so keenly touched by his plight, for it was then surely my own. Yet my faith strengthened my resolve and kept me strong. As I stood silently in contemplation, I finally accepted that it was time for me to pass the light which had been gifted to Anne into Thomas's hands. I turned my head to look at Thomas and said, 'The reform within our faith is still so fragile, but you are in a position to remain as its guardian. And this, my friend, you must do when I am gone. For Mistress Seymour, as we both know, favours the old ways and will seek to turn his majesty away from the truth. Many people in this realm will look to you to champion the Reformation.' I walked back over to where Cranmer knelt, looking down upon him and smiling at him warmly as I said, 'So, my Lord Archbishop, set aside the heavy burden of your guilt. To know that you have never wavered in your heart suffices me well enough and brings me great comfort as my hour approaches.' My friend seized my hand once more, kissing the ring upon my finger again as I sensed a great wave of relief wash over him. Then I indicated that Thomas should stand, before I remembered that he had also come upon the king's business, and so I enquired,

'Now my Lord, you say that you have other matters that touch upon the king's conscience that you must speak of...I pray you to speak plainly of them now.' As one burden had been lifted from his shoulders, almost as swiftly, it was replaced by another. I saw a brooding darkness pass across his face for a second time. Reluctantly, he began to speak,

'Madame, you must forgive me once more. I fear that again I must be the messenger of the most difficult of tidings.' The good Archbishop knew that there was no easy way of saying what he must ask of me, and so came straight the point. 'His grace seeks an annulment of the marriage betwixt the two of you.' For a few seconds I was confused. Being so caught up in Anne's trial and condemnation, I had entirely forgotten that of course, Henry had not finished with Anne. It was not enough to rid himself of her through judicial murder, he needed to scrape away any remnant of her from his life in order to leave the way clear for his marriage to Jane, and more importantly, for their children to inherit the throne. I voiced the word 'annulment' out loud as I tried to come to terms with this new stain upon my honour, as my friend spoke again as if to resolve my confusion. 'His majesty has asked that in the sight of God you confess your prior knowledge of his grace's union with your sister, Mary.'

Ah yes, Mary! How could I forget the role that my own sister would perversely play in the final act of the tragedy between Henry and me? My sister had lain with the king before Henry had set his sights on Anne, and had been subsequently cast aside to make room for me in his affections. I admit that even though I remembered this final twist, I was bewildered and in my confusion, I exclaimed,

'But I do not understand. The king himself showed me the dispensation granted by the Pope that allowed his grace to be joined in wedlock with me, even though he had lain with my sister.'

'In his wisdom, his majesty points out that should both parties accept that the previous relationship with your sister, which was within the forbidden degrees of affinity, in accordance with the Dispensations Act of 1534, the earlier Papal dispensation, is invalid. Such a union, according to canon law is contrary to Holy Scripture and the laws of God.' Thomas added, 'His grace urges you to settle your conscience whilst there is still time, as he now also seeks to do.' I was still struggling with the request that my Lord Archbishop had laid before me, unable to assimilate the enormity of what was being asked of me. One implication began to torment me more than any other.

'But, we entered into the marriage in good faith…and if I were to confess otherwise, then I will disinherit my child! Elizabeth will be declared a bastard!' Thomas cast his eyes to the floor. He had anticipated the pain of Henry's final strike against me, as the arrow of the king's hatred penetrated straight through the centre of its mark. My first response was to cry, 'No! No!' I will not do it.' But like a father who understood my distress but sought to steer me into calm waters, Thomas held up his hand, raising his eyes to meet mine as he explained,

'His majesty has commanded me to tell you that if you confess to me the full knowledge of this impediment, the king, in his great mercy, will consider that you will not be executed, but instead be banished to a nunnery overseas, somewhere like Antwerp.' I searched Thomas' face for the truth for I knew what history had decreed for Anne, and remembered that talk of such banishment cruelly never materialised. Without a flicker of emotion, I asked Thomas directly,

'So says the king. What do you think my Lord? Do you think that the king is honourable in his promise? And what of my brother, and the other men who wait presently to die? Thomas, you are my friend, tell me what truth do you see in this?' Thomas Cranmer took a deep breath then spoke,

'It is possible Madame, but in truth, I think it unlikely. The king perceives himself greatly wronged and is much set on Mistress Seymour. But I have heard whispers amongst the Council that should you so confess, you will be granted a merciful death. Indeed, I hear that already a swordsman from St Omer has been sent for in anticipation of your...' Thomas faltered as he looked away searching for the right word, 'co-operation.' When he looked back at me, I looked squarely into my friend's soulful eyes, eyes that had always shown me kindness and love as I asked in barely a whisper,

'And if I will not confess to this?'

'Then his majesty will exact full retribution on you for your sins, and on those men condemned with you. They will suffer a traitor's death upon the gallows of Tyburn: be hung, drawn, then quartered, whilst you will be burnt at the stake, and your daughter cast out entirely from the king's good graces.' I turned away unable to comprehend the full horror of what I had just heard. Nausea gripped at my throat, and I swallowed hard, breathing deeply, fighting to maintain my equilibrium. When I looked into Thomas's eyes, I knew the gravity of his words and saw him silently implore me to confess as the king commanded. I was terrified for I knew that I held the fate of five men in my hands. I could send them to an excruciating, dishonourable death, or allow them the relative mercy of the axe.

Falling to my knees in front of the altar and clasping my hands together, I prayed fervently to God for guidance for the thought of betraying my daughter was too painful to bear and yet, how could I punish those five innocent men further for my sins. I raised my eyes to behold Christ, and as I did so, I saw it all so clearly in my mind. I saw Elizabeth all grown and resplendent in cloth of gold damask, her red hair flowing freely around her shoulders, as she looked proudly out from behind Boleyn eyes, a sceptre and orb held in either hand. I finally understood and accepted what was there to see all along. Every step of the way, regardless of how I tried to evade Anne's fate, history had continued to be written as it was always decreed. Anne would die but Elizabeth already had her destiny written across the stars and no one, not Henry, nor the Lady Mary, would ever deny Elizabeth her birthright. She would be the greatest queen that England had ever known. I saw then that I could agree to Henry's demands with the assurance that Elizabeth would rise from the ashes of her father's betrayal. Without turning to face Thomas, I spoke clearly and without fear.

'My Lord Archbishop, pray tell his most gracious majesty that I freely and willingly confess that I knew of his grace's relationship with my sister before we were married; that in the eyes of God, our union has never been valid, even though we entered into it in good faith. Tell the king that I agree wholeheartedly to an annulment. All this I confess before you, and before God.' The Archbishop breathed a sigh of relief before I added quietly, 'But know that I say this, Thomas, only to save my brother and those other men condemned from a fate that they have never deserved.' My friend nodded his understanding.

With that, our business was done. I asked Thomas to come forward so that I may receive the sacrament that I had so long been denied. I knew that I had left behind guardians who would watch over Elizabeth, but I know now that she must make her own way, looking in all things to God for guidance until her time, too, will eventually come.

Sometime later Thomas left promising that he would deliver my message of submission to the king and that he would return to hear my final confession should the king insist that I die. And so, in the presence of my friends, the day slipped away all too quickly. I alone knew what history decreed awaited us with the coming sunrise. It was Wednesday, 17 May. It was the day my brother and my friends were to be executed, and the day that my life finally, irrevocably, collapsed around me.

Chapter Forty-Six

The Tower of London,
Tuesday 16 and Wednesday 17 May, 1536

After hearing my confession and saying mass in my oratory, the Archbishop of Canterbury left for Whitehall to relay my words of confession to the king. All things considered, I passed the day before my brother's execution peacefully enough in the company of my beloved friends. Sometimes we reminisced about our carefree days spent in pleasure and goodly sport. Occasionally, we laughed at mere trifles that mattered so much at the time, but of course were of no consequence at all. In between, each of us fell into quiet reflection struggling to comprehend the calamitous events which had struck at the heart of our happy, close-knit sisterhood. Neither Nan nor Margery said anything to me, but their haunted faces spoke of their fear of where they would find the courage to see their friend and mistress die, and how they would pick up the pieces of their own lives in the aftermath.

Later in the day, I entertained Master Kingston at dinner, and was even quite merry for a time, laughing as I said that I thought the king might yet banish me to a nunnery. Of course I never believed it. But when Sir William's face was suddenly rendered with such grim sobriety that I enquired as to what troubled him, he told me flatly that my brother and his co-accused were set to die the next morning on Tower Hill. However, the king in his mercy had ordered their sentences be commuted to beheading with the axe. I could not say that I was happy, but I did feel a great relief in that my co-operation may have contributed to sparing them from the most unspeakable, horrific death. Shortly after his declaration, my dinner guest departed, leaving his ponderous news hanging in my chamber.

The night finally began to close in on us, and faced with the imminent death of the man that I loved so dearly, my mood turned increasingly sombre. I stood silently at the window of my privy chamber looking up into a troubled sky. After weeks of the most glorious weather, storm clouds had gathered over London. In the aftermath of a sultry summer's day, a capacious, burgeoning mass of black clouds hurriedly covered the setting sun, throwing the land into an early dusk, bringing with it an ominous sense of foreboding. I was as sensitised to its coming as any wild animal to the shifting mood of Mother Nature; my body a barometer to the fluctuating pressure of the heavy air which hung about the city. As I watched the White Tower cast in hues of menacing grey, I began to pace restlessly up and down my chamber, unable to find a shred of peace in a mind that was rapidly descending into the same hysteria that had overtaken me on the day that I was first committed to my prison.

I began to panic at the thought of never again seeing those that I truly loved; panic that I would not be able to walk to my death without collapsing in sheer terror; panic that I would never find the courage for which Anne was renowned at the very end of her life. Over and over, without respite, I played the same gory scene in my inflamed mind. I saw the steel blade of the axe hacking at my brother's twitching, bloody body, and then saw my own headless corpse lying in the straw upon the scaffold, the stump of my neck oozing with the last vestiges of life. I knew that night that I was going to die. I tried, oh sweet Jesus, I tried so very hard to stop the trembling in my body, to settle the shaking of a heart that had been greatly agitated by the vexation of my faithless mind. But I was determined not to frighten those ladies who had set aside their own fears to serve their mistress, and so I fell into bed where I could hide my face from their ever-present concern and shield them from my utter desolation.

I lay for some hours in the darkness, terrified of the morning, unable to find a scrap of dry land upon which my shipwrecked mind might clamber ashore. No vestige of safety remained for me, nor would gentle sleep rock me into a peaceful slumber. Instead, as Nan and Margery slept soundly on pallets close to my bed, I lay awake staring above my bed at the opulent canopy emblazoned with Anne's coat of arms. Yet, I no longer had a care for the fine and luxurious objects that surrounded me. Material things were now mere objects from a world to which I had once belonged, and which had once lauded my exalted status as queen. But such things were lost to me. They were passing through my hands like grains of sand in the hour-glass marking the time remaining. As I lay amidst the sound of distant thunder rumbling away to the east, I could only think of a time when my love had been blind.

In my mind's eye, I was no longer alone in the inky blackness, and the canopy above my bed was gone. Instead, I saw Henry leaning over me during our picnic at Windsor Lodge, the sun casting a halo around his head causing me to squint in order to make out his features. His face had shone with radiant love, his words sweet and kind sweeping me up into a dream that was full of hope and of fearless living. Yes, Anne had been unafraid and had pursued a dream of great risk, but of immeasurable reward. Is it madness to confess that I longed to see him again? I would have given anything to turn my head to find him lying next to me as we had done on so many balmy evenings after our love and passion had fused our bodies. I smiled wistfully at the memory, before I thought again on how I had acted rashly in pursuing my love, as if there would never be a price to pay for my actions. I see clearly now how I had cast others into great calamity for my own gain, and there was indeed a ransom to be paid for my carelessness.

My mood chilled as my mind turned away from sunny memories and alighted once more with dark vitriol as I blamed Henry and Daniel for their cold-hearted perfidy. I thought of Jane Seymour at Henry's side, of him touching her like he had once touched me, of showering her freely with his love and affection. I hated Jane for being safe and warm in her own bed waiting to greet the next sunny day as if it would last forever—just as I had so often done before. And for the millionth time, I tied my mind in knots wondering where it all went wrong. When did Daniel decide that I was not worthy of his love? When did Henry lose faith in me—in Anne? When did he first look at me and realise he despised me? Was I there? Did I see it? How could I carry on so blindly, as if everything was always going to be mine by right and in perpetuity? Then I thought of all that I had lost: my status, my honour, my reputation, the men that I had loved, the family that I adored, the wealth and riches that I had once owned—more than one could possibly imagine in a single lifetime. Most harrowing was that I was also to lose my most beloved brother and those friends that had ever been loyal to the Anne Boleyn. Soon I would lose my life.

In my desolation, I craved sanctuary in prayer. So as not to wake my ladies, I carefully peeled back the linen sheets and slid quietly out of bed. I was aware of the warmth of the oak floor boards pressing against the soles of my bare feet, of my fine linen nightshirt brushing gently across my otherwise naked skin. I did not stop to cover myself with a dressing gown as the night was warm. I slipped through the doorway and out into my privy chamber beyond where all was still except for the sound of rain as it pattered against the row of windows, which ordinarily afforded great swathes of light to flood the room. The chamber was cast in shadows as I made my way along its length, as much by intuition as by sight. I was thankful to meet no one; the guards remained outside the external doors leading to and from the queen's lodgings to ensure I could not escape. I made my way across the dais at the high end of my presence chamber before entering my privy closet and closed the door quietly behind me.

Outside the oratory window, I heard the tempest of the storm retreating, sparing London the full force of its fury. Whilst inside the room and upon the altar, a single candle remained alight casting its gentle glow across the chamber's wainscoted interior and expensively tiled floor. I had intended to kneel in prayer before the altar and beseech the good Lord to forgive me my sins and help me find the courage I needed to face the coming day. But I could not set my mind to the task; it was too tormented. My carefully crafted defences were summarily being torn down by the overwhelming reality of my predicament. I leaned back on the door through which I had just entered, my face turned up toward the heavens. Suddenly, it seemed as though my faith could no longer support me; I felt utterly alone, abandoned even by God. How could it have come to this? How could God have destroyed both my lives so completely? Tears brimmed in my eyes once more before I half whispered, half cried in fearful agony,

'Why? Why have you done this to me?' I had tried so hard to be brave, to trust in God for my salvation, but I could no longer hold myself together. I was terrified and utterly exhausted from the battle I had been waging and the pantomime that I had been playing. As my face crumpled in despair, my body slipped slowly down until I found myself slumped in a heap on the ground. I could hardly breathe as deep, guttural sobs washed over me, one after the other. My life no longer seemed worth living—but I could not face dying. In my wretchedness I cried out, once more raising my eyes this time to look upon the crucified Christ, as I begged God,

'Please, help me! I can't do this! Why have you forsaken me? What have I done to deserve this?' Everything that I had known was being swept away. There was no one to help me, no hope to which I might desperately cling. I curled up, my face close to the floor, tears splashing down upon its cool, shiny surface—all hope destroyed.

That was the very moment that finally I let go; let go of trying to be brave, let go of trying to be hopeful, let go of trying to find a solution to my predicament. I knew everything was out of my hands; so I simply surrendered. And it was in that moment that my life was transformed in a way that I had never imagined, never even thought possible. Lying there in the semi-dark, bent over in a pathetic heap of misery, I suddenly felt a mindfulness take hold of my being. I stopped crying and was surrounded by a space which was luminous and exquisitely beautiful. I lifted my head to see if someone had somehow entered my closet and lit up the room, for the darkness that had enshrouded me suddenly vanished. I looked around but no one was there. Yet I hardly noticed as everything in the room seemed to radiate light and bliss. It is incredible for me to explain, but as I slowly lifted myself to kneeling, the chatter of my mind fell away and I saw every episode of both my lives before me, one scene after the other; and what had seemed so tragic just moments before suddenly all seemed perfect. I understood how it was always going to end like this. My actions had brought forth an inevitable sequence of events for which only I could ever be responsible. There was no one to blame, there was no reason to feel betrayed. My mind was perfectly still. Looking about my closet, I took in my world with almost child-like wonderment, as if I had never seen it before. I searched for the anger, the jealousy, and the resentment that just minutes before had so sorely afflicted me. There was nothing, nothing but love and a 'peace that passeth all understanding'.

I sat without moving, floating in an ocean of bliss for what must have been hours. I thought about nothing, but understood everything. It was as if God himself had truly heard my cry for help and had shown me the true nature of life. I saw that the bliss of life would be amplified in the bliss of death—and I no longer felt afraid. Finally, I understood where and why Anne had found her courage. I knew as surely as night follows day that they might end my physical existence, but I had been shown the truth of everlasting life, and this no one could deny me.

As the storm clouds outside my window were chased away, I sat silently watching the first rays of dawn break through the eastern horizon and fill my privy closet with golden sunlight. I was at peace, and upon that historic day, I even felt joy in my heart and a radiant, all-encompassing love that I knew would accompany my brother to the scaffold and into the life that shortly awaited us both, beyond this earthly domain.

And so, when I woke Margery and Nan shortly after dawn, each of them looked at the other, clearly bewildered by my obvious happiness. They even quizzed me, asking me what had happened, for I knew that they sensed a profound shift but could not fathom its exact nature, or from whence it had come. I thought to try and explain, but how could one explain such a transformation which was nothing short of a miracle? In truth, I was struggling to understand it myself. I did not know if this state of grace was temporary, or whether I had crossed a threshold in my consciousness from which there could never be any return. Whatever was the case, by the time Sir William entered my chambers shortly after 9 o'clock on that Wednesday morning, I had long been up; having dressed, taken breakfast and prayed, along with my ladies, for the souls of those gentlemen who were to die outwith the Tower walls on the scaffold erected on Tower Hill. Nan and Madge were greatly distressed, although I was in a place where I could comfort them without reserve, assuring them that the pain my brother and our friends would experience was momentary, and that eternal bliss would be theirs in the sight of the King of Heaven.

When Master Kingston stood before me in my privy chamber, I looked upon him with different eyes, as I was beginning to do with everyone. I could now see so much fear in everybody's hearts that it made me want to weep with compassion. I felt only love for this hardened soldier who had no doubt seen too much blood in his time, and had that morning witnessed yet more. Sir William eyed me warily as I greeted him with genuine warmth and lightness in my voice.

'Sir William, good morrow!' The Constable of the Tower expected to find me distraught, and was greatly perplexed that I stood before him not only composed, but evidentially in a state of considerable joy. Master Constable swept into the usual reverence before righting himself, the faintest furrow of bewilderment giving tell to his inner state of confusion.

'Your Grace, it is my duty to tell you that the king in his mercy has agreed that you will not suffer at the stake, but instead you will be beheaded by the sword. It is anticipated that the swordsmen from St Omer will arrive shortly, and you should prepare yourself for your death upon the morrow.' Oh, I did not want to die, but neither did Sir William's words cause the slightest trace of fear to disturb my inner peace. Thus, I simply nodded my head and said,

'Thank you, Master Kingston.' In truth, I was no longer concerned with my earthly fate to which I had entirely surrendered. Instead, I was concerned for Anne's good name, and whether those men who had suffered for her had died honourably and stood by their innocence and that of their queen. I asked, 'But tell me, Sir William, did my brother and the other innocent men die well? Did they proclaim their innocence?'

'Madame, they died most honourably. Lord Rochford asked God for forgiveness and urged those present to live by the gospel. All stood by their innocence, except Mark, who declared that he had merited his death.'

'Did he not exonerate me before he died of the public infamy relayed upon me?' I felt a heavy weight of sorrow for Mark, who, having failed to retract his confession, had surely perjured his soul. I frowned, shaking my head in sorrow, as I exclaimed this thought aloud, 'Alas! I fear his soul will suffer for it. I ask for God to forgive him and have mercy upon his soul.'

And so I passed my first day of Heaven upon Earth. Whilst Master Kingston urged me to prepare for my death in the morning, I knew that history decreed that as Thursday 17 May dawned, I still had nearly forty-eight hours of precious life left within my hands. And so, as dusk fell, I determined that I would use the time I had left to me to do all that I could to beg forgiveness for my sins, so that when the time came, I could truly walk to the scaffold with an untroubled countenance.

Chapter Forty-Seven

The Tower of London,
Thursday, 18 May 1536

Once more I could not sleep. This time it was not on account of my torment, but those few remaining hours were too precious by far to pass in ignorant slumber. It is not that I cherished the thought of dying, for more than ever in my awakened state I saw just how truly beautiful, yet fragile, life is. How carelessly had I spent my days, and taken so much for granted! I could hardly believe that for so long I had the world at my feet, and had so often expected that yet more should be mine. What inordinate arrogance! How full of vanity and pride had I been? Yet, the woman who had committed such sins was already dead and I sought absolution to make amends. Thus on the Wednesday evening, I put my quill to parchment and scrawled two notes both to be sent via Master Kingston. One requested that my almoner, John Skip, come to me with all haste, regardless of the hour, for I feared that I had little time left and sought his spiritual guidance and comfort. The second was penned to Thomas Cranmer. I urged the Archbishop to come at dawn on the morrow for I specifically wished him to hold mass in my privy closet and hear my final confession. Nan ensured both letters were delivered.

Around two o'clock on the morning of Thursday 18 May, Margery was summoned by a rather hesitant knock on the door of my privy chamber. Despite the early hour, we were all dressed, for I had no intention of retiring to my bed chamber. Nodding toward my friend, I watched her open the door and speak to someone I could not quite see. When Margery stepped aside and announced the arrival of Master Skip, I rose to my feet greatly heartened to see my long-time friend and dutiful servant of God.

'Master Skip, please come forth.' John Skip entered, nodding his acknowledgement to Margery before coming before me and sweeping into a bow, removing his cap as he did so. When he raised his eyes to meet mine, I smiled and said 'I thank you kindly for your pains at such a late hour.'

'Your Grace, I am humbled to be able to serve you at any hour.' He faltered briefly then added, 'I am truly sorry to…' I held my hand up, interrupting him, for I no longer needed condolences. Time was of the essence.

'Father, do not trouble yourself with pity for me; what is done is done. I see that it is the king's wish that I should die and I humbly submit myself to his majesty's will.' I took a couple of steps toward my almoner and in a gentle voice that was firm in my intent, I added, 'There are matters, which press upon my mind, and I will use what little means I have to make amends whilst upon this earth and to seek God's forgiveness. I wish to take the sacrament and for you to hear my confession. I have but little time left to me.' John Skip nodded his understanding. I did not know if I would indeed die on the 'morrow', but should some bizarre twist of fate bring it about, I wanted my soul to be fully prepared. In the still of the night, two shadowy figures slipped into the queen's closet where my almoner heard my confession and, enfolded by His merciful forgiveness for my confessed sins, I prepared my soul for its final pilgrimage home. Yet, I was not done. There were still earthly considerations that I felt compelled to address once the inhabitants of the Tower awoke from their peaceful slumber.

Shortly before dawn, I emerged from my privy closet in order to take a little breakfast. It was another fine morning, the earth barely cooled from the previous day. I asked Mrs Orchard to throw open all the windows in my chamber so that perhaps for the last time, I could enjoy the smell of the fragrant breeze and delight in hearing the dawn chorus sung joyfully from within the privy garden. And whilst a nervous tension emanated from those around me, I remained serene. I found myself placing a hand around my ladies' shoulders and drawing them in to me to assure them that death was not to be feared by good Christians; that I rejoiced to soon be free of all unhappiness and reside in the bliss of everlasting life. I wish I could have taken away their suffering, to make them see what I had come to know, but alas I could not and so provided them with what little comfort I could.

As breakfast was cleared away, another welcome visitor arrived at the queen's lodgings. Somewhat flustered and a little out of breath, Thomas Cranmer had also responded to my summons and entered my privy chamber in an unusual flurry before paying the usual reverence in a hurried bow. I dipped my head courteously then laughed gently saying,

'Do not hurry so my Lord, you are not late. As you can see, I still have my head!' As ever, my humour was met with nervous laughter mixed with a degree of bewildered silence. Those around me struggled to understand that whilst my mirth was black, it was real enough. My soul was the only garden I needed to tend and I found myself disinclined to attach importance to anything else. And so, with this lack of attachment came an easy humour; yet, slightly nonplussed by my remark, Thomas Cranmer faltered before saying,

'Your Majesty, I received your letter and have come as you desire.' I nodded my approval, before turning to Margery and commanding,

'Lady Lee, please go at once and ask Master Kingston and Lady Mary to come hither. The Archbishop is to say mass and I wish to celebrate it in their presence.' Margery dipped a curtsy before scuttling off to find the constable and his wife. I turned back to Thomas. 'Your Grace, mayhap there is little time left for according to Master Kingston I die at nine of the clock. I think to make a start.' To Nan I added, 'When Sir William and Lady Kingston arrive, they should come immediately to my closet.'

I indicated to Thomas that he should follow me into my oratory. As we walked the short distance, Thomas turned to me and proffered,

'Madame, you seem…at ease. In fact, if I may be so bold as to say that I have never seen you looking more beautiful. How…?' My friend struggled to find the words to ask me how I could have alighted upon such a state of grace amongst such desolation. I smiled warmly, replying,

'God, in His infinite grace, has not abandoned me. He has shown me the path to heaven and I feel…' I paused to consider my words, then looked into my friend's troubled eyes adding, '…blessed.' Thomas was a man of deep faith, but even he marvelled at the profound aura of peace that radiated from me. After searching my face for a moment as if he might find the answer written there, he offered,

'Madame, it gladdens my heart immeasurably that you should be so reconciled with your fate for now you surely walk in the presence of God.' By this time, we had reached my small oratory. I invited Anne Wyatt and Madge Shelton to join us in celebration, leaving two empty stools for Master Kingston and the lady who had watched over my incarceration so assiduously. We did not have long to wait as Sir William and Lady Kingston shortly appeared and I indicated for them to take their ease. As Thomas conducted mass, I gave myself whole-heartedly to God, and marvelled at the exquisite beauty of everything that surrounded me.

Amongst the familiar smell of swirling incense and the Latinate chanting of my friend, I reached out silently with my consciousness and touched my brother, assured that though his body was now cold, his spirit was in rapture. On this earthly realm, I sent blessings to my mother, father and sister and most of all to Henry, who I knew needed my forgiveness more than anybody. My death would stain his conscience and weigh heavily upon his mind. I suspected that he would try and hide from the truth, turn away from ultimately taking responsibility for his actions. But there would be nowhere to hide. With my death, and the death of the five men who had already died, the heaviest of penances would hang round his neck, and I shuddered when I thought of the many calamities which would befall him in this lifetime and the next. Finally, it was time to take the sacrament and for Thomas Cranmer to hear my last confession. Sir William, Lady Kingston and my ladies made to leave so that I could be shriven in privacy. In my calm state, I remembered clearly Anne's final determination to have her innocence proclaimed to the world. Thus, I held up my hand and commanded,

'No. I wish you all to stay and hear my confession before the Good Lord.' I noticed some hesitancy for this was an unusual request indeed. Silently they settled themselves once more, whilst I stood gracefully to my feet and moved reverently to the altar where I dropped to my knees upon the crimson cushion. Thomas came forward with the sacrament in his hands. As he stood in from of me, I crossed myself saying,

'In the Name of the Father, the Son and the Holy Spirit.' I began, 'Before dawn, on this very day, I confessed my venial sins before my almoner.'

'And do you now wish to make another confession?'

'Yes, Your Grace, I do.'

'And to what do you wish to confess my child?' With my hands clasped earnestly in prayer, I raised my eyes to look up at my friend. I

570

spoke loud and clear so that all present could hear my words,

'I wish to confess that upon the damnation of my soul, I have never been unfaithful to my lord, the king.' I watched Thomas' eyebrows rise at the boldness of my action, before the faintest smile of confirmation played upon the corners of his lips. If my friend retained any shred of doubt in his heart, it was swept away in that moment. My uncompromising probity lit a light which chased away all shadow of doubt for those who witnessed my oath. To seal the sanctity of my words, I took the sacrament accepting the blood and body of Christ. I turned to Sir William and Lady Kingston and urged, 'Sir William…Lady Mary, you have heard my last confession in the sight of God; go forth and repeat my words to the world. Tell them that I die assured that I will soon sit at the feet of the Lord, for my innocency will always be clear.' I saw their faces and knew that such words so earnestly spoken touched their hearts. I was satisfied that I had done all that I could to propagate the truth and cast yet more doubt upon the weight of slander and infamy that my enemies had worked so hard to heap upon me—upon Anne.

With quiet steadfastness, after mass my ladies helped me change into the gown that I had selected for my execution. It was an English gown of grey damask, trimmed with ermine, and a laced kirtle of crimson taffeta. I stood still to allow them to work without interference as their nimble fingers dressed me for my appointment with death. My senses were now heightened in the extreme, for sometimes, I even felt the warmth of their breath upon me as they came in close to adjust the linen coif upon my head, or place my pearl carcanet hung with a gold '*A*' about my delicate, little neck. Occasionally, I would catch their line of sight and would see the pain that rent apart their hearts reflected there. Each time, I would lightly touch their arm to reassure them, without words, that all would be well.

I was still uncertain if I was to die within the hour, for everything that I knew told me that the day was still mine. Yet, I wanted to be ready in case it was not so. By eight o'clock I was ready and waited patiently, sometime in prayer, whilst other times taking strength as my almoner read aloud from the Gospel. When nine o'clock came and went, Lady Kingston arrived with the news that, as I suspected, I was not to die afore noon. I sent Nan to fetch Master Kingston as, with the five men already dead, the constable's duties had diminished considerably. Within ten minutes, the man with whom I had become so familiar stood before me once more. He looked tired, as well he might; I suspected that since this whole dreadful business began, he had barely a moment to himself.

'Master Kingston, I hearsay I shall not die afore noon, and I am very sorry for I thought to be dead and past my pain.'

'Yes, Madame, I am afraid it is so. The swordsman is on the road from Dover but sadly has not yet arrived. We must postpone your execution until noon.' I accepted Sir William's declaration and simply nodded. In any case, there was nothing that I could do to change the matter. But I was morbidly curious as to what I could expect. In my modern day life, I had read that even decapitation by the sword was not without pain, and so I enquired,

'But pray tell me Master Kingston, will there be much pain for I wish to prepare myself for the blow.' Sir William rocked forward and back on his heels, his hands clasped low before him and shook his head slowly.

'No, Madame, there will be no pain, for the blow is very subtle.' I was not sure that I entirely believed him, for how could he possibly know since he still retained his head. However, I did not want to challenge Sir William's obvious kindness, but nor could I contain my dark humour.

'I heard say the executioner is very good, and I have a little neck!' I did not think on it at the time, such an iconic moment, as I put my hands around my jewel-laden neck and laughed heartily, wishing, longing even for someone to join in. Once more, Sir William and the four ladies who looked on eyed each other nervously for how they might most appropriately react. Eventually my laughter died away, dissolving into the stony silence. With nothing more to say, I dismissed my gaoler and retreated once more into prayer.

Waiting! Waiting! Interminable waiting—for life to begin, for life to end. How ironic that even in the face my execution, Henry still left me waiting, as if six long years had not exacted enough from me. How strange to dance between life and death. Not so far removed that I could

leave behind all earthly suffering, but not so far in death's embrace to know the ultimate bliss. I complained to Master Kingston when he finally admitted what I suspected all along, that I would not die until the morrow. Having been afforded a few more hours upon this Earth in which I might do penance, I took the opportunity to summon Lady Kingston into my presence. I had but one thing on my mind.

Since my condemnation, I had only seen Lady Kingston intermittently as she came by my chambers a couple of times a day to ensure that all was in order within the queen's much reduced household. I had never summoned her before, except with her husband to hear my confession, and certainly never alone. And so, when she came before me in the queen's presence chamber, and I dismissed all my ladies into the adjoining room, she was wary of what I might ask of her. I greeted Lady Kingston upon the dais, beneath the canopy of state which nobody had seen fit to remove. Trying to put Lady Mary at ease, I smiled warmly and said,

'Lady Kingston, I am very grateful for your presence for I wish you to grant the final wish of a condemned woman.' I watched Lady Mary frown, curious that of all people, I should turn to her. I was unperturbed as I stepped aside and with an open arm indicated toward the empty throne. 'Please my lady, do me the honour of taking the seat that I once occupied with such pride.' Lady Kingston recoiled physically from my suggestion, shaking her head vehemently as she protested,

'Nay Madame, it is treason to sit upon this throne which is still yours as God's anointed queen upon this Earth.'

'It is true that in name I am still queen, but all earthly trappings of my life have now departed and tomorrow death will attend to the former. Lady Kingston, fear not to sit upon this chair of estate for you must do so before you can grant me what I desire.' Mary Kingston eyed me suspiciously and without taking her eyes from mine, she stepped forward gingerly scooping up her skirts and lowering herself slowly upon the throne. When she was seated, I moved down onto the floor in front of the dais and fell upon my knees. I watched Lady Kingston's eyes widen in nothing short of shock, as I clasped my hands in front of my chest and begged,

'Good Lady, I beg of you to help me. I beg of you to go before the king's daughter, the Lady Mary, at your first opportunity, sink onto your knees as I have done here today, and most humbly beseech her to forgive me for all the grievous hurts that I have done to her grace. For surely I have done her much wrong in my time—and for this I truly repent.' Never had I spoken with as much fervour or with greater sincerity. I knew Lady Kingston was a staunch supporter of the young woman who I had tormented in my vanity and that she had the lady's ear. For a moment she stared at me, utterly disbelieving of the message that I had most earnestly urged her to convey. Perhaps this day was one of the strangest she had witnessed; a courageous woman, declaring first her innocence before God, and then throwing herself before the throne, craving forgiveness for wrongs so sorely done to a young woman who was Anne's implacable enemy. Yes, death is a great leveller and with my actions, I hoped finally that I might atone for my earthly sins. After a short while, Lady Kingston agreed that when all of this was over, and her duties discharged, she would indeed make the journey to Hunsdon to see the Lady Mary and pass on my words of contrition. I had done all that I could. I gave her my blessing and my thanks, and sombrely withdrew to my privy chamber where I could be alone to contemplate the day ahead.

Just one night remained to me. I spent the evening alone with my friends. In between, I snatched moments of sleep or quietly knelt in prayer, my almoner never far from my side. I prayed to God that my fearlessness would not desert me for on the morrow I would face the *Sword of Calais*.

Chapter Forty-Eight

The Tower of London,
Friday, 19 May 1536

And so it ends. My two deeply flawed and chaotic lives come together in this one moment, a moment that will be forever written in the stars and scorched into the collective memory of this English nation. In both lives, I have experienced moments of sublime happiness and of unimaginable pain and sorrow. Only now do I understand the perfection and beauty of it all; how every moment has been ineffably precious and oh so fleeting!

Everything was bright and clear in my mind. As my ladies made the final adjustments to my gown and headdress, I stared at my face in the polished steel mirror that Madge held up in front of me. It almost took my breath away to see Anne's black eyes stare back into my soul. In times past, I had seen those eyes sparkle with Anne's unique brand of intrepid vivacity, as well as looking drawn and haunted as death and failure stalked her. But now within those eyes, I could see an ocean of peace that seemed to extend for all eternity—a perfect mirror to her blissful soul. Whilst those about me looked pinched and pale from the stress of preparing their mistress to die, Anne had never looked more radiant, more beautiful.

I felt the gold letter 'A' that hung down from my pearl choker with the tips of my fingers, following the smooth outline of the cipher somewhat absentmindedly, as I cast my mind back to another lifetime. I recalled that fateful day when I had first walked across the drawbridge of Hever Castle, innocently thinking that I was simply going to be spending a weekend indulging in a lifelong passion of a young Englishwoman who had long ago captured my imagination, just as she had captured Henry's heart. What had happened to me still defied my understanding. However, now I felt with certainty that we had always been the same soul, reincarnated to live the same tragic love affair with Henry, in a different time, in a different world. Before my incredible adventure began, I remember how much I had longed to walk in Anne's shoes, just to see her face and hear her voice; to know what moved her spirit. And now, it seems I had been allowed to drink more than my fill, and that I would shortly follow in my heroine's footsteps, all the way to the scaffold. How many steps I wondered would it take—one-hundred, two-hundred? Yet, by a miracle that eluded my comprehension, God has taught me how to meet my end, and I was unafraid. The only regret that I would carry with me to the grave was that it took my imminent death to teach me how to live; to see beyond the ordinary befuddlement of our meaningless lives and catch sight of the extraordinary meaning of our existence.

I nodded to Madge to remove the mirror for I was satisfied that, as befitting a queen, I was most regally attired in my English gown of dark grey damask, worn over a crimson, taffeta kirtle, an English hood fixed in place over a netted, white, linen coif that covered my plaited hair. I wished that those who had come to see me die will remember their last vision of Anne as very much an Englishwoman, crowned and anointed by God as an English queen. Having completed their sorry task, my friends stood back; each one, as I commanded, was dressed sombrely in a simple, light-grey gown of taffeta and velvet. Outside my window in the courtyard below, I heard the growing hubbub of people gathering. I looked at the clock; it was ten minutes to eight in the morning. I knew that soon Master Kingston would come knocking at my door.

'Thank you, my friends.' I spoke softly, my eyes unafraid to meet each of theirs in turn. They parted, allowing me to move forward, making my way to my writing desk that stood near the window of my bedchamber. Bright sunlight illuminated a piece of parchment that I had laid there the previous night. I reached out, picking it up between my thumb and forefinger. Scrawled across it in Anne's elegant writing were the last words of love to my mother. I paused to read it once more,

My dear Lady Mother,

In my most humble wise that my poor heart can think, I pray our good Lord bless you.

I could not rest my weary soul until I had written to you of my inestimable love for you and my gratitude for the inexhaustible bounty of a mother's love, of which I have hitherto had so great plenty, such that all the days of my life, I have been most bound to you of all creatures, next to the King's Grace. And I beseech you this, to remember that I will never vary from this thought as long as there is breath left in my body.

This day, I go gladly to God and would be sorry if it were to be any longer. God has kept me and preserved me, and has strengthened my faith, and surely I now know that there is no truer way that leads to the Everlasting Kingdom, than by suffering patiently endured.

So, farewell, my dear mother, and pray for me, as I shall for you, father and for all our friends, that one day, we may merrily meet in heaven. Remembering that I thank you for your great cost, and humbly desiring you, for the salvation of my soul, to forgive me of all my offences that I have done to you. God's blessing to you.

Your humble and loving daughter,

ANNE THE QUENE.

I folded the paper over, placing a kiss upon the parchment, before I turned and held it out toward Margery saying,

'Margery, when I am dead, please take this to my mother. Ensure that she knows of my love and my steadfast assurance of my innocence. Beg her not to grieve for me too deeply and that above all, please tell her I was not afraid, for I fear that will torment her most of all. Tell her that I went to God with joy in my heart.' Margery came over to me, slowly taking the letter from my outstretched arm. She nodded her head silently and I was assured of its delivery, and that my long-time friend would do what she could to comfort my heart-broken mother. I watched her falter, her eyes rising to meet my own, full of unbearable anguish. Oh, I would miss my friend—all my friends so very much! Indeed, it was our parting that caused the greatest heaviness in my heart. How could I ever thank them enough for their bravery, loyalty and enduring friendship? As Margery and I looked deeply into each other's eyes, we suddenly fell into one another's arms, holding on with a tender ferocity that spoke volumes of everything that we had come to mean to each other. And when finally we let go of our embrace, I beckoned over the other three ladies, who were all standing by silently in attendance: Nan, Madge and Anne.

Whilst Nan had always been one of my dearest friends whose happy spirit was easy to love, the adversity that I shared with Margery's sister, and my cousin, Madge, had quickly forged a deep bond of affection between us. I had come to cherish this and now welcomed them easily into my arms. As my ladies approached, I extended my arms wide,

577

inviting all four of them to crowd in as we circled our arms one about the other, our heads close together as many tears were spent. Remaining calm, I said,

'Dear friends, how can I ever thank you for your steadfast love, generous friendship and unswerving loyalty. You will never know how thirsty I was for the sight of you after they brought me here from Greenwich, and what a joyous blessing it was that you were finally returned to me. Your great kindness will be rewarded in heaven, and be assured that when your time comes, I will greet you at the feet of our Lord with a joyful heart.' I was about to say more when on the stairs outside my bedchamber, I heard approaching footsteps scuffing on the wooden steps. We heard the keys jangle in the lock, as the guard outside at the head of the queen's privy stair turned the latch easily, and the heavy oak door swung inwards. Master Kingston appeared dressed in a tawny brown doublet and hose, a black velvet cap upon his greying head. I stepped forward as Sir William bowed in reverence before saying,

'Madame, the time has come.' *The time had come.* How strange that he should summon me to meet my maker using the same words that I had once scrawled in my book of hours—*le temps viendra.* I was reminded of it, no doubt still tucked away in a quiet, sunny place in Hever Castle, unaware of my imminent destruction. I simply nodded and replied,

'Master Kingston, acquit yourself of your charge, for I have long been prepared.' As God is my witness, it was the truth. I turned to my ladies, indicating to Margery that she should place around my shoulders the ermine mantle that I had chosen both to underline Anne's majesty, and to ward off any morning chill that might still be hanging in the air. My friend stepped forward to fasten the cape in place, before stepping back, allowing me to indicate to Sir William that I was ready to follow him. Before we left my chambers, Sir William gave me a purse of twenty pounds for the executioner. I clasped the heavy pouch in my hands, and when we finally left the queen's lodgings, which had been my prison for the last seventeen days, I did not look back; I could not look back. I knew that whatever happened, I must look forward and keep my eyes set on God and the paradise that awaited me.

The queen's privy stair was a wooden staircase that led from the most privy end of the queen's apartments down just fifteen steps into the Tower's inner ward. On the top step, I paused momentarily, closing my eyes as I inhaled deeply. Oh, how sweet it was to know the breath passing in and out of my body! Above me, the sky was flawless; the sun, already high enough to cast its golden rays into the western half of the courtyard. I almost tasted the air, it was fresh and sweet enough to portend a glorious summer's day. I admit that it was difficult to die surrounded by such beauty and knowing that I would never again see another sunrise. When I opened my eyes, I was looking down upon a courtyard bisected along its length by two rows of yeoman of the king's guard. They were paired and facing each other to form a long corridor that extended away from the base of the privy stair toward the Cold Harbour Gate. Each of them stood motionless, swords slung at their sides, a halberd balanced erect in their right hands. Every brawny fellow was dressed in their familiar bright red livery, decorated across their puffed sleeves and skirts with guards of blue velvet; with flat, red felt caps upon their closely-shaven heads. Master Kingston had already reached the bottom of the stairs, so, I picked up my skirts and ran my hand down the smooth wooden rail, descending the stairway carefully, with graceful and sweeping majesty.

At the foot of the stair, I began my final walk, Master Kingston in front of me, my ladies following in pairs behind. One foot in front of the other, the pressure of the earth beneath my feet, the rustle of my taffeta skirts as my hips swayed in their usual elegant fashion, and as we moved out of the shadow cast by the bulk of the queen's lodgings, the gentle warmth of the sun on my back. We made our way along the path that ran alongside the king's jewel house, which was to our right, whilst over to the left, the towering pitched roof of the medieval great hall stood resolutely, a witness to my recent conviction. Having said my goodbyes to my ladies, I quickly gave myself over to the business of dying, of transitioning to another, more ethereal world which lay beyond the veil. As we began to walk, I dropped easily into a state where my mind was virtually empty of chatter. Only occasionally did I break away to turn my head, looking behind me to ensure that my ladies were coping with the stress of their unenviable task.

As our little party reached the south-west corner of the White Tower, we swung right, beneath the imposing Cold Harbour Gate, to begin the gradual climb to the large open space where the scaffold awaited me. The way was lined with yeoman guards, their faces immutable and indifferent to the significance of the day. My eyes moved along studying some of those faces as we passed by, each one chiselled with the story of their extraordinary life. I soon let go of this, for I could not afford to get lost in their drama, or disturb my peace. Taking hold of my skirts once more, we climbed up perhaps fifteen or twenty paces, the hubbub of those gathered to witness Anne's death growing ever louder, until finally, I stepped onto the plateau on the north side of the White Tower.

In front of me, were perhaps 1,000 men and women, all crowded around a scaffold that stood approximately four feet high and draped in macabre black. The avenue of guards held the crowds well back so that I could clearly see it and the three men already standing upon it, who were above the great throng of people. As the first of the expectant crowd caught sight of my arrival, I became aware of a growing hum of babbling voices, whispers at first, as one neighbour turned to the other, pulling on their arm, urging them to take heed that the first queen to be executed in England was approaching. Then voices began to call out from the crowd, 'God bless Your Majesty!', 'May God have mercy upon your soul!' Yet I was undisturbed by the swell of noise. With every step, my soul felt infused with light, all the things that I had once fretted over dropped by the wayside. I walked forward with nothing left to achieve, free from my everyday concerns—the agony of uncertainty, the pain of betrayal, the exhaustion of fighting for my survival. It was over. There was nothing to do but die, and in a strange way, it was such a relief. All I wanted to do was be subsumed by the bliss that had begun to infuse my entire being.

And so, I arrived at the foot of the scaffold. Ahead of me, Master Kingston climbed the steep steps with some awkwardness, his arthritic joints no doubt making heavy work of the sharp ascent. At the top, he paused, turning round to lean down and offer me his hand. I smiled at him warmly, reaching up to accept his kind gesture, feeling the warmth of his rough skin brush against my own smooth and delicate hands. Gathering my skirts in my right hand, I mounted the stairs easily enough, and then suddenly I found myself above the crowd and looking out over a blur faces. However, several of those faces were all too familiar to me. First of these was the rather portly Thomas Audley, Henry's Lord Chancellor, garbed in a fur-lined coat. He eyed me circumspectly but with little emotion, and certainly no pity. Next to him stood the ever imperious Duke of Richmond, raised, for all intents and purposes, as a royal prince and who, just like his father, was full of his own self-importance. As my gaze alighted on his face however, I saw the same deep insecurity alight behind those eyes as I had seen so often in the king's. His vanity and self-aggrandizement merely serving as a mask to cover an overly fragile ego, made unstable by the fact that he could never escape being the king's 'spare'. I pitied the young man, for what a painful burden to bear. Within just a few short weeks, I knew he too would be dead. On Richmond's left, stood another of my sworn enemies, Charles Brandon, Duke of Suffolk. I could not help but salute my Lord Duke for having achieved something that I had never been able to do; for planting the seed of his friendship so deeply in Henry's heart that it would never be plucked out. But I forgave myself. Charles' life with Henry had its beginnings way back in their childhood. They were like two young saplings that had grown together beneath the mighty oak of the Tudor dynasty, their roots becoming inextricably entwined, so that to uproot one would be to mortally wound the other. Anne had never been afforded such a luxury. My gaze then wandered as I noted many of the great men of the land who had gathered to watch me die. All of them eyed me with considerable curiosity. On my far right, I found my Uncle Norfolk standing next to Master Secretary Cromwell in an uneasy, but no doubt temporary, truce. Norfolk looked his usual inscrutable self. No muscle twitched in his jaw and I suspected that he was pleased to finally see the back of his troublesome, intemperate niece. However, if my uncle had thought that Anne was the principal troublemaker in matters of religion, acting behind the scenes as the main protagonist in the dismantling of the England's monasteries, then I reflected with some gentle amusement that he would soon get a shock. Without Anne to challenge Cromwell's growing might, the last check to restrain the Master Secretary's plans for the dissolution of England's great religious houses would be removed. I knew that within months Thomas Cromwell would influence the king to accelerate their final demise in an act of vandalism that would never, and could never, be reversed. Norfolk's beloved Catholicism, the religion which had dominated England for centuries, would be in terminal decline. I turned my attention to Cromwell, I could see that he looked agitated, uncomfortable in his skin, as if he wanted to step out of himself and find refuge elsewhere. I doubted that he had exhaled since this whole affair began; his shining future resting irrefutably on my utter destruction, which I had to admit, he achieved with considerable elegance, even though his soul now stood in great peril on account of it. As I looked about the crowd, to my great relief, I saw none of my family present. I did not want any of them, not even my father—whose actions after my arrest I would never know—to remember me as a bloody, lifeless corpse.

Just seconds passed whilst I surveyed the crowd, the noise gradually abating as I looked at the men who greeted me upon the scaffold. My eyes flicked from one to the other, as each nodded their heads in reverence, still clearly moved by my estate as queen. I dipped my head in turn, grateful of their respectful courtesy, and I wondered which of the men my executioner was. One young lad with a boyish face and fair hair stood toward the back of the scaffold, his hands clasped tidily behind his back. I felt sure it was not him. The other two stood further toward the front. They were older, both well-built and muscular. Each man wore black stockings and a linen shirt rolled up at the sleeves. One of them fixed me with soulful chocolate-brown eyes that seemed deeply moved and filled with kindness. I hovered there for perhaps just two or three seconds before my attention was captured by his feet which wore no shoes. I remembered that Anne's executioner had been so attired. I was sure that this was the famous *Sword of Calais,* Anne's final nemesis. Aware that I had a mind to speak, I turned to Master Kingston and asked,

'Sir William. May I say a few words?' The Constable of the Tower nodded, and with an extended hand indicated that I move forward. Stepping to the side of the straw which was placed in the centre of the scaffold, I walked just two or three paces to the front to look out over the crowd. Finally, the last few errant calls and urgent whispers died away, all eager to hear Anne Boleyn's last words. There was utter silence. It was as if London was holding her breath. Once more I surveyed the crowd seeing easily the newly dug graves of Sir Henry Norris, William Brereton, Sir Francis Weston, and Mark Smeaton in the distance, piled high with fresh dirt in the graveyard of St Peter ad Vincula. The sight briefly caught me off guard, and as I began my final speech to the world, my voice caught in my throat, causing my first words to falter.

'Good…Christian people,' I cleared my throat, gathering myself once more, determined to speak Anne's last words with indomitable courage. 'I have not come here to preach a sermon. I have come here to die. For according to the law, and by the law, I am judged to die, and therefore I will speak nothing against it.' My words seemed to float outwards, above the sea of solemn faces, all of whom beheld a woman shining with tender fearlessness. Satisfied, I allowed myself to meet the eyes of those who stood before me with a smiling countenance. 'I am come hither to accuse no man, nor to speak of that whereof I am accused and condemned to die, but I pray God save the king and send him long to reign over you, for a gentler, nor more merciful prince, was there never,' a murmur of 'God save the King', rippled through the crowd, as a montage of images flashed through my mind. They were almost too fast to me to recognise; of happier times when I had known the generous bounty of Henry's love. I raised my eyes and smiled wistfully, as I added, 'and to me he was ever a good, gentle and sovereign lord. And if any person will meddle with my cause, I require them to judge the best.' I hesitated realising that I was about to speak my last. The final dramatic act in Anne's life required a poignant exit. In a heartfelt plea for the repose of my soul, I said,

'And thus I take my leave of the world and of you all, and I heartily desire you all to pray for me.' For one final time, my gaze fell upon Cromwell who had been the central architect of Anne's demise. I asked God to forgive him. I was interrupted suddenly by the brown-eyed man, who appeared at my side falling to his knees as he begged me,

'Madame, please forgive me for what I must do.' I looked down at the leather pouch I was still holding in my bejewelled hand. I extended it, offering the *Sword of Calais* payment for his swift and accurate work. As he accepted it, I smiled and replied,

'*Mon brave homme, vous êtes entièrement pardonné car la tâche que vous allez accomplir ici aujourd'hui m'ouvrira les portes du paradis.*' I stared into those eyes, which, unlike so many others, seemed unafraid to meet mine. I wondered if through his work, he had learnt to face death, as so many others it seemed, could not.

With the task completed, I turned toward my ladies. Madge was already brimming with tears, and so I spared her further by indicating that Margery and Nan should step forward. This they did, although I could see that it was taking every ounce of self-control that they could muster to remain composed in order to serve their mistress to the end. Margery stepped in front of me to remove my ermine cloak, which she handed back to Nan, before untying the crimson sash at my waist. With trembling hands that only I could see, she began unhooking the front of my English gown. Having worked her way from my waist to my décolletage, the final catch got stuck, her usually agile fingers unable to steady themselves sufficiently to grapple with the tiny object. I laid a hand upon her wrist, causing her to look up from her task.

'It is all right. Do not be concerned, my friend.' She gazed at me in wonderment of my stillness and serenity. I reached up and undid the errant hook, smiling at her warmly before Nan and Margery slipped the gown off my shoulders to reveal the tightly laced crimson kirtle, fashioned with Anne's favourite deep, square-cut neckline. Having laid the cloak over Anne Wyatt's outstretched arms, my two friends unpinned my hood, lifting it off to reveal the netted coif that hid most of Anne's abundant, plaited hair. Their only remaining task was to remove the carcanet which hung about my neck. As Nan unfastened it, I whispered over my shoulder,

'Find a way to get it to Elizabeth; tell her it will bring me to her side whenever she needs me.' My words were too much for my loyal friend who wiped away a tear before stepping backwards. Over my shoulder, I watched them all sink into the lowest curtsies, each defiant of the judgement cast against me and determined to accord me every possible respect. I smiled and mouthed silently, 'thank you', although none of the crowd saw it.

It was time to let them go. I had said my goodbyes. I was finally alone. It was if the world suddenly melted away, and I let go of the very last vestiges of a remarkable life. Picking up my skirts with both my hands, I came forth to kneel upon the straw as Master Kingston directed, only pausing briefly to twist myself about and arrange my skirts over my feet. I was about to settle myself before I was seized by the need to make sure the blow would not come until I was ready. And so I looked up and asked the executioner with all solemnity,

'Master executioner, you will allow me to settle myself before you strike, for I wish to be prepared.'

'Of course, Madame, do not fear.' I nodded, satisfied at his pledge. Turning my head forward, I took one final look at this beautiful world, before closing them and clasping my hands in prayer. With all earnestness, I began to repeat over and over,

'Jesu receive my soul. O Lord God have pity on my soul. To Christ I commend my soul.' When the blow did not come, I hesitated and turned to look toward the executioner. He did not fix my gaze, but instead looked over to my left and called out,

'Boy, fetch my sword!' Instinctively, I turned my head to follow the line of his speech. Then abruptly, I heard a peculiar sound whisper in the air. I had the oddest notion that it was calling out my name. There was the slightest breeze and then a sharp pain exploded through my neck, blinding me with agony. I do not deny it was searing, but then almost as quickly as it had come, it was gone. For just a few, final seconds there was a strangest sensation of falling through the air, then that too rapidly dissipated. Once more, and for the final time, my world descended into blackness.

Epilogue

The Tower of London
19 May 1536 and 2010

I was suddenly everywhere and nowhere all at the same time. My mind was filled with light. I saw my bloody body and severed head lying limp in the straw, my ladies weeping but fiercely defending me from any man who tried to touch me. Finally, I watched the crowds slowly melt away, satisfied that they had seen what they came to witness, the brutal execution of a queen. I was touched by the unswerving loyalty of my grief-stricken friends, who knelt upon the ground, and in amongst their tears, gently wrapped the bloodied corpse of their mistress in a white, linen shroud, before lifting my lifeless form into the arrow chest that would accompany me to the grave.

At the same time, some five hundred years into the future, and on the very same spot, I looked down upon my other body, surrounded by a growing crowd of well-meaning passers-by. In time, I watched the Tower cleared by officials. Curious tourists left reluctantly as they craned their necks in the direction of my already still form in an attempt to witness the unfolding drama. But the bleeding which had occurred in my brain on that second occasion had, as I thought, been catastrophic, taking my life in a matter of minutes. In the same way that Anne Boleyn was scooped up from the ground and carried to her final resting place in the nearby chapel of St Peter ad Vincula, so an ambulance eventually pulled up to retrieve the body that I had so recently discarded. As the people melted away into the mists of time, the Tower, that indomitable fortress of English history, remains a silent witness to the judicial murder of an iconic queen and the death of young woman, who by some extraordinary miracle, had once walked in her shoes.

But I beg you, do not think to grieve for me, or believe that they have destroyed the spirit of Anne Boleyn. You can see my courage living on in the beating heart of anybody who refuses to sacrifice the truth for the comfort of others. You can smell the sweet scent of my love in the summer blossom that flowers in every rose. You can see my grace in the stag that holds your gaze majestically before it melts into a woodland thicket like a shadow. You can taste my freedom in the sight of the white falcon, as she takes flight, soaring over the world like a celestial angel, unfettered by the cares of man.

On the day of my death, my dear friend Thomas Cranmer was heard to say that I would be 'A Queen in heaven.' And so I am.

My name is Anne Boleyn, and I have at last told you my story. I have shown you my innocence, and in this I have found my peace. Finally, I am free.

Glossary

Canterbury Cap: a square, cloth hat with sharp corners, found in the Anglican community and worn by clergy.

Career: a course or progress, especially at full speed; a horse's charge.

Caparisoned: a horse bedecked in rich decorative coverings.

Carpet-Knight: a derogatory, sixteenth century term for a knight whose achievements belong to a lady's boudoir rather than the field of battle.

Charger: the two most common kinds of horse used for jousting were chargers and larger destriers (See below). Chargers were medium-weight horses, bred and trained for agility and stamina.

Curtain Wall: in architecture, an outer covering or wall of a building, non-structural, designed to keep the weather out and the occupants in.

Destrier: one of the two most common type of horses used for jousting. Destriers were heavier than chargers. They were similar to today's Andalusian horse, but not as large as the modern draft horse.

Dronslade: a type of kettle drum; an instrument.

Femme Sole: of French origin; a woman who was given the right to act without recourse to her husband.

Fustian: a variety of heavy woven cloth made of wool or linen used primarily as padding.

Galleting: in architecture, a decorative a technique where small stones are pushed into the mortar whilst it is still soft, producing a pretty ornamental pattern.

Indictment: a legal term for the formal accusation that a person has committed a crime.

Lady Paramount: traditionally appointed to preside at archery tournaments, and to present awards. If there are any disputes that can't be resolved by the judges, the Lady Paramount acts as arbiter.

Lists: the area which contained a jousting event.

Maying: the celebration of May Day.

Nightgown: broadly speaking the Tudor equivalent of a dressing gown.

Pair of Bodies (Bodies): a lady's garment that roughly equates to a modern day corset, but which was usually not boned or stiffened. Its purpose was to give definition to the décolletage by pushing up the breasts.

Parlement: the old word for Parliament.

Platts: A Tudor term for architectural plans.

Postdromal: the period of time immediately after an epileptic seizure.

Quire: in architecture, the area of a church or cathedral usually in the western part of the chancel between the nave and the altar, designed to accommodate the liturgical singers.

Sarcenet: a fine, soft fabric, often of silk, made in plain or twill weave and used especially for linings.

Stays: see 'Pair of Bodies' above.

Sedilia: (the plural of Lat. *sedile*, seat), in ecclesiastical architecture, the term used to describe stone seats, usually to be found on the south side of an altar, often in the chancel, for the use of the officiating priests. The seat is often set back into the main wall of the church itself.

SHO: Senior House Officer – a junior grade of medical staff in the British National Health Service

String Course: in architecture is a projecting course of brickwork or stone that runs horizontally around a building, typically to emphasize the junction between floors, or just below the eaves.

Swiving: Tudor slang term meaning 'screwing', having sex with.

Tambour: a drum.

Yule Log: the Yule Log was a Viking tradition. Although burned especially throughout the festive period, good luck demanded that part of it would be kept behind at the end of the festivities to light the following year's log.

NOTES

Part IV
Chapter One:

Henry and Anne used the honeysuckle and acorns motif, the meaning of which is as described in the book. The description of Anne's counterpane derives from contemporary descriptions of what soft furnishings graced Anne's apartments.

The queen's bed chamber and privy chamber roughly occupy where the current queen's ballroom exists in Windsor Castle: taken from the floor plans in Simon Thurley's, *The Royal Palaces of Tudor England.*

Anne was invested as Marquess of Pembroke at Windsor Castle on 1 September 1532. It was a singular honour, as she was the first female and last noblewoman to hold the male title, with all its hereditary rights.

The ages, appearances and family ties of the Anne's ladies-in-waiting described in this scene reflect, as accurately as possible, the known facts. Many of Anne's ladies were related to her through the extensive families of her father and mother, giving and a multitude of aunts, uncles and cousins at court.

Elizabeth Wood, Lady Boleyn, is known to have had a difficult relationship with her niece. She was one of the ladies placed to attend Anne in the Tower after her arrest, and from Anne's comments, we know that she 'loved her not'.

Anne and her sister-in-law, Lady Jane Rochford, had an amicable relationship up to the end of 1534. It was to Jane that Anne turned when she tried to get rid of the mistress that Henry took during 1534. However, she has gained a notorious reputation of having spoken against her husband, George Boleyn, and Anne after their arrest. It has always intrigued me as to why and how this relationship went so sour, and what role Jane actually played in their downfall. Many have conjectured that she was deeply jealous of George's relationship with his sister, and I have attempted to explore how this may have come about. However, the truth remains elusive.

The layout of the royal chamber described is as would have been expected in the royal Tudor household. Very often, the royal wardrobe was located close to, or underneath, the king or queen's bedchamber for convenience. The flat presses and mannequins were used to store clothes.

The scene in which Anne and Henry hear mass in the king's privy closet is fictional. The decoration, layout, dimensions and purpose of the closet are based on contemporary paintings, floor plans from Henry's great houses, and descriptions in Simon Thurley's book, *The Royal Palaces of Tudor England.*

The Book of Hours in which Anne and Henry inscribed passages in their own hand is housed in the British Library in London.

Contrary to popular belief, there is some evidence from contemporary accounts that Thomas Boleyn was reluctant to see Anne married to the king. I have assumed that he was not against the union *per se*, but that he wished it to take place against the backdrop of approval from the Holy See. This would ensure that any children from the marriage were legitimate. There is some suggestion that a marriage may have been planned either before or during the

590

Calais trip. The ferocious argument between Henry and Anne about the matter is entirely fictional, but the words that Henry uses to placate Anne's disquiet about delays in the legitimising of their relationship are taken from one of the love letters written by the king to his sweetheart.

The Henry VII tower at Windsor Castle houses the library but is not open to the general public.

At about this time, Henry took back the queen's jewels from Katherine, much to her disgust and reluctance. The scene in which Henry presents them to Anne is entirely fictitious.

The clothes worn by Anne at her investiture as Marquess of Pembroke are as described in contemporary accounts. These accounts also include the names of those who attended Anne in the procession.

The route taken by Anne to the king's presence chamber, (which is currently the garter throne room at Windsor Castle), where Anne was invested as Marquess is not known. From floor plans of the castle dating from the Tudor period, I have projected a most-likely route.

Chapter Two:
The royal party left Greenwich on 4 October 1532, taking the route as described. The king ordered that 300 of the royal party should travel separately to the main court, avoiding the plague which had broken out in Rochester.

As far as I am aware, the first recorded use of the queen's barge by Anne is for her coronation procession in May 1533. The use of the queen's royal barge in this scene is purely conjectural.

Anne was attended by around thirty ladies during the Calais trip and we know the names of some from the account of the lavish banquets and entertainment at the Staple Hall in Calais. These have been included for authenticity, wherever possible.

Mark Smeaton was a groom of the king's privy chamber at this time, although we do not know when he was first introduced to Anne.

The sonnet whose answer is ANNA was written by Thomas Wyatt and is thought to have referred to Anne Boleyn.

The changing personal circumstances of relationships, marriages and pregnancies of Anne's ladies are factual.

Bridget Tyrwhitt (nee Wiltshire) is an important character in Anne's story in relation to the evidence used by the Crown against Anne during her trial in May 1536. She was a very good friend of Anne's, one of the Boleyn's Kentish neighbours. Her matrimonial history, and the visit of Henry and Anne to Stone Place on the way to Calais, did occur. Sir Robert Tyrwhitt was a friend of Charles Brandon, (whilst Nicolas Harvey, her first husband, was a strong supporter of Anne). I have inferred a potential issue of allegiance in order to make sense of a rift between the two women, and to explain the contents of a crucial letter that was written by Anne to Bridget during the short period of time when Anne signed herself as the Marquess of Pembroke. However the argument between Anne and Lady Tyrwhitt at Stone Place is entirely fictional.

Chapter Three:

After Stone Place, Anne and Henry travelled to Shurland Abbey, as guests of Sir Thomas Cheney; then on to Canterbury, to the home of Sir Christopher Hales, Henry's Attorney general.

The appearance of Thomas Cromwell is taken from his iconic portrait; his background and history is as described in the book.

Lord William Sandys was Henry's Lord Chamberlain at the time. I have found no evidence that he particularly plotted against Anne. However, he was a conservative in faith, therefore more of a supporter of Katherine than Anne credits him for in the novel.

.Anne famously made her appearance to the French court in Calais in a dance with several other ladies at the banquet held in the Staple Hall, one of the finest buildings in Calais. The author's conjecture that Anne had a defining hand in the arrangements would fit with her dramatic and creative flair.

Chapter Four:
We do not know whether Henry and Anne used Dover Castle before going to and arriving from Calais. However, contemporary accounts describe repairs to the drawbridge at Dover Castle 'against the king's coming'. Therefore, I have assumed that the castle was their base.

Nobody knows for sure whether Anne remained chaste at the French court, but the weight of current opinion seems to suggest she remained a virgin. However, she may well have learnt other creative ways of pleasing a man, an idea supported by Henry's comments that he had had enough of her 'French ways' after Anne was accused of adultery, treason and incest in 1536.

The *Swallow* was the name of the ship which carried Henry and Anne to Calais.

The letter written by Anne to Lady Bridget is real. I have applied creative licence to explain what may have transpired. Bridget eventually became Anne's chief lady of the bedchamber.

The scene in which Anne talks with Charles Brandon on the deck of The *Swallow* is fictional but the sentiments reflect their respective positions on religious change.

The history of Calais, the layout of its streets, key buildings and surrounding countryside are all factual. Sadly, the remnants of old Calais were almost entirely obliterated during heavy WWII bombing. The tower which once formed part of the Town Hall remains as the *Tour de Guet*.

The description of the reception, processional entry into the town, and thanksgiving at the Church of St Nicolas are factual.

The royal party were housed at The Exchequer where Anne had a palatial suite of seven rooms. A floor plan of the building from the 1540s still survives, and this has been used in the later descriptions of Anne's lodgings.

Primero was a card game played in the Tudor period. There is plenty of evidence that Anne often beat Henry at cards as sums paid to her were recorded in the *Privy Purse Expenses of Henry VIII*.

Anne received gifts of sweet cherries, grapes and pears from Anne de Montmorency.

There are no known portraits, or physical descriptions, of Jane Rochford.

Mary Boleyn, Anne's sister, is listed in the *Privy Purse Expenses of Henry VIII* as Lady Mary Rochford, although her married name was Carey.

There is enormous controversy about George Boleyn's sexual inclinations, fuelled by Retha Warnicke in her biography, *The Rise and Fall of Anne Boleyn*. This notion was further propagated in the recent Showtime series *The Tudors*. I believe George was not gay and note a reference in a contemporary poem which speaks of him deflowering many a maiden. I adhere to my feeling that women were amongst George's great passions in life.

The scene in which Jane Rochford confesses her difficulties with George is part of my fictional interpretation of Lady Rochford's resentment toward her husband, and why she seems to have spoken against George and Anne in 1536.

Chapter Five:
On 16 October 1532, the Duke of Norfolk, accompanied by various noblemen, rode out to meet Anne de Montmorency, in order to discuss the forthcoming rendezvous between the two monarchs.

The details of the hunt and how it might have been expected to progress have been researched and verified by a modern day falconer.

Anne owned a copy of Jacques Lefèvre d'Étaples book entitled, *Epistles and Gospels for the Fifty-two Weeks of the Year* and was inscribed by her brother. It must have been presented after the elevation of Anne as Marquess of Pembroke because of the way in which George Boleyn addresses his sister; *To the right honourable lady, the Lady Marchioness of Pembroke*.

On 21 October 1532, Henry set out to meet Francis I of France.

The tapestry which illustrates the marriage of Mary Tudor, Henry's sister, to the elderly King Louis XII of France currently hangs in Hever Castle. Anne and Mary Boleyn were part of Mary Tudor's entourage, and so it is thought that they are probably depicted in it, although which of the figures represents them remains a mystery.

Chapter Six:
The firing of shot to welcome the king back to Calais is as described.

At the meeting in Calais, Francis pledged to write to the Pope, in support of Henry's marriage to Anne and urged him not to fear the Emperor's reprisals should he grant the King of England his divorce; the two king's also agreed fight the Turks together.

Francis dispatched the Provost of France to Anne with a gift of a large diamond as described; the fashioning of it into a pendant brooch is fiction.

The entertainments of Sunday 27 October 1532 are as described. The location and architectural features of the Staple Inn are based on known street maps of Tudor Calais, floor plans and old images of the gatehouse. The gatehouse was destroyed during WWII bombing raids. The site of the gatehouse is found today at the corner of the *Rue de Duc de Guise* and the *Rue Marie Tudor*.

There are contemporary details of the decoration of the banqueting hall at the Staple Inn on Sunday 27 October, and the sartorial outfits worn by each monarch, and those of Anne and her ladies; we also have the names of the ladies who danced with Anne.

The Black Prince's ruby was worn by Henry in a collar of precious jewels at that banquet and is on view today in the Crown Jewels at the Tower.

The layout of the Exchequer is based on a floor plan of the building from around 1540.

We do not know when Henry and Anne consummated their relationship, but most historians agree that it was either in Calais, or on their return to London from Dover.

Chapter Seven:

When the weather suddenly turned in Calais, Henry ordered a great number of courtiers to return to London, leaving a much smaller party in Calais. Some historians think that this was almost like a honeymoon for Anne and Henry.

Thomas Cromwell was one of the courtiers to leave Calais early. That he was going home to prepare for Anne and Henry's betrothal is pure conjecture.

The meeting between Anne, Thomas Cromwell and George in the queen's privy closet at the Exchequer in Calais is fictional.

The storm which hit Calais, and the subsequent impact on those vessels that had already set sail for England, is based in fact.

Chapter Eight:

Henry and Anne's progress back through Kent is factual; they arrived at Greenwich Palace on 26 November 1532.

Nobody knows when exactly the relationship between Henry and Anne began to unravel. I believe it was a very gradual process that began at some point when Anne became betrothed, or married, to Henry. At this time, the qualities that so endeared her to Henry as his lover became liabilities in a wife, who was expected to be submissive and unquestioning; not character traits one would ever associate with Anne Boleyn. However, it was a long path, involving a number of complex factors, which ultimately led Henry to lose faith in Anne, and eventually abandon her.

Thomas Cranmer left Mantua on 19 November 1532, and returned directly to England to take up his position as Archbishop of Canterbury. The appointment was influenced by the Boleyns; Anne, in particular.

The scene in which George Boleyn escorts Anne to her husband's bedchamber, the arrangement of the chambers, and their likely interiors, are based in fact. The content of the scene is fictitious, although it is believed that given the date of Elizabeth Tudor's birth, it is likely that she was conceived at around this time; that is during the first two weeks of December.

Chapter Nine:

All of Henry's nobles were required to attend court for celebrations, such as Christmas. Only the excuses described were an acceptable reason for non-attendance.

Christmas 1532 was the first Christmas that Anne presided over the court as queen in all but name.

The scene in which Anne Boleyn confronts the Duke of Norfolk is fictitious. However, we do know that Norfolk's initial support for the match between the king and his niece had waned considerably by this point. They had clashed on several occasions, perhaps as a result of Anne's volatile temper. We do not know exactly when Thomas Howard withdrew his support for his niece. However, with her growing influence over the king eclipsing his own, my view is that by 1533, their relationship had largely broken down.

The Christmas decorations and festivities described are all contemporary to sixteenth century England.

George Zouche married Nan Gainsford in 1533.

We do not know exactly who was at court that Christmas, and very little is known about Mary's movements during her sister's tenure as Henry's consort-in-waiting, and then as queen. Until Mary's secret marriage to William Stafford, I have assumed that she shared her time between waiting upon her younger sister and attending to her country estates.

Mary Boleyn's first husband, William Carey died during the outbreak of the sweat in 1528. Without the permission of her family, she married Master William Stafford, who was a soldier and part of the entourage that travelled with Henry and Anne to Calais in 1532. The speculation is that this is when Mary possibly met William. Thus, as the novel suggests, they would have been in the midst of their courtship during Christmas 1532.

We do not know for sure if Henry VIII was the father of Mary Boleyn's two children, Catherine and Henry. However, the wardship of the young Henry Carey was granted to Anne Boleyn, and we do know that part of his education took place in a distinguished Cistercian monastery. Both of these practices were quite normal for the time, and would have been seen as highly advantageous for Henry's future.

As Anne was rapidly becoming the most senior member of the Boleyn household, it would be reasonable for her to take up the role of matching-making and finding her sister a suitable new husband.

Chapter Ten:
The king and queen would normally hear mass in their privy closets. However, on the great feast days of the year, full ceremonial regalia would be worn and they would process to the chapel royal in full view of the court.

There was little love lost between Princess Mary and Anne. We can only imagine the strained, and possibly fiery, conversations which passed between Henry and Anne regarding Mary, and her refusal to accept Anne as Henry's new wife and queen.

Margery was pregnant as described in the early months of 1533.

The meeting between Anne and Joan Champernowe is fictitious. We do not know whether Kat Champernowe (later Kat Ashley), was Joan's sister or cousin; historians are divided. I believe Kat was Joan's cousin. Her age and physical description are based on known facts. Please view Kat's portrait at: http://en.wikipedia.org/wiki/Kat_Ashley

The dimensions and function of the banqueting hall at Greenwich, or at any of Henry's great houses, is as described. We do not know how the hall was decorated for festivities of Twelfth Night; however, we do know that the banqueting hall was like an empty stage, dressed appropriately to fit the occasion. In 1527, Hans Holbein painted a magnificent canvas ceiling which inspired me to create the one described in the book. The Christmas decorations, the rituals and ceremonies, and the type of food brought forth during the banquet are all based upon contemporary descriptions of how wealthy Tudors celebrated Christmas.

It is well know that Kat Champernowe served the infant Princess Elizabeth and stayed loyally by her side for the rest of her life. I wanted to explore how that bond of loyalty might have been established. This scene begins that exploration.

The physical description of the Countess of Worcester, and how I have portrayed her character, were inspired firstly from the effigy upon her tomb, which can be viewed by following the link below, (under the entry for Elizabeth Browne), as well as the few remaining fragments of contemporary descriptions of her behaviour. See:

http://www.kateemersonhistoricals.com/TudorWomenBrooke-Bu.htm

Chapter Eleven:

Katherine presented Henry a New Year's gift of a gold cup, which the king rejected.

The festivities held on January 6 1533, for Twelfth Night, were amongst the grandest ever seen and extra kitchens were set up in the nearby tiltyard, adjacent to the banqueting hall.

The scene in which Anne meets with Thomas Cranmer for the first time in the privy gallery at Greenwich is entirely fictional. We do know that Thomas Cranmer was one of Anne's most devoted and loyal supporters. It is also recorded that Cranmer was reluctant initially to take up his post. The physical description of Thomas Cranmer is taken from a portrait painted by Gerlache Flicke in the mid-1540s. See:

http://en.wikipedia.org/wiki/File:Thomas_Cranmer_by_Gerlach_Flicke.jpg

As ever, the description of Anne moving about Greenwich Palace is based upon the floor plan described in Simon Thurley's book, *The Royal Palaces of Tudor England*. This is also true of the position and dimensions of the King's presence chamber at Greenwich.

We know that Anne Boleyn presented a set of Tyrolean boar spears to Henry as his New Year's gift in 1532/1533.

Chapter Twelve:

At this time, Cromwell was working feverishly to put the finishing touches to the bill known as the Act of Appeals which was to go before Parliament in early February.

At some point between Twelfth Night, which was spent at Greenwich Palace, and 25 January, (when we know that Anne and Henry were married at Whitehall) the court transferred to Westminster. Thomas Cranmer was lodged at Canon Row, and Cromwell within the heart of the palace.

Cranmer's appointment to the See of Canterbury was made public on Friday, 24 January 1533.

Great mystery surrounds Anne's marriage to Henry. Ambassador Chapuys' account is that Anne's family were present, and that Thomas Cranmer conducted the service. However, Cranmer denied all knowledge of the event until two weeks after it had taken place. In a letter which he wrote to a Master Hawkins, he confirms that the wedding date was 'St Paul's day last', the 25 January. It has always seemed strange to me that Anne's family were not present, and I have accounted for this by their absence from court, and the last-minute arrangements made for the ceremony. I have also found it strange that Anne Savage was the only female attendant. Other than in relation to this ceremony, she is mentioned little in Anne's story and, in fact, leaves court in April of the same year to marry Lord Berkeley; apparently she did not return. There is no evidence that she remained close to Anne. Were they two close friends who later fell out? Was Anne Savage the only suitable person present to stand in as chief bridesmaid? I do not know the answer to this perplexing question. However, the description given of Anne Savage's age and her temperament are based upon contemporary descriptions.

Both Margaret Wyatt and Joan Champernowe gave birth in 1533 (the exact dates are not known) which explains their absence from court in early 1533.

I have relied upon one of the most widely accepted versions of events detailed by Nicolas Harpsfield, a Catholic priest, stating that the marriage took place in January 1533 was conducted by a Mr Roland Lee, the king's chaplain, with Sir Henry Norris, Thomas Heneage and Anne Savage, later the Lady Berkeley, present as witnesses. Historians have surmised that it would have been improper to have Cranmer conducting the marriage when he was simultaneously involved in dissolving Henry's union with Katherine.

The wedding ceremony is believed to have taken place before dawn in the upper chamber of the newly constructed Holbein Gate. Simon Thurley describes this chamber as one of the king's privy libraries in *Whitehall Palace: an Architectural History of the Royal Apartments 1242-1690*.

Anne would have had to maintain the greatest secrecy on the day and so to get to the Holbein Gate, her most likely route would have been through the king's privy chambers; therefore, she must have passed through the king's closet, the lantern room, and the long privy gallery which connected the king's apartments to the Holbein Gate. The interior decoration of the gallery is based upon accounts given in contemporary descriptions again from Simon Thurley's book, *Whitehall Palace: an Architectural History of the Royal Apartments 1242-1690*. The staircase described descending to the great garden also existed and this was later called the Adam and Eve stair.

The dress I described Anne wearing for her wedding is based on her iconic portrait in which she is wearing her pearl 'B' necklace. The description of the interior decoration of the library and the garments worn by Henry at his wedding are also fictional, although based on the fashions of the day.

The gallery and stairs used to ascend to the upper chamber of the Holbein Gate did exist as described.

Nicolas Harpsfield describes an exchange that took place between Dr Roland Lee and the king before the ceremony, in which he questioned the king's permission to marry (much as it is described in the novel).

The description of the king's privy chamber at Whitehall, in terms of its dimensions, layout and positioning, is based on an extant drawing of a fireplace by Holbein (undoubtedly intended for a royal residence). We do not know if this fireplace was built, and if it was, in which palace it was built.

The interior of the king's privy closet at Whitehall is based on architectural evidence in terms of its dimensions, position and layout. However, other than the position of the window and the presence of a large lantern, for which it is eponymously named, the decoration is conjecture. The writing desk described belonged to Henry, and exists to this day.

The description of Anne being painted by Holbein is fictitious. However, we do know that Holbein returned to England in 1532, and that both Thomas Cromwell and Anne Boleyn were keen patrons of his work. There are no extant contemporary Holbein portraits of Anne. Some historians, such as Professor Eric Ives, believe that it is inconceivable that she did not sit for him, and that at some point, a full length portrait would have been commissioned.

Thomas Audley was appointed as Henry's Chancellor on 26 January 1533.

Chapter Thirteen:
Parliament opened on 4 February, 1533. We do not know the whereabouts of Anne's family up to and around this time.

If we accept the account of Anne's marriage, then we find her parents, brother and sister absent from the ceremony. There is no known reason for this. The storyline that I have used explaining their absence from court is entirely conjecture.

We know that on 7 February 1533, the Earl of Wiltshire quarrelled with the Earl of Rutland regarding his resistance to supporting the Act of Appeals, and that, subsequently, Rutland fell into line and supported the new Act.

Stephen Vaughan is thought to have acted as an intermediary between Thomas Cromwell and Anne Boleyn, supporting the cause of known reformers who had fallen upon difficult times. It is true that Anne intervened on behalf of Thomas Patmore, the Parson of Hadham in Hertfordshire, who had been languishing in the Lollard's Tower at Lambeth Palace for two years, on account of his faith. As a result, Thomas was subsequently released.

Chapter Fourteen:
.George Boleyn and the Duke of Norfolk left England on 13 March 1533, on a diplomatic mission to inform King Francis of Anne's marriage to the King. They returned for Elizabeth's christening in September of that year.

The detailed description of the privy gardens at Whitehall is based on Simon Thurley's book, *Whitehall Palace: an Architectural History of the Royal Apartments 1242-1690.'* Other details are drawn from the contemporary portrait, *The Family of Henry VIII* which is thought to have been painted in the king's presence chamber at Whitehall. Views of the privy garden can be seen in the distance through the two archways on either side of the picture.

The privy garden was converted into the Preaching Place during the reign of Edward VI.

.

Chapter Fifteen:

Thomas Cranmer was consecrated as Archbishop of Canterbury on 30 March 1533.

Anne's household of approximately 200 was appointed at some time toward the end of March. We do not know exactly how much say Anne had in these appointments. Some were from earlier connections, people who shared Boleyn sympathies and/or reformist tendencies, such as George Taylor. Others, are less obvious, and I have surmised that these appointments may have been made by the king (who had to sanction and had ultimate control over all the queen's household appointments), or influenced by Cromwell. However, whether this is true or not, is unknown.

The appointments of gentlemen to Anne's senior administrative and religious roles were as described in this book. There were three categories of attendants to the queen: the queen's ladies were the so-called 'great ladies', who were the most senior noble women in the land, and were present mainly at great state and official occasions; the next category were the ladies-in-waiting, by and large wives of peers, who assisted the queen with her most intimate of tasks; then came her maids of honour, who were largely younger, unmarried ladies, and chamberers, and the lowest in rank. All the names mentioned are known to have attended upon Anne in one of these capacities.

Lady Tyrwhitt was appointed lady of the bedchamber before her death in 1534. Some accounts mention Margaret Wyatt as mistress of the wardrobe; others appoint Margery Horsman to this role. Margaret Filiol, also known as Mistress Stonor, occupied the role of mother of the maids for each of Henry's wives. No other named appointments could be identified by the author.

It is not clear if Jane Seymour left court after being dismissed from Katherine of Aragon's household which was sometime in the summer of 1532; nor when she was re-appointed to Anne's household. What seems more certain is that she was introduced by Sir Francis Bryan, who was a family friend. The scene in which Anne first meets Mistress Jane, and subsequently confronts the king regarding the appointment, is entirely fictitious.

An inventory taken after the death of Henry VIII listed a pair of matching sleeves (from a lady's gown) of 'white satin, embroidered over with pearled, gold acorns and honeysuckles, whilst matching sleeves were tied with ten pairs of aiglets of gold'. Ives states that these surely belonged to Anne Boleyn, on account of the acorns and honeysuckles, used commonly as a cipher by Henry and Anne. As ladies sleeves often matched their kirtle, I have designed a fictional dress based on this inventory item.

The dimensions, placement of windows and doors in the queen's presence chamber, as well as its imprint upon Wolsey's original chamber, are based on Simon Thurley's book, *Whitehall Palace: an Architectural History of the Royal Apartments, 1242-1690*. The interior decoration is entirely conjectural, based upon contemporary descriptions and paintings of other public chambers at Henry's great houses.

The description of the king's presence chamber at Whitehall is also based on Simon Thurley's *Whitehall Palace: an Architectural History of the Royal*

Apartments, 1242-1690. Further detail is drawn from the contemporary portrait, *The Family of King Henry VIII*, which is believed to show the king upon his throne, with his family, in this chamber at Whitehall Palace.

During Anne's ascendancy, it seems that there were strong ties between her and Sir Francis Bryan, whom she promoted to gain favour with the king. He was subsequently appointed as one of Henry's gentlemen of the privy chamber. However, it seems that at some point, Sir Francis and Anne must have fallen out for he was one of those individuals who played an active part in her downfall in 1536; Cromwell gave him the nickname '*the Vicar of Hell*'. The reason for this turnabout is not known and my story-line is that it ties in with Anne's treatment of Mistress Jane is entirely conjecture.

Chapter Sixteen:
The Moost Happi was Anne's motto adopted in 1533, prior to her coronation.

Anne Boleyn kept a copy of Tyndale's English version of the Bible in her privy apartments for all to see. Such books were regarded as heretical, and technically according to the law, this was still the case. This must have been an event of enormous significance to Anne and her contemporaries.

Towards the end of March, Anne Boleyn's household as queen was finally established, prior to her being presented to the court on Easter Eve, Saturday, 12 April 1533 at Greenwich Palace. We also know that she lectured members of her household together and instructed them upon the manner of behaviour which she deemed appropriate for setting a good example to all. The qualities that she insisted upon, and some of the structure of the speech Anne gives to her household in the novel, are based upon contemporary records.

During Easter week, 1533, Katherine of Aragon, was instructed that she must no longer style herself as 'queen', and that she was henceforth to be known as the Princess Dowager of Wales.

The Imperial ambassador, Eustace Chapuys, had an audience with Henry on Maundy Thursday, two days prior to Anne being presented to the court as queen. A conversation along the lines of that described in the novel did occur between them. Neither Anne, nor Henry, would have known about the ambassador's behind-the-scenes activity. During these months, Chapuys urged his master, the Holy Roman Emperor, to wage war upon England.

Anne was presented to the court by attending mass in the chapel royal at Greenwich on Easter Eve, 12 April 1533. She was attended by sixty ladies, with as great a pageantry as ever was seen for Katherine. However, we have no more detail than this, so the content of the scene is fictional. Anne's process through the palace is based on the floor plans of Greenwich, and the most likely route taken by the queen from her privy apartments to the chapel royal.

The scene in which Anne entertains the king, the French ambassador, (Jean de Dinteville) and his friend, the Bishop of Tarbes, (Georges de Selve) is fictional. We do know that Georges was in England from around the end of March/beginning of April to sometime in May 1533. Holbein's masterpiece, known as, *The Ambassadors* depicts these two friends during this time. Some have projected that this painting has a direct reference to Anne Boleyn and her presentation to the court as queen at Greenwich, on account of the date shown by the dial in the picture. However, according to John North in his book, *The Ambassadors' Secret: Holbein and the World of the Renaissance,* the date on the dial refers to Good Friday, not Easter Eve. I could find no reference connecting this portrait to Anne Boleyn. Both Thomas Cromwell and Anne Boleyn were great patrons of Holbein.

Chapter Seventeen:

On 23 May 1533, Frances Brandon, the elder daughter of Mary Tudor and Charles Brandon, was married to the young Henry Grey, Marquess of Dorset. Henry VIII was the principal guest of honour, although Anne did not attend, sensitive to her difficult relationship with her sister-in-law. The fate of Francis' family is as described in the novel.

Mary Tudor, Queen of France and Duchess of Suffolk, died at the Suffolk's residence, Westhorpe Hall, on 25 June 1533. She was 37 years old.

On 23 May 1533 Archbishop Cranmer and the court at Dunstable found Henry VIII's marriage to Katherine of Aragon to be null and void. His marriage to Anne was declared valid just the day before the Coronation festivities were due to begin, on 28 May 1533.

Anne's daughter Elizabeth did pronounce the words, '*A Dominum factum est illud, et est mirabile in oculis notris*' upon hearing of her succession from her half-sister, Mary, at Hatfield Palace in Hertfordshire. This scene in which Anne speaks these words first is, however, entirely fictional but it meant to capture what might have inspired Elizabeth's later words.

Chapter Eighteen:

The description of Anne's route from her privy apartments at Greenwich to the waterfront is fictional. However, the layout of the rooms through which she passes is as in Simon Thurley's book, *The Royal Palaces of Tudor England.*

The account of the river pageant that greeted Anne at Greenwich and her subsequent arrival at the Tower, on 29 May 1533, is taken from a contemporary description written by the chronicler, Edward Hall. See http://www.archive.org/stream/hallschronicleco00halluoft#page/798/mode/2up

Anne spoke publically of her thanks upon her arrival at the Tower, however, the exact speech was not recorded. The speech in this chapter is inspired by a contemporary letter, written on behalf of the queen, announcing her happiness at the arrival of the newly born Princess Elizabeth in September of that year.

The description of the newly rebuilt and refurbished royal apartments at the Tower of London is based on the fabulous reconstruction which can be viewed on YouTube at: http://www.youtube.com/watch?v=HZcYl2D2a9s.

The description of the now lost great hall at the Tower of London is based on another, contemporaneous hall, built by Henry III in Winchester, which still stands today. The detail of the remaining interiors is based on floor plans detailed in Simon Thurley's book, *The Royal Palaces of Tudor England*, and contemporary descriptions of the royal apartments at the Tower.

The Duke of Norfolk and George Boleyn were dispatched to France on 28

May 1533,for the reasons described in this book and, therefore, George Boleyn was absent from his sister's coronation.

When I began writing about Anne's pregnancy, I was unsure about whether sex was considered appropriate during the time that a woman was with child. My research concluded that sexual intercourse was not prohibited, although one contemporary account describes that it should be done with great care!

Chapter Nineteen:

The description of the Norman Chapel of St John in the Tower of London is based in fact. It is the oldest church in the City's capital, and was the place where Knights of the Bath were invested during the medieval period.

The investiture ceremony for the Knights of the Bath was a part of the celebrations of Anne's coronation. This was a great honour, as it usually only occurred to celebrate the crowning of a reigning monarch.

The layout of the privy garden at the Tower of London is as described.

Chapter Twenty:

The details of events described in this chapter: the creation of the Knights of the Bath and Knights Bachelor, the progress of the coronation procession, the general decoration of the city, and excerpts from various pageants are all from contemporary accounts.

The description of the robes that Anne wore for her coronation, including her headdress and how she wore her hair, is based largely on the account of the chronicler, Edward Hall. The description of the procession, those who took part, their dress and their order in the procession is based in fact. However, I have taken the liberty of assigning names to those ladies who are described as following Anne in attendance upon their queen.

The description of Westminster, the palace, the abbey and surrounding buildings, is based upon the following illustrations: see
http://www.flickr.com/photos/20631910@N03/2651119856/
http://en.wikipedia.org/wiki/File:Westminster_16C.jpg

Chapter Twenty-One:

A deathbed confession from Lady Bridget Tyrwhitt was used as evidence against Anne at her trial in May 1536; two years after Bridget had died.

The arrival of Anne at the queen's stair, part of the old Palace of Westminster, her progress through the queen's privy apartments and St Stephen's Chapel, are conjectural. However, as Anne departed from Westminster Hall, via the queen's privy stair, on her way to Whitehall the previous evening, it seems most likely that this would have been the route on her return the following day.

The description of the decoration and layout of Westminster Hall was as described in the novel and is based upon the account of the chronicler, Edward Hall, as well as Professor Eric Ives' research and interpretation, described in his book, *The Life and Death of Anne Boleyn.*

A blue carpet was laid between the dais in Westminster Hall and the high altar in the Abbey of Westminster. It was tradition that monarch's walked barefoot in an act of reverence and humility from the said hall to their place of crowning in the abbey. We do not know if Anne followed this tradition. However, based on the fact that everything else was followed according to tradition in order to underline Anne's regal status, I have assumed she would also have walked barefoot.

The procession is broadly correct and is again based on the accounts of the Tudor chronicler Edward Hall, and that of Eric Ives.

The ancient crown of St Edward the Confessor, eponymously named for the eleventh century king, its form and decoration, and subsequent loss, is as described. An image of the original crown can be seen in the link below to the portrait of Charles I, the last English King to wear it before it was melted down. See: http://en.wikipedia.org/wiki/File:Crown_Henry_VII.JPG

The layout and description of the abbey, the positioning of King Edward's chair for Anne's coronation, its form and decoration, are as described. The coronation chair is today on display at Westminster Abbey.

The description of the *sacrarium* in Westminster Abbey is as it would have been on the day of Anne's Coronation. The existing altar screen does not seem to have been in place in the sixteenth century, and so it is likely that the shrine of St Edward the Confessor would have been much more visible than it is today. In the sixteenth century, the Westminster Retable was the decorative screen positioned directly behind the high altar. At the time of the dissolution it was dismantled and incorporated into furniture, then 'rediscovered' in the eighteenth century. It can still be seen on display in the Abbey's Museum. See

http://en.wikipedia.org/wiki/Westminster_Retable

Henry observed the coronation ceremony in the presence of the French and Venetian ambassadors. His privacy was provided by a lattice screen, although its exact position within the abbey at the time remains unknown.

The coronation ceremony has remained largely unchanged for nearly 1000 years. The order of Anne's coronation was not recorded in contemporary accounts; however, we can assume that it closely mirrored the traditional format. In the pre-reformation era, this would have been set in the context of the Roman Catholic Mass. Some accounts do exist, including those of the Edward Hall and in a letter written by Thomas Cranmer. These give us fragments of Anne's role during the coronation itself. This is where we hear of Anne prostrating herself in front of the altar, before being anointed and crowned, largely as described in the novel. The garments that were placed about her in the novel have been based on the Coronation robes used in today's ceremony. It is unclear to me whether such garments were also used during the medieval period. Once crowned, Anne would have received the sacrament before withdrawing, as described.

Chapter Twenty-Two:

On the 28 June 1533, Anne was presented with a sumptuous litter and three mules as a wedding present from King Francis I. This was presented to George Boleyn in Paris, and subsequently delivered to the queen at Greenwich by the French ambassador. Chapuys records the presence of a second man called 'Esq St Jullien'. In his dispatches to the emperor, Eustace Chapuys describes meeting these two gentlemen on the way back from delivering their gift, but he was 'unable to hear any news of importance'.

Mary Tudor, Queen of France and Duchess of Suffolk died at Westhorpe Hall on Tuesday, 25 June. Certainly, Katherine and Mary still refused to surrender their titles and accept Anne as Henry's new wife and queen.

There is a suggestion in contemporary documents, notably in the 1,000 line poem of Lancelot de Carles, written in 1536 that the late stages of pregnancy were difficult (this is also alluded to in Ives, p183). It is said that Henry had, 'been at his wit's end, even hoping for a miscarriage if it would save Anne's life'. The syndrome of pre-eclampsia—or elevated blood pressure occurring during pregnancy—is as described. From this point forward, I have based the descriptions of what occurred during Anne's final weeks of pregnancy in relation to this medical condition.

Chapter Twenty-Three:

On 30 July 1533, Ambassador Chapuys wrote to the Emperor that, 'the better to conceal from her the disagreeable intelligence from Rome, the king, under plea of going to the chase, left Windsor the other day and went to Guildford, whither he has summoned his Privy Councillors and several doctors and canonists.'

Clearly Anne was left at Windsor on, or about, 28 July 1533. It seems that she was unaware of the news from Rome, and given that the pair had been little parted, I have imagined that Anne may have been concerned that her husband had left to chase something more than a hind! It is interesting to note that in some historical texts, there is the story of Henry having his first affair whilst Anne was still pregnant with Elizabeth. Eric Ives points out that this story appears to have come from a misreading of the original sources, and that Henry actually remained faithful to Anne throughout her first pregnancy.

On 11 July 1533, Ambassador Chapuys writes to the Emperor that instructions were sent to Katherine's household that, 'it could only be arrogance, selfishness, or inordinate vainglory that could induce her [Katherine] now to assume or use the title of queen... [That the king] was legitimately divorced from her, and married to another who has since been crowned with due solemnity. And, moreover, that she was singularly mistaken if she thought that he could, as long as he lived, ever go back to her'. I have woven into the plot that part of the pressure that the king put on Katherine and his daughter, came from Anne herself.

We know that Mary Boleyn attended her sister's coronation. However, after this time her exact whereabouts is unknown until she surfaces again at court, pregnant and married to William Stafford in the summer of 1534. We do not know where Mary was during this time and can only surmise that she came and went from court (see my previous notes for Chapter 9). We have no idea if any member of the Boleyn family knew anything of William Stafford before that fateful summer of 1534. Therefore, the storyline in which Anne seeks to make a match for Mary (with the Earl of Oxford), and subsequently finds out about her lover, is entirely fictional. The character of John, 15th Earl of Oxford had indeed been a widower for some five years at that point. Interestingly, he was also the first protestant Earl of Oxford.

Anne left Windsor on Thursday, 21 August 1533. The royal couple stayed at Whitehall Palace for the weekend. They then left for Greenwich on Tuesday, 26 August, when Anne underwent the ceremony of 'taking to her chamber', as described in the novel. Normally, a royal confinement would begin four to six weeks before the expected delivery date. There has been much debate as to why Anne appeared to take to her chambers only ten days before Elizabeth's delivery. This could mean that Elizabeth was significantly premature, or Anne got her dates wrong. However, if we take the date of Anne's conception to the first two weeks of December (as described by historians such as Ives), Elizabeth's birth date of around 7 September becomes more acceptable. We do not know if any difficulties that Anne experienced later in her pregnancy (as alluded to in de Carles), accounted for her taking to her chambers later than might have been expected. Therefore, the story-line describing the circumstances and events at, and surrounding, Anne's confinement is conjecture.

Richard Bartlett was Anne's physician in 1533.

Margaret Beaufort, Henry VIII's grandmother, established the rules for a royal confinement in the *Rayalle Book*, or Royal Book. The type of furnishings and conditions kept within the Queen's Privy Chamber are as described in the book. The walnut bed and the pallet bed, covered with a crimson canopy and used for giving birth, are known to have belonged to Anne Boleyn. An extant account describing the preparations of the queen's lying-in chamber indicate that the false roof hung with arras, the cupboard bedecked with plate, and the tapestries depicting St Ursula and the 11,000 virgins were to be found in Anne's bedchamber during her confinement.

Chapter Twenty-Four:

At the outset of this section, I would like to take the opportunity to issue a hearty thanks to a number of my devoted Facebook fans who kindly offered up their experiences of pregnancy and birth, some of which have been included in this novel.

The lantern clock described at the beginning of this chapter is in the private collection of Her Majesty Queen Elizabeth II in the royal library at Windsor.

Building on the storyline that Anne experienced complications in the late stages of pregnancy, I think that Anne chose to induce her labour. Today induction would be used for women suffering from pre-eclampsia, when the life or the baby or mother is endangered. *Obstetrics and Gynaecology in Tudor and Stuart England*, states that midwives at the time knew how to induce labour by perforating the amniotic sac. Depending on the instrument used, it was not without risk of infection. The obstetric practices that I describe in this chapter are contemporary with the time.

It has been a suggested that a Nan Cobham might have been Anne's midwife. However, as far as I'm aware the name of her midwife has been lost in time. Thus the character of Margaret Symons is entirely fictional.

We know that Elizabeth was born between three and four o'clock in the afternoon on Sunday, 7 September 1533.

Chapter Twenty-Five:

In Tudor England, a woman normally stayed in confinement for approximately forty days following delivery of her child. After this time, the religious ceremony of 'churching' marked a watershed in which she re-entered society and the marital bed. It seems that Henry and Anne were back together somewhat earlier, as they are reported together again by 15 October 1533.

Anne had a strong and close relationship with her daughter, and, defying all convention, initially breastfed her baby, rather than using a wet nurse. However, Henry forbade this practice.

Most historians agree that Henry was bitterly disappointed with the birth of a daughter. He put a brave face on matters by stating that, 'sons would follow'.

We do not know exactly what happened between Henry and Anne following Elizabeth's birth. We do know that by Christmas 1533, the king kept court which was as 'merry and as lusty as ever'. One suspects that the announcement of Anne's second pregnancy around this time may well have been influential in this significant change in mood. Thus my storyline of how the relationship between Anne and Henry unfolds in the weeks immediately following the birth of their daughter is conjecture, although I have tried to align this as closely as possible with the known facts.

Henry kept a library on the second floor of the donjon at Greenwich Palace. The general layout and contents of the library are taken from contemporary descriptions of the Greenwich library, specifically, and is in line with the known appearance of the king's libraries at that time.

The appearance of bound manuscripts is as described in the text. *Les Miroir des Dames* is a medieval manuscript still in existence today, and was produced for the purpose described in this book.

Lady Mary was forcefully removed from Beaulieu to Hertford Castle at this time and at the same time, Lord Rochford was granted possession of the Palace of Beaulieu.

The Duke of Richmond and the Earl of Surrey returned in Norfolk's wake, taking longer to travel back through France, arriving in England, sometime in October. The reason for their recall is as described in the book. However, to smooth diplomatic relations, the excuse that Richmond had reached a marriageable age facilitated his withdrawal from France, without causing undue political angst. He was married to Lady Mary Howard on either the 25 or 26 November 1533.

Chapter Twenty-Six:

The figure of George Boleyn is somewhat elusive and I have portrayed him as I believe he was probably seen by his contemporaries; much liked, highly gifted in many noble pursuits, and probably overly fond of women. We do not know if George Boleyn had affairs, although I believe that this would be in keeping with his character. Indeed, various possible illegitimate lines have been raised by historians and other interested parties, in the past. These will be touched upon later in the notes section. We know that one of the maids who first made accusations against Anne in May 1536 was a Nan Cobham.

However, there are five contenders for the honour of being the paramour of George who betrayed Anne. They are:

➤ Anne Bray, Baroness Cobham. This Anne Cobham was an attendant horsewoman at Anne Boleyn's coronation on 1 June 1533, and was married to Thomas Wyatt's brother-in-law, Sir George Brooke. They lived at Cobham Hall in Kent and had ten children.

➤ Anne Cobham who served as a lady-in-waiting to Catherine Parr in 1547.

➤ The widow Anne Cobham who was granted lands in 1540 which used to belong to Syon Abbey.

➤ The Anne Cobham who was married to Sir Edward Borough, 2nd Baron Borough of Gainsborough, although it is thought that she died in the late 1520s.

➤ Anne Boleyn's midwife who, historian Retha Warnicke, cites as the diminutive 'Nan' possibly Cobham, but 'makes it unlikely that she was of aristocratic birth'.

I have made the most of this ambiguity to deliberately fail to identify which of these Nan Cobhams I have woven into the plot as being that 'one maid more', so as not to unjustly accuse the innocent.

Lady Mary Howard married Henry Fitzroy, Duke of Richmond, Somerset and Earl of Nottingham on either the 25 of 26 November 1533. They were married at Hampton Court, although, unfortunately, I was unable to identify whether this took place in the chapel royal or in one of the king or queen's privy closets.

I have as faithfully as possible adhered to the facts relating to the site, state of the buildings, redevelopment and remodelling of Hampton Court as principally described by Simon Thurley in his extensive article on Hampton Court, *'Henry VIII and the Building of Hampton Court: A Reconstruction of the Tudor Palace'*, and in his book, *The Lost Tudor Palaces of England* and other related sources.

The vows spoken at the wedding ceremony of Lady Mary and Henry Fitzroy are taken from a contemporary account of the marriage between Henry VIII and Catherine Parr. I have used these contemporary Henrician marriage vows as a template for the ceremony between Henry Fitzroy and Lady Mary.

In 1533, the great hall at Hampton Court Palace was being completely rebuilt, and would not have been available to accommodate a wedding feast.

It was about this time that it was decided that the new Princess of Wales should be established in her own household at Hatfield in Hertfordshire. I am not aware that we know of the extent of Anne's involvement in determining this arrangement, or reaction to it. Therefore, my storyline in which Anne is initially greatly disturbed by this thought is perhaps in line with what we know of her character as a devoted mother, but is entirely fictional.

The scene in which Henry and Anne make love, and conceive another child, is entirely fictional. However, we do know that Anne must have become pregnant for a second time at around this time, for by sometime in December her pregnancy seems to have been known at court.

Chapter Twenty-Seven:

As ever, the court resided at Greenwich Palace for the Christmas festivities of 1533.

The layout of the palace and gardens, including the great orchard, is based on existing architectural evidence and plans of the palace. The tradition of New Year's gift giving is as described in the novel.

Lady Bridget Tyrwhitt died in January 1534. As far as I'm aware, there is no known cause of death, and so the storyline in which she catches pneumonia, and dies suddenly, is entirely fictional.

Lady Bridget made a deathbed confession about Anne's morals which, in conjunction with an earlier letter sent (previously documented) to her by Anne in 1532, was used as evidence against the queen in May 1536. However, we do not know to whom Lady Bridget was supposed to have made her deathbed confession.

Chapter Twenty-Eight:

Anne Gainsford gave birth to her first child, John Zouche, on 27 August 1534. This means that she must have conceived the child somewhere in the first week of December, assuming that her pregnancy went to term.

The description of the queen's long gallery at Whitehall Palace is based on contemporary accounts, as well as later paintings of the Tudor Palace of Whitehall, and archaeological evidence. Once again, Simon's Thurley's book, *Whitehall Palace: an Architectural History of the Royal Apartments, 1240 to 1690* and his book on *The Royal Palaces of Tudor England* were primary sources for this information.

This is the English translation to 'Helas Madame', attributed to Henry VIII:

> *Alas, my lady, whom I love so,*
> *let me be your humble servant;*
> *your humble servant I shall always be,*
> *and for as long as I live, I will love only you.*

The king's physician, Dr William Butts, and Thomas Cranmer were all part of the evangelical faction at court, and were known to be allies and friends of Anne's. Nicolas Bourbon was plucked out of a Paris jail on account of Anne's influence, and came to live in England where he lodged with Dr Butts; Anne paid for his upkeep. I found two sources that give dates for his arrival in England, one in May 1534 and the other in May 1535. So, it is possible that this sequence of events happened a year later than I suggest in the novel. However the basic nature of these events, and the involvement of Anne in supporting reformers in difficulty, is real enough.

The position, purpose and description of the gilt chamber are based on contemporary accounts.

On 20 January 1534, Sir Francis Bryan wrote a letter from Whitehall Palace to Honor, Lady Lisle, that the gift of her little toy dog, Purkoy, had been well received by the queen, who had stolen it from his arms within half an hour.

We know that Henry seems to have taken his first mistress during his

relationship with Anne in the spring of 1534. *The Imperial Lady*, as she's referred to in contemporary letters, seems to have been a beautiful woman, who had a strong allegiance with the Lady Mary (and therefore we can assume Katherine and the conservative faction). The identity of this lady remains a mystery. Kate Emerson who has done extensive research on Tudor women has suggested that her favourite candidate is a certain Elizabeth (or Bess) Harvey (Hervey). See
http://www.kateemersonhistoricals.com/TudorWomenIndex.htm.

However, very little seems to be known even of this lady, although David Starkey's book *Six Wives: The Queens of Henry VIII* recounts that Bess Hervey was in service to Anne Boleyn, and on 'friendly terms' with Sir Francis Bryan. I used this in the storyline to explain her introduction at court. The description of her and her family connections are entirely fictional.

Chapter Twenty-Nine:

The Parliamentary session began on 15 January 1534, and the Act of Succession was passed on 23 March 1534. The nature of this act, as described by Thomas Cromwell in his conversation with Anne, draws upon the original wording which can be read online.

The description of the great garden and the view of the palace to the north are as described in this chapter.

Thomas Cromwell was made Principal Secretary to the King in April 1534. It would be a pivotal position over the next few years of Henry's reign. The suggestion that Anne had a hand in commending Thomas Cromwell for this honour is purely fictional, but plausible, given that the Boleyn's had strongly supported Thomas's rise at court.

Henry's most favoured courtiers would often have lodgings close to the king; such arrangements have been detailed at Hampton Court and Greenwich Palace. However the arrangement at Whitehall is undocumented, and therefore my description of the allocation of these lodgings is fictional.

There is much debate as to the nature of the relationship between George Boleyn and his wife, Jane. They do not seem to have been particularly close, and did not have children. George's character suggests that he enjoyed the company of women, other than his wife, at court, although there is no factual evidence that George did have an affair. Some historians believe that George Boleyn, who became the Dean of Lichfield Cathedral in 1576, could well have been his son. Furthermore, there is the tombstone at Kilkenny Castle in Ireland which claims that two daughters of George Boleyn's son lie buried there. There has been a considerable amount of investigation by the Anne Boleyn community as to the veracity of this story, but no firm conclusion has been reached. I have drawn upon this mystery, and the apparent character of George Boleyn, to suggest that he had an affair and at least one illegitimate child. I must reiterate, however, this storyline is entirely fictional.

Chapter Thirty:

Henry and Anne visited Eltham Palace at Easter 1534, in order to see their infant daughter, Elizabeth. We do not know the exact dates.

The sketch of the cradle described at the beginning of this chapter is thought to have been executed by Holbein, in anticipation of the coming of the new prince later in the year.

The descriptions of the layout of the palace, the gardens, and the panorama from the palace, are from contemporary accounts and from later archaeological excavations of Eltham recorded after it had fallen into decay.

The exact dates of Joan Champernowe's pregnancy are not known. However, it is known that she gave birth to a boy, Douglas, in 1534.

The Life of Jane Dormer: Duchess of Feria gives a contemporary account of the famous meeting between Anne and the Lady Mary in the chapel at Eltham Palace in Easter 1534. The description of the event is taken directly from this account, although, sadly, not all the details of the encounter between the two women were recorded.

Chapter Thirty-One:

I have portrayed the building works at Hampton Court as Anne would have likely seen them during the summer of 1534. At this time, the building of the queen's privy apartments was well underway. Unfortunately, Anne would never occupy the completed lodgings.

The descriptions of the long gallery at Hampton Court are taken directly from contemporary accounts, both in terms of its structure, layout, interior decor, and proximity in connection to the king's privy apartments.

Many historians refer to the loss of Anne's second child as a miscarriage, as she had not taken to her chamber before losing the baby. However, medically speaking a stillbirth is any death of a child after the 28th week of pregnancy. It seems that having conceived sometime in November, everything had gone well with Anne's second pregnancy. *The Letters and Papers of Henry VIII* show that the king and queen were 'merry' as late as 26 June 1534, when they were staying at Hampton Court Palace. However, between seven and eight months gestation, Anne's baby seems to have died. I personally believe that Warnicke's account of what happened next is the most logical and thorough that I have read. She writes that: '...Sometime after 26 June but before 2 July she [Anne] was delivered of a stillborn child. On 2 July, Henry decided to go without her on his already delayed summer progress. The decision of the royal couple to separate at this time can only be viewed as extraordinary.'

Henry left Hampton Court suddenly on 2 July, summoning Cromwell and the Duke of Norfolk to meet him at the More as described. Soon after, the decision was made to cancel the forthcoming trip to Calais. I agree with Warnicke, that this was done under false pretences; that is that the queen would be stressed and unsettled if her husband left her alone at this crucial time. The royal couple subsequently remained apart for nearly a month. Again, *Letters and Papers* indicate that the two were due to meet just a few days hence, on 28 July at Guildford, where Sir William Fitzwilliam was keeper of the park. There is no evidence to suggest that this did not happen, but also there is no confirmed presence of Anne at court until late September, (when the court reached Oxfordshire), and when Chapuys comments that the queen no longer appeared to be pregnant.

There is complete silence in contemporary accounts about what happened during this time; about how Anne may have lost her baby, under what circumstances, and the surely frightful impact that had on her, Henry and on their relationship. Most historians believe that this child was probably a boy, on account of Henry's later comments (in 1536) that Anne had been 'unable to bear him sons'. The use of the plural is understood to mean that this stillbirth, and the later miscarriage in 1536, was of dead, male foetuses. Thus, with so much unknown, the account that I have given is entirely fictional. However the following should be borne in mind:

1. Statistically speaking, stillbirths usually occur due to a problem within the womb, rather than a genetic abnormality. Many people, I believe erroneously, continue to attribute the loss of Anne's second child to a genetic abnormality. Statistically, such abnormalities are the commonest cause of miscarriage only during the early months of pregnancy and not in the final trimester. Although I am aware of other theories for the loss of Anne's second child, including the Rhesus blood group theory, I have stayed true to the statistical likelihood that the most common event causing death of a child at this stage in pregnancy is a condition known as placental abruption.

2. The writing, which touches on all matters relating to the loss of Anne's baby and the psychological and physical impact that this would likely have had on her, comes from my conversations with the Stillbirth and Neonatal Death Charity (SANDS: http://www.uk-sands.org/), who were incredibly helpful in assisting me in understanding the devastating impact of this kind of event upon a mother, as well as some of the unpalatable and difficult physical experiences in giving birth to a dead child.

Overall, I believe that this event, the later dismissal of her pregnant sister, Mary, from court and the fact that the king renewed his amours for the 'Imperial Lady' around this time, meant that these few months in the late summer/early autumn of 1534 were incredibly traumatic for Anne. Because of the lack of factual information, they have sadly been much glossed over in non-fiction books. My hope is that these chapters, surrounding the death of Anne's second child, will highlight just how dramatic and pivotal these events were in Anne's life and court career.

Chapter Thirty-Two:

The Letters and Papers of Henry VIII reveal that from the beginning of September, the court was lodged at the Palace of Woodstock, in Oxfordshire, and that Henry then appears to have transferred his court to The Old Palace of Langley, which lay some ten miles to the west. According to Simon Thurley, it was common practice for the king to leave the majority of the court at one place, in this case Woodstock, and seek greater privacy at one of the nearby hunting lodges, here at Langley. Assuming, that Anne did accompany the king after they met up in Guildford, there is a strong likelihood that she was present with him at Woodstock and Langley in the early autumn of that year.

There is little extant information regarding the appearance of the palace. Its location and its environs, however, would have been as described. I have included one or two snippets of information that we have in extant accounts (such as in *The History of the King's Works*). Over and above this, I have assumed the usual layout of a medieval/Tudor palace, with the privy apartments arranged around a central courtyard.

There were two significant events in and around September 1534. Firstly, Mary Boleyn arrived at court married and pregnant. From the information gathered during my research of Anne's stillbirth, it is clear that women who have experienced a stillbirth or neonatal death find it incredibly difficult to be around pregnant women or new-born babies. I believe that Mary's condition would have greatly distressed Anne—after her miscarriage just weeks earlier. Secondly, to make matters worse, Mary Boleyn brought great shame on the family by marrying without the queen's permission, and below her status. Combined, these events, and the fact that Henry resumed his liaison with his mistress, produced an explosive combination. It goes some considerable way to shed more light on Anne's dramatic reaction to her sister's appearance at court, and her subsequent banishment in disgrace.

It is clear from Chapuys' letters, that the 'Imperial Lady' proclaimed to Lady Mary that her troubles 'would soon be over'. We also know that in October of that year, Lady Jane Rochford was expelled for conspiring with the queen to get rid of the said lady from court. There are no contemporary accounts of what this conspiracy was about or exactly when it took place.

Part V
Chapter Thirty-Five:
The original great gatehouse of Hampton Court Palace was five stories high. The top two stories were dismantled some-time between 1771-73, due to structural instability.

Base Court is the first courtyard that one enters upon coming into Hampton Court Palace. It was built by Cardinal Wolsey and houses thirty separate lodgings for guests and courtiers. The grandest guests and courtiers were lodged in double fronted accommodation, the lesser ones in single rooms.

The court beyond Base Court is known as Clock Court. Here, the grandest apartments, including the royal apartments, were built by Cardinal Wolsey. The three tiered lodgings built for Henry, Katherine and the Princess Mary, still exist today, although as the novel describes, the interiors have been greatly modified. Many of the rooms are not open to the general public.

Although the rebuilding of the great hall at Hampton Court Palace was well underway during Anne's time, it was not completed until 1535. It was the last of the medieval, royal, great halls to be built in England.

The original ceiling was painted in vivid colours but in the 1920s, they were stripped to expose the roof timbers, as we see them today.

Today, a set of Henry VIII's original tapestries hang in the great hall. During the Tudor period, such fine and hugely expensive tapestries were generally only hung to decorate the hall during great celebrations, such as for the christening of Prince Edward in 1537.

The storyline in which Anne revisits the grave of Anne Boleyn's stillborn son is entirely fictional. We do not know what happened to the body of this child. A stillborn baby would often be incinerated, or buried alongside a dead female relative.

Part VI

Chapter Thirty-Eight:
Sunday, 30 April was a critical day for Anne Boleyn. A series of events, which I will not detail here, had led to the commission of 'oyer and terminer' being set up for the counties of Middlesex and Kent on 24 April. The purpose of such commissions was to collect evidence of serious and treasonable crimes. It is likely that the commissioners listed (which included Anne's father, Sir Thomas) were not initially aware, nor informed, that they were being called. It is also unknown whether Henry was even aware that these commissions had been established; it is possible that Cromwell was the instigator. On the 27 April, Parliament was also unexpectedly recalled; the same one which would later confirm the annulment of Henry's marriage.

It is unclear when exactly Anne quarrelled with Sir Henry Norris; possibly on Saturday the 29 or early on Sunday, 30 April, but the essence of the events are as described: Anne first arguing with Sir Henry, then urging him to swear that she was a good woman to her almoner, John Skip. Sometime after, she took Elizabeth in her arms in order to speak, or more likely plead, with Henry. A witness to this conversation was Alexander Ales, a Scottish Lutheran, who many years later confided to Queen Elizabeth I that he had seen Anne in a heated exchange with Henry at Greenwich. The king had been looking down from an open window onto the great courtyard below. Elizabeth had been in Anne's arms, and clearly Henry was angry. We do not know what was said in this exchange, but one can easily imagine that Anne knew something was terribly wrong; that perhaps gossip might have reached the king's ears of her earlier argument with Henry Norris.

Nan Cobham was the first of three women to allegedly make allegations against the queen.

Sometime on 30 April, Mark Smeaton was taken, or perhaps went of his own accord, to Master Secretary Cromwell's house in Stepney. Stepney is about a couple of miles north-west of Greenwich, north of the River Thames. It seems to have been done under the greatest secrecy.

A great banquet was held on the evening of 30 April as part of the May Day celebrations. By all accounts, Henry treated Anne entirely as normal and showed no evidence of the coming storm.

Chapter Thirty-Nine:
Frances de Vere, Countess of Surrey, gave birth to the future fourth Duke of Norfolk on 10 March 1536. He would later be executed for treason by Anne's daughter, Elizabeth, on 2 June 1572, when he was 36 years of age.

The Privy Council meeting went on to late in the night on Sunday, 30 April. This has been described as unusual and portentous in light of the events unfolding at court. Following the conclusion of the Council meeting, the long planned trip by the king and queen to Calais (due to set out on the following day), was indefinitely postponed.

It is unclear exactly how much Sir Thomas Boleyn knew of events which were gathering apace towards the end of April. He was on Henry's Privy Council, and was Lord Privy Seal; one might readily assume that to some degree, he was aware that all was not well. His name is also included as one of the men serving on the Royal Commission of oyer and terminer for the counties of Kent and Middlesex. However, historians have pointed out that while panel members had been appointed on 24 April, they may not have initially been made aware of the inclusion. Therefore, we do not know exactly when, and to what extent, Sir Thomas became actively involved in the commission, whose purpose was to gather evidence against the accused.

Lady Jane Rochford's involvement in the fall of her sister-in-law and husband is disputed. There is great debate amongst historians as to the real nature of the relationship between George and his wife (as previously noted), and indeed between Anne and Jane. Many have postulated that Lady Rochford was jealous of her sister-in-law, particularly, the close relationship between Anne and her brother. At one point, we know that Anne and Jane seemed to have been relatively close, with Jane helping to secure the removal of the king's one-time mistress in the autumn of 1534. Jane was subsequently banished from court. We do not know whether this had anything to do with the deteriorating relationship between the two women. I have postulated that it did play a role, in combination with Jane's prickly character and tendency towards brittleness and jealousy. We also know that in 1535, Jane Rochford ended up in the Tower for a short period of time, having demonstrated with other women against Queen Anne. Clearly, by this stage the two sisters-in-law had fallen out. Jane's family was sympathetic toward the Lady Mary which may have made it easy in the end for Jane to switch her allegiance from her Boleyn relatives. Another possibility is that Cromwell forced Jane's confession. The fact that Master secretary Cromwell looked after Jane following Anne's fall, certainly suggests that she cooperated in one way or another in the prosecution of Anne and the men who were to die with the queen.

The 'Lady of Worcester' has been described in contemporary sources as being the first person to put forth allegations against the queen. However, it seems that Anne and Lady Elizabeth were close and so, this leaves us with yet another mystery as to why Elizabeth might turn against her friend. We have testimony from Anne herself that they were close. Upon Anne's committal to the Tower, she was concerned for Elizabeth's welfare, and that of her unborn child. We know that Elizabeth's brother, Anthony Browne, was no friend of Anne's, and neither was her brother-in-law, Sir William Fitzwilliam. Contemporary sources described how the Countess was upbraided by her brother for her behaviour, Lady Elizabeth replying that 'it was no worse than the queen's'. Ives states in his biography of Anne that he believes that these were passing comments made by the Countess and taken up and embellished by men who wished to undo Anne and the Boleyn faction. I agree with Ives; it may well be the case that history has done a great disservice to Elizabeth, Countess of Worcester.

There was a spectators' gallery which ran between the two, five story tiltyard towers at Greenwich.

We do not know exactly who took part in the tilt that day and who sat with the king and queen as spectators (other than that of the roles of Lord Rochford and Sir Henry Norris – see below).

Descriptions of how a tiltyard would typically appear, and the order of ceremony, were taken from an account of an actual joust described in, '*The Tournament: Its Period and Phases* by R. Coltman Clephan.
http://archive.org/stream/cu31924029810862#page/n11/mode/2up

Lord Rochford led the 'challengers' and Sir Henry Norris led the 'answerers' during the May Day joust of 1536. We also have a contemporary account of Sir Henry Norris's horse refusing to run at the tilt, and Henry subsequently allowing Sir Henry to ride one of his own horses.

The Spanish Chronicle speaks of the 'handkerchief incident', which I have chosen to include in the novel. I do not think that this is mentioned in other sources and so must be treated with a degree of circumspection.

Contemporary accounts suggest that all had seemed well between the king and queen until late in the day, just before the joust was due to close. At this point, a note arrived for Henry. Having read it, he subsequently stalked off, never to see Anne again. We do not know what happened to Anne after Henry departed. I have assumed that in a state of great agitation and confusion, she returned to the queen's apartments at Greenwich.

One puzzling aspect of this part of Anne's story is the role of her almoner, John Skip. Anne seems to have trusted Skip, having given him the task of preaching a damning sermon, essentially aimed at the likes of Cromwell, on 2 April 1536. After her arrest, her almoner certainly seems to have been with her in the Tower, and possibly accompanied her to the scaffold. It was to John Skip that Anne sent Sir Henry Norris to swear that she was a 'good woman', following her argument with Henry around 30 April. However, he seems to have taken this information directly to Sir Edward Baynton. Although Anne's Lord Chamberlain, Sir Edward had long been a friend of Katherine of Aragon. It is likely that Sir Edward then passed this information on to those willing to use it against the queen. I have struggled with whether John Skip did this deliberately or inadvertently. In the novel, I have erred on the side of his innocence, and that like the Countess of Worcester, no malice or harm was intended. However, the scene in which Master Skip confesses his concern that the information would be used against Anne is entirely fictional.

George Boleyn, Lord Rochford, was arrested at Westminster; he had been with the king and his sister at Greenwich just the day before. We can only assume that he went after Henry at some point, possibly to try and intercede on his sister's behalf. I have included this storyline in the novel, but the actual scene where George and Anne say their final goodbyes, is fictitious.

Sadly, we do not know which ladies were left with Anne during her final few days, or even hours at Greenwich. Obviously, I am assuming it is those who were most loyal to Anne, and therefore, I have placed those who were closest to Anne throughout the course of this novel at the queen's side.

The scene between Anne Boleyn and Sir Thomas Boleyn is entirely fictional as we do not know when she last saw her father. We do not know the whereabouts of Anne's mother before or after her arrest. We do know, though, from one of William Kingston's letters reporting on Anne from the Tower, that the Earl of Wiltshire was at Westminster on 2 May. We do not know what he was doing there, or whether he tried to intercede for his children.

Chapter Forty:

Henry Fitzroy, Duke of Richmond and Somerset, died six weeks after Anne's execution, at the age of seventeen. It has long been assumed that the cause of his death was tuberculosis, and that a miniature of the duke, dressed in bedclothes, suggests that he had been unwell for some time prior to his demise. This is the version of events I have followed in the novel. However, other historians have suggested that his death was much more sudden than this, occurring as the result of an acute pulmonary infection. Mary Howard, Duchess of Richmond and Somerset, never married again.

Prior to her arrest on 2 May, Anne had been watching a game of real tennis at Greenwich. Recent archaeological evidence has uncovered the likely position of a tennis play in the south-west corner of the palace precinct. With Princess Elizabeth still in the palace, I have assumed that an anxious mother, uncertain of her future, may well have wished to spend time with her daughter. The scenes pertaining to the interaction between mother and daughter are entirely fictional. The layout and citing of gardens and buildings is drawn from what is known of the layout of palace precinct at Greenwich.

Sometime prior to dinner, the main midday meal in Tudor England, a messenger arrived as Anne watched the game of tennis. She was commanded to go before members of the Privy Council where the charges of adultery were laid against her, and told that three men had also been arrested. She was also informed that Mark Smeaton and Sir Henry Norris had confessed to committing adultery with her. Anne defended herself but to no avail. She was sent back to her apartments under arrest, there to await further instructions.

We do not know whether the Privy Council Chamber was at Greenwich Palace; unlike Whitehall and Hampton Court Palace where the location of the council chamber is well established. Its description is inspired by the council chamber at Hampton Court, which is open to the public.

Norfolk, Fitzwilliam and Paulet were the three councillors who Anne first faced as her accusers. The appearance, profiles, history and sympathies are as described in the novel.

The scene in which Anne says goodbye to her ladies is fictional; we do not know if Anne had any time to pen letters to members of her family.

At about two o'clock in the afternoon, a delegation from the Privy Council arrived in Anne's presence chamber, where her dinner was being cleared. Her arrest warrant was read by Norfolk and she was conducted to the Tower. We know that she would have been taken through Greenwich Palace to the river, where a barge was awaiting her at the privy stair. The only information we have about the barge journey was that crowds did indeed throng to watch the queen being conducted to her imprisonment, and that Norfolk was heard to say once more, 'tut-tut' and speak of those men who had accused her. We also know that the barge appears to have left Greenwich not long after 2 o'clock in the afternoon, but Anne did not arrive at the Tower until 5 o'clock. It is a mystery as to why the journey took so long. I have hypothesised that in error, the oarsmen ended up rowing against the tide, although in truth, there is no accepted explanation for this time delay.

Anne was received at the Tower via the privy stair and court gate (now known as the Byward Tower). She did not enter the Tower through the now infamous Traitor's Gate, as it was subsequently named. The queen was conveyed to her prison by a delegation of lords, as described, and received by Sir Edward Walsingham, Deputy Lieutenant of the Tower. Some accounts have Sir William Kingston travelling in the barge with the queen, others have Anne being met by him once within the Tower precinct.

Having remained composed and calm throughout, Anne is said to have collapsed on the cobblestones under by the Byward Gate.

Chapter Forty-One:
General note: Descriptions of the layout of the royal apartments at the Tower of London are based on contemporary drawings and archaeological evidence. We know that Anne Boleyn was housed in these royal lodgings after she was imprisoned in the Tower on 2 May 1536. She remained there until her execution. Many of the events outlined during Anne's incarceration, and the conversations held in the Tower, come from a series of letters written by Sir William Kingston to Master Secretary Cromwell reporting on the queen, as he had been directed. The remains of these (sadly they are not complete), are to be found in *The Letters and Papers of Henry VIII*, which can be read online.

I have read what contemporary accounts exist of the time from Anne's arrest to her death, and believe that the queen passes through four psychological states; these states are well known from twentieth century research into human reaction to loss. Broadly speaking, they can be classified as; shock, anger, denial/bargaining and acceptance. As you will see later, I also postulate that during this final stage, Anne experiences a profound spiritual transformation as a result of being subjected to major adversity. This is a now well-known psychological theory developed by Professor Steve Taylor at the University of Leeds and is known as SITE—Suffering Induced Transformational Experiences (See notes on chapter forty-six). If this did occur, it puts a radically different view upon how Anne perceived her last few hours/days upon this Earth.

Finally, many of the words spoken by Anne in this final part are her actual words as recorded by Sir William Kingston during her imprisonment. Whilst we have the words, we do not have the context; much of this, by necessity, has been imagined by the author.

Although Anne's usual household was left behind at Greenwich, not only was she lodged as a queen, but she was appointed four ladies in waiting, two chamberers, two grooms and an usher. The four ladies appointed were placed there as spies of Cromwell, and had little love for their mistress. Sadly, the information on these ladies is relatively scant, but is as presented in the novel. We do not have contemporary portraits of any of these ladies, but there is a stained-glass window showing the appearance of Anne Boleyn, Lady Shelton and a marble effigy showing the figure of Margaret Dymock. Both of these artefacts were used to inspire my descriptions of the ladies in question.

From her arrival in the Tower, Anne requested that the sacrament be placed in her oratory (privy closet). This was not possible as Anne was a woman accused of adultery and had not confessed to her sins and therefore, the sacrament could not put in place as she requested.

Anne requested the presence of her almoner, John Skip. Although, it seems, he was also withheld from her service. This left her with no priest to conduct mass; hence I assume she turned to her private devotions.

The conversation between Anne, Sir William Kingston and Lady Kingston (in the presence of Lady Boleyn and Margaret Dymock) is fictional, but the words that pass between Sir William and Anne are as reported in one of William Kingston's undated letters.

Chapter Forty-Two:

This chapter weaves into the storyline the famous letter, reputedly written to Henry by *The Lady in the Tower* [Anne] dated 6 May 1536. It was found sometime after Cromwell's execution in his papers. Some believe it was Anne's final letter to her husband, in which she sets forth the case for her innocence and appeals for justice and clemency for the men accused with her. A huge debate rages around its authenticity. It certainly is not in Anne's handwriting, but may have been dictated by her. Others have argued that Anne's fierce tone is too reckless at a time when Henry's fury could well unleash itself on her living relatives. But it certainly does have Anne's spirit flowing through it, and if anyone would write to the king thus, then it would have been Anne. I personally believe it has basis in fact and, therefore, have included it here.

The chapter opens with a letter from Henry to Anne, borne by a messenger who Anne refers to as her 'ancient and professed enemy'. We do not know who this person was; that it was Sir William Fitzwilliam is conjecture. However, the opening lines of the *Lady in the Tower* letter certainly intimates that if the letter is based on a lost original, Henry had been in contact with Anne, offering her some kind of plea bargain, which she goes on to vehemently reject. If there was such a message, this has been lost to time, and so the letter from Henry is fiction, but uses words and phrases extracted from other documents, contemporary to the letter, in order to keep its tone authentic.

Chapter Forty-Three:

We do not know if Anne was allowed to walk in the privy garden during her imprisonment. Certainly, her daughter would be allowed the privilege during her, but Elizabeth was not awaiting trial as Anne was. Thus, this scene is fictional.

Mary Orchard's appointment as chamberer during Anne's imprisonment, and her relationship to Anne and the Boleyns is as described in the book. Little is known about her sadly, but we can imagine that she was of enormous comfort to Anne, in amongst ladies that 'loved her not'.

A delegation of Privy Councillors and Archbishop Cranmer arrived at the Tower to confront Anne in order to extract a confession from the queen. As there is a gap in William Kingston's letters, it is unclear as to exactly when this interview took place. I have set it on 7 May; it may well be a little later.

Once more, the words Anne uses are as recorded in contemporary records. The setting for this meeting in the queen's presence chamber is conjecture.

Chapter Forty-Four:

Note: Certain aspects relating to the legal process of Anne Boleyn's trial were extracted from an excellent article entitled, *The Law as the Engine of State: The Trial of Anne Boleyn* by Margery S. Schauer and Frederick Schauer. This article discusses a rarely highlighted notion that Jane Boleyn should have also been charged with treason, as she knew of her sister-in-law's treasonable words but did not report them immediately to the authorities.

The clothes worn by Anne at her trial are from contemporary records.

We have no idea of how Anne's relationship developed with her ladies as her imprisonment progressed. My suggestion that in some way Anne's courage and steadfastness inspired a thawing of the relationship between herself and Lady Boleyn is a work of fiction.

Anne and her brother were tried in the king's great hall at the Tower on Monday, 15 May 1536. Around 2,000 people witnessed this momentous event in English history. The general layout of the hall, the wooden stands erected, and positions of the prisoner and Council during the trail are as described.

It is well know that both Anne and her brother acquitted themselves admirably at their respective trials. Psychologically, it seems that Anne had come a long way since her nervous collapse following her imprisonment. I believe that all the evidence suggests that having passed through both shock and anger at events, Anne was approaching the final stage of grieving and loss, that of acceptance.

According to Tudor law, once accused, the onus was on the defendant to prove himself or herself not guilty. It is also true that in cases of treason, the prisoner had no prior knowledge of the evidence that would be brought against them, nor would they have any counsel to advise or defend them against the charges. The odds were certainly stacked in favour of the prosecution, and it was rare for a defendant to be acquitted.

It is true that the indictments included many dates when Anne was not physically present at the place or time that she was supposed to have committed adultery.

The legal process of a sixteenth century trial for treason has been gleaned from, *The Law as the Engine of State: The Trial of Anne Boleyn* (see above).

The indictments laid against Anne are based in fact, to which Anne pleaded 'not guilty' as described in the book.

The jury was, of course, heavily weighted against Anne. There is controversy over whether Anne's father, Thomas Boleyn, was present. His name does not appear on the list of jury members from a surviving contemporary document; however, some of the names are missing. It is possible that Thomas Boleyn is one of those names. I personally, have never been convinced of his presence at Anne Boleyn's trial, and have elected to follow the evidence that does exist, suggesting he did not have to face condemning two of his children to death.

The role of the 1352 statute in Anne's case is described in, *The Law as the Engine of State: The Trial of Anne Boleyn.*

Testimony provided by ladies of Anne's bedchamber is as described.

Unusually for a case of this gravity, no witnesses were brought to testify. It is not known why this was so, but it did undermine the strength of the prosecution's case. *The Law as the Engine of State: The Trial of Anne Boleyn* concludes that the case brought against Anne Boleyn would never stand up to scrutiny in a modern day court, but was legal in the context of the sixteenth century legal system.

The words Anne used to defend herself were never recorded; just that her defence was admirable, and that she stood more 'accused that convicted'. Thus the words spoken in this book by Anne are fictional.

The guilty verdict was unanimous and Anne was by her Uncle Norfolk as described. Her response to the conviction was recorded in contemporary documents and is related here.

Chapter Forty-Five:

There is great controversy over whether Anne was allowed to have her own ladies attend her following her conviction. Ives argues that there is no evidence to suggest that this was the case. Other historians believe that the assertion that Anne was attended by 'four maids' upon the scaffold, must preclude the four relatively elderly women who had been attending Anne since her imprisonment. I agree with the latter argument, particularly since her maids were recorded as shedding many tears as they wrapped up the bloody body of their mistress in preparation for burial. It is hard to imagine ladies who had been happy to spy on Anne being greatly distressed at her demise. Thus, I have Anne's personal friends and supporters return to her side after she had been condemned to death, but I stress the truth remains elusive.

The request of Mary Howard, the Duchess of Richmond, to attend Anne at the Tower is fictional.

Anne Boleyn is noted to have made one reference to her mother shortly after her arrest; she lamented that Elizabeth Boleyn would surely die of sorrow, making passing reference to the countess's ill health. However, the extent of any communication between Anne and members of her family during her imprisonment is not known.

Only Thomas Cranmer attempted to intervene on Anne's behalf with Henry, in a letter to the king. However, Cromwell had isolated the king, preventing all but a few of Henry's most trusted councillors from gaining access to him during the whole of Anne's imprisonment.

Cranmer was summoned from Knole, and was called away from writing to the king, in order to attend the Star Chamber for the purposes described.

The location of Mary Boleyn during the whole of her sister's and brother's incarceration is unknown. It is thought that at some point after her banishment from court, she lived in Calais with her husband, William Stafford. However, whether she was there in May 1536, is unknown.

The day after Anne's conviction, Thomas Cranmer visited Anne, for reasons unknown. However, the next day, Anne's marriage was annulled at Lambeth Palace. Anne's sentence was commuted from burning to beheading with the sword; her brother, and those sentenced to die with him, were to suffer the axe and not death by the horrific process of hanging, drawing and quartering. Did Cranmer offer Anne a deal? Did Henry offer clemency, including a possible inducement that would save Anne's life (as detailed), in return for a confession that that the marriage had never been lawful? We simply do not know. So, the scene in which Cranmer visits Anne and puts these things to her is conjecture on the author's part.

After Anne's death, Cromwell and Cranmer would do much to foster the early reformation in which Anne had played such a pivotal part. Cranmer died a martyr to his faith, burnt at the stake in Oxford, during the reign of Mary I.

Chapter Forty-Six:

I have long been fascinated by Anne's courage as she met her death, and in particular, a number of rather strange comments by those made about her during her final days, as well as by eye-witnesses who saw her walk to the scaffold. One states that, 'the queen had never looked more beautiful'. William Kingston describes how Anne appears to 'take much pleasure in death'. Such comments, and a chance reading of an article by Professor Steve Taylor of Leeds University on SITE (Suffering Induced Transformational Experiences), led me into unchartered territory. I saw the distinct possibility that Anne underwent a now well recognised, and very distinct, psychological transformation in the hours / days before her death. To read the full article about Anne Boleyn and SITE, please go to my FB page at:

https://www.facebook.com/notes/le-temps-viendra-a-novel-of-anne-boleyn/long-prepared-to-die-the-transformation-of-anne-boleyn/124368997642610

Anyone who experiences a SITE has their normal ego structures torn down, and accesses a higher state of consciousness that knows only love and peace. I believe that this is the explanation for Anne's profound aura of calm acceptance that brought forth a radiant beauty, commented on by those who saw her during her last few hours upon this Earth. Of course, I must stress that we will never know the truth of the matter, but it aligns with how Anne appeared to outside observers at the very end of her life.

The conversation between Anne and Sir William about the deaths of Lord Rochford, Sir Henry Norris, William Brereton, Francis Weston and Mark Smeaton is recorded in contemporary accounts; the words are purportedly real enough, although the scene itself is an invention of the author's imagination.

Chapter Forty-Seven:

Thomas Cranmer heard Anne's last confession on the morning of 18 May 1536; she knew she was soon to die. However, her appointment with the swordsman from St Omer / Calais would not to happen for another twenty-four hours, on the morning of 19 May. However, this confession was pivotal as Anne insisted it was witnessed. We know that Sir William Kingston was present as he later reported it. He did not mention other witnesses in his dispatches, but this does not necessarily mean that there were none. In this account, I have also included Lady Kingston and two of Anne's ladies. The impact that this must have had on underlining Anne's innocence to her contemporaries should not be underestimated. It was a private confession, directly stating her innocence before God. To perjure one's soul in such a way was unthinkable to a sixteenth century mind.

Chapter Forty-Eight:

The clothes that Anne reportedly wore to her execution are as described; with the exception of the carcanet or necklace, which is a fictional addition. We do not know if she wore any jewellery. There is a portrait of Elizabeth I that now hangs in Hampton Court Palace wearing a pearl necklace with an *A* pendant which many believe once belonged to her mother.

The letter written by Anne to be given to her mother is fictional, but draws upon phraseology taken from extant Tudor letters, including the one written by Thomas More, just before his own execution the previous year.

Anne's words upon the arrival of Master Kingston in her chambers are her own.

Anne paid £20 to her executioner which was the usual practice.

Anne's walk to the scaffold site is as detailed. The scaffold stood to the north of the White Tower as described, and not where the modern day monument to the executed stands on Tower Green; this is a Victorian myth.

Around 1,000 people gathered to see Anne die; amongst them many of the king's nobles and councillors, as described.

There are differing accounts of Anne's death; some have John Skip, her almoner accompanying her to the scaffold, others do not. Others have Anne being blindfolded, whilst some do not. There are also different accounts of Anne's scaffold speech, so the absolute truth eludes us. Anne was executed by a single strike of the sword at 8 am on Friday, 19 May, whilst kneeling upon the scaffold. It is said that Anne did look round at the executioner, and that the *Sword of Calais* distracted her by calling out to a boy for his sword. When Anne looked toward the boy, the sword was drawn out from under the straw behind her; the headsman decapitating her with one blow.

Chapter Forty-Nine:

Reportedly distressed, Anne's ladies stripped her body and placed her remains in an arrow chest as no coffin had been made ready for the queen. She was buried that afternoon next to her brother in the nearby chapel of St Peter ad Vincula.

Cranmer did speak of Anne as a 'queen in heaven' on the day of her execution.

CPSIA information can be obtained at www.ICGtesting.com
Printed in the USA
LVOW08s1219130614

389939LV00001B/118/P